Welles-Turner
Memorial Library
Glastonbury, CT 06033

W9-BDA-464

DISCARDED BY
WELLES-TURNER MEMORIAL LIBRARY
GLASTONBURY, CT

DISCARDED BY
WELLES-TURNER MEMORIAL LIBRARY
GLASTONBURY, CT

DISCARDED BY
WELLES-TURNER MEMORIAL LIBRARY
GLASTONBURY, CT

WILLIAM MAXWELL

WILLIAM MAXWELL

LATER NOVELS AND STORIES
The Château
So Long, See You Tomorrow
Stories and Improvisations 1957–1999

THE LIBRARY OF AMERICA

Volume compilation, notes, and chronology copyright © 2008 by
Literary Classics of the United States, Inc., New York, N.Y.
All rights reserved.
No part of this book may be reproduced commercially
by offset-lithographic or equivalent copying devices without
the permission of the publisher.

The Château; *So Long, See You Tomorrow*; selections from *All the
Days and Nights: The Collected Stories of William Maxwell* copyright
© 1961, 1980, 1995 by William Maxwell. Used by permission of
Alfred A. Knopf, a division of Random House, Inc.

"Grape Bay (1941)"; "The Room Outside"; selections from *The Old
Man at the Railroad Crossing and Other Tales*; "Perfection";
"Mushrooms"; "The dancing"; "The education of Her Majesty
the Queen"; "Newton's law"; "Nearing Ninety"; Preface to
The Château; Preface to *So Long, See You Tomorrow*; "Remarks
upon accepting the Gold Medal in Fiction from the American
Academy of Arts and Letters" copyright © 1966, 1988, 1992,
1994, 1995, 1997, 1998, 1999 by William Maxwell. Used by
permission of the William Maxwell Estate.

"What you can't hang on to," copyright © 2001 by William
Maxwell, from *The Element of Lavishness*.
Reprinted by permission of Counterpoint.

The paper used in this publication meets the
minimum requirements of the American National Standard for
Information Sciences—Permanence of Paper for Printed
Library Materials, ANSI z39.48—1984.

Distributed to the trade
in the United States by Penguin Putnam Inc.
and in Canada by Penguin Books Canada Ltd.

Library of Congress Control Number: 2008923668
ISBN 978-1-59853-026-1

First Printing
The Library of America—184

Manufactured in the United States of America

CHRISTOPHER CARDUFF
SELECTED THE CONTENTS AND WROTE THE NOTES
FOR THIS VOLUME

Contents

THE CHÂTEAU

For $\left\{\begin{array}{l} \text{E. B.} \\ \\ \text{E. C.} \\ \\ \text{M. O'D.} \\ \\ \text{F. S.} \\ \\ \text{W. S.} \end{array}\right.$

Contents

". . . wherever one looks twice there is some mystery."
ELIZABETH BOWEN,
A World of Love

"And there stand those stupid languages, helpless as two bridges that go over the same river side by side but are separated from each other by an abyss. It is a mere bagatelle, an accident, and yet it separates. . . ."
RAINER MARIA RILKE,
letter to his wife, September 2, 1902,
from Paris

". . . a chestnut that we find, a stone, a shell in the gravel, everything speaks as though it had been in the wilderness and had meditated and fasted. And we have almost nothing to do but listen. . . ." RILKE, *letter to his friend Arthur*
Holitscher, December 13, 1905, from
Meudon-Val-Fleury

Part One

Leo and Virgo

Chapter 1

THE big ocean liner, snow white, with two red and black slanting funnels, lay at anchor, attracting sea gulls. The sea was calm, the lens of the sky was set at infinity. The coastline— low green hills and the dim outlines of stone houses lying in pockets of mist—was in three pale French colors, a brocade borrowed from some museum. The pink was daybreak. So beautiful, and no one to see it.

And on C Deck: Something had happened but what he did not know, and it might be years before he found out, and then it might be too late to do anything about it. . . . Something was wrong, but it was more than the mechanism of dreaming could cope with. His eyelids opened and he saw that he was on shipboard, and what was wrong was that he was not being lifted by the berth under him or cradled unpleasantly from side to side. He listened. The ship's engines had stopped. The straining and creaking of the plywood walls had given way to an immense silence. He sat up and looked through the port-hole and there it was, across the open water, a fact, in plain sight, a real place, a part of him because he could say he had seen it. The pink light was spreading, in the sky and on the water. Cherbourg was hidden behind a long stone breakwater —an abstraction. He put his head clear out into the beautiful morning and smelled land. His lungs expanding took in the air of creation, of the beginning of everything.

He drew his head back in and turned to look at the other berth. How still she was, in her nest of covers. Lost to the world.

He put his head out again and watched a fishing boat with a red sail come slowly around the end of a rocky promontory. He studied the stone houses. They were more distinct now. The mist was rising. Who lives in those houses, he thought, whose hand is at the tiller of that little boat, I have no way of knowing, now or ever. . . .

He felt a weight on his heart, he felt like sighing, he felt wide open and vulnerable to the gulls' cree-cree-creeing and the light on the water and the brightness in the air.

9

The light splintered and the hills and houses were rainbow-edged, as though a prism had been placed in front of his eyes. The prism was tears. Some anonymous ancestor, preserved in his bloodstream or assigned to cramped quarters somewhere in the accumulation of inherited identities that went by his name, had suddenly taken over; somebody looking out of the port-hole of a ship on a July morning and recognizing certain char-acteristic features of his homeland, of a place that is Europe and not America, wept at all he did not know he remembered.

The cabin steward knocking on their door woke her.

"Thank you," he called. Then to his wife: "We're in France. Come look. You can see houses." He was half dressed and shaving.

They stood at the porthole talking excitedly, but what they saw now was not quite what he had seen. The mist was gone. The sky was growing much brighter. And they had been no-ticed; two tenders were already on their way out to the liner, bringing more gulls, hundreds of them.

"So beautiful!" she said.

"You should have seen it a few minutes ago."

"I wish you'd wakened me."

"I thought you needed the sleep," he said.

Though they had the same coloring and were sometimes mistaken for brother and sister, the resemblance was entirely a matter of expression. There was nothing out of the ordinary about his features, nothing ordinary about hers. Because she came of a family that seemed to produce handsomeness no matter what hereditary strains it was crossed with, the turn of the forehead, the coloring, the carving of the eyelids, the fine bones, the beautiful carriage could all be accounted for by people with long memories. But it was the eyes that you no-ticed. They were dark brown, and widely spaced, and very large, and full of light, the way children's eyes are, the eye-brows naturally arched, the upper eyelids wide but not heavy, not weighted, the whites a blue white. If all her other features had been bad, she still would have seemed beautiful because of them. They were the eyes of someone of another Age, their expression now gentle and direct, now remote, so far from calculating, and yet intelligent, perceptive, pessimistic, without guile, and without coquetry.

"I don't remember it at all," she said.

"You probably landed at Le Havre."

"I mean I don't remember seeing France for the first time."

"It could have been night," he said, knowing that it bothered her not to be able to remember things.

Mr. and Mrs. Harold Rhodes, the tags on their luggage read.

A few minutes later, hearing the sound of chains, he went to the porthole again. The tenders were alongside, and the gulls came in closer and closer on the air above the tenders and then drifted down like snow. He heard shouting and snatches of conversation. French it had to be, but it was slurred and unintelligible. A round face appeared, filling the porthole: a man in a blue beret. The eyes stared solemnly, unblinking, without recognition as the face on the magic-lantern slide moved slowly to the left and out of sight.

On shore, in the customs shed at seven thirty, they waited their turn under the letter R. She had on a wheat-colored traveling suit and the short black cloth coat that was fashionable that year and black gloves but no hat. He was wearing a wrinkled seersucker suit, a white broadcloth shirt, a foulard tie, and dusty white shoes. He needed a haircut. The gray felt hat he held in his hand was worn and sweat-stained, and in some mysterious way it looked like him. One would have said that, day in and day out, the hat was cheerful, truthful, even-tempered, anxious to do what is right.

How she looked was, Barbara Rhodes sincerely thought, not very important to her. She did not look like the person she felt herself to be. It was important to him. He would not have fallen in love with and married a plain girl. To do that you have to be reasonably well satisfied with your own appearance or else have no choice.

He was thin, flat-chested, narrow-faced, pale from lack of sleep, and tense in his movements. A whole generation of loud, confident Middle-Western voices saying: *Harold, sit up straight . . . Harold, hold your shoulders back . . . Harold, you need a haircut, you look like a violinist* had had no effect whatever. Confidence had slipped through his fingers. He had failed to be like other people.

On the counter in front of them were two large suitcases, three smaller ones, a dressing case, and a huge plaid dufflebag.

"Are you sure everything is unlocked?" she asked.

Once more he made all the catches fly open. The seven pieces of luggage represented a triumph of packing on her part and the full weight of a moral compromise: it was in his nature to provide against every conceivable situation and want, and she, who had totally escaped from the tyranny of objects when he married her, caught the disease from him.

They stood and waited while a female customs inspector went through the two battered suitcases of an elderly French-woman. Everything the inspector opened or unfolded was worn, shabby, mended, and embarrassingly personal, and the old woman's face cried out that this was no way to treat some-one who was coming home, but the customs inspector did not hear, did not believe her, did not care. There was the book of regulations, which one learned, and then one applied the reg-ulations. Her spinsterish face darkened by suspicion, by anger, by the authority that had been vested in her, she searched and searched.

"What shall I tell her if she asks me about the nylon stockings?" Barbara Rhodes said.

"She probably won't say anything about them," he an-swered. "If she does, tell her they're yours."

"Nobody has twelve pairs of unused nylon stockings. She'll think I'm crazy."

"Well, then, tell her the truth—tell her they're to give to the chambermaid in hotels in place of a tip."

"But then we'll have to pay duty on them!"

He didn't answer. A boy of sixteen or seventeen was plucking at his coat sleeve and saying: "Taxi? Taxi?"

"No," he said firmly. "We don't want a taxi. One thing at a time, for God's sake."

The wind was off the harbor and the air was fresh and stim-ulating. The confusion in the tin-roofed customs shed had an element of social excitement in it, as if this were the big affair of the season which everybody had been looking forward to, and to which everybody had been asked. More often than not, people seemed pleased to have some responsible party pawing through their luggage. In the early spring of 1948 it had seemed to be a question of how long Europe would be here— that is, in a way that was recognizable and worth coming over to see. Before the Italian elections the eastbound boats were half empty. After the elections, which turned out so much better than anybody expected, it took wire-pulling of a sustained and anxious sort to get passage on any eastbound boat of no matter what size or kind or degree of comfort. But they had made it. They were here.

"Taxi?"

"I wish I hadn't brought them now," she whispered.

Tired of hearing the word "taxi," he turned and drove the boy away. Turning back to her, he said: "I think it would probably look better if we talked out loud. . . . What has she got against that poor woman?"

"Nothing. What makes you think exactly the same thing wouldn't be happening if the shoe were on the other foot?"

"Yes?" he said, surprised and pleased by this idea.

He deferred to her judgments about people, which were not infallible—sometimes instead of seeing people she saw through them. But he knew that his own judgment was never to be trusted. He persisted in thinking that all people are thin-skinned, even though it had been demonstrated to him time and time again that they are not.

In the end, the female customs inspector made angry chalk marks on the two cheap suitcases. The old woman's guilt was not proved, but that was not to say that she was innocent; nobody is innocent.

When their turn came, the inspector was a man, quick and pleasant with them, and the inspection was cursory. The question of how many pairs of stockings a woman travels with didn't come up. They were the last ones through the customs. When they got outside, Harold looked around for a taxi, saw that there weren't any, and remembered with a pang of remorse the boy who had plucked at his coat sleeve. He looked for the boy, and didn't see him either. A hundred yards from the tin customs shed, the boat train stood ready to depart for Paris; but they weren't going to Paris.

Two dubious characters in dark-blue denim—two comedians—saw them standing helplessly beside their monumental pile of luggage and took them in charge, made telephone calls (they said), received messages (perhaps) from the taxi stand at the railroad station, and helped them pass the time by alternately raising and discouraging their hopes. It was over an hour before a taxi finally drew up and stopped beside the pile of luggage, and Harold was not at all sure it hadn't arrived by accident. Tired and bewildered, he paid the two comedians what they asked, exorbitant though it seemed.

The taxi ride was through miles of ruined buildings, and at the railway station they discovered that there was no provision in the timetables of the S.N.C.F. for a train journey due south from Cherbourg to Mont-Saint-Michel. The best the station agent could offer was a local at noon that would take them southeast to Carentan. At Carentan they would have to change trains. They would have to change again at Coutances, and at Pontorson. At Pontorson there would be a bus that would take them the remaining five miles to Mont-Saint-Michel.

They checked their luggage at the station and went for a walk. Most of the buildings they saw were ugly and pock-marked by shellfire, but Cherbourg was French, it had sidewalk cafés, and the signs on the awnings read *Volailles & Gibier* and *Spontex* and *Tabac* and *Charcuterie*, and they looked at it as carefully as they would have looked at Paris. They had coffee at a sidewalk café. They inquired in half a dozen likely places and in none of them was there a public toilet. The people they asked could not even tell them where to go to find one. He went into a stationery store and bought a tiny pocket dictionary, to make sure they were using the right word; also a little notebook, to keep a record of their expenses in. Two blocks farther on, they came to a school and stood looking at the children in the schoolyard, so pale and thin-legged in their black smocks. Was it the war? If they had come to Europe before the war, would the children have had rosy cheeks?

He looked at his wrist watch and said: "I think we'd better not walk too far. We might not be able to find our way back to the station."

She saw a traveling iron in a shop window and they went in and bought it. They tried once more—they tried a tearoom with faded chintz curtains and little round tables. The woman at the cashier's desk got up and ushered Barbara to a lavatory in the rear. When they were out on the sidewalk again, she said: "You should have seen what I just saw!"

"What was it like?"

"It was filthy. And instead of a toilet there was a stinking hole in the floor. I couldn't believe it."

"I guess if you are a stranger, and homeless, you aren't supposed to go to the bathroom in France. Are you all right?"

"Yes, I'm perfectly all right. But it's so shocking. When you think that women with high heels have to go in there and stand or squat on two wooden boards. . . ."

They stopped to look in the window of a bookstore. It was full of copies of "Gone With the Wind" in French.

The local train was three coaches long. At the last minute, driven by his suspicions, he stepped out onto the platform, looked at the coach they were in, and saw the number 3. They were in third class, with second-class tickets. The fat, good-natured old robber who had charged them five hundred francs for putting them and their luggage in the wrong car was nowhere in sight, and so he moved the luggage himself. His head felt hollow from lack of sleep, and at the same time he was excited, and so full of nervous energy that nothing required any exertion.

The train began to move. Cherbourg was left behind.

The coach was not divided into compartments but open, like an American railway car. Looking out of the train window, they saw that the sky was now overcast. They saw hedgerows enclosing triangular meadows and orchards that were continually at a slant and spinning with the speed of the train. House after house had been shelled, had no windows or roof, had been abandoned; and then suddenly a village seemed to be intact. They saw poppies growing wild on the railroad embankment and could hardly believe their eyes. That wonderful intense color! They were so glad they had seen them. They saw a few more. Then they saw red poppies growing all through a field of wheat—or was it rye? They saw (as if seeing were an art and the end that everything is working toward) a barn with a sign painted on it: *Rasurel.*

Their eyes met, searching for some relief from looking so

intently at the outside world. "We're in France," he said, and
let his hand rest lightly in hers. The train came to a stop. They
looked for the name on the station: *Valognes.* They saw flower
beds along the station platform. Blue pansies. "*Pensées,*" it said
in the pocket dictionary. They saw a big blond man with blue
eyes and bright pink cheeks. They saw a nice motherly woman.
They saw a building with a sign on it: *Café de la Gare.* The station was new. In a moment this tiny world-in-itself was left
behind. He looked at his watch.

"What time do we change?" she asked, smothering a yawn.

"At two. It's now seventeen minutes of one."

"We'd better not fall asleep."

He felt his right side and was reassured; his wallet and their
passports were in his inside coat pocket, making a considerable
bulge. "Is it the way you remembered it?" he asked anxiously.
"I know there weren't any ruined buildings, but otherwise?"

"Yes. Except that we were in a car."

That other time, she was with her father and mother and
two brothers. They went to England first. They saw Anne
Hathaway's cottage, and Arlington Row in Bibury, and Oxford, and Tintern Abbey. And because she was sick in bed with
a cold, they left her alone in the hotel in London while they
went sight-seeing, and she had a wonderful afternoon. The
chambermaid brought her hot lemonade with whisky in it, and
it was the first time she had ever had any whisky, and the chambermaid took a liking for her and gave her a gold locket, which
she still had, at home in her blue leather jewel case.

After England, they crossed the Channel and spent two
weeks in Paris, and then they drove to Concarneau, which they
loved. In her snapshot album there was a picture of them all,
walking along a battlement at Carcassonne. That was in 1933.
The hem of her skirt came halfway to her ankles, and she was
twelve years old.

"What is Cinzano?" she asked.

"An apéritif. Or else it's an automobile."

. . . five, six, seven. Knowing that nothing had been left
behind, he nevertheless could not keep from insanely counting
the luggage. He looked out of the train window and saw roads
(leading where?) and fields. He saw more poppies, more or-

chards, a church steeple in the distance, a big white house. Could it be a château?

The yawn was contagious, as usual.

"Where do you suppose the Boultons are now?"

"Southampton," he said. "Or they might even be home. They didn't have far to go."

"It was funny our not speaking until the last day—"

"The last afternoon."

"And then discovering that we liked them so much. If only we'd discovered them sooner." Another yawn.

"I have their address, if we should go to England."

"But we're not."

She yawned again and again, helplessly.

They no longer had to look at each hedgerow, orchard, field, burning poppy, stone house, barn, steeple. The landscape, like any landscape seen from a train window, was repetitious. Just when he thought he had it all by heart, he saw one of Van Gogh's little bridges.

Her chin sank and sank. He drew her over against him and put her head on his shoulder, without waking her. His eyes met the blue eyes of the priest across the aisle. The priest smiled. He asked the priest, in French, to tell him when they got to Carentan, and the priest promised to. Miles inland, with his eyes closed, he saw the gulls gliding and smelled salt water.

His eyelids felt gritty. He roused himself and then dozed off again, not daring to fall sound asleep because they had to change trains. He tried willing himself to stay awake, and when that didn't work, he tried various experiments, such as opening his eyes and shutting them for a few seconds and then opening them again immediately. The conductor came through the car examining tickets, and promised to tell him when the train got to Carentan. Though the conductor seemed to understand his French, how can you be sure, speaking in a foreign language, that people really have understood you? . . . The conductor did come to tell them, when the train was slowing down, on the outskirts of Carentan, but by that time the luggage was in a pile blocking the front of the coach, and they were standing beside it, ready to alight.

What should have been a station platform was, instead, a

long, long rock pile. Looking up and down it as the train drew to a stop he saw that one of his fears, at least, was justified: there were no porters. He jumped down and she handed him the lighter suitcases, but the two big ones she could not even lift. The other passengers tried to get by her, and then turned and went toward the other end of the coach—all except a red-headed man, who saw that they were in trouble and without saying a word took over, just as Harold was about to climb back on the train.

What a nice, kind, *human* face . . .

All around them, people were stepping from rock to rock, or leaping, and it was less like changing trains than like a catastrophe of some kind—like a shipwreck. The red-haired man swung the dufflebag down expertly and then jumped down from the train himself and hurried off before they could thank him. Until that moment it had not occurred to Harold to wonder how much time they would have between trains.

He stopped a man with a light straw suitcase. "Le train à Coutances?"

"Voie D!" the man shouted over his shoulder, and when they didn't understand, he pointed to the entrance to an underpass, far down the rock pile. "De ce côté-là."

"Oh my God!"

"Why aren't there any porters?" she asked, looking around. "There were porters in Cherbourg."

"I don't know!" he said, exasperated at her for being logical when they were faced with a crisis and action was what was called for. "We'll have to do it in stages." He picked up the big brown suitcase, and then, to balance it, two smaller ones. "You stay here and watch the rest of the luggage until I get back."

"Who is going to watch those?" she demanded, pointing at the suitcases he had just picked up. "What if somebody takes them while you are coming back for more?"

"We'll just have to hope they don't."

"I'm coming with you." She picked up two more suitcases.

"No, don't!" he exclaimed, furious at not being allowed to manage the crisis in his own way. "They're too heavy for you!"

"So are those too heavy for you."

Leaving the big white suitcase and the dufflebag (two thousand cigarettes, safety matches, soap, sanitary napkins, Kleenex,

razor blades, cold cream, cleaning fluid, lighter fluid, shoe polish, tea bags, penicillin, powdered coffee, cube sugar, etc.—a
four months' supply of all the things they had been told they
couldn't get in Europe so soon after the war) behind and un-
guarded, they stumbled along in the wake of the other passengers, some of whom were now running, and reached the
underpass at last, and went down into it and then up another
long flight of steps onto Track D, where their train was
waiting.

"How *can* they expect people to do this?" she exclaimed indignantly.

Track D was an ordinary station platform, not another rock
pile, and all up and down the train the doors of compartments
were slamming shut. "It's like a bad dream," he said.

He left her standing with the luggage beside a second-class
carriage and ran back down into the underpass, his footsteps
echoing against the cold concrete walls. When he emerged
onto Track A again, the train from Cherbourg was gone. Far
down the deserted rock pile he saw the big white suitcase and
the dufflebag; they hadn't been stolen. From that moment it
was not merely France he loved.

He swung the dufflebag onto his shoulder and picked up
the suitcase. It weighed a ton. The traveling iron, he thought.
And Christ knows what else . . . His heart was pounding,
and he had a stitch in his side. As he staggered up the steps of
the underpass out onto Track D again, he saw that she was the
only person left on the platform, beside the last open compartment door.

"Hurry!" she called. (As if he weren't!)

He thought surely the train would start without them, not
realizing that it was full of ardent excitable people who would
have thrown themselves in front of the engine if it had. They
leaned out of all the windows all up and down the train,
shouting encouragement to the American tourists, shouting to
the conductor and the brakeman that Monsieur was here,
finally, but still had to get the luggage on.

When the luggage had been stowed away in the overhead
racks, they sat trembling and exhausted and knee to knee with
six people who did not speak a word of English but whom
they could not under the circumstances regard as strangers. A

well-dressed woman with a little boy smiled at them over the child's head, and they loved her. They loved her little boy, too. Looking out of the train window, they saw the same triangular meadows and orchards as before, the same tall hedgerows, and poppies without number growing in the wheat.

"It was very nice of that man to hand the suitcases down to you," she said.

"Wasn't it."

"I don't know what we'd have done without him."

"I don't either."

"What an experience."

Conscious that by speaking English to each other they were separating themselves from the other people in the compartment, and not wanting to be separated from them, they lapsed into silence. He made himself stop counting the luggage. After a time, the man directly across from them—a farmer or a laborer, judging by his clothes and his big, misshapen, callused hands—took down a small cardboard suitcase. They saw that it contained a change of underwear, a clean shirt, a clean pair of socks, a loaf of bread, a sausage, and a bottle of red wine that had already been uncorked. The sausage was offered politely around the compartment and politely refused. With dignity the man began to eat his lunch.

"What time is it?" Barbara asked.

Harold showed her his watch. If only there were porters in the station in Coutances . . . He looked searchingly at the other faces in the compartment. He was in love with them all.

There were no porters in the railway station at Coutances, and the crisis had to be gone through all over again, but nothing is ever as bad the second time. The station platform was not torn up, and he did not wait for somebody to see that they were in difficulty; instead, he turned and asked for help and got it. As he shook hands with one person after another, looking into their intelligent French eyes and thanking them with all his heart, he began to feel as if an unlimited amount of kindness had been deposited somewhere to his account and he had only to draw on it. Coupled with this daring idea was an even more dangerous one: he was becoming convinced by what had happened to them that in France things are different, and people more the way one would like them to be.

At Pontorson he saw a baggage truck and helped himself to it, thinking that this time he had surely gone too far and an indignant station agent would come running out and make a scene. No one paid any attention to him. The bus parked in front of the station said *Le Mont-Saint-Michel* over the windshield but it was empty, and they discovered from a timetable posted on the wall nearby that it did not leave for an hour and a half. He looked at her drawn, white face and then walked out into the middle of the station plaza in search of a taxi. The square was deserted. For a moment he did not know what to do. Then he saw a bus approaching and hailed it. The bus came to a stop in front of him, and he saw the letters *St. Servan–St. Malo* and that there were no passengers.

"Nous cherchons un hôtel," he said when the driver put his head close to the open window. "Nous avons beaucoup de bagages, et il n'y a pas de taxi. . . . Ma femme est malade," he lied, out of desperation, and then corrected it in favor of the truth. "Elle est très fatiguée. Nous désirons—"

The door swung open invitingly and he hopped in. The big bus made a complete turn in the middle of the square and came to a stop in front of the pile of luggage. He jumped out and ran into the station and found Barbara, and they got in the bus, which went racing through the very narrow, curving streets, at what seemed like sixty miles an hour, and stopped in front of a small hotel. The driver refused to take any money, shook hands, and drove on.

Harold took the precaution of looking the hotel up in the Guide Michelin. "Simple mais assez confortable," it said. He stuffed the Michelin back in his raincoat pocket.

The hotel was old and dark and it smelled of roasting coffee beans. The concierge led them up a flight of stairs and around a corner, to a room with windows looking out on the street. The room was vast. So was the double bed. So was the adjoining bathroom. There was no difficulty about hot water. The concierge took their passports and went off down the hall.

"Whenever I close my eyes I see houses without any roofs," he said.

"So do I."

"And church steeples." He loosened his tie and sat down to take off his shoes. "And Cinzano signs."

The automatic images fell on top of one another, as though they were being dealt like playing cards.

"There's something queer about this bed," she said. "Feel it."

"I don't have to. I can see from here. I don't think we'll have any trouble sleeping, though."

"No."

"The way I feel, I could sleep hanging from a hook."

While she was undressing, he went into the bathroom and turned on both faucets. Above the sound of the plunging water, he heard her saying something to him from the adjoining room. What she said was, she was glad they hadn't gone on to Mont-Saint-Michel.

"I am too," he called back. "I don't think I could bear it. If I saw something beautiful right now, I'd burst into tears. The only thing in the world that appeals to me is a hot bath."

The waitress was at the foot of the stairs when they came down, an hour later. "Vous désirez un apéritif, monsieur-dame?"

She hadn't the slightest objection to their sitting at one of the tables outdoors, in front of the hotel, and before they settled down, he raced back upstairs and got the camera and took Barbara's picture. He managed to get in also the furled blue and white striped umbrella, the portable green fence with geraniums and salvia growing in flower boxes along the top and bottom, and the blue morning-glories climbing on strings beside the hotel door.

"Quel apéritif?" demanded the waitress, when the camera had been put away. Finding that they didn't know, because they had had no experience in the matter, she took it upon herself to begin their education. She returned with two glasses and six bottles on a big painted tin tray, and let them try one apéritif after another, and, when they had made their decision, urged them to have the seven-course dinner rather than the five; the seven-course dinner began with écrevisses.

"Ecrevisses" turned out to be tiny crawfish, fried, with tartar sauce. There were only two other guests in the dining room, a man and a woman who spoke in such low tones and were so absorbed in each other that it was quite clear to anyone who had ever seen a French movie that they were lovers.

As the waitress changed their plates for the fourth time,

Barbara said: "Wonderful food!" The color had come back
into her face.

"Wonderful wine," Harold said, and asked the waitress what
it was that they were drinking. The wine was Algerian and had
no name, so he couldn't write it down in his little notebook.

When they went up to their room, the images started coming
once more. Their eyelids ached. They felt strung on wires.

The street outside their window was as quiet as a cemetery.
They undressed and sank sighing into the enormous bed, so
like a mother to them in their need of rest.

After ten o'clock there was no sound in the little hotel, and no
traffic in the street. The night trucks passed by a different
route.

At midnight it rained. Between three and four in the morning, the sky cleared and there were stars. The wind was off the
sea. The air was fresh. A night bird sang.

The sleepers knew nothing whatever about any of this. One
minute they were dropping off to sleep and the next they
heard shouting and opened their eyes to broad daylight. When
they sat up in bed they saw that the street was full of people,
walking or riding bicycles. The women all wore shapeless long
black cotton dresses. An old woman went by, leading her cow.
Chickens and geese. Goats. The shops were all open. A man
with a vegetable cart was shouting that his string beans were
tender and his melons ripe.

"It's like being in the front row at the theater," she said.
"How do you feel?"

"Wonderful."

"So do I. Do you think if I pressed this button anything
would happen?"

"You mean like breakfast?"

She nodded.

"Try it," he said with a yawn.

Five minutes later there was a knock at the door and the
waitress came in with a breakfast tray. "Bonjour, monsieur-
dame."

"Bonjour, mademoiselle," he said.

"Avez-vous bien dormi?"

"Oui, merci. Très bien. Et vous?"

"Moi aussi."

"Little goat, bleat. Little table, appear," Harold said as the door closed after her. "Have some coffee."

After breakfast, they got up and dressed. She packed while he was downstairs paying the bill. The concierge called a taxi for them.

"I hate to leave that little hotel," she said, looking back through the rear window as they drove off.

"I didn't mean for the taxi to come quite so soon," he said. "I was hoping we could explore the village first."

But he was relieved that they were on their way again. Six days on shipboard had made him hungry for movement. They rode through the flat countryside with their faces pressed to the car windows.

"Just look at that woodpile!"

"Look how the orchard is laid out."

"Never mind the orchard, look at the house!"

"Look at the vegetable garden."

Look, look. . . .

Though they thought they knew what to expect, at their first glimpse of the medieval abbey they both cried out in surprise. Rising above the salt marshes and the sand flats, it hung, dreamlike, mysterious, ethereal. "Le Mont-Saint-Michel," the driver said respectfully. As the taxi brought them nearer, it changed; the various parts dissolved their connection with one another in order to form new connections. The last connection of all was with the twentieth century. There were nine chartered sight-seeing buses outside the medieval walls, and the approach to the abbey was lined on both sides of the street with hotels, restaurants, and souvenir shops.

The concierge of the Hôtel Mère Poulard was not put out with them for arriving a day late. Their room was one flight up, and they tried not to see the curtains, which were a large patterned design of flowers in the most frightful colors. Without even opening their suitcases, they started up the winding street of stairs. Mermaid voices sang to them from the doorways of the open-fronted shops ("Monsieur-dame . . . monsieur-dame . . .") and it was hard not to stop and look at everything, because everything was for sale. He bought two tickets for the conducted tour of the abbey, and they stood a little to one side, waiting for the tour to begin.

"Did you ask for a guide who speaks English?"

He shook his head.

"Why not?"

"I don't think there are any," he said, arguing by analogy from the fact that there were no porters in the railway stations.

"The other time, we always had a guide who spoke English."

"I know, but that was before the war."

"You could ask them if there is one."

But he was reluctant to ask. Instead, he studied the uniformed guides, trying to make out from their faces if they spoke English. At last he went up to the ticket booth and the ticket seller informed him disapprovingly—rather as if he had asked if the abbey was for sale—that the guides spoke only French.

It was their first conducted tour and they tried very hard to understand what the guide said, but names, dates, and facts ran together, and sometimes they had to fall back on enjoying what their eyes saw as they went from room to room. What they saw—stone carvings, stone pillars, vaulting, and archways —seemed softened, simplified, and eroded not only by time but also by the thousands and thousands of human eyes that had looked at it. But in the end, reality failed them. They felt that some substitution had been effected, and that this was not the real abbey. Or if it was, then something was gone from it, something that made all the difference, and they were looking at the empty shell.

They stood in front of the huge fireplace in the foyer of their hotel and watched the famous omelets being made. With their own omelet they had a green salad and a bottle of white wine, which was half a bottle too much. Half drunk, they staggered upstairs to their room and fell asleep in the room with the frightful curtains, to the sound of the omelet whisk. When they woke, the afternoon was half gone. Lying in one another's arms, dreamy and drained, they heard a strange new sound, and sat up and saw through the open casements the sea come rushing in. Within twenty minutes all the surrounding land but the causeway by which they had come from Pontorson was under water. They waited for that too to be covered, but this wonderful natural effect, so often described by earlier travelers, the tide at Mont-Saint-Michel, had been tampered with. The island was not an island any more; the water did not cover the tops of the sight-seeing buses; it did not even cover their hubcaps.

But another tide rising made them turn away from the window. All afternoon, while they were making love and afterward, whether they were awake or asleep, the omelet whisk kept beating and the human tide came and went under their window: tourists from Belgium, tourists from Denmark and Sweden and Switzerland, tourists from Holland, Breton tourists in embroidered velvet costumes, tourists from all over France.

In the evening, they dressed and went downstairs. The omelet cook was again making omelets in front of the roaring wood fire. Harold found out from the concierge that there was no provision in the timetable of the S.N.C.F. for a quick, easy journey by train from Mont-Saint-Michel to Cap Finisterre. They would have to go to Brest, which they had no desire to see, changing trains a number of times along the way. At Brest they could take a bus or a local train to Concarneau.

They stepped out of the hotel into a surprising silence. The cobblestone street was empty. The chartered buses were all gone.

Turning their back on the street of stairs, they followed the upward-winding dirt paths, and discovered the little gardens, here, there, and everywhere. They stood looking down on the salt marshes and the sandbars. Above them the medieval abbey hung dreamlike and in the sky, and that was where they were also, they realized with surprise. The swallows did not try to sell them anything, and the sea air made them excited. Time had gone off with the sight-seeing buses, and they were free to look to their heart's content. Stone towers, slate roofs, half-timbered houses, cliffs of cut stone, thin Gothic windows and crenelated walls and flying buttresses, the rock cliffs dropping sheer into the sea and the wet sand mirroring the sky, cloud pinnacles that were changing color with the coming on of night, and the beautiful past, that cannot quite bear to go but stands here (as it does everywhere, but here especially) saying *Good-by, good-by*. . . .

Shortly before noon the next day, they returned to Pontorson by bus, left their luggage at the hotel, where their old room was happily waiting for them, and went off sight-seeing. The bus driver was demonically possessed. Dogs, chickens, old people, and children scattered at the sound of his horn. The people who got on at villages and crossroads kept the bus waiting while they delivered involved messages to the driver or greeted those who were getting off. Bicycles accumulated on the roof of the bus. Passengers stood jammed together in the aisles. On a cool, cloudy, Wednesday afternoon, the whole countryside had left home and was out enjoying the pleasures of travel.

St. Malo was disappointing. Each time they came to a gateway in the ramparts of the old town, they stopped and looked in. The view was always the same: a street of brand-new boxlike houses that were made of stone and would last forever. They took a motor launch across the harbor to Dinard, which seemed to be made up entirely of hotels and boarding houses, all shabby and in need of paint. The tide was far out, the sky was a leaden gray, the wind was raw. At Concarneau it would be colder still.

They bought postcards to prove to themselves later that they had actually been to Dinard, and tried to keep warm by walking. They soon gave up and took the launch back across the harbor. Something that should have happened had not happened; they had been told that Dinard was charming, and they had not been charmed by it, through no fault of theirs. And St. Malo was completely gone. There was nothing left that anybody would want to see. The excursion had not been a success. And yet, in a way, it had; they'd had a nice day. They'd enjoyed the bus ride and the boat ride and the people. They'd enjoyed just being in France.

They had the seven-course dinner again, and, lying in bed that night, they heard singing in the street below their window. (Who could it be? So sad . . .)

In the morning they explored the village. They read the

inscriptions in the little cemetery and, in an atmosphere of extreme cordiality, cashed a traveler's check at the mairie. They
stared in shop windows. A fire broke out that was like a fire in
a dream. Smoke came pouring out of a building; shopkeepers
stood in their doorways watching and made comments about
it, but did not try to help the two firemen who came running
with a hose cart and began to unreel the hose and attach it to
a hydrant in a manhole. Though they couldn't have been
quicker or more serious about their work, after twenty minutes
the hose was still limp. The whole village could have gone up
in flames, and for some strange reason it didn't. The smoke
subsided, and the shopkeepers withdrew into their shops. Barbara saw a cowhide purse with a shoulder strap in the window
of a leather shop, and when they reappeared a few minutes
later, she was wearing the purse and he was writing "purse—
1850 fr." in his financial diary.

They went back to the hotel and the waitress drew them
into the dining room, where she had arranged on an oak sideboard specimens of woodcarving, the hobby of her brother,
who had been wounded in the war and could not do steady
work. The rich Americans admired but did not buy his chef-
d'œuvre, the art-nouveau book ends. Instead, trying not to
see the disappointment in her eyes, they took the miniature
sabots (500 fr.), which would do nicely for a present when they
got back home and meanwhile take up very little room in their
luggage. The concierge inquired about their morning and they
told him about the fire. A sliding panel in the wall at the foot
of the stairs slid open. The cook and the kitchenmaid were also
interested.

Upstairs in their room, he said: "I don't suppose we ought
to stay here when there are a thousand places in France that
are more interesting."

"I could stay here the rest of my life," Barbara said.

They did nothing about leaving. They squandered the
whole rest of the day, walking and looking at things. As for
their journey to Brittany, they would do better to go inland,
the concierge said; at Rennes, for example, they could get an
express train from Paris that would take them straight through
to Brest.

The next morning, they closed their suitcases regretfully and

paid the bill (surprisingly large) and said good-by to the waitress, the chambermaid, the cook, and the kitchenmaid, all of
whom they had grown fond of. Their luggage went by pushcart to the railway station, and they followed on foot, with the
concierge. Out of affection and because he was sorry to see
them go, the concierge was keeping them company as long as
possible, and where else would they find a concierge like him?
    When they got off the train in Rennes, the weather had
grown colder. There was no train for Brest until the next day,
and so they walked half a block to the Hôtel du Guesclin et
Terminus. Rennes was an ugly industrial city, and they wished
they were in Pontorson. An obliging waiter in the restaurant
where they ate dinner gave Barbara the recipe for Palourdes
farcies. "Clams, onions, garlic, parsley," Harold wrote in his
financial diary. It was raining when they woke the next
morning. Their hotel room was small and cramped and a peculiar shape. Only a blind person could have hung those curtains with that wallpaper. They could hardly move for their
luggage, which they hated the sight of. What pleasure could
they possibly have at the seashore in this weather? They decided to go farther inland, to Le Mans, in the hope that it
would be warmer. When they got there, they could decide
whether to take the train to Brest or one going in the opposite
direction, to Paris. But they had not planned to be in Paris
until September, and perhaps they would like Le Mans enough
to stay there a week. They had arranged to spend the two
weeks after that as paying guests at a château in Touraine.
    Late that same afternoon, pale and tired after two train
journeys—Le Mans was hideous—they stood in the lobby of
the Hôtel Univers in Tours, watching the profile of the concierge, who was telephoning for them and committed heart
and soul to their cause. With the door of the phone booth
closed, they couldn't hear what he said to the long-distance
operator, but they could tell instantly by the way he shed his
mask of indifference that he was talking to someone at the
château. They watched his eyes, his expression, his sallow
French face, for clues.
    The call was brief. The concierge put the receiver back on its
hook and, turning, pushed open the glass door. "I talked to
Mme Viénot herself," he said. "It's all right for you to come."

"Thank God," Harold said. "Now we can relax."

Taking Barbara's arm above the elbow, he guided her across the lobby to the street door. Outside, a white-gloved policeman directed the flow of Saturday-afternoon bicycle traffic around the orange and green flower beds in the middle of a busy intersection.

"I think I've seen that building before," she said, meaning the Hôtel de Ville, directly across the street. He consulted a green Michelin guide to the château country that he had bought in the railway station in Le Mans. The Hôtel de Ville was not starred, and the tricolor flags that hung in clusters along the façade, between caryatids, were old and faded. This was true everywhere they went, and it had begun to trouble him. In the paintings they were always vivid and fresh. Was something not here that used to be here and everywhere in France? Had they come too late?

The cathedral (**) and the Place Plumereau (*) and the Maison de Tristan (*) all appeared to be at a considerable distance, and since it was late in the afternoon and they did not want to walk far, they decided in favor of the leafy avenue de Grammont, which was wide enough to accommodate not only an inner avenue of trees but also a double row of wooden booths hemmed in by traffic and the streetcar tracks. Unable to stop looking, they stared at the patrons of sidewalk cafés and stood in front of shop windows. What were "rillettes de Tours"? Should they buy a jar?

Eventually they crossed over into the middle of the street and moved from booth to booth, conscientiously examining pots and pans, pink rayon underwear, dress materials, sweaters, scarves, suspenders, aprons, packets of pins and needles, buttons, thread, women's hats, men's haberdashery, knitted bathing suits, toys, stationery, romantic and erotic novels, candy, shoes, fake jewelry, machine-made objets d'art, the dreadful dead-end of the Industrial Revolution, all so discouraging to the acquisitive eye that cannot keep from looking, so exhausting to the snobbish mind that, like a machine itself, rejects and rejects and rejects and rejects.

With their heads aching from all they had looked at, they found their way back to the hotel. Tours was very old, and they had expected to like it very much. They had not expected it to be a big modern commercial city, and they were disappointed. But that evening they were given a second chance. They went for a walk after dinner and came upon a street fair all lit up with festoons of electric lights and ready to do business with the wide-eyed and the young, who for one reason and another (the evening was chilly, the franc not yet stabilized) had stayed away. There was only a handful of people walking up and down the dirt avenues, and they didn't seem eager to part with their money. The ticking lotto wheels stopped time after time on the lucky number, the roulette paid double, but no one carried off a sexy lamp, a genuine oriental rug, a kewpie doll. In this twilight of innocence, nobody believed enough in his own future to patronize the fortune-telling machine. No sportif character drew a bead on the plastic ducks in the shooting gallery. The festooned light bulbs were noticeably small and dim. With no takers, the familiar enticements were revealed in the light of their true age—tired, old, worn out at last.

"It makes me feel bad," Harold said. He loved carnivals. "They can't keep going much longer, if it's always like this."

He stepped up to a booth, bought two tickets for the little racing cars that bump, and entered the sum of twenty francs in his financial diary. Only one other car had somebody in it—a young man and his girl. When Harold and Barbara bumped into them, the young man wheeled around and came at them again with so much momentum that it made their heads jerk. He was smiling unpleasantly. It crossed Harold's mind that there was something here that was not like the French movies —that they had been bumped too hard because they were Americans. He saw the young man preparing to come at them again, and steered his own car in such a way that they couldn't be reached. But unless you did bump somebody, the little cars were not exciting. And all the empty ones, evoking a gaiety that ought to have been here and wasn't, reminded them of their isolation as tourists in a country they could look at but never really know, the way they knew America. They bought a bag of white taffy, which turned out to be inedible, and then stood looking at the merry-go-round, the Ferris wheel, the flying swings, the whip—all of them empty and revolving inanely up, down, and around. The carnival occupied a good-sized city block, and in its own blighted way it was beautiful.

He said soberly: "It's as if the secret of perpetual motion that my Grandmother Mitchell was always talking about had been discovered at last, and nobody cared."

But somebody did care, somebody was enjoying himself—a little French boy, wide awake and on his own at an hour when, in America at least, it is generally agreed that children should be asleep in their beds. Since he did not have to pay for his pleasure, they assumed that he was the child of one of the concessionaires. They tried to make friends with him and failed: he had no need of friends. Liberty was what he cared about— Liberty and Vertigo. He climbed on the merry-go-round and in a moment or two the baroque animals began to move with a slow, dreamlike, plunging gait. The little boy sat astride a unicorn. He rose in the stirrups and reached out with a long pole for the stuffed rabbit that dangled just out of reach. Time after time, trying valiantly, he was swept by it.

"I'd take *him*," Barbara said wistfully.

"So would I, but he's not to be had, for love or money."

The merry-go-round went faster and faster, the calliope showed to what extremes music can go, and eventually, in accordance with the mysterious law that says: *Whatever you want with your whole heart and soul you can have*, the stuffed rabbit was swept from its hook (the little boy received a prize—a genuine ruby ring—and ran off in search of something new) and the Americans turned away, still childless.

She asked for a five-franc piece to put in the fortunetelling machine. The machine whirred initially and produced through a slot a small piece of cardboard that read: "En apparence tout va bien pour vous, mais ne soyez pas trop confiant; l'adversité est en train de venir. Les morts, les séparations, sont indiqués. Dans les procès vous seriez en perte. La maladie est sérieuse." She turned and discovered the little French boy at her elbow. Curiosity had fetched him. She showed him the fortune and he read it. His brown eyes looked up at her seriously, as if trying to decide what effect these deaths, separations, and lawsuits would have on her character. She asked him if he would like to keep it and he shook his head. She tucked the cardboard in her purse.

"C'est votre frère?" the little boy asked, indicating Harold.

"Non," she said, smiling, "il est mon mari."

His glance shifted to the bag of candy. When she put it into his hands, he said politely that he couldn't accept it. But he did, with urging. He took it and thanked her and then ran off. They stood watching while a bearded man, the keeper of a roulette wheel, detained him. The little boy listened intently (to what? a joke? a riddle?) and then he suddenly realized what was happening to him and escaped.

"I think he all but fell in love with you," Harold said. "If he'd been a little older or a little younger, he would have."

"He fell in love with the candy," Barbara said.

They made one more circuit of the fair. The carnival people had lost the look of wickedness. Their talent for not putting down roots anywhere, and for not giving the right change, and for sleeping with one eye open, their sexual promiscuity, their tattooed hearts, flowers, mermaids, anchors, and mottoes, their devout belief that all life is meaningless—all this had not been enough to sustain them in the face of too much history. They were discouraged and ill-fed and worried, like everybody else.

He bought some cotton candy. Barbara took two or three licks and then handed it to him. Pink, oversweet, and hairy, it hadn't changed; it was just the way he remembered it from his childhood. Wisps clung to his cheeks. He couldn't finish it. He got out his handkerchief and wiped his chin. "Shall we go?" he asked.

They started walking toward the exit. The whole failing enterprise was as elegiac as a summer resort out of season. They looked around one last time for the little French boy but he had vanished. As they passed the gypsy fortuneteller's tent, Harold felt a slight pressure on his coat sleeve. "All right," he said. "If you want to."

"Just this once," she said apologetically.

He disliked having his fortune told.

The gypsy fortuneteller sat darning her stocking by the light of a kerosene lamp. It turned out that she had lived in Chicago and spoke English. She asked Barbara for the date of her birth and then, nodding, said "Virgo." She looked inquiringly at Harold. "Scorpio," he said.

The gypsy fortuneteller looked in her crystal ball and saw that he was lying. He was Leo. Raising her eyes, she saw that he had kept his hands in his pockets.

She passed her thin brown hand over the crystal ball twice and saw that there was a shadow across their lives but it was not permanent, like the shadows she was used to finding. No blackened chimneys, no years and years of wandering, no loved one vanished forever into a barbed-wire enclosure, no savings stolen, no letters returned unopened and stamped *Whereabouts Unknown*. Whatever the trouble was, in five or six years it would clear up.

She took Barbara Rhodes's hand and opened the fingers (beautiful hand) and in the lines of the palm discovered a sea voyage, a visitor, popularity and entertainment, malice she didn't expect, and a triumph that was sure to come true.

Chapter 2

THE Americans were last in line at the gate, because of their luggage, and as the line moved forward, he picked up a big suitcase in each hand and wondered which of the half-dozen women in black waiting outside the barrier would turn out to be Mme Viénot. And why was there no car?

The station agent took their tickets gravely from between Harold's teeth, and as he walked through the gate he saw that the street was empty. He went back for the dufflebag and another suitcase. When the luggage was all outside they stood and waited.

The sign on the roof of the tiny two-room station said: *Brenodville-sur-Euphrone.* The station itself had as yet no doors, windows, or clock, and it smelled of damp plaster. The station platform was cluttered with bags of cement and piled yellow bricks. Facing the new station, on the other side of the tracks, was a wooden shelter with a bench and three travel posters: the Côte D'Azur (a sailboat) and Burgundy (a glass of red wine) and Auvergne (a rocky gorge). Back of the shelter a farmyard, with the upper story of the barn full of cordwood and the lower story stuffed with hay, served as a poster for Touraine.

They waited for five minutes by his wrist watch, and then he went back inside and consulted the station agent, who said that the Château Beaumesnil was only two and a half kilometers outside the village and they could easily walk there. But not with the luggage, Harold pointed out. No, the station agent agreed, not with their luggage.

There was no telephone in the station and so, leaving the dufflebag and the suitcases on the sidewalk where they could keep an eye on them, they walked across the cobblestone street to the café. He explained their situation to the four men sitting at a table on the café terrace, and learned that there was no telephone here either. One of the men called out to the proprietress, who appeared from within, and said that if Monsieur would walk in to the village, he would find several shops open, and from one of these he could telephone to the château.

Standing on the sidewalk beside the luggage, Barbara followed Harold with her eyes until the street curved off to the left and he disappeared between two slate-roofed stone houses. He was gone for a long, long time. Just as she was beginning to wonder if she would ever see him again, she heard the rattle of an approaching vehicle—a noisy old truck that wheezed and shook and, to her surprise, turned into the station platform at the last minute and drew to a stop beside her. The cab door swung open and Harold hopped out.

In the driver's seat was a middle-aged man who looked like a farmer and had beautiful blue eyes.

"I was beginning to worry about you," she said.

"This is M. Fleury. What a time I've had!"

Sitting in the back of the truck, on the two largest suitcases, they were driven through the village and out into open country. The grain was turning yellow in the fields, and they saw poppies growing along the roadside. The dirt road was rough and full of potholes, and they had to keep turning their faces away to keep from breathing in the dust.

"This is too far to walk even without the luggage," he said.

"I'll have to wash my hair," she said. "But it's beautiful, isn't it?"

Before long they had a glimpse of the château, across the fields. The trees hid it from view. Then they turned in, between two gate posts, and drove up a long curving cinder drive, and saw the house again, much closer now. It was of white limestone, with tall French windows and a steep slate roof. Across the front was a raised terrace with a low box hedge and a stone balustrade. To the right of the house there was an enormous Lebanon cedar, whose branches fell like dark-green waves, and a high brick wall with ornamental iron gates. To their eyes, accustomed to foundation planting and wisteria or rose trellises, the façade looked a little bare and new. The truck went through the gate and into a courtyard and stopped. For a moment they were aware of how much racket the engine made, and then M. Fleury turned the ignition off to save gasoline, and after that it was the silence they heard. They sat waiting with their eyes on the house and finally a door burst open and a small, thin, black-haired woman came hurrying out. She stopped a few feet from the truck and nodded bleakly to M. Fleury, who touched his beret but said nothing. We must look very strange sitting in the back of the truck with our luggage crammed in around us, Harold thought. But on the other hand, it was rather strange that there was no one at the station to meet them.

They had no way of knowing who the woman was, but she must know who they were, and so they waited uneasily for her to speak. Her eyes moved from them to the fresh Cunard Line stickers on their suitcases. "Yes?" she said coldly in English. "You wanted something?"

"Mme Viénot?" Barbara asked timidly.

The woman clapped her hand to her forehead. "Mme Rhodes! Do forgive me! I thought— Oh how extraordinary! I thought you were middle-aged!"

This idea fortunately struck all three of them as comical. Harold jumped down from the truck and then turned and helped Barbara down. Mme Viénot shook hands with them and, still amazed, still amused at her extraordinary mistake, said: "I cannot imagine what you must think of me. . . . We were just starting to go to the station to meet you. M. Carrère very kindly offered his car. The Bentley would have been more comfortable, perhaps, but you seem to have managed very well by yourselves." She smiled at the camion.

"We thought of telephoning," Barbara said, "but there was no telephone in the station, and at the Café de la Gare they told us—"

"We can't use the telephone after eleven o'clock on Sundays," Mme Viénot interrupted. "The service is cut off. So even if you had tried to reach us by telephone, you couldn't have." She was still smiling, but they saw that she was taking them in—their faces, their American clothes, the gray dust they were powdered with as a result of their ride in the open truck.

"The stationmaster said we could walk," Barbara said, "but we had the suitcases, so I stayed with them, at the station, and my husband walked into the village and found a store that was open, a fruit and vegetable store. And a very nice woman—"

"Mme Michot. She's a great gossip and takes a keen interest in my guests. I cannot imagine why."

"—told us that M. Fleury had a truck," Barbara finished.

Mme Viénot turned and called out to a servant girl who was watching them from a first-floor window to come and take the suitcases that the two men were lifting from the back of the truck. "So you found M. Fleury and he brought you here. . . . M. Fleury is an old friend of our family. You couldn't have come under better auspices."

Harold tried to prevent the servant girl from carrying the two heaviest suitcases, but she resisted so stubbornly that he let go of the handles and stepped back and with a troubled expression on his face watched her stagger off to the house. They were much too heavy for her, but probably in an old country like France, with its own ideas of chivalry and of the physical strength and usefulness of women, that didn't matter as much as who should and who shouldn't be carrying suitcases.

"You are tired from your journey?" Mme Viénot asked.

"Oh, no," Barbara said. "It was beautiful all the way."

She looked around at the courtyard and then through the open gateway at the patchwork of small green and yellow fields in the distance. Taking her courage in both hands, she murmured: "Si jolie!"

"You think so?" Mme Viénot murmured politely, but in English. A man might perhaps not have noticed it. Barbara's next remark was in English. When Harold started to pay M. Fleury, Mme Viénot exclaimed: "Oh dear, I'm afraid you don't understand our currency, M. Rhodes. That's much too much. You will embarrass M. Fleury. Here, let me do it." She took the bank notes out of his hands and settled with M. Fleury herself.

M. Fleury shook hands all around, and smiled at the Americans with his gentian-blue eyes as they tried to convey their gratitude. They were reluctant to let him go. In a country where, contrary to what they had been told, no one seemed to speak English, he had understood their French. He had been their friend, for nearly an hour. Instinct told them they were not going to manage half so well without him.

The engine had to be cranked five or six times before it caught, and M. Fleury ran around to the driver's seat and adjusted the spark.

"I never hear the sound of a motor in the courtyard without feeling afraid," Mme Viénot said.

They looked at her inquiringly.

"I think the Germans have come back."

"They were here in this house?" Barbara asked.

"We had them all through the war."

The Americans turned and looked up at the blank windows. The war had left no trace that a stranger could see. The courtyard and the white château were at that moment as peaceful and still as a landscape in a mirror.

"It looks as if it had never been any other way than the way it is now," Harold said.

"The officers were quartered in the house, and the soldiers in the outbuildings. I cannot say that we enjoyed them, but they were correct. 'Kein Barbar,' they kept telling us—'We are not barbarians.' And fancy, they expected my girls to dance with them!"

Mme Viénot waited rather longer than necessary for the irony to be appreciated, and then with a hissing intake of breath she said: "It's exciting to be in the clutches of the tiger . . . and to know that you are quite helpless."

The truck started up with a roar, and shot through the gateway. They stood watching until it disappeared from sight. The silence flooded back into the courtyard.

"So delicious, your arriving with M. Fleury," Mme Viénot said.

He searched through his coat pockets for a pencil and the little notebook, wherein the crises were all recorded: "Rennes départ 7ʰ50 Le Mans 10ʰ20, départ 11ʰ02," etc. Also the money paid out for laundry, hotel rooms, meals in restaurants, and conducted tours. This was a mistake, he thought. We shouldn't have come here. . . . He wrote: "100 fr transportation Brenodville-sur-Euphrone to chateau" and put the pencil and notebook back in his breast pocket.

Mme Viénot was looking at him with her head cocked to one side, frankly amused. "I wonder what it was that made me decide you were middle-aged," she said. "Why, you're *babies!*"

He started to shoulder the dufflebag and she said: "Don't bother with the luggage. Thérèse will see to it." Linking her arm cozily through Barbara's, she led them into the house by the back door and along a passageway to the stairs.

When they reached the second-floor landing, the Americans glanced expectantly down a long hallway that went right through the center of the house, and then saw that Mme Viénot had continued on up the stairs. She threw open the door on the left in the square hall at the head of the stairs and said: "My daughter's room. I think you'll find it comfortable."

Harold waited for Barbara to exclaim "How lovely!" and instead she drew off her black suede gloves. He went to the window and looked out. Their room was on the front of the château and overlooked the park. The ceiling sloped down on that side, because of the roof. The wallpaper was black and white on a particularly beautiful shade of dark red, and not like any wallpaper he had ever seen.

"Sabine is in Paris now," Mme Viénot said. "She's an artist. She does fashion drawings for the magazine *La Femme Elégante*. You are familiar with it? . . . It's like your *Vogue* and *Harper's Bazaar*, I believe. . . . We dine at one thirty on Sunday. That won't hurry you?"

Barbara shook her head.

"If you want anything, call me," Mme Viénot said, and closed the door behind her.

There was a light knock almost immediately, and thinking that Mme Viénot had come back to tell them something, Barbara called "Come in," but it was not Mme Viénot, it was the blond servant girl with the two heaviest suitcases. As she set them down in the middle of the room, Barbara said "Merci," and the girl smiled at her. She came back three more times, with the rest of the luggage, and the last time, just before she turned away, she allowed her gaze to linger on the two Americans for a second. She seemed to be expecting them to understand something, and to be slightly at a loss when they didn't.

"Should we have tipped her?" Barbara asked, when they were alone again.

"I don't think so. The *service* is probably *compris*," Harold said, partly because he was never willing to believe that the simplest explanation is the right one, and partly because he was confused in his mind about the ethics of tipping and felt that, fundamentally, it was impolite. If he were a servant, he would resent it; and refuse the tip to show that he was not a servant. So he alternated: he didn't tip when he should have and then, worried by this, he overtipped the next time.

"I should have told her that we have some nylon stockings for her," Barbara said.

"Or if it isn't, I'll do something about it when we leave," he said. "It's too bad, though, about M. Fleury. After those robbers in Cherbourg it would have been a pleasure to overtip him—if four hundred francs was overtipping, which I doubt. She was probably worrying about herself, not us." Trying one key after another from Barbara's key ring with the rabbit's foot attached to it, he found the one that opened the big brown suitcase. "What about the others?" he asked, snapping the catches.

"Maybe we'll run into him in the village," Barbara said. "Just that one and the dufflebag." She took the combs out of her hair, which then fell to her shoulders. "The rest can wait."

He carried the dufflebag into the bathroom, and she changed from her suit into a wool dressing gown, and then began transferring the contents of the large brown suitcase, a pile at a time, to the beds, the round table in the center of the room, and the armoire. She was pleased with their room. After the violent curtains and queer shapes of the hotel rooms of the past week, here was a place they could settle down in peacefully and happily. An infallible taste had been at work, and the result was like a wax impression of one of those days when she woke lighthearted, knowing that this was going to be a good day all day long—that whatever she had to do would be done quickly and easily; that the telephone wouldn't ring and ring; that dishes wouldn't slip through her nerveless hands and break; that it wouldn't be necessary to search through the accumulation of unanswered letters for some reassurance that wasn't there, or to ask Harold if he loved her.

Standing in the bathroom door, with his shirt unbuttoned and his necktie trailing from one hand, he surveyed the red room and then said: "It couldn't be handsomer."

"It's cold," she said. "I noticed it downstairs. The whole house is cold."

He glanced at the fireplace. The ornamental brass shield over the opening was held in place with screws and it looked permanent. There was no basket of wood and kindling on the hearth. In her mind the present often extended its sphere of influence until it obscured the past and denied that there was going to be any future. When she was cold, when she was sad, she was convinced that she would always be sad or cold and there was no use doing anything about it; all the sweaters and coats and eiderdown comforters and optimism in the world would not help, and all she wanted him to do was agree that they would not help. Unfortunately, she could not get him to agree. It was a basic difference of opinion. He always tried to do something. His nature required that there be something practical you could do, even though he knew by experience that it took some small act of magic, some demonstration of confidence or proof of love, to make her take heart, to make her feel warm again.

"Why don't you take a hot bath? You've got time if you hurry," he said, and turned to the bookcase. Because there were times when he was too tired, or just couldn't produce any proof of love, or when he felt a deep disinclination to play the magician. At other times, nothing was too much trouble or exhausted his strength and patience.

His finger, in the pursuit of titles, stopped at Shaw and Wells, in English; at Charles Morgan and Elizabeth Goudge, in French, and so inconsistent from the point of view of literary taste with the first two; at *La Mare au Diable*, which he had read in high school and could no longer remember anything about; at *Le Grand Meaulnes*, which he remembered hazily. The letters of Mme de Sévigné (in three small volumes) he had always meant to read some time. The *Fables* of La Fontaine, and the *Contes*, which were said to be indecent. A book of children's songs, with illustrations by Boutet de Monvel. A book of the religious meditations of someone that he, raised a Presbyterian, had never heard of. He said: "Say, whose books *are* these, do you suppose?" and she answered from the bathroom in a shocked voice: "Why, there's no hot water!"

"Let it run," he called back.

"There's no water to let run."

He went into the bathroom and tried both faucets of the immense tub. Nothing came out of them, not even air.

"It's the war," he said.

"I don't see how we can stay here two weeks without a bath," Barbara said.

He moved over to the washstand. There the cold-water faucet worked splendidly but not the faucet marked *chaud.*

"She said in her letter 'a room with a bath.' If this is what she means, I don't think it was at all honest of her."

"Mmmm."

"Aud I don't see any toilet."

They looked all around the room, slowly and carefully. There was one door they hadn't opened. He opened it confidently, and they found themselves staring into a shallow clothes closet with three wire coat hangers on the metal rod. They both laughed.

"In a house this size there's bound to be a toilet somewhere," he said, by no means convinced that this was true.

They washed simultaneously at the washbowl, and then he put on a clean shirt and went out into the hall. He listened at the head of the stairs. The house was steeped in silence. He put his head close to the paneling of the door directly opposite theirs, heard nothing, and placed his hand on the knob. The door swung open cautiously upon a small lumber room under the eaves. In the dim light he made out discarded furniture, books, boxes, pictures, china, bedclothes, luggage, a rowing machine, a tin bidet, a large steel engraving of the courtyard and Grand Staircase of the château of Blois. He closed the door softly, struck with how little difference there is in the things people all over the world cannot bring themselves to throw away.

The remaining door of the third-floor hall revealed a corridor, two steps down and uncarpeted. The fresh paint and clean wallpaper ended here, and it seemed unlikely that their toilet would be in this wing of the house, which had an air of disuse, of decay, of being a place that outsiders should not wander into. The four dirty bull's-eye windows looked out on the back wing of the château. There were doors all along the corridor, but spaced too far apart to suggest the object of his search, and at the end the corridor branched right and left, with more doors that it might be embarrassing to open at this moment. He opened one of them and saw a brass bed, made up, a painted dresser, a commode, a rag rug on the painted floor, a single straight chair. He had ended up in the servants' quarters.

Retracing his steps, he listened again at the head of the stairs. The house was as still as houses only are on Sunday. When he opened the door of their room, Barbara had changed back into her traveling suit and was standing in front of the low dresser. "I couldn't find it," he said.

"Probably it's on the second floor." She leaned toward the mirror. She was having difficulty with the clasp of her pearls. "But it's funny she didn't tell us."

"She has dyed hair," he said.

"Sh-h-h!"

"What for?"

"There may be someone in the room across the hall."

"I looked. It's full of old junk."

She stared at him in the mirror. "Weren't you afraid there'd be somebody there?"

"Yes," he said. "But how else was I going to find it?"

"I don't believe that she was about to go to the station to meet us."

"Do you think she forgot all about us?"

"I don't know."

He put on a coat and tie and stood waiting for her.

"I'm afraid to go downstairs," she said.

"Why?"

"We'll have to speak French and she'll know right away that Muriel helped me with those letters. She'll think I was trying to deceive her."

"They don't expect Americans to speak idiomatic French," he said. "And besides, she was trying to overcharge us."

"You go down."

"Without you? Don't be silly. The important thing is you got her to figure the price by the week instead of by the day. She probably respects you more for it than she would have if we—"

"Do you think if we asked for some wood for the fireplace—"

"I don't know," he said doubtfully. "Probably there isn't any wood."

"But we're right next door to a forest."

"I know. But if there's no hot water and no toilet— Anyway, we're in France. We're living the way the French do. This is what goes on behind the high garden walls."

"I don't trust her," Barbara said.

"Fortunately, we don't have to trust her. Come on, let's go."

Chapter 3

As they descended the stairs, they listened for the sound of voices, and heard the birds outside. The second-floor hall was deserted. In the lower hall, at the foot of the stairs, they were confronted with two single and two double curtained French doors. One of the single doors led to the passageway through which Mme Viénot had brought them into the front part of the house. He opened one of the double doors, and they saw a big oval dining table. The table was set, the lights in the crystal chandelier were turned on, the wine and water carafes were filled. "At least we're not late for dinner," he said, and pulled the door to.

The other single door opened into a corner room, a family parlor. Two large portraits in oil of the epoque of Louis XV; a radio; a divan with a row of pillows; a fireplace with a Franklin stove in front of it; a huge, old-fashioned, square, concert-grand piano littered with family photographs. In the center of the room, a round table and four straight chairs. The windows looked out on the courtyard and on the park in front of the château.

He crossed the room to examine the photographs. "Mme Viénot has changed surprisingly little in the last quarter of a century," he said. His eyes lingered for a moment on the photograph of a thin, solemn schoolboy in the clothes of a generation ago. "Dead," he said softly. "The pride of the family finished off at the age of twelve or thirteen."

"How do you know that?" Barbara asked from the doorway.

"There are no pictures of him as a grown man."

As he deferred to her judgment of people, so she deferred to his imagination about them, which was more concrete than hers, but again not infallible. (Maurice Bonenfant died at the age of twenty-seven, by his own hand.)

They went back into the hall and tried again. This time when the door swung open, they heard voices. The doorway was masked by a folding screen, and there was just time as they emerged from behind it to be aware that they were in a long pink and white room. Mme Viénot rose to greet them, and then led them around the circle of chairs.

"My mother, Mme Bonenfant . . ." (a very old woman)

"Mme Carrère . . ." (a woman of fifty)

"M. Carrère . . ." (a tall, stoop-shouldered man, who was slightly older)

"And M. Gagny . . . who is from Canada . . ." (a young man, very handsome, with prematurely gray hair and black eyebrows)

When the introductions had been accomplished, the old woman indicated with a smile and a slight gesture that Barbara was to take the empty chair beside her, and Harold sat down next to Mme Viénot.

Perceiving that their arrival had produced an awkward silence, he leaned forward in his chair and dealt with it himself. He began to tell them about his search through the village for the house of M. Fleury. "Je ne comprends pas les directions que Mme Michot m'a données, et par consequence il me faut demander à tout le monde: 'Où est la maison de M. Fleury—du côté de là, ou du côté de là?' On m'a dirigé encore . . . et encore je ne comprends pas. Alors . . . je demande ma question à un petit garçon, qui me prendre par la main et me conduire chez M. Fleury, tout près de la bureau de poste. . . . Je dis 'merci' et je frappe à la porte. La porte ouvre un très peu. C'est Mme Fleury qui l'ouvre. Je commence à expliquer, et elle ferme la porte dans ma figure."

He saw that the tall middle-aged man was amused, and breathed easier.

"Le garçon frappe à la porte," he continued, "et la porte ouvre un peu. C'est le fils de M. Fleury, cette fois. Il écoute. Il ne ferme pas la porte. . . . Quand j'ai fini, il me dit 'Un instant! Attendez, monsieur!' . . . J'attends, naturellement. J'attends et j'attends. . . . La porte ouvre. C'est M. Fleury lui-même, les pieds en bas, pas de souliers. . . . J'explique que madame et les baggages sont à la gare et que nous désirons aller au château. . . . Il entend. Il est très sympathique, M. Fleury, très gentil. Il envoie son fils en avant pour prendre le clef du garage où le camion repose. Le garage est fermé parce que c'est dimanche. . . . Et puis, nous commençons. M. Fleury—" He paused, unable to remember the word for "pump," and realized that he was out in deep water. "—M. Fleury pompe l'air dans les tires, et moi, je lève quelques sacs de grain qui sont dans le derrière du camion. Le camion est plus vieil que le Treaty de Versailles. . . . Plusier années plus vieil. Et le fils de M. Fleury versait un litre de petrol dans le tank, que est empty, et l'eau dans le radiator. . . ."

Out of the corner of his eyes, he saw Mme Viénot nervously unfolding her hands. Was the story going on too long? He tried to hurry it up, and when he couldn't think of the French word he fell back on the English, which he hopefully pronounced as if it were French. Sometimes it was. The camion that antedated the Treaty of Versailles shuddered and shook and came to life, and the company burst out laughing. Harold sat back in his chair. He had pulled it off, and he felt flooded with pleasure.

There was a pause, less awkward than before. Mme Bonenfant confided to Barbara that she was eighty-three and a great-grandmother.

Mme Viénot said to Harold: "M. Gagny has just been telling us why General de Gaulle is not held in greater esteem in London."

"So many noble qualities," M. Carrère said in French, "so many of the elements of true greatness—all tied to that unfortunate personality. My older brother went to school with him, and even then his weaknesses—especially his vanity—were apparent."

The conversation shifted to the Mass they had just come from. It had a special interest in that the priest, who was saying his first Mass, was a boy from the village. Mme Viénot explained parenthetically to the Americans that, since the war, young men of aristocratic family, really quite a number of them, were turning to the priesthood or joining holy orders. It was a new thing, a genuine religious awakening. There had been nothing like it in France for more than two generations.

The Americans were conscious of the fact that the gray-haired young man could have talked to them in English and, instead, continued to speak to the others in French. The rather cool manner in which he acknowledged the introduction implied that he felt no responsibility for or interest in Americans.

Harold looked around at the room. It was a long rectangle, with a fireplace at either end. The curtains and the silk uphol-stery were a clear silvery pink. The period furniture was light and graceful and painted a flat white, like the molding and the fireplaces, which were identical. So were the two horizontal mirrors over the Adam mantelpieces. In the center of the room, four fluted columns and a sculptured plant stand served as a reminder that in France neo-classicism is not a term of re-proach. Along one side of the room, a series of French doors opened onto the terrace and made the drawing room well lighted even on a gray day. The circle of chairs where they were sitting now was in front of one of the fireplaces. At the other end of the room, in front of the other fireplace, there were two small sofas and some chairs that were not arranged for conver-sation. In its proportions and its use of color and the taste with which it was furnished, it was unlike any drawing room he had ever seen. The more he looked at it, the more strange and beautiful it became.

The sermon had exceeded the expectations of the company, and they continued to talk about it complacently until the servant girl opened the hall doors and removed the folding screen. The women rose and started toward the dining room. M. Carrère had to be helped from his chair, and then, leaning on his cane, he made his way into the hall. Harold, light-headed with the success of his story, waited for the Canadian to precede him through the doorway. The Canadian stopped too, and when Harold said: "After you," he changed. Right in front of Harold's eyes he stopped being a facsimile of a French-man and became exactly like an American. With his hand on Harold's shoulder, he said: "Go on, go on," goodnaturedly, and propelled him through the door ahead of him.

In the dining room Harold found himself seated between Mme Carrère and old Mme Bonenfant. Mme Carrère was served before him, and he watched her out of the corner of his eye, and was relieved to see that there was no difference; table manners were the same here as at home. But his initial at-tempts to make conversation met with failure. Mme Carrère seemed to be a taciturn woman, and something told him that any attempt to be friendly with her might be regarded as being over-friendly. Mme Bonenfant either did not understand or was simply not interested in his description of the terraced gardens of Mont-Saint-Michel.

George Ireland, the American boy who had spent the previous summer at the château and was indirectly responsible for their being here now, had said that it was one of his duties to keep Mme Bonenfant's water glass filled. Harold saw that there was a carafe of water in front of him and that her glass was empty. Though she allowed him to fill it again and again during dinner, she addressed her remarks to M. Carrère.

As the soup gave way to the fish and the fish in turn to the entree, the talk ranged broadly over national and international politics, life in Paris before the war, travel in Spain and Italy, the volcanic formations of Ischia, the national characteristics of the Swiss. In his effort to follow what was being said around the table, Harold forgot to eat, and this slowed up the service. He left his knife and fork on his plate and, too late, saw them being carried out to the pantry. A clean knife and fork were brought to him with the next course. Mme Viénot interrupted the flow of wit and anecdote to inquire if he understood what was being said.

"I understand part of it," he said eagerly.

A bleak expression crossed her face. Instead of smiling or saying something reassuring to him, she looked down at her plate. He glanced across the table at Barbara and saw, with surprise, that she was her natural self.

After the dessert course, Mme Viénot pushed her chair back and they all rose from the table at once. Mme Carrère, passing the sideboard, lifted the lid of a faïence soup tureen and took out a box of Belgian sugar. The Canadian kept his sugar in a red lacquer cabinet in the drawing room, and Mme Viénot hers and her mother's in the writing desk in the petit salon. Harold excused himself and went upstairs to their room. Strewing the contents of the dufflebag over the bathroom floor, he finally came upon the boxes of cube sugar they had brought with them from America. When he walked into the drawing room, the servant girl had brought the silver coffee service and Mme Viénot was measuring powdered coffee into little white coffee cups.

The Canadian lit a High Life cigarette. Harold, conscious of the fact that their ten cartons had to last them through four months, thought it might be a good idea to wait until he and Barbara were alone to smoke, but she was looking at him expectantly, and so he took a pack from his coat pocket, ripped the cellophane off, and offered the cigarettes to her and then around the circle. They were refused politely until he came to Mme Viénot, who took one, as if she was not quite sure what it might be for but was always willing to try something new.

"I think the church is in Chartres," Barbara said, and he knew that she had been talking about the little church at the end of the carline. There were two things that she remembered particularly from that earlier trip to France and that she wanted to see again. One was a church, a beautiful little church at the end of a streetcar line, and the other was a white château with a green lawn in front of it. She had no idea where either of them was.

"You don't mean the cathedral?" Mme Viénot asked.

"Oh, no," Barbara said.

Though there were matches on the table beside her, Mme Viénot waited for Harold to return and light her cigarette. Her hand touched his as she bent over the lighted match, and this contact—not accidental, he was sure—startled him. What was it? Was she curious? Was she trying to find out whether his marriage was really pink and happy or blue like most marriages?

"There is no tram line at Chartres," she said, blowing a cloud of smoke through her nostrils. "I ought to know the château, but I'm afraid I don't. There are so many."

And what about M. Viénot, he wondered. Where was he? Was he dead? Why had his name not come up in the conversation before or during dinner?

"It was like a castle in a fairy tale," Barbara said.

"Cheverny has a large lawn in front of it. Have you been there?" Mme Viénot asked. Barbara shook her head.

"I have a brochure with some pictures of châteaux. Perhaps you will recognize the one you are looking for. . . . You are going to be in France how long?"

"Until the beginning of August," Barbara said. "And then we're going to Switzerland and Austria. We're going to Salzburg for the Festival."

"And then to Venice," Harold said, "and down through Italy as far as Florence—"

"You have a great deal in store for you," Mme Viénot said. "Venice is enchanting. You will adore Venice."

"—and back through the Italian and French Rivieras to Paris, and then home."

"It is better not to try to see too much," Mine Viénot said. "The place one stays in for a week or ten days is likely to be the place one remembers. And how long do you have? . . . Ah, I envy you. One of the most disagreeable things about the Occupation was that we were not permitted to travel."

"The luggage is something of a problem," he said.

"What you do not need you can leave here," she said.

Tempting though this was, if they left their luggage at the château they would have to come back for it. "Thank you. I will remember if we . . ." He managed not to commit them to anything.

The Canadian was talking about the Count of Paris, and it occurred to Harold that for the first time in his life he was in the presence of royalists. His defense of democracy was extremely oblique; he said: "Is the Count of Paris an intelligent man?"—having read somewhere that he was not.

"Unfortunately, no," Mme Viénot said, and smiled. "Such an amusing story is going the round. It seems his wife was quite ill, and the doctors said she must have a transfusion—you say 'transfusion' in English?—or she would die. But the Count wouldn't give his consent. He kept them waiting for two whole days while he searched through the Almanach de Gotha."

"It was a question of blue blood?"

She nodded. "He could not find anyone with a sufficient number of royal quarterings in his coat of arms. In the end he had to compromise, I believe, and take what he could get." She took a sip of coffee and then said: "Something similar happened in our family recently. My niece has just had her first child, and two days after it was born, she commenced hemorrhaging. They couldn't find her husband—he was playing golf—so the doctor went ahead and arranged for a transfusion, without his consent—and when Eugène walked in and saw this strange man—he was a very common person—sitting beside his wife's bed, he was most upset."

"The blood from a transfusion only lasts forty-eight hours," Harold said, in his own peculiar way every bit as much of a snob as the Count of Paris.

"My niece's husband did not know that," Mme Viénot said. "And he did not want his children to have this person's blood in their veins. My sister and the doctor had a very difficult time with him."

On the other side of the circle of chairs, M. Carrère said that he didn't like Germans, to Mme Bonenfant, who was not defending them.

Mme Viénot took his empty cup and put it on the tray. Turning back to Harold and Barbara, she said: "France was not ready for the war, and when the Germans came we could do nothing. It was like a nightmare. . . . Now, of course, we are living in another; we are deathly afraid of war between your country and the Union of Soviet Republics. You think it will happen soon? . . . I blame your President Roosevelt. He didn't understand the Russian temperament and so he was taken in by promises that mean nothing. The Slav is not like other Europeans. . . . Some years ago I became acquainted with a Russian woman. She was delightful to be with. She was responsive and intelligent. She had all the qualities one looks for in a friend. And yet, as time went on, I realized that I did not really know her. I was always conscious of something held back."

She was looking directly at Harold's face but he was not sure she even saw him. He studied her, while she took a sip of coffee, trying to see her as her friend the Russian woman saw her—the pale-blue eyes, the too-black hair, the rouged cheeks. She must be somewhere in Proust, he thought.

"Never trust a Slav," she said solemnly.

And what about the variations, he wondered. There must be variations, such as never trust an Englishman; never trust a Swede. And maybe even never trust an American?

"Are French people always kind and helpful to foreigners?" he asked. "Because that has been our experience so far."

"I can't say that they are, always," Mme Viénot said. She put her cup and saucer on the tray. "You have perhaps been fortunate."

She got up and moved away, leaving him with the feeling

that he had said something untactful. His own cup was empty, but he continued to hold it, though the table was within reach.

M. Gagny was talking about the British royal family. He knew the Duke of Connaught, he said, and he had danced with the Princess Elizabeth, but he was partial to the Princess Margaret Rose.

Mme Viénot sat down beside her mother, patted her dry mottled hand, and smiled at her and then around at the company, lightly and publicly admitting her fondness.

M. Carrère explained to Barbara that he could speak English, but that it tired him, and he preferred his native tongue. Mme Carrère's English was better than his, but on the other hand he talked and she didn't. Mme Bonenfant did not know English at all, though she spoke German. And the Canadian was so conspicuously bilingual that his presence in the circle of chairs was a reproach rather than a help to the Americans. Harold told himself that it was foolish—that it was senseless, in fact—to make the effort, but nevertheless he couldn't help feeling that he must live up to his success before dinner or he would surrender too much ground. A remark, a question addressed directly to him, he understood sufficiently to answer, but then the conversation became general again and he was lost. He sat balancing the empty cup and saucer in his two hands, looked at whoever was speaking, and tried to catch from the others' faces whether the remark was serious or amusing, so that he could smile at the right time. This tightrope performance and fatigue (they had got up early to catch the train, and it had already been a long day) combined to deprive him of the last hope of understanding what was said.

Watching him, Barbara saw the glazed look she knew so well—the film that came over his eyes whenever he was bored or ill-at-ease. As she got ready to deliver him from his misery, it occurred to her suddenly how odd it was that neither of them had ever stopped to think what it might be like staying with a French family, or that there might be more to it than an opportunity to improve their French.

"Could you understand them?" he asked, as soon as they were behind the closed door of their room.

She nodded.

"I couldn't."

"But you talked. I was afraid to open my mouth."

This made him feel better.

"There's a toilet on this floor, at the far end of the attic corridor. I asked Mme Bonenfant."

"Behind one of the doors I was afraid to open," he said, nodding.

"But it's out of order. It's going to be fixed in a day or two. Meanwhile, we're to use the toilet on the second floor."

They undressed and got into their damp beds and talked drowsily for a few minutes—about the house, about the other guests, about the food, which was the best they had had in France—and then fell into a deep sleep. When they woke, the afternoon was gone and it was raining softly. He got into her bed, and she put her head in the hollow of his shoulder.

"I wish this room was all there was," he said, "and we lived in it. I wish it was ours."

"You wouldn't get tired of the red wallpaper?"

"No."

"Neither would I. Or of anything else," she said.

"It's not like any room that I've ever seen."

"It's very French."

"What is?" he asked.

"Everything. . . . Why isn't she here?"

"Who?"

"The French girl. If this was my room, I'd be living in it."

"She's probably having a much better time in Paris," he said, and looked at his wrist watch. "Come on," he said, tossing the cover back. "We're late."

After dinner, Mme Viénot led her guests into the family parlor across the hall. The coffee that Harold was waiting for did not appear. He and Barbara smoked one cigarette, to be sociable, and then wandered outside. It had stopped raining. They walked up and down the gravel terrace, admiring the house and the old trees and the view, which was gilded with the evening light. They were happy to be by themselves, and pleased with the way they had managed things—for they might, at this very moment, have been walking the streets of Le Mans, or freezing to death at the seashore, and instead they were here. They would be able to include this interesting place

among the places they had seen and could tell people about
when they got home.

From the terrace they went directly to their room, their
beautiful red room, whose history they had no way of knowing.

The village of Brenodville was very old and had interesting
historical associations. The château did not, if by history you
mean kings and queens and their awful favorites, battles and
treaties, ruinous entertainments, genius harbored, the rise and
fall of ambitious men. Its history was merely the history of the
family that had lived in it tenaciously, generation after generation. The old wing, the carriage house, the stables, and the
brick courtyard dated from the seventeenth century. Around
the year 1900, the property figured in still another last will and
testament, duly signed and sealed. Beaumesnil passed from the
dead hands of a rich, elderly, unmarried sportsman, who seldom used it, into the living, eager hands of a nephew who had
been sufficiently attentive and who, just to make things doubly
sure, had been named after him. Almost the first thing M.
Jules Bonenfant did with the fortune he had inherited was to
build against the old house a new wing, larger and more formal in design. From this time on, instead of facing the carp
pond and the forest, the château faced the patchwork of small
fields and the River Loire, which was too far away to figure in
the view. For a number of years, the third-floor room on the
left at the head of the stairs remained empty and unused.
Moonlight came and went. Occasionally a freakish draft blew
down the chimney, redistributing the dust. A gray squirrel got
in, also by way of the chimney, and died here, while mud wasps
beat against the windowpanes. The newspapers of 1906 did
not penetrate this far and so the wasps never learned that a
Captain Alfred Dreyfus had been decorated with the Légion
d'Honneur, in public, in the courtyard of the artillery pavilion
at St. Cyr. In September of that same year, Mme Bonenfant
stood on the second-floor landing and directed the village
paperhanger, with his scissors, paste, steel measuring tape, and
trestle, up the final flight of stairs and through the door on the
left. When the room was finished, Mlle Toinette was parted
from a tearful governess and found herself in possession of a
large bedroom that was directly over her mother's and the
same size and shape. The only difference was that the ceiling

sloped down on one side and there was one window instead
of two. With different wallpaper and different furniture, the
room was now her younger daughter's. So much for its history. Now what about the two people who are asleep in it?
Who are they? What is their history?

Well, where to begin is the question. The summer he spent
in bed with rheumatic fever on an upstairs sleeping porch? Or
the street he lived on—those big, nondescript, tree-shaded,
Middle Western white houses, beautiful in the fall when the
leaves turned, or at dusk with the downstairs lights turned on,
or in winter when the snow covered up whatever was shabby
and ugly? Should we begin with the tree house in the back
yard or with the boy he was envious of, who always had money
for ice-cream cones because his mother was dead and the
middle-aged aunt and uncle he lived with felt they had no
other way to make it up to him? Given his last name, Rhodes,
and the time and place he grew up in, it was inevitable that
when he started to go to school he should be called Dusty.
Some jokes never lose their freshness.

It helps, of course, to know what happened when they were
choosing up sides and he stood waiting for his name to be
called. And about the moment when he emerged into the public eye for the first time, at the age of six, in a surgical-cotton
wig, knee britches, buckles on his shoes, and with seven other
costumed children danced the minuet in the school auditorium.

The sum total of his memories is who he is, naturally. Also
the child his mother went in to cover on her rounds, the last
thing at night before she went to bed—the little boy with his
own way of sleeping, his arm around some doll or stuffed
animal, and his own way of recognizing her presence through
layers and layers of sleep. Also the little boy with a new navy-
blue suit on Easter Sunday, and a cowlick that would not stay
down. Then there is that period when he was having his teeth
straightened, when he corresponded with postage-stamp companies. The obedient, sensible, courteous ten-year-old? Or the
moody boy in his teens, who ate them out of house and home
and had to be sent from the table for talking back to his father?
Take your choice, or take both of them. His mother's eyes, the
Rhodes nose and mouth and chin; the Rhodes stubbornness,

his mother said. This book belongs to Harold Rhodes, Eighth Grade, Room 207, Central School. . . . And whatever became of those boards for stretching muskrat skins on, the skins he was going to sell and make a fortune from? Or his magic lantern and his postcard projector? Or his building blocks, his Boy Scout knife, his school report cards? And that medicine-stained copy of *Mr. Midshipman Easy*? And the Oz books? Somewhere, all these unclaimed shreds of his personality, since matter is never entirely lost but merely changes its form.

As a boy of thirteen he was called up on the stage of the Majestic Theater by a vaudeville magician, and did exactly what the magician told him (under his breath) to do; even though the magician told him out loud not to do it, and so made a monkey of him, and the audience rocked with perfectly kind laughter. Since then he hasn't learned a thing. The same audience would rock with the same laughter if he were called up on the stage of the Majestic Theater tomorrow. Fortunately it has been torn down to make a parking lot.

In college he was responsive, with a light in his eye; he was a pleasure to lecture to; but callow, getting by on enthusiasm because it came more natural to him than thinking, and worried about his grades, and about the future, and because, though he tried and tried, he could not break himself of a shameful habit. If he had taken biology it would have been made clear to him that he too was an animal, but he took botany instead.

But who is he? which animal?

A commuter, standing on the station platform, with now the *Times* and now the *Tribune* under his arm, waiting for the 8:17 express. A liberal Democrat, believing idealistically in the cause of labor but knowing few laborers, and a member in good standing of the money-loving class he was born into, though, as it happens, money slips through his fingers. A spendthrift, with small sums, cautious with large ones. Who is he? Raskolnikov—that's who he is.

Surely not?

Yes. Also Mr. Micawber. And St. Francis. And Savonarola. He's no one person, he's an uncountable committee of people who meet and operate under the handy fiction of his name. The minutes of the last meeting are never read, because it's

still going on. The committee arrives at important conclusions
which it cannot remember, and makes sensible decisions it
cannot possibly keep. For that you need a policeman. The
committee members know each other, but not always by their
right names. The bachelor who has sat reading in the same
white leatherette chair by the same lamp with the same cigarette box within reach on the same round table for so long
now that change is no longer possible to him—that Harold
Rhodes of course knows the bridegroom with a white carnation in his buttonhole, sipping a glass of champagne, smiling,
accepting congratulations, aware of the good wishes of everybody and also of a nagging doubt in the back of his mind. Just
as they both know the head of the family, the born father, with
the Sunday paper scattered around him on the living-room
rug, smiling benignly at no children after three years of marriage. And the child of seven (in some ways the most mature of
all these facets of his personality) who is being taken, with his
hand in his father's much bigger hand, to see his mother in the
hospital on a day that, as it turned out, she was much too sick
to see anyone.

What does he—what do all these people do for a living?

Does it matter?

Certainly.

After two false starts he now has a job with a future. He is
working for an engraving firm owned by a friend of his father.

What did he do, where was he, during the war?

He wasn't in the war . . . 4F. He has to be away from Barbara, traveling, several times a year, but the rest of the time he
can be home, where he wants to be. His hours are long, but he
has already had two raises, and now this four months' leave of
absence, proof that his work is valued.

And who is she? whom did he marry?

Somebody who matches him, the curves and hollows of her
nature fitting into all the curves and hollows of his nature as, in
bed, her straight back and soft thighs fit inside the curve of his
breast and belly and hips and bent legs. Somebody who looks
enough like him that they are mistaken occasionally for brother
and sister, and who keeps him warm at night, taking the place
of the doll that he used to sleep with his arm around: Barbara
Scully. Barbara S. Rhodes, when she writes a check.

And what was her childhood like?

Well, where to begin is again the question. At the seashore? Or should we take up, one after another, the dogs, the nurse-maids? Or the time she broke her arm? She was seven when that happened. Or the period when she cared about nothing but horses? Or that brief, heartbreaking, first falling in love? Or the piles of clothes on the bed, on the chairs in her room, all with name tapes sewed on them, and the suitcases waiting to be filled?

Or should we open that old exercise book that by some accident has survived?

"One day our mother gave the children a party.

There were fourteen merry girls and boys at the party.

They played games and raced about the lawn with Rover.

But John fell from a tree and broke his arm.

Mother sent a boy to bring the doctor.

The doctor set the arm and said that it would soon be better.

Was not John a brave boy to bear the pain as he did."

Three times 269 is not 627, of course; and neither does 854 minus 536 equal 316. But it is true that there are seven days in the week, and that all the children must learn their lessons. Also that it is never the raveled sleeve of just one day's care that sleep knits up. She should have been at home nursing her baby, and instead here they both are in Europe. And every month contains doomed days, such sad sighs, the rain that does not rain, and blood that is the color of bitter disappointment when it finally flows. This is the lesson she is now learning.

The shadow that showed up in the crystal ball?

Right. And all the years he was growing up, he would have liked to be somebody else—an athlete, broad-shouldered, blond, unworried, and popular. Even now he avoids his reflection in mirrors and wants to be liked by everybody. Not loved; just liked. On meeting someone who interests him he goes toward that person unhesitatingly, as if this were the one moment they would ever have together, their one chance of knowing each other. He is curious and at the same time he is tactful. He lets the other person know, by the way he listens, by the sympathetic look in his brown eyes, that he wants to know everything; and at the same time the other person has the reassuring suspicion that Harold Rhodes will not ask questions it would be embarrassing to have to answer. He tries to attach people to him, not so that he can use them or so that they will add to his importance but only because he wants them to be a part of his life. The landscape must have figures in it. And it never seems to occur to him that there is a limit to the number of close friendships anyone can decently and faithfully accommodate.

If wherever you go you are always looking for eyes that meet your eyes, hands that do not avoid touching or being touched by you, then you must have more than two eyes and two hands; you must be a kind of monster. If, on meeting someone who interests you, you go toward them unhesitatingly as if this is the only moment you will ever have for knowing each other, then you must learn to deal with second meetings that aren't always successful, and third meetings that are even less satisfactory. If on your desk there are too many unanswered letters, the only thing to do is to write to someone who hasn't written to you lately. And if sometimes, hanging by your knees head down from a swinging trapeze high under the canvas tent, you find too many aerial artists are coming toward you at a given moment and you have to choose one and let the others drop, you can at least try not to see their eyes accusing you of an inhuman betrayal you did not mean and cannot avoid. Harold Rhodes isn't a monster, he doesn't try to escape the second meetings, he answers some of the letters, and he spends a great deal of time, patience, and energy inducing performers with hurt feelings to climb the rope ladder again and fling themselves across the intervening void. Some of them do and some of them don't.

That's all very interesting, but just exactly what are these two people doing in Europe?

They're tourists.

Obviously. But it's too soon after the war. Traveling will be much pleasanter and easier five years from now. The soldiers have not all gone home yet. People are poor and discouraged. Europe isn't ready for tourists. Couldn't they wait?

No, they couldn't. The nail doesn't choose the time or the circumstances in which it is drawn to the magnet.

They would have done better to do a little reading before they

came, so they would know what to look for. And they could at least
have brushed up on their French.

They could have, but they didn't. They just came. They are
the first wave. As Mme Viénot perceived, they are unworldly,
and inexperienced. But they are not totally so; there are certain
areas where they cannot be fooled or taken advantage of. But
there is, in their faces, something immature, reluctant—

You mean they are Americans.

No, I mean all those acts of imagination by which the cupboard is again and again proved to be not bare. And putting so
much faith in fortunetelling. Playing cards, colored stones,
bamboo sticks, birthday-cracker mottoes, palmistry, the signs
of the zodiac, the first star—she trusts them all, but only with
a partial trust. Each new prognostication takes precedence
over the former ones, and when the cards are not accommo-
dating, she reshuffles them and tells herself a new fortune. Her
right hand lies open now, relaxed on the pillow, her palm ready
and waiting for a fortuneteller who can walk through locked
doors and see in the dark.

Unaccustomed to sleeping in separate beds, they toss and
turn and are cold and have tiring dreams that they would not
have had if their two bodies were touching. But they won't be
here long, or anywhere else. Ten days in Paris after they leave
here. A night in Lausanne. Six days in Salzburg. Four days in
Venice. Four more days in Florence. Ten days in Rome, a
night in Pisa, two days in San Remo . . . No place can hold
them.

And it is something that they are turned towards each other
in their sleep. It means that day in and day out they are com-
panionable and happy with one another; that they have identical (or almost) tastes and pleasures; and that when they diverge
it is likely to be in their attitude toward the world outside their
marriage. For example, he thinks he does not believe in God,
she thinks she does. If she is more cautious about people than
he is, conceivably this is because in some final way she needs
them more. He needs only her. Parted from her in a crowd he
becomes anxious, and in dreams he wanders through huge
houses calling her name.

Chapter 4

"WHAT time is breakfast?" he asked, rising up from his bed. She did not know. They had forgotten to ask about breakfast. They saw that it was a dark, rainy Monday morning. They washed in ice-cold water, dressed, and went downstairs. He peered around the folding screen, half expecting the household to be assembled in the drawing room, waiting for them. The beautiful pink and white room was deserted, and the rugs were rolled up, the chairs pushed together. In the dining room, the table was set for five instead of seven, and their new places were pointed out to them by their napkin rings. Talking in subdued tones, they discovered the china pitcher of coffee under a quilted cozy, and, under a large quilted pad, slices of bread that were hard as a rock and burned black around the edges from being toasted over a gas burner. The dining-room windows offered a prospect of wet gravel, long grass bent over by the weight of the rain, and dripping pine branches. The coffee was tepid.

"I think it would have been better if we hadn't got her to lower the price," he said suddenly.

"Did she say anything about it?"

He shook his head. "The amount she asked was not exorbitant."

"It was high. Muriel said it was high. She lived in France for twenty years. She ought to know."

"That was before the war. In the total expenses of the summer, it wouldn't have made any difference, one way or the other."

"She said it was not right, and that it was a matter of principle."

"Muriel, you mean? I know, but the first two or three days after we got off the boat, I consistently undertipped people, because I didn't know what the right amount was, and I didn't want us to look like rich Americans throwing our money around, and in every case they were so nice about it."

"How do you know you undertipped them?"

"By the way they acted when I gave them more."

"Mme Viénot has a romantic idea of herself," Barbara said. "The way she flirts with you, for instance . . ."

He took the green Michelin guide to the château country from his coat pocket and put it beside his plate. After a week of sight-seeing, any other way of passing the time seemed unnatural.

"You're sure she was flirting with me?"

"Certainly. But it's a game. She's attempting to produce, with your help, the person she sees herself as—the worldly, fascinating adventuress, the heroine of *Gone with the Wind*."

He filled their cups again and offered her the burned bread, which she refused. Then he opened the guidebook and began to turn the pages as he ate. Programmes de voyage . . . Un peu d'histoire . . . wars and maps . . . medieval cooking utensils . . . The fat round towers of Chaumont, and Amboise as it was in the sixteenth century.

"How old do you think Gagny is?" Barbara said.

"I don't know. He varies so. Somewhere between twenty-three and thirty-five."

More maps. Visite rapide . . . Visite du Château . . .

"Why isn't he married?"

"People don't have to get married," he said. "Sometimes they just—"

Rain blew against the windowpanes, so hard that they both turned and looked.

"Besides, he's in the diplomatic service," Harold said. "He can't just marry any pretty girl he feels like marrying. He needs a countess or somebody like that, and I suppose they won't have him because he isn't rich."

"How do you know he isn't rich?"

"If he were rich he wouldn't *be* here. He'd be somewhere where the sun is shining."

Behind his back a voice said: "Good morning!" and Mme Viénot swept into the dining room, wearing a dark-red housecoat, with her head tied up in a red and green Liberty scarf. She sat down at the head of the table. "You slept well? . . . I'm so glad. You must have been very tired after your journey." She placed her box of sugar directly in front of her, so there could be no possible misunderstanding, and then said: "What a pity it is raining again! M. Gagny is very discouraged about the weather, which I must say is not what we are accustomed to in July."

"Is it bad for the grain?" Harold asked.

Mme Viénot lifted the quilted pad and considered the burned bread with a grimace of disapproval. "Not at this time of year. But my gardener is worried about the hay." She peered into the china pitcher and her eyebrows rose in disbelief. "Perhaps it is only a shower. I hope so." She picked up the plate of toast and pushed her chair back. "The cook, poor dear, forgot to moisten the bread. I don't care for it when it is hard like this." Taking the pitcher also with her, she went out to the kitchen.

"We shouldn't have had a second cup," Barbara whispered.

"I think it was all right," he said.

"But she looked—"

"I know. I saw it. Coffee is rationed, but surely that wasn't coffee. . . . There wasn't enough for the others, in any case."

"You won't forget to speak to her about the beds, will you?" Barbara said. "I wrote her that we wanted a room with a *grand lit*, and if she didn't have anything but twin beds, it was up to her to tell us. And she didn't."

"No," he agreed, shifting in his chair, the uneasy male caught between two females.

"And the bicycles . . . You don't think she overheard what we were saying?"

"It wouldn't matter, unless she was standing out in the hall the whole time."

"She could have been."

They sat in wary silence until the pantry door opened.

"We must plan some excursions for you," Mme Viénot said. "You are in the center of one of the most interesting parts of France. The king used to come here with the court, for the hunting. They each had their own château and it was marvelous."

"We want to see Azay-le-Rideau," he said, "and Chinon, and Chenonceau—"

"Chinon is a ruin," Mme Viénot said disapprovingly. "Unless you have some particular reason for going there—" She surveyed the table and then got up again and pried open the door of the sideboard with her table knife. They heard a faint exclamation and then: "Within twenty-four hours after I open a jar of *confitures* it is half gone."

"Do have some," she said as she sat down again. "It is plum."

They both refused.

"Chenonceau is ravishing," Mme Viénot said, and helped herself sparingly to the jam. "It belonged to Diane de Poitiers. She was the king's mistress. She adored Chenonceau, and Catherine de Médicis took it away from her and gave her Chaumont instead."

He asked the reason for this exchange.

"She was jealous," Mme Viénot explained, with a shrug.

"But couldn't the king stop her?"

"He was killed in a tournament."

"Are the châteaux within walking distance?" Barbara asked.

"Alas, no," Mme Viénot said.

"But we can bicycle to some of them?" he asked.

In one of the two polite letters that arrived before they left New York, Mme Viénot had assured them that bicycles would be waiting for them when they arrived. Now she filled their cups and then her own and said plaintively: "I inquired about bicycles for you in the village, and it appears there aren't any. Perhaps you can arrange to rent them in Blois. Or in Tours. Tours is a dear old city—you know it?"

"We were there overnight," Barbara said.

"You saw the cathedral?"

Barbara shook her head.

"You must see the cathedral," Mme Viénot said. "The old part of the city was badly damaged during the war. Whole blocks went down between the center of town and the river. So shocking, isn't it?"

The servant girl appeared with a plate of fresh toast that had not been burned and the china pitcher, now full of steaming hot coffee. Mme Viénot remarked in French to the surrounding air that someone in the house was extremely fond of *confitures*, and with a sullen look Thérèse withdrew to the kitchen.

"Now, with the rubble cleared away," Mme Viénot said cheerfully, "you can have no idea what it was like. . . . The planes were American."

For a whole minute nobody said anything. Then Harold

said: "Riding on the train we saw a great deal of rebuilding.
Everywhere, in fact."

"Our own people raised the money for the new bridge at
Tours," Mme Viénot said. "Naturally we are very proud of it.
They are of stone, the new buildings?"

He nodded. "There's one thing, though, I kept noticing,
and that is that the openings—the windows and doors—were
all the same size. Do they have to do that? The new buildings
look like barracks."

"In Tours all the new buildings are of stone. It would have
been cheaper to use wood, but that would have meant sacrificing the style of the locality, which is very beautiful," Mme
Viénot said firmly, and so prevented him from pursuing a subject that, he now perceived, might well be painful to her. Probably it wasn't possible to rebuild, exactly as they were before,
houses that had been built hundreds of years ago, and added
onto and changed continually ever since.

He said: "Is there a taxi in the village?"

"There is one," Mme Viénot said. "A woman has it, and I'm
afraid you will find her expensive. I'm sorry we haven't a car to
offer you. We sold our Citroën after the war, thinking we
could get a new one immediately, and it was a dreadful mistake. You can take the train, you know."

"From Brenodville?"

She nodded. Rearranging her sleeves so they wouldn't trail
across her plate, she said: "I used to go to parties at Chaumont
before the war. The Princesse de Broglie owned it then. She
married the Infant Louis-Ferdinand, of Spain, and he was not
always nice to her." She looked expectantly at them and seemed
to be waiting for some response, some comment or anecdote
about a royal person they knew who was also inconsiderate.
"The Princesse was a very beautiful woman, and immensely
rich. She was of the Say family—they manufacture sugar—and
she wanted a title. So she married the Prince de Broglie, and he
died. And then in her old age she married the Infant, and
mothered him, and gave parties to which everyone went, and
kept an elephant. The bridge at Chaumont is still down, but
there is a ferry, I am told. I must find out for you how often
it goes back and forth. . . . The Germans blew up all the

bridges across the Loire, and for a while it was most inconvenient."

"How do we get to Chenonceau?" Harold asked.

"You take a train to Amboise, and from there you take a taxi. It's about twelve kilometers."

"And there are lots of trains?"

"There are two," Mme Viénot said. "One in the morning and one at night. I'll get a schedule for you. Before the war, the mayor of Brenodville was a member of the Chamber of Deputies and we had excellent service; all the fast trains between Paris and Nantes stopped here. . . . Amboise is also worth seeing. Léonard de Vinci is buried there. And during the seventeenth century, there was an uprising—it was the time of the Huguenot wars—and a great many men were put to death. They say that Marie Stuart and the young king used to dine out on the battlements at Amboise, in order to watch the hangings."

"What about buses?"

"I don't think you'll find the bus at all convenient," Mme Viénot said. "You have to walk a mile and a half to the highway where it passes, and usually it is quite crowded." Then as the silence in the dining room became prolonged: "I've been meaning to ask you about young George Ireland. We grew very fond of him while he was here, and he was a great favorite in the village. What is he doing now?"

"George is in school," Harold said.

"But now, this summer?"

"He's working. He's selling little dolls. He showed them to us the last time we were at the Irelands' for dinner. A man and a woman this high . . . You wind them up and they dance around and around."

"How amusing," Mme Viénot said. "He sells them on the street corner?"

"To tobacco stores, I believe."

"And is he successful?"

"Very. He's on his way to becoming a millionaire."

Mme Viénot nodded approvingly. "When he arrived, he didn't know a word of French, and it was rather difficult at first. But he spoke fluently by the end of the summer. We also discovered that he was fond of chocolate. He used to ride into the village after dinner and spend untold sums on candy and sweetmeats. And he was rather careless with my *bicyclette*. I had to have it repaired after he left. But he is a dear, of course. That reminds me—I haven't answered his mother's letter. I must write her today, and thank her for sending me two such charming clients. It was most kind of her. I gather that she knows France well?"

Harold nodded.

"Such an amusing thing happened—I must tell you. My younger daughter became engaged last summer, and before she had quite made up her mind, George came to me and said that Sabine must wait until he could marry her. Fancy his thinking she would have him? I thought it was very fresh—a fifteen-year-old boy!"

"He speaks of you all—and of the place—with great affection," Harold said.

"It was a responsibility," Mme Viénot said. "There are so many kinds of trouble a boy of that age can get into. You're quite sure you won't have anything more? Some bread, perhaps? Some more coffee?" She rolled her napkin and thrust it through the silver ring in front of her, and pushed her chair back from the table. "When George left, he kissed me and said: 'You have been like a mother to me!' I thought it sweet of him—to say that. And I really did feel like his mother."

As they were moving toward the door, he said hurriedly: "We've been meaning to ask you— Is there some way we could have hot water?"

"In your room? But of course! Thérèse will bring it to you. When would you like it? In the evening, perhaps?"

"At seven o'clock," Barbara said.

"I could come and get it myself," he said. "Or would that upset them?"

"Oh, dear no!" Mme Viénot exclaimed. "I'm afraid that wouldn't do. They'd never understand in the kitchen. You must tell Maman about the *poupées*. She will be enchanted."

"*Porc-épic* is French for porcupine," he announced. He was stretched out on the chaise longue, in the darkest corner of their room, reading the green Michelin guide to the château country. "The porcupine with a crown above it is the attribute—emblem, I guess it means—of Louis XII. The emblem of François premier is the salamander. The swan with an arrow sticking through its breast is the emblem of Louise of Savoy, mother of François premier. And it's also the emblem of Claude de France, his wife. Did you know we have a coat of arms in our family?"

"No," Barbara said. "You never told me." She had covered the towel racks in the bathroom with damp stockings and lingerie, and was now sitting at the kidney-shaped desk, with her fur coat over her shoulders and the windows wide open because it was no colder outside than it was in, writing notes to people who had sent presents to the boat. There were letters and postcards he should have been writing but fortunately there was only one pen.

"The ermine is Anne of Brittany and Claude de France," he said, turning back to the guidebook.

"Why does she have two emblems?"

"Who?"

"Claude de France. You said—"

"So she does . . . Ummm. It doesn't say. But it gives the genealogy of the Valois kings, the Valois-Orléans, the Valois-Angoulême, and the Bourbons through Louis XIV. . . . Charles V, 1364–1380, married Jeanne de Bourbon. Charles VI, 1380–1422, married Isabeau de Bavière. Charles VII—"

"Couldn't you just read it to yourself and tell me about it afterward?"

"All right," he said. "But it's very interesting. Charles VIII and Louis XII both married Anne of Brittany."

"The salamander?"

"No, the ermine. I promise not to bother you any more." But he did, almost immediately. "Listen to this, I just want to read you the beginning paragraph. It's practically a prose poem."

"Is it long?"

" 'Between Gien and Angers, the banks of the Loire and the affluent valleys of the great river present an incomparable ensemble of magnificent monuments.' That's very good, don't you think? Don't you think it has sweep to it? 'The châteaux, by their number, their importance, and their interest appear in the foreground. Crammed with art and history, they occupy the choicest sites in a region that has a privileged light—' "

"It looks like just any gray day to me," she said, glancing out at the sky.

"Maybe the light is privileged and maybe it isn't. The point is you'd never find an expression like that in an American guidebook. . . . 'The landscapes of the Loire, in lines simple and calm'—that's very French—'owe their seductiveness to the light that bathes them, wide sky of a light blue, long perspectives of a current that is sometimes sluggish, tranquil streams with delicate reflections, sunny hillsides with promising vineyards, fresh valleys, laughing flower-filled villages, peaceful visions. A landscape that is measured, that charms by its sweetness and its distinction—' "

He yawned. The guidebook slipped through his fingers and joined the pocket dictionary on the rug. After a minute or two, he got up and stood at the window. The heavy shutters opened in, and the black-out paper was crinkled and torn and beginning to come loose. Three years after the liberation of France, it was still there. No one in a burst of happiness and confidence in the future had ripped it off. Germans, he thought, standing where he stood now, with their elbows on the sill. Looking off toward the river that was there but could not be seen. Lathering their cheeks in front of the shaving stand . . . Did Mme Bonenfant and Mme Viénot eat with their unwelcome guests, or in the kitchen, or where?

It had stopped raining but the air was saturated with moisture and the trees dripped. In the park in front of the château, the gardener and his wife and boy were pulling the haystacks apart with their forks and spreading the hay around them on the wet ground. He was tempted to go down and offer his services. But if they wouldn't understand in the kitchen, no doubt they wouldn't understand outdoors either.

"What time is it?" Barbara asked.

"Quarter of eleven. How time flies, doesn't it. Are you warm enough?"

"Mmmm."

"It's like living at the bottom of the sea."

He left the window and stood behind her, reading as she

wrote. She had started a letter to her mother and father. The quick familiar handwriting moved across the page, listing the places they had been to, describing the château and the countryside and the terribly interesting French family they were now staying with. The letter seemed to him slightly stepped up, the pleasures exaggerated, as if she were trying to conceal from them (or possibly from herself) the fact that they were not as happy in their present surroundings as they had been in the Hôtel Ouest et Montgomery in Pontorson.

He moved on to the big round table in the center of the room. Among the litter of postcards, postage stamps, and souvenirs, a book caught his eye. Mme Viénot had come upon him in the drawing room after breakfast, and had made a face at the book he was looking at—corrections, additions, and objections to the recently issued grammar of the French Academy—and had said, with a smile: "I don't really think you are ready for that kind of hair-splitting." Taking the book out of his hands, she had given him this one instead. It was a history of the château of Blois. He opened it in the middle, read a paragraph, and then retired to the chaise longue.

Barbara finished her letter, folded it, and brought it to him to read. "Is it all right?"

"Mmmm," he said.

"Should I do it over?"

"No," he said. "It's a very nice letter. Why should you do it over? It will make them very happy."

"You don't like it."

"Yes, I do. It's a fine letter." The insincerity in his voice was so marked that he even heard it himself.

"There isn't a thing wrong with that letter," he said, earnestly this time. "There's no point in writing it over." But she had already torn it in half, and she went on tearing it in smaller pieces, which she dropped in the wastebasket.

"I didn't mean for you to do that!" he exclaimed. "Really, I didn't!" And a voice in his head that sounded suspiciously like the voice of Truth asked if that wasn't exactly what he had wanted her to do. . . . But why, he wondered. What difference did it make to him what she wrote to her father and mother? . . . No difference. It was just that they were shut up together in a cold house, and it was raining.

She sat down at the desk and took a blank sheet of paper and began over again. Ashamed of his petty interfering, he watched her a moment and then retrieved the pocket dictionary from the rug and placed it on the chaise longue beside his knees. While he was trying to untangle the personal and political differences of Henri III and the Duc de Guise, he raised his eyes from the print and observed Barbara's face, bent over her letter. Her face, on every troubled occasion, was his compass, his Pole Star, the white pebbles shining in the moonlight by which Hop-O'-My-Thumb found his way home. When she was happy she was beautiful, but the beauty came and went; it was at the mercy of her feelings. When she was unhappy she could be so plain it was frightening.

After a short while—hardly five minutes—she pushed the letter aside and said, quite cheerfully: "It's stopped raining. Should we go for a walk?"

They went downstairs and through the drawing room and outdoors without seeing anyone. Something kept them from quite liking the front of the house, which was asymmetrical and bare to the point of harshness. They looked into the courtyard at the carriage house, the stables, the high brick wall, and windows they had now looked out of. They followed the cinder drive around the other end of the house. Climbing roses and English ivy struggled for possession of the back wing, which had a much less steeply sloping roof and low dormers instead of bull's-eyes.

The drive took them on up a slope, between two rain-stained statues, and past a pond that had been drained, and finally to another iron gate. Peering through the bars, they saw that there was no trace of a road on the other side. Nothing but the forest. They tried the gate; it was locked. They turned and looked back, and had an uncomfortable feeling that eyes were watching them from the house.

On the way down again, they stopped and looked at the statues. They looked again at the clock that straddled the roof tree of the back wing. It had stopped at quarter of twelve. But quarter of twelve how long ago? And why was there no water in the pond? Seen from the rear, the whole place cried out that there had once been money and the money was gone, frittered away.

They noticed a gap in the hedge, and, walking through it, found themselves in a huge garden where fruit trees, rose trees, flowers, and vegetables were mingled in a way that surprised and delighted them. So did the scarecrow, which was dressed in striped morning trousers and a blue cotton smock. Under the straw hat the stuffed head had sly features painted on it. They saw old Mme Bonenfant at the far end of the garden, and walked slowly toward her. By the time they arrived at the sweet-pea trench her basket was full. She laid her garden shears across the long green stems and took the Americans on a tour of the garden, pointing out the espaliered fruit trees and telling them the French names of flowers. She did not understand their schoolroom French. They felt shy with her. But the tour did not last very long, and they understood that she was being kind, that she wanted them to feel at home. Leading them to some big fat bushes that were swathed in burlap against the birds, she told them to help themselves to the currants and gooseberries, and then she went on down the garden path to the house.

A few minutes later they left the garden themselves and followed the cinder drive down to the public road, where they turned left, in the opposite direction from the village. The road led them past fields on one side and the forest on the other. They came to a farmhouse and an excitable dog, detecting an odor that was not French, barked furiously at them; then to an opening in the forest, where a wagon track wound in through tall oak trees and out of sight. They left the road and followed the wagon track. The tree trunks were green with moss and there was no underbrush, which made the forest look unreal. The ground under their feet was covered with delicate ferns. Barbara kept stooping to gather acorns. These had a high polish and a beautiful shape and were smaller than the acorns she was accustomed to. Her pockets were soon full of them.

"We don't have to stay," she said, turning and looking at him.

"No," he agreed doubtfully. He was relieved, now she had given voice to his own uneasiness. But at the same time, how could they leave? "Of course we don't," he said. "Not if we don't want to."

"But we said we'd stay two weeks. What if she's counting on that, and has turned other people away?"

"I know."

"So in a way, we're bound to do what we said we'd do."

"We could tell her, I guess," he said. "The trouble is, we'll never have anywhere else as good a chance to learn to speak French."

"That's true."

"And later we may be glad we stuck it out. We may find when we get to Paris that it is possible to talk to people in a way that we haven't been able to, so far."

"So let's stay," she said.

"We'll try it for a few days, and then if it doesn't work, we can leave."

There seemed to be no end to the forest. After a short while they turned back, not because they were afraid of getting lost —there was only one road—but the way swimmers confronted with the immensity of the ocean swim out a little way and then, though they could easily swim farther, give way to a nameless fear and turn and head for the shore.

As they came back up the cinder drive, they saw the Canadian pacing the terrace in front of the château and staring up at the sky. The clouds had coalesced for the first time in several days, and the sun was trying to break through.

Away from the French, he seemed perfectly friendly, and willing to acknowledge the fact that Canada is right next to the United States.

"I congratulate you," he said, smiling.

"On what?" Harold asked.

"On the way you made your escape last night, after dinner. The evenings are very long."

"Then we ought to have stayed?" Barbara said.

"You have established a precedent. From now on, they expect you to be independent."

"But we didn't mean to," Harold said, "and if it was really impolite—"

"Oh, yes," Gagny said, smiling. "I quite understood, and the others did too. There was no comment."

"Are *you* expected to remain with them after dinner?" Harold persisted.

"As Americans you are in an enviable position," Gagny said, ignoring the question. Still smiling, he held the door open for them to pass into the drawing room, where Mme Carrère, with tortoise-shell glasses on, sat reading a letter. In her lap were half a dozen more. Mme Viénot was also reading a letter. Mme Bonenfant was reading *Le Figaro*, without glasses.

"Sabine has seen the King of Persia," Mme Viénot announced. And then, turning the page: "There is to be an illumination on Bastille Day. . . . I inquired about ration stamps for you in the village, M. Rhodes, and it seems you must go to Blois and apply for the stamps in person. I'm going there tomorrow afternoon. I could take you to the ration bureau."

"Oh, fine," he said.

"I'm sorry to put you to this trouble, but I do need the stamps."

On the way upstairs, Barbara said: "Do you think we ought to write to the Guaranty Trust Company and have our mail forwarded here?"

"I don't know," he said. "I can't decide."

The first thing they saw when they walked into their room was the big bouquet of pink and white sweet peas on their table. "Aren't they lovely!" Barbara exclaimed, and as she put her face down to smell the flowers, he said: "Let's wait. We've only been gone ten days, and that way there'll be more when we do get it."

"Think of her climbing all the way up here to bring them to us," Barbara said, and then, as she began to brush her hair: "I'm glad we decided to stay."

M. Carrère had breakfast in his room and came downstairs for the first time shortly before lunch. He walked with a cane, and Mme Carrère had to help him into his chair, but once seated he ignored his physical infirmity and so compelled the others to ignore it also. Mme Viénot explained privately to the Americans that he was recovering from a very serious operation. His convalescence was fulfilling the doctors' best hopes. He had gained weight, his appetite was improved, each day he seemed a little stronger. In her voice there was a note of wonder. So many quiet country places he could have gone to, she seemed to be saying, and he had come to her, instead.

He was not like anybody they had ever seen before. Though he seemed a kind man, there was an authority in his manner that kind men do not usually have. His face was long and equine. His eyes were set deep in his head. His hands were extraordinary. You could imagine him playing the cello or praying in the desert. When he smiled he looked like an expert old circus clown. He did not appear to want the attention of everybody when he spoke, and yet he invariably had it, Harold noticed. If he was aware of the dreary fact that there are few people who are not ready to take advantage of natural kindness in the eminent and the well-to-do, it did not bother him. The overlapping folds of his eyelids made his expression permanently humorous, and his judicious statements issued from a wide, sensual, shocking red mouth.

M. Carrère's great-grandfather, Mme Viénot said, had financed the building of the first French railway. M. Carrère himself was of an order of men that was becoming extremely rare in France today. His influence was felt, his taste and opinions were deferred to everywhere, and yet he was so simple, so sincere. To know him informally like this, to have the benefit of his conversation, was a great privilege.

She did not say—she did not have to say—that it was a privilege they were ill-equipped to enjoy.

Mme Carrère, quiet in her dress and in her manner, with black eyes and a Spanish complexion and neat gray hair parted in the middle, looked as if she were now ready for the hard, sharp pencil of Ingres—to whom, it turned out, her great-grandparents had sat for their portrait. She sat in a small armchair, erect but not stiff or uneasy, and for the most part she listened, but occasionally she added a remark when she was amused or interested by something. To Harold Rhodes's eyes, she had the look of a woman who did not need to like or be liked by other people. She was neither friendly nor unfriendly, and when her eyes came to rest on him for a second, what he read in them was that chance had brought them all together at the château, and if she ever met up with him elsewhere or even heard his name mentioned, it would again be the work of chance.

Unable to say the things he wanted to say, because he did not know how to say them in French, able to understand only a minute part of what the others said, deprived of the view from the train window and the conducted tour of the remnants of history, he sat and watched how the humorous expression around M. Carrère's eyes deepened and became genuine amusement when Mme Bonenfant brought forth a *mot*, or observed Mme Carrère's cordiality to Mme Viénot and her mother, not with the loving eye of a tourist but the glazed eye of a fish out of water.

He thought of poor George Ireland, stranded in this very room and only fifteen years old. If I could lie down on the floor I'd probably understand every word they're saying, he thought. Or if I could take off my shoes.

M. Carrère made a point of conversing with the Americans at the lunch table. They were delighted with his explanation of the phrase "entre la poire et le fromage" and so was Mme Viénot, who said: "I hope you will remember what M. Carrère has just said, because it is the very perfection of French prose style. It should be written down and preserved for posterity."

M. Carrère had recently paid a visit to his son, who was living in New York. He had seen the skyscrapers, and also Chicago and the Grand Canyon, on his way to the West Coast. "I could converse with people vis-à-vis but not when the conversation became general, and so I missed a great deal that would have been of interest to me. I found America fascinating," he added, looking at Harold and Barbara as if it had all been the work of their hands. "I particularly liked the 'ut doaks that are served everywhere in your country." They looked blank and he repeated the word, and then repeated it again impatiently: "'ut doaks, 'ut doaks—le saucisson entre les deux pièces de pain."

"Oh, you mean hot dogs!" Barbara said, and laughed.

M. Carrère was not accustomed to being laughed at. The resemblance to a clown was accidental. "'ut doaks," he said defensively, and subsided. The others sat silent, the luncheon table under a momentary pall. Then the conversation was resumed in M. Carrère's native tongue.

Chapter 5

THE Bentley was waiting in front of the house when they got up from the table and went across the hall for their coffee. As the last empty cup was returned to the silver tray, Mme Carrère rose. Ignoring the state of the weather, which they could all see through the drawing-room windows, she helped M. Carrère on with his coat, placed a lilac-colored shawl about his shoulders, and handed him his hat, his pigskin gloves. Outside, the Alsatian chauffeur held the car door open for them, and then arranged a fur robe about M. Carrère's long, thin legs. With a wistful look on their faces, the Americans watched the car go down the drive.

As they turned away from the window, Mme Viénot said: "I have an errand to do this afternoon, in the next village. It would make a pleasant walk if you care to come."

Off they went immediately, with the Canadian. Mme Viénot led them through the gap in the hedge and down the long straight path that bisected the potager. Over their heads storm clouds were racing across the sky, threatening to release a fresh downpour at any moment. She stopped to give instructions to the gardener, who was on his hands and knees among the cabbages, and the walk was suspended a second time when they encountered a white hen that had got through the high wire netting that enclosed the chicken yard. It darted this way and that when they tried to capture it. With his arms spread wide, Gagny ran at the silly creature. "Like the Foreign Office, she can't bear to commit herself," he said. "Steady . . . steady, now . . . Oh, blast!"

When the hen had been put back in the chicken yard, where she wouldn't offer a temptation to foxes, they resumed their walk. The path led past an empty potting shed with several broken panes of glass, past the gardener's hideous stucco villa, and then, skirting a dry fountain, they arrived at a gate in the fence that marked the boundary of Mme Bonenfant's property. On the other side, the path joined a rough wagon road that led them through a farm, and the farm provoked Mme

Viénot to open envy. "It is better kept than my garden!" she exclaimed mournfully.

"In Normandy," Harold said, "in the fields that we saw from the train window, there were often poppies growing. It was so beautiful!"

"They are a pest," Mme Viénot said. "We have them here, too. They are a sign of improper cultivation. You do not have them in the fields in America? . . . I am amazed. I thought they were everywhere."

He decided that this was the right moment to bring up the subject of the double bed in their room.

"We never dreamed that it would take so long to recover from the Occupation," she said, as if she knew exactly what he was on the point of saying, and intended to forestall him. "It is not at all the way it was after the Guerre de Quatorze. But this summer, for the first time, we are more hopeful. Things that haven't been in the shops for years one can now buy. There is more food. And the farmers, who are not given to exaggeration, say that our wheat crop is remarkable."

"Does that mean there will be white bread?" he asked.

"I presume that it does," Mme Viénot said. "You dislike our dark bread? Coming from a country where you have everything in such abundance, you no doubt find it unpalatable."

Ashamed of the abundance when his natural preference was to be neither better nor worse off than other people, he said untruthfully: "No, I like it. We both do. But it seemed a pity to be in France and not be able to have croissants and brioches."

They had come to a fork in the road. Taking the road that led off to the right, she continued: "Of course, your government has been most generous," and let him agree to this by his silence before she went on to say, in a very different tone of voice: "You knew that in order to get wheat from America, we have had to promise to buy your wheat for the next ten years —even though we normally produce more wheat than we need? One doesn't expect to get something for nothing. That isn't the way the world is run. But I must say you drive a hard bargain."

And at that moment Hector Gagny, walking a few feet behind them, with Barbara, said: "We're terribly restricted, you know. Thirty-five pounds is all we can take out of England for travel in a whole year, and the exchange is less advantageous than it is with your dollars."

What it is like, Harold thought, is being so stinking rich that there is no hope of having any friends.

Walking along the country road in silence, he wondered uneasily about all the people they had encountered during their first week in France. So courteous, so civilized, so pleasant; so pleased that he liked their country, that he liked talking to them. But what would it have been like if they'd come earlier—say, after the last excitement of the liberation of Paris had died down, and before the Marshall Plan had been announced? Would France have been as pleasant a place to travel in? Would the French have smiled at them on the street and in train corridors and in shops and restaurants and everywhere? And would they have been as helpful about handing the suitcases down to him out of train windows? In his need, he summoned the driver of the empty St. Malo–St. Servan bus who was so kind to them, the waitress in the hotel in Pontorson, the laborer who had offered to share his bottle of wine in the train compartment, the nice woman with the little boy, the little boy in the carnival, M. Fleury and his son—and they stood by him. One and all they assured Harold Rhodes solemnly in their clear, beautiful, French voices that he was not mistaken, that he had not been taken in, that the kindness he had met with everywhere was genuine, that he had a right to his vision.

"Americans love your country," he said, turning to look directly at the Frenchwoman who was walking beside him. "They always have."

"I am happy to hear it," Mme Viénot said.

"The wheat is paid for by taxation. *I* am taxed for it. And everybody assumes that it comes to you as a gift. But there are certain extremely powerful lobbying interests that operate through Congress, and the State Department does things that Americans in general sometimes do not approve of or even know about. With Argentina, and also with Franco—"

"Entendu!" Mme Viénot exclaimed. "It is the same with us. The same everywhere. Only in politics is there no progress. Not the slightest. Whatever we do as individuals, the government undoes. If France had no government at all, it would do much better. No one has faith in the government any more."

"There is nothing that can be done about it?"

"Nothing," she said firmly. "It has been this way since 1870."

As they walked along side by side, his rancor—for he had felt personally attacked—gradually faded away, and they became once more two people, not two nationalities, out walking. Everything he saw when he raised his eyes from the dirt road pleased him. The poppy-infested fields through which they were now passing were by Renoir, and the distant blue hills by Cézanne. That the landscape of France had produced its painters seemed less likely than that the painters were somehow responsible for the landscape.

The road brought them to a village of ten or twelve houses, built of stone, with slate roofs, and in the manner of the early Gauguin. He asked if the village had a name.

"Coulanges," Mme Viénot said. "It is very old. The priest at Coulanges has supernatural powers. He is able to find water with a forked stick."

"A peach wand?"

"How did you know?" Mme Viénot asked.

He explained that in America there were people who could find water that way, though he had never actually seen anyone do it.

"It is extraordinary to watch," she said. "One sees the point of the stick bending. I cannot do it myself. They say that the priest at Coulanges is also able to find other things—but that is perhaps an exaggeration."

A mile beyond the village, they left the wagon road and followed a path that cut diagonally through a meadow, bringing them to a narrow footbridge across a little stream. On the other side was an old mill, very picturesque and half covered with climbing blush roses. The sky that was reflected in the millpond was a gun-metal gray. A screen of tall poplars completed the picturesque effect, which suggested no special painter but rather the anonymous style of department-store lithographs and colored etchings.

"It's charming, isn't it?" Mme Viénot said.

"Is it still used as a mill?" Harold asked.

"Indeed yes. The miller kept us in flour all through the war. He has a kind of laying mash that is excellent for my hens. I have to come and speak to him myself, though. Otherwise, he isn't interested."

When she left them, they stood watching some white ducks swimming on the surface of the millpond.

The Canadian said, after quite some time: "Why did you come here?" It was not an accusation, though it sounded like one, but the preface to a complaint.

"We wanted to see the châteaux," Barbara said. "And also—"

"Mmmm," Gagny interrupted. "I'd heard about this place, and I thought it would be nice to come here, but I might as well have stayed in London. There hasn't been one hour of hot sunshine in the last five days."

"We were hoping to rent bicycles," Barbara said. "She wrote us that it had been arranged, and then this morning at breakfast she—"

"There are no bicycles for rent," Gagny said indignantly.

"I know there aren't any in the village," Barbara said. "But in Blois?"

He shook his head.

"Then I guess we'll have to go by train," she said.

"It's no use trying to get around by train. It will take you all day to visit one château."

"But she said—"

"If you want to see the châteaux, you need a car," he said, looking much more cheerful now that his discouragement was shared.

They saw Mme Viénot beckoning to them from the door of the mill.

"If this weather keeps up," Gagny said as they started toward her, "I'm going to pack my things and run up to Paris. I've told her that I might. I have friends in Paris that I can stay with, and Wednesday is Bastille Day. It ought to be rather lively."

"I've just had a triumph," Mme Viénot said. "The miller has agreed to let me have two sacks of white flour." The Americans looked at her in surprise, and she said innocently: "I'm not sure that it is legal for him to sell it to me, but he is very attached to our family. I'm to send my gardener around for it early tomorrow morning, before anyone is on the road."

Instead of turning back the way they had come, she led

them across another footbridge and they found themselves on a public road. Walking four abreast, they reached the crest of a long ridge and had a superb view of the valley of the Loire.

Turning to Barbara, Mme Viénot said: "When did you come out?"

"Come out?" Barbara repeated blankly.

"Perhaps I am using the wrong expression," Mme Viénot said. "I am quite out of the habit of thinking in English. Here, when a young girl reaches a certain age and is ready to be introduced to society—"

"We use the same expression. I just didn't understand what you meant. . . . I didn't come out."

"It is not necessary in America, then?"

"Not in the West. It depends on the place, and the circumstances. I went to college, and then I worked for two years, and then I got married."

"And you liked working? So does Sabine. I must show you some of her drawings. She's quite talented, I think. When you go to Paris, you must call on her at *La Femme Elégante*. She will be very pleased to meet two of my guests, and you can ask her about things to see and do in Paris. There is a little bistro that she goes to for lunch—no doubt she will take you there. The clientele is not very distinguished, but the food is excellent, and most reasonable, and you will not always want to be dining at Maxim's."

Harold opened his mouth to speak and then closed it; Mme Viénot's smile made it clear that her remark was intended as a pleasantry.

"I think I told you that my daughter became engaged last summer? After some months, she asked to be released from her engagement. She and her fiancé had known each other since they were children, but she decided that she could not be happy with him. It has left her rather melancholy. All her friends are married now and beginning to have families. Also, it seems her job with *La Femme Elégante* will terminate the first of August. The daughter of one of the editors of the American *Vogue* is coming over to learn the milieu, and a place has to be made for her."

"But that doesn't seem fair!" Barbara exclaimed.

Mme Viénot shrugged. "Perhaps they will find something else for her to do. I hope so."

The road led them away from the river, through fields and vineyards and then along a high wall, to an ornamental iron gate, where the Bentley was waiting. The gatehouse was just inside, and Mme Viénot roused the gatekeeper, who came out with her. His beret was pulled down so as to completely cover his thick gray hair, and he carried himself like a soldier, but his face was pinched and anxious, and he obviously did not want to admit them. Mme Viénot was pleasant but firm. As they talked she indicated now the lane, grown over with grass, that led past the gatehouse and into the estate, now the car that must be allowed to drive up the lane. In the end her insistence prevailed. He went into the gatehouse and came out again with his bunch of heavy keys and opened the gates for the Bentley to drive through.

The party on foot walked in front of the car, which proceeded at a funeral pace. Ahead of them, against the sky, was the blackened shell of a big country house with the chimneys still standing.

It looks like a poster urging people to buy war bonds, Harold thought, and wondered if the planes were American. It turned out that the house had been destroyed in the twenties by a fire of unknown origin. At the edge of what had once been an English garden, the chauffeur stopped the car, and M. and Mme Carrère got out and proceeded with the others along a path that led to a small family chapel. Inside, the light came through stained-glass windows that looked as if they had been taken from a Methodist church in Wisconsin or Indiana. The chapel contained four tombs, each supporting a stone effigy.

With a hissing intake of breath Mme Viénot said: "Ravissant!"

"Ravissant!" said M. and Mme Carrère and Hector Gagny, after her.

Harold was looking at a vase of crepe-paper flowers in a niche and said nothing. The chapel is surely nineteenth-century Gothic, he thought. How can they pretend to like it?

The effigies were genuine. Guarded by little stone dogs and

gentle lap lions, they maintained, even with their hands folded in prayer, a lifelike self-assertiveness. Looking down at one of them—at the low forehead, the blunt nose, the broad, brutal face—he said: "These were very different people."

"They were Normans," Mme Viénot said. "They fought their way up the rivers and burned the towns and villages and then settled down and became French. He's very beautiful, isn't he? But not very intelligent. He was a crusader."

There was no plaque telling which of the seven great waves of religious hysteria and tourism had picked the blunt-nosed man up and carried him all the way across Europe and set him down in Asia Minor, under the walls of Antioch or Jerusalem. But his dust was here, not in the desert of Lebanon; he had survived, in any case; the tourist had got home.

"What I brought you here to see," Mme Viénot said, "is the *prieuré* on the other side of the garden. I don't know the word in English."

"Priory," Barbara said.

"The same word. How interesting!"

While they were in the chapel, it had commenced to sprinkle. They hurried along a garden path. The garden still had a few flowers in it, self-sown, among the weeds and grass. Except for the vaulting of the porch roof, the priory looked from the outside like an ordinary farm building. The entrance was in the rear, down a flight of stone steps that M. Carrère did not attempt. He stood under the shelter of the porch, leaning on his cane, looking ill and gray. When they were around the corner of the building, Harold asked Mme Carrère if the expedition had been too much for him and she said curtly that it had not. Her manner made it as clear as words would have that, though he had the privilege of listening to M. Carrère's conversation, he did not know him, and Mme Carrère did not see that he had, therefore, any reason to be interested in the state of her husband's health. He colored.

The key that Mme Viénot had obtained from the gatekeeper they did not need after all. The padlock was hanging open. The two young men put their weight against the door and it gave way. When their eyes grew accustomed to the feeble light, they could make out a dirt floor, simple carving on the capitals of the thick stone pillars, and cross-vaulting.

Barbara was enchanted.

"It is considered a jewel of eleventh-century architecture," Mme Viénot said. "There is a story— It seems that one of the dukes was ill and afraid he would die, and he made a vow that if he recovered from his sickness he would build a prieuré in honor of the Virgin. And he did recover. But he forgot all about the prieuré and thought of nothing but his hawks and his hounds and hunting, until the Virgin appeared in a dream to someone in the neighborhood and reminded him, and then he had to keep his promise."

The interior of the building was all one room, and not very large, and empty except for an object that Harold took for a medieval battering ram until Mme Viénot explained that it was a wine press.

"In America," he said, "this building would have been taken apart stone by stone and shipped to Detroit, for Henry Ford's museum."

"Yes?" Mme Viénot said. "Over here, we have so many old buildings. The museums are crammed. And so things are left where they happen to be."

He examined the stone capitals and walked all around the wine press. "What became of the nuns?" he asked suddenly.

"They went away," Mme Viénot said. "The building hasn't been lived in since the time of the Revolution."

What the nuns didn't take away with them other hands had. *If you are interested in those poor dead women*, the dirt floor of the priory said—*in their tapestries, tables, chairs, lectuaries, cooking utensils, altar images, authenticated and unauthenti-cated visions, their needlework, feuds, and forbidden pets, go to the public library and read about them. There's nothing here, and hasn't been, for a hundred and fifty years.*

On the way home the walking party was caught in a heavy shower and drenched to the skin.

Dressing hurriedly for dinner, Barbara said: "It's so like her: 'Thérèse will bring you a can—what time would you like it?' and then when seven o'clock comes, there isn't a sign of hot water."

"Do you want me to go down and see about it?"

"No, you'd better not."

"Maybe she does it on purpose," he said.

"No, she's just terribly vague, I've decided. She only half listens to what people are saying. I wouldn't mind if we were on a camping trip, but to be expected to dress for dinner, to have everything so formal, and not even be able to take a bath! Do you want to button me up in back? . . . I've never seen anyone look as vague as she does sometimes. As if her whole life had been passed in a dream. Her eyelids come down over her eyes and she looks at us as if she couldn't imagine who we were or what we were doing here."

"M. Carrère likes Americans, but Mme Carrère doesn't. I don't think she likes much of anybody."

"She likes the Canadian."

"Does she?"

"She laughs at his jokes."

"I don't think Gagny's French is as good as he thinks it is. It's an exaggeration of the way the others speak. Almost a parody."

"M. Carrère speaks beautiful French."

"He speaks French the way an American speaks English. It just comes out of him easily and naturally. Gagny shrugs his shoulders and draws down the corners of his mouth and says 'mais oui' all the time, and it's as if he had picked up the mannerisms of half a dozen different people—which I guess you can't help doing if the language isn't your own. At least, I find myself beginning to do it."

"But it *is* his language. He's bilingual."

"French-Canadian isn't the same as French." He pulled his tie through and drew the knot snugly against his collar. "While you are trying to make the proper sounds and remember which nouns are masculine and which feminine, the imitation somehow unconsciously— M. Carrère's *English* is something else again. His pronunciation is so wide of the mark that sometimes I can't figure out what on earth he's talking about. ''ut doaks, 'ut doaks!' And so impatient with us for not understanding."

"I shouldn't have laughed at him," Barbara said sadly. "I was sorry afterward. Because our pronunciation must sound just as comic to the French, and they never laugh at us."

*

At dinner, Mme Viénot's navy-blue silk dress was held together at the throat by a diamond pin, which M. Carrère admired. He had a passion for the jewelry of the Second Empire,
he said. And Mme Carrère remarked dryly that there was only
one thing she would do differently if she had her life to live
over again. She let her husband explain. In the spring of 1940,
as they were preparing to escape from Paris by car, she had entrusted her jewel case to a friend, and the friend had handed it
over to the Nazis. The few pieces that she had now were in no
way comparable to what had been lost forever. Even so, Barbara had to make an effort to keep from looking at the emerald solitaire that Mme Carrère wore next to her plain gold
wedding ring, and she was sorry that she had listened to
Harold when he suggested that she leave everything but a
string of cultured pearls in the bank at home.

Having established a precedent, the Americans were concerned to live it down. They remained in the petit salon with
the others, after dinner. The company sat, the women with
sweaters and coats thrown over their shoulders, facing the
empty Franklin stove. Observing that Gagny smoked one cigarette and then no more, the Americans, not wanting to be responsible for filling the room with smoke, denied the impulse
each time it recurred, and sometimes found to their surprise
that they had a lighted cigarette in their hand.

While Hector Gagny and M. Carrère were solemnly discussing the underlying causes of the defeat of 1940, the present weakened condition of France, and the dangers that a
reawakened Germany would present to Europe and the rest of
the world, a quite different conversation was taking place in
the mirror over the mantelpiece. Harold Rhodes's reflection,
leaning forward in his chair, said to Mme Viénot's reflection:
"I am not accustomed to bargaining. It makes me uneasy. But
we have a friend who lived in France for years, and she said—"

"Where in France?" Mme Viénot's reflection interrupted.

"In Paris. They had an apartment overlooking the Parc
Monceau."

"The Monceau quarter is charming. I wouldn't mind living
there myself."

"She said it was a matter of principle, and that in traveling
we must keep our eyes open and not be above bargaining or

people would take advantage of us . . . of our inexperience. It was she who told us to ask you to figure the price by the week instead of by the day, but if I had it to do over again, I wouldn't listen to her. I'd just pay you what you asked for, and let it go at that."

Instead of giving him the reassurance he wanted, Mme Viénot's reflection leaned back among the sofa pillows, with her hand to her cheek. It would have been better, he realized, not to have brought the matter up at all. It was not necessary to bring it up. It had been settled before they ever left America. In his embarrassment he turned for help to the photograph of the schoolboy on the piano. "What I am trying to say, I guess, is that it's one thing to live up to your principles, and quite another thing to live up to somebody else's idea of what those principles should be."

"My likeness is here among the others," the boy in the photograph said, "but in their minds I am dead. They have let me die."

"The house is cold and damp and depressing," Barbara Rhodes's reflection said to the reflection of M. Carrère. "Why must we all sit with sweaters and coats over our shoulders? Why isn't there a fire in that stove? I don't see why we all don't get pneumonia."

"People born to great wealth—"

All the other reflections stopped talking in order to hear what M. Carrère's reflection was about to say.

"—are also born to a certain kind of human deprivation, and soon learn to accept it. For example, those letters that arrive daily, even in this remote country house—letters from my lawyer, from my financial advisors, from bankers and brokers and churchmen and politicians and the heads of charitable organizations, all read and acknowledged by Mme Carrère, lest they tire me (which indeed they would). The expressions of personal attachment, of concern for my health, are judged according to their sincerity, in most instances not great, and a few are read aloud to me, lest I think that no one cares. I am accustomed to the fact that in every letter, sooner or later, self-interest shows through. I do not really mind, any more. Music is my delight. When I want companionship, I go to the Musée des Arts Décoratifs and look at the porcelains and the period furniture."

"I used to have a friend—" Mme Bonenfant's reflection said. "She has been dead for twenty years: Mme Noë—"

"Mme Noë?" M. Carrère interrupted. "I knew her also. That is, I was taken to see her as a young man."

"Mme Noë was fond of saying, and of writing in letters and on the flyleaf of books: 'Life is something more than we believe it to be.'"

"Since my illness," M. Carrère said, "I have become aware for the first time of innumerable—reconciliations, I suppose one would call them, that go on around us all the time without our noticing it. Again and again, Mme Carrère hands me something just as I am on the point of asking for it. And in her dreams she is sometimes a party to financial transactions that I am positive I have not told her about. . . . But it is strange that you should speak of Mme Noë. I was thinking about her this very afternoon as I stood looking at that grass-choked garden and that house gutted by fire. She was quite old when I was taken to see her. And she asked me all sorts of questions about myself that no one had ever asked me before, and that I went on answering for days afterward."

"She had that effect on everyone," Mme Bonenfant said.

"I remember that she led me to a vase of flowers and we talked."

"And what did you say?" Barbara Rhodes asked.

"I said something that pleased her," M. Carrère said, "but what it was I can no longer remember. All I know is that it was not at all like the sort of thing I usually said. And when she left me to speak to someone else, I did not have the feeling that I was being abandoned. Or that she would ever confuse me afterward with anyone else. . . . She is an important figure in the memoirs of a dozen great men, and reading about her the same question always occurs to me. What manner of woman she was really, if you made no claim on her, if you asked for nothing (as she asked for nothing) but merely sat, silent, content merely to be there beside her, and let her talk or not talk, as she felt like doing, all through a summer afternoon, none of them seem to know."

"She was frail," Mme Bonenfant said. "She was worn out by ill-health, by the demands, the endless claims upon her time and energy—"

"Which she must have encouraged," M. Carrère said.

"No doubt," Mme Bonenfant said. "By temperament she was not merely kind, she was angelic, but there was also irony. Once or twice, toward the end of her life, she talked to me about herself. It seems she suffered always from the fear that, wanting only to help people, she nevertheless unwittingly brought serious harm to them. This may have been true but I do not know a single instance of it. For my own part, I am quite content to believe that life is nothing more than our vision of it—of what we believe it to be. Tacitus says that the phoenix appears from time to time in Egypt, that it is a fact well verified. Herodotus tells the same story, but skeptically."

"At the Council of Nicaea," M. Carrère said, "three hundred and eighteen bishops took their places on their thrones. But when they rose as their names were called, it appeared that they were three hundred and nineteen. They were never able to make the number come out right; whenever they approached the last one, he immediately turned into the likeness of his neighbor."

"Before Harold and I were married," Barbara said, "a woman in a nightclub read our palms, and she said Leo and Virgo should never marry. Their horoscopes are in conflict. If they love each other and are happy it is a mistake. . . . That's why he doesn't like fortunetellers. I don't think our marriage is a mistake, but on the other hand, sometimes I lie awake between three and four in the morning, planning dinner parties and solving riddles and worrying about curtains that don't hang straight in the dark, and about my clothes and my hair, and about whether I have been unintentionally the cause of hurt feelings. And about Harold, sound asleep beside me and sharing not only the same bed but some of my worst faults. . . . Does anybody know the answer to the riddle that begins: 'If three people are in a room and two of them have a white mark on their forehead—' "

"The answer to the riddle of why I am not married," Hector Gagny said, "is that I am. And my wife hates me."

"So did the woman I gave my jewel case to," Mme Carrère said. "But I didn't know it."

"She has all but ruined my career," Gagny said. "She is beautiful and willful and perverse, and in her own way quite wonderful. But she makes no concessions to the company she finds herself in, and I sit frozen with fear of what may come out of her mouth."

"Do not despair," Mme Bonenfant said. "Be patient. Your wife, M. Gagny, may only be acting the way she does out of the fear that you do not love her."

"In the beginning we seemed to be happy, and only after a while did it become apparent that there were things that were not right. And that they were not ever going to be right. I began to see that behind the fascination of her mind, her temperament, there was some force at work that was not on my side, and bent on destroying both of us. But what is it? Why is she like that?"

"Though there was only two years difference in our ages," Mme Viénot said, "my mother held me responsible for my brother's safety when we were children. I used to have nightmares in which something happened to him or was about to happen to him. When we played together, I never let go of his hand."

"Maurice was delicate," Mme Bonenfant said.

"He cried easily," Mme Viénot said. "He was always getting his feelings hurt. My daughter Sabine is very like him in appearance. I only hope that her life is not as unhappy as his."

"I see that you haven't forgiven me," the boy in the photograph said. "I failed to distinguish myself in my studies but I made three friendships that were a credit to me, and I died bravely. It took me almost an hour to kill myself. . . . Now I am an effect of memory. When you have completely forgotten me, I assume that I will pass on to other places."

"They say that people who talk about committing suicide never actually do it," Mme Viénot said. "Maurice was the exception. When his body was brought home for burial we were warned that it would be better not to open the coffin."

"It was an accident," Mme Bonenfant said.

"And M. Viénot?" Harold Rhodes asked the boy in the

photograph. "Why does nobody speak of him? His name is never mentioned."

"Do not interrupt," the boy in the photograph said. "They are speaking of me—of what happened to me."

At quarter of eleven, when the Americans went upstairs, they found a large copper can in their bathroom. The temperature of the water in the can was just barely warm to the touch.

Lying awake in the dark, she heard the other bed creak.

"Are you awake?" she whispered, when he turned again.

He was awake.

"We don't have to stay," she said, in a small, sad voice.

"If it's no good I think we could tell her that we're not happy and just leave." He sat up and rearranged the too-fat pillows and then said: "It's funny how it comes and goes. I have periods of clarity and then absolute blankness. And my mind gets so tired I don't care any more what they're saying." The bed creaked as he turned over again. He tried to go to sleep but he had talked himself wide awake. "Good night. I love you," he said. But it didn't work. This declaration, which on innumerable occasions had put his mind at rest, had no effect because she was not in his arms.

"It isn't simply the language," he said, after several minutes of absolute silence. "Though that's part of it. There's a kind of constraint over the conversation, over everything. I think they all feel it. I think it's the house."

"I know it's the house," she said. "Go to sleep."

Five minutes later, the bed creaked one last time. "Do I imagine it," he asked, "or is it true that when they speak of the Nazis—downstairs, I mean—the very next sentence is invariably some quite disconnected remark about Americans?"

Chapter 6

THE village of Brenodville was too small and unremarkable to be mentioned in guidebooks, and derived its identity from the fact that it was not some other village—not Onzain or Chouzy or Chailles or Chaumont. It had two principal streets, the Grande Rue and the avenue Gambetta, and they formed the letter T. The avenue Gambetta went from the Place de l'Eglise to the railway station. The post office, the church, the mairie, and the cemetery were all on the Grande Rue. So was the house of M. Fleury. It ought to have given some sign of recognition, but it didn't; it was as silent, blank, secretive, and closed to strangers as every other house up and down the village street. While they stood looking at it, Mme Viénot came out of the post office and caught them red-handed.

"You are about to pay a call on M. Fleury?"

"We weren't even sure this was where he lived," Harold said, blushing. "The houses are all alike."

"That is the house of M. Fleury. You didn't make a mistake," Mme Viénot said. "I think it is unlikely that you will find him at home at this hour, but you can try."

After an awkward moment, during which they did not explain why they wanted to pay a call on M. Fleury, she got on her bicycle and pedaled off down the street. Watching the figure on the bicycle get smaller and smaller, he said: "She's going to be soaked on the way home. Look at the sky."

"A hundred francs was probably enough," Barbara said. "In a place as small as this."

"It would reflect on her, in any case," he said.

"And if he isn't there, we'd have to explain to his wife."

"Let's skip it."

They bought stamps at the post office, and wondered, too late, if the postmistress could read the postcards they had just mailed to America. The woman who sold them a sack of plums to eat in their room may have been, as Mme Viénot said, a great gossip, but she did not gossip with them. They tried unsuccessfully to see through, over, or around several garden gates. With the houses that were directly on the street, shutters or lace curtains discouraged curiosity. They stood in the vestibule of the little church and peered in. Here there was no barrier but their own Protestant ignorance.

The Grande Rue was stopped by a little river that was a yard wide. Wild flags grew along the water's edge. A footbridge connected an old house on this side with its orchard on the other. They decided that the wooden shelter on the river bank was where the women brought their linen to be washed in running water.

"I don't suppose you could have a washing machine if you wanted to," he said.

"No, but you'd have other things," she said. "You'd live in a different way. You wouldn't want a washing machine."

The sky had turned a greenish black while they were standing there, and now a wind sprang up. Out over the meadows a great abstract drama was taking place. In the direction of Pontlevoy and Montrichard and Aignan, the bodies and souls of the unsaved fell under the sway of the powers of darkness, the portions of light in them were lost, and the world became that much poorer. In the direction of Herbault and St. Amand and Selommes, all glorious spirits assembled, the God of Light himself appeared, accompanied by the aeons and the perfected just ones. The angels supporting the world let go of their burden and everything fell in ruins. A tremendous conflagration consumed meadows and orchard, and on the very brink of the little river, a perfect separation of the powers of light and darkness took place. The kingdom of light was brought into a condition of completeness, all the grass bent the same way. Darkness should, from this time on, have been powerless.

"We'd better start home," Barbara said.

On the outskirts of the village they had to take shelter in a doorway. The rain came down in front of their faces like a curtain. At times they couldn't even see through it. Then the sky began to grow lighter and the rain slackened.

"If we had a car," he said, "it would be entirely different. We wouldn't feel cooped up. The house is damp and cold. The books accumulate on the table in our room and I read a few sentences and my mind gets tired of translating and having to look up words and begins to wander."

"A lot of it's our fault," she said, "for not speaking French."

"And part of it isn't our fault. It wasn't like this anywhere else. With time hanging heavy on our hands, we always seem to be hurrying, always about to be late to lunch or dinner. We ask for a double bed and nothing is done about it, and she says nothing *can* be done about it because of the lamp. What actually has the lamp got to do with it? We didn't ask for a lamp. Nothing is done about anything we ask for in the way of comfort or convenience. And neither is it refused. The hot water arrives while we're at dinner. The cook's bicycle is too frail for us to borrow, and we can't borrow hers because it has just been repaired. The buses and trains run at the wrong time, the taxi is expensive. George Ireland showed me a snapshot of the horse hitched up to a dog cart, but that was last summer. Now the horse is old and needed in the garden. When I try to find her to ask her about some arrangement, she's never anywhere. I don't even know where her room is."

"Did you hear her say 'I like your American custom of not shaking hands in the morning'?"

"They shake hands at *breakfast*?"

"Apparently."

"The cozy atmosphere of the breakfast table is a fabrication that we are supposed to accept and even contribute to," he went on, "as the other guests politely accept and support the fiction that Mme Viénot and her mother are the very cream of French society and lost nothing of importance when they lost their money."

"Perhaps they *are* the cream of French society," Barbara said.

"From the way Mme Viénot kowtows to Mme Carrère, I would say no. Mme Viénot is a social climber and a snob. And that's another thing. Yesterday evening before dinner, Mme Carrère asked the Canadian to call on them. In Paris."

"And did he accept?"

"He behaved like a spaniel that has just been petted on the head."

"Probably if you were French the Carrères would be very useful people to know."

"I found myself wondering whether—before they go on Monday—they would invite *us* to call on them," he said.

"Do you want to see the Carrères in Paris?"

"I don't care one way or the other."

"Our French isn't good enough," she said. "Besides, I don't think they do that sort of thing over here. It isn't reasonable to expect it of them."

"Who said anything about being reasonable? He gave Gagny his card, and I want him to do the same thing to us. And it isn't enough that he should invite us to call on him at his office. I want us to be invited to their home."

"We have nothing to say to them here. What point is there in carrying it any farther?"

"No point," he said. "There's no excuse for our ever seeing them again, except curiosity."

They saw that they were being stared at by a little boy in the open doorway of the house across the street.

"If they did ask us, would you go?"

"No," he said.

"It would be interesting to see their apartment," she said, and so, incriminating herself, sharing in his dubious desires, made him feel better about having them.

"They give me the creeps," he said. "Mme Carrère especially."

"What did she say that hurt your feelings?"

"Nothing."

"It isn't raining so hard," Barbara said.

He stepped out of the shelter of the doorway with his palm extended to the rain.

"We might as well be starting back or we'll be late again," he said.

He took off his coat and put it around her shoulders. As they went off down the street, she tried not to listen to what he was saying. In the mood he was in, he exaggerated, and his exaggerations gave rise to further exaggerations, and helplessly, without wanting to, analyzing and explaining and comparing one thing with another that had no relation to it, he got farther and farther from the truth.

They stopped to look at a pink oleander in a huge tub. The blossoms smelled like sugar and water.

"As soon as we're outside," he said, "in the garden or stopping to pick wildflowers along the road or like now—the moment we're off somewhere by ourselves, everything opens up like a fan. And as soon as we're indoors with them, it closes."

"We could go to Paris," she said.

"With the Canadian?"

"If you like."

"And be there for Bastille Day? That's a wonderful idea. We could run up to Paris and come back after two or three days."

"Or not come back," she said.

At lunch Mme Viénot said: "We should leave the house by two o'clock."

But when two o'clock came, they were on the terrace, leaning against the stone balustrade, and she had not appeared.

"I'd go look for her," he said, "if it weren't so much like looking for a needle in a haystack."

"Don't talk so loud," Barbara said, glancing up at an open window directly above them.

"I'm not talking loud. I'm practically whispering."

"Your voice carries."

He noticed that she was wearing a cotton dress and said: "Are you going to be warm enough?"

"I meant to bring a sweater."

He jumped down and started across the terrace, and she called after him: "The cardigan."

He pushed the door open and saw a small elderly woman standing in an attitude of dramatic indecision beside the white columns that divided the drawing room in half. She was wearing a tailored suit with a high-necked silk blouse. A lorgnette hung by a black ribbon from her collar. Her hair was mouse-colored. Like the old ladies of his childhood she wore no rouge or lipstick. She saw him at the same moment that he saw her, and advanced to meet him, as if his sudden appearance had resolved the question that was troubling her.

"Straus-Muguet," she said.

He put out his hand and she took it. To his surprise, she knew his name. She had heard that he was staying in the house, and she had been hoping to meet him. "J'adore la jeunesse," she said.

He was not all that young; he was thirty-four; but there was no one else in the room that this remark could apply to, and so he was forced to conclude that she meant him. He looked into her eyes and found himself in another climate, the one he had been searching for, where the sun shines the whole day long, the prevailing wind is from the South, and the natives are friendly.

She was not from the village, he decided on the way upstairs. She was a lady, but a lady whose life had been lived in the country; a character out of Chekhov or Turgenev. Probably she belonged in one of the big country houses in the neighborhood and was a family friend—a lifelong friend of old Mme Bonenfant, who had come to call, to spend the afternoon in quiet reminiscences over their embroidery or their knitting, with tea and cake at the proper time, and, at parting, the brief exchange of confidences, the words of reassurance and continuing affection that would make it seem worth while, for both of them, to go on a little longer.

When he came back with the sweater, the drawing room was empty and Mme Viénot and the Canadian were standing on the terrace with Barbara. Walking at a good pace they covered the two kilometers to the concrete highway that followed the river all the way into Blois. The bus came almost immediately and was crammed with people.

"I'm afraid we won't get seats," Mme Viénot said. "But it's only a ten-minute ride."

There was hardly room to breathe inside the bus, and all the windows were closed. Harold stood with his arm around Barbara's waist, and craned his neck. His efforts to see out were defeated everywhere by heads, necks, and shoulders. It took him some time to determine which of the passengers was responsible for the suffocating animal odor that filled the whole bus. It was twenty-five minutes before they saw the outskirts of Blois.

Threading her way boldly between cyclists, Mme Viénot led them down the rue Denis Papin (inventor of the principle of the steam engine), through the Place Victor Hugo, up a long ramp, and then through a stone archway into the courtyard of the château, the glory of Blois. They saw the octagonal staircase, the chapel, and a splendid view, all without having to purchase tickets of admission. Then they followed her back down the ramp, through the crowded narrow streets, to a charcuterie, where she bought blood sausage, and then into the bicycle shop next door, where they saw a number of bicycles, none of which were for rent. They saw the courtyard of the ancient Hôtel d'Alluye, built by the treasurer of François premier, but did not quite manage to escape out onto the sidewalk before the concierge appeared. While Harold stood wondering if they should be there at all and if the concierge would be as unpleasant as she looked, Hector Gagny extracted fifty francs from his wallet and the threat was disposed of. Climbing a street of stairs, they saw the cathedral. There they separated. Gagny went off in search of a parfumerie, and Mme Viénot took the Americans to the door of the ration bureau and then departed herself to do some more shopping. They stood in line under a sign—*Personnes Isolées*—that had for them a poignancy it didn't have for those who were more at home in the French language. They could not get ration coupons because Harold had not thought to bring their passports.

When they emerged from the building, they saw that it was at one end of a long terrace planted in flower beds, with a view over the lower part of the city. Leaning against a stone balustrade, with his guidebook open in front of him, he started to read about the terrace where they now were.

"What's that?" Barbara asked.

He looked up. At the far end of the terrace a crowd had gathered. The singing came from that direction. They listened intently. It sounded like children's voices.

"It's probably something to do with Bastille Day," he said, and stuffed the guidebook in his raincoat pocket, and they hurried off down the gravel paths.

For tourists who fall in love with the country they are traveling in, charms of great potency are always at work. If there is a gala performance at the Opéra, they get the last two tickets. Someone runs calling and gesturing the whole length of the train to find them and return the purse that was left on a bench on the station platform. And again and again they are drawn, as if by wires, to the scene that they will never be able to forget as long as they live.

At first the Americans stood politely on the outskirts of the crowd, thinking that they had no right to be here. But then they worked their way in gradually, until at last they were clear inside.

The children, dressed all in white, had no leader, and did not need one. They had been preparing for this occasion for years. Their voices were very high, pure, on pitch, thoroughly drilled, and happy. Music heard in the open air is not like music in a concert hall. It was as if the singing came from one's own heart.

Remember what the lark sounds like, said the stones of the Bishop's Palace. *Try for perfection.* . . .

Try for joy, said the moss-stained fountain.

Do not be afraid to mark the contrasts if it is necessary, said the faded tricolor. *But do not let one voice dominate.* . . . *Remember that you are French. Remember that in no other country in the world do children have songs that are as beautiful and gay and unfading as these.* . . .

The exact sound of joy is what you must aim for. . . .

. . . of a pure conscience . . .

. . . of an enthusiastic heart . . .

"Oh, oh, oh," Harold exclaimed under his breath, as if he had just received a fatal wound.

Full of delight but still exact and careful and like one proud voice the children sang: "Qui n'avait jam-jam-jamais naviGUÉ!"

He looked at Barbara. They shook their heads in wonder.

"They must be very old songs," he whispered.

Turning, he studied the adults, dressed in somber colors and shabby suits, but attentive, critical, some of them probably with ears only for the singing of a particular child. They appeared to take the songs for granted. This is what it means to be French, he thought. It belongs with the blue, white, and red flags and the careful enunciation and the look of intelligence in every eye and the red poppies growing in the wheat. These songs are their birthright, instead of "London Bridge Is Falling Down. . . ."

The children finished singing and marched off two by two, and the crowd parted to let in some little boys, who performed a ferocious staff dance in which nobody got hurt; and then six miniature couples, who marched into the open space and formed a circle. The boys had on straw hats, blue smocks, and trousers that were too large for them. The little girls wore white caps and skirts that dragged the ground and in some instances had to be held up with a safety pin. At a signal from an emaciated man with a violin, the gavotte began. In the patterns of movement, and quite apart from the grave self-conscious children who danced, there was a gallantry that was explicitly sexual, an invitation now mocked, now welcomed openly. But because they were only eight-year-olds, the invitation to love was like a melody transposed from its original key and only half recognizable. Suddenly he turned and worked his way blindly toward the outer edge of the crowd. Barbara followed him out into the open, where a group of fifteen-year-old girls in diaphanous costumes waited to go on. If the sight of a foreigner wiping his eyes with his handkerchief interested them, they did not show it. They stretched and bent over, practicing, or examined the blackened soles of their feet, or walked about in twos and threes. He saw that Barbara was looking at him anxiously and tried to explain and found he could not speak. Again he had to take his handkerchief out.

"There's Mme Viénot," Barbara said.

Turning, he saw her hurrying toward them between the flower beds. Ignoring his condition, she said: "M. and Mme Carrère are waiting in the pâtisserie," and hurried them off down the gravel path.

The pastry shop was down below, in the rue de Commerce, and it was crowded and noisy. Cutting her way through clots of people, squeezing between tables, frustrating waitresses with trays, Mme Viénot arrived at the large round table in the rear of the establishment where M. and Mme Carrère and Mme Bonenfant were waiting, their serenity in marked contrast to the general noise and confusion. Mme Carrère invited Harold and Barbara to sit down, and then she allowed her eyes to roam over the room, as if something were about to happen of so important a nature that talk was not necessary. Mme Bonenfant asked if they had found Blois a beautiful city and was pleased when he said that they preferred Brenodville. The village was charming, she agreed; very old, and just the way a village should be; she herself had great affection for it. Mme Viénot went off in search of M. Gagny, and for the next ten minutes M. Carrère devoted himself to the task of capturing a busboy and ordering a carafe of "fresh" water. Human chatter hung in the air like mist over a pond.

They saw that Mme Viénot had returned, with the Canadian. She stopped to confer with the proprietress and he came straight back to their table. He had found the parfumerie, he explained as he sat down, but it did not have the kind of perfume his mother had asked him to get for her. The proprietress of the pâtisserie nodded, shrugged, and seemed in no way concerned about what Mme Viénot was saying to her. Arriving at the table in the rear, Mme Viénot said: "She's going to send someone to take our order." She sat down, glanced at her watch nervously, and said: "The Brenodville bus leaves at seven minutes to six and it is now after five," and then explained to the Americans that the pâtisserie was well known.

The water arrived, was tested, was found to be both cool and fresh. They sat sipping it until a waitress came to find out what they wanted. This required a good five minutes of animated conversation to decide. The names meant nothing to Barbara and Harold, and since they could not decide for themselves, Mme Carrère acted for them; Mme Rhodes should have *demi-chocolat et demi-vanille* and M. Rhodes *chocolat-praliné*. The ices arrived, and with them a plate of pâtisseries—cream puffs in the shape of a cornucopia, strawberry tarts, little cakes that were rectangular, diamond-shaped, or in layers, with a soft filling of chocolate, or with almond paste or whipped cream. The enthusiasm of the Americans was gratifying to the French, who agreed among themselves that the pâtisseries, though naturally not what they had been before the war, were acceptable. "If you consider that they have not been made with white flour," M. Carrère said, "and that the ices have to be flavored with saccharine . . ."

Harold was conscious of a genuine cordiality in the faces around the table. They were being taken in, it seemed; he and Barbara were being initiated into the true religion of France.

The *addition*, on a plate, was placed in front of M. Carrère, who motioned to Harold to put his wallet away. In America, he said, he had been treated everywhere with such extraordinary kindness. He was grateful for this opportunity of paying it back.

There was a crowd waiting in the rue Denis Papin for the

bus, but they managed to get seats. Six o'clock came and nothing happened; the driver was outside stowing bicycles away on the roof. More people kept boarding the bus until the aisle was blocked. Sitting beside Barbara, with his hand in hers, Harold saw Gagny get up and give his seat to a colored nun, but it did not occur to him to follow this example, and he was hardly aware of when the bus started at last. The children's voices, high, clear, and only half human, took him far outside his ordinary self. He felt as if he were floating on the end of a long kite string, the other end of which was held by the hand that was, in actuality, touching his hand. He did not remember anything of the ride home.

When the household assembled before dinner, Harold saw that the elderly woman who had introduced herself to him earlier in the afternoon was still here, and he was pleased for her sake that she had been asked to stay and eat with them. In that first glimpse of her, standing beside the white columns in the drawing room, she had seemed uneasy and as if she was not sure of her welcome. He sat down beside her now, ready to take up where they had left off. She leaned toward him and confessed that it was the regret of her life that she had never learned English. She had a nephew—or a godson, he couldn't make out which—living in America, she said, and she longed to go there. Harold began to talk to her about New York City, in French, and after a minute or two she shook her head. He smiled and sat back in his chair. Her answering smile said that though they were prevented from conversing, they needn't let that stand in the way of their being friends. He turned his head and listened to what Mme Bonenfant was saying to M. Carrère.

". . . To them the entry into Paris was a perfectly agreeable occasion, and they insisted on showing us snapshots. They could see no reason why we shouldn't enjoy looking at them."

"The attitude is characteristic," M. Carrère said. "And extraordinary, if you think how often their own country has been invaded. . . . I had an experience . . ."

In his mind Harold still heard the children's voices. Mme Viénot addressed a remark to him, which had to be repeated before he could answer it. He noticed that Mme Straus-Muguet was wearing a little heart encrusted with tiny diamonds, on a fine gold chain. So appropriate for her.

M. Carrère's experience was that a Nazi colonel had sent for him, knowing that he was ill and would have to get up out of bed to come, and had then kept him waiting for over an hour in his presence while he engaged in chit-chat with another officer. But then he committed an error; he remarked on the general lack of cultivation of the French people and the fact that so few of them knew German. With one sentence, in the very best *hoch Deutsch*, M. Carrère had reduced him to confusion.

"I have a friend," Mme Viénot said, "who had a little dog she was very fond of. And the German officers who were quartered in her house were correct in every way, and most courteous to her, until the day they left, when one of them picked the little dog up right in front of her eyes and hurled it against the marble floor, killing it instantly."

It's their subject, Harold thought. This is what they are talking about, everywhere. This is what I would be talking about if I were a Frenchman.

Mme Straus-Muguet described how, standing at the window of her apartment overlooking the Etoile, peering through the slits of the iron shutter, with the tears running down her face, she had watched the parade that she thought would never end. "Quelle horreur!" she exclaimed with a shiver, and Harold checked off the first of a whole series of mistaken ideas about her. She was not a character out of Turgenev or Chekhov. Her life had not been passed in isolation in the country but at the center of things, in Paris. She had been present, she said— General Weygand had invited her to accompany him to the ceremony at the Invalides, when the bronze sarcophagus of Napoléon II, which the Nazis had taken from its crypt in Vienna, was placed beside the red porphyry tomb of his father, Napoléon Ier.

The room was silent, the faces reflecting each in its own way the harsh wisdom of history.

Since she was a friend of General Weygand, it was not likely that she was socially unsure in the present company, Harold said to himself. He must have been mistaken. He turned to Mme Viénot and explained that they were thinking of going up to Paris with M. Gagny in the morning, and would probably return on Friday. To his surprise, this plan met with her enthusiastic approval. He asked if they should pack their clothes, books, and whatever they were not taking with them, so that the suitcases could be removed from their room during the three days they would be gone.

"That won't be necessary," Mme Viénot said, and he took this to mean that they would not be charged during their absence, and was relieved that this delicate matter had been settled without his having to go into it. For the first time, he found himself liking her.

She offered to telephone the hotel where they were planning to stay, and make a reservation for them. As she went toward the hall, M. Carrère called out the telephone number. The hotel was around the corner from their old house, he said, and he knew it well. During the war it had been occupied by German officers.

Mme Bonenfant reminded Barbara that there was to be an illumination on the night of July 14, and Harold took out his financial notebook and wrote down the route that Mme Carrère advised them to follow: if they began with the Place de la Concorde and the Madeleine, and then went on to the Place de l'Opéra, and then to the Place du Théâtre Français and the Comédie Française, with its lovely lamps, and then to the Louvre, and finally Notre Dame reflected in the river, they would see all the great monuments, the city at its most ravishing.

They got up and went in to dinner, and something that Mme Straus-Muguet said during the first course made Harold realize at last that she was not a caller but a paying guest like them. He looked across the table at her, at the winking reflections of the little diamond-encrusted heart, and thought what a pity it was that she should have come to stay at the château just as they were leaving.

When the company left the dining room, Mme Straus-Muguet excused herself and went upstairs and brought back down with her a box of *diamonoes*. She asked Harold if he knew this delightful game and he shook his head.

"I take it with me everywhere I go," she said.

Mme Bonenfant removed the cover from the little round table in the center of the petit salon, and the ivory counters were dumped onto the green felt center. While Mme Straus-Muguet was explaining the rules of the game to Barbara, Mme Viénot captured M. Carrère and then indicated the place beside her on the sofa where Harold was to sit.

The Canadian, Mme Carrère, Mme Bonenfant, Barbara, and Mme Straus-Muguet sat down at the table and commenced playing. The game, a marriage of dominoes and anagrams, was agreeable and rather noisy. M. Carrère excused himself and went upstairs to read in bed.

Mme Viénot, reclining against the sofa cushions with her hand to her temple, defended the art of conversation. "The young people of today are very different from my generation," she said, setting Harold a theme to develop, a subject to embroider, as inclination or experience prompted. "They are serious-minded and idealistic, and concerned about the future. My daughter's husband works until eleven or twelve every night at his office in the Ministry and Suzanne sits at home and knits for the children. At their age, my life was made up entirely of parties and balls. Nobody thought about the future. We were having too good a time."

She sat up and rearranged the pillows. Her face was now disturbingly close to his. He shifted his position.

"My nephew maintains that we were a perverted generation," Mme Viénot said cheerfully, "and I dare say he is right. All we cared about was excitement. . . ."

Though he was prevented from going toward the gaiety in the center of the room, he was aware that Mme Carrère had come out of her shell at last and, pleased with the extent of Barbara's vocabulary, was coaching her.

"I'm no good at anything that has to do with words," the Canadian said mournfully. "When something funny happens to me, I never can put it in a letter. I have to save it all up until I go home."

Mme Bonenfant was slower still, and kept the others waiting, and had to be shown where her pieces would fit into the meandering diagram. Mme Straus-Muguet was quick as lightning, and when Barbara completed a word, she complimented her, seized her hand, called her "chérie," taught her an idiom to go with the word, and put down a counter of her own—all in thirty seconds.

*

"Mme Carrère loves words," Barbara said later as she was transferring four white shirts from the armoire to an open suitcase. "Any kind of abstraction. Anything sufficiently intellectual that she can apply her mind to it. When we started to play that game she became a different person."

"I saw that she was. Gagny asked us to have lunch with him on Thursday at a bistro he goes to. He said it was quite near our hotel."

"Did you say we would?"

He shook his head. "I left it up in the air. I wasn't sure that was what we'd most want to be doing."

"Did you enjoy your conversation with Mme Viénot?"

"It was interesting. I had a different feeling about the house tonight. And the people. I'm glad we decided not to leave."

"So am I."

"All in all, it's been a nice day."

"Very."

He pulled the covers back and jumped into bed.

"They seemed very pleased with us when I said we were thinking of going up to Paris. . . . As if we were precocious children who had suddenly grasped an idea that they would have supposed was too old for us."

"I expect they'd all like to be going up to Paris in the morning," Barbara said.

"Or as if we had found the answer to a riddle. Or managed to bring a long-drawn-out parlor game to an end."

Chapter 7

THE Canadian did not appear at breakfast, and Mme Viénot did not offer any explanation of why he was not coming, but neither did she appear to be surprised, so he must have spoken to her. Either his threats had been idle and he had no friends in Paris who were waiting for him with open arms, or else he was avoiding a long train journey in their company. If he was, they did not really care. They were too lighthearted, as they sipped at their peculiar coffee and concealed the taste of the bread with marmalade, to care about anything but their own plans. They were starting on a train journey across an entirely new part of France. They were going to have to speak French with all kinds of strangers, some of whom might temporarily become their friends. They were going to change trains in Orléans, and at the end of their journey was Paris on Bastille Day. They could hardly believe their good fortune.

The taxi was old, and the woman who sat behind the wheel looked like a man disguised as a woman. Mme Viénot stood in the open doorway and waved to them until they were out of sight around the corner of the house. As the taxi turned into the public road, they looked back but they could not see the house from here. He felt the bulge in his inside coat pocket: passports, wallet, traveler's checks. He covered Barbara's gloved hand with his bare hand, and leaned back in the seat. "This is more like it," he said.

"Just where is the Hôtel Vouillemont?" Harold said when they were out in the street in front of the Gare d'Austerlitz.

Barbara didn't know.

He managed to keep from saying: "How can you not know where it is when you spent two whole weeks there?" by saying instead: "I should have asked Mme Viénot." But she was aware of his suppressed impatience with her, and sorry that she couldn't produce this one piece of helpful information for him when he, who had never been to Europe before, had got them in and out of so many hotels and railroad stations. Actually she could have found it all by herself, simply by retracing her steps.

It was the only way she ever found her way back to some place she didn't know the location of. Back through three years of being married to him, and two years of working in New York, to the day she graduated from college, and from there back to the day she sat watching her mother and Mrs. Evans sewing name tapes on the piles of new clothes that were going off with her to boarding school, and then back to the time when the walls of her room were covered with pictures of horses, and so finally to the moment when they were leaving the Hôtel Vouillemont to go to the boat train—which was, after all, only what other people do, she thought; only they do it in their minds, in large jumps, and she had to do it literally.

She tried, anyway. She thought very carefully and then said: "I think it's not far from the Louvre."

They went into the Métro station, and there he found an electrified map and began to study it.

Also, she thought, when she was here before, it was with her father, who had an acutely developed sense of geography and never got lost in strange cities, any more than in the woods. Instead of trying to figure out for themselves where they were, they always stood and waited for him to make up his mind which was north, south, east, and west. As soon as he had arrived at the points of the compass, he started off and they followed, talking among themselves and embroidering on old jokes and keeping an eye on him without difficulty even in crowds because he was half a head taller than anybody else.

Harold pushed a button, lights flashed, and he announced: "We change trains at Bastille."

With a sense that they were journeying through history, they climbed the steps to the platform. They were delighted with the beautiful little toy train, all windows and bright colors and so different from the subway in New York. They changed at Bastille and got off at Louvre and came up out onto the sidewalk. The big forbidding gray building on their left was the Louvre, Barbara was positive, but there was no dancing in the street in front of it. A short distance away, they saw another building with a sign *Louvre* on it, but that turned out to be a department store. It was closed. All the shops were closed. Paris was as empty and quiet as New York on a Sunday morning. They listened. No sound of distant music came from the side streets. Neither did a taxi. Their suitcases grew heavier with each block, and at the first sidewalk café they sat down to rest. A waiter appeared, and Harold ordered two glasses of red wine. When he had drunk his, he got up and went inside. The interior of the café was gloomy and ill-lit, and he was glad he had left Barbara outside. It was clearly a tough joint. He asked if he could see the telephone directory and discovered that there was more than one, and that they were compiled according to principles he didn't understand, and in that poor light the Hôtel Vouillemont did not seem to be listed in any of them. So he appealed to the kindness of Madame la Patronne, who left the bar untended and came over to the shelf of telephone books and looked with him.

"The Hôtel Vouillemont?" she called out, to the three men who were standing at the bar.

"In the rue Boissy d'Anglas," Harold said.

"The rue Boissy d'Anglas . . ."

"The rue Boissy d'Anglas?"

"The rue Boissy d'Anglas."

One of them remembered suddenly; it was in the sixteenth arrondissement.

"No, you are thinking of the rue Boissière," the waiter said. "I used to help my cousin deliver packages for a shop in the sixteenth arrondissement, and I know the quarter well. There is no Hôtel Vouillemont."

The three men left their drinks and came over and started thumbing through the telephone directories. The waiter joined them. "Ah!" he exclaimed. "Here it is. The Hôtel Vouillemont . . . It's in the rue Boissy d'Anglas."

"And where is that?" Harold asked.

The waiter peered at the directory and said: "The eighth arrondissement. You got off too soon. You should have descended at Concorde."

"Is that far from here?"

They all five assured him that he could walk there.

"But with suitcases?"

"In that case," Madame said, "you would do well to return to the Métro station."

He shook hands all around, hesitated, and then took a chance. It didn't work; they thanked him politely but declined the invitation to have a glass of wine with him. So his instinct must have been wrong.

"Is there any way that one can call a taxi?" he asked.

The waiter went to the door with him and showed him which direction they must go to find a taxi stand. Harold shook hands with him again, and then turned to Barbara. "We should have descended at Concorde," he said, and picked up the suitcases. "It's miles from here."

The taxi driver knew exactly where the Hôtel Vouillemont was, and so they could sit back and not worry. They peered through the dirty windows at Paris. The unfamiliar streets had familiar names—the rue Jean-Jacques Rousseau; the rue Marengo. They caught a glimpse down a long avenue of the familiar façade of the Opéra. The arcades of the rue de Rivoli were deserted, and so were the public gardens on the other. side of the street. So was the Place de la Concorde. The sky over the fountains and the Egyptian obelisk was cold and gray. The driver pointed out the American Embassy to them, and then they were in a dark, narrow street. The taxi stopped.

"He's made a mistake," Barbara said. "This isn't it."

"It says 'Hôtel Vouillemont' on the brass plate," Harold said, reaching for his wallet. And then, though he disliked arguments, he got into one with the taxi driver. Mme Viénot had said he must refuse to pay more than the amount on the meter. The driver showed him a chart and explained that it was the amount on the chart he must pay, not the amount on the meter. Harold suggested that they go inside and settle the matter there. The driver got out and followed him into the hotel, but declined to help with the suitcases. To Harold's surprise, the concierge sided with the driver, against Mme Viénot.

Still not sure they hadn't cheated him, he paid the driver what it said on the chart and turned back to the concierge's desk. If it turned out that the concierge was dishonest, he was not going to like staying at the Hôtel Vouillemont. He studied the man's face, and the face declined to say whether the person it belonged to was honest or dishonest.

While he was registering, Barbara stood looking around her at the lobby. She could not even say, as people so often do of some place they knew as a child, that it was much smaller than she remembered, because she didn't remember a thing she

saw. She wondered if, all these years, she could have misremembered the name of the hotel they stayed in. It was not
until they were in the elevator, with their suitcases, that she
knew suddenly that they were in the right hotel after all. She
remembered the glass elevator. No other hotel in the world
had one like it. It was right out in the center of the lobby, and
it had a red plush sofa you could sit down on. As they rose
through the ceiling, the past was for a moment superimposed
on the present, and she had a wonderful feeling of lightness—
as if she were rising through water up to the surface and sunshine and air.

Their room was warm, and when they turned on the faucets
in the bathroom, hot water came gushing out of the faucet
marked *chaud*. They filled the tub to the brim and had a bath,
and dressed, and went off down the street to have lunch at a
restaurant that Barbara remembered the name of: Tante
Louise. Like the glass elevator, the restaurant hadn't changed.
After lunch they strolled. Harold stopped at a kiosk and
bought a map-book of Paris by arrondissements, so that he
wouldn't ever again be caught not knowing where he was and
how to get to where he wanted to go. They looked in the
windows of the shops in the rue St. Honoré, full of beautiful
gloves and scarves, and purses that probably cost a fortune.

They were in Paris at last, and aware that they should have
been happy, but there was no indication anywhere that Paris
was happy. No dancing in the streets, no singing, no decorations, no flags, even. They discovered the Madeleine and the
American Express and Maxim's, none of which gave off any
effervescence of gaiety, and finally, toward the end of the
afternoon, they gave up searching for Paris on Bastille Day,
since it appeared to be only an idea in their minds, and went
back to their hotel.

That evening, before it was quite dark, they set off to see the
illuminations. They were encouraged when they saw that the
streets had begun to fill up with people. They went first to
the Place de la Concorde, and admired the light-soaked fountains and the flood-lighted twin buildings. With lights trained
on it, the Madeleine, at the end of the rue Royale, no longer
looked quite so gloomy and Roman. They were about to start
off on the route that Mme Carrère had recommended, when a

skyrocket exploded and long yellow ribbons of light fell down the sky. So, instead, they joined the throngs of people hurrying toward the river. For half an hour they stood in the middle of the Pont de la Concorde, looking now at the fireworks and now at the upraised, expectant French faces all around them. Bouquet after bouquet of colored lights exploded in the sky and in the black water. They decided that, rather than retrace their steps, they would reverse the directions Mme Carrère had given them. This turned out to be a mistake. They rushed here and there, got lost, doubled back on their route, and wasted a good deal of time changing trains in the Métro. And they never did see the lighted lamps of the Comédie Française.

At one o'clock, exhaustion claimed them. They were lost again, and a long way from home. They asked directions of a gendarme, who hurried them into a Métro station just in time to catch the last train back to Concorde.

The address of the editorial offices of *La Femme Elégante* turned out to be a courtyard, and the entrance was up a short flight of steps. They gave the receptionist their name and, as they waited for Sabine Viénot to appear, Harold's eyes roamed around the small foyer, trying to make out something, anything, from the little he saw—nobly proportioned doors with heavy molding painted dove gray, nondescript lighting fixtures, and dove-gray carpet. When Mme Viénot spoke of her daughter's career, her tone of voice suggested that she was at the forefront of her profession. But then she had showed them some of her daughter's work—thumbnail sketches of dress patterns buried in the back of the magazine. The girl who came through the doorway and shook hands with them was very slight and pale and young, with observant blue eyes and brown hair and a high, domed forehead, like the French queens in the *Petit Larousse*.

Harold started to explain who they were and she said that she knew; her mother had written to her about them. "You can speak English if you prefer," she said. "I speak it badly but— They are all well in the country?"

Barbara nodded.

"I'm afraid you haven't had very nice weather. It has been cold and rainy here, also. You arrived in Paris when?"

"Yesterday," Barbara said.

"But we didn't see any dancing in the streets," Harold said. "Last night at midnight we saw a crowd of people singing and marching in the square in front of Notre Dame, but they were Communists, I think. Anyway, there was no dancing."

"In Montmartre you would have seen it, perhaps," the French girl said. "Or the Place Pigalle."

They couldn't think what to say next.

"Mother has written how much she enjoyed having you with her," the French girl said.

"We are returning to Brenodville tomorrow," Harold said, "and your mother asked us to let you know the train we are taking. She thought you might also be intending to—"

"I may be going down to the country tomorrow," the French girl said thoughtfully. "I don't know yet."

"We're taking the four o'clock train," he said. "Your mother suggested that we might all three take one taxi from Blois."

"That is very kind of you. Perhaps I could telephone you tomorrow morning. You are staying where?"

"It's quite near here, actually." He tore a leaf out of his financial diary, wrote down the name of their hotel, and held it out to her. She glanced at the slip of paper but did not take it from him. They shook hands, and then she was gone.

Standing on the sidewalk, waiting for the flow of traffic to stop so they could cross over, he said: "I thought at first she was like her mother—like what Mme Viénot was at that age. But she isn't."

"Not at all," Barbara said.

"Her voice made me realize that she wasn't."

"She has a lovely voice—so light. And silvery."

"She has a charming voice. Something of the French intonation carries over into her English, of course. But it's more than that, I think. It's an amused voice. It has a slight suggestion of humor, at no one's expense. As if she had learned to see things with a clarity that—that was often in excess of whatever need there was for seeing things clearly. And the residue had turned into something like amusement."

"But she didn't ask us to lunch."

"I know."

They went to the Guaranty Trust Company and were di-

rected to the little upstairs room where their mail was handed
to them.

"So what do we do now?" Barbara asked when they were
outside again.

He looked at his watch. They had spent a considerable part
of their first twenty-four hours in Paris walking the streets. He
was dog-tired, his feet hurt, and Notre Dame in daylight faced
the wrong way. For the moment, they were satiated with
looking, and ready to be with someone they knew, it didn't
matter how slightly, so long as they could talk about what they
had seen, ask questions, and feel that they were a part of the
intense sociability that they were aware of everywhere around
them. Paris on the day after Bastille Day was not a deserted
city. Also the sun was shining, and it was warm; it was like
summer, and that lifted their spirits.

He said: "What about having lunch with Gagny at that
bistro he told us about?"

"But we don't know where it is."

"Rue de Castellane." He consulted the plan of Paris by arrondissements. "It's somewhere behind the Madeleine . . .
L17." He turned the pages. "Here it is. See?"

She pretended to look at the place he pointed out to her on
the map, and then said: "If you're sure it's not too far."

The rue de Castellane proved to be farther than it appeared
to be on the map, and when they got there, they found two,
possibly three, eating places that answered to Gagny's description. Also, they were not very clear in their minds about the
distinction between a bistro and a restaurant. They walked
back and forth, peering at the curtained windows and trying
to decide. They took a chance on one, the smallest. Gagny had
said that it was a hangout of doubtful characters, and that
there was sometimes brawling. The bistro was very quiet, and
it looked respectable. They were shown to the last free table.
Harold ordered an apéritif, and they settled down to read their
mail from home, unaware that they were attracting a certain
amount of attention from the men who were standing at the
bar. Thugs and thieves do not, of course, wear funny hats or
emblems in their buttonholes, like Lions and Elks, and some
types of human behavior have to be explained before they are
at all noticeable. The bistro was what Hector Gagny had said it

was. In her letter about him, the cousin of the Canadian Ambassador failed to inform Mme Viénot of something that she happened to know, and that he didn't know she knew. It was in his folder in the Embassy files: he had a taste for low company. He enjoyed watching heated arguments, stage after stage of intricate insult, so stylized and at the same time so personal, all leading up to the point where the angry arguers could have exchanged blows—and never did. He also enjoyed being the unengaged spectator to situations in which the active participants must feel one another out. His eyes darting back and forth between their eyes, he measured accurately the risk taken, and then calculated enviously the chance of success.

In places the police knew about, Gagny never disguised his education, or pretended to be anything but an observer. He sat, well dressed, well bred, quiet, and conspicuous, with his glass of wine in front of him, until the *type* who had been eying him for some time disengaged himself from the others and wandered over and was invited to sit down at his table.

"We're terribly restricted, you know," Gagny would tell the character with franc notes to be converted into dollars or, if worst came to worst, pounds sterling. "I mean to say, thirty-five pounds is all we're allowed to take out of England." Or, as he handed the pornographic postcards back to their owner: "Why do the men all have their shoes and socks on?" The *type*, a cigarette hanging from his lips and sometimes a question hanging in his eyes, would begin to talk. After a moment or two, Gagny would interrupt him politely in order to signal to the waiter to bring another glass.

In exchange for the glimpses of high life that he offered casually, not too much or too many at a time, he himself was permitted glimpses into the long corridor leading down, where crimes are committed for not very much money, or out of boredom, or because the line between feeling and action has become blurred; where the gendarme is the common enemy, and nobody knows the answer to a simple question, and danger is ever-present, the oxygen in the wine-smelling, smoke-filled air.

Only in France did Gagny allow himself this sort of diversion. In London it was not safe. He might be followed. His name was in the telephone directory. And he might have the bad luck to run into some acquaintance who also had a taste for low company.

Also, it was a matter of the Latin sensibility as compared with Anglo-Saxon. Oftener than not in Paris the *type* proved to be gentle, amiable, confused and more than willing (though the occasion for this had never presented itself) to pass over into the world of commonplace respectability. His education may have been sordid, pragmatic, and one-sided, but at least it had taught him how to stay alive, and he had a story to tell, invariably. Gagny had a story to tell, too, but he refrained from telling it. The *types* understood this. They were responsive, they understood many things—states of feeling, human needs, gradations of pleasure, complexities of motive—that people of good breeding unfortunately do not.

The sense of unreality—the dreadful recognition that he belonged not to the white race but to the pink or gray—that often came over him at official functions, among people of the highest importance and social distinction, he never experienced in any place where there was sawdust on the floor. He enjoyed the tribute that was paid to his social superiority (sometimes it only lasted a second, but it was there, nevertheless—a flicker of incredulity that he should be talking to them) and also their moment of vanity, encouraged by his lack of condescension. Though their fingernails were dirty and their clothes had been bought and worn by somebody else, they thought well of themselves; they were not apologetic. As a rule they understood perfectly what he wanted of them, and when he had checked the *addition* and put the change in his pocket notebook, they clapped him on the shoulder, smiling at his way of doing business, and went back to theirs. Now and then, misunderstanding, they offered him their friendship—were ready to throw in their lot, such as it was, with his, whatever that might prove to be. And when this offer was not accepted, they became surly or abusive, and it was a problem to get rid of them.

The Americans passed their letters back and forth, and when they were all read, Harold glanced at his watch again and said: "It looks as if he isn't coming."

Before he could catch the eye of the waitress, they saw Gagny, and saw that he had already seen them, but it was a very different Gagny from the one they had known in the country—erect and handsome and as wildly happy as if he had just succeeded in extricating himself from a long-standing love affair with a woman ten years older than he, and very demanding, given to emotional scenes, threats, tears, accusations that could only be answered in bed. He was delighted that they had kept their engagement with him. He had checked in at his hotel, he said, and come straight here, hoping to find them. They had been missed, he told them cheerfully. Mme Viénot and Mme Carrère had agreed that the house was not the same without the Americans. Then, seeing the look of surprise on their faces, he said: "You can believe me. I never make anything up." He surveyed the bar, in one fleeting glance, and for this afternoon renounced its interesting possibilities.

The waitress came and stood beside the table.

"Let me order for you," Gagny said, "since I know the place. And this is *my* lunch."

"Oh no it's not!" Harold cried.

"Oh yes it is!"

By the time the pâté arrived, they were all three talking at once, exchanging confidences, asking questions, being funny. The Americans found it a great relief to confide to someone their feelings about staying at the château, and who was in a better position to understand what they meant than someone who had seen them floundering? But if they had only known what he was really like . . .

He kept saying "Well exactly!" and they kept saying "I know. I know." They talked steadily through course after course. They finished the carafe of red wine and Gagny ordered a second, and cognac after that. The bistro was empty when they finally pushed their chairs back from the table. In spite of the adverse exchange, Gagny seized the check and would not hear of any other arrangement.

The sun was shining in the street outside. Gagny had an errand to do in the rue St. Honoré, and they walked with him as far as the rue Boissy d'Anglas. He was their favorite friend, and they felt sure that he was just as fond of them, but when the moment came for exchanging addresses, they were all three silent.

Standing on the street corner, Gagny smiled at the blue sky

and then at them, and said: "You don't happen to know where Guerlain is, by any chance?"

"Just one moment," Harold said, "I'll look it up." He brought out his plan of Paris and began thumbing the pages. "'Théâtres et spectacles . . . cabarets artistiques . . . cinémas . . .'"

"You won't find it in there," Gagny said.

"'Cultes,'" Harold read. "'Eglises Catholiques . . . Chapelles Catholiques Etrangères . . . Rite Melchite Grec' . . . Certainly it's in here. 'Eglises Luthériennes . . . Eglises réformées de France . . . Eglises protestantes étrangères . . . Science Chrétienne . . . Eglise Adventiste . . . Eglises Baptistes . . . Eglises Orthodoxes . . . Culte Israélite, Synagogues . . . Culte Mahométan, Mosquée . . . Facultés, Ecoles Supérieures . . .'"

Barbara put a restraining hand on his arm, and he looked up and saw that Gagny was ten feet away, in lively conversation with an English couple—friends, obviously—who had just arrived in Paris, by car, they said, from the south of France. They were very brown.

After a few minutes they said good-by and went off down the street. Gagny rejoined Harold and Barbara and said with a note of pure wonder in his voice: "They had beautiful weather the whole time they were on the Riviera."

"We came up out of the Métro," Harold said earnestly, all that wine having caught up with him at last, "and there it was right in front of us, with searchlights trained on the flying buttresses, and it was facing the *opposite* direction from Cleopatra's Needle and the Place de la Concorde."

"You're sure about that?" Gagny said, looking at him affectionately.

"Positive," Harold said.

"Well, old chap, all I can say is, there's something wrong somewhere."

"*Terribly* wrong," Harold said.

"I'd love to help you straighten it out," Gagny said. "But not this afternoon. I've got to buy perfume for my mother. Cheerio."

*

They spent all Friday morning at the Louvre and had lunch sitting on the sidewalk looking at the Comédie Française, but it was broad daylight and the lamps were not lighted; it was impossible to imagine what they were like at night. By not doing what they were told to do they had missed their one chance of having this beautiful experience. There was not going to be another illumination the whole rest of the summer.

They went back to the Louvre, and barely left time to check out of their hotel and get to the station. Sabine Viénot had not called, and they did not see her on the station platform. On the train they amused themselves by filling two pages of the financial diary with a list of things they would like to steal from the Louvre. Harold began with a Romanesque statue of the Queen of Sheba, and then took *The Lacemaker* by Vermeer, and *Lot and His Daughters* by Lucas van Leyden, and some panels by Giotto. Barbara took a fragment of a Greek statue— the lower half of a woman's body—and a section of the frieze of the Parthenon, and a Bronzino portrait. He took a Velásquez, a Goya, a Murillo, some Fra Angelico panels, *La Belle Ferronière*, and a fragment of a horse's head. She took two Rembrandts, a Goya, an El Greco crucifixion, and a Bruegel winter scene. . . . And so on and so on, as the shadows outside the train window grew longer and longer. When the compartment began to seem oppressive, they stood in the crowded corridor for a while. They saw a church spire that was like the little church in Brenodville, and here and there on the line of hills a big country house half hidden by trees, and sometimes they saw the sky reflected in a river. When they grew tired of standing, they ground out their cigarettes and went back into their compartment and read. From time to time they raised their eyes to observe the other passengers or the sunset.

Mme Viénot had said that she was expecting some relatives on Friday, and would Harold look around for them when he got off the train? But there was no one in the railway station in Blois who appeared uncertain about where he was going or to be looking for two Americans. The taxi brought them by a back road through the forest instead of by the highway along the river, and this reminded Harold of something. "We thought they would come from the direction of the highway," Mme. Bonenfant had said, "and they came through the forest instead." He turned and looked back. There were no Germans in the forest now, but would it ever be free of them? Was that why the gate was kept locked?

It was just getting dark when they turned into the drive and saw the lights of the house. Leaving their suitcases in the hall, they walked past the screen and into the drawing room. Mme Viénot and her mother and M. and Mme Carrère and Mme Straus-Muguet were all sitting around the little table in front of the fireplace. Seeing their faces light up with pleasure and expectancy, Harold thought: Why, it's almost as if we had come home. . . .

"We've been waiting dinner for you," Mme Viénot said as she shook hands with them. "How did you like Paris?"

"Did anyone ever not like Paris?" Harold said.

"And you were comfortable at the Vouillemont?"

He laughed. "Once we found it, we were comfortable," he said.

"And the weather?"

"The weather was beautiful."

"Sabine telephoned this evening," Mme Viénot said, on the way into the dining room. "She tried to reach you, it seems, after you had gone. I'm afraid she does not have a very exact idea of time."

"But she wasn't on the train with us? We looked for her—"

"She is coming next week end instead," Mme Viénot said as he drew her chair out for her. "I hope you didn't give yourself any anxiety on her account?"

He shook his head.

"She enjoyed meeting you," Mme Viénot said.

"We enjoyed meeting her," he said, and then, since she seemed to be waiting for something more: "She's charming."

Mme Viénot smiled and unfolded her napkin.

He noticed that there were two people handing the soup plates around the table—Thérèse and a boy of seventeen or eighteen, in a white coat, with thick glasses and slicked-down hair. His large hands were very clean but looked like raw meat. He served unskillfully, in an agony of shyness, and Harold wondered if Mme Viénot had added a farm boy to her staff.

As always, he could speak better when he was sure he had an audience. ". . . There we were in the Métro," he said, "with no idea of what station to get off at, or what arrondissement our hotel was in."

"I should have told you," Mme Viénot said. "I'm so sorry. And this time you didn't have M. Fleury to take you there."

"Barbara thought it was somewhere near the Louvre—"

"Oh dear no! You should have descended at Concorde."

"So we discovered. But we got off at the Louvre, instead, and walked two or three blocks until we came to a sidewalk café, and the waiter showed me where the telephone books were, but there were so many and I couldn't make head nor tail of them, so he and the proprietress and everybody there dropped what they were doing and thumbed through telephone directories and finally the waiter found it."

"I should have thought anyone could have told you where it is," M. Carrère said. "It is very well known."

"*They* didn't know about it. . . . I tried to buy them all a drink before I left—they had been so kind—and they refused. Was that wrong? In America it would not have been wrong."

"Not at all," Mme Viénot said. "Another time just say: 'I insist that you have a glass of wine with me,' and the offer will be accepted. But it wasn't at all necessary."

"I wish I'd known that."

"They were no doubt happy to have been of assistance to you. And you found your hotel?"

"We took a taxi," he said. "And the fares have gone up. They have a chart they show you. I remembered that you had said not to pay more than the amount on the meter, and when the driver got angry I made him come into the hotel with me and the concierge straightened it out. After that, whenever we took a taxi I was careful to ask the driver if I had given him enough."

"But they will cheat you!" Mme Viénot exclaimed.

"They didn't. I knew from the chart what it *should* be, and added the tip, and they none of them asked for more."

"Perhaps they found you sympathetic," Mme Bonenfant said.

"It was pleasanter than arguing."

He saw that Mme Straus-Muguet was looking at him and he said to her with his eyes: *I was afraid you wouldn't be here when we got back.* . . .

Mme Viénot lifted her spoon to her lips and then exclaimed. Turning to Barbara, she said: "My cook gave notice while you were gone. The new cook, poor dear, is very nervous. Last night there was too much salt in everything, so I spoke to her about it, and tonight there is no salt whatever in the soup. Do I dare speak to her again?" She turned to M. Carrère, who said, his clown's eyes crinkling: "In your place I don't think I should. It might bring on something worse."

"I hope you will be patient with her," Mme Viénot said. "She has a sister living in the village, whom she wanted to be near. The boy is her son. He has had no experience but she begged me to take him on so that he can learn the métier and they can hire themselves out as a couple. . . . Tell us what happened to you in Paris."

"We spent all our time walking the streets," Barbara said, "and looking in shop windows."

"They are extraordinary, aren't they?" Mme Carrère agreed. "Quite like the way they were before the war."

"And we had lunch with M. Gagny," Harold said.

"Yes? You saw M. Gagny?" Mme Viénot said, and Mme Carrère asked if they had followed her directions on the night of the illumination. Harold hesitated, and then, not wanting to spoil her pleasure, said that they had. He had a feeling that she knew he was not telling the truth. She did not attempt to catch him out, but the interest went out of her face.

As he and Barbara were undressing for bed, they remarked upon a curious fact. They had hoped before they came here that a stay at the château would make them better able to deal with what they found in Paris, and instead a stay of three days in Paris had made them able, really for the first time, to deal with life in the château. Neither of them mentioned their reluctance to leave Paris, that afternoon, or the fact that their room, after the comforts of the hotel, seemed cold and cheerless. Thérèse had again forgotten to bring them a can of hot water; the fan of experience was already beginning to close, and in Paris it had opened all the way.

Chapter 8

THEY spent Saturday morning in their room. Barbara filled the washbasin with cold water and while she washed and rinsed and washed again, Harold sat on the edge of the tub and told her about the murder of the Duc de Guise, in the château of Blois, in the year 1588.

"He got in, and then he found he couldn't get out. . . . He was warned on the Grand Staircase, but by that time it was too late; there were guards posted everywhere. He asked for the Queen, who could have saved him, and she didn't come. He sent his servant for a handkerchief, as a test, and the servant didn't come back. . . . Are you listening to me?" he demanded above the sound of the soapy water being sucked down the drain.

"Yes, but I've got to change the water in the sink."

"You don't have to make so much noise. . . . Everywhere he looked, people avoided meeting his eyes. He had just come from the bed of one of the Queen's ladies-in-waiting."

"Which queen was this?"

"Not Queen Victoria. Catherine de Médicis, I think. Anyway, it was two days before Christmas. And he was cold and hungry. He stood in front of the fireplace, warming himself and eating some dried prunes, I guess it was. It's hard to make out, from that little dictionary. The council of state convened, and they told him the King had sent for him. So he left the room—"

At this point Barbara left the bathroom and went to the armoire. Harold followed her. "The eight hired assassins in the next room bowed to him," he said, helping himself to a piece of candy from the box on the table. "I suppose it comes from living in the same house with *her*, but somebody's been at the chocolates while we were away."

"Oh, I don't think so," Barbara said, and closed the doors of the armoire and went back to the bathroom with a nightgown and a slip, which she added to the laundry in the washbasin.

"Want to bet?"

"It doesn't matter if they did."

"I know it doesn't. But I don't think it was Thérèse, even so."

"Who else could have?"

"Somebody that likes chocolate. . . . He got as far as the door to the King's dressing room, and saw that there were more of them, at the end of the narrow passageway, waiting for him with drawn swords in their hands."

"Poor man!"

"Mmm. Poor man, indeed—he was responsible for the Massacre of St. Bartholomew. It took forty men to do him in. He was huge and very powerful. And when it was all over, the King bent down cautiously and slapped his face."

"After he was *dead*?"

"Yes. Then he went and told his mother. What people!"

"If you knew what it is like to wash silk in cold water!" Barbara said indignantly.

"Why do you do it, then? I could go down and ask them for a can of hot water?"

There was no answer.

He wandered back into the bedroom, and stood looking around the room, seeing it with the eyes of the person who took the chocolates. Not Mme Bonenfant. The flowers hadn't been changed. And anyway, she wouldn't. Not the houseboy, in all probability. He was new, and he had no reason to be in this part of the house. Mme Viénot? Who else? If they were curious about her, why shouldn't she be curious about them?

She had stood in the doorway waving to them until the taxi disappeared around the corner of the house. And then what happened? Was she relieved? Was she happy to see them go? He put himself in her shoes and decided that he would have been relieved for a minute or two, and then he would have begun to worry. He would have been afraid that they would find in Paris what they were looking for—they were tourists, after all—and not come back. He had offered to have the luggage packed so that it could be removed from their room, and if she remembered that, she would surely think they had planned not to come back, and that in a day or so she would get a letter saying they'd changed their plans again, and would she send their luggage, which was all packed and ready, to the Hôtel Vouillemont. . . . Only the luggage was not packed, of course. And what she must have seen when she threw open the door of the room was that they had left everything—clothes, books, all their possessions, scattered over the room. There was a half-finished letter on the desk, and the box of Swiss chocolates open on the table. The room must have looked as if they had left it to go for a walk.

He stood reading the letter, which had lain on the pad of the writing desk since last Tuesday. It was to Edith Ireland, of all people. Barbara was thanking her for the book and the bottle of champagne she had sent to the boat. Barbara's handwriting was very dashing, and not very legible, because of a tendency to abbreviate and leave off parts of letters, but if you were patient you could get the hang of it, and no doubt Mme Viénot had.

On the table, beside a pile of guidebooks, were three pages—also in Barbara's handwriting—of a diary she was keeping. The entries covered the period from July 11, when they came to the château from Tours, through July 13, the day before they went up to Paris. He turned away from the table, relieved and grinning.

She had a façade that she retired behind when she was with strangers—the image of an unworldly, well-bred, charming-looking, gentle young woman. The image was not even false to her character; it merely left out half of it. Who could possibly have any reason to say anything rude or unkind to anyone so shy and unsure of herself? Nobody ever did.

It was the façade that was keeping the diary.

When they went down to lunch they learned that Mme Viénot's relatives had arrived sometime during the morning. The dining-room table was larger by two leaves to accommodate them and there were three empty chairs. Two of them were soon filled, by a middle-aged woman and a young man. The cook's son brought two more soup plates, and Mme Viénot said: "How do you find Maman? Doesn't she look well?"

"She is more beautiful than ever," the young man said, his face totally without expression, as if it had been carved out of a piece of wood and could not change.

"The weather has been most discouraging here," Mme Viénot said.

"In Paris it is the same. Rain day after day," the young man said. "One hears everywhere that it is the atomic bomb that is responsible. I myself think it is by analogy with the political climate, which is damp, cold, unhopeful. . . . Alix said to tell you that she is giving Annette her bottle. She will be down presently."

"Perhaps she can manage some slight adjustment of the baby's schedule which will permit her to come to meals at the usual time," Mme Viénot said. "It is not merely the empty chair. It upsets the service. . . . Your father and mother are well?"

"My father is having trouble with his eyes. It is not cataracts, though it seems that the difficulty may be progressive. It is a question of the arteries not carrying enough food to the optic nerve. Maman is well—at least, well enough to go to weddings. There has been a succession of them. My cousin Suzanne, in Brittany. And Philippe Soulès. You remember that de Cléry girl everyone thought was a mental defective? She has turned out to be the clever one of the family. They are going to live with his parents, it seems. And my Uncle Eugène, for the third time. Or is it the fourth? And Simone Valéry. Maman has been thinking of taking a job. She has been approached by Jacques Fath. She has just about decided to say no. It is rather an amusing idea, and if she could come and go as she pleased— but it seems they would expect her to keep regular hours, and she is quite incapable of that. Besides, she has set her heart on a trip to Venice. In August."

"The Biennale?"

"No, another wedding. I have not seen Jean-Claude. I read about him in *Figaro*. And Georges Dunois had lunch with him last Wednesday in London. Georges asked me to pay you his devoted respects. He said Jean-Claude has aged."

"The responsibility is, of course, very great," Mme Viénot said modestly, and then turning to Barbara: "We are discussing my son-in-law, who is in the government."

"He now looks twenty-two or three, Georges said."

"Suzanne writes that he is being sent to Oran, on an important mission, the details of which she is not free to disclose."

"Naturally."

"She is expecting another child in November."

"She is my favorite of the entire family, and I am not sure I would recognize her if I saw her. I never see her, not even at those functions where one would have supposed her husband's career might be affected by her absence. Proving that the Ministry is helpless without him."

"She is absorbed in her family duties," Mme Viénot said.

"So one is told. As for Jean-Claude, one hears everywhere that he is immensely valued, successful, happy, and— Ah, there you are."

The young woman who sat down in the chair next to Barbara was very fair, and her blue eyes had a look of childlike sweetness and innocence. She acknowledged the introductions in the most charming French accent Harold had ever heard, and then said: "I did not expect to be down for another quarter of an hour, but she went right off to sleep. She was exhausted by the trip, and so many new sensations."

Harold decided that he liked her, and that he didn't like the man, who seemed to have a whole repertoire of manners—one (serious, intellectual) for M. Carrère; another (simpering, mock-gallant) for Mme Viénot; another (devoted, simple, respectful) for Mme Bonenfant; and still another for Barbara, whose hand he had raised to his lips. Harold was put off by the hand-kissing (though Barbara was not; she did not, in fact, turn a hair; where had she learned that?) and by the limp handshake when he and the young Frenchman were introduced and the look of complete indifference now when their eyes met across the table.

At two o'clock, when they came downstairs from their room, Mme Straus-Muguet was waiting for them in the second-floor hall at the turn of the stairs. Speaking slowly and distinctly, the way people do when they are trying to impress careful instructions on the wandering minds of children, she asked if they would do an errand for her. She had overheard them telling Mme Viénot that they were going to Blois this afternoon. On a scrap of paper she had written the name of a confiserie and she wanted them to get some candy for her, a particular kind, a delicious bonbon that was made only at this shop in Blois. She gave Barbara the colored tinsel wrapper it came in, to show the confiseur, and a hundred-franc note. They were to get eight pieces of candy—six for her and two for themselves.

This time the bus was not crowded. They found seats together and all the way into town sat looking out of the window at scenery that was simple and calm, as Harold's guidebook said—long perspectives of the river, with here and there a hill, some sheep, a house, two trees, women and children wading, and then the same hill (or so it seemed), the same sheep, the same house, the same two trees, like a repeating motif in wallpaper. It was a landscape, one would have said, in which no human being had ever raised his voice. They went straight to the ration bureau and stood in line at the high counter, with their green passports ready, and were quite unprepared for the unpleasant scene that took place there. A grim-faced, gray-haired woman took their passports, examined them efficiently, and then returned them to Harold with ration stamps for bread, sugar, etc. She also said something to him in very rapid French that he did not understand. Speaking as good French as he knew how to speak, he asked her if she would please repeat what she had said, and she shrieked furiously at him in English: "They're for ten days only!"

They stood staring at each other, her face livid with anger and his very pale. Then he said mildly: "If you ever come to America, you will find that you are sometimes obliged to ask the same question two or three times." And because this remark was so mild, or perhaps because it was so illogical (the woman behind the counter had no intention ever of setting foot out of France, and if by any stretch of the imagination she did, it would not be to go to a country that so threatened the peace of the world), there was no more shouting. He went on looking directly into her eyes until she looked away.

Outside, standing on the steps of the building, he said: "Was it because we are taking food out of the mouths of starving Frenchmen?"

"Possibly," Barbara said.

"But we haven't seen anybody who looked starving. And they *want* American tourists. The French government is anxious to have them come."

"I know. But she isn't the French government."

"Maybe she hates men." His voice was unsteady and he felt weak in the knees. "Or it could be, I suppose, that her whole life has been dreadful. But the way she spoke to us was so—"

"It's something that happens to women sometimes," Barbara said. "An anger that comes over them suddenly, and that they feel no part in."

"But why?"

She had no answer.

If it is true that nothing exists without its opposite, then the thing they had just been exposed to was merely the opposite of the amiability and kindness they had encountered everywhere in France. Also, the gypsy fortuneteller had promised Barbara malice she didn't expect.

Facing the ration bureau was a small open-air market, and they wandered through it slowly, looking at straw hats, cotton dresses, tennis sneakers, and cheap cooking utensils. They were unable to get the incident out of their minds, though they stopped talking about it. The day was blighted.

From the market they made their way down into the lower part of the city, and found Mme Straus's candy shop. They also spent some time in the shop next door, where they bought an intermediate French grammar, two books on gardening, and postcards. Then they walked along the street, dividing their attention between the people on the sidewalk and the contents of shop windows, until they arrived at the ramp that led up to the château.

They stood in the courtyard, looking at the octagonal staircase and comparing what the Michelin said with the actuality in front of them. Because it was getting late and they weren't sure they wanted to join a conducted tour—they were, in fact, rather tired of conducted tours—they walked in the opposite direction from the sign that said *guide du château*, and toward the wing of Gaston d'Orléans. Harold put his hand out and tried a doorknob. It turned and the door swung open. They walked in and up a flight of marble stairs, admiring the balustrades and the ceiling, and at the head of the stairs they came upon two large tapestries dealing with the Battle of Dunkerque —a previous battle, in the seventeenth century, judging by the costumes and theatrical-looking implements of war. The doors leading out of this room were all locked, and so they made their way down the stairs again, trying other doors, until they were out in the courtyard once more. They were just in time to see two busloads of tourists from the American Express stream out of the wing of Louis XII and crowd into the tiny blue and gold chapel. The tourists were with a guide and the guide was speaking English.

Standing under an arcade, surrounded by their countrymen, Barbara and Harold learned about the strange life of Charles d'Orléans, who was a poet and at fifteen married his cousin, the daughter of Charles VI. She had already been married to Richard II of England, when she was seven years old. The new marriage did not last long. She died in childbirth, and the poet remarried, lost the battle of Agincourt, and was imprisoned for twenty-five years, after which, a widower of fifty, he again married—this time a girl of fourteen—and surrounded himself with a little court of artists and writers, and at seventy-one had at last, by his third wife, the son he had waited more than fifty years for.

"I see what you mean about having a guide who speaks English," Harold said as they followed the crowd back across the courtyard and up a flight of steps to the Hall of State. They were waiting to learn about that, too, when the guide came over to them and asked Harold to step outside for a moment, with Madame.

He was about thirty years old, with large dark intelligent eyes, regular features, a narrow face cleanly cut, and dark skin. An aristocratic survival from the time of François premier, Harold thought as they followed the guide across the big room, with the other tourists looking at them with more interest than they had shown toward the Hall of State. He did not know precisely what to expect, or why the guide had singled them out, but whatever he wanted or wanted to know, Harold was ready to oblige him with, since the guide was not only a gentleman but obviously a far from ordinary man.

Though the guide made his living taking American tourists through historical monuments, he did not understand Americans the way he understood history. If you are as openhanded as they mostly are, you cannot help rejoicing in small accidental economies, being pleased when the bus conductor fails to collect your fare, etc., and it doesn't at all mean that you are trying to take advantage of anybody. The guide asked them if they were members of his party, and Harold said no, and the guide said would they leave the château immediately by that little door right down there?

The whole conversation took place in English, and so Harold had no trouble understanding what the guide said, but for a few seconds he went right on looking at the Frenchman's face. The expression in the gray eyes was contempt.

Blushing and angry, with the guide and with himself (for he had had in his wallet the means of erasing this embarrassment as completely as if it had never happened), he made his way down the ramp with Barbara, past the château gift shop, and into the street.

It was too soon for the bus, and so they turned in at the pâtisserie, and ordered tea and cakes, and found that they had no appetite for them when they came. They got up and left, and a few minutes later had a third contretemps. The bus driver, misunderstanding Harold's "deux" for "douze," gave him the wrong change and would not rectify his mistake or let them get on the bus until everybody else had got on. So they had to stand, after being first in line at the bus stop.

"So far," he said, peering through the window at the river, "we've had very few experiences like what happened this afternoon, and they were really the result of growing confidence. We were attempting to behave as if we were at home."

Out of consideration for his feelings, Barbara did not point out that this was only partly true; at home he was neither as friendly nor as trusting as he was here, and he did not expect strangers to be that way with him. She herself did not mind what had happened half as much as she minded having to come down to dinner in a dress that she had already worn three times.

Mme Straus-Muguet was waiting for them on the stairs. She praised them for carrying out her errand so successfully, in a city they did not know well, and invited them to take an apéritif with her before lunch on Sunday morning. She seemed subdued, and as if during their absence in Paris she had suffered a setback of some kind—a letter containing bad news that her mind kept returning to, or unkindness where she least expected it.

Feeling tired and bruised by their own series of setbacks, they hurried on up the stairs, conscious that the house was cold and there would not be any hot water to wash in and they would have to spend still another evening trying to understand people who could speak English but preferred to speak French.

From the conversation at the lunch table, Harold had pieced together certain facts about Mme Viénot's relatives. The blonde young woman with the charming low voice and the beautiful accent was Mme Viénot's niece, and the young man was her husband. Listening and waiting, he eventually found out their names: M. and Mme de Boisgaillard. And they had brought with them not only their own three-months-old baby but Mme de Boisgaillard's sister's two children, who were too young to come to the table, and a nursemaid. But when they sat down to dinner he still did not know who the middle-aged woman directly across from him was. There was something that separated her from everybody else at the table. Studying her, he saw that she wore no jewelry of any kind, and her blue dress was so plain and inexpensive-looking that he wasn't absolutely sure that it wasn't a uniform—in which case, she was the children's nurse. Or perhaps M. de Boisgaillard's mother, he decided; a woman alone in the world, and except for her claim on her son, without resources. Now that he was married, the claim was, of course, much slighter, and so she was obliged to be grateful that she was here at all. No one spoke to her. Thinking that it might ease her shyness, her feeling of being (as he was) excluded from the conversation, he smiled directly at her. The response was polite and impersonal, and he decided that, as so often was the case with him, she was past rescuing.

He listened to the pitch, the intonations, of Mme de Bois-gaillard's voice as if he were hearing a new kind of music, and decided that there were as many different ways of speaking French as there were French people. Because of her voice he would have trusted absolutely anything she said. But he trusted her anyway, because of the naturalness and simplicity of her manner. Looking at her, he felt he knew her very well, without knowing anything at all about her. It was as if they had played together as children. Her husband's voice was rather high, thin, and reedy. It was also the voice of someone who knows exactly what to respect and what to be contemptuous of. So strange that two such different people should have married . . .

Mme de Boisgaillard spoke English fluently. In an undertone, with a delicate smile, she supplied Barbara, who sat next to her, with the word or phrase that would limit the context of an otherwise puzzling statement or explain the point of an amusing remark. Harold clutched at these straws eagerly. When Mme Viénot translated for them, it was usually some word that he knew already, and so she was never the slightest help. He watched M. de Boisgaillard until their eyes met across the table. The young Frenchman immediately looked away, and Harold was careful not to look at him again.

Mme Viénot was eager to learn whether her nephew thought the Schumann cabinet would jump during September. The young man and M. Carrère both thought it would— not because of a crisis, easy though it was to find one, but because of political squabbles that were of no importance except to the people directly involved.

"Why would they wait until September?" Harold asked. "Why not in August?"

"Because August is the month when Parliament takes its annual vacation," Mme Viénot said. "No government has ever been known to jump at this time of year. They always wait until September."

The joke was thoroughly enjoyed, and Mme Straus-Muguet nodded approvingly at Harold for having made it possible.

After the dessert course, napkins were folded in such a way as to conceal week-old wine stains and then inserted in their identifying rings.

Barbara saw that Mme Straus was aware that she had been looking at her, and said: "I have been admiring your little diamond heart."

"You like it?" Mme Straus said. From her tone of voice one would almost have supposed that she was about to undo the clasp of the fine gold chain and present the little heart, chain and all, to the young woman at the far end of the table. However, her hands remained in her lap, and she said: "It was given to me by a friend, long long ago," leaving them to decide for themselves whether the fiery little object was the souvenir of a romantic attachment. Mme Viénot gave her a glance of frank disbelief and pushed her chair back from the table.

The ladies left the dining room in the order of their age. Harold started to follow M. Carrère out of the room and to his surprise felt a hand on his sleeve, detaining him. M. de Boisgaillard drew him over to the other side of the room and asked him, in French, how he liked it at the château. Harold started to answer tactfully and saw that the face now looking down into his expected a truthful answer, was really interested, and would know if he was not candid; so he was, and the Frenchman laughed and suggested that they walk outside in the garden.

He opened one of the dining-room windows and stepped out, and Harold followed him around the corner of the house and through the gap in the hedge and into the potager. With a light rain—it was hardly more than a mist—falling on their shoulders, they walked up and down the gravel paths. The Frenchman asked how rich the ordinary man in America was. How many cars were there in the whole country? Did American women really rule the roost? And did they love their husbands or just love what they could get out of them? Was it true that everybody had running water and electricity? But not true that everybody owned their own house and every house had a dishwasher and a washing machine? Did Harold have any explanation to offer of how, in a country made up of such different racial strains, every man should be so passionately interested in machinery? Was it the culture or was it something that stemmed from the early days of the country—from its colonial period? How was America going to solve the Negro problem? Was it true that all Negroes were innately musical? And were they friendly with the white people who exploited them or did they hate them one and all? And how did the white people feel about Negroes? What did Americans think of Einstein? of Freud? of Stalin? of Churchill? of de Gaulle? Did they feel any guilt on account of Hiroshima? Did they like or dislike the French? Had he read the Kinsey Report, and was it true that virtually every American male had had some homosexual experience? And so on and so on.

The less equipped you are to answer such questions, the

more flattering it is to be asked them, but to answer even superficially in a foreign language you need more than a tourist's vocabulary.

"You don't speak German?"

Harold shook his head. They stood looking at each other helplessly.

"You don't speak *any* English?" Harold said.

"Pas un mot."

A few minutes later, as they were walking and talking again, the Frenchman forgot and shifted to German anyway, and Harold stopped him, and they went on trying to talk to each other in French. Very often Harold's answer did not get put into the right words or else in his excitement he did not pronounce them well enough for them to be understood, the approximation being some other word entirely, and the two men stopped and stared at each other. Then they tried once more, and impasses that seemed hopeless were bridged after all; or if this didn't happen, the subject was abandoned in favor of a new subject.

It began to rain in earnest, and they turned up their coat collars and went on walking and talking.

"Shall we go in?" the Frenchman asked, a moment later.

As they went back through the gap in the hedge, Harold said to himself that it was a different house they were returning to. By the addition of a man of the family it had changed; it had stopped being matriarchal and formal and cold, and become solid and hospitable and human, like other houses.

At the door of the petit salon, they separated. Harold took in the room at a glance. M. Carrère sat looking quite forlorn, the one man among so many women. And did he imagine it or was Mme Viénot put out with them? There was an empty chair beside Mme de Boisgaillard and he sat down in it and tried once more to follow the conversation. He learned that the woman he had taken for the children's nurse or possibly M. de Boisgaillard's mother was Mme de Boisgaillard's mother instead; which meant that she was Mme Viénot's sister and had a perfect right to be here. What he had failed to perceive, like the six blind men and the elephant, was that she was deaf and so could not take part in general conversation. During dinner she did not even try, but now if someone spoke directly to her she

adjusted the pointer of the little black box that she held to her
ear as if it were a miniature radio, and seemed to understand.

When the others retired to their rooms at eleven o'clock,
Eugène de Boisgaillard swept the Americans ahead of him,
through a doorway and down a second-floor hall they had not
been in before, and they found themselves in a bedroom with
a dressing room off it. They stood looking down at the baby,
who was fast asleep on her stomach but escaped entirely from
the covers, at right angles to the crib, with her knees tucked
under her, her feet crossed like hands, her rump in the air.

Her mother straightened her around and covered her, and
then they tiptoed back into the larger room and began to talk.
Mme de Boisgaillard translated and summarized quickly and
accurately, leaving them free to go on to the next thing they
wanted to say.

Unlike M. Carrère, Eugène de Boisgaillard did not hate all
Germans. His political views were Liberal and democratic. He
was also as curious as a cat. He wanted to know how long
Harold and Barbara had been married, and how they had met
one another, and what part of America they grew up in. He
asked their first names and then what their friends called them.
He asked them to call him by his first name. And then the
questions began again, as if the first thing in the morning he
and they were starting out for the opposite ends of the earth
and there was only tonight for them to get to know each
other. Once, when a question was so personal that Harold
thought he must have misunderstood, he turned to Mme de
Boisgaillard and she smiled and shook her head ruefully and
said: "I hope you do not mind. That is the way he is. When I
think he cannot possibly have said what I think I have heard
him say, I know that is just what he did say."

At her husband's suggestion, she left them and went downstairs to see what there was in the larder, and they were surprised to discover that without her they couldn't talk to each
other. They waited awkwardly until she came into the room
carrying a tray with a big bowl of sour cream and four smaller
bowls, a sugar bowl, and spoons.

Eugène de Boisgaillard pointed to the empty fireplace and
said: "No andirons. Does the one in your room work?"

Harold explained that it had a shield over it.

"During the Occupation the Germans let the forests be depleted—intentionally—and so one is allowed to cut only so much wood," Mme de Boisgaillard said, "and if they used it now there would not be enough for the winter. Poor Tante! She drives herself so hard. . . . The thing I always forget is what a beautiful smell this house has. It may be the box hedge, though Mummy says it is the furniture polish, but it doesn't smell like any other house in the world."

"Have your shoes begun to mildew?" Eugène de Boisgaillard said.

Barbara shook her head.

"They will," he said.

"You will drive them away," Mme de Boisgaillard said, "and then we won't have anyone our age to talk to."

"We will go after them," Eugène de Boisgaillard said, "talking every step of the way. The baby's sugar ration," he said, saluting the sugar bowl.

Sweetened with sugar, the half-solidified sour cream was delicious.

"Have you enjoyed knowing M. Carrère?" Eugène asked.

Harold said that M. Carrère seemed to be a very kind man.

"He's also very rich," Eugène said. "Everything he touches turns into more money, more gilt-edged stock certificates. He is a problem to the Bank of France. Toinette has a special tone of voice in speaking of him—have you noticed? Where does she place him, I wonder? On some secondary level. Not with Périclès, or Beethoven. Not with Louis XIV. With Saint-Simon, perhaps . . . In the past year I have learned how to interpret the public face. It has been very useful. The public face is much more ponderous and explicit than the private face and it asks only one question: 'What is it you want?' And whatever you want is unfortunately just the thing it isn't convenient for you to be given. . . . Do you get on well with your parents, Harold?"

He listened attentively to Alix's translation of the answer to this question and then said: "My father is very conservative. He has never in his whole life gone to the polls and voted."

"Why not?" Barbara asked.

"His not voting is an act of protest against the Revolution."

"You don't mean the Revolution of 1789?"

"Yes. He does not approve of it."

Tears of amusement ran down Harold's cheeks and he reached for his handkerchief and wiped them away.

"What does your father do?" Barbara asked.

"He collects porcelain. That's all he has done his whole life."

In a moment Harold had to get his handkerchief out again as Eugène launched forth on the official and unofficial behavior of his superior, the Minister of Planning and External Affairs.

At one o'clock the Americans stood up to go, and, still talking, Eugène and Alix accompanied them down the upstairs hall until they were in their own part of the house. Whispering and tittering like naughty children, they said good night. Was Mme Viénot awake, Harold wondered. Could she hear them? Did she disapprove of such goings on?

Eugène said that he had one last question to ask.

"Don't," Alix whispered.

"Why not? Why shouldn't I ask them? . . . Is there a double bed in your room?"

Harold shook his head.

"I knew it!" Eugène said. "I told Alix that there wouldn't be. Don't you find it strange—don't you think it is *extraordinary* that all the double beds in the house are occupied by single women?"

They said good night all over again, and the Americans crept up the stairs, which, even so, creaked frightfully. When Barbara fell asleep, Harold wrapped the covers around her snugly and moved over into his own damp bed and lay awake for some time, thinking. What had happened this evening was so different from anything else that had happened to them so far on their trip, and he felt that a part of him that had been left behind in America, without his realizing it, had now caught up with him. He thought with wonder how far off he could be about people. For Eugène was totally unlike what he had seemed at first to be. He was not cold and insincere but amusing and unpredictable, and masculine, and direct, and intelligent, and like a wonderful older brother. Knowing him was reason enough for them to come back time after time, through the years, to France. . . .

Chapter 9

A t breakfast the next morning, Mme Viénot's manner with the Americans did not convey approval or disapproval. She urged on them a specialty of the countryside—bread with meat drippings poured over it—and then, folding her napkin, excused herself to go and dress for church. Harold asked if they could go to church also, and she said: "Certainly."

At ten thirty the dog cart appeared in front of the house, with the gardener in the driver's seat and his white plow horse hitched to the traces. It had been arranged that Barbara should go to church in the cart with Mme Straus-Muguet and Alix and Eugène; that Mme Bonenfant should ride in the Bentley with M. and Mme Carrère; that Harold and Mme Viénot should bicycle. She rode her own, he was given the cook's, which got out of his control, in spite of Mme Viénot's repeated warnings. Unaccustomed to bicycles without brakes, he came sailing into the village a good two minutes ahead of her.

They were in plenty of time for Mass, but instead of going directly to the little church she went to Mme Michot's, where she stood gazing at the fruit and vegetables, her expression a mixture of disdain and disbelief, as if Mme Michot were trying to introduce her to persons whose social status was not at all what they pretended. Madame Michot's tomatoes were inferior and her plums were too dear. In the end she bought two lemons, half a pound of dried figs, and some white raisins that were unaccountably cheap.

As they came out of the little shop, she explained that she had one more errand; her seamstress was making her a green silk dress that was to have the New Look, and it had been promised for today.

At the seamstress's house, Mme Viénot knocked and waited. She knocked again. She stood in the street and called. She stopped and questioned a little girl, who told her reluctantly where the seamstress had said she could be found. Mme Viénot looked at her wrist watch. "I really don't see why she couldn't have been home!" she exclaimed. "We are already quite late for church, and it means going clear to the other side of the village."

Once more they got on their bicycles. As they were riding side by side over the bumpy cobblestones, she remarked that the village was older than it looked. "There is a legend— whether it is true I cannot say—that Jeanne d'Arc, traveling toward Chinon with her escort of three or four soldiers, arrived at Brenodville at nightfall and was denied a lodging by the monks."

"Why?"

"Because of her sex, no doubt."

"Where did she go?" Harold asked.

"She slept in a farmhouse, I believe."

He looked around for Gothic stonework and found, here and there, high up out of harm's way, a small gargoyle at the end of a waterspout, a weathered stone pinnacle, a carved lintel, or some other piece of medieval decoration, proving that the story was at least possible. The houses themselves—sour, secretive, commonplace-looking—said that if Jeanne d'Arc were to come again in the middle of the twentieth century, she would get the same inhospitable reception, and not merely from the monks but from everybody.

The house where the little girl had said the seamstress said she could be found was locked and shuttered, and no one came to the door. At five minutes of twelve, they arrived at the vestibule of the church. Mme Viénot genuflected in the aisle outside the family pew and then moved in and knelt beside her mother. Harold followed her. Half kneeling and half sitting, he tried not to look so much like a Protestant. The drama on the altar was reaching its climax. A little silver bell tinkled. The congregation spoke. (Was it Latin? Was it French?) Mme Viénot struck her flat chest three times and seemed to be asking for something from the depths of her heart, but though he listened intently, he could not hear what it was; it was lost in the asking of other low voices all around them. The bell tinkled again and again, insistently. There was a moment of hushed expectation and then the congregation rose from their knees with a roaring sound that nobody paid any attention to, filled the aisle, streamed out of the chill of the little church into the more surprising chill of a cold gray July day, and, pleased that an essential act was done, broke out into smiles and conversation.

Harold waited beside the two bicycles while Mme Viénot went into the stationer's for her mother's *Figaro*. He looked around for Mme Straus-Muguet, not sure whether she had meant them to meet her here in the village after church or where. And if he saw her beckoning to him, how would he escape from Mme Viénot? Mme Straus was nowhere in sight now, and he had made two trips downstairs after breakfast without encountering her.

When Mme Viénot took a long, thin, empty wine bottle out of her saddlebag and went into still another shop, he followed her out of curiosity and was introduced to M. Canourgue, whose stock was entirely out of sight, under a wooden counter or in the adjoining room. She counted out more ration coupons, and explained that Harold was American and a friend of M. Georges who was so fond of chocolates. The wine bottle went into the back room and came back full of olive oil. Mme Viénot bought sardines, and this and that. When they were outside in the street again, Harold saw that the canvas saddlebag of her bicycle was crammed, and so he took the bottle from her and placed it carefully on its side in his saddle bag, which was empty.

As they rode home, he asked where she had learned English and she said: "From my governess . . . And in England."

Her education had been rounded off with a year in London, during which she had lived with a private family. She admired the British, she said, but did not particularly like them. "They dress so badly, in those ill-fitting suits," she said. He waited, hoping that she would say that she liked Americans, but she didn't.

They dismounted in the courtyard and wheeled their bicycles into the kitchen entry, where Mme Viénot let out a cry of distress. He saw that she was looking at his saddlebag, and said: "What's the matter?" She pointed to the wine bottle lying on its side. "The cork has come out," she said, in the voice of doom.

He started to apologize, and then realized that she wasn't paying any attention to what he said. She had picked up the bottle and was examining the outside, turning it around slowly. It was dry. They examined the saddlebag. Not a drop of oil had been spilled! He learned a new French phrase—"une espèce de miracle"—and used it frequently in conversation from that time on.

Mme Straus-Muguet was in the drawing room, with M. and Mme Carrère and Mme Bonenfant and Barbara and Alix and Eugène. They had all been invited to take an apéritif with her on Sunday morning. An unopened bottle of Martinique rum stood on the little round table. Thérèse brought liqueur glasses and the corkscrew. The rum loosened tongues, smoothed away differences of background, of age, of temperament, of nationality. The conversation became animated; their eyes grew bright. Thérèse removed the screen, and they all rose and, still talking, floated on a wave of intense cordiality through the hall and into the dining room, where the long-promised poulet awaited them. As Harold unfolded his clean napkin, he decided that life in the country was not so bad, after all.

The gaiety did not quite last out the meal. The nine people around the table sank back, one after another, into their ordinary selves. There had been no real, or at least no lasting, change but merely a sleight-of-hand demonstration. As some people know how to make three balls appear and disappear and a whole flock of doves fly out of an opera hat, Mme Straus-Muguet knew how to lift a dead social weight. Out of the most unpromising elements she had just now constructed an edifice of gaiety, an atmosphere of concert pitch. Shreds of her triumph lasted until teatime, when Mme Viénot surrendered the silver teapot to her, and she presided—modestly, but also as if she were accustomed to having this compliment paid her.

Sitting with the others, in the circle of chairs at one end of the drawing room, Barbara listened to what Alix and Eugène were saying to each other. His train left at six, and there were last-minute instructions and reminders, of a kind that she was familiar with, and that made her feel she knew them intimately merely because the French girl was saying just what she herself might have said in these circumstances.

"You know where the bread coupons are?"

"You put them in the desk, didn't you?"

"Yes. You'll have to go and get new ones when they expire. Do you think you will remember to?"

"If I don't, my stomach will remind me."

"I have arranged with Mme Emile to buy ice for you, and butter once a week. And if you want to ask someone to dinner, Françoise will come and cook it for you. She will be there Fridays, to clean the apartment and change the linen on your bed. Can you remember to leave a note for the laundress? I meant to do it and forgot. She is to wash your dressing gown. Is it late?"

"There is plenty of time," Eugène said, glancing at his wrist watch.

"If it should turn hot, leave the awning down at our window and close the shutters, and it will be cool when you come home at night. It might be better to leave all the shutters closed—but then it will be gloomy. Whatever you think best. And if you are too tired after work to write to me, it will be all right. I will write to you every day. . . ."

A few minutes more passed, and then he stood up and started around the circle, shaking hands and saying good-by. His manner with M. and Mme Carrère was simply that of a man of breeding. And yet beneath the confident surface there was something a little queer, Harold thought, watching them. Was Eugène trying to convey to them that his father would not have permitted them to be introduced to him?

When he arrived at Harold and Barbara, he smiled, and Harold said as they shook hands: "We'll see you on Friday."

Eugène nodded, turned away, and then turned back to them and said: "You are coming up to Paris—"

"Next Sunday."

"Good. We will all be taking the train together. That is what I had hoped. And where will you stay?"

Harold told him.

"Why do you spend money for a hotel," Eugène said, "when there is room in my mother-in-law's apartment?"

Harold hesitated, and Eugène went on: "I won't be able to spend as much time with you as I'd like, but it will be a pleasure for me, having you and Barbara there when I come home at night."

"But it will make trouble for you."

"It will be no trouble to anyone."

Harold looked at Barbara inquiringly, and misinterpreted her answering look.

"In that case—" he began, and before he could finish his sentence she said: "Can we let you know later?"

"When I come down next week end," Eugène said, and bent down to kiss Mme Bonenfant's frail hand.

Harold thought a slight shadow had passed over his face when they did not accept his invitation, and then he decided that this was not so. The relations between them were such that there was no possibility of hurt feelings or any misunderstanding.

Later, Barbara said that she would have been delighted to accept the invitation except for one thing: it should have come from Alix's mother. "Or at least he should have made it clear that Mme Cestre had been consulted before he invited us. And also, perhaps we ought to be a little more cautious; we ought to know a little more what we're getting into."

"Eugène enjoyed talking to you so much," Alix said, in the petit salon after dinner. "It was a great pleasure to him to find you here. He learned many things about America which interested him."

"The things he wanted to know about, most of the time I couldn't tell him," Harold said. "Partly because nobody knows the answer to some of his questions, and partly because I didn't know the right words to explain in French the way things are. Also, there are lots of things I should know that I don't. Sometimes we couldn't understand each other at all, and when I was ready to give up he would insist that I go on. And eventually, out of my floundering, he seemed to understand what it was I was trying to say. I've never had an experience quite like it."

"Eugène is very intuitive. . . . I have been telling him that he ought to learn English, and until now he hasn't cared to take the trouble. But it distressed him that I could speak to you in your language, badly though I do it, and he—"

"Your English is excellent."

"I am out of the habit. I make mistakes in grammar. Eugène has decided to go to the Berlitz School and learn English, so that when you come back to France he will be able to talk to you. So you see, you have accomplished something which I try to do and couldn't."

She turned away in order to repeat to her mother a remark of M. Carrère's that had pleased the company. Mme Cestre's face lit up. She was reminded of an observation of her husband's that in turn pleased M. Carrère. Alix waited until she saw that this conversation was proceeding without her help and then she turned back to Harold. "Eugène was so excited to learn that you have been married three years. We thought you were on your wedding journey."

"How long have you been married?"

"A little over a year. Eugène thought that in marriage, after a while, people changed. He thought they grew less fond of one another, and that there was no way of avoiding it. When he saw you and your wife together, the way you are with each other, it made him more hopeful."

"Where did you meet?" Harold said, to change the subject. He was perfectly willing to discuss most subjects but not this, because of a superstitious fear that his words would come back to him under ironical circumstances.

"When the Germans came," she said, "my father was in the South, and we were separated from him for some time. We were here with my grandmother. But as soon as we were able, we joined my father in Aix-en-Provence, and it was there that I met Eugène. He was different from the boys I knew. I thought he was very handsome and intelligent, and I enjoyed talking to him. At that time he was thinking of taking holy orders. I felt I could say anything to him—that he was like my brother."

"That's what he seems like to me," Harold said. "Like a wonderful older brother, though actually he is younger than I am."

"Do you have any brothers and sisters?"

"One brother," he said. "When we were growing up, we couldn't be left together in the back seat of the car, because we always ended up fighting. But now we get along all right."

"It never occurred to me that Eugène would want me to love him," she said. "When he asked me to marry him, I was surprised. I was not sure I would marry. I don't know why, exactly. It just didn't seem like something that would happen to me. . . . As a child I always played by myself."

"So did I," Harold said.

"I lived in a world of my own imagination. . . . When I grew older I began to notice the people around me. I saw that there were two kinds—the bright and the stupid—and I decided that I would choose the bright ones for my friends. Later on, I was disappointed in them. Clever people are not always kind. Sometimes they are quite cruel. And the stupid ones very often are kind."

"Then what did you do?"

"I had to choose my friends all over again. . . . I have a sister. The two small children we brought with us are hers. She is two years younger than I, and for a long time I was hardly aware of her. One day she asked me who is my best friend, and I named some girl, and she began to cry. She said: '*You* are *my* best friend.' I felt very bad. After that we became very close to each other."

Mme Viénot addressed a question to her, and Alix turned her head to answer. If I only had a tape recording of the way she says "father," "brother," and "other," Harold thought, smiling to himself. When she turned back to him, he said: "It must have been very difficult—the Occupation, I mean."

"We lived on turnips for weeks at a time. I cannot endure the sight of one now."

She saw that her grandmother was watching them and said in French: "I have been telling Harold how we lived on turnips during the Occupation." It was the first time she had used his Christian name, and he was pleased.

Mme Bonenfant had an interesting observation to make: perpetual hunger makes the middle-aged and the elderly grow thinner, as one would expect, but the young become quite plump.

Was that why she thought she would never marry, he wondered.

"The greatest hardship was not being allowed to write letters," Alix said.

"The Germans didn't allow it?"

"Only postcards. Printed postcards with blanks that you filled in. Five or six sentences. You could say that so-and-so had died, or was sick. That kind of thing. We used to make up names of people that didn't exist, and we managed to convey all sorts of information that the Germans didn't recognize, just by filling in the blanks."

"Did my niece tell you that during the Occupation she and my sister hid a girl in their apartment in Paris?" Mme Viénot said. "The Gestapo was looking for her."

"She was a school friend," Alix explained. "I knew she was in the Résistance, and one day she telephoned me and asked if she could spend the night with me. I told her that it wasn't convenient—that I had asked another girl to stay with me that night. And after she had hung up, I realized what she was trying to tell me."

"How did you manage to reach her again?"

"I sent word, through a little boy in the house where she lived. She came the next night, and stayed four months with us."

"I was in and out of the apartment all the time," Mme Viénot said, "and never suspected anything. I saw the girl occasionally and thought she had come to see Alix."

"We didn't dare tell anyone," Alix said, "for her sake."

"After the war was over, my sister told me what had been going on right under my nose," Mme Viénot said. "But it was very dangerous for them, you know. It might have cost them their lives."

Mme Cestre raised her hearing aid to her ear, and Alix leaned toward her mother and explained what they were talking about.

"She was rather imprudent," Mme Cestre said mildly.

"She went out at night sometimes," Alix said. "And she told several people where she was hiding. She enjoyed the danger of their knowing."

"Were many people you know involved in the Résistance?" Harold asked.

"In almost every French family something like that was going on," Mme Viénot said.

A silence fell over the room. When the conversation was resumed, Harold said: "There is something I have been wanting to ask you: when people do something kind, what do you say to them?"

"'Merci,'" Alix said.

"I know, but I don't mean that. I mean when you are really grateful."

" 'Merci beaucoup.' Or 'Merci bien.' "

"But if it is something really kind, and you want them to know that you—"

"It is the same."

"There are no other words?"

"No."

"In English there are different ways of saying that you are deeply grateful."

"In French we use the same words."

"How do people know, then, that you appreciate what they have done for you?"

"By the way you say it—by your expression, the intonation of your voice."

"But that makes it so much more difficult!" he exclaimed.

"It is a question of sincerity," she said, smiling at him as if she had just offered him the passkey to all those gates he kept trying to see over.

Chapter 10

O N Monday morning the Bentley appeared in front of the château for the last time. The chauffeur carried the luggage out, and then a huge bouquet of delphiniums wrapped in damp newspaper, which he placed on the floor of the back seat. Mme Viénot, Mme Bonenfant, Harold, Barbara, and Alix accompanied M. and Mme Carrère out to the car. Harold watched carefully while Mme Carrère was thanking Mme Viénot for the flowers and the quart of country cream she held in her hand. They did not embrace each other, but then Mme Carrère was not given to effusiveness. The fact that she didn't speak of seeing Mme Viénot again in Paris might mean merely that it wasn't necessary to speak of it. One thing he felt sure of—there was not one stalk of delphinium left in the garden.

The necessary handshaking was accomplished, and Mme Carrère got into the back seat of the car. M. Carrère put his hand in his pocket and drew out his card, which he handed Harold. It was a business card, but on the back he had written the address and telephone number of the apartment in the rue du Faubourg St. Honoré. As Harold tucked the card in his wallet, he felt stripped and exposed, a small boy in the presence of his benign, all-knowing father. If they found themselves in any kind of difficulty, M. Carrère said, they were to feel free to call on him for help. What he seemed to be saying (so kind was the expression in the expert old clown's eyes, so comprehending and tolerant his smile) was that human thought is by no means as private as it seems, and all you need in order to read somebody else's mind is the willingness to read your own. With his legend intact and his lilac-colored shawl around his shoulders, he leaned forward one last time and waved, through the car window.

Waving, Harold said: "I hope the drive isn't too much for him."

"They are going to stop somewhere for lunch and a rest," Mme Viénot said. Already, though the car had not yet turned into the public road, she seemed different, less conventional, lighter, happier. "They are both very dear people," she said, but he could not see that she was sorry to have them go.

"We are thinking of going to Chaumont this afternoon," he said.

"And you'd like me to arrange about the taxi? Good. I'll tell her to come at two."

"Alix is coming with us," he went on, and then, spurred by his polite upbringing: "We hope you will come too." He did not at all want her to come; it would be much pleasanter with just the three of them. But in the world of his childhood nobody had ever said that pleasure takes precedence over not hurting people's feelings, even when there is a very good chance that they don't have any feelings. "If the idea appeals to you," he said, hoping to hear that it didn't. "Perhaps it would only be boring, since you have seen the château so many times."

"I would enjoy going," Mme Viénot said. "And perhaps the taxi could bring us home by way of Onzain? I have an errand there, and it is not far out of the way."

But if Mme Viénot was coming to Chaumont with them, what about poor Mme Straus-Muguet? Wouldn't she feel left out?

"And will you please invite Mme Straus-Muguet for us," he said.

"Oh, that won't be necessary," Mme Viénot exclaimed. "It is very nice of you to think of it, but I'm sure she doesn't expect to be asked, and it will make five in the taxi."

When he insisted, she agreed reluctantly to convey the invitation, and a few minutes later, meeting him on the stairs, she reported that it had been accepted.

The taxi came promptly at two, and all five of them crowded into it, and still apologizing cheerfully to one another for taking up too much space they arrived at a point directly across the river from Chaumont, which was as far as they could go by car. The ferry was loading on the opposite shore, and Alix and Mme Viénot did not agree about where it would land. After they had scrambled down the steep sandbank to the water's edge, they saw some hikers and cyclists waiting a hundred yards upstream, at the exact spot where Mme Viénot had said the ferry would come. She and Harold began to help Mme Straus-Muguet up the bank again. The two girls took off their shoes and waded into the water. The sound of their voices and their laughter made him turn and look back. Alix tucked the hem of her skirt under her belt. Then the two girls waded in deeper and deeper, with their dresses pulled up and their white thighs showing.

There are certain scenes that (far more than artifacts dug up out of the ground or prehistoric cave paintings, which have a confusing freshness and newness) serve to remind us of how old the human race is, and of the beautiful, touching sameness of most human occasions. Anything that is not anonymous is all a dream. And who we are, and whether our parents embraced life or were disappointed by it, and what will become of our children couldn't be less important. Nobody asks the name of the athlete tying his sandal on the curved side of the Greek vase or whether the lonely traveler on the Chinese scroll arrived at the inn before dark.

He realized with a pang that he had lost Barbara. He was up here on the bank helping an old woman to keep her balance instead of down there with his shoes and stockings off, and so he had lost her. She had turned into a French girl, a stranger to him.

The girls' way was blocked by a clump of cattails. They stopped and considered what to do. Then, taking each other by the hand, they started slowly out into still deeper water. . . . The water was too deep. They could not get around the cattails without swimming, and so they turned back and went the rest of the way on dry land.

The ferryboat coming toward them from the opposite shore was long and narrow, and the gunwales were low in the water. When it was about fifty yards from the bank, the ferryman turned off the outboard motor, which was on the end of a long pole, and lifted it out of the water. The boat drifted in slowly. Harold did not see how it could possibly hold all the people who were now waiting to cross over—hollow-cheeked, pale, undernourished hikers and cyclists, dressed for *le sport*, in shorts and open-collared shirts, with their sleeves rolled up. The slightest wind would have blown them away like dandelion fluff.

They pulled the prow of the boat up onto the mud bank and took the bicycles carefully from the hands of the ferryman. When the passengers had jumped ashore, the hikers and cyclists stood aside politely while the party from the château went on board. Mme Viénot and Mme Straus-Muguet sat in the stern, in the only seat there was. Barbara and Alix perched on the side of the boat, next to them. Harold stood among the other passengers. Under the ferryman's direction a dozen bicycles were placed in precarious balance. The boat settled lower and lower as more people, more bicycles with loaded saddle bags came on board. There were no oars, and the ferryman, on whom all their lives depended, was a sixteen-year-old boy with patches on his pants. He pushed his way excitedly past wire wheels and bare legs, shouting directions. When everybody was on board, he shoved the boat away from the shore with his foot, all but fell in, ran to the stern, making the boat rock wildly, and lowered the outboard motor. The motor caught, and they turned around slowly and headed for the other shore.

"This boat is not safe!" Mme Viénot told the ferryman, and when he didn't pay any attention to her she said to Barbara: "I shall complain to the mayor of Brenodville about it. . . . The current is very treacherous in the middle of the river."

Mme Straus-Muguet took Barbara's hand and confessed that she could not swim.

"Harold is a very good swimmer," Barbara said.

"M. Rhodes will swim to Mme Straus and support her if the boat capsizes," Mme Viénot decided.

"Très bien," Mme Straus-Muguet said, and called their attention to the scenery.

Harold's mind ran off an unpleasant two-second movie in which he saw himself in the water, supporting an aged woman whose life was nearly finished, while Barbara, encumbered by her clothes, with no one to help her, drowned before his eyes.

Out in the middle of the river there was a wind, and the gray clouds directly over their heads looked threatening. Mme Straus-Muguet was reminded of the big painting in the Louvre of Dante and Virgil crossing the River Styx. She was so gallant and humorous, in circumstances a woman of her age could hardly have expected to find herself in and few would have agreed to, that she became a kind of heroine in the eyes of everyone. The cyclists turned and watched her, admiring her courage.

The shore they had left receded farther and farther. They were in the main current of the river for what seemed a long long time, and then slowly the opposite shore began to draw nearer. They could pick out details of houses and see the people on the bank. As Harold stepped onto the sand he felt the triumph and elation of a survivor. The ferryboat had not sunk after all, and he and everybody in it were braver than they had supposed.

The climb from the water's edge up the cliff was clearly too much for a woman in the neighborhood of seventy. Mme Straus-Muguet took Harold's arm and clung to it. With now Alix and now Barbara on her other side supporting her, she pressed on, through sand, up steep paths and uneven stone stairways, stopping again and again to exclaim to herself how difficult it was, to catch her breath, to rest. Her face grew flushed and then it became gray, but she would not hear of their turning back. When they were on level ground at last and saw the towers and drawbridge of the château, she stopped once more and exclaimed, but this time it was pleasure that moved her. "You do not need to worry any more about me," she said. "I am quite recovered."

While they were waiting for the guide, she bought and presented to Harold and Barbara a set of miniature postcards of the rooms they were about to see. She called Barbara's attention to the tapestries in the Salon du Concert before the guide had a chance to speak of them. Confronted with a glass case containing portrait medallions by the celebrated Italian artist Nini, she said that she had a passion for bas-relief and could happily spend the rest of her life studying this collection. They were shown the dressing table of Catherine de Médicis, and Mme Straus insisted on climbing the steep stone staircase to the tower where the Queen had learned from her astrologer the somber fate in store for her three sons who would sit on the throne of France: one dead of a fever, within a year of his coronation, one the victim of melancholy, and one of the assassin's dagger. As Mme Straus listened to this story, her sensitive face reflected the surprise and then the consternation of Catherine de Médicis, whose feelings she, a mother, could well appreciate, though they were separated by four centuries. Mme Viénot congratulated the guide on his diction and his knowledge of history, and Mme Straus-Muguet congratulated him on the view up and down the river. She was reluctant to leave the stables where the elephant had been housed, but perfectly willing to return to the river bank and for the second time in one day risk death by drowning.

The taxi was where they had left it. It had waited all afternoon for them, time in Brenodville being far less dear than gasoline. Mme Viénot's errand took them a considerable distance out of their way but gave them an opportunity to see the villages of Chouzy and Onzain. The grain merchant at Onzain was away, and his wife refused to let Mme Viénot have the laying mash she had come for. They rode home with two large sacks of inferior horse feed tied across the front and back of the taxi.

That evening before dinner, Harold heard a knock and went to the door. Mme Straus entered breathing harshly from the stairs. "What a charming room!" she exclaimed.

She was leaving tomorrow morning, to go and stay with friends at Chaumont, and she wanted to give them her address and telephone number in Paris. "When you come," she said, squeezing Barbara's hand, "we will have lunch together, and afterward take a drive through the city. It will be my great pleasure to show it to you."

She had brought with her two books—two thin volumes of poetry, which they were to read and return to her when they met again—and also some letters. They lay mysteriously in her lap while she told them about the convent in Auteuil where she now lived. She was most fortunate that the sisters had taken her in; the waiting list was long. And the serenity was so good for her.

She looked down at the letters in her lap. They were from Mme Marguerite Mailly, of the Comédie Française, whose Phèdre and Andromaque were among the great performances of the French theater. Mme Straus considered these letters her most priceless possession, and took them with her wherever she went. Mme Mailly's son, such a gifted and handsome boy,

so intelligent, was only eighteen when his plane was shot down
at the very beginning of the war.

"I too lost a son in this way," Mme Straus said.

"Your son was killed in the war?" Harold asked.

"He died in an airplane accident in the thirties," Mme
Straus-Muguet said. The look in her eyes as she told them this
was not tragic but speculative, and he saw that she was considering their chaise longue. Because she knew only too well the
dangers of giving way to immoderate grief, she had been able,
she said, to lead her friend gently and gradually to an attitude
of acceptance. She opened her lorgnette and, peering through
it, read excerpts from the actress's letters, in which Mme
Mailly thanked her dear friend for pointing out to her the one
true source of consolation.

Harold read the inscription on the flyleaf of one of the
books (the handwriting was bold and enormous) and then several of the poems. They seemed to be love poems—incestuous
love sonnets to the actress's dead son, whose somewhat girlish
countenance served as a frontispiece. But when would he ever
have time to read them?

"I'm afraid something might happen to them while they're
in our possession," he said. "I really don't think we ought to
keep them."

But Mme Straus was insistent. They were to keep the two
volumes of poetry until they saw her again.

The next morning, standing in the foyer, with her suitcases
around her on the black and white marble floor, she kept the
taxi waiting while she thanked Mme Viénot elaborately for her
hospitality. When she turned and put out her hand, Harold
bent down and kissed her on the cheek. Her response was pure
pleasure. She dropped her little black traveling bag, raised her
veil, said: "You have made it possible for me to do what I have
been longing to do," and with her hands on both his shoulders kissed him first on one cheek and then on the other.

"Voilà l'amour," Mme Viénot said, smiling wickedly. The
remark was ignored.

Mme Straus kissed Barbara and then, looking into their eyes
affectionately, said: "Thank you, my dear children, for not allowing the barrier of age to come between us!"

Then she got into the taxi and drove off to stay with her

friends at Chaumont. In order that her friends here should not be totally without resource during her absence, she was leaving behind the box of *diamonoes.*

That afternoon, Barbara and Harold and Alix took the bus into Blois. The Americans were paying still another visit to the château; Harold wanted to see with his own eyes the rooms through which the Duc de Guise had moved on the way to his death. They suggested that Alix come with them, but she had errands to do, and she wanted to pay a visit to the nuns at the nursery school where she had worked during the early part of the war. They would gladly have given up the château for the nursery school if she had asked them to go with her, but she didn't ask them, and she refused gently to meet them for tea at the pâtisserie. They did not see her again until they met at the end of the afternoon. She was pushing a second-hand baby carriage along the sidewalk and they saw that she was radiantly happy.

"It is a very good carriage," she said, "and it was cheap. Eugène will be very pleased with me."

The baby carriage was hoisted on top of the bus, and they took turns pushing it home from the highway. Alix pointed out the house of Thérèse's family, and in a field Harold saw a horse-drawn reaper. "Why, I haven't seen one of those since I was a child!" he said excitedly, and then proceeded to describe to Alix the elaborate machine that had taken its place.

It was a nice evening, and they were enjoying the walk. "I hope you will decide to stay in our apartment," Alix said suddenly. "It would be so pleasant for Eugène. It would mean company for him."

They did not have to answer because at that moment they were passing a farmhouse and she saw a little boy by the wood-shed and spoke to him. He was learning to ride a bicycle that was too big for him. She left the baby carriage in the middle of the road and went over to give him some pointers.

When they got home, the Americans went straight to their room, intending to rest before dinner. Harold had just got into bed and pulled the covers up when they heard a knock. Barbara slipped on her dressing gown, and before she got to the door it opened. Though one says the nail is drawn to the magnet, if you look very closely you see that the magnet is also drawn to the nail. Mme Viénot had come to tell them about her visit to the mayor of Brenodville.

". . . I said that the ferry at Chaumont was extremely dangerous, and that some day, unless something was done about it, a number of people would lose their lives. . . . You won't believe what he said. The whole history of modern France is in this one remark. He said"—her eyes shone with amusement—"he said: 'I know but it's at Chaumont.' . . . How was your afternoon?"

She sat down on the edge of Harold's bed, keeping him a prisoner there; he was stark naked under the covers.

Since she did not seem concerned by the fact that his shoulders and arms were bare, he did his best to forget this, and she went on talking cozily and cheerfully, as if their intimacy were long established and a source of mutual pleasure. He realized that, with reservations and at arm's length, he really did like her. She was intelligent and amusing, and her pale-blue eyes saw either everything or nothing. Her day was full of small but nevertheless remarkable triumphs. In spite of rationing and shortages of almost everything you could think of, the food was always interesting. Though the house was cold, it was also immaculately clean. And there were never any awkward pauses in the conversations that took place in front of the empty Franklin stove or around the dining-room table.

She told them how she had searched for and finally found the wallpaper for this room; and about the picturesque fishing villages and fiords of Ile d'Yeu, where, in happier circumstances, the family always went in August, for the sea air and the bathing; and about the year that Eugène and Alix had spent in Marseilles. Rather than be a fonctionnaire in Paris, Eugène chose to work as a day laborer, carrying mortar and rubble, in Marseilles. They lived in the slums, and their evenings were spent among working people, whom he hoped to educate so that France would have a future and not, like Italy, merely a past. He was not the only young man of aristocratic family to dedicate himself to the poor in this way; there were others; there was, in fact, a movement, which was now losing its impetus because the church had not encouraged it. Eugène should perhaps have taken holy orders, as he once

thought seriously of doing. It was in his temperament to go
the whole way, to go to extremes, to become a saint. Shortly
before the baby was born, they came back to Paris. Alix did
not want their child to grow up in such sordid surroundings.
He was not very happy in his job at the Ministry of Planning
and External Affairs, and Mme Viénot could not help thinking
that both of them were less happy than they had been before,
but the decision was, of course, the only right one. And after
all, if one applied oneself, and had the temperament for it, one
could do very well in the government. Her son-in-law, for
instance— "I hope you didn't repeat to M. Carrère what I said
about his being talked about as the future Minister of Finance?"

Harold shook his head.

"I'm afraid it was not very discreet of me," she said. "Jean-
Claude is quite different from the rest of his family, who are
charming but hors de siècle."

"Does that mean 'old-fashioned'?"

"They are gypsies."

"Real gypsies? The kind that travel around in wagons?"

"Oh mercy no, they are perfectly respectable, and of a very
old family, but— How shall I put it? They are unconventional.
They come to meals when they feel like it, wear strange
clothes, stay up all night practicing the flute, and say whatever
comes into their minds. . . . Is there a word for that in English?"

"Bohemian," Barbara said.

"Yes," Mme Viénot said, nodding. "But not from the country of Bohemia. His mother is so amusing, so unlike anyone
else. Sometimes she will eat nothing but cucumbers for weeks
at a time. And Jean-Claude's father blames every evil under
the sun on the first Duke of Marlborough—with perhaps some
justice but not a great deal. There are too many villains of our
own époque, alas. . . . I am keeping you from resting?"

Reassured, she stayed so long that they were all three late for
dinner. The box of *diamonoes* remained unopened on Mme
Viénot's desk in the petit salon, and the evening was given
over, as before, to the game of conversation.

*

On Wednesday morning the cook prepared a picnic lunch and the Americans took the train to Amboise. There was a new bridge across the river at Amboise, and so they did not have to risk their lives. After they had seen the château they went and peered into the little chapel where Leonardo da Vinci either was or was not buried.

Down below in the village, Harold saw a row of ancient taxis near the Hôtel Lion d'Or, and arranged with the driver of the newest one to take them to Chenonceau, twelve kilometers away. After they had eaten their lunch on the river bank, they went back to where the row of taxis had been and, mysteriously, there was only one and it was not their taxi, but the man Harold had talked to was sitting in the driver's seat and seemed to be waiting for them. It was a wood-burning taxi, and for the first few blocks they kept looking out of the back window at the trail of black smoke they were leaving in their wake.

Crossing a bridge on the narrow dirt road to Chenonceau, they passed a hiker with a heavy rucksack on his back. The driver informed them that the hiker was a compatriot of theirs, and Harold told him to stop until the hiker had caught up with them. He was Danish, not American, but on finding out that he was going to the château, Harold invited him into the car anyway. He spoke English well and French about the way they did.

The taxi let them out at an ornamental iron gate some distance from the château itself. They stayed together as far as the drawbridge, and then suddenly the Dane was no longer with them or in fact anywhere. Half an hour later, when they emerged from the château with a dozen other sight-seers, they saw him standing under a tree that was far enough away from the path so that they did not have to join him if they did not care to. The three of them studied the château from all sides and found the place where they could get the best view of the inverted castle in the river. The formal gardens of Catherine de Médicis and Diane de Poitiers were both planted in potatoes. A small bronze sign said that the gardens had been ruined by the inundation of May 1940, and since the river flowing under the château at that moment was only a few inches deep, they took this to be a reference to the Germans, though as a matter of fact it was not. They rode back to Amboise in the wood-burning taxi and, sitting on the bank of the Loire, Harold and Barbara shared what was left of their lunch and a bottle of red wine with the Dane, who produced some tomatoes for them out of his rucksack and told them the story of his life. His name was Nils Jensen, he was nineteen years old, and he had cut himself off from his inheritance. It had been expected that he would go into the family business in Copenhagen and in-stead he was studying medicine. He wanted to become a psy-chiatrist. He could only bring a small amount of money out of Denmark, and so he was hiking through France. Harold saw in his eyes that there was something he wanted them to know about him that he could not say—that he was well bred and a gentleman. He did not need to say it, but he was a gentleman who had been living largely on tomatoes and he badly needed a bath and clean clothes.

He had not yet decided where he was going to spend the night; he might stay here; but if he went on to Blois he would be taking the same train they were taking. He had not yet seen the château of Amboise, and so they said good-by, provision-ally. The Americans went halfway across the bridge and down a flight of stairs to a little island in the middle of the river, and there they walked up and down in a leafy glade, searching for just some small trace of the Visigoths and the Franks who, around the year 500 A.D., met here and celebrated a peace treaty, the terms of which neither army found it convenient to honor.

At the railroad station, Harold and Barbara looked around for Nils Jensen, and Harold considered buying third-class tick-ets, in case he turned up later, but in the end decided that he was not coming and they might as well be comfortable. When the train drew in, there he was. He appeared right out of the ground, with a second-class ticket in his hand—bought, it was clear, so that he could ride with them.

The god of love could be better represented than by a little boy blindfolded and with a bow and arrow. Why not a mem-ber of the Actors' Equity, with his shirt cuffs turned back, an impressive diamond ring on one finger, his long black hair heavily pomaded, his magic made possible by a trunkful of ac-cessories and a stooge somewhere in the audience. Think of a

card—any card. There is no card you can think of that the foxy
vaudeville magician doesn't have up his sleeve or in a false
pocket of his long coattails.

The train carried them past Monteux, past Chaumont on
the other side of the river. There was so much that had to be
said in this short time, and so much that their middle-class upbringing prevented them from saying or even knowing they
felt. The Americans did not even tell Nils Jensen—except with
their eyes, their smiles—how much they liked being with him
and everything about him. Nils Jensen did not say: "Oh I
don't know which of you I'm in love with—I love you both!
And I've looked everywhere, I've looked so long for somebody I could be happy with. . . ." Nevertheless, they all three
used every minute that they had together. The train, which
could not be stopped, could not be made to go slower, carried
them past Onzain and Chouzy. At Brenodville they shook
hands, and Angle A and Angle B got out and then stood on
the brick platform waving until the train took Angle C (as talented and idealistic and tactful and congenial a friend as they
were ever likely to have) away from them, with nothing to
complete this triangle ever again but an address in Copenhagen that must have been incorrectly copied, since a letter
sent there was never replied to.

Walking through the village, with the shadows stretching
clear across the road in front of them, they saw windows and
doors that were wide open, they heard voices, they met people
who smiled and spoke to them. They thought for a moment
that the man returning from the fields with his horse and his
dog was one of the men who were sitting on the café terrace
the day they arrived, and then decided that he wasn't. Coming
to an open gate, they stopped and looked in. There was no
one around and so they stood there studying the courtyard
with its well, its neat woodpile, its bicycle, its two-wheeled
cart, its tin-roofed porch, its clematis and roses growing in
tubs, its dog and cat and chickens and patient old farm horse,
its feeding trough and watering trough, so like an illustration
in a beginning French grammar: *A* is for *Auge*, *B* is for *Bicyclette*, *C* is for *Cheval*, etc.

When they were on the outskirts of the village, they saw
Mme Viénot's gardener coming toward them in the cart and

assumed he had business in the village. He stopped when he was abreast of them, and waited. They stood looking up at him and he told them to get in. Mme Viénot had sent him, thinking that they would be tired after their long day's excursion. They *were* tired, and grateful that she had thought of them.

In the beautiful calm evening light, driving so slowly between fields that had just been cut, they learned that the white horse was named Pompon, and that he was thirty years old. The gardener explained that it was his little boy who had taken Harold by the hand and led him to the house of M. Fleury. They found it easy to talk to him. He was simple and direct, and so were the words he used, and so was the look in his eyes. They felt he liked them, and they wished they could know him better.

On the table in their room, propped against the vase of flowers, was a letter from Mme Straus-Muguet. The handwriting was so eccentric and the syntax so full of flourishes that Harold took it downstairs and asked Alix to translate it for them. Mme Straus was inviting them to take tea with her at the house of her friends, who would be happy to meet two such charming Americans.

He watched Alix's face as she read the protestations of affection at the close of the letter.

"Why do you smile?"

She refused to explain. "You would only think me uncharitable," she said. "As in fact I am."

He was quite sure that she wasn't uncharitable, so there must be something about Mme Straus that gave rise to that doubtful smile. But what? Though he again urged her to tell him, she would not. The most she would say was that Mme Straus was "roulante."

He went back upstairs and consulted the dictionary. "Roulante" meant "rolling." It also meant a "side-splitting, killing (sight, joke)."

Reluctantly, he admitted to himself, for the first time, that there was something theatrical and exaggerated about Mme Straus's manner and conversation. But there was still a great gap between that and "side-splitting." Did Alix see something he didn't see? Probably she felt that as Americans they had a right to their own feelings about people, and did not want to spoil their friendship with Mme Straus. But in a way she *had* spoiled it, since it is always upsetting to discover that people you like do not think very much of each other.

When he showed Barbara the page of the dictionary, it turned out that she too had reservations about Mme Straus. "The thing is, she might become something of a burden if she attached herself to us while we're in Paris. We'll only be there for ten days. And I wouldn't like to hurt her feelings."

Though they did not speak of it, they themselves were suffering from hurt feelings; they did not understand why Alix would not spend more time with them. For reasons they could not make out, she was simply inaccessible. They knew that she slept late, and she was, of course, occupied with the baby, and perhaps with her sister's children. But on the other hand, she had brought a nursemaid with her, so perhaps it wasn't the children who were keeping her from them. Perhaps she didn't want to see any more of them. . . . But if that were true, they would have felt it in her manner. When they met at mealtime, she was always pleased to see them, always acted as if their friendship was real and permanent, and she made the lunch and dinner table conversation much more enjoyable by the care she took of them. But why didn't she want to go anywhere with them? Why did she never seek out their company at odd times of the day?

She was uneasy about Eugène—that much she did share with them. She had hoped that he would write and there had been no letter. Harold suggested that he might be too busy to write, since the government had jumped after all, without waiting this time for the August vacation to be over. He asked if the crisis would affect Eugène's position, and she said that, actually, Eugène had two positions in the Ministry of Planning and External Affairs, neither of which would suffer any change under a different cabinet, since they were not that important.

The dining-room table was now the smallest the Americans had seen it and, raising her hearing aid to her ear, Mme Cestre took part in the conversation.

Alix explained that her mother's health was delicate; she was a prey to mysterious diseases that the doctors could neither cure nor account for. There would be an outbreak of blisters on the ends of her fingers, and then it would go away as suddenly as it had come. She had attacks of dizziness, when the floor seemed to come up and strike her foot. She could not stand to be in the sun for more than a few minutes. Alix herself thought sometimes that it was because her mother was so good and kind—really much kinder than anybody else. Beggars, old women selling limp, tarnished roses, old men with a handful of pencils had only to look at her and she would open her purse. She could not bear the sight of human misery.

Leaning toward her mother, Alix said: "I have been telling Barbara and Harold how selfish you are."

Mme Cestre raised the hearing aid to her ear and adjusted the little pointer. The jovial remark was repeated and she smiled benignly at her daughter.

When she entered the conversation, it was always abruptly, on a new note, since she had no idea what they were talking about. She broke in upon Mme Bonenfant's observation that there was no one in Rome in August—that it was quite deserted, that the season there had always been from November through Lent—with the observation that cats are indifferent to their own reflection in a mirror.

"Dogs often fail to recognize themselves," she said, as they all stared at her in surprise. "Children are pleased. The wicked see what other people see . . . and the mirror sees nothing at all."

Or when Alix was talking about the end of the war, and how she and Sabine suddenly decided that they wanted to be in Paris for the Liberation and so got on their bicycles and rode there, only to be sent back to the country because there wasn't enough food, Mme Cestre remarked to Barbara: "My husband used to do the packing always. I did it once when we were first married, but he had been a bachelor too long, and no one could fold coatsleeves properly but him. . . . It is quite true that when I did it they were wrinkled."

It was hard not to feel that this note of irrelevance must be part of her character, but once she was oriented in the conversation, Mme Cestre's remarks were always pertinent to it, and interesting. Her English was better than Alix's or than Mme Viénot's, and without any trace of a French accent.

Sometimes she would sit with her hearing aid on her lap, content with her own thoughts and the perpetual silence that her deafness created around her. But then she would raise the hearing aid to her ear and prepare to re-enter the conversation.

"Did Alix tell you that I am writing a book?" she said to her sister as they were waiting for Thérèse and the boy to clear the table for the next course.

"I didn't know you were, Maman," Alix said.

"I thought I had told you. It is in the form of a diary, and it consists largely of aphorisms."

"You are taking La Rochefoucauld as your model," Mme Bonenfant said approvingly.

"Yes and no," Mme Cestre said. "I have a title for it: 'How to Be a Successful Mother-in-Law.' . . . The relationship is never an easy one, and a treatise on the subject would be useful, and perhaps sell thousands of copies. I shall ask Eugène to criticize it when I am finished, and perhaps do a short preface, if he has the time. I find I have a good deal to say. . . ."

"My sister also has a talent for drawing," Mme Viénot said. "She does faces that are really quite good likenesses, and at the same time there is an element of caricature that is rather cruel. I do not understand it. It is utterly at variance with her nature. Once she showed me a drawing she had done of me and I burst into tears."

Thursday was a nice day. The sun shone, it was warm, and Harold and Barbara spent the entire afternoon on the bank of the river, in their bathing suits. When they got home they found a scene out of *Anna Karenina*. Mme Bonenfant, Mme Viénot, Mme Cestre, and Thérèse were sitting under the Lebanon cedar, to the right of the terrace, with their chairs facing an enormous burlap bag, which they kept reaching into. They were shelling peas for canning.

Alix was in the courtyard, making some repairs on her bicycle. She had had a letter from Eugène. "He sends affectionate greetings to you both," she said. "He is coming down to the country tomorrow night. And Mummy asked me to tell you, for her, that it would give her great pleasure if you would stay in the apartment while you are in Paris."

This time the invitation was accepted.

After dinner, Mme Viénot opened the desk in the petit salon and took out a packet of letters, written to her mother at the château. She translated passages from them and read other passages in French, with the pride of a conscientious historian. Most of the letters were about the last week before the liberation of the city. The inhabitants of Paris, forbidden to leave their houses, had kept in active communication with one another by telephone.

"But couldn't the Germans prevent it?" Harold asked.

"Not without shutting off the service entirely, which they didn't dare to do. We knew everything that was happening," Mme Viénot said. "When the American forces reached the southwestern limits of the city, the church bells began to toll, one after another, on the Left Bank, as each section of the city was delivered from the Germans, and finally the deep bell of Notre Dame. In the midst of the street fighting I left the apartment, to perform an errand, and found myself stranded in a doorway of a house, with bullets whistling through the air around me." In the letter describing this, she neither minimized the danger nor pretended that she had been involved in an act of heroism. The errand was a visit, quite essential, to her dressmaker in the rue du Mont-Thabor.

On Friday afternoon, Mme Viénot rode with Harold and Barbara in their taxi to Blois, where they parted. She went off down the street with an armful of clothes for the cleaner's, and they got on a sight-seeing bus. They chose the tour that consisted of Chambord, Cheverny, and Chaumont instead of the tour of Azay-le-Rideau, Ussé, and Chinon, because Barbara, looking through the prospectus, thought she recognized in Cheverny the white château with the green lawn in front of it. Cheverny did have a green lawn in front of it but it was not at all like a fairy-tale castle, and Chambord was too big. It reminded them of Grand Central Station. Since they had already seen Chaumont, they got the driver to let them out at the castle gates, and stood looking around for a taxi that would take them to the house of Mme Straus-Muguet's friends. It turned out that there were no taxis. The proprietor of the restaurant across the road did not know where the house was, and it was rather late to be having tea, so instead they sat for a whole hour on the river bank, feeling as if they had broken through into some other existence. They watched the sun's red reflection on the water, the bathers, the children building sand castles, the goats cropping and straying, and the next two trips of the ferryboat; and then it was time for them to cross over, themselves, and take the train home.

Though they were very late, dinner was later still. They sat in the drawing room waiting for Eugène and Sabine to arrive.

When they met again at the château, Harold's manner with Mme Viénot's daughter was cautious. He was not at all sure she liked him. He and Eugène shook hands, and there was a flicker of recognition in the Frenchman's eyes that had in it also a slight suggestion of apology: at the end of a long day and a long journey, Harold must not expect too much of him. Tomorrow they would talk.

As Sabine started toward the stairs with her light suitcase, Mme Viénot said: "The Allégrets are giving a large dinner party tomorrow night. I accepted for you." Then, turning to Harold and Barbara: "My daughter is very popular. Whenever she is expected, the telephone rings incessantly. . . . You are included in the invitation, but you don't have to go if you don't want to."

"Are Alix and Eugène going?" he asked.

"Yes."

He and Barbara looked at each other, and then Barbara said: "Are you sure it is all right for us to go?"

"Quite sure," Mme Viénot said. "The Allégrets are a very old family. They are half Scottish. They are descended from the Duke of Berwick, who was a natural son of the English King James II, and followed him into exile, and became a marshal of France under Louis XIV."

During dinner, Eugène entertained them with a full account of the fall of the Schumann government. Day after day the party leaders met behind closed doors, and afterward they posed for the photographers on the steps of the Palais Bourbon, knowing that the photographers knew there was nothing of the slightest importance in the brief cases they held so importantly. What made this crisis different from the preceding ones was that no party was willing to accept the portfolios of Finance and Economics, and so it was quite impossible to form a government.

"But won't they have to do something?" Harold asked.

"Eventually," Mme Viénot said, "but not right away. For a while, the administrative branches of the government can and will go right on functioning."

"In my office," Eugène said, "letters are opened and read, and copies of the letters are circulated, but the letters are not answered, because an answer would involve a decision, and all decisions, even those of no consequence, are postponed, or better still, referred to the proper authority, who, unfortunately, has no authority. I have been working until ten or eleven o'clock every night on a report that will never be looked at, since the man who ordered it is now out of office."

At that moment, as if the house wanted to point out that there is no crisis that cannot give way to an even worse situation, the lights went off. They sat in total darkness until the pantry door opened and Thérèse's sullen peasant face appeared, lighted from below by two candles, which she placed on the dining-room table. She then lit the candles in the wall sconces and in a moment the room was ablaze with soft light. Looking at one face after another, Harold thought: This is the way it must have been in the old days, when Mme Viénot and Mme Cestre were still young, and they gave dinner parties, and the money wasn't gone, and the pond had water in it, and everybody agreed that France had the strongest army in Europe. . . . In the light of the still candle flames, everyone was beautiful, even Mme Viénot. As her upper eyelids descended, he saw that that characteristic blind look was almost (though not quite) the look of someone who is looking into the face of love.

At the end of dinner she pushed her chair back and, with a silver candlestick in her hand, she led them across the hall and into the petit salon, where they went on talking about the Occupation. It was the one subject they never came to the end of. They only put it aside temporarily at eleven o'clock, when, each person having been provided with his own candle, they went up the stairs, throwing long shadows before and behind them.

Chapter 11

"A vez-vous bien dormi?" Harold asked, and Eugène held up his hand as if, right there at the breakfast table, with his hair uncombed and his eyes puffy with sleep, he intended to perform a parlor trick for them. Looking at Barbara, he said: "You don't lahv your hus-band, do you?" and to Harold's astonishment she said: "No."

He blushed.

"I mean yes, I do love him," Barbara said. "I didn't understand your question. Why, you're speaking *English!*"

Delighted with the success of his firecracker, Eugène sat down and began to eat his breakfast. He had enrolled at the Berlitz. He had had five lessons. His teacher was pleased with his progress. Still in a good humor, he went upstairs to shave and dress.

Thérèse brought the two heaviest of the Americans' suitcases down from the third floor, and then the dufflebag, and put them in the dog cart. Mme Viénot had pointed out that the trip up to Paris would be less strenuous if they checked some of their luggage instead of taking it all in the compartment with them. Harold and the gardener waited until Eugène came out of the house and climbed up on the seat beside them. Then the gardener spoke to his horse gently, in a coaxing voice, as if to a child, and they drove off to the village. At the station, Eugène took care of the forms that had to be filled out, and bought the railroad tickets with the money Harold handed him, but he was withdrawn and silent. Either his mood had changed since breakfast or he did not feel like talking in front of the gardener. When they got back to the château, Harold went upstairs first, and then, finding that Barbara was washing out stockings in the bathroom and didn't need him for anything, he went back downstairs and settled himself in the drawing room with a book. No one ever used the front door—they always came and went by the doors that opened onto the terrace—and so he would see anybody who passed through the downstairs. When Eugène did not reappear, Harold concluded that he was with Alix and the baby in the back wing of the house, where it did not seem proper to go in search of him, since he had been separated from his family for five days.

It was not a very pleasant day and there was some perverse influence at work. The village electrician could not find the short circuit, which must be somewhere inside the walls, and he said that the whole house needed rewiring. And Alix, who was never angry at anyone, was angry at her aunt. She wanted to have a picnic with Sabine and the Americans on the bank of the river, and Mme Viénot said that it wasn't convenient, that it would make extra work in the kitchen. This was clearly not true. They ate lunch in the dining room as usual, and at two thirty they set out on their bicycles, with their bathing suits and towels and four big, thick ham sandwiches that they did not want and that Mme Viénot had made, herself.

The sunshine was pale and watery and without warmth. They hid the bicycles in a little grove between the highway and the river, and then withdrew farther into the trees and changed into their bathing suits. When Barbara and Harold came out, they saw Alix and Sabine down by the water. Eugène was standing some distance away from them, fully dressed, and looking as if he were not part of this expedition.

"Aren't you going in?" Harold called, and, getting no answer, he turned to Alix and said: "Isn't he going in swimming with us?"

She shook her head. "He doesn't feel like swimming."

"Why not?"

"He says the water is dirty."

Then why did he bring his bathing suit if he didn't feel like swimming in dirty water, Harold wondered. Didn't he know the river would be dirty?

The water was also lukewarm and the current sluggish. And instead of the sandy bottom that Harold expected, they walked in soft oozing mud halfway up to their knees, and had to wade quite far out before they could swim. Alix had a rubber ball, and they stood far apart in the shallow water and threw it back and forth. Harold was self-conscious with Sabine. They had not spoken a word to each other since she arrived. The ball passed between the four of them now. They did not smile. It felt like a scene from the Odyssey. When the rubber ball came to him, sometimes, aware of what a personal act it was, he threw it to Sabine. Sometimes she sent it spinning across the water to him. But more often she threw it to one of the two girls. He didn't dislike or distrust her but he couldn't imagine what she was really like, and her gray wool bathing suit troubled him. It was the cut and the color of the bathing suits that are handed out with a locker key and a towel in public bathhouses, and he wondered if she was comparing it with Barbara's, and her life with what she imagined Barbara's life to be like.

From down river, behind a grove of trees, they heard some boys splashing and shouting. On the other bank, sheep appeared over the brow of the green hill, cropping as they came. Farther down the river, out of sight, was Chaumont, with its towers and its drawbridge. Then Amboise, and back from the river, on a river of its own, Chenonceau. Much farther still were those other châteaux that he knew only by their pictures in the guidebook—Villandry and Luynes and Langeais and Azay-le-Rideau and Ussé and Chinon. And no more time left to see them.

They stopped throwing the ball, and he waded in deeper and started swimming. The current in the channel was swifter but it did not seem very strong, even so, and he wanted to swim to the other bank, but he heard voices calling—"Come back!" (Barbara's voice) and "Come back, it's dangerous!" (Alix's voice) and so, reluctantly, rather than cause a fuss, he turned around. "People have drowned near here," Alix said as he stood up, dripping, and walked toward them. "And there is quicksand on the other bank."

They wiped their feet on the grass and then, using their towels, managed to get the mud off. Near the highway, two girls with bicycles and knapsacks were putting up a small tent for the night. Eugène stood watching them. The bathers went into the grove to dress and came out and sat on the ground and dutifully, without appetite, ate the thick ham sandwiches. Alix called to Eugène to come and join them and he replied that he was not hungry.

"Why is Eugène moody?" Sabine asked.

"He is upset because he has to wear a tweed coat to the Allégrets' party," Alix said.

"But so do I!" Harold exclaimed.

"No one expects you to have a dinner coat," she said gently. "It is quite all right. If Eugène had known, he could have brought his dinner coat down with him. That is why he is angry. He thinks I shouldn't have accepted without consulting him. Also, he is angry that there aren't enough bicycles."

"Aren't there?" Sabine asked.

"There are now," Alix said. "Eugène went and borrowed two from the gardener. But it annoys him that he should have to do that—that there aren't bicycles enough to go round."

She herself had long since reverted to her usual cheerful, sweet-tempered self.

Harold went into the trees and brought out the bicycles and they started home, the three girls pedaling side by side, since the highway was empty. After a quarter of a mile, Harold slowed down until Eugène drew abreast of him, and they rode along in what he tried to feel was a comfortable silence. The afternoon had been a disappointment to him, and not at all what he expected, but perhaps, now that they were alone, Eugène would open up—would tell him why he was in such an unsociable mood. For it couldn't be the coat or the bicycles. Something more serious must have happened. Something about his job, perhaps.

Eugène began to sing quietly, under his breath, and Harold rode a little closer to the other bicycle, listening. It was not an old song, judging by the words, but in the tune there was a slight echo of the thing that had moved him so, that day in Blois. When Eugène finished, Harold said: "What's the name of that song you were singing?"

"It's just a song," Eugène said, with his eyes on the road, and pure, glittering, personal dislike emanating from him like an aura.

The painful discovery that someone you like very much does not like you is one of the innumerable tricks the vaudeville magician has up his sleeve. Think of a card, any card: now you see it, now you don't. . . .

Struggling with the downward drag of hurt feelings, as old and familiar to him as the knowledge of his name, Harold kept even with the other bicycle for a short distance, as if nothing had happened, and then, looking straight ahead of him, he pedaled faster and moved ahead slowly until he was riding beside the three girls.

The bicycles were brought out of the kitchen entry at six o'clock, and just as they were starting off, Mme Viénot appeared with three roses from the garden. Alix pinned her rose to the shoulder of her dress, and so did Sabine, but Barbara fastened hers in her hair.

"How pretty you look!" Mme Viénot said, her satisfied glance taking in all three of them.

With Eugène leading and Harold bringing up the rear, and the girls being careful that their skirts did not brush against the greasy chain or the wire wheels, they filed out of the courtyard and then plunged directly into the woods behind it. There were a number of paths, and Eugène chose one. The others followed him, still pushing their bicycles because the path was too sandy to ride on. After a quarter of a mile they emerged from the premature twilight of the woods into the open country and full daylight. Eugène took off his sport coat, folded it, and put it in the handlebar basket. Then he got on his bicycle and rode off down a dirt road that was not directly accessible to the château. Harold disposed of his coat in the same way. At first they rode single file, because of the deep ruts in the road, but before long they came to a concrete highway, and the three girls fanned out so that they could ride together. The two men continued to ride apart. Sometimes they all had to get off and push their bicycles uphill as the road led them up over the top of a long arc. At the crest, the land fell away in a panorama—terraced vineyards, the river valley, more hills, and little roads winding off into he wondered where—and they mounted their bicycles and went sailing downhill with the wind rushing past their ears.

"Isn't this a lovely way to go to a party?" Barbara said as Harold overtook her. "It's so unlike anything we're used to, I feel as if I'm dreaming it."

"Are you getting tired?" Alix called to them, over her shoulder.

"Oh no!" Barbara said.

"How far is it?" Harold asked.

"About five miles," Alix said.

"Such a beautiful evening," he said.

"Coming home there will be a moon," Alix said.

Just when the ride was beginning to seem rather long, they left the highway and took a narrow lane that was again loose sand and that forced them to dismount for a few yards. Pushing their bicycles, they crossed a small footbridge and started up a steep hill. When they got to the top, they had arrived. The Americans saw a big country house of gray stone with castellated trimming and lancet windows and a sweep of lawn in front of it. The guests—girls in long dresses, young men in dinner jackets—were standing about in clusters near a flight of stone steps that led up to the open front door.

The party from the château left their bicycles under a grape arbor at the side of the house. The two men put on their coats, and felt their ties. The girls straightened their short skirts, tucked in stray wisps of hair, looked at their faces in pocket mirrors and exclaimed, powdered their noses, put on white gloves. In front of the house, Alix and Eugène and Sabine were surrounded by people they knew, and Harold and Barbara were left stranded. It was a party of the very young, they perceived; most of the guests were not more than eighteen or nineteen. How *could* Mme Viénot have let them in for such an evening!

"I foresee one of the longest evenings of my entire life," Harold said out of the corner of his mouth.

Just when he was sure that Alix had abandoned them permanently, she came back and led them from group to group. The boys, thin and coltlike, raised Barbara's hand two thirds of the way to their lips, without enthusiasm or gallantry. The gesture was not at all like hand-kissing in the movies, but was, instead, abrupt, mechanical: they *pretended* to kiss her hand.

Alix was called away, and the Americans found themselves stranded again but inside the party this time, not outside. They struck up a conversation in French with a dark-haired girl who was studying music; then another conversation, in English, with a girl who said that she wanted to visit America. They talked about America, about New York. Alix returned, bringing a blond young man who was very tall and thin. An old and very dear friend of hers and Eugène's, she said. He bowed, started to say something, and was called away to answer a question, and didn't return. Then Alix too left them.

Barbara began to talk to another young man. Harold turned and gave his attention to the view—an immense sweep of marshland, the valley of the Cher, now autumn-colored with the setting sun. He looked back at the house, which was Victorian Gothic, and nothing like as handsome as Beaumesnil. It was, in fact, a perfectly awful house. And he was the oldest person he could see anywhere.

Once when he was a small child, he had had an experience like this. He must have been about six years old, and he was visiting his Aunt Mildred, who took him with her on a hay-ride party. But that time he was the youngest; he was the only child in a party of grownups; and so he opened his mouth and cried. But it didn't change anything. The hay-ride party went on and on and on, and his aunt was provoked at him for crying in front of everybody.

There was a sudden movement into the house, and he looked around for Alix and Sabine, without being able to find them. And then he saw Barbara coming toward him, against the flow of people up the stone steps to the front door. With her was a young man whom he liked on sight.

"I am Jean Allégret," the young man said as they shook hands. "Your wife tells me you are going to Salzburg for the Festival. I was stationed there at the end of the war. It is a beautiful city, but sad. It was a Nazi headquarters. Don't be surprised if— You are to sit with me at dinner." Taking Harold by the arm he led him toward the stone steps.

As they passed into the house, Harold looked around for Barbara, who had already disappeared in the crowd. He caught a glimpse of rooms opening one out of another; of large and small paintings on the walls, in heavy gilt frames; of brocade armchairs, thick rugs, and little tables loaded with *objets*. The house had a rather stiff formality that he did not care for. In the dining room, the guests were reading the place cards at a huge oval table set for thirty places. Jean Allégret led him to a small table in an alcove, and then left him and returned a moment later, bringing a tall pretty blonde girl in a white tulle evening dress. She looks like a Persian kitten, Harold thought as he acknowledged the introduction. The girl also spoke English. Jean Allégret held her chair out for her and they sat down.

"In America," Harold said as he unfolded his napkin, "this would be called 'the children's table.'"

"I saw a great deal of the Americans during the war," Jean Allégret said. "Your humor is different from ours. It is three-quarters fantasy. Our fantasy is nearly always serious. I understand Americans very well. . . ."

Harold was searching for Barbara at the big table. When he found her, he saw that she was listening attentively, with her head slightly bowed, to the very handsome young man on her right. He felt a twinge of jealousy.

"—but children," Jean Allégret was saying. "I never once found an American who knew or cared what they were fighting about. And yet they fought very well. . . . What you are doing in Germany now is all wrong, you know. You make friends with them. And you will bring another war down on us, just as Woodrow Wilson did."

"Where did you get that idea?" Harold asked, smiling at him.

"It is not an idea, it is a fact. He is responsible for all the mischief that followed the Treaty of Versailles."

"That is in your history books?"

"Certainly."

"In our history books," Harold said cheerfully, "Clemenceau and Lloyd George are the villains, and Wilson foresaw everything." He began to eat his soup.

"He was a very vicious man," Jean Allégret said.

"Wilson? Oh, get along with you."

"Well, perhaps not vicious, but he didn't understand European politics, and he was thoroughly wrong in his attitude toward the German people. My family has a house in the north of France, near St. Amand-les-Eaux. It was destroyed in 1870, and rebuilt exactly the way it was before. My grandfather devoted his life to restoring it. In 1914 it was destroyed again, burned to the ground, and my father rebuilt it so that it was more beautiful than before. Thanks to the Americans, I am now living in a farmhouse nearby, because there is no roof on the house my father built. I manage the farms, and when it is again possible, I will rebuild the house for the third time. My life will be an exact repetition of my father's and my grand-father's."

"Does it have to be?" Harold asked, raising his spoon to his lips.

"What do you mean?"

"Why not try something else? Let the house go."

"You are joking."

"No. Everyone has dozens of lives to choose from. Pick another."

"I am the eldest son. And if the house is destroyed a fourth time, I will expect my son to rebuild it. But if the Americans were not such children, it wouldn't have to be rebuilt."

"We didn't take part in the war of 1870," Harold said mildly. "And we didn't start either of the last two wars."

The Frenchman pounced: "But you came in too late. And you ruined the peace by your softness—by your idealism. And now, as the result of your quarrel with the Russians, you are going to turn France into a battlefield once more. Which is very convenient for you but hard on us."

Harold studied the blue eyes that were looking so intently into his. Their expression was simple and cordial. In America, he thought, such an argument was always quite different. By this time, heat would have crept into it. The accusations would have become personal.

"What would you have us do?" he asked, leaning forward. "Stay out of it next time?"

"I would have you take a realistic attitude, and recognize that harshness is the only thing the German people understand."

"And hunger."

"No. They will go right back and do it over again."

Harold glanced at the girl who was sitting between them, to see whose side she was on. Her face did not reveal what she was thinking. She took a sip of wine and looked at the two men as if they were part of the table decorations.

Caught between the disparity of his own feelings—for he felt a liking for Jean Allégret as a man and anger at his ideas—Harold was silent. No matter what I say, he thought, it will sound priggish. And if I don't say anything, I will seem to be agreeing.

"It is true," he said at last, "it is true that we understand ma-

chinery better than we understand European politics. And I
do not love what I know of the German mentality. But I have
to assume that they are human—that the Germans are human to
this extent that they sleep with their wives"—was this going
too far?—"and love their children, and want to work, at such
times as they are not trying to conquer the world, and are sometimes discouraged, and don't like growing old, and are afraid
of dying. I assume that the Japanese sleep with their wives,
the Russians love their children and the taste of life, and are
sometimes discouraged, don't like growing old, and are afraid
of—"

"You don't think that your niggers are human," Jean Allégret said triumphantly.

"Why not? Why do you say that?"

"Because of the way you treat them. I have seen it, in Normandy. You manage them very well."

"We do not manage them at all. They manage us. They are
a wonderful people. They have the virtues—the sensibility, the
patience, the emotional richness—we lack. And if the distinction between the two races becomes blurred, as it has in Martinique, and they become one race, then America will be
saved."

"They are animals," the Frenchman said. "And you treat
them like animals."

The girl stirred, as if she were about to say something. Both
men turned toward her expectantly.

"I prefer a nigger to a Jew," she said.

At the end of the meal, the guests at the large table pushed
their chairs back. Barbara Rhodes, turning away from the
young man who had bored her so with his handsome empty
face, his shallow eyes that did not have the thing she looked
for in people's eyes but only vanity, glanced toward the little
table in the alcove. She saw Harold rise, still talking (what
could they have found to talk about so animatedly all through
dinner?) and draw the little table toward him so that the girl
could get up. . . . *Oh no!* she cried as the table started to tilt
alarmingly. She saw the Frenchman with a quick movement try
to stop it but he was on the wrong side of the table and it was
too late. There was an appalling crash.

"Une table pliante," a voice said coolly beside her.

Unable to go on looking, she turned away, but not before she had seen the red stain, like blood, on the beautiful Aubusson carpet, and Harold, pale as death, standing with his hands at his side, looking at what he had done.

"These ideas of yours are foolish and will not work," Jean Allégret said an hour later.

"Perhaps not," Harold said.

They were sitting on a bench on the lawn, facing the lighted windows but in the dark. On another bench, directly in front of them, Barbara and Sabine and another girl whose name Harold didn't know were sitting and talking quietly. There were five or six more people here and there, on the steps, in chairs, or on other benches, talking and watching the moon rise. The others were inside, in the library, dancing to the music of a portable record player.

"Perhaps they *are* foolish," he said, "but I prefer them, for my own sake. If it is foolish to think that all men are brothers, it is at least more civilized—and more agreeable—than thinking that all men—you and I, for instance—are enemies, waiting for a chance to run a bayonet through each other's back."

The wine had made him garrulous and extravagant in speech; also, he had done much less than the usual amount of talking since they had landed in France, and it gave him the feeling of being in arrears, of having a great deal backed up that he urgently needed to say.

"If it is really a question of that," he went on, "then I will get up and turn around and—since I like you too much to put a bayonet in your back—offer you my back instead. Hoping that you won't call my bluff, you understand. Or that something will distract your attention long enough for me to—"

"Very dear, your theories. Very gentle and sweet and impossible to put into practice. Nevertheless, you interest me. You are not the American type. I didn't know there were Americans like that."

"But that's what I keep telling you. Exactly what I am *is* the American type."

"You have got everything all wrong, but your ideas interest me."

"They are not my ideas. I have not said one original thing all evening."

"I like you," Jean Allégret said. "And if it were possible, if there was the slightest chance of changing human nature for the better, I would be on your side. But it does not change. Force is what counts. Idealism cannot survive a firing squad. . . . But in another way, another world, maybe, what you say is true. And in spite of all I have said, I believe it too. I am an artist. I paint."

"Seriously?"

"Excuse me," the Frenchman said. "I neglect my duties as a host. I will be back in a moment." He got up and went across the lawn and into the house.

The moon was above the marshes now, round and yellow and enormous. The whole sky was gilded by it. The house was no longer ugly. By this light you could see what the Victorian architect had had in mind. Harold stood behind Barbara, with his hand on her shoulder, listening to the girls' conversation. Then, drawn by curiosity, he went up the steps and into the house, as far as the drawing-room door. The fruitwood furniture was of a kind he had little taste for, but around the room were portraits and ivory miniatures he would have liked to look at. But would it (since the French were said to be so reluctant to ask people into their homes) be considered an act of rudeness for him to go around looking at things all by himself?

He turned back toward the front door and met Jean Allégret in the hall. "Oh there you are," the Frenchman said. "I was looking for you."

They went and sat down where they had been before, but turned the bench around so that they could watch the moon rising through the night sky.

"I do not like the painting of our time," Jean Allégret said. "It is sterile and it has nothing to do with life. What I paint is action. I stand and watch a man cutting a tree down, a farmer in the field, and I love the way he swings the ax blade, I see every motion, and it's that motion that interests me—not color or design. It's life I want to paint."

"You are painting now?"

"I have not painted since the war. I am rebuilding what was destroyed, you understand. I cannot do that and also paint.

The painting is my personal life, which has to give way to the responsibilities I have inherited."

"You are not married?"

The Frenchman shook his head. "When the house is rebuilt and the farms are under cultivation again, then I will find a wife who understands what I expect of her, and there will be children."

"And she must expect nothing of you? There can be no alteration of your ideas to fit hers?"

"None whatever. I do not approve of American ideas of how to treat women. They are gallant only on the surface. You lose control over your women. And you have no authority over your children or your home. You continually divorce and remarry and make a further mess of it."

"Modern marriage is very complicated."

"It need not be."

Harold saw Eugène stop in front of Barbara and say something. After a moment he walked away. He did not appear to be having a good time. The tweed coat, Harold thought.

Turning to Jean Allégret, he said: "You do not know my name, do you?"

The Frenchman shook his head.

"Very good," Harold said. "I have a suggestion to make. Suppose I do not tell you my name. Some day you may find that you cannot go on carrying the burden of family responsibilities, or that you were wrong in laying aside your personal life. And you may have to drop everything and start searching for what you once had. Or for something. Everybody at one time or another has to go on a search, and if I do not tell you my name, or where I live, then you will have an object to search for, an excuse. America is a large country, it may take years and years to find me, but while you are searching you will be discovering all sorts of things, you will be talking to people, having experiences, and even if you never find me— You don't like my idea?"

"It's completely impractical. Romantic and charming and impractical—a thoroughly American idea."

"I suppose it is," Harold said. He took his financial diary out of his pocket and wrote his name and forwarding address in Paris and their address in America. Then he tore the page out and handed it to the Frenchman, and went over to the bench where the three girls were sitting. They looked up as he approached.

"Do you want to come and join us?" he asked.

"Are you having a pleasant conversation?" Barbara asked.

"Very."

"Then I think I'll stay here. We're talking about America."

"When you come back to Paris in September," Jean Allégret said as Harold sat down, "I'd like very much to have you come and stay with me in the country. At my own place, I mean. This is my uncle's house, you understand."

Harold noticed that he had said "you," not "you and your wife."

"We'd like to very much," he said.

"We could have some shooting. It's very primitive, you understand. Not like this. But I think you will find it interesting. Actually," Jean Allégret said, his voice changing to accommodate a note of insincerity, "I am young to have taken on so large a responsibility. I'm only twenty-seven, you know." Behind the insincerity was the perfectly sincere image that he projected on the screen of his self-approval—of the man who lays aside his youth prematurely.

Like those people who, weeping at the grave of a friend, have no choice but to dramatize the occasion, Harold thought, and search around in their mind for a living friend to write to, describing how they stood at the grave, weeping, etc. The grief is no less real for requiring an audience. What the person doubts and seeks confirmation of is his own reality.

"There are six farms to manage," the Frenchman went on, "and I am—in spite of my lack of experience—in the position of a father to the village. They wanted to make me mayor. They bring all their problems to me, even their marital problems. I am also working with the boys. . . . The whole life of the community was destroyed, and slowly, a little at a time, I am helping them rebuild it. But it means that I have very little time to myself, and no time for painting. If the Communists take over, I will be the first to be shot, in our village."

"Are there many?"

"Five or six."

"And you know who they are?"

"Certainly. They have nothing against me personally, but if I am successful I will defeat their plans, and so I will be the first person taken out and shot. But you must come and see my village. . . . I want to give you my address, before I forget it."

Harold produced the financial diary again and while the Frenchman was writing, he sat looking at the dancers framed by the lighted windows. He still felt amazed and numb when he thought of what happened in the dining room, but most of the time he didn't think about it. A curtain had come down over his embarrassment. After a startled glance at the wreckage of the children's table, the guests had politely turned away and filed from the room as if nothing had happened. Jean Allégret went to the kitchen and came back with a damp cloth and scrubbed at the wine stain in the rug. Harold started to pick up the broken glass and found himself gently pushed out of the dining room. The sliding doors closed behind him. In a few minutes, Jean Allégret reappeared and brushed his apology aside—it was nothing, it was all the fault of the table pliante—and took him by the arm and led him outdoors and they went on talking.

Now, when the financial diary and the pencil had been returned to him, Harold said: "Would you take me inside and show me the house? I didn't want to walk around by myself looking at things. Just the two rooms they're dancing in."

To his surprise, the Frenchman stood up and said stiffly: "I will speak to my uncle."

"If it means that, never mind. I don't want to bother anyone. I just thought you could take me around and tell me about the portraits, but it isn't in the least important."

"I will speak to my uncle. It is his house."

Twice in one evening, Harold thought with despair. For it was perfectly clear from the gravity with which his request had been received that it was not the light thing he had thought it was.

Jean Allégret conducted him up the steps and into the hall and said: "Wait here." Then he turned and went back down the steps. Watching through the open doorway, Harold saw him approach a tall elderly man who was standing with a group of people in the moonlight. He bent his head down attentively while Jean Allégret spoke to him. Then, instead of turning and coming toward the house, they left the group and walked up and down, talking earnestly. A minute passed, and then another, and another. Harold began to feel more and more conspicuous, standing in the lighted hall as on a stage, in plain sight of everyone on the terrace. He had already been *in* those two rooms. The others were dancing there now. And he could have looked at the pictures, the tapestries, the marble statuary, by himself, if he hadn't been afraid that it would be bad-mannered. And in America people were always pleased when you asked to see their house.

Uncle and nephew made one more complete turn around the terrace, still talking, and apparently arrived at a decision, for they turned suddenly and came toward the house. Jean Allégret introduced Harold to his uncle and then left them together. M. Allégret spoke no English. He was about sixty, taller than Harold, dignified, and soft-spoken. For a minute or two he went on making polite conversation. Then he said abruptly, as if in reply to something Harold had just said: "Vous prenez un intérêt aux maisons?"

"Je prends un intérêt dans cette maison. Mais—"

"Alors." Turning, M. Allégret led him over to a lithograph hanging on the wall beside the door into the salon. "Voici un tableau d'une chasse à courre qui a eu lieu ici en mille neuf cent sept," he said. "La clef indique l'identité des personnes. Voici le Kaiser, et auprès de lui est le Prince Philippe zu Eulenberg . . . le Prince Frédéric-Guillaume . . . la Princesse Sophie de Württemberg, portant l'amazone noire, et le roi d'Angleterre . . . Mon père et ma mère . . . le Prince Charles de Saxe . . . avec leurs chasseurs et leurs laquais. Le tableau a été peint de mémoire, naturellement. Ces bois de cerf que vous voyez le long du mur. . . ."

At eleven o'clock Alix came toward the circle in the library, where Harold and four or five young men were talking about French school life, and said: "Eugène thinks it is time we went home."

Harold shook hands around the circle and then sought out Jean Allégret.

"We have to go," he said, "and I wanted to be sure I said good night to all your cousins. Would you take me around to them? I am not sure which—"

This request presented no difficulties. Barbara and Harold said good night to Mme Allégret, to various rather plain young girls, and to M. Allégret, who came out of the house with them. The others were waiting with the bicycles, under the grape arbor. Jean Allégret and his uncle conducted the party from the château along the driveway as far as the place where it dropped steeply downhill, and there they said good night. Harold and Jean Allégret shook hands warmly, one last time. Calling good night, good night, they coasted down the hill, through the dark tunnel of branches, with the dim carbide bicycle lamps barely showing the curves in the road, and emerged suddenly into bright moonlight. Dismounting at a sandy patch before the bridge, Harold risked saying to Eugène: "Did you have a pleasant evening?"

"No. They were too young. There was no one there who was very interesting." His voice in the moonlight was not unfriendly, but neither was it encouraging.

Out on the main road, Harold pedaled beside Barbara, whose lamp was brighter than his. "Wasn't it awful about the folding table?" he said.

"It wasn't your fault."

"I felt terrible about it, but they were so kind. They just closed the doors on it, and it was exactly as if it had never happened. But I keep thinking about the broken china and glasses that can never be replaced probably. And that stain on the carpet."

"What were you talking about?"

"I don't remember. Why?"

"I just wondered."

"They attacked poor dead Woodrow Wilson. And then they started on the Jews and Negroes. I thought France was the one country where Negroes were accepted socially. They sounded just like Southerners. What was it like at dinner?"

"All right. I didn't like the boy I sat next to."

"He was very handsome."

"He is coming to America on business, and he thought we could be useful to him. I didn't like him at all."

"And Alix's friend, who sat on the other side of you?"

"He was nice, but he was talking to Alix."

"I had a lovely time. And I saw the house. Jean Allégret's uncle showed me all through the downstairs, as far as the kitchen, and then he took me upstairs, through all the bedrooms, which were wonderful. It was like a museum. And in a dressing room I saw the family tree, painted on wood. It was interminable. It must have gone back at least to Charlemagne. And then we went outside and saw the family chapel. Jean Allégret wants us to come and stay with him up near the Belgian border. . . . Did you have a nice evening? Afterward, I mean?"

"All except for one thing. I think I hurt Eugène's feelings. He came and asked me to dance with him and I refused. I was interested in what Sabine was saying, and I didn't feel like dancing at the moment, and I'm afraid he was offended."

"He probably understood. . . . They don't use the chapel as a chapel any more. They keep wine in it."

"And I don't think Sabine had a very good time," Barbara said. "She sat with Alix or me all evening, and the boys didn't ask her to dance. I don't understand it. She's very pretty, and Mme Viénot said that she was so popular and had so many invitations."

"The money," he said.

"What money?"

They were overtaking Alix, and so he did not answer. The winding road was almost white, the distant hills were silver, and they could see as well as in daylight. They rode now in single file, now all together.

"Think of going five miles to a party on bicycles," Barbara said to Harold, "and coming home in the moonlight!"

In a high, thin, eerie voice, Sabine began to sing: "Au clair de la lune, mon ami Pierrot, prête-moi ta plume pour écrire un mot . . ." The tune was not the one the Americans knew, and they drew as near to her as their bicycles permitted. After that she sang "Cadet Rouselle a trois maisons qui n'ont ni poutres ni chevrons . . ." and they were so taken with the three houses that had no rafters, the three suits, the three hats, the three big dogs, the three beautiful cats, that they begged her to sing it again. Instead she told them a ghost story.

In a village near here, she said, but a long time ago, there was a schoolmaster who drove himself into a frenzy trying to teach reading and writing and the catechism to boys who wanted to be out working in the fields with their fathers. He had a birch cane, which he used frequently, and an expression which he used still more. Whenever any boy didn't know his lesson, the schoolmaster would say: "One dies as one is born. There is never any improvement." Then he'd reach for his birch rod.

One rainy autumn evening when he got home, he discovered that he had left his examination books at the school. And though he could have waited until next day to correct them, he was so anxious to find what mistakes his pupils had made that he went back that night, after his supper. A waning moon sailed through black clouds, and the wind whipped his cloak up into the air, and the familiar landscape looked different, as everything does on a windy autumn night. And when he opened the door of the schoolhouse, he saw that one of the pupils was still there, sitting on his bench. "Don't you even know enough to go home?" he shouted. "One dies as one is born." And the boy said, in a voice that chilled the schoolmaster's blood: "I was never born, and therefore I cannot die." With that he vanished.

Now I know what she's like, Harold thought. This is her element—telling ghost stories. And this filtered moonlight. All this silveriness.

The supernatural shouldn't be understood too well; it should have gaps in it for you to think about afterward. . . . What he missed because he didn't know the words or because their bicycles swerved, drawing them apart for a moment, merely added to the effect.

The next day, the schoolmaster was very nervous when he came to teach the class. He looked at each face carefully, and saw with relief only the usual ones. But one thing was not usual. André, who had never in his life recited, knew his whole day's lesson without a fault. Growing suspicious, the schoolmaster stopped calling on him. Even then the hand waved in the air, so anxious was he to recite. That evening, the schoolmaster walked home the long way round, and stopped at

André's house, and learned that he was sick in bed. So then he knew.

After that, somebody always knew his lesson, and it wasn't long before the boys caught on. One at a time they played hookey, knowing that whatever it was—a ghost, a fairy, an uneasy spirit—would come to school that day looking exactly like them, and recite and recite. The schoolmaster grew thin. He began to make mistakes in arithmetic and to misspell words. He would start to say: "One dies as one is—" and then be afraid to finish. Finally, unable to stand the strain any more, he went to the curé one morning before school and told him his troubles. The curé reached for his hat and coat, and filled a small bottle with holy water from the font. "There is only one way that a person can be born," he said, "and that is in Jésus-Christ. When the possessed boy—because it can only be a case of possession—stands up to recite, I will baptize him." And that's what happened. The schoolmaster called on one boy who didn't know his lesson after another, until he came to Joseph, who was a great doltish boy with arms as long as an ape's. And when Joseph began to name the kings of France without a single mistake, the curé said: "In nomine patris et filii et spiritus sanctus," and uncorked the vial of holy water and flung it all in his face. The boy looked surprised and went on reciting. When he had finished, he sat down. There was no change in his appearance. The schoolmaster and the curé rushed off to Joseph's house and it was as they feared: Joseph was not there. "Isn't he at school?" his mother asked, in alarm.

"Yes, yes," the curé said, "he's at school," and they left without explaining.

As they were going through the wood, the curé said: "There is only one thing you can do. You must adopt this orphaned spirit, give him your name, and make him your legal heir." When they came out of the wood they went to the mairie and began to fill out the necessary adoption papers, which took all the rest of the day. When they finished, the maire took them, looked at them blankly, and handed them back. There was no writing on the documents they had spent so much time filling out.

So when the class opened the next day, the boys saw to their surprise that the schoolteacher was not at his desk in the front of the room but sitting on the bench that was always reserved for dunces. They were afraid to titter because of his birch rod, and when he saw their eyes go to it he got up and broke the rod over his knee. Then they sat there and waited. Finally one of the boys summoned enough courage to ask: "What are we waiting for?" "For the schoolmaster," the man said. "I have tried very hard to teach you, but I had a harsh unloving father and I never learned how to be a father to anybody else, and so you boys learn nothing from me. But I have learned something from the spirit that takes your place on the days when you are absent, and I know that he should be teaching you, and I am waiting now in the hope that he will come and teach us all."

After a time, Joseph left his seat and went to the desk and in a voice of the utmost sweetness began to conduct the lesson.

"Are you the spirit?" the boys asked.

"No, I am Joseph," he said.

"Then how is it you know the lesson?"

"I learned it last night. It took me a long time and it was very hard, but now I know it."

The next day, the same thing happened, only it was André who went to the front of the class. And right straight through the room, they took turns, each day a different boy, until it was the schoolmaster's turn. Looking very pale, he stood in front of them once more, and they waited, expecting him to say: "One dies as one is born." Instead, he began to hear the lesson, which they all knew. "But are you really the schoolmaster, or are you the spirit that takes our place?" they asked. "I am the schoolmaster," the man said sadly. "One dies as one is born, and I was born a man. But through the grace of Heaven, one is—one can hope to be of the company of spirits." That was the last time they ever heard him utter this familiar expression, though he stayed at his desk and taught them patiently, in a voice of the utmost gentleness and reasonableness, from that time on.

If the ride to the party seemed long, the ride home was too brief. Harold found himself pushing his bicycle into the darkness of the woods behind Beaumesnil long before he expected to. The courtyard, like everywhere else, was flooded with moonlight. There was a lighted kerosene lamp on the kitchen table. All the rest of the château was either white in the moonlight or in total shadow.

They piled their bicycles in a heap in the kitchen entry. Alix lit the other lamps that had been left for them. In a procession, they went through the pantry and the dining room to the stairs and parted in the second-floor hallway. They were relaxed and sleepy and easy with each other; even Eugène. It was as if they had come home from any number of parties in just this way ("Good night") and were all one family ("Good night, Barbara") and knew each other's secrets ("Good night, good night") and took for granted the affection that could be heard in their voices. ("It was lovely, wasn't it? . . . I hope you sleep well. . . . Good night. . . .")

Chapter 12

O N Sunday morning, Harold sat tense and ready, his week-old, wine-stained, really horrible-looking napkin rolled and inserted in its ivory ring. He refused another cup of coffee and pretended to be following the history of the Allégret family that Mme Viénot was telling with so much pleasure. He was waiting for her to leave the table. When she pushed her chair back, he got up also and followed her out into the hall.

"If it would be convenient," he began, "if there is time before church, that is, could we—"

"Yes, of course," Mme Viénot said, as if she were grateful to him for reminding her of something she should have thought of, herself. She led the way through the pink and white drawing room to a room beyond it, a study, which Harold had not been in before. Composed and businesslike, she indicated a chair for him and sat down at the flat-topped mahogany desk in the center of the room. To be embarrassed by a situation one has deliberately contrived to bring about in one's own interests is not realistic; is not intelligent; in short, is not French. As Mme Viénot opened a drawer and drew out a blank sheet of paper, she saw that his eyes were focused on the wall directly behind her and said: "That is a picture of Beaumesnil as it was when my father inherited it. As you see, it was a small country house. I find it rather charming. Even though the artist was not very talented. As a painting it is rather sentimental. . . . I spoke to my cook about the pommes de terre frites."

He looked blank.

"You remember that Mme Rhodes asked for the recipe— and it was as I suspected. She is unwilling to divulge her secret. They are so peculiar in this respect."

"It doesn't matter," he said.

"I'm sorry. I would have liked to have got it for her. You came here on the eleventh—"

He nodded.

"—and today is Sunday the twenty-fifth. That makes two full weeks—"

His eyes opened wide. So they were being charged, after all, for the three days they were in Paris.

"—and one day," Mme Viénot concluded.

They had arrived at one o'clock; they would be leaving for the train at three thirty this afternoon. The extra day was two and a half hours long.

A moment later, Mme Viénot interrupted her writing to say: "I did not think it proper to allow M. Carrère to pay for the ices and the pâtisseries that afternoon in Blois. Your share of the *addition* came to a hundred and eighty francs." The amount was written down, while he tried to reconcile M. Carrère's pleasant gesture toward America with the fact that he had afterward allowed the cost of the gesture to be deducted from his bill and added onto theirs. Only in dreams are such contradictions reconciled; in real life, fortunately, it isn't necessary. Nothing was deducted for the ten or eleven meals they had not taken at the château, or for the taxi ride to Blois that Mme Viénot had shared with them. The taxi to and from the ferry, the day they went to Chaumont, was six hundred francs. He had not intended that Mme Viénot, Mme Straus-Muguet, and Alix should have to pay a share of this amount; he would not have allowed it. Apparently it was, as Alix said, a question of sincerity. But *had* M. Carrère allowed her to deduct their ices and pastry from his bill? It did not seem at all like him. And had Mme Straus-Muguet been charged for her share of the taxi to and from the ferry at Chaumont?

The sense of outrage, clotted in his breast, moved him to fight back, and the form his attack took was characteristic. In one of her letters she had written them that the *service* was included. He offered her now a chance to go the whole hog.

"What about the cook and Thérèse and Albert?"

"I shall give them something," Mme Viénot said.

But will she, he wondered.

The sheet of paper that she handed across the desk read:

Note de Semaine de M. Harold Rhodes
   2 semaines
   + 1 jour   32,100 f
   5 téléphones   100 f
   Goûter è Blois   180 f
   Laundry   125 f
                        payé le 24 Juillet 48
   Château Beaumesnil
   Brenodville s/Euphrone

With the pen that she offered to him he wrote the date and his signature on four American Express traveler's checks—a fifty, two twenty-fives, and a ten—and handed them to her as he wrote.

"Will you also give me a statement that you have cashed these four checks?"

"Is that necessary?" Mme Viénot asked.

"For the customs," he said. "The amount we brought in is declared in our passports, and the checks have to be accounted for when we leave."

"I have been advised not to put down the money I receive from my clients, when I make out my tax statement," Mme Viénot said. "If they do not ask to see the statement when you go through customs, I would appreciate your not showing it."

He agreed to this arrangement.

She opened a little metal box and produced four hundred-franc notes, a fifty, a twenty-five, and two tens, and gave them to him. He folded the huge paper currency and put it in his coat pocket. With the traveler's checks neatly arranged in front of her, she said: "It has been a great pleasure having you. . . . I hope that when you come again it will be as friends."

He said nothing. He had paid the full amount, which was perhaps reasonable, since he had not asked outright if they would be charged for the three days they were in Paris. If she had really felt kindly toward them, or had the slightest impulse toward generosity or fairness, she could have made some slight adjustment. She hadn't, and he was therefore not obliged to pretend now.

His eyes met hers in a direct glance and she looked away. She picked up the checks and put them down again, and then said: "There is something I have wanted to tell you, something

I would like to explain. But perhaps you guessed— We have not always lived like this."

"I understand that."

"There has been a *drame* in our family. Two years ago, my husband—"

She stopped talking. Her eyes were filled with tears. He leaned forward in his chair, saw that it was too late for him to say anything, and then sat back and waited for the storm of weeping to pass. He could not any more help being moved, as he watched her, than if she had proved in a thousand ways that she was their friend. Whatever the trouble was, it had been real.

Five minutes later he closed the door of their third-floor room and said: "I almost solved the mystery."

"What mystery?" Barbara asked.

"I almost found out about M. Viénot. She started to tell me, when I finished paying her—"

"Did she charge us for the full two weeks?"

"How did you know that? And then she started to tell me about *him*."

"What happened to him?"

"I don't know," he said. "I didn't let her tell me."

"But *why*, if she wanted to tell you?"

"She broke down. She cried."

"Mme Viénot?"

He heard the sound of wheels and went to the window. The dog cart had come to a stop in front of the château, and the gardener was helping Mme Bonenfant up into the seat beside him. She sat, dressed for church, with her prayerbook in her hand.

Harold turned away from the window and said: "I could feel something. She changed, suddenly. She started searching for her handkerchief. And from the way she looked at me, I had a feeling she was asking me to deliver her from the situation she had got herself into. So I told her she didn't need to tell me about it. I said I was interested in people, that I observed them, but that I never asked questions."

"But are you sure she changed her mind about telling you?"

"Not at all sure. She may have been play-acting. I may have

given her the wrong cue, for all I know. But she didn't cry on purpose. That much I'm sure of."

Leaning on his elbows, he looked out at the park. The hay stacks were gone, and the place had taken on a certain formality. He saw how noble the old trees were that lined the drive all the way out to the road. The horse restlessly moved forward a few paces and had to be checked by the gardener, who sat holding the reins. Mme Bonenfant arranged her skirt and then, looking up at the house, she called impatiently.

From somewhere a voice—light, unhurried, affectionate, silvery—answered: "Oui, Grand'maman. A l'instant. Je viens, je viens . . ."

"What an idiotic thing to do," Barbara said. "Now we'll never know what happened to him."

"Yes we will," he said. "Somebody will tell us. Sooner or later somebody always does."

On Sunday afternoon, an hour before it was time to start for the train, Mme Viénot said to her American guests: "Would you like to see the house?"

Alix and Mme Bonenfant went with them. The tour began on the second floor at the head of the stairs, with Mme Bonenfant's bedroom, which was directly under theirs. The counterpane on the huge bed was of Persian embroidery on a white background. The chair covers were of the same rich material. They were reminded of the bedchamber of Henri IV at Cheverny. The bedroom at Beaumesnil smelled of camphor and old age, and the walls were covered with family photographs. As they were leaving the room, Harold glanced over at the bedside table and saw that the schoolboy whose photograph was on the piano in the petit salon had not been finished off at the age of twelve; here he was, in the uniform of the French army.

They saw the two rooms that had been occupied by M. and Mme Carrère and that would have been theirs, Mme Viénot said, if they had come when they originally planned. And at the end of the hall, they were shown into Mme Cestre's room, on which her contradictory character had failed to leave any impression whatever. The curtains, the bedspread were green and white chintz that had some distant connection with water lilies.

Mme Viénot's room, directly across the hall from her mother's but around a corner, where they had never thought to search for her, was much smaller, and furnished simply and apparently without much thought. It was dominated not by the bed but by the writing desk.

Mme Viénot opened a desk drawer and took out some post-cards. "I think you have no picture of Beaumesnil," she said.

"We took some pictures with our camera," Barbara said, "but they may not turn out. We're not very good at taking pictures."

"You may choose the one you like best," Mme Viénot said.

They looked through the cards and took one and handed the others to Mme Viénot, who gave them to her mother as they were going along the second-floor passageway that connected the two parts of the house. Mme Bonenfant gave the cards back to Barbara, saying: "Keep them. Keep all of them."

Alix did not speak of the fact that they had already seen her room. It almost seemed that the room itself, as they stood in the doorway looking in, was denying that that illicit evening had ever taken place. They passed on to the bare, badly furnished room that had been Mme Straus-Muguet's. It was so much less comfortable than their own third-floor room or than any of the rooms they had just seen that Harold wondered if a deliberate slight had been involved. As Mme Viénot closed the door she said dryly: "It seems Mme Straus saw your room and she has asked for it when she comes back in August. I do not think I can see my way clear to letting her have it."

But why did Mme Viénot not want her to have their room, he wondered. Unless Mme Straus was unwilling to pay what they had paid, or perhaps was unable to pay that much. And if that was so, should they allow her to entertain them in Paris?

In this back wing of the house there was a box-stair leading up to a loft that had once been used as a granary. It still smelled of the dust of grain that had been stored there, though it was empty now, except for a few old-fashioned dolls (whose dolls, he wondered; how long ago had their place been usurped by children?) and, in the center of the high dim room, the wooden works of the outdoor clock.

They were quite beyond repair, Mme Viénot said, but the wooden cogwheels had turned, the clock had kept time, as recently as her girlhood. The pineapple-shaped weights were huge, and a hole had had to be cut in the floor for them to rise and descend through. Standing in this loft, Harold had the feeling that they had penetrated into the secret center of the house, and that there were no more mysteries to uncover.

As always at the end of a visit, there was first too much time and then suddenly there was not enough and they were obliged to hurry. Alix and Eugène had already started out for the village on foot. The gardener's bicycles having been returned to him, again there weren't enough to go round. The Americans took one last survey of the red room, free of litter now, the armoire and the closet empty, the postcards, guidebooks, and souvenirs all packed, the history of the château of Blois and the illustrated pamphlet returned to their place downstairs. The dying sweet peas in their square vase on the table in the center of the room said: *It is time to go.* . . .

"Where will we find another room like this?" he said, and closed the door gently on that freakish collection of books, on the tarnished mirrors, the fireplace that could not be used, the bathtub into which water did not flow, the map of Ile d'Yeu, the miniatures, the red and black and white wallpaper, the now familiar view, through that always open window, of the bottom of the sea. As he started down, he thought: *We will never come here again.* . . .

Mme Viénot was waiting for them at the foot of the stairs, and they followed her along the back passageway by which they had first entered the house, around a corner, and then another corner. A door opened silently, on the right, and Harold found himself face to face with a maniacal old woman, who clawed at his coat pocket and for a second scared him out of his wits. It was the cook. He was seeing the cook at last, and she had put something in his pocket. Too astonished to speak, he pressed a five-hundred-franc note into her hand, and she withdrew behind the door. He glanced ahead of him and saw Mme Viénot's skirt disappearing around the next corner. He was more than half convinced that she had seen—that she had eyes in the back of her head. She must, in any case, have sensed that something strange was going on. But when he caught up with her in the courtyard, she made no reference to what had happened in the corridor and, blushing from the sense of com-

plicity in a deception he did not understand, he also avoided
any mention of it.

Mme Bonenfant and Mme Cestre were waiting outside with
the two children, whom the Americans had scarcely laid eyes
on, and Alix's baby in her stroller. The Americans shook hands
with their hostess, with Mme Bonenfant, with Mme Cestre.
They disposed of the dressing case and the two small suitcases
among the three of them. Sabine kissed her mother and grandmother, and then, mounting their bicycles, waving and calling
good-by, they rode out of the courtyard, past the Lebanon
cedar that was two hundred years old, and down the cinder
drive.

Harold did not dare look at the piece of paper until they had
turned into the road and there was no possibility of his being
seen from the house. He let Barbara and Sabine draw ahead
and then, balancing a suitcase with one hand, he put his other
into his pocket. By all the rules of narration it should have
been a communication from M. Viénot, a prisoner somewhere
in the attic, crying out for help through his only friend, the
cook. It was, instead, a recipe for French-fried potatoes, and
with it, on another piece of paper three inches square, a note:

Si, par hasard, M. et Mme Rhodes connaissaient quelqu'un desirant
du personnel français mon fils et moi partirions très volontiers à
l'Etranger. Voici mon addresse Mme Foëcy à St. Claude de Diray
Indre-et-Loire. . . .

So he was not so far off, after all. It was the cook who
wanted them to rescue her, from Mme Viénot and the unhappy country of France.

In all the fields between the château and the village, the grain
had been cut and stacked. The scythe and the blades of the
reaper had spared only those poppies that grew along the road,
among the weeds and the wildflowers. The *bluets* had just
come into flower.

"My sister was married at Beaumesnil," Sabine said, "and
because of the Occupation we couldn't have the kind of
flowers that are usual at weddings, so, half an hour before the
ceremony, the bridesmaids went out and picked their own
bouquets, at the side of the road."

"It sounds charming," Barbara said.

"It was." Sabine swerved to avoid a rut. "There were some people from the village present, and they thought that if my sister had field flowers for her wedding it must be the fashion. Since that time, whenever there is a wedding in Brenodville the bride carries such a bouquet."

The note of condescension he heard in her voice was unconscious, Harold decided, and had nothing to do with the fact that she belonged to one social class and the village to another but was simply the smiling condescension of the adult for the child. He kept turning to look back at the château, so white against the dark woods. Since he couldn't do what he would have liked to do, which was to fold it up and stuff it in the suitcase and take it away with him, he tried to commit it to memory.

Then they were at the outskirts of Brenodville, and it looked as if the whole village had come out to meet them and escort them to their train. Actually, as he instantly realized, it was simply that it was Sunday afternoon. The people they met spoke to Sabine and sometimes nodded to the Americans. They cannot not know who we are, he thought, and at that moment someone spoke to him—a middle-aged man in a dark-blue Sunday suit, with his two children walking in front of him and his wife at his side. Surprised and pleased, Harold answered: "Bonjour, monsieur!" and when they were past, he turned to Sabine and asked: "Who is that?"

"That was M. Fleury."

He looked back over his shoulder to see if their old friend had stopped and was waiting for him to ride back, but M. Fleury had kept on walking.

"Have I got time to ride back and speak to him?" he said.

"You did speak to him," Barbara said.

"But I didn't recognize him. He looked so different."

The girls were talking and didn't hear him.

Riding past the cemetery, he took one last look at the monuments, which were surely made of papier-mâché, and at the graves decorated with a garish mixture of real and everlasting wreaths and flowers. As for the village itself, in two weeks' time they had come to know every doorway, every courtyard, every purple clematis, climbing rose, and blue morning-glory vine between here and the little river.

In the cobblestone square in front of the mairie they turned left, into a street that led them downhill in the direction of the railway station, and soon overtook Eugène, striding along by himself, with his coat on one arm and in the other hand his light suitcase. Alix was not with him. Harold looked around for her and saw that she wasn't anywhere. He slowed down, ready to ride beside Eugène. Receiving no encouragement, he rode on.

"What do we do with the bicycles?" he asked, when the two girls caught up with him.

"Someone will call for them," Sabine said.

On the station platform, he saw their two big suitcases and the dufflebag, checked through to Paris. The smaller suitcases they could manage easily with Eugène's help, even though they had to change trains at Blois. Traveling with French people, there would be no problems. He wouldn't have to ask the same question four different times so that he would have four answers to compare.

Eugène arrived, and drew Sabine aside, and stood talking to her farther down the platform, where they were out of earshot. Harold turned to Barbara and said in a low voice: "Where is Alix?"

"I don't know," she answered.

"Something must have happened."

"Sh-h-h."

"It's very queer," he said. "She didn't say good-by. There is only one direct way home—the way we came—and we didn't meet her, so she must have wanted to avoid us."

"Possibly."

"Do you think they quarreled?"

"Something has happened."

"Do you think it has anything to do with us?"

"What could it have to do with us?"

"I don't know," he said.

When Sabine came and joined them on the station platform, he thought: Now she will explain, and everything will be all right again. . . . But her explanation—"Alix has gone home.

She said to say good-by to you"—only deepened his sense of something being held back.

The station was surrounded by vacant land, and the old station still existed, but in the form of a low mound covered with weeds. Harold kept looking off in the direction of the château, thinking that he might see Alix; that she might suddenly appear in the space between two buildings. She didn't appear. Eugène remained standing where he was. The bell started to ring, though there was no train as far as the eye could see down the perfectly straight tracks in the direction of Blois, Orléans, and Paris or in the direction of Tours, Angers, and Nantes. The ringing filled the air with intimations of crisis. The four men seated on the terrace of the Café de la Gare paid no attention to it, which meant that they were either stone deaf or long accustomed to this frightful sound.

After five minutes the station agent appeared. He walked the length of the brick platform and, cranking solemnly, looking neither at the avenue Gambetta on his right nor at the bed of blue pansies on his left, let down the striped gates and closed the street to traffic.

A black poodle leaning out of the window of the house next to the café waited hopefully for something to happen, with its paws crossed in an attitude that was half human. The woolly head turned, betraying a French love of excitement, and the poodle watched the street that led toward the river. The bell went on ringing but with less and less conviction, like a man giving perfectly good advice that he knows from past experience will not be followed. Just when it seemed that nothing was ever going to happen, there was a falsetto cry and the four men on the terrace turned their heads in time to see the train from Tours rush past the café and come to a sudden stop between the railway station and the travel posters. Carriage doors flew open and passengers started descending. They reached up for suitcases that were handed down to them by strangers. They shouted messages to relatives who were going on to Blois, remembered a parcel left on the overhead rack, were alarmed, were reassured (the parcel was on the platform), held small children up to say good-by, or hurried to be first in line at the gate.

Eugène found a third-class compartment that was empty,

and they got in, and he pulled the door to from the inside. Harold let the glass down and kept his head out, with all the other heads, until the train had carried them past the place where they had waited for the bus. Having seen the last of the country he wanted especially to remember, he sat down. Barbara and Sabine were talking about their schools. He waited to see what Eugène would do. Eugène had a book in his coat pocket, and he took it out and read until the train drew into the station at Blois.

Eugène made his way along the crowded cement platform, and Harold followed at his heels, and the two girls tagged along after him, as relaxed as if they were shopping. Suddenly they came upon a group of ten or twelve of the guests at the Allégrets' party. Their youth, their good looks, their expensive clothes and new English luggage made them very noticeable in the drab crowd. Harold would have stopped but Eugène kept on going. Several of them nodded or smiled at Harold, whose eyes, as he spoke to them, were searching for Jean Allégret. He was there too, a little apart from the others. Harold started to put the suitcase down and shake hands with him, and then realized that he had just that second received all that was coming to him from Jean Allégret—a quick, cold nod.

Fortunately, the suitcases were still in his hands and he could keep on walking. He remembered but did not resort to a trick he had learned in high school: when you made the mistake of waving to somebody you did not know or, as it sometimes happened, somebody you knew all right but who for some unknown reason didn't seem to know you, the gesture, caught in time, could be diverted; the direction of the hand could be changed so that what began as a friendly greeting ended as smoothing the hair on the side of your head. Bewildered, he took his stand beside Eugène, a hundred feet further along the platform.

In giving him the money to buy Sabine's ticket, Mme Viénot had explained that third class was just as comfortable as second and only half as expensive. The second part of this statement was true, the first was not. He didn't look forward to a four-hour ride, on a hot July night, on wooden slats.

Just before the train drew in, the announcer's voice, coming over the loud-speaker system, filled the station with the sound

of rising panic, as if he were announcing not the arrival of the
Paris express, stopping at Orléans, etc., etc., but something
cataclysmic—the fall of France, the imminent collision of the
earth and a neighboring planet. When the train drew to a stop,
they were looking into an empty compartment. Again Eugène
closed the door from the inside, to discourage other passengers from crowding in. Just before the train started, the door
was wrenched open and a thin, pale young man—Eugène and
Alix's friend—looked in. Behind him, milling about in confusion, was the house party. Surely *they're* not traveling third
class, Harold thought.

Eugène told them there was room for four in the compartment. After a hurried consultation, they decided that they did
not want to be separated. Leaning out of the window, Harold
saw them mount the step of a third-class carriage farther along
the train. Were they all as poor as church mice, he wondered.
The question could not be asked, and so he would never know
the answer.

As the train carried them north through the evening light,
Sabine and Barbara and Harold whiled away a few miles of the
journey by writing down the names of their favorite books. *A
Passage to India*, he wrote on the back of the envelope that
Sabine handed to him. Barbara took the envelope and wrote
Fear and Trembling. He gave Sabine the financial diary and on
a blank page she wrote *Le Silence de la Mer*, while he looked
over her shoulder. "Vercors," she wrote. And then, "un petit
livre poétique." Barbara wrote *Journey to the End of the Night*
on the back of the envelope. He took it and wrote *To the
Lighthouse*. He glanced carefully at Eugène, who was sitting
directly across from him. Eugène looked away. *A Sportsman's
Notebook*, he wrote, and turned the envelope around so that
Sabine could read it.

Shortly after that, Eugène got up and went out into the corridor and stood by an open window. After Orléans, Barbara
and Sabine went out into the corridor also and stood by another window, and when Barbara came back into the compartment she said in a low voice: "I asked Sabine if she knew what
was the matter with Eugène, and she said he was moody and
not like other French boys." Though, during the entire journey, Eugène had nothing whatever to say to the three people

he was traveling with, he had a long, pleasant, animated conversation with a man in the corridor.

In the train shed in Paris, they met up with the house party again, and this time Jean Allégret acknowledged the acquaintance with a smile and a wave of his hand, as if not he but his double had had doubts in the station at Blois about the wisdom of accepting an American as a friend.

Harold put his two suitcases down and searched through his pockets for the luggage stubs. After four hours of ignoring the fact that he was being ignored, it was difficult to turn casually as if nothing had happened and ask where he should go to see about the two big suitcases and the dufflebag. Eugène shrugged, looked impatient, looked annoyed, looked as if he found Harold's French so inaccurately pronounced and so ungrammatical that there was no point in trying to understand it, and Harold felt that his education had advanced another half-semester. (Though there is only one way of saying "Thank you" in French, there are many ways of being rude, and you don't have to stop and ask yourself if the rudeness is sincere. The rudeness is intentional, and harsh, and straight from the closed heart.)

Too angry to speak, he turned on his heel and started off to find the baggage office by himself. He had only gone a short distance when he heard light footsteps coming after him. Sabine found the right window, took the stubs from him, gave them to the agent, and in her calm, soft, silvery voice dictated the address of her aunt's apartment.

The four of them took the Métro, changed at Bastille, and stepped into a crowded train going in the direction of the Porte de Neuilly. More and more people got on. Farther along the aisle a man and a woman, neither of them young, stood with their arms around each other, swaying as the train swayed, and looking into each other's eyes. The man's moist mouth closed on the woman's mouth in a long, indecent kiss, after which he looked around with a cold stare at the people who were deliberately not watching him.

Harold and Barbara found themselves separated from Sabine and Eugène. Barbara whispered something that Harold could not hear, because of the train noise. He put his head down.

"I said 'I think we'd better go to the Vouillemont.'"

"So do I. But I'm a little worried. It's after eleven o'clock, and we have no reservations."

"If there's no room at the Vouillemont, we can go to some other hotel," she said. "I'd rather spend the night on a park bench than put up with this any longer."

"But why did he ask us?"

"Something is wrong. He's changed his mind. Or perhaps he enjoys this sort of thing."

"The son of a bitch. You saw what happened when I asked him where to go about the big suitcases? . . . The only reason I hesitate at all is Alix and Mme Cestre. I hate to have them know we were—"

"He may not tell them what happened."

"But Sabine will."

The train rushed into the next station. They peered through the window and saw the word *Concorde*. Over the intervening heads, Eugène signaled that they were to get off.

Harold set the suitcases down and extended his hand. "We'll leave you here," he said stiffly. "Good night."

"But why?" Eugène demanded, astonished.

"The hotel is near this station, and we don't want to put you to any further trouble. Thank you very much."

"For what?"

"For taking care of us on the way up to Paris," Harold said. But then he spoiled the effect by blushing.

There was a brief silence during which both of them struggled with embarrassment.

"I am extremely sorry," Eugène said, "if I have given you any reason to think—"

"It seemed to us that you are a trifle distrait," Harold said, "and we'd rather not put you to any further trouble."

"I am not distrait," Eugène said. "And you are not putting me to any trouble whatever. The apartment is not being used. There is no need for you to go to a hotel."

A train drew in, at that moment, and Harold had the feeling afterward that that was what decided the issue, though trains don't, of course, decide anything. All decisions are the result of earlier decisions; cause, as anyone who has ever studied Beginning Philosophy knows, is another way of looking at effect. They got on the train, and then got off several stations farther along the line, at the Place Pierre-Joseph Redouté. A huge block of granite in the center of the square and dark triangular buildings, with the streets between them leading off in six directions like the rays of a star, were registered on Harold's mind as landmarks he would need to know if they suddenly decided to retrace their steps.

Sabine took her suitcase from Eugène. Then she shook hands with Barbara and Harold. "I am leaving you here," she said, and walked off down a dark, deserted avenue.

The other three turned into a narrow side street, and the Americans stopped when Eugène stopped, in front of the huge door of an apartment house. The door was locked. He rang the bell and waited. There was a clicking noise and the door gave under the pressure of his hand and they passed through a dimly lighted foyer to the elevator. Eugène put the suitcases into it, indicated that Harold and Barbara were to get in also, pressed the button for the sixth floor, and stepped out. "It only holds three," he said. "And with the suitcases it would not rise."

He shut the elevator door, and as they went up slowly, they saw him ascending the stairs, flight after flight. He was there in time to open the elevator door for them. He let them into the dark apartment with his key and then proceeded down the hall, turning on lights as he went, to the bedroom they were to occupy. "It is our room when Alix is here," he explained.

"But we don't want to put you out of your room," Harold protested.

"During the summer I prefer to sleep in the study," Eugène said.

He showed them the toilet, in a separate little room off the hall, and the bathroom they were to use. The gas hot-water heater was in the other bathroom, and he led them there and showed them how to turn the heater on and off when they wanted a bath.

They went back to the room that was to be theirs, and Eugène opened the window and unlatched the metal shutters and pushed them outward, letting in the soft night air. They saw that the room opened onto an iron balcony. Eugène removed the pillows from a big studio couch, and then he drew the

Kelly-green bedspread off and folded it and put it over the back of a chair. They watched him solemnly, as if he were demonstrating the French way to fold a bedspread. He showed them how to unhook the pillow covers and where the extra blankets were, and then he said good night. During all this, everybody was extremely polite, as if they had tried everything else and found that nothing works but politeness and patience.

Chapter 13

IN the first luminous quarter-hour of daylight, the Place Pierre-Joseph Redouté in the 16th arrondissement of Paris was given over to philosophical and mathematical speculation. The swallows skimming the wet rooftops said: *What are numbers?*

The sky, growing paler, said: *What is being when being becomes morning?*

What is "five," asked the birds, *apart from "five" swallows?*

The French painter and lithographer who belonged in the center of the Place and who from his tireless study of natural forms might have been able to answer those questions was unfortunately not there any more; he had been melted down and made into bullets by the Germans. The huge block of rough granite that was substituting for him said: *Matter is energy not in motion*, and the swallows said: *Very well, try this, then, why don't you . . . and this . . . and this . . .*

Though proof was easy and the argument had long ago grown tiresome, the granite refrained. But it could not resist some slight demonstration, and so it gave off concentric circles of green grass, scarlet salvia, curbing, and cobblestone.

The wide, wet, empty streets that led away from the Place Redouté like the rays of a star or the spokes of a wheel also at the very same time returned to it—returned from the Etoile, the Place d'Iéna, the Place Victor Hugo, the Trocadéro, and the Bois de Boulogne. The sky went on turning lighter. The pissoir, ill-smelling, with its names, dates, engagements, and obscene diagrams, said: *Everything that happens, in spite of the best efforts of the police, is determined by the space co-ordinates x, y, and z, and the time co-ordinate t.*

God is love, said the leaves on the chestnut trees, and the iron church bell filled the air with a frightful clangor.

Across an attic window in the rue Malène a workshirt hanging on a clothesline to dry grew a darker blue as it absorbed the almost invisible rain.

On the other side of the street, at the same sixth-floor level, a pair of metal shutters folded back gave away the location of a bedroom. The sleepers, both in one bed, were turned toward each other. She moved in her sleep, and he put his hand under her silken knees and gathered them to his loins and went on sleeping. Shortly afterward they turned away from each other, as if to demonstrate that in marriage there is no real resting place. Now love is gathered like great long-stemmed summer flowers, now the lovers withdraw from one another to nourish secretly a secret life. He pulls the blanket and sheet closer, shutting off the air at the back of his neck. She has not committed the murder, the police are not looking for her, and there is just time, between the coming and going of the man in the camel's-hair coat and the footsteps outside the door, to hide the papers. But where? If she puts them inside a book, they will be found, even though there are so many books. She will explain and they will not listen. They will not believe her. And he is asleep, dreaming. She has no one to stand by her when they come. She goes to the closet and finds there the camel's-hair coat worn by the murderer, who knew she was innocent and good, and slipped in and out of the apartment without being seen, and so who will believe her? . . . *Help! Help!* takes the form of a whimper.

Across the room a long-deferred, often-imagined reconciliation is taking place on the wall, behind glass. The Prodigal Son, wearing a robe of stone, kneels on one knee before the Prodigal Father. One arm reaches out and touches the old man's side. One arm, upraised, touches his face. The old man sits, bearded, with a domed forehead, a large stone mouth, blunt nose, and eyes nearly closed with emotion. He has placed one hand against the young man's head, supporting it, but not looking (why is that?) at the face that is looking up at his with such sorrow and love.

The iron balcony, polished by the rain, turns darker, shines, collects puddles. Water dripping from the eaves is caught in the first fold of the awnings.

The sleepers' breath is shallow. His efforts to take her in his arms meet with no response. He cannot blame her for this because she is asleep. The sky goes on turning lighter and whiter. It has stopped raining. A man (out of whose dream?) comes up the rue Malène and, noiseless as a cat, his vibrations sinister, crosses the Place Redouté and disappears down the same street that Sabine Viénot took. But that was last night and now it is morning.

Crowded to the extreme edge of the bed by his half-waking and half-sleeping lust, she turns.

"Are you awake?" he says softly.

"Yes."

"We're back in Paris."

"So I see."

Beside the door to the hall a bookshelf, too far away to read the titles. Then an armchair, with her dress and slip draped over the back and on the seat her bra, panties, and stockings in a soft heap. Her black wedge-soled shoes. Back of the chair a photograph—a detail of sculpture from a medieval church.

"Why the Prodigal Son?"

There is no answer from the other side of the bed.

He continues his investigation of the room. A low round table, elaborately inlaid, with two more period chairs. The radiator, and then the French windows. The room is high up, above the treetops, and there are windows directly across the way, an attic floor above that, and a portion of blue sky. Love in a garret. A door leading into the next room. A little glass table with knick-knacks on it. Another chair. On this chair, his clothes. Beside it his huge shoes—careless, scuffed, wide open, needing to be shined. Then the fireplace, with a mirror over it. Then an armchair, with the green spread and pillow covers and bolster piled on it. And over the bed an oil painting, a nude lying on a bed, plump, soft-fleshed, blonde. Alix—but not really. It is eighteenth century. He turns over.

"She was living for his return," he said. "That's all she talked about. And then when he came, they quarreled."

"Perhaps they didn't quarrel. Perhaps they just said good-by and she went back to the château."

"Then why was she avoiding us? It doesn't make sense. She must not have gone home by the road that goes past the cemetery. She probably didn't want us to see that she had been crying. All week long she kept waiting for a letter and there wasn't any letter."

"He called."

"That's true. I forgot that he called on Thursday. But all week end he wasn't himself. He wouldn't go swimming. And he didn't have a good time at the party. Did she?"

"Apparently."

"And the rest of the time, they were off somewhere by themselves. In the back part of the house . . . You don't think it has something to do with us?"

"No."

"I feel that it must have something to do with us. . . . She may not have wanted us here, sleeping in their bed and all."

"She said she was very glad."

"Then it must be all right. She wouldn't lie about it, just to be polite. If they quarreled, I can understand his not wanting to talk afterward. But in that case, why the long cheerful conversation with the man in the corridor?"

She turned over on her back and looked at the ceiling. "It's an effort for them. They have to choose their words carefully in order to make us understand."

"It's an effort for us too."

"They may not always feel like making the effort."

"Nothing was too much effort at first. . . . Did Sabine say 'Eugène is not like other French boys'? That may be what she meant—that he was friendly one minute and not the next. Or maybe when his curiosity is satisfied, he simply isn't interested any more. . . . I suppose the streets of Paris are safe, but I felt very queer watching her go off alone at that time of night. You think she got home all right?"

"Oh yes."

"I would have offered to take her home myself, but I didn't see how I could leave you, at that point. . . . How can she go on being nice to him?"

"She knows him better than we do."

He turned back again and, finding that she was curled up in a ball and he couldn't get at her, he put his hand between her knees. He felt her drifting back into sleep, away from him.

"What time is it?"

He drew his bare arm out from under the covers and looked at his wrist watch. "Five minutes of eight. Why?"

"Breakfast," she said. "In a strange kitchen."

He sat up in bed. "Do you wish we'd gone to a hotel?"

"We're here. We'll see how it works out."

"I could call the Vouillemont. . . . I didn't know what to do last night. He seemed genuinely apologetic. . . . If we never had to see him again, it would be simpler. But the suitcases are coming here."

She pushed the covers aside and started to get up, and then, suddenly aware of the open window and the building across the street, she said: "They can see us in bed."

"That can't be of much interest to anybody. Not in Paris," he said, and, naked as he was, he went to the curtained windows and closed them. In the dim underwater light they dressed and straightened up the room, and then they went across the hall to the kitchen. She was intimidated by the stove. He found the pilot light and turned on one of the burners for her. The gas flamed up two inches high. They found the teakettle and put water on to boil and then searched through the icebox. Several sections of a loaf of dark bread; butter; jam; a tiny cake of ice. In their search for what turned out to be the right breakfast china but the wrong table silver, they opened every cupboard door in the kitchen and pantry. While she was settling the teacart, he went back across the hall to their bedroom, opened one of the suitcases, and took out powdered coffee and sugar. She appeared with the teacart and he opened the windows.

"Do you want to call Eugène?"

He didn't, but it was not really a question, and so he left the room, walked down the hall to the front of the apartment, hesitated, and then knocked lightly on the closed door of the study. A sleepy voice answered.

"Le petit déjeuner," Harold said, in an accent that did credit to Miss Sloan, his high-school French teacher. At the same time, his voice betrayed uncertainty about their being here, and conveyed an appeal to whatever is reasonable, peace-loving, and dependable in everybody.

Since ordinary breakfast-table conversation was impossible, it was at least something that they were able to offer Eugène the sugar bowl with their sugar in it, and the plate of bread and butter, and that Eugène could return the pitcher of hot milk to them handle first. Eugène put a spoonful of powdered coffee into his cup and then filled it with hot water. Stirring, he said:

"I am sorry that my work prevents me from doing anything with you today."

They assured him that they did not expect or need to be entertained.

Harold put a teaspoonful of powdered coffee in his cup and filled it with hot water, and then, stirring, he sat back in his chair. The chair creaked. Every time he moved or said something, the chair creaked again.

Eugène was not entirely silent, or openly rude—unless asking Harold to move to another chair and placing himself in the fauteuil that creaked so alarmingly was an act of rudeness. It went right on creaking under his own considerable weight, and all it needed, Harold thought, was for somebody to fling himself back in a fit of laughter and that would be the end of it.

Through the open window they heard sounds below in the street: cartwheels, a tired horse's plodding step, voices. Harold indicated the photograph on the wall and asked what church the stone sculpture was in. Eugène told him and he promptly forgot. They passed the marmalade, the bread, the black-market butter, back and forth. Nothing was said about hotels or train journeys.

Eugène offered Harold his car, to use at any time he cared to, and when this offer was not accepted, the armchair creaked. They all three had another cup of coffee. Eugène was in his pajamas and dressing gown, and on his large feet he wore yellow Turkish slippers that turned up at the toes.

"Ex-cuse me," he said in Berlitz English, and got up and left them, to bathe and dress.

The first shrill ring of the telephone brought Harold out into the hall. He realized that he had no idea where the telephone was. At that moment the bathroom door flew open and Eugène came out, with his face lathered for shaving, and strode down the hall, tying the sash of his dressing gown as he went. The telephone was in the study but the ringing came from the hall. Between the telephone and the wall plug there was sixty feet of cord, and when the conversation came to an end, Eugène carried the instrument with him the whole length of the apartment, to his bathroom, where it rang three more times while he was shaving and in the tub. Before he left the apartment he knocked on their door and asked if there was anything he could do for them. Harold shook his head.

"Sabine called a few minutes ago," Eugène said. "She wants you and Barbara to have dinner with her tomorrow night."

He handed Harold a key to the front door, and cautioned him against leaving it unlocked while they were out of the apartment.

When enough time had elapsed so that there was little likelihood of his returning for something he had forgotten, Harold went out into the hall and stood looking into one room after another. In the room next to theirs was a huge cradle, of mahogany, ornately carved and decorated with gold leaf. It was the most important-looking cradle he had ever seen. Then came their bathroom, and then a bedroom that, judging by the photographs on the walls, must belong to Mme Cestre. A young woman who looked like Alix, with her two children. Alix and Eugène on their wedding day. Matching photographs in oval frames of Mme Bonenfant and an elderly man who must be Alix's grandfather. Mme Viénot, considerably younger and very different. The schoolboy. And a gray-haired man whose glance—direct, lifelike, and mildly accusing—was contradicted by the gilt and black frame. It was the kind of frame that is only put around the photograph of a dead person. Professor Cestre, could it be?

With the metal shutters closed, the dining room was so dark that it seemed still night in there. One of the drawing-room shutters was partly open and he made out the shapes of chairs and sofas, which seemed to be upholstered in brown or russet velvet. The curtains were of the same material, and there were some big oil paintings—portraits in the style of Lancret and Boucher.

Though, taken individually, the big rooms were, or seemed to be, square, the apartment as a whole formed a triangle. The apex, the study where Eugène slept, was light and bright and airy and cheerful. The window looked out on the Place Redouté—it was the only window of the apartment that did. Looking around slowly, he saw a marble fireplace, a desk, a low bookcase of mahogany with criss-crossed brass wire instead of glass panes in the doors. The daybed Eugène had slept in, made up now with its dark-brown velours cover and pillows. The portable record player with a pile of classical records beside it. Beethoven's Fifth was the one on top. Da-da-da-dum . . . Music could not be Eugène's passion. Besides, the records were dusty. He tried the doors of the bookcase. Locked. The titles he could read easily through the criss-crossed wires: works on theology, astral physics, history, biology, political science. No poetry. No novels. He moved over to the desk and stood looking at the papers on it but not touching anything. The clock on the mantelpiece was scandalized and ticked so loudly that he glanced at it over his shoulder and then quickly left the room.

The concierge called out to them as they were passing through the foyer. Her quarters were on the right as you walked into the building, and her small front room was clogged with heavy furniture—a big, round, oak dining table and chairs, a buffet, with a row of unclaimed letters inserted between the mirror and its frame. The suitcases had come while they were out, and had been put in their room, the concierge said.

He waited until they were inside the elevator and then said: "Now what do we do?"

"Call the Vouillemont, I guess."

"I guess."

Rather than sit around waiting for the suitcases to be delivered, they had gone sight-seeing. They went to the Flea Market, expecting to find the treasures of Europe, and found instead a duplication of that long double row of booths in Tours. Cheap clothing and junk of every sort, as far as the eye could see. They looked, even so. Looked at everything. Barbara bought some cotton aprons, and Harold bought shoestrings. They had lunch at a sidewalk café overlooking the intersection of two broad, busy, unpicturesque streets, and coming home they got lost in the Métro; it took them over an hour to get back to the station where they should have changed, in order to take the line that went to the Place Redouté. It was the end of the afternoon when he took the huge key out of his pocket and inserted it into the keyhole. When he opened the door, there stood Eugène, on his way out of the apartment. He was wearing sneakers and shorts and an open-collared shirt, and in his hand he carried a little black bag. He did not explain where he was going, and they did not ask. Instead, they went on down the hall to their room.

"Do you think he could be having an affair?" Barbara asked, as they heard the front door close.

"Oh no," Harold said, shocked.

"Well, this is France, after all."

"I know, but there must be some other explanation. He's probably spending the evening with friends."

"And for that he needs a little bag?"

They went shopping in the neighborhood, and bought two loaves of bread with the ration coupons they had been given in Blois, and some cheese, and a dozen eggs, and a bag of oranges from a peddler in the Place Redouté—the first oranges they had seen since they landed. They had Vermouth, sitting in front of a café. When they got home Harold was grateful for the stillness in the apartment, and thought how, under different circumstances, they might have stayed on here, in these old-fashioned, high-ceilinged rooms that reminded him of the Irelands' apartment in the East Eighties. They could have been perfectly happy here for ten whole days.

He went down the hall to Eugène's bathroom, to turn on the hot-water heater, and on the side of the tub he saw a pair of blue wool swimming trunks. He felt them. They were damp. He reached out and felt the bath towel hanging on the towel rack over the tub. Damp also. He looked around the room and then called out: "Come here, quick!"

"What is it?" Barbara asked, standing in the doorway.

"I've solved the mystery of the little bag. There it is . . . and there is what was in it. But where do people go swimming in Paris? That boat in the river, maybe."

"What boat?"

"There's a big boat anchored near the Place de la Concorde, with a swimming pool in it—didn't you notice it? But if he has time to go swimming, he had time to be with us."

She looked at him in surprise.

"I know," he said, reading her mind.

"I don't know what I'm going to do with you."

"It's because we are in France," he said, "and know so few people. So something like this matters more than it would at home. Also, he was so nice when he *was* nice."

"All because I didn't feel like dancing."

"I don't think it was that, really."

"Then what was it?"

"I don't know. I wish I did. The tweed coat, maybe. The thing about Eugène is that he's very proud."

And the thing about hurt feelings, the wet bathing suit pointed out, is that the person who has them is not quite the innocent party he believes himself to be. For instance—what about all those people Harold Rhodes went toward unhesitatingly, as if this were the one moment they would ever have together, their one chance of knowing each other?

Fortunately, the embarrassing questions raised by objects do not need to be answered, or we would all have to go sleep in the open fields. And in any case, answers may clarify but they do not change anything. Ten days ago, high up under the canvas roof of the Greatest Show on Earth, thinking *Now . . .* Harold threw himself on the empty air, confidently expecting that when he finished turning he would find the outstretched arms, the taped wrists, the steel hands that would catch and hold him. And it wasn't that the hands had had to catch some other flying trapeze artist, instead; they just simply weren't there.

He lit the hot-water heater, went back to their room, threw open the shutters, and stepped out on the balcony. He could see the Place Redouté, down below and to the left, and in the other direction the green edge of the Bois de Boulogne. The street was quiet. There were trees. And there was a whole upper landscape of chimney pots and skylights and trapdoors leading out onto the roof tops. He saw that within the sameness of the buildings there was infinite variety. When Barbara joined him on the balcony, he said: "This is a very different neighborhood from the Place de la Concorde."

"Do you want to stay?" she asked.

"Do you?"

"I don't know."

"I do and I don't want to stay," he said. "I love living in this apartment instead of a hotel. And being in this part of Paris."

"I don't really think we ought to stay here, feeling the way we do about Eugène."

"I know."

"If we are going to leave," she said, "right now is the time."

"But I keep remembering that we wanted to leave the château also."

"Mmm."

"And that we were rewarded for sticking it out. And probably would be here. But I really hate him."

"I don't think we'd be seeing very much of him. The thing I regret, and the only thing, is leaving that kitchen. It isn't like any kitchen I ever cooked in. Everything about it is just right."

"Yes?" he said, and turned, having heard in her voice a sound that he was accustomed to pay attention to.

"If we could only take our being here as casually as *he* does," she said.

He leaned far out over the balcony, trying to see a little more of the granite monument. "Let's not call the hotel just yet," he said. "The truth is, I don't want to leave either."

They had dinner in a restaurant down the street and went to a movie, which turned out to be too bad to sit through. They walked home, with the acid green street lights showing the undersides of the leaves and giving their faces a melancholy pallor. Since it was still early, they sat down at a table in front of the café in the Place Redouté and ordered mineral water.

"In Paris nobody is ever alone," Barbara said.

He surveyed the tables all around them, and then looked at the people passing by. It was quite true. Every man had a woman, whom he was obviously sleeping with. Every woman had her arm through some man's arm. "But how do you account for it?" he asked.

"I don't."

"The Earthly Paradise," he said, smiling up into the chestnut trees.

They sat looking at people and speculating about them until suddenly he yawned. "It's quarter of eleven," he said. "Shall we go?"

He paid the check and they got up and went around the corner, into the rue Malène. Just as he put out his hand to ring the bell, a man stepped out of a small car that was parked in front of their door. They saw, with surprise, that it was Eugène. He made them get into the car with him, and after a fashion—after a very peculiar fashion—they saw Paris by night. It was presumably for their pleasure, but he drove as if he were racing somebody, and they had no idea where they were and they were not given time to look at anything. "Jeanne d'Arc, Barbara!" Eugène cackled, as the car swung around a gilded monument on two wheels. Now they were in a perfectly ordinary street, now they were looking at neon-lighted night clubs. "La Place Pigalle," Eugène said, but they had no idea why he was pointing it out to them. Politely they peered at a big windmill without knowing what that was either.

The tour ended in Montmartre. Eugène managed to park the car in a street crowded with Chryslers and Cadillacs. Then he stood on the sidewalk, allowing them to draw their own conclusions from the spectacle provided by their countrymen and by the bearded and sandaled types (actors, could they be, dressed up to look like Greenwich Village artists of the 1920's?) who circulated in the interests of local color. He showed them the lights of Paris from the steps of the Sacré-Coeur, and then all his gaiety, which they could only feel as an intricate form of insult, suddenly vanished. They got in the car and drove home, through dark streets, at a normal rate of speed, without talking. And perhaps because he had relieved his feelings, or because, from their point of view, he had done something for them that (even though it was tinged with ill-will) common politeness required that he do for them, or because they were all three tired and ready for bed, or because the city itself had had an effect on them, the silence in the car was almost friendly.

Chapter 14

THE ringing of an electric bell in the hour just before day-light Harold heard in his sleep and identified: it was the ting-a-ling of the Good Humor Man. He wanted to go right on dreaming, but someone was shaking him. He opened his eyes. The hand that was shaking him so insistently was Barbara's. The dark all around the bed he did not recognize. Then that, too, came to him: they were in Paris.

"There's someone at the door!" Barbara whispered.

He raised himself on his elbows and listened. The bell rang twice more. "Maybe it's the telephone," he said. He could feel his heart racing as it did at home when the telephone woke them—not with its commonplace daytime sound but with its shrill night alarm, so suggestive of unspecified death in the family, of disaster that cannot wait until morning to make itself known. If it was the telephone they didn't have to do anything about it. The telephone was in the study.

"No, it's the door."

"I don't see how you can tell," he said, and, drunk with sleep, he got up out of bed and stumbled out into the pitch-dark hallway, where the ringing was much louder. He had no idea where the light switches were. Groping his way from door to door, encountering a big chair and then an armoire, he arrived at a jog in the hallway, and then at the foyer. After a struggle with the French lock, he succeeded in opening the front door and peered out at the sixth-floor landing and the stairs, dimly lighted by a big window. Confused at seeing no one there, he shut the door, and had just about convinced himself that it was a mistake, that he had dreamed he heard a bell ringing somewhere in the apartment, when the matter was settled once and for all by a repetition of the same silvery sound. So it *was* the telephone after all. . . .

He started across the foyer, intending to wake Eugène, who must be sleeping the sleep of the dead. Before he reached the door of the study a new sound stopped him in his tracks: someone was beating with both fists on a door. Feeling like the blindfolded person who is "it" in a guessing game, he retraced his steps down the dark hallway, as far as the door into the kitchen. The pounding seemed to come from somewhere quite near. He crossed the threshold and to his surprise and horror found that he was walking barefoot in water. The kitchen floor was awash, and there was another sound besides the voices and the pounding—a sound that was like water cascading from a great height. He found the back door and couldn't unlock it. Angry excited voices shouted at him through the door, and try as he might, turning the huge key back and forth and pulling at the spring lever that should have released the lock, he couldn't get the door open. He gave up finally and ran back into the hallway, shouting "Eugène!"

Even so, Eugène did not waken. He had to open the study door and go in and, bending over the bed, shake him into sensibility.

"Il y a un catastrophe!" Harold said loudly.

There was a silence, and then Eugène said, without moving: "Une catastrophe?"

The pounding was resumed, the bell started ringing again, and Eugène sat up and reached for his dressing gown. Harold turned and ran back to the kitchen. Awake at last, he managed to get the door open. The concierge and a boy of fifteen burst in upon him. They were both angry and excited, and he had no idea what they were saying to him. The single word "inondation" was all he understood. The concierge turned the kitchen light on. Harold listened to the cascade. A considerable quantity of water must be flowing over the red-tiled floor and out the door and down six flights of the winding metal stair that led down into the courtyard, presumably. And maybe from there the water was flowing into the concierge's quarters. In any case, it was clear that she blamed him, a stranger in the apartment, for everything.

Eugène appeared, with his brocade dressing gown over his pajamas, and his massive face as calm and contained as if he were about to sit down to breakfast. Without bothering to remove the Turkish slippers, he waded over to the sink and stood examining the faucets. He and the concierge and the boy carried on a three-way conversation that excluded foreigners by its rapidity, volubility, and passion. They turned the faucets on and off. With their eyes, with their searching hands, they followed the exposed water pipes around the walls of the kitchen, and, passing over the electric hot-water heater, arrived eventually at a small iron stove—for coal, apparently, and not a cooking stove. (There were three of those in the kitchen.) It was cylindrical, five feet high, and two feet in diameter, with an asbestos-covered stove pipe rising from the top and disappearing into a flue in the wall. The concierge bent down and opened the door of the ash chamber. From this unlikely source a further quantity of water flowed out over the floor and down the back stairs. For a moment, as if he had received the gift of tongues, Harold understood what Eugène and the concierge and the boy were saying. Eugène inquired about the apartment directly below. The people who lived there were away, the concierge said, and she had no key; so there was no way of knowing whether that apartment also was being flooded. A plumber? Not at this hour, she said, and looked at Harold balefully. Then she turned her attention to the pipes in the pantry, and Eugène stood in front of the electric hot-water heater, which was over the sink. Yesterday morning he had put the plug into the wall socket and explained that the heater took care of the hot water for the dishes. He said nothing about removing the plug when they were finished, and so, remembering how the light in the elevator and the light on the sixth-floor landing both extinguished themselves, barely leaving time to reach the door of the apartment before you were in total darkness, they had left the heater in charge of its own current. Foolishly, Harold now saw, because it must be the heater. Unless by some mischance he had forgotten to turn the gas off after Barbara's bath, last night. He distinctly remembered turning the gas off, and even so the thought was enough to make him have to sit down in a chair until the strength came back into his knees. Once more he inquired if the flood was something that he and Barbara had done. Eugène glanced around thoughtfully, but instead of answering, he joined the search party in the pantry. Cupboard doors were opened and shut. Pipes were examined. Hearing the word "chauffage" again and again from the pantry, Harold withdrew to the bathroom at the end of the hall, expecting to discover the worst— the gas heater left burning all night, a burst pipe, and water everywhere. The heater was cold and the bathroom floor was dry. He was on the point of absolving himself of all responsibility for the inundation when a thought crossed his mind—a quite hideous thought, judging by the expression that accompanied it. He went down the hall past the kitchen and opened the door of the little room that contained the toilet.

As a piece of plumbing, the toilet was done for. It only operated at all out of good will. Last night, while they were getting ready for bed, he had heard it flushing, and then flushing again, and again; and thinking to avoid just such a situation as had now happened, he got the kitchen stepladder, climbed up on it, reached into the water chamber, and closed the valve, intending to open it when they got up in the morning. By so doing, he now realized, he had upset the entire system. It could only be that; they hadn't been near the iron boiler in the kitchen from which water so freely flowed. And it was only a question of time before the search, now confined to the pantry, would lead Eugène, the concierge, and the boy to the real source of the trouble. Nevertheless, like Adam denying the apple, he climbed up on the stepladder and opened the valve. The water chamber filled slowly and then the pipes grew still.

As he reached the kitchen door, the search party brushed past him and went into Eugène's bathroom. Harold turned and went back to their bedroom. Barbara had got up out of bed and was sitting at the window, with her dressing gown wrapped around her, smoking a cigarette.

"Look up the word 'chauffage,'" he said. "The dictionary is in the pocket of my brown coat," and he went on down the hall. Ignoring the gas heater, Eugène searched for and found a valve behind the tub. As soon as the valve was closed, the bathtub began to fill with rusty red water gurgling up out of the drainpipe. He hurriedly opened the valve, and the water receded, leaving a guilty stain.

"'Chauffage' means heating or a heating system," Barbara said, as Harold came into the bedroom. He closed the door behind him.

"Did he say it was our fault?" she asked.

"I asked him five times and just now he finally said 'Heureusement oui.'"

"That doesn't make any sense, 'heureusement oui.'"

"I know it doesn't, but that's what he said. It *must* be our fault. We ought never to have come here."

The voices and the heavy footsteps passed their door, returning to the kitchen, and wearily he went in pursuit of them. They still had not found the valve that controlled the water pipes, and the cascade down the back stairs was unabated. The landing and the stair well were included in the area under investigation. Locating a new valve, Eugène left his sodden Turkish slippers inside the kitchen door and went into the front of the apartment; opened the door of the huge sculptured armoire and took out a cigar box; opened the cigar box and took out a pair of pliers.

"There is something I have to tell you," Harold said. "I'm awfully sorry but last night the toilet didn't work properly and so I got the kitchen stepladder and . . ."

Eugène listened abstractedly to this confession and when it was finished he asked where Harold had put the stepladder. Then he went into the little room where the toilet was, picked up the stepladder, and carried it out to the back landing. With the pliers, standing on the stepladder, he closed a valve in the pipeline out there. He and the concierge and the boy listened. Their faces conveyed uncertainty, and then hope, and then triumph, as the sound of falling water began to diminish. It took some time and further discussion, a gradual letting down of tension and a round of congratulations, before the concierge and the boy left. Eugène put away the stepladder and picked up the mop. As he started mopping up the red tiles, Harold said: "Barbara and I will clean the kitchen up."

Eugène stopped and stared at him, and then said: "The floor will be dirty unless it is mopped." They stood looking at each other helplessly. He must think we don't understand anything at all, Harold thought.

"I'm very sorry that your sleep has been disturbed," Eugène said.

Harold studied his face carefully, thinking that he must be speaking sarcastically. He was not. The apology was sincere. Once more, with very little hope of a sensible answer, Harold asked if they had caused the trouble.

"This sort of thing happens since the war," Eugène said.

"The building is old and needs new plumbing. Now that the water is turned off, there is nothing more that we can do until the plumber comes and fixes the leak."

"Was it caused by turning the water off in the toilet?"

Eugène turned and indicated the little iron stove, inside which a pipe had burst, for no reason.

"Then it wasn't our fault?"

For a few seconds Eugène seemed to be considering not what Harold had just said but Harold himself. He looked at him the way cats look at people, and did something that cats are too polite ever to do: he laughed. Then he turned and resumed his mopping.

Standing on the balcony outside their room, Harold lit a cigarette. Barbara was in bed and he couldn't tell whether she was asleep or not. The swallows were darting over the roof tops. Directly below him, so straight down that it made him dizzy to look, an old man was silently searching through the garbage cans. On the blue pavement he had placed four squares of blue cloth, and when he found something of value he put it on one or the other of them.

The stoplights at the intersection at the foot of the hill changed from red to green, from green to red. The moon, in its last quarter, was white in a pearly pink sky. The discovery that it was not their fault had come too late. They had had so much time to feel they were to blame that they might just as well have been. Too tired to care any longer, he left the balcony and got into bed. A moment later, he got up and took his wallet out of his coat and found a five-hundred-franc note and then returned to the balcony. When the old man looked up he would make signals at him. Though he waited patiently, the old man did not look up. Instead, he tied his four pieces of cloth at the corners and went off down the street, which by now had admitted it was morning.

Awakened out of a deep sleep by a silvery sound, Harold sat up in bed. It was broad daylight outside. The telephone? he thought wildly. The front door? Or the back? Whatever it was, Barbara was sleeping right through it.

He got up and followed his own wet footprints down the gray carpeting until he came to the foyer. This time when he opened the front door someone was there—the concierge, smiling and cordial, with three blond young men. One of them had a brief case, and they didn't look at all like plumbers. The concierge asked for M. de Boisgaillard, and Harold knocked on the study door and fled.

Ten minutes later, he heard a faint tap on their door.

"Yes?"

As he sat up in bed, the door opened and Eugène came in. Keeping his voice low because Barbara was still asleep, he said: "The people you let in— They just arrived in Paris this morning, from Berlin." He hesitated.

Harold perceived that Eugène was telling him this because there was something they could do for him. Eugène was not in the habit of asking for favors, and it was painful for him to have to now. What he was going to say would alter somewhat the situation between them and him, but he was going to say it anyway.

"They have no money, and they haven't had any breakfast."

"You'd like Barbara to make breakfast for them?" Harold asked, and found himself face to face with his lost friend, Eugène the way he used to be before that picnic on the banks of the Loire.

Bread, oranges, marmalade, eggs, honey—all bought the afternoon before, and with their money. Nescafe in the big suitcase, sugar cubes in the small one. All the wealth of America to feed the hungry of Europe.

"There is plenty of everything," he said.

"Plenty?" Eugène repeated, unconvinced.

"Plenty," Harold said, nodding.

"Good."

The image of a true friend was dimmer; was fading like a rainbow or any other transitory natural phenomenon, but it was still visible. When Eugène left, Harold woke Barbara, and as he was hurriedly getting into his clothes he began to whistle. It was their turn to do something for Eugène. And if they cared to, they could be both preoccupied and moody as they went about it.

When Barbara wheeled the teacart into Mme Cestre's drawing room, the four heads were raised. The four men rose, and the Germans clicked their heels politely as Eugène presented them to her and then to Harold, who had come in after her. All three were pale, thin, and nervous. One had pink-tinted rimless glasses, and one had ears that stuck straight out from his head, and one was tall and blond (the pure Nordic abstraction, the race that never was) with wide, bony shoulders, concave chest, hollow stomach, and the trousers of a much heavier man hanging from his hip bones.

"Do sit down," Barbara said.

Herr von Rothenberg, the Nordic type, spoke French and English fluently, and the two others told him what they wanted to say and he translated for them. They had traveled as far as the French border by plane, and from there by train. They had arrived in Paris at daybreak.

"We were very surprised," Herr von Rothenberg said to the Americans. "We did not expect to find Paris intact. We had understood that it was largely ruins, like London and Berlin."

He was not entirely happy that Paris had been spared. It offended his sense of what is fair. But he did not say this; it only came out in his voice, his troubled expression.

The Germans politely took the cups that Eugène handed them, but allowed their coffee to grow cold. Barbara had to urge it on them, and point again and again to the bread and butter on their plates, before they could bring themselves to eat. Their extreme delicacy in the presence of food seemed to say: *It was most kind of M. de Boisgaillard to offer us these cigarettes, and surely something is to be gained from a discussion of the kind we are having, between the people who have lost a war and those who, for reasons history will eventually make clear, have won it. But as for eating—we do not care to impose on anyone, we are accustomed to being faint with hunger, we have much more often than not, the last few years, gone without breakfast. We would prefer to continue with what M. de Boisgaillard was saying about the establishment of a central bureau that would have control over credit and . . .*

In the end, though, the bread was eaten, the coffee was drunk, and on two of the plates there was a pile of orange peelings. The third orange remained untouched. Barbara looked inquiringly from it to the young man whose ears stuck out, and whose orange it was. He smiled at her timidly and then looked at Eugène, who was telephoning and ignored his appeal. Pointing to the orange, the young man whose ears stuck out said, in halting English: "The first in twelve years." He hesitated and then, since Eugène was still talking into the telephone and Barbara was still waiting and the orange had not been snatched from him, said: "I have a wife. And ten days ago a baby is born. . . . Could I take this orange with me, to give to her?"

Barbara explained that there were more oranges, and that he could eat this one. He put it in his pocket, instead.

Eugène was trying to find a place for the Germans to stay. They listened to the one-sided telephone conversations with a sympathetic interest, as if it were the welfare of three other young men he was devoting himself to with such persistence.

Finally, as the morning dragged on, the Americans excused themselves and left the drawing room, taking the teacart with them.

"Terrible," Harold said.

"Terrible," she agreed.

"I didn't know there were Germans like that."

"Did you hear what he said about the orange?"

"Yes, I heard. We must remember to send some back with them."

"But what will become of them?"

"God knows."

"Do you think they were Nazis?"

"No, of course not. How could they have been? Probably they never even heard of Hitler."

At noon, Barbara wheeled the teacart out of the kitchen again, and down the hall to Mme Cestre's drawing room, which was now murky with cigarette smoke. The men sprang to their feet and waited for her to sit down, but she shook her head and left them. She and Harold ate in the kitchen, sitting on stools. They had just finished cleaning up when Eugène appeared in the doorway.

"I am much obliged to you, Barbara," he said. "It is a very great kindness that you do for me."

"It was nothing," she said. "Did you find a place for them to stay?"

He shook his head. "I have told them that they can stay here. But you will not have to do this any more. I have made other arrangements. The person who comes in by the day when we are all here will cook for them. Her name is Françoise. She is a very nice woman. If you want anything, just tell her and she will do it for you. I did not like to ask her because her son was in a concentration camp and she does not like Germans."

"But what are they doing in Paris?" Harold asked.

"They are trying to get to Rome," Eugène said. "They want to attend an international conference there. Arrangements had been made for them to go by way of Switzerland, but they decided to go by way of Paris, instead. They used up their money on train fare. And unfortunately in all of Paris no one knows of a fund that provides for an emergency of this kind or a place that will take them in. Herr von Rothenberg I met at an official reception in Berlin, last year. He is of a very good family. The other two I did not know before. . . . You have Sabine's address? She is expecting you at eight."

The address that Eugène gave them turned out to be a modern apartment building on a little square that was named after a poet whose works Harold had read in college but could no longer remember; they had joined with the works of three other romantic poets, as drops of water on a window pane join and become one larger drop. A sign by the elevator shaft said that the elevator was out of order. They rang Sabine's bell and started climbing. Craning his neck, he saw that she was waiting for them, six floors up. She called down over the banister: "I'm sorry you have such a long climb," and he called up: "Are you as happy to see us as we are to see you?"

She had on a little starched white apron, over her blouse and skirt. She shook hands with them, took the flowers that Barbara held out to her, and, looking into the paper cone, exclaimed: "Marguerites! They are my favorite. And a book?"

"*A Passage to India*," Harold said. "We saw it in the window of a bookstore."

"I will be most interested to read it," she said. "This is my uncle's apartment—did Eugène tell you? The family is away now. I am here alone. My uncle collects paintings and objets d'art. There is a Sargent in the next room. . . . I must put these beautiful flowers in water. You will not mind if I am a little distracted? I am not used to cooking."

She and Barbara went off to the kitchen together, and Harold stood at the window and peered down at the little square. Then he started around the room, looking at Chinese carvings and porcelains and at the paintings on the walls. When the two girls came back with a bottle of Cinzano and glasses, he was standing in front of a small Renoir.

"It's charming, isn't it?" Sabine said.

"Very," he said.

"In my aunt's apartment there is a bookcase with art books in it— Have you found it yet?"

"In the front hall," he said. "By the study door. But it's locked."

"I know where the key is kept," she said, but before she had a chance to tell him, the doorbell rang. "Are you comfortable in the rue Malène?" she asked as she started toward the hall.

Harold and Barbara looked at each other.

"Something has happened since I saw you?" Sabine asked.

"A great deal has happened," he said. "It's a very long story. We'll tell you later."

The young man she introduced to them was in his middle twenties, small, compact, and alert-looking, with hair as black as an Indian's and dark skin. For the first few minutes, he was self-conscious with the Americans, and kept apologizing for his faulty English. They liked him immediately, encouraged him when he groped for a word, assured him that his English was fine, and in every way possible took him under their wing, enjoying all his comments and telling him that they felt as if they already knew him. The four-sided conversation moved like a piece of music. It was as if they had all agreed beforehand to say only what came into their heads and to say it instantly, without fear or hesitation. In her pleasure at discovering that Sabine had such a handsome and agreeable young man on a string, Barbara was more talkative than usual. She was witty. She made them all laugh. Sabine was astonished to learn of the presence of three Berliners in her aunt's apartment, and said doubtfully: "I do not think that my aunt would like it, if she knew."

"But if you saw them!" Harold exclaimed. "So pale, so thin. And as sensitive as sea horses." Then he began to tell the story of the burst water pipe.

They sat down to dinner at a gateleg table in the drawing-room alcove. The Americans dug out of the young Frenchman that he was in the government. From his description of his job, Harold concluded that it was to read all the newspaper articles and summarize them for his superior, who based his statements to the press on them. This explanation the Frenchman rejected indignantly; it was he who prepared the statements for the press. Looking at him, Harold thought that if he had had to draw up a set of requirements for a husband for Sabine, they would have added up to the young man across the table. Though he must be extremely intelligent to hold down a position of responsibility at his age, there was nothing pompous in his manner or his conversation. He was simply young and quick-witted and unsuspicious. They felt free to tease him, and he defended himself without attacking them or being anything but more agreeable. The evening flew by, and when they left at eleven, they tried to do it in such a way that he wouldn't feel he had to leave too. But he left with them, and as they were passing under a street lamp in the avenue Victor Hugo, they learned that he was not the person they thought he was; he was Sabine's brother-in-law, Jean-Claude Lahovary.

"Mme Viénot told us about you," Barbara said.

"Yes?"

"She told us about your family," Barbara said.

Oh no, Harold begged her silently. *Don't say it. . . .*

But Barbara was a little high from the wine, and on those rare occasions when she did put her trust in strangers, she was incautious and wholehearted. As if no remark of hers could possibly be misunderstood by him, she said: "She said your mother was hors de siècle."

The Frenchman looked bewildered. Harold changed the subject. Exactly how offensive the phrase was, he didn't know, and he hadn't been able to tell from Mme Viénot's tone of voice because her voice was always edged with one kind of cheerful malice or another. Trying to cover up Barbara's mistake he made another.

"Do you know what you remind me of?" he asked, though

an inner voice begged him not to say it. (He too had had too much wine.)

"What?" the Frenchman asked politely.

"An acrobat."

The Frenchman was not pleased. He did not consider it a compliment to be told that he was like an acrobat. The tiresome inner voice had been right, as usual. Though table manners are the same in France, other manners are not. We shouldn't have gone so far with him, the first time, Harold thought. Or been quite so personal.

The conversation lost its naturalness. There were silences as they walked along together. They quickly became strangers. As they crossed one of the streets that went out from the Place Redouté, they were accosted by a beggar, the first Harold had seen in Paris. Always an easy touch at home, he waited, not knowing if beggars were regarded cynically by the French, and also not wanting to appear to be throwing his American money around. The future minister of finance reached in his pocket quickly and brought out a hundred-franc note and gave it to the beggar, and so widened the misunderstanding: the French have compassion for the poor, Americans do not, was the only possible conclusion.

They shook hands at the entrance of the Métro and said good night. Still hoping that something would happen at the last minute, that he would give them a chance to repair the damage they had done to the evening, they stood and watched him start down the steps, turn right, and disappear without looking back. Though they might read his name years from now in the foreign-news dispatches, this was the last they would ever see of Mme Viénot's brilliant son-in-law.

As they were walking home, past shuttered store fronts, Barbara said: "I shouldn't have said that about his mother, should I?"

"People are very touchy about their families."

"But I meant it as a compliment."

"I know."

"Why didn't he realize I meant it as a compliment?"

"I don't know."

"I liked him."

"So did I."

"It's very sad."

"It doesn't matter," he said, meaning something quite different—meaning that there was nothing either of them could do about it now.

He called out who they were as they passed through the foyer of the apartment building. They went up in the elevator, and the hall light went out just as he thrust his key at the keyhole. He stepped into the dark apartment and felt around until he found the light switch. The study door was closed and so was the door of Mme Cestre's bedroom.

Lying in bed in the dark, looking through the open window at the one lighted room in the building across the street, he said: "What it amounts to is that you cannot be friends with somebody, no matter how much you like them, if it turns out that you don't really understand one another."

"Also—" he began, five minutes later, and was stopped by the sound of Barbara's soft, regular breathing. He turned over and as he lay staring at the lighted room he felt a sudden first wave of homesickness come over him.

Chapter 15

THE first daylight, whitening the sky and making the windows shine, revealed that the three Berliners had spent the night in Mme Cestre's bedroom. Their threadbare, unpressed, spotty coats and trousers, neatly folded, were on three chairs. Also, their shirts and socks and underwear, which had been washed without soap. Two of them slept in the narrow bed, with their mouths open like dead people and their breathing so quiet they might have been dead. The third slept on the floor, with a rug under him, his head on the leather brief case, his pink-tinted glasses beside him, and Mme Cestre's spare comforter keeping him from catching pneumonia. So pale they were, in the gray light. So unaggressive, so intellectual, so polite even in their sleep. *Oh heartbreaking—what happens to children,* said the fruitwood armoire, vast and maternal, bound in brass, with brass handles on the drawers, brass knobs on the two carved doors. The dressing table, modern, with its triple way of viewing things, said: *It is their own doing and redoing and undoing.*

"Bonjour, monsieur-dame," said the tall, full-bosomed woman with carrot-colored hair and a beautiful carriage. She raised the front wheels of the teacart and then the back, so that they did not touch the telephone cord. When she had gone back to the kitchen, Harold said: "There are plates and cups for three, which can only mean that he is having breakfast with us."

"You think?" Barbara said.

"By his own choice," Harold said, "since there is now someone to bring him a tray in his room."

They sat and waited. In due time, Eugène appeared and drew the armchair up to the teacart.

It was a beautiful day. The window was wide open and the sunlight was streaming in from the balcony. Eugène inquired about their evening with Sabine, and the telephone, like a spoiled child that cannot endure the conversation of the grownups, started ringing. Eugène left the room. When he came back, he said: "It is possible that I may be going down to

237

the country on Friday. A cousin of Alix is marrying. And if I do go—as I should, since it is a family affair—it will be early in the morning, before you are up. And I may stay down for the week end."

They tried not to look pleased.

He accepted a second cup of coffee and then asked what they had done about getting gasoline coupons. "But we don't need them," Harold said, and so, innocently, obliged Eugène to admit that he did. "I seldom enjoy the use of my car," he said plaintively, "and it would be pleasant to have the gasoline for short trips into the country now and then."

He reached into his bathrobe pocket and brought out a slip of paper on which he had written the address of the place they were to go to for gasoline coupons.

"How can we ask for gasoline coupons if we don't have a car?" Harold said.

"As Americans traveling in France you are entitled to the coupons whether you use them or not," Eugène said. "And the amount of gasoline that tourists are allowed is quite considerable."

Harold put the slip of paper on the teacart and said: "Could you tell us— But there is no reason you should know, I guess. We have to get a United States Army visa to enter Austria."

"I will call a friend who works at the American Embassy," Eugène said, rising. "He will know."

Five minutes later, he was back with the information Harold had asked for.

Walking past the open door of the dressing room, Harold saw the Germans for the first time that morning. They were crowded around Eugène, and pressing on him their latest thoughts about their predicament. He avoided looking at whoever was speaking to him, and his attention seemed to be entirely on the arrangement of his shirt tails inside his trousers.

Later he stopped to complain about them, standing in the center of the Americans' room, with the door open, so that there was a good chance that he might be overheard. It was already too late for the Germans to get to the conference in Rome in time to present their credentials, he said. Their places would be taken by alternates.

"What will they do?" Harold asked. "Turn around and go home?"

"There are other conferences scheduled for other Italian cities," Eugène said, "and they hope to be allowed to attend one of these. Unfortunately, there isn't the slightest chance of their getting the visas they need to cross the Italian border. The whole thing is a nuisance—the kind of silliness only Germans are capable of."

Though Eugène was bored with the Germans' dilemma and despised them personally for having got themselves into it, they had thrown themselves on his kindness, and it appeared that he had no choice but to go on trying to help them.

The Americans spent the morning getting to know parts of Paris that are not mentioned in guidebooks. The address on Eugène's slip of paper turned out to be incorrect; there was no such number. Harold was relieved; he had dreaded exposure. The information about where to go to get the Austrian visa was also wrong. They talked to the concierge of the building, who gave them new and explicit directions, and in a few minutes they found themselves peering through locked doors at the marble foyer of an unused public building. Eventually, by asking a gendarme, they arrived at the Military Permit Office. There they stood in line in a large room crowded with people whom no country wanted and whom France could not think what to do with. When Harold produced their American passports, the man next to him turned and looked at him reproachfully. All around them, people were arguing tirelessly with clerks who pretended (sometimes humorously) not to understand what they wanted, not to speak German or Italian, not to know that right there on the counter in front of them was the rubber stamp that would make further argument unnecessary. As Harold and Barbara went from clerk to clerk, from the large room on the first floor to a smaller office on the third floor, and finally outdoors with a new address to find, they began to feel less and less different from the homeless people around them, even though they had a perfectly good home and were only trying to get to a music festival. At the right place at last, they were told that they had to leave their passports with the application for their visas, which would be ready the next day.

After lunch, they walked through the looking glass, leaving the homeless on the other side, and spent the afternoon sight-seeing. They took the Métro to the Place du Trocadéro, descended the monumental stairs of the Palais de Chaillot, went through the aquarium, and then strolled across the Pont d'Iéna in the sunshine.

At the top of the Tour Eiffel there was a strong wind and they could not bear to look straight down. All that they remembered afterward of what they saw was the colored awnings all over Paris. They took a taxi home, and as they went down the hall to their own room they could hear the Germans talking to each other, behind the closed door of theirs.

Meeting Herr Rothenberg in the hall, they learned that he and his friends had spent the day going the rounds of the embassies and consulates.

"But you ought to be seeing Paris," Harold said. "It's so beautiful."

"We will come back and see the museums another time," Herr Rothenberg said, smiling and quite pleased with the Paris they had seen.

Shortly afterward, he appeared at their door and said that Françoise had gone home and could they please have some bread and butter and coffee?

Harold followed Barbara into the kitchen and as she was putting the kettle on he said: "Do you suppose they don't realize that all those things are rationed?"

"I don't know," she said, "but let's not tell them."

"All right. I wasn't going to. It just occurred to me that maybe the national characteristics were asserting themselves."

"I'm so in love with this kitchen," Barbara said. "If it were up to me, I'd never leave."

The two Americans and the three Germans had coffee together in Mme Cestre's drawing room, with the shutters open and the light pouring in. The Germans showed Barbara snapshots of their wives, and Harold wrote their names and addresses in his financial diary, and then they all went out on the balcony so that Barbara could take the Berliners' pictures. They stood in a row before her, three pale scarecrows stiffly composed in attitudes that would be acceptable to posterity.

Still in a glow from the success of the tea party, Harold went down into the Place Redouté and found the orange peddler and bought a bag of oranges from him, which he then presented to Herr Rothenberg at the door of their room, with a carefully prepared little speech and three thousand-franc notes, in case the Germans found themselves in need of money on the next lap of their journey. The effect of this act of generosity was partly spoiled because, out of a kind of Anglo-Saxon politeness they were unfamiliar with, he didn't give them a chance to finish their speeches of gratitude. But at all events the money got from his wallet into theirs, where it very much needed to be.

At twenty-five minutes after six, he walked into the study with a calling card in his hand and stood by Eugène's desk, waiting until his wrist watch and the clock on the mantelpiece agreed that it was half-past six. On the back of the card Mme Straus-Muguet had scrawled the telephone number of the convent in Auteuil, and "coup de fil à 6h½." During the three and a half weeks that they had been in France he had managed, through the kindness of one person and another, not to have to talk over the telephone. He would just as soon not have done it now.

A woman's voice answered. He asked to speak to Mme Straus-Muguet and the voice implored him not to hang up. He started to say that he had no intention of hanging up, and then realized by the silence that if he did speak no one would hear him. It was a long, long discouraging silence that extended itself until he wondered why he continued to hold the telephone to his ear. At last a familiar voice said his name and he was enveloped in affectionate inquiries and elaborate arrangements. Mme Straus's voice came through strong and clear and he had no trouble understanding her. They were to meet her on Saturday evening at eight thirty sharp, she said, on the corner of the rue de Berry and the avenue des Champs Elysées. They would dine at the restaurant of her goddaughter and afterward go to the theater to see Mme Marguerite Mailly.

"At the Comédie Française?" he asked. They had not yet crossed that off their list.

Mme Mailly had had a disagreement with the Comédie Française, Mme Straus said, and had left it to act in a modern comedy. The play had had an enormous success, and tickets

were impossible to obtain, but knowing that they were arriving in Paris this week, she had written to her friend, and
three places for the Saturday performance would be waiting at
the box office.

"I don't know that we should do that," Barbara said doubtfully, when he told her about the arrangements. "It sounds so
expensive, and she may not be able to afford it."

"I don't know that I'm up to dissuading her," he said.
"Tactfully, I mean, over the telephone, and in French. Besides,
it is no longer 6h½, and if I called her back I probably wouldn't
reach her. Do *you* want to call her?"

"No, I don't"

"Maybe she'll let us pay for the dinner," he said.

At breakfast the next morning, Eugène surprised them by saying, as he passed his coffee cup across the tray to Barbara: "I
am having a little dinner party this evening. You are free? . . .
Good. I have asked Edouard Doria. He is Alix's favorite
cousin. I think you will like him."

From the way he spoke, they realized that he was giving the
dinner party for them. But why? Had Alix asked him to? And
were the Berliners invited?

Meeting them in the hall, a few minutes later, Harold
stepped aside to let them pass. They greeted him cheerfully,
and when he inquired about their situation, they assured him
that progress was being made, in the only way that it could
be made; their story was being heard, their reasons considered. What they wanted was in no way unreasonable, and so
in time some action, positive or negative, surely must result
from their efforts. Meanwhile, there were several embassies
they did not get to yesterday and that they planned to go to
today. . . .

Harold stood outside the dining-room door and listened
while Eugène consulted with Françoise about the linen, the
china, the menu. They reached an agreement on the fish and
the vegetable. There would be oysters, then soup. He left the
soup to her discretion. For dessert there would be an ice,
which he would pick up himself on the way home.

The Americans left the apartment in the middle of the
morning, and crossed over to the Left Bank. They walked

along the river as far as Notre Dame, and had lunch under an awning, in the rain. In the window of a shop on the Quai de la Mégisserie they saw a big glass bird cage, but how to get it home was the question. Also, it was expensive, and the little financial diary kept pointing out that, even though they had no hotel bill to pay, they were spending quite a lot of money on taxis, flowers, books, movies, and food.

As they came through the Place Redouté, they picked up the Kodak films they had left to be developed. They were as surprised by what came out as if they had had no hand in it. Some of the pictures were taken on shipboard, and some in Pontorson and Mont-Saint-Michel. But there was nothing after that until the one of Beaumesnil, with the old trees rising twice as high as the roofs, and a cloud castle in the sky above the real one. The best snapshot of all was a family picture, taken on the lawn, their last morning at the château. This picture was mysterious in that, though the focus was sharp enough, there was so much that you couldn't see. Alix's shadow fell across Mme Bonenfant's face. There was only her beautiful white hair, and her hand stretched out to steady herself against the fall all old people live in dread of. Alix's hair blacked out the lower part of Harold's face, and what you could see of him looked more like his brother. Barbara had taken the picture and so she wasn't in it at all. A shadow from a branch overhead fell across the upper part of Mme Cestre's face, leaving only her smile in bright sunlight and the rest in doubt. The two small children they had hardly set eyes on were nevertheless in the picture, and Mme Viénot was wearing the green silk dress with the New Look. Beside her was a broad expanse of white that could have been a castle wall but was actually Eugène's shirt, with his massive face above it looking strangely like Ludwig van Beethoven's. And Sabine, on the extreme right, standing in a diagonal shaft of light that didn't come from the sun but from an inadvertent exposure as the film was being taken from the camera.

"I don't see how we could not have taken more than one roll in all this time," Barbara said.

"We were too busy looking."

"We have no picture of Nils Jensen. Or of Mme Straus-Muguet."

"With or without a picture, I will never forget either of them."

"That's not the point. You think you remember and you don't."

When they got home, she made him go straight out on the balcony where, even though it was late in the afternoon and the light was poor, she took a picture of him in his seersucker suit and scuffed white shoes, peering down into the rue Malène, and he took one of her in her favorite dress of black and lavender-blue, with the buildings on the far side of the Place Redouté showing in the distance and in the foreground a sharply receding perspective of iron railing and rolled-up awnings.

There were no sounds from behind the closed door of Mme Cestre's room. Nothing but a kind of anxious silence. Were they gone? Had somebody at last reached for a rubber stamp?

The Germans were not at the dinner party, and Eugène did not mention them all evening. The dinner party was not a success. The food was very good and so was the wine, and Alix's cousin was young and likable, but when he spoke to the Americans in English, Eugène fidgeted. Barbara never came out from behind the shy, well-bred young woman whom nobody could ever have any reason to say anything unkind to, and Harold did not want to repeat the mistake they had made with Jean-Claude Lahovary, and so he did not proceed as if this was the one moment he and Edouard Doria would ever have for knowing each other (though as a matter of fact it was). He did not ask personal questions; he tried to speak grammatically when he spoke French; he waited to see what course the evening would take. In short, he was not himself. Edouard Doria sat smiling pleasantly and replied to the remarks that were addressed to him. Eugène did not explain to his three guests why he had thought they would like one another, and neither did he take the conversation into his own hands and make tears of amusement run down their cheeks with the outrageous things he said. As the evening wore on, the conversation was more and more in French, between the two Frenchmen.

*

In the morning, the study door was open and the room itself neat and empty. All through breakfast the Americans breathed the agreeable air of Eugène's absence from the apartment, and they kept assuring each other that he would not possibly return that night; it was a long hard journey even one way.

When Harold took the mail from Mme Emile there were several letters for M. Soulès de Boisgaillard, which he put on the table in the front hall, by the study door, and one for M. et Mme Harold Rhodes. It was from Alix, and when Barbara drew it out of the envelope, they saw that she had put a four leaf clover in it.

"'. . . I was so sad not to say good-by to you at the station on Sunday. But I love writing to you now. It was delightful to know you both, and I wish you to go on in life loving more and more, being happier and happier, and making all those you meet feel happy themselves, as you did here—'"

"Oh God!" Harold exclaimed.

Barbara stopped reading and looked at him.

"Read on," he said.

"'We miss you a lot. Do write and give some of your impressions of Paris or Italy. And I hope we shall see one another very often in September. I should like to be in Paris with you and Eugène now. I hope you have at least nice breakfasts. I suppose you are a little too warm—but I will know all that on Friday as Mummy and I will join Eugène in the train for Tours. Good-by, dear you two, and my most friendly thoughts. Alix.'"

He put the four-leaf clover in his financial diary, and then said: "It's a nice letter, isn't it? So affectionate. It makes me feel better about our staying here. At least her part wasn't something we dreamed."

"If she were here, it would be entirely different," Barbara said.

"Do you think he will tell her how he has acted?"

"No, do you? . . . On the other hand, she may not need to be told. That may be the reason she waited so long to speak about our staying here."

"But the letter doesn't read as if she had any idea."

"I don't think she has."

They went and stood in the kitchen door, talking to

Françoise, who was delighted with the nylon stockings that Barbara presented to her. Holding up a wine bottle, she showed them how much less than a full liter of milk (at twenty-four times the price of milk before the war) they had allowed her for the little one, who fortunately was now in the country, where milk was plentiful. They told her about their life in America, and she told them about her childhood in a village in the Dordogne. They asked if the Germans had gone, and she said no. She had given them their dinner the night before, in their room.

"What a queer household we are!" she exclaimed, rolling her eyes in the direction of Mme Cestre's room. "Nobody speaks anybody else's language and none of us belong here." But they noticed that she was pleasant and kind to the Germans, and apparently it did not occur to them that she might have any reason to hate them. They did not hate anyone.

The door to Mme Cestre's room was open, and the sounds that came from it this morning were cheerful; those mice, too, were enjoying the fact that the cat was away. The Americans left their door open also, and were aware of jokes and giggling down the hall.

"When we need butter, speak to Mme Emile," Eugène had said, and so Harold went downstairs and found her having a cup of coffee at her big round table. She rose and shook hands with him and he took out his wallet and explained what he had come for. While she was in the next room he looked at the copy of *France Soir* spread out on the dining table. The police had at last tracked down the gangster Pierrot-le-Fou. He had been surprised in the bed of his mistress, Catherine. The dim photograph showed a young man with a beard. Reading on, Harold was reminded of the fire in Pontorson. No doubt the preparations had been just as extensive and thorough, and it was a mere detail that the gangster had got away. Mme Emile returned with a pound of black-market butter, which she wrapped in the very page he had been reading, and since her conscience seemed perfectly clear, his did not bother him, though he supposed they could both have been put in jail for this transaction.

Shortly afterward, he went off to pick up their passports and

the military permit to enter Austria, and when he returned at
two o'clock, he found Barbara half frantic over a telephone call
from Mme Straus-Muguet. "I didn't want to answer," she
said, "but I was afraid it might be you. I thought you might be
trying to reach me, for some reason. I tried to persuade her to
call back, but she said she was going out, and she *made* me
take the message!"

What Barbara thought Mme Straus had said was that they
were to meet her on the steps of the Madeleine at five.

They left the apartment at four, and took a taxi to the bank,
where they picked up their mail from home. Then they wandered through the neighborhood, going in and out of shops,
and at a quarter of five they took up their stand at the top of
the flight of stone steps that led up to the great open door of
the church. For the next twenty minutes they looked expectantly at everybody who went in or out and at every figure that
might turn out to be Mme Straus-Muguet approaching
through the bicycle traffic. The more they looked for her, the
less certain they were of what she looked like. Suddenly Barbara let out a cry; her umbrella was no longer on her arm. She
distinctly remembered starting out with it, from the apartment, and she was fairly certain she had felt the weight of the
umbrella on her arm as she stepped out of the taxi. She could
not remember for sure but she thought she had laid it down in
the china shop, in order to examine a piece of porcelain.

They left the steps of the Madeleine, crossed through the
traffic to the shop, and went in. The clerk Barbara spoke to
was not the one Harold had wanted her to ask. No umbrella
had been found; also, the clerk was not interested in lost umbrellas. As they left the shop, he said: "Don't worry about it.
You can buy another umbrella."

"Not like this one," she said. The umbrella was for traveling, folded compactly into a third the usual length, and
could be tucked away in a suitcase. "If only we'd gone to the
Rodin Museum this afternoon, as we were intending to," she
said. "I'd never have lost it there."

He went back to the Madeleine and waited another quarter
of an hour while she walked the length of the rue Royale,
looking mournfully in shop windows and trying to remember

a place, a moment, when she had put her umbrella down, meaning to pick it up right away. . . .

"I'm sure I left it in the china shop," she said, when she rejoined him.

"It's probably in that little room at the back, hidden away, this very minute. . . ."

He led her through the bicycle traffic to a table on the sidewalk in front of Larue's and there, keeping one eye on the steps of the church, they had a Tom Collins. It was possible, they agreed, that Barbara had misunderstood and that Mme Straus might have been waiting (poor old thing!) on the steps of some other public monument. Or it could have been another day that they were supposed to meet her.

"But if it turns out that I did get it right and that she's stood us up, then let's not bother any more with her," Barbara said. "We have so little time in Paris, and there is so much that we want to do and see, and I have a feeling that she will engulf us."

"We've already said we'd have dinner with her and go to the theater, tomorrow night."

"If she knows so many people, why does she bother with two Americans? She may be making a play for us because we're foreigners and don't know any better."

"To what end?"

"Oh, I don't know!" Barbara exclaimed. "I don't like it here! Should we go?"

She was always depressed and irritated with herself when she lost something—as if the lost object had abandoned her deliberately, for a very good reason.

The waiter brought the check, and while they were waiting for change, Harold said: "She may call this evening."

They crossed the street one last time, to make sure that their eyes hadn't played tricks on them. There were several middle-aged and elderly women waiting on the steps of the Madeleine, any one of whom could have explained the true meaning of resignation, but Mme Straus-Muguet was not among them.

That night, when they walked into the apartment at about a quarter of eleven, after dinner and another movie and a very pleasant walk home, the first thing they saw was that the mail on the hall table was gone. The study door was closed.

"Oh *why* couldn't he have stayed!" Barbara whispered, behind the closed door of their room. "It was so nice here without him. We were all so happy."

Chapter 16

"ALIX sent you her love," Eugène said when he joined them at breakfast.

He did not explain why he had not stayed in the country, or describe the wedding. They were all three more silent than usual. The armchair, creaking and creaking, carried the whole burden of conversation. It had come down to Eugène from his great-great-grandfather. In a formal age that admired orators, military strategists, devout politicians, and worldly ecclesiastics, Jean-Marie Philippe Raucourt, fourth Count de Boisgaillard, had been merely a sensible, taciturn, unambitious man. He lived in a dangerous time, but, having bought his way into the King's army, he quickly bought his way out again and put up with the King's displeasure. He avoided houses where people were dying of smallpox and let no doctor into his own. He made a politic marriage and was impatient with those people who prided themselves on their understanding of the passions. He had children both in and out of wedlock, escaped the guillotine, noticed that there were ways of flattering the First Consul, and died at the age of fifty-two, in secure possession of his estates. His son, Eugène's great-grandfather, was a Peer and Marshal of France under the Restoration. Eugène's grandfather was an aesthete, and his taste was the taste of his time. He collected grandiose allegorical paintings and houses to hang them in, married late in life, and corresponded with Liszt and Clara Schumann. His oldest son, Eugène's uncle, had a taste for litigation. The once valuable family estates were now heavily mortgaged and no good to anyone, and the house at Mamers stood empty. But scattered over the whole of France were the possessions of the fourth Count de Boisgaillard—beds and tables and armchairs (including this one), brocades, paintings, diaries, letters, books, firearms—and through these objects he continued, though so long dead, to exert an influence in the direction of order, restraint, the middle ground, the golden mean. But even he had to give way and became merely a name, a genealogical link, one of thousands, when the telephone started ringing. Seeing Eugène in his study, with his hat on the back of his head and the call going on and on in spite of his impatience and the air of distraction that increased each time he glanced over his shoulder at the clock, one would have said that there was no end to it; that it was a species of blackmail. The telephone seemed to know when he left the apartment. Once he was out the front door, it never rang again all day.

At nine o'clock, Mme Emile brought up the morning's mail, and Eugène, leafing through it, took out a letter and handed it to Harold, who ripped the envelope open and read the letter standing in the hall:

Petite Barbara Chérie
Petit Harold Chéri

I am a shabby friend for failing to keep my word yesterday evening, and not coming to the rendezvous! But a violent storm prevented me, and no taxi in the rain. I was obliged to mingle my tears with those of the sky. Forgive me, then, petits amis chéris. . . . Yes, I say "chéris," for a long long chain of tenderness will unite me to you always! It is with a mother's heart that I love you both! My white hairs didn't frighten you when we met at "Beaumesnil," and at once I felt that a very sincere sympathy was about to be established between us. This has happened by the grace of God, for your dear presence has given back to me my twentieth year and the sweetness of my youth, during which I was so happy! . . . but after! . . . so unhappy! May these lines bring you the assurance of my great and warm tenderness, mes enfants chéris. Je vous embrasse tous deux. Votre vieille amie qui vous aime tant—

Straus-Muguet

This evening on the stroke of 8h½ if possible.

He put the letter in the envelope and the envelope in his pocket, and said: "Did you ever hear of a restaurant called L'Etoile du Nord?"

"Yes," Eugène said.

"What is it like?"

"It's a rather night-clubby place. Why do you ask?"

"We're having dinner there this evening, with Mme Straus-Muguet."

Eugène let out a low whistle of surprise.

"Is it expensive?"

"Very."

"Then perhaps we shouldn't go," Harold said.

"If she couldn't afford it, she wouldn't have invited you," Eugène said. "I have been making inquiries about her, and it seems that the people she says she knows definitely do not know her."

Harold hesitated, and then said: "But why? Why should she pretend that she knows people she doesn't know?"

Eugène shrugged.

"Is she a social climber?" Harold asked.

"It is more a matter of psychology."

"What do you mean?"

"Elle est un peu maniaque," Eugène said.

He went into the study to read his mail, and Harold was left with an uncomfortable choice: he could believe someone he did not like but who had probably no reason to lie, or someone he liked very much, whose behavior in the present instance . . . He took her letter out and read it again carefully. Mme Straus's hair was not white but mouse-colored, and though the sky had been gray yesterday afternoon, it was no grayer than usual, and not a drop of rain had fallen on the steps of the Madeleine.

When he and Barbara went out to do some errands, they saw that a lot more of the rolling metal shutters that were always pulled down over the store fronts at night had not been raised this morning, and in each case there was a note tacked up on the door frame or the door of the shop explaining that it would be closed for the "vacances." Every day for the last three days it had been like this. Paris seemed to be withdrawing piecemeal from the world. At first it didn't matter, except that it made the streets look shabby. But then suddenly it did matter. There were certain shops they had come to know and to enjoy using. And they could not leave Harold's flannel trousers at the cleaners, though it was open this morning, because it would be closed by Monday. The fruit and vegetable store where they had gone every day, for a melon or lettuce or tomatoes, closed without warning. Half the shops in the neighborhood were closed, and they had to wander far afield to get what they needed.

Shortly after they got home, there was a knock on their door, and when Barbara opened it, there stood the three

Berliners in a row. They had come to say good-by. Herr
Rothenberg and the one whose ears stuck out were going
home. The one with the pink glasses had managed to get himself sent to a conference in Switzerland. There was something
chilling in their manner that had not been there before; now
that they were on the point of returning to Germany, they
seemed to have become much more German. When they had
finished thanking the Americans for their kindness, they took
advantage of this opportunity to register with these two citizens of one of the countries that were now occupying the Fa-
therland their annoyance at being made a political football
between the United States and the U.S.S.R.

And the war? Harold asked silently as they shook hands.
And the Jews?

And then he was ashamed of himself, because what did he
really know about them or what the last ten years had been like
for them? Herr Doerffer and Herr Rothenberg and Herr
Darmstadt were in all probability the merest shadow of true
Prussian aggressiveness, and its reflection in them was undoubtedly something they were not aware of and couldn't
help, any more than he could help disliking them for being
German. And feeling as he did, it would have been better—
more honest—if he had not acted as if his feelings toward
them were wholly kind. They carried away a false impression of
what Americans were like, and he was left with a feeling of his
own falseness.

As they stepped out of the taxi at eight thirty Saturday
evening, they saw a frail ardent figure in a tailored suit, waiting
on a street corner with an air of intense conspiratorial expectancy. She's missed her calling, Harold thought as he was
paying the driver; we should be spies meeting in Lisbon, and
recognizing each other by the seersucker suit and the little
heart encrusted with diamonds.

Mme Straus embraced Barbara and then Harold, and taking
each of them by the arm, she guided them anxiously through
traffic and up a narrow street. With little asides, endearments,
irrelevancies, smiling and squeezing their hands, she caught
them up in her own excitement. The restaurant was air-
conditioned, the décor was nautical; the whole look of the

place was familiar but not French; it belonged in New York, in the West Fifties.

They were shown to a table and the waiter offered a huge menu, which Mme Straus waved away. From her purse she extracted a scrap of paper on which she had written the dinner that—with their approval—she would order for them: a consommé, broiled chicken, dessert and coffee. They agreed that before the theater one doesn't want to stuff.

When the matter of the wine had been disposed of, she made them change seats so that Barbara was sitting beside her ("close to me") and Harold was across the table ("where I can see you"). She demanded that they tell her everything they had seen and done in Paris, all that had happened at the château after her departure.

Barbara described—but cautiously—their pleasure in staying in Mme Cestre's apartment, and added that they had grown fond of Mme de Boisgaillard.

"An angel!" Mme Straus-Muguet agreed. "And Monsieur also. But I do not care for *her*. She is not *gentille*. . . ." They understood that she meant Mme Viénot.

"Do you know anything about M. Viénot?" Harold asked. "Is he dead? Why is his name never mentioned?"

Mme Straus did not know for sure, but she thought it was— She tapped her forehead with her forefinger.

"Maniaque?" Harold asked.

She nodded, and complimented them both on the great strides they had made in speaking and understanding French.

Under her close questioning, he began to tell her, hesitantly at first and then detail by detail, the curious situation they had let themselves in for by accepting the invitation to stay in Mme Cestre's apartment. No one could have been more sane in her comments than Mme Straus, or more sympathetic and understanding, as he described Eugène's moods and how they themselves were of two minds about everything. A few words and it was all clear to her. She had found herself, at some time or another, in just such a dilemma, and there was, in her opinion, nothing more trying, or more difficult to feel one's way through. But what a pity that things should have turned out for them in this fashion, when it needn't have been like that at all!

Having found someone who understood their ambiguous situation, and did not blame them for getting into it, they found that it could now be dismissed, and it took its place, for the first time, in the general scheme of things; they could see that it was not after all very serious. Mme Straus was so patient and encouraging that they both spoke better than they ever had before, and she was so eager to hear all they had to tell her and so delighted with their remarks about Paris that she made them feel like children on a spree with an indulgent aunt who was ready to grant every wish that might occur to them, and whose only pleasure while she was with them was in making life happy and full of surprises. This after living under the same roof with kindness that was not kind, consideration that had no reason or explanation, a friend who behaved like an enemy or vice versa—it would be hard to say which. And she herself spoke so distinctly, in a vocabulary that offered no difficulty and that at moments made it seem as if they were all three speaking English.

Mme Straus was dissatisfied with the consommé and sent it back to the kitchen. The rest of the dinner was excellent and so was the wine. As Harold sat watching her, utterly charmed by her conversation and by her, he thought: She's a child and she isn't a child. She knows things a child doesn't know, and yet every day is Bastille Day, and at seventy she is still saying *Ah!* as the fountains rise higher and higher and skyrockets explode.

While they were waiting for their dessert, Mme Straus's goddaughter came over to the table, with her husband. They were introduced to Harold and Barbara, and shook hands and spoke a few words in English. The man shook hands again and left. Mme Straus's goddaughter was in her late thirties, and looked as if she must at some time have worked in a beauty parlor. Harold found himself wondering on what basis godparents are chosen in France. It also struck him that there was something patronizing—or at least distant—in the way she spoke to Mme Straus. Though Mme Straus appeared to rejoice in seeing her goddaughter again, was full of praise for the food, for the service, and delighted that the restaurant was so crowded with patrons, the blonde woman had, actually, nothing to say to her.

When they had finished their coffee, Mme Straus summoned

the waiter, was horrified at the sight of Harold's billfold, and insisted on paying the sizable check. She hurried them out of the restaurant and into a taxi, and they arrived, by a series of narrow, confusing back streets, at the theater, which was in an alley. Mme Straus inquired at the box office for their tickets. There was a wait of some duration and just as Harold was beginning to grow alarmed for her the tickets were found. They went in and took their seats, far back under the balcony of a small shabby theater, with twelve or fifteen rows of empty seats between them and the stage.

Mme Straus took off her coat and her fur, and gave them to Barbara to hold for her. Then she gave Harold a small pasteboard box tied with yellow string and Barbara her umbrella, and sat back ready to enjoy the play. With this performance, she explained, the theater was closing for the month of August, so that the company could present the same play in Deauville. Pointing to the package in Harold's lap, she said that she had bought some beautiful peaches to present to her friend when they went backstage; Mme Mailly was passionately fond of fruit. He held the carton carefully. Peaches were expensive in France that summer.

Only a few of the empty seats had been claimed by the time the house lights dimmed and went out. Mme Straus leaned toward Barbara in the dark and whispered: "When you are presented to Mme Mailly, remember to ask for her autograph."

The curtain rose upon a flimsy comedy of backstage bickering and intrigue. The star, a Junoesque and very handsome woman, entered to applause, halfway through the first scene. She played herself—Mme Marguerite Mailly, who in the play as in life had been induced to leave the Comédie Française in order to act in something outside the classic repertory. The playwright had also written a part for himself into the play— the actress's husband, from whom she was estranged. Their domestic difficulties were too complicated and epigrammatic for Harold to follow, and the seats were very hard, but in the third act Mme Mailly was given a chance to deliver—on an off- stage stage—one of the great passionate soliloquies of Racine. An actor held the greenroom curtain back, and the entire cast of the play listened devoutly. So did the audience. The voice offstage was evidence enough of the pleasure the Americans had been deprived of when Mme Mailly decided to forsake the classics. It was magnificent—full of color, variety, and pathos. The single long speech rose up out of its mediocre setting as a tidal wave might emerge from a duck pond, flooding the flat landscape, sweeping pigsties, chicken coops, barns, houses, trees, and people to destruction.

The play never recovered from this offstage effect, but the actress's son was allowed to marry the ingénue and there was a reconciliation between the playwright and Mme Mailly, who, Harold realized as she advanced to the apron and took a series of solo curtain calls, was simply too large for the stage she acted on. The effect was like a puppet show when you have unconsciously adjusted your sense of scale to conform with small mechanical actors and at the end a giant head emerges from the wings, the head of the human manipulator, producing a momentary surprise.

The lights went on. Mme Straus, delighted with the comedy, gathered up her fur, her umbrella, her coat, and the present of fruit. She spoke to an usher, who pointed out the little door through which they must go to find themselves backstage. They went to it, and then through a corridor and up a flight of stairs to a hallway with four or five doors opening off it and one very bright light bulb dangling by its cord from the ceiling. Mme Straus whispered to Harold: "Don't forget to tell her you admire her poetry. You can tell her in English. She speaks your language beautifully."

Four people had followed them up the stairs. Mme Straus knocked on the door of the star's dressing room, and the remarkable voice answered peremptorily: "Don't come in!"

Mme Straus turned to Harold and Barbara and smiled, as if this were exactly the effect she had intended to produce.

More people, friends of the cast, came up the stairway. The little hall grew crowded and hot. The playwright came out, wearing a silk dressing gown, his face still covered with grease paint, and was surrounded and congratulated on his double accomplishment. Mme Straus knocked once more, timidly, and this time the voice said: "Who is it?"

"It's me," Mme Straus said.

"Who?" the voice demanded, in a tone of mounting irritation.

"It's your friend, chérie."

"Who?"

"Straus-Muguet."

"Will you please wait. . . ." The voice this time was shocking.

Harold looked at Mme Straus, who was no longer confident and happy, and then at Barbara, who avoided his glance. All he wanted was to push past the crowd and sneak down the stairs while there was still time. But Mme Straus-Muguet waited and they had no choice but to wait with her until the door opened and the actress, large as Gulliver, bore down upon them. She nodded coldly to Mme Straus and looked around for other friends who had come backstage to congratulate her. There were none. Barbara and Harold were presented to her, and she acknowledged the introduction with enough politeness for Barbara to feel that she could offer her program and Mme Straus's fountain pen. The actress signed her name with a flourish, under her silhouette on the first page. When Harold told her that they had read her poems, she smiled for the first time, quite cordially.

Mme Straus tore the string off the pasteboard carton and presented it open to her friend, so that Mme Mailly could see what it contained.

"No, thank you," Mme Mailly said. And when Mme Straus like a blind suppliant continued to show her peaches, the actress said impatiently: "I do not care for any fruit." Her manner was that of a person cornered by some nuisance of an old woman with whom she had had, in the past and through no fault of her own, a slight acquaintance, under circumstances that in no way justified this intrusion and imposition on her good nature. All this Harold could have understood and perhaps accepted, since it took place in France, if it hadn't been for one thing: in his raincoat pocket at that moment were two volumes of sonnets, and on the flyleaf of one of them the actress had written: "To my dear friend, Mme Straus-Muguet, whose sublime character and patient fortitude, as we walked side by side in the kingdom of Death, I shall never cease to remember and be grateful for. . . ."

In the end, Mme Mailly was prevailed upon to hold the pasteboard box, though nothing could induce her to realize that it was a present. The stairs were spiral and treacherous, requiring all their attention as they made their way down them cautiously. The passageway at the foot of the stairs was now pitch dark. By the time they found an outer door and emerged into the summer night, Mme Straus had had time to rally her forces. She took Barbara's arm and the three of them walked to the corner and up the avenue de Wagram, in search of a taxi. No one mentioned the incident backstage. Instead, they spoke of how clever and amusing the play had been. As they parted at the taxi stand, Harold gave Mme Straus the two books that were in his coat pocket, and she said: "I'm glad you remembered to ask for her autograph. You must preserve it carefully."

On Sunday morning, Eugène showed his membership card at the gate in the stockade around the swimming pool in the Bois de Boulogne. Turning to Harold, he asked for their passports.

"You have to have a passport to go swimming?" Harold asked in amazement.

"I cannot get you into the Club without them," Eugène said patiently.

"I don't have them. I'm so sorry, but it never occurred to me to bring them. In America . . ."

With the same persistence that he had employed when he was trying to arrange for food and lodging for the Berliners, Eugène now applied himself to persuading the woman attendant that it was all right to let his American guests past the gate. The attendant believed that rules are not made to be broken, and the rule of the Racing Club was that no foreigner was to be admitted without proof of his foreignness. There are dozens of ways of saying no in French and she went through the list with visible satisfaction. Eugène, discouraged, turned to Harold and said: "It appears that we will have to drive home and get your passports."

"But the gasoline— Couldn't we just wait here while you go in and have a swim?" Harold asked, and then he started to apologize all over again for causing so much trouble.

"I will try one last time," Eugène said, and, leaving them outside the gate, he went in and was gone for a quarter of an hour. When he came back he brought with him an official of

the Club, who told the attendant that it was all right to admit
M. de Boisgaillard's guests.

Harold and Barbara followed Eugène into a pavilion where
the dressing rooms were. There they separated, to meet again
outside by the pools, in their bathing suits. Though he had
seen French bathing slips at Dinard, Harold was astonished all
over again. They concealed far less than a fig leaf would have,
and the only possible conclusion you could draw was that in
France it is all right to have sexual organs; people are supposed
to have them. Even so, the result was not what one might have
expected. The men and women around him, standing or lying
on canvas mats and big towels or swimming in the two pools,
were not lightened and made happier by their nakedness, the
way people are when they walk around their bedroom without
any clothes on, or the way children or lovers are. Standing by
herself at the shallow end of one of the pools was a woman
with a body like a statue by Praxiteles, but the two young men
who were standing near her looked straight past her, discontented with everything but what they themselves exposed. It
was very dreamlike.

Having argued energetically for half an hour to get Harold
and Barbara into the Club, Eugène stretched out in a reclining
chair, closed his eyes, and ignored them. Sitting on the edge of
the pool with his feet in the water, Harold thought: So this is
where he comes every afternoon. . . . What does he come
here for? The weather was not really hot. And what about his
job? And what about Alix? Did she know that this was how he
spent his free hours?

From time to time, Eugène swam, or Harold and Barbara
dived into the deeper pool and swam. But though they were
sometimes in the water at the same time, Eugène didn't swim
with them or even exchange remarks with them. Nothing in
the world, it seemed—no power of earth, air, or water—could
make up to him for the fact that he had had to go to the Allégrets' dressy party in a tweed jacket.

The sun came and went, behind a thin veil of clouds. Harold
was not quite warm. He offered Barbara his towel and she
wouldn't take it, so he sat with it around his shoulders and
looked at the people around him and thought that this was a

place that, left to himself, he would never have succeeded in imagining, and that the world must be full of such surprises.

Barbara went into the pool once more, and this time Harold stayed behind. Instinct had told him that something was trying to break through Eugène's studied indifference. Instinct was wrong, apparently. Eugène's eyes stayed closed, in spite of all there was to stare at, and he said nothing. Barbara came back from the pool, and Harold saw that she was cold and suggested that she go in and dress. "In a minute," she said. He tried to make her take his bath towel and again she refused. He looked at Eugène and thought: *He's waiting for someone or something. . . .*

Suddenly the eyelids opened. Eugène looked around him mildly and asked: "How well do you know George Ireland?"

"I know his parents very well, George hardly at all," Harold said. "Why?"

"I thought you might be friends."

"There is a considerable difference in our ages."

"Oh?" Eugène said. And then: "Have you had enough swimming, or would you like to stay a little longer? I do not think the sun is coming out any more."

"It's up to you," Harold said. "If you want to stay, we'll go in and get dressed and wait for you."

"I am quite ready," Eugène said.

They drove home to the apartment, and Barbara made lunch for them. They ate sitting around the teacart in the bedroom. Eugène congratulated Barbara on her mastery of the French omelet, and she flushed with pleasure. "It's the stove," she said. "They don't have stoves like that in America."

The swimming and the food made them drowsy and relaxed. The silences were no longer uncomfortable. Without any animation in his voice, almost as if he were talking about people they didn't know, Eugène began to talk about Beaumesnil and how important it was that the château remain in the family, at whatever cost. When his daughter came of age and was ready to be introduced to society, the property at Brenodville must be there, a visible part of her background. Seeing it now, he said, they could have no idea of what it was like before the war. He himself had not seen it then, but he had seen other houses like it, and knew, from stories Alix had told him, what it used to be like in her childhood.

The Americans had the feeling, as they excused themselves to dress and keep an appointment with Mme Straus, that Eugène was reluctant to let them go, and would have spent the rest of the day in their company. The last two days he had been quite easy with them, most of the time, but they couldn't stop thinking that they shouldn't be here in the apartment at all, feeling the way they did about him. Against their better judgment, they had come here when they knew that they ought to have gone to a hotel. Tempted by the convenience and the space, and by the game of pretending that they were living in Paris, not just tourists, they had stayed on—paying a certain price, naturally. During those times when they were with Eugène, they avoided meeting his eyes, or when they did look directly at him, it was with a carefully prepared caution that demonstrated, alas, how easily he could have got through to them if he had only tried.

At five o'clock that afternoon, while Barbara waited in a taxi, Harold went into the convent in Auteuil and explained to the nun who sat in the concierge's glass cage that Mme Straus-Muguet was expecting them. He assumed that men were not permitted any farther, and that they would all three go out for tea. The nun got up from her desk and led him down a corridor and into a large room with crimson plush draperies, a black and white marble floor, too many mirrors, and very ugly furniture. There she left him. He stood in the middle of the room and looked all around without finding a single object that suggested Mme Straus's taste or personality. Surprised, he sat down on a little gilt ballroom chair and waited for her to appear. He felt relieved in one respect; the room was so large that in all probability they didn't need to worry for fear Mme Straus couldn't afford to entertain them at an expensive restaurant.

It was at least five minutes before she appeared. She greeted him warmly and, as he started to sit down again, explained that they were going to take tea upstairs in her chamber; this room was the public reception room of the convent. He picked up his hat, went outside, paid the taxi driver, and brought Barbara back in with him. The rest of the building turned out to be bare, underfurnished, and institutional. Mme Straus led them up so many flights of stairs that she had to stop once or twice, gasping, to regain her breath. Harold stopped worrying about her financial condition and began to worry about her heart. It *couldn't* be good for a woman of her age to climb so much every day.

"I am very near to heaven," she said with a wan smile, as they arrived on the top floor of the building. They went down a long corridor to her room, which was barely large enough to accommodate a bed, a desk, a small round table and, crowded in together, three small straight chairs. The window overlooked the convent garden, and opening off the room there was a cabinet de toilette, the walls of which were covered with photographs. Mme Straus opened the door of her clothes closet and brought out a box of pastries. Then she went into the cabinet de toilette and came out with goblets and a bottle of champagne. There being no ice buckets in the convent, she had tried to chill the champagne by setting it in a washbasin of cold water.

They drank to each other, and then Mme Straus, lifting her glass, said: "To your travels!" And then nobody said anything.

Barbara asked the name of a crisp sweet pastry.

"Palmiers," Mme Straus said—from their palm-leafed shape —and apologized because there were no more of them. She opened a drawer of the desk and brought out two presents wrapped in tissue paper. But before she allowed them to open their gifts, she made Barbara read aloud the note that accompanied them: "Mes amis chéris, before we part I want you to have a souvenir of France and of a new friend, but one who has loved you from the beginning. Jolie Barbara, in wearing these clips give a thought to the one who offers them. Harold, smoke a cigarette each day so that the smoke will come here to rejoin me."

The Americans were embarrassed by the note and by the fact that they had not thought to bring Mme Straus a present, but she sat back with the innocent complacency of an author who has enjoyed the sound of his own words, and did not appear to find anything lacking to the occasion.

Barbara put the mother-of-pearl clips on her dress, which

wasn't the kind of dress you wear clips with, and so they looked large and conspicuous. Harold emptied a pack of cigarettes into the leather case that was Mme Straus's gift to him. He never carried a cigarette case, and this one was bulky besides. He hoped his face looked sufficiently pleased.

He and Barbara stood in the door of the cabinet de toilette while Mme Straus showed them the framed photographs on the walls of that tiny room—her dead son, full-faced and smiling; and again with his wife and children; various nieces and goddaughters, including the one they had met the night before; and another, very pretty girl who was a member of the corps de ballet at the Opéra. The last photograph that Mme Straus pointed out was of her daughter, who did not look in the least like her. The old woman said, with her face suddenly grave: "A great egoist! Her heart is closed to all tenderness for her mother. She refuses to see me, and replies to my communications through her lawyer."

After a rather painful silence, Harold asked: "Was your son like you?"

"But exactly!" she exclaimed. "We were alike in every respect. His death was a blow from which I have never recovered."

Harold turned and looked at the picture of him. So pleasure-loving, so affectionate, so full of jokes and surprises that were all buried with him.

When they sat down again, she showed them a small oval photograph of herself at the age of three, in a party dress, kneeling, and with her elbows on the back of a round brocade chair. A sober, proud child, with her bangs frizzed, she was looking straight at the click of the shutter. Mme Straus explained that in her infancy she had been called "Minou." Barbara expressed such pleasure in the faded photograph that Mme Straus took it to her desk, wrote "Minou à trois ans" across the bottom, and presented it to her. Then she asked Harold to bring out from under the bed the pile of books he would find there. He got down on his hands and knees, reached under, and began fishing them out: Mme Mailly's verses, the memoirs of General Weygand in two big volumes handsomely bound, and, last of all, the plays of Edmond Rostand, volume after volume. The two books of verse were passed from hand to hand and admired, as if Harold and Barbara had never seen them before. The General's memoirs had an inscription on the flyleaf and looked highly valued but unread. Mme Straus explained that she had enjoyed Rostand's friendship during a prolonged stay in the South of France. Each volume was inscribed to the playwright's charming companion, Mme Straus-Muguet; and Mme Straus described to Harold and Barbara the moonlit garden in which the books were presented to her, on a beautiful spring night shortly before the First World War. "These are my treasures," she said, "which I have no place to keep but under the bed."

When the books were returned to their place of safekeeping, they went downstairs and walked in the garden. It was a gray day, and from the rear the convent looked dreary and like a nursing home. The only other person in the garden was a young woman who was sitting on a bench reading a newspaper. As they approached, Mme Straus explained that it was one of her dearest friends, a charming Swedish girl. They were presented to her, and the Swedish girl acknowledged the introduction blankly and went on reading her newspaper.

They sat down on a bench in the far end of the garden, but after a minute or two the chill in the evening air made them get up and walk again. Barbara suggested that Mme Straus come out and have dinner with them. There was a little restaurant nearby, Mme Straus said, very plain and simple, where she often went. The food was excellent, and she was sure they would find it agreeable.

The restaurant was dirty, and they sat under a harsh, white overhead light. The waitress, whom Mme Straus addressed by her Christian name, was brusque with her, and the food was not good. They were all three talked out.

On the way back to the convent, Mme Straus saw a lighted pastry shop, rushed in, bought all the palmiers there were, and presented them to Barbara. Still not satisfied with what she had given the Americans, she opened her purse while they were standing on a street corner waiting for their bus and took out two religious stamps that were printed on white tissue paper. She gave one to Harold and the other to Barbara. The design was Byzantine—the Virgin and the Christ child, with two tiny angels hovering like birds, one on either side of the

Virgin's rounded shoulders. The icon from which the design was taken was in a church in Rome, Mme Straus said, where they must go and pray for her. Meanwhile, the stamps, through their miraculous efficacy, would conduct her two dear children safely on their journey and bring them back to her in September.

Chapter 17

O N the fourth of September, with their faces pressed to the window of the San Remo–Nice motorbus, they saw a little harbor surrounded by cliffs. They saw the masts of fishing boats. They saw a bathing beach. They turned their heads and saw, on the other side of the road, a small three-story hotel. "Since we don't have any hotel reservation in Nice," he said, "what about staying here?" She nodded, and, rising from his seat, he pulled the bell cord. The bus came to a stop on the brow of the next hill, and the driver, handing the suitcases down to Harold, said: "Monsieur, that was a very good idea you just had."

The small hotel could accommodate them, and sent a bus-boy back with Harold to help with the luggage. When Harold tipped him, he also asked if the tip was sufficient, and the boy looked at him the way people do at someone who is obviously running a fever. Then, serene and amused, he smiled, and said: "Mais oui." In Beaulieu nobody worried about anything.

Very soon Harold and Barbara stopped worrying also. Right after breakfast, they went across the road to the beach. They read for a while, and then they stretched out on the sand and surrendered themselves to the sun. When it grew hot they swam, with their eyes open so that they could watch their shadows on the sandy floor of the harbor. Barbara walked slowly up the beach and back again, searching for tiny pieces of broken china which the salt waves had rounded and faded and made velvet to the touch. She was collecting them, and she kept sorting over her collection, comparing and discarding, saving only the best of these treasures that no one else cared about. Harold sat watching her and eavesdropping. At first the other people on the beach thought Barbara had lost something: a ring, perhaps. And one of the life guards offered his help. When they found out that it was only an obsession, they paid no more attention to her searching. They did not even make jokes about it. If Harold grew tired of looking at sunbathers, he looked at the cliffs, or at the sails on the horizon. Or he got up and went into the water.

By noon they were ravenous. After a long heavy nap they got dressed, yawning, and went out again. They walked the streets of Beaulieu, stopping in front of shop windows or to stare at the huge, empty Hôtel Bristol. They found a café that sold American cigarettes. They bought fruit in an open-air market. They went to the English tea shop. They had a quick swim before dinner. In the evening they sat in a canvas tent on the beach, drinking vermouth and dancing, or watching the hotel chambermaids dancing with each other or with the life guards, to a three-piece band that played "Maria de Bahia" and "La Vie en Rose." Or they walked, under a canopy of stars, with the warm sea wind accompanying them like an inquisitive dog. Now and then they stopped to smell some garden that they could not see: box and oleander, bay leaves, night-blooming stock.

One afternoon they took a bus into Nice to see what they were missing. Half an hour after they had stepped off the bus they were on their way back to Beaulieu. Nice was like Miami, they decided, without ever having been to Miami.

They walked all the way around Cap Ferrat. Behind one of the high, discolored stucco walls was the villa of Somerset Maugham; behind which was the question. Instead of becoming friends with Somerset Maugham, they took up with a couple fifteen years older than they were—a cousin of Mme la Patronne and his English wife. The four of them climbed the Moyenne Corniche and saw Old Eze; lingered in the dining room of the Hôtel Frisia, drinking brandy and Benedictine; went to Monte Carlo and saw the botanical gardens. In the Casino at Beaulieu, Barbara won four hundred francs at roulette, and a life of gambling opened before her.

On all the telephone poles there were posters announcing a Grand Entertainment under the Auspices of the Jeunesse de Beaulieu. Harold and Barbara went. Nothing could have kept them away. The Grand Entertainment was in a big striped circus tent. The little boy from the carnival in Tours came and sat at their table—or if it was not that exact same little boy, it was one just like him, his twin, his double. They supplied him with confetti and serpentines and admiration, and he supplied them with family life. The orchestra played "Maria de Bahia" and "La Vie en Rose." Fathers danced with their two-year-old daughters tirelessly. At midnight the little boy's real mother claimed him. Harold and Barbara stayed till the end, dancing. When they rang the bell of their hotel at two o'clock in the morning, the busboy let them in, his eyes pink with sleep, his good night unreproachful. He was their friend. So was the single waiter in the dining room. Also the chambermaids, and—but in a more reserved fashion—Mme la Patronne.

Their hotel room was small and bare but it looked out over the harbor. Undressing for bed, Harold would step out onto their balcony in his bathrobe, see the lanterns hanging from the masts of fishing boats, hear God knows what mermaid singing, and reach for his bathing slip. At night the water was full of phosphorescence. They slept the sleep of stones. The man in the camel's-hair coat could not find them. Those faint lines in her forehead, put there prematurely by riddles at three a.m., by curtains that did not hang straight in the dark, by faults there was no correcting, disappeared. With his lungs full of sea air, he held himself straighter. "I feel the way I ought to have felt when I was seventeen and didn't," he said. Their skin grew darker and darker. Their faces bloomed. The very bed they made love on was like a South Sea Island.

They should never have left Beaulieu, but they did; after ten days, he went and got bus tickets, and she packed their suitcases, and he went downstairs and paid the bill, and early the next morning they stood in the road, waiting for the bus to Marseilles. It is impossible to say why people put so little value on complete happiness.

They arrived at Marseilles at five o'clock in the evening. The city was plastered with posters advertising the annual industrial fair, and they were turned away from one hotel after another. They decided that the situation was hopeless, and Harold told the taxi driver to take them to the railway station. The next train to anywhere left at seven thirty a.m. They drove back into the center of town and tried more places. While Harold was standing on the sidewalk, wondering where to go next, a man came up to him and handed him a card with the name of a hotel on it. Harold showed the card to the taxi driver, who tore it up. Though they had no place to stay, they had a friend; the driver had taken them under his protection; their troubles were his. He remained patient and optimistic. After another

hour and a half, Harold dipped a pen into an inkwell and
signed the register of the Hôtel Splendide. It had a hole right
down through the center of the building, because the elevator
shaft was being rebuilt. The lobby was full of bricks and mortar and scaffolding, and their room was up five flights and expensive, but they knew how lucky they were to have a roof
over their heads. And besides, this time tomorrow they would
be in Paris.

They went for a walk before dinner and found the Old Port,
but whatever was picturesque had been obliterated by the repeated bombings. They saw some sailboats along an esplanade
that could have been anywhere, and left that in favor of a
broad busy boulevard with shops. After a few blocks they
turned back. As a rule, the men who turned to stare at Barbara
Rhodes in public places were generally of a romantic disposition or else old enough to be her father. Even more than her
appearance, her voice attracted and disturbed them, reminding
them of what they themselves had been like at her age, or
throwing them headlong into an imaginary conversation with
her, or making them wonder whether in giving the whole of
their affection to one woman they had settled for less than
they might have got if they had had the courage and the
patience to go on looking. But this was not true here. In the
eyes that were turned toward her, there was no recognition of
who she was but only of the one simple use that she could be
put to.

Harold had the name of a restaurant, and the shortest way
to it was an alley so dark and sinister-looking that they hesitated to enter it, but it was only two blocks long and they could
see a well-lighted street at the other end, and so they started
on, and midway down the alley encountered a scene that made
their knees weak—five gendarmes struggling to subdue a filthy,
frightened, ten-year-old boy. At the corner they came upon
the restaurant, brightly lighted, old-fashioned, glittering, clean.
The waiters were in dinner jackets, and the food was the best
they had had in Europe. They managed to relegate to the warehouse of remembered dreams what they had just seen in the
alley; also the look of considered violence in faces they did not
ever want to see again.

*

The porter who carried their heavy luggage through the Gare Montparnasse informed them that there was a taxi strike in Paris. He put the luggage down at the street entrance, and pointed to the entrance to the Métro, directly across the street. "If you'll just help me get these down into the station," Harold said. The porter was not permitted to go outside the railway station, and left them stranded in the midst of their seven pieces of luggage. Though they had left the two largest suitcases here in Paris with the American Express, during their travels they had acquired two more that were almost as big. Harold considered moving the luggage in stages and found that he didn't have the courage to do this. Somewhere—in Italy or Austria or the South of France—he had lost contact with absolutes, and he was now afraid to take chances where the odds were too great. While they stood there helplessly at the top of a broad flight of stone steps, discussing what to do, a tall, princely man with a leather strap over his shoulder came up to them and offered his services.

"Yes," Harold said gratefully, "we do need you. If you'll just help me get the suitcases across the street and down into the Métro—" and the man said: "No, monsieur, I will go with you all the way to your hotel."

He draped himself with the two heaviest suitcases, using his strap, and then picked up three more. Harold shouldered the dufflebag, and Barbara took the dressing case, and they made their way through the bicycles and down the stairs. While they stood waiting for a train, the Frenchman explained that he was not a porter by profession; he worked in a warehouse. He had been laid off, the day before, and he had a family to support, and so he had come to the railway station, hoping to pick up a little money. At this moment, he said, there were a great many people in Paris in his circumstances.

At his back there was a poster that read, incongruously: *L'Invitation au Château.* Harold thought of Beaumesnil. Then, turning, he looked up into the man's eyes and saw that they were full of sadness.

Each day, the Frenchman said, things got a little worse, and they were going to continue to get worse. The only hope was that General de Gaulle would come back into power.

"Do you really think that?" Harold said, concerned that a

man of this kind, so decent and self-respecting, so courteous, so willing to take on somebody else's heavy suitcases while weighted down by his own burdens, should have lost all faith in democracy.

They talked politics all the way to the Concorde station, and made their way up the steps and across the rue de Rivoli and past the Crillon and down the narrow, dark, rue Boissy d'Anglas. In the lobby of the Hôtel Vouillemont, the Frenchman divested himself of the suitcases, and Harold paid him, and shook hands with him, and thanked him, and thought: *It isn't right to let him go like this when he is in trouble*, but did let him go, nevertheless, and turned to the concierge's desk, thinking that their own troubles were over, and learned that they were just beginning. They had wired ahead for a reservation but the concierge was not happy to see them. The delegates to the General Assembly of the United Nations, the secretarial staff, the delegates' families and servants—some three thousand people—had descended on Paris the day before, and the Hôtel Vouillemont was full; all the hotels were full. How long did monsieur expect to stay? . . . Ah no. Decidedly no. They could stay here until they had found other accommodation, but the sooner they did this the better.

So, instead of unpacking their suitcases and hanging up their clothes and having a long hot bath and deciding where to have dinner their first night back in Paris, they went out into the street and started looking for a hotel that would take them for five weeks. Avoiding the Crillon and places like it that they knew they couldn't afford, they went up the rue du Mont-Thabor and then along the rue de Castiglione. They would have been happy to stay in the Place Vendôme but there did not seem to be any hotels there. They continued along the rue Danielle Casanova and turned back by way of the rue St. Roch. Nobody wanted them. If only they'd thought to arrange this in July. If they'd only been able to imagine what it would be like . . . But in July they could have stayed anywhere.

Early the next morning, they started out again.

Harold removed his hat and with a pleasant smile said: "Bonjour, madame. Nous désirons une chambre pour deux personnes . . . pour un mois . . . avec un—"

"Ah, monsieur, je regrette beaucoup, mais il n'y a rien." The patronne's face reflected satisfaction in refusing something to somebody who wanted it so badly.

"Rien du tout?"

"Rien du tout," she said firmly.

He did not really expect a different answer, though it was possible that the answer would be different. Once he had been refused, nothing was at stake, and he used the rest of the conversation to practice speaking French. Within the narrow limits of this situation, he was becoming almost fluent. He even tried to do something about his accent.

"Mais la prochaine semaine, peut-être?"

"La semaine prochaine non plus, monsieur."

"C'est bien dommage."

He glanced around the lobby and at the empty dining room and at the glass roof over their heads. Then he considered the patronne herself—the interesting hair-do, the flinty eyes, the tight mouth, the gold fleur-de-lys pin that had no doubt belonged to her mother, the incorruptible self-approval. She was as well worth studying as any historical monument, and seemed to be made of roughly the same material.

"C'est un très joli hôtel," he said, and smiled experimentally, to see whether just this once the conversation could be put on a personal or even a sexual basis. All such confusions are, of course, purely Anglo-Saxon; the patronne was not susceptible. He might as well have tried to charm one of her half-dozen telephone directories.

"Nous aurions été très contents ici," he said, with a certain pride in the fact that he was using the conditional past tense.

"Ah, monsieur, je regrette infiniment qu'il n'y a rien. L'O.N.U., vous savez."

"Oui, oui, l'O.N.U." He raised his hat politely. "Merci, madame."

"De rien, monsieur." The voice was almost kind.

"Nothing?" Barbara asked, when he got outside. She was standing in front of a shop window.

"Nothing. This one would have been perfect." Then he studied the shop window. "That chair," he said.

"I was looking at it too."

"It would probably cost too much to ship it home, but we could ask, anyway." He put his hand to the door latch. The door was locked.

They started on down the street, looking for the word "hôtel." The weather was sunny and warm. Paris was beautiful.

In the middle of the morning, they sat down at a table under an awning on a busy street, ordered café filtre, and stretched their aching legs. Barbara opened her purse and took out the mail that they had picked up at the bank but not taken the time to read. They divided the letters between them. It was not a very good place to read. The noise was nerve-racking. Every time a big truck passed, the chairs and tables and their two coffee cups shook.

"Here's a letter from the Robertsons," she said.

"Are they still here?" he asked, looking up from his letter with interest.

Among the American tourists whom the Austrian government had billeted at a country inn outside Salzburg because the hotels in town were full of military personnel there was an American couple of the same age as Harold and Barbara and so much like them that at first the two couples carefully avoided each other. But when day after day they ate lunch at the same table and swam in the same lake and took the same crowded bus into Salzburg, it became more and more difficult and finally absurd not to compare notes on what they had heard or were going to hear. The Robertsons had no hotel reservations in Venice, and so Harold told them where he and Barbara were staying. And when they got to Venice they were welcomed in the hotel lobby by the Robertsons, who had already been there two days and showed them the way to the Piazza San Marco. With the mail that was handed to Harold at the American Express in Rome there was a note from Steve Robertson: he and Nancy were so sorry to miss them, and they must be sure and go to the Etruscan Museum and the outdoor opera at the Baths of Caracalla. The note that Barbara now passed across the table contained the name and telephone number of the Robertsons' hotel in Paris.

He finished reading the mail that was scattered over the table and then said suddenly: "I don't think we are going to find anything."

"What will we do?"

"I don't know," he said. He signaled to the waiter that he was ready to pay the check. "Close our suitcases and go home, I guess."

After lunch they started out again. There was only one small hotel in the neighborhood of the Place Redouté and it was full. Rien, monsieur. Je regrette beaucoup. They tried the Hôtel Bourgogne et Montana, the Hôtel Florida, the Hôtel Continental. They tried the Hôtel Scribe, and the Hôtel Métropolitain, and the Hôtel Madison. The Hôtel Louvre, the Hôtel Oxford et Cambridge, the Hôtel France et Choiseul . . . Rien, monsieur. Je n'ai rien . . . rien du tout . . . pas une seule chambre pour deux personnes avec salle de bains, pas de grand lit . . . Absolument rien . . . And all the while in his wallet there was that calling card, which he had saved as a souvenir. Used properly, the card of M. Carrère would have got them into any hotel in Paris, no matter how crowded. He never once thought of it.

From their room in the Hôtel Vouillemont, Harold called the Robertsons' hotel. The voice that answered said: "Ne quittez pas," and then after several minutes he heard another voice that was like an American flag waving in the breeze. "Dusty? How wonderful! You must come right over! It's our last night in Paris, we're taking the boat train in the morning, and what could be more perfect?"

The Robertsons' hotel was on the other side of the river, in the rue de l'Université, and as Harold and Barbara walked up the street from the bus stop, they saw Steve coming to meet them. He was smiling, and he embraced them both and said: "Paris is marvelous!"

"If you have a place to lay your head," Harold said.

They told him about the trouble they had been having, and he said: "Let's go talk to the proprietor of our hotel. We're leaving in the morning. I'm sure you can have our room. You'll love it there, and it's dirt cheap." The proprietor said that he would be happy to let them have the Robertsons' room, but for one night only. So they went on upstairs.

"Oh, it's just marvelous!" Nancy said as she kissed them. "We've had the most marvelous two weeks. I know it's a terrible thing to say but neither of us want to go home. We're both heartsick at the thought of leaving Paris. Wasn't Rome wonderful!"

The Robertsons had friends who were living here and spoke perfect French and had initiated them into the pleasures of the Left Bank. They took Barbara and Harold off to have dinner at a place they knew about, where the proprietor gave the women he admired a little green metal souvenir frog, sometimes with a lewd compliment. He was considered a character. The restaurant was full of students, and Harold and Barbara felt they were on the other side of the moon from the Place Redouté, where they belonged.

Saturday morning, Harold came down in the elevator alone, and, avoiding the reproachful look of the concierge as he passed through the lobby on his way to the street door, went to the Cunard Line office to see if their return passage could be changed to an earlier date, and was told that they were fortunate to be leaving as soon as the middle of October; the earliest open sailing was December first.

"I think it's a sign," Barbara said.

"We might as well take what we have," he said. "While we have it."

They got into a taxi and went back to the Left Bank and fanned out through the neighborhood of St. Germain-des-Prés—the rue Jacob, the rue de l'Université, the rue des Saints Pères, the rue des Beaux-Arts . . . The story was always the same. Their feet ached, their eyes saw nothing but the swinging hotel sign far up the street. Harold had tried to get Barbara to stay in their room while he walked the streets, but she insisted on keeping him company.

At one o'clock she said: "I'm hungry," and he said: "Shall we try one more?" The concierge was eating his lunch when they walked into the hotel lobby. The smell of beef casserole pierced the Americans to the heart. It was the essence of everything French, and it wasn't for them.

When they returned to their hotel, the concierge called to Harold. Expecting the worst, he crossed the lobby to the desk. The concierge handed him a letter and Harold recognized Steve Robertson's tiny, precise handwriting. Inside there was an advertisement clipped from that morning's Paris *Herald*.

The Hôtel Paris-Dinard, in the rue Cassette, had a vacancy—a room with a bath.

They moved across the river the first thing Sunday morning, and by lunchtime their suitcases were unpacked and stored away under the bed, their clothes were hanging in the armoire, the washbasin in the bathroom was full of soaking nylon, the towel racks were full, the guidebooks were set out on the rickety little table by the window, and they had all but forgotten about that monotonous dialogue between the possessor and the dispossessed, which began: "Nous désirons une chambre pour deux personnes . . ."

The hotel was very quiet, there were no other Americans staying there, and they were delighted with the room and the view from their window. They were up high, in the treetops, and could see through the green leaves the greener dome of a church. They looked down into a walled garden directly across the street from the hotel. The room was not large, but it was not too small, and it was clean and quiet and had a double bed and a bathroom adjoining it, and it was not expensive. Fortune is never halfhearted when it decides to reverse itself.

The green dome was in their guidebooks; it was the Church of the Ancient Convent of the Carmelites. During the Reign of Terror, a hundred and sixteen priests had had their throats cut on the church steps, and every morning, in the darkness and the cold just before dawn, Harold was wakened by a bell tolling, so loud and so near that it made his heart race wildly. Barbara slept through it. Leo is sleepy at night and easily wakened in the morning; the opposite is true of Virgo.

When the bell stopped tolling, he drifted off. Three hours later the big breakfast tray was deposited on their laps, before they were wholly awake or decently clothed. Though white flour was illegal, by paying extra they could have, with their coffee, croissants made of white flour. They were still warm from the bakery oven. Through the open window came the massed voices of school children in the closed garden, so like the sound of noisy birds. After they had finished their breakfast they fell asleep again, and when they woke, the street was quiet; the children had been swallowed up by the school. At recess time they reappeared, but the racket was never again so vivid during the rest of the day.

The owner of the hotel sat at a high desk in the lobby, behind his ledger, and nodded remotely to them as they came and went. If they turned right when they emerged from the hotel, they came to a street of religious-statuary shops, which took them into the Place St. Sulpice, with its fountain and plane trees and heavy baroque church. If they turned left, they came to the rue Vaugirard, which was busier, and if they turned left again, they eventually came to the Palais du Luxembourg and the gardens. Sitting on iron chairs a few feet away from the basin where the children sailed their boats, they read or looked at the faces—narrow, unhandsome compared to the Italian faces they had left behind, but intense, nervously alive. Or they got up and walked, past the palace, between the flower beds, down one of the formal avenues.

In an alley off the Place St. Sulpice they found the perfect restaurant, and they went there every day, for lunch or dinner or both. Harold held the door open for Barbara, and they were greeted as they came in—by madame behind her desk and then by monsieur with his hands full of plates—and went on into the back room, where they usually sat at the same table in order to be served by a waiter called Pierre, who took exquisite care of them and smiled at them as if he were their affectionate older brother. Here in this small square room, eating was as simple and as delightful as picking wildflowers in a wood. They had artichokes and pâté en croûte, green peas and green beans from somebody's garden, and French-fried potatoes that were rushed to their table from the kitchen. They had little steaks with Béarnaise sauce, and pheasant, and roast duck, and sweetbreads, and calf's liver, and brains, and venison. They had raspberries and pears and fraises des bois and strawberry tarts, and sometimes with their dessert Pierre smuggled them whipped cream. They drank Mâcon blanc or Mâcon rouge. They ate and drank with rapture, and, strangely, grew thinner and thinner.

Though there were always people in the Place St. Sulpice, they almost never saw anybody in the rue Cassette. It had not always been so quiet. Walking home one day they saw there wasn't a single house that didn't have pockmarks that could

only have been made by machine-gun bullets in the summer of
1944.

They learned to use the buses, so that they could see the
upper world of Paris when they went out, instead of the
underworld of the Métro. They also walked—down the rue
Vaugirard to the Odéon and then down the rue de l'Odéon to
the boulevard St. Germain; down the boulevard St. Germain
to the Place St. Germain-des-Prés. Over and over, as if this
were a form of memorizing, they walked in the rue Bonaparte
and the rue Jacob, in the rue Dauphine and the rue du
Cherche-Midi, in the rue Cardinale and the Carrefour de
l'Odéon, in the rue des Ciseaux and the rue des Saints Pères,
in the boulevard St. Germain and the boulevard Raspail.

In their hurry to move into a hotel that wanted them, they
neglected to leave behind their new address. Their first piece
of mail, forwarded by the bank, was a letter from Mme Straus-
Muguet:

Sunday

Dear Little Friends:

What a disappointment! I passed by your hotel a little while ago and
you had taken flight this very morning. But where? And how to rejoin
you? Have you returned to the country? In short, a word guiding me,
I beg of you, for I am leaving for Sarthe for six days, and I had so
much hoped to spend this past week with you. Well, that's life! But
your affectionate Minou is so sorry not to see you, and fondly embraces you both!

Straus-Muguet

Harold called the convent in Auteuil, and was told that
Mme Straus-Muguet had left. Barbara wrote and told her
where they were, and that they would be here until the nineteenth of October. She also wrote to Alix, who answered immediately, inviting them down to the country for the week
end.

"Do you think that means we're to pay or are we really invited?" he said.

"I don't know. Do you want to go? I'd just as soon."

"No," he said. "I don't want to leave Paris."

They heard a gala performance of *Boris Godounov* at the
Opéra, with the original Bakst settings and costumes. On a

rainy night they got into a taxi and drove to the Opéra Comique. The house was sold out but there were folding seats. Blocking the center aisle, and only now and then wondering what would happen if a fire broke out, they heard *Les Contes d'Hoffman.*

They went to the movies, they went to the marionette theater in the Champs-Elysées. They went to the Grand Guignol. They went to the Cirque Médrano.

"What I like about living in Paris," he said, "is planning ahead very carefully, so that every day you can do something or see something that you wouldn't do if you weren't here."

"That isn't what *I* like," Barbara said. "What I like is *not* to plan ahead, but just see what happens. Couldn't we do that for a change?"

"All right," he said. But his heart sank at the thought of leaving anything to chance. The days would pass, would be frittered away, and suddenly their five weeks in Paris would be used up and they wouldn't have seen or done half the things they meant to. He managed to forget what she had said. He waited impatiently for each new issue of *La Semaine de Paris* to appear on the kiosks, and when it did, he studied it as if he were going to have to pass an examination in the week's plays, concerts, and movies. They did not understand one word in fifty of Montherlant's *La Reine Morte*, and during the first intermission he rushed out into the lobby to buy a program; but they were in France, the rest of the audience did not need a résumé of the plot, the program was not helpful.

At Cocteau's *Les Parents Terribles* the old woman who opened the door of their box for them came back while the play was going on and tried to oust them from their seats in order to put somebody else in them. With one eye on the stage—the mother was in bed with a cold, the grown son was kneeling on the bed, he accused, she admitted to remorse, incest was in the air—Harold fought off the ouvreuse. They were in their right seats, and indignation made him as eloquent as a Frenchman would have been in these circumstances. But by the time the enemy had retired and he was free to turn his attention to the play, the remarkable love scene was over.

Barbara went off by herself one morning, while he stayed

home and wrote letters. When she came back, she reported that she had found a store with wonderful cooking utensils—just the kind of thin skillets that were in Mme Cestre's kitchen and that she had been looking for for years.

"I would have bought them," she said, "except that I decided they would take up too much room in the luggage. . . . Now I'm sorry I didn't."

"Where was this shop?" he asked, reaching for his hat.

She didn't know. "But I can find my way back to it," she said.

It was a virtuoso performance, up one street and down the next, across squares and through alleys, beyond the sixth arrondissement and well into the fifth. At last they came on the shop she was searching for. They bought four skillets, a nutmeg grater, a salad basket, some cooking spoons, a copper match box to hang beside the stove, and a paring knife. In the next street, they came upon a bookshop with old children's books and Victorian cardboard toy theaters. They bought the book of children's songs with illustrations by Boutet de Monvel that was in the bookcase of the red room at Beaumesnil. While Barbara was trying to decide between the settings for *La belle au bois dormant* and *Cendrillon*, he said suddenly: "Where did Sabine sleep while we were occupying her room?"

"In the back part of the house, probably. Why?"

"Or one of those dreary attic rooms," he said. "It's funny we never thought about it at the time. Do you think she minded our being in her room?"

That evening while Barbara was dressing, he gave M. le Patron the number of the apartment in the rue Malène and waited beside the bed, with the telephone held to his ear. The phone rang and rang. But she's too thin, he thought, watching her straighten the seam of her stockings. She isn't getting enough rest. . . .

Reaching into the armoire, she began pushing her dresses along the rod. She could hardly bear to put any of them on any more.

"Mme Viénot's affectionate manner with you I took at the time to be disingenuous," he said. "Looking back, I think that it wasn't."

The cotton print dress she had bought in Rome was out of

season. The brown, should she wear, with a green corduroy
jacket? Or the lavender-blue?

"I think she really did like us. And that we totally misjudged
her character," he said.

She chose the brown, which had a square neck and no
sleeves, and so required the green jacket. "We didn't misjudge
her character."

"How do you know?"

"From one or two remarks that Alix made."

"They do not answer," M. le Patron said.

In her letter Alix had said that she would be coming back to
Paris soon, but a week passed, and then two, and there was still
no answer when they called the apartment in the rue Malène.
One morning they made a pilgrimage to the Place Redouté
and stood looking affectionately around at the granite monument, the church, the tables piled on top of each other in front
of the café, the barber shop. Standing in the rue Malène, they
saw that all the windows of Mme Cestre's apartment were
closed, and the shutters as well. "Shall we go in and ask when
they are coming back?" Barbara said.

Mme Emile shook hands cordially but had no news. They
were all away, she said. Monsieur also. She did not know when
they were returning.

"Do you think she wrote and the letter got lost in the mails?"
Barbara asked as they were walking toward the bus corner.

"I don't know," he said. "I don't think so. Perhaps their
feelings were hurt that we didn't accept the invitation to come
down to the country."

"We should have gone," Barbara said with conviction.

"But then we would have had to leave Paris."

"What do you think really happened?"

"You mean the 'drame'? They lost their money."

"But how?" Barbara said.

"There are only about half a dozen ways that a family that
has money can lose it. They can run through it—"

"I don't think they did."

"Neither do I," he said. "Or they can lose it through
inflation—which could have happened, because the franc used
to be twenty to the dollar before the war. But then what about
the drama? Maybe they were swindled out of it."

"Not Mme Viénot, surely."
"Well, something," he said.

Summer departed without their noticing exactly when this
happened. Fall was equally beautiful. It was still warm in the
daytime. The leaves were turning yellow outside their window.
He started wearing pajamas because the nights were cold. So
was their room when they got up in the morning. Soon, even
in the middle of the day it was cool in the shade, and they kept
crossing the street to walk in the sun. They discovered the
Marché St. Gemain, and wandered up and down the aisles
looking with surprise at the wild game and enjoying the color
and fragrance and appetizingness of the fruit and vegetables.
They walked all the way down the rue de Varennes, and saw
the Rodin Museum and Napoleon's tomb. They took a bus
to the Jardin des Plantes and walked there. They took the
Métro to the Bois de Vincennes. Walking along the Left Bank
of the Seine in the late afternoon, they examined the bookstalls, but with less interest than they had shown in the shabby
merchandise in the avenue de Grammont in Tours. The apparatus of rejection was fatigued; they only looked now at what
there was some possibility of their wanting, and the bookstalls
were too picked-over.

Coming home on the top of a bus just as the lights were
turned on in the shops along the Boulevard St. Germain, they
saw a china shop, and got off the bus and went inside and
bought two small ash trays of white porcelain, in the shape of
an elm and a maple leaf.

Barbara bought gloves in the rue de Rivoli, and in a little
shop in the rue St. Honoré she found a moss-green velours hat
with a white ostrich feather that curled charmingly against her
cheek. It was too small, and after the clerk had stretched it
Barbara knew suddenly that it was not right. It was too cos-
tumy. But the clerk and Harold both begged her to take it,
and so, against her better judgment, she did.

He was looking for the complete correspondence of Flaubert, in nine volumes, and this was not easy to find and gave
him an excuse to stop in every bookstore they came to.

In a little alley off the rue Jacob they saw a small house with
a plaque on it: *Ici est mort Racine.* Across the door of a butcher

shop in the rue Vaugirard they saw a deer hanging head down, with a sign pinned to its fur: *Will be cut up on Thursday.*

They took the train to Versailles, and walked all the way around the palace and then a little way into the park, looking for the path to the Petit Trianon. They couldn't find it, but came instead upon a fountain with a reclining goddess whose beautiful vacant face was turned to the sky. Leaves came drifting down and settled on the surface of the pool and sailed around the statue like little boats. For the few minutes that they stood looking at the fountain, they were released from the tyranny of his wristwatch and the calendar; there was no time but the time of statues, which seems to be eternity, though of course they age, too, and become pitted, lose a foot or a hand, lichen grows in the folds of their drapery, their features become blurred, and what they are a statue of nobody knows any longer.

Finding themselves in the street where Jean Allégret lived, they stopped and rang his bell. There was no answer. Harold left a note for him, in the mailbox. There was no answer to that, either.

Passing through the Place St. Sulpice on their way home, they raised their eyes to the lighted windows and wondered about the people who lived there. As far as they could see, nobody wondered about them.

The woman who had helped Barbara write those two mildly misleading letters to Mme Viénot had also given Harold the name and telephone number of two old friends from the period when she and her husband were living in Paris. One was a banker. She had not heard anything from him for a long time and she was worried about him. The other was her doctor. Both men were cultivated and responsive and just the sort of people Harold and Barbara would enjoy knowing. Harold called the Hanover Bank and learned that the banker was dead. Then he telephoned the doctor, and the doctor thanked him for giving him news of his friends in America and hung up. Harold looked at the telephone oddly, as if it must in some way be to blame. As for their own French friends, he had been conscious for some time of how completely absent they were—Alix, Sabine, Eugène, Jean Allégret, Mme Straus. Not one word from any of them.

Though they were very happy in Paris, they were aware that a shadow hung over the city. The words "crise" and "grève" appeared in the newspaper headlines day after day. The taxi strike had lasted two weeks. One day the Métro was closed, because of a strike. Two days later, to save coal, the electric utilities shut off all power for twelve hours, and as a result the elevator in their hotel did not run and their favorite restaurant was lit by acetylene lamps. Tension and uncertainty were reflected in the faces they saw in the streets.

They made one more attempt to find the château with the green lawn in front of it—they went to Fontainebleau. They enjoyed seeing the apartment of Mme de Maintenon and Napoleon's little bathtub, and from across the water the château did look like a fairy-tale palace, but not the right one. It was too large, and it was not white.

When they got back to their hotel, M. le Patron handed them a letter. Mme Straus-Muguet's handwriting dashed all the way across the face of the envelope, which was postmarked *Sarthe*:

My dear little friends, what contretemps all along the line, since I miss you at every turn! Because of the beautiful weather I have not had the courage to remain in Paris, and here I am in paradise! Sun, flowers, and the dear nuns, who are so good to me! But let us put an end to this game of hide-and-seek. I must return to Paris on Thursday, the fourteenth, but if it is necessary I shall advance the date of my return in order to see you. What are the sorties, plays, operas that will be performed on these dates, and what would you like to see? Find this out in *La Semaine* or from the billboards, and write me at once if between the fifteenth and your departure there is to be a Wednesday soirée de ballet, for I will then write immediately to Paris to the Opéra. If I return on Sunday—the eleventh that would be—is that better for you? Have you still many things to do before the final departure? And from where do you sail? And on what boat? Behind all these questions, my dear children, is only the desire to please you and see you again before the complete separation that will be so hard for me to bear. . . . I will continue to write to your present hotel, and do not change without telling me. What have you done up to this moment that was delightful and interesting? I so much wanted to show you all the beautiful things—but you have already seen many of them! . . . Au revoir, dear little friends. I clasp you to my heart,

both of you, and embrace you with all my tenderness—the tenderness
of a friend and of a mother.

Madame Minou
Straus-Muguet
October 4

There was no ballet between the twelfth and the nineteenth,
and so Harold got seats for *Le Roi d'Ys* instead. He wrote to
Mme Straus that they had seats for the opera for the four-
teenth of October and were looking forward to her return.
Also that they were enjoying Paris very much, and that on
Sunday they were going to Chartres for the day.

Chartres was wonderful; it was one of the high points of
their whole trip. There was no streetcar line, just as Mme
Viénot had said, and so no little church at the end of it, but
they got off the train and found that it was only a short walk to
the cathedral from the station. To their surprise, in the whole
immense interior there was no one. The greatest architectural
monument of the Middle Ages seemed to be there just for
them. The church was as quiet as the thoughts it gave rise to.
They stood and looked at the stained-glass prophets, at the
two great rose windows, at the forest of stone pillars, at the dim,
vaulted ceiling, at a little side altar with lighted candles on it.
They felt in the presence of some vast act of understanding.
When they spoke it was in whispers. Their breathing, their
heartbeat, seemed to be affected.

They climbed one of the towers, and saw what everybody in
Chartres was doing. Then they went down and had a very
good lunch in a little upstairs restaurant, where they were the
only patrons, and walked through the old part of town until
dusk. They went back to the cathedral, and walked all the way
around it, and came upon the little vegetable garden in the
rear; like every other house in Chartres, it had its own potager.
This time, when they went inside, there was no light at all in
the sky, and it was a gray evening, besides. The stained-glass
windows were still glorious, still blazing with their own color
and their own light.

"Nothing from Alix?"

"Nothing," he said, and sat down on the edge of the bed,

ripped open an envelope, and commenced reading a long letter from Mme Straus-Muguet.

"What does she say?" Barbara asked when he turned the first page.

"I'll start at the beginning: *'Sunday . . . Mes petits enfants chéris, I am sad at heart at the thought that you are going to leave France without my being able to find you again—'*"

"No! She's not coming?"

"*'—and embrace you with all my heart. But it is impossible'*—underlined—*'for me to return the fourteenth donc pas d'opéra le R.'*—whatever that means."

"Let me see," she said, looking over his shoulder. "*'There-fore not of the opera* Le Roi d'Ys' . . . But she said for you to get tickets. What will we do with the extra one?"

"Take Sabine," he said, "if she's here by then. *'. . . but there is at Mans a charity fête for "the work of the prisons" of my dear Dominicans, of which I occupy myself so much. It takes place Sunday the seventeenth and Monday the eighteenth, and it will be only after the twentieth that I will be returning! . . . And to say that during eight days in August I was alone in Paris! Then my poor dears, understand my true chagrin at not seeing you again, and just see how all the events are against us! Of more I was'*—Is that right?"

"Let me see . . . *'de plus j'étais à une heure de Chartres . . . all the more since I was only one hour from Chartres and it was there that I would have been able to join you . . .'*"

He continued: "*'And you would have passed the'* . . . or *'we'* would. Her handwriting is really terrible. *'. . . passed the day together. You would even have been able to come to Mans, city so interesting, superb cathedral! That all that is lacking, my God, and to say that in this moment (nine o'clock in the morning) when I am writing you, you are perhaps at Chartres. But where to find you? . . . Little friends, it is necessary to combler mon chagrin'*—what's 'combler'?"

"You'll have to look it up," Barbara said. "The dictionary is in my purse."

The dictionary was not in the purse but in the desk drawer.

"'Combler' means 'to fill up,' 'to overload,' 'to heap,'" he said. "*'. . . it is necessary to try to heap my sorrows by a kindness on your part. It is of yourselves to make photographs, tous les deux*

ensemble, and to send me your photo with dédicace'—dedication
—*'underneath. 19 rue de la Source, that will be a great joy for
me, and at Paris there are such good photographers. Make inquiries about them and'*—it could be 'épanchez.'"

"Exaucez," Barbara said, and read from the dictionary.

"'Exaucer: to grant, give ear to, answer the prayer of someone.'"

"'. . . *grant the prayer that I make of you. You will be thus
with me, in my chamber that you know, and I will look at you
each day, and that will be to me a great happiness. . . . Thank
you in advance! . . . I am enchanted that you are going to the
Opéra to hear* Le Roi d'Ys—*so beautiful, so well sung, such
beautiful music. But to avoid making the queue at the
location'*—the box office, I guess she means—*'do this: go take
your two places at the Opéra at the office of the disection—'"*

"That can't be right," Barbara interrupted.

"'. . . *direction,' then. 'Boulevard Haussman. Enter by the
large door which is in back of the Opéra. On entering, at right
you will see the concierge, M. Ferari. He will point out the office
of M. Decerf or his secretary Nelle'*—no, Mlle.— *'Simone cela de
ma part. Both are my friends, and you will have immediately
two good places à la corbeille'*—But we have the seats already,
and it took exactly ten minutes in line at the box office, and
they're the best seats in the opera house . . . *'where it is necessary to be to see all, salle et scène. I'm writing to M. Decerf by
this same courier to reserve you two places, and it is Wednesday
morning at eleven o'clock that it is necessary to go there to take
them. In this fashion all will go well and I will be tranquil about
you. Servez-vous de mon nom dans tout l'Opéra et à tout le
monde. . . . In mounting to the premier étage, to the office of
M. Decerf (they speak English, both of them), speak to M. Georges,
on arriving, de ma part. He will lead you to M. Decerf. I hope I
have explained sufficiently the march to follow to arrive à bien,
and to all make my good compliments. . . . On your arrival in
New York I pray you to write me immediately to tell me your voyage is well passed. Such is my hope, and above all do not leave
alone in France your Maman Minou, who loves you so much and
has so many regrets. But "noblesse oblige" says the proverb, and to
the title of president I owe to be at my post. I will send you tomorrow the book of Béthanie Fontanelle's work of the prisons. Perhaps*

they will go one day to America. I know the Mauretania, *splendid boat, and I am going to make the crossing with you—in my thoughts. Et voilà, mes petits amis . . . a long letter that you are going to find too long, perhaps, but I was desirous of writing to you. An idea comes to me: if you have the time Saturday or Sunday to come to Le Mans, a train toward eight o'clock in the morning brings you here at eleven. We will lunch together, and that evening a train takes you to Paris, arriving at nine o'clock.'* That makes seven hours on the train. *'Mais c'est peut-être grosse fatigue pour vous. Anyway, at need you may telegraph me at Arnage, Straus, Sarthe. Au revoir, au revoir, mes chéris, je vous embrasse de tout mon coeur et vous aime tendrement. . . . Madame Minou.'"*

He closed the window, and the cries from the school yard became remote.

"Chartres isn't a very big place," Barbara said thoughtfully. "And there is only one thing that people go there to see. She could probably have found us all right, if she had come. But anyway, I'm not going to Le Mans."

"The trains may not even be running," he said. "There is a railroad strike about to begin at any minute. We might get there and not be able to get back. Also, I never wanted to hear *Le Roi d'Ys.* I wanted to hear *Louise* and they aren't giving it this week. *Le Roi d'Ys* was entirely Mme Straus's idea."

"I can't bear it!" Barbara exclaimed. "It's so sad. *'Use my name all through the Opéra, and to everybody. . . .'"*

The book on the prison work of the Dominican nuns did not arrive, and neither did Harold search out the office of M. Decerf and tell him they already had three tickets for *Le Roi d'Ys.* He could not believe that Mme Straus had written to the manager of the Paris Opéra, any more than he could believe that after a stay of three weeks in Arnage she was in charge of a charity bazaar in Le Mans; or that it is possible for it to rain on the sixteenth arrondissement of Paris and not on the eighth. As the gypsy fortuneteller could have told him, this was perhaps not wise. The only safe thing, if you have an ingenuous nature, is to believe everything that anybody says.

In spite of his constant concern that she dress warmly enough, Barbara caught a cold. They were both showing signs of a general tiredness, of the working out of the law of diminishing returns. There were still days when they enjoyed themselves as keenly as they had in the beginning, but the enjoyment was never quite complete; they enjoyed some things and not others; they couldn't any more throw themselves on each day as if it were a spear. Also, their appetite was beginning to fail. They found that once a day was all they could stand to eat in the little restaurant in the alley off the Place St. Sulpice. They bought bread and cheese and a bottle of wine, and ate lunch in their room, and at dinnertime were embarrassed by the welcome they received when they walked into the back room of the restaurant. Or they avoided going there at all.

Sometimes he dreamed in French. He found, at last, the complete correspondence of Flaubert. In a shop in the Place St. Sulpice he saw a beautiful book of photographs of houses on the Ile St. Louis, but it cost twenty dollars and he did not buy it. Their American Express checkbook was very thin, and he had begun to worry about whether they were going to come out even.

Barbara saw a silk blouse in the window of a shop in the rue Royale, and they went inside, but she shook her head when the clerk told her the price. The clerk suggested that, since they were Americans, all they had to do was get their dollars changed on the black market and then the blouse would be less expensive, but Harold delivered a speech. "Madame," he said, "j'aime la France et je ne prends pas avantage du marché noir." The clerk shook hands with him and with tears in her eyes said: "Monsieur, il n'y a pas beaucoup." But she didn't reduce the price of the blouse.

Barbara's cold got worse, and she had to go to bed with it. Harold stopped at the desk and asked if her meals could be sent up to her until she was feeling better. The hotel no longer served meals, but M. le Patron and his wife ate in the empty dining room, and so he knew that what he was asking for was possible, though it meant making an exception. One of the ways of dividing the human race is between those people who are eager to make an exception and those who consider that nothing is more dangerous and wrong. M. le Patron brusquely refused.

Burning with anger, Harold started off to see what could be

done in the neighborhood. Their restaurant was too far away; the food would be stone-cold by the time he got back with it; and so he tried a bistro that was just around the corner, in the rue Vaugirard, and the bartender sent him home with bread and cheese and a covered bowl of soup from the pot-au-feu. It was just the kind of food she had been longing for. After that, he ate in the bistro and then took her supper home to her. Shopping for fruit, he discovered a little hole-in-the-wall where the peaches were wrapped in cotton and where he and the proprietress and her grown daughter discussed seriously which pear madame should eat today and which she should save till tomorrow.

He kept calling the apartment in the rue Malène and there was never any answer. It was hard not to feel that there had been a concerted action, a conspiracy, and that the French, realizing that he and Barbara had got in, where foreigners are not supposed to be, had simply put their heads together and decided that the time had come to push them out. It was not true, of course, but that was what it felt like. And it wasn't wholly not true. Why, for example, didn't Alix write to them? She knew they were only going to be here eight days longer, and still no word came from her; no message of any kind. Was she going to let them go back to America without even saying good-by?

The next morning, as if someone at the bank were playing a joke on them, there was a letter, but it was from Berlin, not Brenodville. It was an old letter that had followed them all around Europe:

Dear Mr. Rhodes:
    A few days before, we returned to Berlin, only our friend Hans got clear his journey to Switzerland at the consulate in Baden-Baden. And now I want to thank you and Mrs. Rhodes once more, also in the name of my wife and of my children. You can't imagine how they enjoyed the oranges and the chocolate and the fishes in oil and the bananes, etc; many of these things they never saw before. They begged me to send you their thanks and their greetings and a snapshot also "that the friendly uncle and the friendly aunt from America may see how we look." (I beg your pardon if the expression "aunt" in U.S.A. is less usual than in Germany for a friend of little children.)
    In Paris I was glad that I could report you over the circumstances

under which we are living and working. But I am afraid that we saw one side only of the problem. We came from a poor and exhausted country into a town that seemed to be rich and nearly untouched by the war. And personally we were in a rather painful situation. So it could happen that we grew more bitter and more pessimist than it is our kind.

We told you from the little food rations—but we did not speak from all the men and women who try to get a little harvest out of each square foot bottom round the houses or on the public places. We did not speak from the thousands who leave Berlin each week end trying to get food on the land, who are hanging on the footboards or on the buffers of the railway or wandering along the roads with potatoes or corn or fruit. We did not speak from all those who are working every day in spite of want of food or clothes or tools. And we did not speak from the most important fact, from all the women who supply their husbands and their children and know to make something out of a minimum of food and electricity and gas, and only a small part of all these women is accustomed to such manner of living by their youth.

To me it seems to be the greatest danger in Germany: on the one side the necessity to live under rather primitive conditions—on the other side the attempts of an ideology to make proletarians out of the whole people with the aim to prepare it for the rule of communisme. A people within such a great need is always in the danger to loose his character, to become unsteady. And the enticement from the other side is very dangerous.

And another point seems important to me: there are two forms of democracy in Germany, the one of the western powers, the other of communisme in the strange form of "Volksdemokratie." It is not necessary to speak about this second form, but also the first is not what we need. The western democracy may be good for the western countries. Also the German people wants to bear the whole responsibility for his government, but it is not prepared to do so. It is very dangerous to put it into a problem that it cannot solve. Our people needs some decades of political education (but it does not need instructors which try to feed it with their own ideas and ideologies) and in the meantime it ought to get a strong government of experts assisted by a parliament with consultative rights only. German political parties incline to grow dogmatical and intolerant and radical—even democratical parties—and it is necessary to diminish their influence in administration and legislative and, later on, specially in foreign affairs.

I am sure that my opinion is very different from the opinion of the most Germans but I don't believe in the miracle of the majority.

Dear Mr. Rhodes, I suppose you are smiling a little about my manner of torturing your language, but I am sure that you hear what I want to say and that you will not be inconvenienced by the outside appearance.

May ask you for giving my respects to Mrs. Rhodes?

Would you allow me to write you then and now.

Always your faithfully
Stefan Doerffer.

"Let's see the picture of the children," Barbara said when he had finished reading the letter to her.

The children were about four and six. Both were blond and sturdy. The little girl looked like a doll, the boy reminded Harold of those fat Salzburgers whose proud stomachs preceded them and whose wives followed two steps behind, carrying the luggage. It was partly the little boy's costume—he had on what looked like a cheap version of Bavarian lederhosen—and partly his sullen expression, which might have been nothing more than the light the picture was taken by or a trick of the camera, but it made him look like a Storm Trooper in the small size. The children's feet were partly covered by a large square block of building stone. It could have been ruins or a neglected back yard. The little boy's hands made it clear that he was only a child and that there was no telling what kind of German he would be when he grew up.

"I don't feel like being their uncle," Harold said as he put the letter back in its envelope. "'A strong government of experts, assisted by a parliament with consultative rights only . . .' It's all beyond me. It depresses me."

"Why should it depress you?" Barbara said. "It's a truthful letter."

"But they haven't learned anything—anything at all. He feels sorry for the German women but not a word about the others, all over the world. Not a word about who started it. Not a word about the Jews."

"What can he say? They're dead. Maybe he doesn't speak about it because he can't bear to."

"He could say he was sorry."

"Maybe. But you aren't a Jew. What right have you to ask for or receive an apology in their name? And how do you know they would accept his apology if he said it? I wouldn't—not if it was my relatives that were sent to the gas chambers."

"I don't know," he said sadly. "I don't know anything. All I know is I'm tired, and I guess I'm ready to go home."

She looked at him, to see if he really meant it. He didn't. But she was ready to go home, and had been for some time. In Beaulieu her period was five days late. This disappointment she was not able to leave behind her in the South of France. She woke to it every morning, and it confronted her in the bathroom mirror when she washed her face. For his sake she concealed the weight on her heart and did not allow herself so much as a sigh. But more and more her pleasure was becoming second-hand, the reflection of his.

Chapter 18

JUST when they had got used to the idea that they had been cast out, and had managed to accept it philosophically, they discovered that they were not cast out; there had been no change in the way that the French felt about them.

Sabine was the first to call. Harold asked about Alix, and Sabine said that they were back too—they had all come up from the country together.

And while he was out doing an errand, Alix called and asked them to tea on Monday.

"What did she sound like?" he asked.

"Herself," Barbara said.

"You didn't hear anything in her voice that might indicate she was hurt or anything?"

"No. She was just affectionate, as always."

"Perhaps we imagined it," he said. "It will be so nice to see them and the apartment again. Did she say Eugène would be there?"

"She said he wouldn't be there."

The next morning, Barbara heard him say: " 'My dear little friends, do not come to Le Mans,' " and called out from the bathroom, where she was brushing her teeth: "It's too far!"

"Nobody's going to Le Mans," he said, and doubled over with laughter.

"Then what are you talking about?"

"Mme Straus. She's coming after all. Just listen: *'Tuesday . . . Mes petits amis chéris, Do not come to LeMans'*—underlined—*'It is I who will arrive in Paris Saturday evening, Gare Montparnasse, at six o'clock. I have arranged all in order to see you . . .'"*

In the same mail, there was an invitation from Jean Allégret, who had been in the country, and had just returned to Paris and found their note, and was inviting them to have dinner with him at his club on Friday.

"Do you want to?" Barbara asked dubiously.

"It might be interesting," Harold said.

His pajamas had split up the back and, later that morning,

he went out to buy a new pair. When he came back, he showed them to her and said: "Look—they're made of parachute cloth."

"Not really?"

"So the clerk said. I guess they don't have anything else. Anyway, something wonderful happened. I asked him if they weren't too large and he looked at me and said no, they were the normal size. . . . In France *I'm* the normal size. *Not* football players. The first time in my life anybody has ever said that. . . . It's so beautiful out. No matter which direction you look. The clerk was the normal size too. Everything in France is normal. It doesn't seem possible that Tuesday morning we're going to get on a train and— Except that maybe we won't. The railway strike is supposed to start Monday or Tuesday."

"What will we do if there are no trains?"

"There probably will be," he said.

"Would you like to stay?"

"A few days longer, you mean?"

"No, for good."

"We can't," he said soberly. "There is no way that it is possible, or reasonable. And besides, they tried that, in the twenties, and it didn't work. In the end they all had to come home."

He read in *La Semaine de Paris* the plays that were to be performed at the Comédie Française and the Odéon, the movies, the concerts, for the first three days after they would be gone. Like a man sentenced to execution, he had a sudden stabbing vision of the world as it would be without him. The day after they left, there was to be a performance of *Louise* at the Comique.

And he was haunted by that book he felt he shouldn't buy— the book of photographs of the old houses on the Ile St. Louis. And by the Ile St. Louis itself. Every time he went across the river, there it was, in plain sight, just beyond the Ile de la Cité. He kept trying to get there, and instead he found himself going to the American Express, getting a haircut, cashing traveler's checks, standing at the counter at the Cunard Line. These errands all seemed to take more time than they would have at home, and time—time running out—was what he kept having to deal with.

It did not interest him to wonder if he could stay, if there was after all some way of arranging this, because he did not want to stay here as an observer, an outsider, an expatriate; he was too proud to do that. He wanted to possess the thing he loved. He wanted to be a Frenchman.

When he got home in the late afternoon, a group of school boys would be having choir practice out of doors under the trees in the school yard. There was no music teacher—only an older boy with a pitch pipe—and the singing that rose from the walled garden was so beautiful that it made him hold his head in his hands. This and other experiences like it (the one-ring circus on the outskirts of Florence; the big searchlight from the terrace of Winkler's Café picking out a baroque church, which they then ran through the streets to, and then moving on to a palace, and then to a fountain—all the churches and palaces and fountains of Salzburg, bathed in lavender-blue light; the grandiose Tiepolo drawn in white chalk on the pavement of the Via Ventidue Marzo in Venice by a sixteen-year-old boy out of another century, who began his work at eight in the morning and finished at four in the afternoon and was rewarded with a hatful of lira notes; arriving in Venice at midnight, leaving Pisa at six in the morning, taking an afternoon nap in Rome, eating ice cream under a canvas awning by the Lake of Geneva during a downpour; the view from the Campanile at Siena in full sunshine—a medieval city constructed on the plan of a rose; the little restaurant on a jetty in San Remo, where they ate dinner peering out through the rain at the masts of fishing boats; the carnival in Tours, the Grand Entertainment in Beaulieu, dinner at Iznard, dinner at Doney's, the dinner with Sabine at Le Vert Galant, just before they left for Switzerland, with the river only a few yards from their table, and with their vision concentrated by the candle flame until they saw only their own three faces, talking about what they believed, what they thought, what they felt—so intently that they did not know exactly when it got dark or even at what point the tables all around them were taken by other diners. And so on, and so on)—these ecstatic memories were, he thought, what made the lines in his face, and why he had lost so much weight. He felt that he was slowly being diminished by the succession of experiences that he had responded to with his whole heart and that seemed to represent something that belonged to him, and that he had not had, and, not having, had been starved for all his life, without knowing it. He was being diminished as people are always diminished who are racked with love, and that it was for a place and not a person was immaterial.

Jean Allégret's club was in a little narrow street behind the Chamber of Deputies, and they did not allow enough time to get there from their hotel, and had trouble finding it, and when they walked into the courtyard, half an hour late, Jean Allégret was standing on the steps of the building. They felt that he felt that in not being punctual they had been guilty of rudeness, and so the evening began stiffly. Through dinner, they talked about Austria and Italy, and he talked about his farm—about how the people he was living with—the two old gardeners who had been in the family for fifty years—were sick, and would have to go, since they could not help him any longer, and he did not know who he would find to do his cooking, for he could not do it himself; and about the water system, which would be running at the end of the month; and about his efforts to bring a few improvements to his little village. There was no doctor or chemist nearer than four miles, and he had decided that there must be a dispensary. With the help of the men and boys of the place, he had fixed up an old uninhabited house, and got two nuns to come there, and provided them with supplies. The money they needed for this had been raised through benefits—plays given by boys and girls, bicycle races, that sort of thing; and a few days ago they had celebrated the hundredth case treated there. In his spare time he had been drawing, doing sketches of rabbits, pheasants, wild ducks, stags, wild boars, or of people working in the fields or going to market. Someday, perhaps, he would publish some of them in a book.

The club was an army-officer's club, and he had done murals for it, which he showed them after dinner. Looking at the people around them, they thought: This is not at all the sort of place Americans usually see. . . . Neither was it very interesting. Then they sat down again and, over a glass of brandy, went on talking. But something was missing from the conversation. There were moments when they had to work to make it go. Why does it have to go, Harold wondered. *Because it went before* was the answer. His eyes came to rest on one figure after another at the nearby tables—the neat blond mustache, the trim military carriage, the look of cold pride.

He heard Barbara saying: "They gave Gluck's *Orpheus* in the Riding Academy, and there was a wonderful moment. The canvas roof was rolled back without our knowing it, and as Orpheus emerged from the Underworld we saw the lights of Salzburg. . . ."

Jean Allégret nodded politely, and Harold thought: Has she left out something? The music, of course. The most important part of all.

"*Orpheus* is a beautiful opera," he said, but Jean Allégret's expression did not change.

There is something he's not saying, Harold thought, and that's why the evening has gone this way. Instead of listening, he watched Jean Allégret's face. It told him nothing, and he decided that, as so often happened, he was imagining things that did not really exist.

"In the mountains," Jean Allégret was saying, "the political struggle and all the unsolved problems of modern life belong to a tiny lost spot over there in the evening fog, miles away in the bottom of the valley . . . the last village. We slept in any deserted hut or rolled up in our blankets in a hole between rocks. Our only concern was the direction of the winds, the colors of the sunset, the fog climbing from the valley, the bucks always on the top of the following peak . . ."

"My older brother loved to hunt," Harold said.

Jean Allégret turned and looked at him with interest.

"He took me rabbit hunting with him when I was about eight years old. It was winter, and very cold, and there was deep snow on the ground. I still remember it vividly. We got up at five o'clock in the morning, to go hunting, and he missed three rabbits in a row. I think it flustered him, having me there watching him. And he swore. And then we went home."

It seemed hardly worth putting beside a shooting expedition in the Pyrenees, but Harold, too, was holding something back, and it was: *I never had a gun. I never wanted one. I always thought I couldn't bear to kill anything. But once when we were staying in the country—this was after Barbara and I were married—there was a rabbit in the garden every day, and it was doing a lot of damage, and I killed it with a borrowed shotgun, and I didn't feel anything. People are so often mistaken about themselves. . . .*

Though they were close enough to have reached out and touched each other (and it would perhaps have been better if they had) the broad Atlantic Ocean lay between them. That first conversation, under the full moon, had been so personal and direct that it left no way open for increasing intimacy, and so they had reverted; they had become an aristocratic Frenchman and an American tourist.

Outside on the steps of the building, they thanked Jean Allégret for a very pleasant evening, and shook hands, and at the last possible moment the brandy brushed Harold's hesitations aside and spoke for him: "There were no brown-eyed people in Austria."

"Why not?" Jean Allégret said.

"You know why not," Harold said solemnly.

"Yes, I'm afraid I do," Jean Allégret said, after a moment.

"I kept looking for them everywhere. All dead. No brown-eyed people left. Terrible!" And then: "It was all right before, and now it isn't. . . . Home, I'm talking about . . . not Austria. I didn't know about any other place. Or any other kind of people. I didn't have to make comparisons. I will never be intact again."

"In the modern world," Jean Allégret said gently, "nobody is intact. It is only an illusion. When you are home, you will forget about what it is like here. And be happy, as you were before."

"No I won't!"

"Well, you will be busy, anyway," Jean Allégret said, looking into Harold's eyes, the same person, suddenly, that he had been on that moon-flooded terrace in the Touraine. Having reached each other at last, they shook hands once more, and Jean Allégret said: "If you come back to France one day, come and spend a few days with me."

With Sabine they did not feel any constraint. She came to their hotel on Saturday evening, and they took her to the restaurant in the alley off the Place St. Sulpice. She had a job, she told them. She was going to work for an elderly man who published lithographic reproductions of paintings and some art books. The salary was a little less than she had been earning at *La Femme Elégante*, but it was work that she would enjoy doing, she liked the man she would be working for, and perhaps it might lead to something better, in time. The job was to start on the first of November, and she had come up to Paris a few days early.

She was wearing the same white silk blouse and straight skirt that she invariably wore. Doesn't she have any other clothes, Harold wondered. But it turned out to be one of those things men don't understand; the white silk blouse was beautifully tailored, Barbara said later, and right for any occasion.

There were no awkward silences, because they never ran out of things to say. The few things Sabine told them about herself were only a beginning of all there was to tell, and each time they were with her they felt they knew her a little better. But there was something elusive about her. The silvery voice that was just right for telling stories and the faintly mysterious smile, though charming in themselves, were also barriers. It is possible to see the color of flowers by moonlight, but you can never quite read a book.

While Pierre was changing the plates, Harold said suddenly: "Would you like to hear a ghost story? . . . In Marseilles, all the hotels were full, because of a big fair of some kind, and we went to one after another, and finally one that the taxi driver had never heard of, and he didn't even think it was a hotel, but it was listed in the Michelin, so I made him stop there and I got out and went inside. There was no hotel sign, and when I opened the door and walked in off the street, there wasn't any lobby either. Nothing but a spiral stairway. I decided the lobby must be one flight up. On the second floor there was a landing, but no doors led from it. So I went on, and while I was climbing the stairs I heard footsteps."

"This is not a true story?" Sabine said. "You are inventing it just to please me?"

"No, no, it all happened. . . . Someone was climbing the stairs ahead of me. I called out and there was no answer. I stood still and listened. The footsteps continued, and I felt the hair rise on the back of my neck. I went a little farther, and when there were still no doors, I stopped again. This time there wasn't any sound. My heart was pounding. I could feel somebody up there waiting for me to climb the last few steps. I turned and ran all the way down the stairs and burst through the doorway into the open air. . . . What was it, do you think? Was it really a hotel?"

"I think it was a nightmare," Sabine said.

"But I was wide awake."

"One is, sometimes," she said, and he thought of the drama that had happened in her family. He had a feeling that if he leaned forward at that moment and asked: "What *did* happen?" she would tell them. But the next course arrived, and put an end to the possibility.

Sabine said to Barbara: "Where did you find your little heart?"

The little heart was of crystal, bound with a thin band of gold, and Barbara had noticed it in the window of an antique shop in Toulon, during the noon bus stop. "It wasn't very expensive," she said. "Do you think it's a child's locket? Do you think I shouldn't wear it?"

"No, it's charming," Sabine said. "And perfectly all right to wear."

"Do you remember," Barbara said, "that little diamond heart that Mme Straus always wore?"

They began to talk about the gloves and scarves and purses in the window of Hermès, and he picked up his fork and started eating.

After dinner they walked through the square and back to the hotel, and sat on the big bed, leaning against the headboard or the footboard, with their legs tucked under them, talking, until eleven thirty. He knew that Sabine liked Barbara, and had always liked her, but as he was walking her to the Métro station he realized with surprise that she liked him too. She could not say so, directly and simply, as Alix said such things; it came out, instead, in her voice, in the way she listened to his account of their last days in Paris, and how queer he felt about going home. It was something he had been refusing to think about, but apparently he had been carrying the full weight of it around, because now that he had spoken to somebody about it, he felt lighter. He had the feeling that, no matter what he told her, she would get it right; she wouldn't go off with a totally wrong idea of what he was feeling or thinking.

He was going to take her all the way to her door but she wouldn't let him. At the entrance to the Métro, they stopped and he started to say good-by, under a street lamp, and she said: "I will be at my aunt's house on Monday."

"Oh, that's good," he exclaimed. "Then I won't say good-by. . . . I keep trying to get to the Ile St. Louis. It's as if my life depended on it. As if I *must* see it. And every day something keeps me from going there. What is it like?"

"From the Ile St. Louis there is a beautiful view of the back of Notre Dame," she said. "Voltaire lived there for a while. So did Bossuet. And Théophile Gautier, and Baudelaire, and Daumier. In the Ile St. Louis you feel the past around you, more than anywhere else in Paris. The houses are very old, and the streets are so silent. Perhaps you will go there tomorrow. . . ."

He suggested to Mme Straus, over the telephone on Sunday morning, that she take a taxi directly to their hotel, and she said Mon dieu, she would be taking the bus, and that they should meet her at one o'clock in front of the church of St. Germain-des-Prés, which was only five minutes' walk from where they were staying.

Barbara was still dressing when the time came to start out to meet her, and since Mme Straus was usually prompt and they did not want to keep her waiting outside on a damp, raw day, he went on ahead. As he crossed the boulevard St. Germain, he saw standing in front of the church a figure that could have been Mme Straus; he wasn't sure until he had reached the sidewalk that it wasn't. In the two months since they had seen her, her face had grown dim in his mind. The old woman at the foot of the church steps was poorly dressed, and when he got closer to her, he saw she had a cigar box in her hand. The purpose of the cigar box became clear when people began to pour out of the church at the conclusion of the service. Harold stood in a doorway where he could keep an eye on the buses arriving from Auteuil and from across the river. One bus after another arrived, stopped, people got off and other people got on, but still no Mme Straus.

The beggarwoman was also not having much luck. About

one person in fifty, he calculated. He found himself judging
the people who came out of the church solely in relation to
her. Those who gave her something were nice, were good,
were kind. Those who ignored her outstretched box, or were
annoyed, or raised their eyebrows, or just didn't see her, he
disliked. He watched a young woman who was helping an
older woman down the steps—mother and daughter, they must
be. So like Alix, he thought. The young woman didn't notice
the box at first, and then when she did see it, she immediately
smiled at the old woman, stopped, opened her purse—all in
such a way that there could be no questioning her sincerity
and goodness of heart. As for the others, perhaps they had
been stopped by too many beggars, or knew the old woman
was a fraud, or just didn't have ten francs to spare.

He kept expecting the old woman to come over to him, and
she did finally. She came over and spoke to him—a rushing
speech full of bitterness and sly derision at the churchgoers—
that much was clear—though most of it he could not understand. He looked at her and listened, and smiled, and didn't
say anything, thinking that she must know by his clothes that
he was an American, and waiting for her to present the box.
She didn't, and so he didn't put his hand in his pocket and
draw out his folded French money. Something more personal
was happening between them. Either he was serving her well
enough by listening so intently to what she said, or else she
recognized in him a character somehow on the same footing
with her—a beggar holding out his hand for something if not
for money, a fraud, a professional cheat of some kind, at odds
with society and living off it, a blackmailer, a thief—somebody
the police are interested in, or if not the police then the charity
organizations. . . . A poor blind tourist, that's what he was.

While he was listening, his eyes recorded the arrival of Mme
Straus-Muguet. She stepped down to the cobblestones from
the back platform of a bus, and as he went toward her, looking
at her clothes—her fur piece, her jaunty hat with a feather, her
lorgnette swinging by its black ribbon—he wondered how he
could, even at a distance, have mistaken the old beggar woman
with the cigar box and a grievance against society for their
faithful, indomitable, confusing friend.

Her voice, her greeting, her enthusiasm, the pressure on his arm were all affectionate and unchanged. She could not bear to leave the vicinity of such a famous church, the oldest church in Paris, without going inside for a moment. They stood in the hushed empty interior, looking down the nave at the altar and the stained-glass windows, and then they came out again. As they were crossing the street, she said that she knew the quarter well. Her sister had an apartment in the boulevard Raspail, and as a child she had lived in the rue Madame, a block from their hotel.

"But you are thin!" she exclaimed.

"Too much aesthetic excitement," he said jokingly, and she said: "You must eat more!"

Barbara was waiting for them in the rue des Canettes. Mme Straus kissed her, admired Barbara's new hat, and then, turning, perceived that she knew the restaurant; she had dined here before, with satisfaction. As they walked in, monsieur and madame bowed and smiled respectfully at Mme Straus and then approvingly at Harold and Barbara for having at last got themselves a sponsor. Pierre led them to their regular table, and recommended the pâté en croûte. Mme Straus ordered potage instead. The restaurant was unusually crowded, and the waiters were very busy. Though Barbara had explained to Mme Straus that Pierre was their friend, she called "Garçon!" loudly. And when he left what he was doing and came over to their table, she complained because the pommes de terre frites weren't hot. He hurried them away and came back with more that had just been taken from the spider. She continued to be condescending to him, but as if she were acting for Harold and Barbara—as if this were one more lesson they ought to learn. He kept his temper but something passed between them, an exchange of irritable glances and cutting phrases that the Americans could not follow and that made them uneasy. They felt left out. Pierre and Mme Straus were like two members of the same family who know each other's sore spots and can't resist aggravating them. As Pierre hurried off to bring the filtered coffees, Mme Straus assured them that their friend was an intelligent boy. And a few minutes later, when Harold got up and went into the front room to pay the check, Pierre stopped, on his way past, and remarked gravely (but kindly, as if what he was about to say was dictated solely by concern for them):

"Your guest—that old lady—is not what she pretends to be. The girl you brought yesterday—*she's* the real thing."

After lunch they walked in the square, and Mme Straus pointed out that the fountain, which they had never really looked at before, was in commemoration of Bossuet, Fénelon, Massillon, and Fléchier—the four great bishops who should have been but were not made cardinals. "How they must have hated each other!" she exclaimed merrily.

Barbara took a snapshot of Harold and Mme Straus standing in front of the fountain, and then they walked to their hotel. She approved of their room and of the view, and asked how much they paid. She considered seriously the possibility of taking a room here. She was in mortal terror lest the nuns raise the price of her small chamber among the roses, in which case she could no longer afford to stay there.

They left the hotel and wandered up the rue Vaugirard to the Luxembourg Gardens, and walked up and down looking at the flower beds, the people, the Medici fountain, the balloon man, the children sailing their boats in the shallow basin. A gas-filled balloon escaped, and they followed it with their eyes. Since we last saw her, Harold thought, there has been a change—if not in her then in her circumstances.

Mme Straus kept looking at her wrist watch, and at five o'clock she hurried them out of the Gardens and up the street to a tea shop, where she had arranged for her grandson Edouard to meet them. Edouard was seventeen and in school; he was studying to be an engineer, Mme Straus said, and he had only one desire—to come to America.

After so big a lunch, they had no appetite. Barbara crumbled but did not eat her cupcake. Harold slowly got his tea and three cakes down. Edouard did not appear. Mme Straus sat with her back to the wall and glanced frequently at the doorway. Conversation died a dull death. There was no one at the surrounding tables, and the air was lifeless. The tea made them feel too warm. Done in by so much walking and talking, or by Edouard's failure to show up for the tea party, Mme Straus reached out for her special talent, and for the first time in their experience it was not there. She sat, silent and apparently distracted by private thoughts. She roused herself and said how disappointed Edouard would be, not to make their acquaintance. Something must have happened, of a serious nature; nothing else would account for his absence. And a few minutes later she considered the possibility that he had gone to the cinema with friends. Harold found himself wondering whether it is possible to read the mind of someone who is thinking in a language you don't understand. What he was thinking, and did not want Mme Straus to guess that he was thinking, was: Does Edouard exist? And if there really is an Edouard, does he regard his grandmother with the same impatience and undisguised contempt as the celebrated actress, her friend, to whom she is so devoted?

Mme Straus called for the check, and either misread the amount or absent-mindedly failed to put down enough to pay for the tea and cakes and *service*. The waitress pointed out the mistake, and while it was being rectified, Harold looked the other way, for fear he would see more than Mme Straus intended them to see.

They parted from her at dusk. She announced that she was coming to the boat train on Tuesday, to see them off. As they stood on a corner of the boulevard St. Germain, waiting for the bus, she pointed out the Cluny Museum to them, and was shocked that they hadn't heard of it.

The bus came and she got on it and went up the curving steps. Waving to them from the top of the bus, she was swept away.

"Do you think he forgot?" Barbara asked as they started on down the street.

"I don't even think he exists," Harold said. "But does *she*, is the question. You don't think she is something we made up?"

"No, she exists."

They crossed over, so that she could look in the window of a shoe shop.

"So courageous," he said. "Always taking life at the flood. . . . But what is she going to do— Who or what can she turn to, now that the flood has become a trickle?"

The last day was very strange. He had hoped that there would be time to go to the Ile St. Louis in the morning, and instead he found himself on the top of a bus going down the rue Bonaparte with another suitcase to leave at the steamship office. The sun was shining, the air was cool, and there was a kind of brilliance over everything. The bus turned left and then right and went over the Pont du Carrousel, and as he looked up and down the river, the sadness that he had managed to hold at arm's length for the last four days took possession of him.

The bus went through the south gate of the Louvre and out into the sunshine again and stopped to take on passengers. The whole of the heart of Paris lay before him—the palace, the geometrical flower beds, the long perspective down the gardens, which had been green when he came and were now autumn-colored, the people walking or bicycling, the triumphal arch, the green statues, the white gravel, the grass, the clouds coming over from the Left Bank in a procession. Looking at it now, so hard that it made his eyes burn and ache, he knew in his heart that what he loved was here, and only for the people who lived here; it wasn't anywhere else. *I cannot leave!* he cried out silently to the old buildings and the brightness in the air, to the yellow leaves on the trees, and to the shine that was over everything. *I cannot bear it that all this will be here and I will not be. . . . I might as well die. . . .*

At noon they turned into the rue des Canettes for the last time. When Harold had finished ordering, he made a little farewell speech to Pierre and, after the waiter had gone off to the kitchen, thought: How foolish of me. . . . What does he care whether we love France or not? . . . But then, though they had asked for Perrier water, Pierre brought three wine glasses and a bottle of Mâcon rouge. First he assured them that the wine would not be on their bill, and then he opened the bottle ceremoniously, filled their two glasses, and poured a little wine into his. They raised their glasses and drank to each other, and to the voyage, and to the future of France. Pierre went on about his work, but from time to time he returned, with their next course or merely to stand a moment talking to them. They dallied over lunch; they had a second and then a third cup of coffee. They were the last clients to leave the restaurant, and the wine had made them half drunk, as usual. They shook hands with Pierre and said good-by. They stopped to shake hands with the other waiter, Louis, and again, in the

front room with Monsieur and Madame, who wished them
bon voyage. As they stepped out into the street, they heard
someone calling to them and turned around. It was Pierre. He
had shed his waiter's coat and he drew them into the restaurant across the street, to have a cognac with him. Then they
had another round, on Harold, and before he and Barbara
could get away, Louis joined them, as jealous as a younger
brother, insisting that they have a cognac with him. Harold
said no, saw the look of hurt on both men's faces, and said:
"Why not?"

Pierre went off, and came back a few minutes later with his
wife, who worked in a nearby department store. The two
women talked to each other, in English. They had one last
round, and shook hands, and said good-by, and the Americans
promised to come back soon.

They got into a taxi and went to the bank. With the floor
tilting dangerously under him, Harold stood in line and
grinned foolishly at the teller who counted out his money.

To clear their heads, they rode to the Place Redouté on the
top of a bus, and they were able to walk straight by the time
they stopped to shake hands with Mme Emile, on their way
into the building.

"Are you all right?" Barbara asked as they stepped into the
elevator.

"Yes. How about you?"

"I'm all right," she said. "But we probably smell to high
heaven of all that we've been drinking."

"It can't be helped," he said, and pressed the button.

Alix was just the same, and they were very happy to see her,
but the apartment was different. With the shutters thrown
back in the drawing room, it was much lighter and brighter
and more cheerful.

Shortly after they arrived, Mme Viénot came in, with
Sabine, and took possession of the conversation. While she sat
listening, Barbara had a question uppermost in her mind, and
it was why didn't Mme Viénot or Alix or Mme Cestre mention
the soap? Didn't it ever arrive? Or weren't they as pleased with
it as she had thought they would be?

Harold was telling how they couldn't find the Simone
Martinis in Siena and finally gave up and climbed the bell

tower of the very building the paintings were in, without knowing it. When he finishes I'll ask them, she thought, but she didn't because by that time she had another worry on her mind: what if Françoise should show Alix the stockings she had given her, which were the same kind that Barbara had presented to Alix and Mme Cestre and Mme Viénot in the country, and that they had been so pleased with. She wished now the stockings had been of a better quality. She had economized on them, but she could not explain this without bringing in the fact that they were to give to the chambermaids in hotels in place of a tip.

"You must excuse me," Alix said. "I am going to get the tea things."

"Can I help?" Barbara asked, but Alix did not hear her, and so she sat back in her chair. The thing she had hoped was that she would have one last look at the kitchen. It was very queer, having to act like a guest in a place where they were so much at home. Neither Alix nor Mme Cestre made any reference to the fact that she and Harold had spent ten days in this apartment. One would almost have thought that they didn't know it. Or that it hadn't really happened.

Speaking very distinctly, Harold said to Mme Cestre: "In Italy I saw with my own eyes how fast the earth is turning. We went to hear *Traviata*. It was out of doors—it was in the Baths of Caracalla—and during the second act the moon came up so fast that it was almost alarming to watch. Within five minutes from the time it appeared above the ruins it was high up in the sky."

"You saw St. Peter's? And the Vatican?" Mme Viénot asked.

Right after she had finished her tea, she rose and shook hands with her sister, and then with Barbara and Harold. In the hall she presented her cheek to Alix to be kissed, and said: "Good-by, my dear. I'll call you tomorrow afternoon, before I leave for the country. . . . I won't say good-by now, M. Rhodes. I am seeing someone off on the boat train tomorrow —a cousin who is going to America on the *Mauretania* with you."

"You think the boat train will be running?" he asked.

"For your sake, I hope it is," Mme Viénot said. "You must be quite anxious."

"I have a present for you," Sabine said as she was shaking hands with them. "I am making you a drawing, but it isn't quite finished."

"We'd love to have one of your drawings," Barbara said.

"Maman will bring it to the train tomorrow."

When she and Mme Viénot had left, the others sat down again, and the Americans waited until a polite interval had passed before they too got up to go.

Mme Cestre told them that she had been at Le Bourget when Lindbergh's plane appeared out of the sky.

"You were in that vast crowd?" Harold said.

"Yes. It was very thrilling," she said. "I will never forget it. I was quite close to him as they carried him from the field."

Harold thought he heard someone moving around in the study, and looked at Alix, to see if she too had heard it. She said: "I also have a present for you." She opened a door of the secretary and took out a small flat package wrapped in tissue paper and tied with a white ribbon. This present gave Barbara a chance to ask about the soap.

"I should have thanked you," Alix said. "Oh dear, you will think we are not very grateful. We thought it might be from you. But there are also some other people, cousins who are now traveling in America, who could have sent it, and so I was afraid to speak about it. . . . Mummy, you were right. It was Barbara—that is, it was Barbara's mother who sent us the beautiful package of soap!"

On their way out of the building, they shook hands one last time with Mme Emile, who wished them bon voyage, and when they were outside in the street, Barbara opened the little package. It was a book—a charming little edition of Flaubert's *Un Coeur Simple* with hand-colored illustrations. On the fly-leaf, Alix had written their names and her name and the date and the words: "Really with all my love."

"Wasn't that nice of her," Barbara said. And then, as they were crossing the square: "What about dinner?"

"Are you hungry?" he asked.

She shook her head. "There was somebody in the study."

"I know," he said. "Eugène."

"You think?"

"Who else."

"Françoise, maybe."

"What would she be doing in there?"

"I don't know. Do you feel like walking?" she asked.

"All right. . . . He gave me four Swiss francs, to buy sugar for him in Switzerland. I didn't do it."

"Why not?"

"It would have been a lot of trouble, and it turned out that we didn't have much time. Also, I didn't feel like doing it."

"Do you still have the money?" she asked.

"Yes. It's not very much. About a dollar. I guess we can forget about it."

They turned and took one last look at the granite monument.

"Do you think there was something going on that we didn't know about?" he said.

"Like what?"

"That's just it, I have no idea what."

"If you mean the 'drama' that—"

"I don't mean the 'drama.' That was two or three years ago. I mean right now, this summer."

"There would be no reason for them to tell us if there was," she said thoughtfully.

"No," he agreed.

"You think they're all right? You don't think they're in any kind of serious trouble, all of them?"

"Maybe not all of them. Maybe just Alix and Eugène. It would explain a lot of things. The way he was with us. And why they stayed in the country so long. I don't suppose we'll ever know what it was."

"Then you think there was something?"

"Yes," he said.

"So do I."

"Even when we thought we were on the inside," he said, "we weren't really. Inside, outside, it's nothing but a state of mind, I guess. . . . Except that if you love people, you can't help wanting to—"

"Alix is having another baby."

He took her hand as they walked along but said nothing. He was not sure at this moment what her feelings were, and he did not want to say something that would make her cry in the street.

They skipped dinner entirely and instead took the Métro halfway across Paris to a movie theater that was showing *Le Diable au Corps*. Harold wanted to see it, and they had missed it when they were here in the summer, and it had not been showing anywhere since they got back. In America it would be cut.

They were half an hour early, and walked up and down, rather than go in and sit in an empty theater. Over the ticket booth there was an electric bell that rang insistently and continuously; the whole street was filled with the sound. They looked at all the shop windows on both sides of the street. He glanced at his wrist watch. It was still twenty minutes before it would be time to go inside, and at the thought of twenty minutes more of that dreadful ringing, and then the hocus-pocus and the delay that always went on in French movie theaters, and people passing through the aisles selling candy, while they waited and waited for the picture to begin, he suddenly stopped, swallowed hard, and, taking Barbara's arm, said: "Let's go home. I can't stand that sound. . . . And even if we do wait, I won't be able to enjoy the movie. I've had all I can manage. I'm through. I can't take in any more."

They arrived at the Gare St. Lazare, with their hand luggage, an hour early. The boat train was running. It was due to leave at eleven ten, and they would get to Cherbourg about five. They walked down the platform, looking for their carriage and compartment, and found it. Barbara waited in the train, while Harold walked up and down outside. Magazine and fruit vendors had come to see them off, and a flower girl whose pushcart was covered with bouquets of violets, but there was no sign of Mme Straus. Minute after minute passed. The platform grew crowded. There was a sense of growing excitement. Harold wandered in and out among the porters and the passengers, who, standing in little groups along the track, were nearly all Americans. For the first time in four months it didn't require any effort on his part to overhear scraps of conversation. He didn't like what he heard. The voices of his compatriots were loud, and what they said seemed silly beyond endurance. It was like having home thrown at him.

At three minutes of eleven, he gave up all hope of finding

Mme Straus in the crowd that was milling around on the platform and started back to their coach, telling himself that it didn't matter that she had failed to come. It wasn't so much that she was insincere as that she loved to arouse expectations it wasn't always convenient or even possible to satisfy, when the time came. . . . Only it did matter, he thought, still searching for her among the faces. Now that they were leaving, he wanted some one person out of a whole country that they had loved on first sight and never stopped loving—he wanted somebody to be aware of the fact that they were leaving, and come to say good-by.

At the steps of their carriage he took one last look around and saw her, talking agitatedly to one of the train guards. He was close enough that he could hear her asking the guard to point out the carriage of M. and Mme Rhodes. The guard shrugged. Harold went up to her and took hold of her elbow, and she cried: "Ah, chéri!" and kissed him.

She had been delayed. She thought that she would never find them in the crowd.

Barbara saw Mme Straus from the train window and came out onto the platform. Mme Straus kissed her and then presented her with a farewell gift, a pasteboard box containing palmiers. "They're to eat on the train," she said.

Edouard's mother had been taken ill on Sunday afternoon and he couldn't leave her. He was sorry to have missed them.

She wanted to see their compartment, so they mounted the steps and went down the corridor and showed her their reserved seats and their luggage, safely stowed away on the overhead rack.

"By the window," she said approvingly. "Now that I have it firmly in mind, I can go with you." She squeezed their hands in both of hers.

They went outside again and stood talking together on the platform. Mme Viénot appeared out of the crowd, with a boutonniere for Barbara. "From the garden at Beaumesnil," she said. She and Mme Straus greeted each other with the comic cordiality of two women who understand the full extent of their mutual dislike and are not concerned about it. Then, turning to Barbara and Harold, she said: "Sabine had something that she wanted me to bring you—a drawing. But she didn't get it finished in time. She said to tell you that she would be mailing it to you. I saw it. It is quite charming. It is of the old houses on the Ile St. Louis. . . . Au revoir, my dears. Have a good trip home."

She went off to rejoin her cousin.

The train guards called out a warning, and Mme Straus embraced them both one last time and urged them back on the train. When they sat down, she was at the window, dabbing her eyes with a tiny white handkerchief. They tried to carry on a conversation in pantomime.

She said something but they couldn't hear what it was. Harold said something back and she shook her head, to show that she didn't understand. They got up and went down the corridor to the end of the car. The door was still open. Mme Straus was there waiting, with the tears running down her cheeks. They leaned down and touched her hands, as the train began to move. For reasons that there was now no chance of their knowing, she clung to them, hurrying along beside the slowly moving train, waving to them, calling good-by. When she could no longer find them among the other heads and waving arms they could see her, still waving her crumpled handkerchief, old, forsaken, left in her own sad city, where the people she knew did not know her, and her stories were not believed even when they were true.

Part Two

Some Explanations

Chapter 19

IS THAT ALL?
    Yes, that's all.
    But what about the mysteries?
You mean the "drama" that Mme Viénot didn't tell Harold
Rhodes about?
    And where M. Viénot was.
Oh, that.
    And why Hector Gagny didn't go up to Paris with the Ameri-
cans. And why Alix didn't say good-by to them at the station.
And why the actress was so harsh with poor Mme Straus-Muguet,
when they went backstage. And why that woman who kept the
fruit and vegetable shop—Mme Michot—was so curious about
what was going on at the château.
    I don't know that any of those things very much matters.
They are details. You don't enjoy drawing your own conclusions about them?
    Yes, but then I like to know if the conclusions I have come to are
the right ones.
    How can they not be when everything that happens hap-
pens for so many different reasons? But if you really want to
know why something happened, if explanations are what you
care about, it is usually possible to come up with one. If necessary, it can be fabricated. Hector Gagny didn't go up to Paris
on Bastille Day because Mme Carrère invited him to go driving
with them, and he was perfectly happy to put off his departure
until the next day. And the reason that Mme Michot was so
curious is that her only daughter was married and had left
home, and M. Michot had left home, too, years before, in a
crowded box car bound for the German border, and there had
been no word from him since. It is only natural that, having to
live with an unanswered question of this kind, she should occupy her mind with other questions instead. . . . But if you
concentrate on details, you lose sight of the whole. The Americans fell in love with France, the way Americans are always
doing, and they had the experience of knowing some French
people but not knowing them very well. They didn't speak

French, which made it difficult, and they were paying guests, and the situation of the paying guest is peculiar. It has in it something of the nature of an occupation by force. Once they were home, they quickly forgot a good many of the people they met abroad and the places they stayed in, but this experience with a French family, and the château, and the apartment in Paris, they couldn't forget. Hearing the blast that departing liners give as they turn in the Hudson River, Harold Rhodes raised his head and listened for a repetition of the sound. For those few seconds his face was deeply melancholy. And he took a real hatred—briefly—to an old and likable friend whose work made it possible for him to live in Paris. Neither of these things needs explaining. As for those that do, when you explain away a mystery, all you do is make room for another.

Even so. If you don't mind.

No, I don't mind. It's just a question of where to begin.

Begin with the drama.

Which one?

Were there two?

There was a drama that occurred several years before the Americans came to stay at the château, and there was another, several years after. One was a tragedy, the other was a farce. They don't belong together, except as everything that happens to somebody, or to a single family, belongs together. In that case, though, there is no question of why anything happened, but only what happened, and what happened then, and what happened after that—all of it worth looking at, as a moral and a visual spectacle.

Well, what happened to the money, then?

That's the first drama. You're sure you want to hear about it? . . . "Somebody will tell us," Harold said, and sure enough somebody did. A cousin turned up, in New York, and called Mrs. Ireland, who invited her to lunch. She was the same age as Sabine and Alix, but a rather plain girl, and talkative. And what she talked about was the sudden change in the situation of the family at Beaumesnil. She said that shortly after the war ended, M. Viénot sold all the securities that Mme Bonenfant had been left by her husband, who was a very rich man, and bought shares in a Peruvian gold mine. The stocks and bonds he disposed of were sound, and the gold mine proved to be a swindle.

Then he was a crook?

It may have been nothing more than a mistake in judgment. . . . The cousin said that he himself profited by the transaction, but then she may not have got the facts straight. People seldom do.

But how could he have profited by reducing his wife's family from affluence to genteel poverty? It doesn't make any sense.

No, it doesn't, does it? Neither did his explanations. So Mme Viénot left him and went to live with her mother. But quite recently Barbara had a letter from Sabine in which she said that her mother and father were living in Oran, and Beaumesnil was closed. So they must have gone back together again.

The day young George Ireland arrived to spend the summer, M. Viénot turned up at the château, in an Italian sports car, with a blonde on the seat beside him. She was young, George said. And pretty. They were invited to stay for lunch, and they did, and drove back to Paris that night.

How extraordinary.

After which Mme Viénot communicated with him only through her lawyer, but Sabine continued to see her father, and so did her sister. The family could only suppose that his reason had been affected, what he did was so out of character, so unlike the man he had always been. And since Mme Bonenfant had always loved him like a son, she particularly clung to this explanation of his disastrous behavior. But there were certain signs they ought to have paid attention to. He had begun to wear less conservative clothes. He drove his car recklessly, was inattentive and irritable, sighed in his sleep, and showed a preference for the company of young people. He had even ceased to look like the man he used to be. These changes were gradual, of course, and they saw him with the eyes of habit.

So much for the tragedy. The second drama, the farce, began when two men appeared at the door one day and asked to speak to Mme Viénot. They said that they had heard in the village that she took guests and they wanted to stay at the château. Mme Viénot said that surely the person who told them this also told them that she only took guests who came to her with a proper introduction. They said they'd be back in an hour with a proper introduction and Mme Viénot said that she was sorry they had had this long walk for nothing, and shut the door on them. After lunch, at the moment when Thérèse should have appeared in the drawing room with the coffee tray, she appeared without the coffee tray, and informed Mme Viénot that the cook wanted to speak to her. This was unprecedented, and Mme Viénot foresaw, as she excused herself, that on the cook's face too there would be a look of fright.

This was Mme Foëcy?

This was a different cook. Mme Foëcy was there only that summer. She was not in the habit of staying very long in any one establishment. . . . The same two men had turned up at the kitchen door, it seems, and asked for something to eat. The cook gave them a sandwich but wouldn't let them come inside. They wanted her to leave the kitchen window open that night, so they could get into the house. She threatened to call out for help, and so they left. That same afternoon, at teatime, Mme Viénot saw the gardener hovering in the vicinity of the drawing room windows.

As soon as she could, she slipped outside. The gardener was in a state of excitement. He too had had a visit, and the two men said that there was a treasure hidden somewhere in the house.

No!

Gold bullion. Left by the Germans, because they didn't have the means or the time to take it with them.

And was it true?

It is true that there was such a rumor in the village. The same story was told of other country houses after the war, and probably had its origin in a folk tale. The story varied, according to who told it. Sometimes the treasure was buried in the garden, in the dead of night. Sometimes it was hidden inside the walls. Great importance was attached to the fact that no member of Mme Bonenfant's family had ever denied this story, but actually it had never reached their ears.

The gardener told the men he would help them. He agreed to leave a cellar window open for them, but not that night. It was not a good time, he said; the house was full of people. And if they'd wait until there was no one here but the women, their chances would be better. They decided upon a signal, and as soon as the two men were off the property, the gardener came to find Mme Viénot.

Then what happened?

She went to the police, and together they worked out a plan. The only men in the house, Eugène and Mme Viénot's son-in-law, Jean-Claude Lahovary, were to leave as conspicuously as possible in Eugène's car and come back after dark, on foot. The gardener would hang the lantern in the potting shed—the signal that had been agreed upon—and the police would be nearby, waiting for a telephone call saying that the robbers were actually inside the house. It was all very melodramatic and like a British spy movie, except for one characteristically French touch. When the police cars came up the drive, they were blowing their sirens.

So the robbers got away?

No, they were caught. They must not have heard the sirens. Or else they were confused, or couldn't find their way out of the house in the dark. They were convicted of housebreaking, and sentenced to a term in jail. At the trial it came out that one of them had had some education; he had been a government clerk. Later, in the woods back of Beaumesnil, somebody found the remains of a campfire, and it was assumed that the robbers hid out there, while they were waiting for the signal.

What an amazing story.

Yes, isn't it. What would you like to know about next?

I think I'd like to know about Eugène why he acted the way he did. Was he in the study, the day the Americans came to say good-by?

Of course.

And Alix knew that he was there?

Her hearing was excellent. It was her mother who suffered from deafness. There was no one Eugène could not make love him if he chose to, but he blew hot and cold about people. He blew hot and they mistook it for friendship; he blew cold and they had to learn, in self-defense, to despise him. This deadly, monotonous pattern did not occur with his wife. In spite of his belief that married people change and grow less fond of one another with time, this did not happen in his case. Their marriage had its ups and downs, like all marriages, but it did not become absent-minded or perfunctory. Would you like to see them sleeping together?

Well, I don't know that I—

It's quite all right. No trouble at all. The workshirt hanging across the attic window has been replaced by a potted geranium, and the Prodigal Son is gone. Someone, unable to stand the sight of so much raw emotion any longer, took it down and put it away in a closet. If you look closely, you will see that the fauteuil that belonged to Eugène's great-great-grandfather has been mended. The dresses and skirts in the armoires throughout the apartment are of a different length, and Alix and Eugène have three children now. But certain things are the same: the church bell, the rays of the star arriving and departing simultaneously, and whoever it is that at daybreak comes through the rue Malène and silently searches through the garbage cans for edible peelings, cheese rinds, moldy bread, good rags, diamond rings, broken objects that can be mended, shoes with holes in their soles, paper, string, and other treasures often found in just such refuse by old men and women with the will to live. The sky, growing lighter, says: *What is being but being different, night from day, the earth from the air, the way things were from the way things are?* The newspaper lying in the gutter announces that a turning point has been reached in the tide of human affairs, and the swallows, skimming the rooftops—

I've really had enough of those swallows.

For some reason, I never grow tired of them. The swallows, in their quick summarizing trip over the rooftops prove conclusively that there *is* no point of turning, because turning is all there is—constant, never-ending patterns of turning.

The shutters are open, the awnings are rolled. Alix and Eugène are sleeping with their backs turned to each other but touching. When she moves in her sleep, his body accommodates itself to the change without waking. Now they are facing each other. Of his forearm, shoulder, and cheek he makes a soft warm box for her head. Over her bent knees he extends protectively a relaxed weightless leg. Shortly afterward they turn away from each other. In their marriage also there is no

real resting place; one partner may dominate, may circum-
scribe, the actions of the other, briefly, but nothing is fixed,
nothing is final.

His moods—what were they all about?

Those recurring periods of melancholy, of a kind of darkness
of the soul, had nothing to do with her.

What did they have to do with?

Money, chiefly. Money that is lost becomes a kind of magic
mirror in which the deprived person sees himself always in the
distorted landscape of what might have been. When they were
living in Marseilles, Eugène did not think about money, largely
because everyone else was poor also. But in Paris he was reminded continually that his father had always lived in a certain
way, and so had his grandfather, and he would have liked to live
in the same way himself and he couldn't, and never would be
able to, because they have made no provision for him to do this.

Shouldn't they have?

Perhaps.

Then why didn't they?

Life was beautiful, and they thought it couldn't go on being
this way—about this they were quite right—and in any case it
would have meant sacrificing their pleasure and they needed
their pleasures; they needed all of them. His father's desk was
a mosaic of unpaid bills, which he never disturbed. When he
wanted to write a letter, he used his wife's desk.

What about Alix? Did she mind it that they were poor?

Not for herself. But she listened carefully to what Eugène
had to say about rich young men like Jean Allégret and René
Simon, and what she perceived was that it was not the money
itself but that he felt the loss of it had cast a shadow over their
lives so dense that they could not be seen. They were no longer
part of the world. They did not move among people who
counted. They might as well be the children of shopkeepers.

*It would have been better if she had not made him give up his
work among the poor in Marseilles.*

She didn't. That was only Mme Viénot's idea of what happened. Since he had renounced his spiritual vocation in order
to marry her, she was prepared to give up everything for his
sake, but unfortunately it turned out that he did not really

have a spiritual vocation. If he had, he would not have taken it so to heart when the men he was trying to educate failed him by falling asleep over the books he lent them, or by getting drunk and beating their wives, or simply by not understanding what it was that he wanted from them. Two or three years later, he threw himself into politics in the same high-minded way. He dedicated every free moment to working for the M.R.P.—the Mouvement Républicain Populaire, the Catholic reform party. Then he decided that all political efforts were futile, and found himself once more committed to nothing, nothing to cling to, no foothold, and totally outside the life around him. And though he was patient—no one was ever more patient—he was not always easy to live with. Or pleasant to people. Anyone in trouble could count on his help, and the telephone rang incessantly, but he had no friends. If he met someone he liked, someone who interested him, he was intensely curious, direct, personal, and charming. And then, his curiosity satisfied, he was simply not interested any more. The friends of his school days called up, made arrangements to see him, were startled by what they found, and didn't return.

That painful train journey, do you remember? the time he went up to Paris with Sabine and the Americans? What really happened?

He had quarreled with Alix on the way to the station, just as the Americans thought, and the quarrel was about them. After a few days of staying in the apartment by himself, he had found that he liked being alone, and he was sorry he had invited them. On the way to the station he proposed to Alix that she tell the Americans that it was not convenient to have them stay in the apartment at this time, and she refused. He said he would tell them himself, then, and she said that she could at least not be present when he did. After she left him, he decided that instead of telling the Americans outright that he didn't want them, he could make them understand, from his behavior, that he had changed his mind about having them.

And they didn't understand.

No, they did understand, and started to go to the Hôtel Vouillemont. But in the Métro, when they tried to leave him, he changed his mind again. For a moment, he felt something like affection for them. He continued to teeter in this fashion, between liking and not liking them, the whole period of their stay in the apartment.

But why did he act the way he did? Was it because Barbara did not dance with him? She really should have. It was inexcusable, her refusing to dance with him at the Allégrets' party.

She would have danced with him, except that he was so sullen when he asked her. But that wasn't why he changed.

Was it something Harold did?

It was something he was, I think.

What was he?

A young man with a beautiful wife and the money to spend four months traveling in Europe. An American. A man with a future, and no shadow across his present life.

But that isn't what his life was like.

No, but that's what it looked like, from the outside.

It was also wrong of them, very wrong, not to accept Alix's invitation to come down to the country for the week end. And not to call on M. and Mme Carrère, after M. Carrère had given Harold his card, was—

True. Perfectly true. Their behavior doesn't stand careful inspection. But on the other hand, you must remember that they were tourists. This is not the way they behaved when they were at home. And it is one thing to hand out gold stars to children for remembering to brush their teeth and another to pass moral judgment on adult behavior. So much depends on the circumstances.

In short, it is something you don't feel like going into. Very well, what happened to Hector Gagny?

He divorced his wife, and married a woman with a half-grown boy, and she made him very happy. I always felt that his first wife was more—but she was impossible, as a wife. Or at least as a wife for him. The little boy in the carnival is grown up now and has a half interest in the merry-go-round. The gypsy fortuneteller dealt herself the ace of spades. Anybody or anything else you'd like to know about?

That drawing Sabine was going to send to the Americans. Did it ever arrive?

Yes, it arrived, about a month after Harold and Barbara got home, and with it was a rather touching letter, written the day they took the boat train:

Here is the little drawing promised, I hope it will not oblige you to lengthen your list for the douane!— Thanks still for all your kindness— You don't know what it meant for me, nor what both of you meant to me—. It's difficult to explain specially in English—. I think you represent like Aunt Mathilde and Alix an atmosphere *kind*, gay and harmonious, where everything is in its real place. And seeing you was a sort of rest through the roughness of existence, a bit like putting on fairy shoes.

Perhaps did you guess there was, a few years ago, a sad drama in our family. Since then many things changed, and I lived in one place and then in another—missing baddly that sort of atmosphere I just described. That's why perhaps I bored you a bit like Mme Straus, in trying to see you often— I am very sorry if I did. But you know: qu'il est encore plus difficile de diriger ses bons mouvements que ses mauvais, car, contrairement à ces derniers on ne peut jamais prévoir exactement leur résultat. En tout cas sachez que vous m'avez fait grand plaisir. . . .

It is so curious how, in the history of a family, you have one drastic change after another, all in a period of two or three years, and then for a long long time afterward no change at all. Sabine continued to live now in this place and now in that. The one place where she was always welcome at any time, and for as long as she cared to stay there, the apartment in the rue Malène, she would not make use of. But she turned up fairly often, and stayed just long enough to take her bearings by what she found there. "You will stay and eat with us?" Mme Cestre would say, but she did not urge her. And a few minutes later, Alix would say: "Françoise has set a place for you. . . . Well, come and sit down with us anyway," and Françoise waited and when the others were halfway through dinner she brought in a plate of soup, which Sabine allowed to grow cold in front of her, and then absent-mindedly ate. And then she went home—only it wasn't home she went to but the apartment of a cousin or an uncle or an old school friend of her grandmother's; and the bed she slept in was only a few feet away from an armoire that was crammed with somebody else's clothes.

But the family stood by her. And people were kind; very kind. ("Such a pleasure to have you, dear child"—until the end of the month, when this large room overlooking the avenue Friedland would be required for a granddaughter whose parents were traveling in Italy, and who was therefore coming here for the school holidays.) And Sabine was still invited to the larger parties, but when she went, wearing the one dress she had that was suitable, what she read on the faces of older women—friends of her mother or her grandmother, women she had known all her life—was: "It is a pity that things turned out the way they did, but you do understand, don't you, that you are no longer a suitable match for any of the young men in our family?"

And did she mind?

The way children mind a bruise or a fall. She cried sometimes, afterward, but she did not mind deeply. She did not want the kind of life that a "brilliant" marriage would have opened up to her. And the waters did not close over her head, though there was every reason to think that they would. Or perhaps there wasn't every reason to think that. It all depends on how you look at things. She did have talent; it was merely slow in revealing itself. And failure—real failure—has a way of passing over slight, pale, idealistic girls with observant eyes and a high domed forehead, in favor of some victim who is too fortunate and whose undoing therefore offers a chance for contrast and irony. You know those marvelous windows in Paris?

In the Sainte Chapelle, you mean? And the rose windows of Notre Dame?

No. They're marvelous too, God knows. But I meant the windows of the shops in the rue St. Honoré and the place Vendôme. She had a talent for designing window displays that were original and had humor and appealed to the Parisian mind. For example, she did a small hospital scene, in which the doctor and the patient in bed and the nurses were all perfume bottles dressed up like people. It created a small stir. She worked very hard, but her work was valued. The hours were long, and sometimes she overtaxed her strength. The family worried about her lungs. But she was well paid. And happy in her work. And she did not have to go to a fortuneteller because Eugène had a way of sardonically announcing the future. It was a gift the family stood in some fear of. "Would you like to know what is going to happen to Sabine?" he demanded one day. "She is going to be introduced to a man without any papers. Of good family, but dispossessed; a refugee. And he will not become a French citizen because he is a patriot and cannot bring himself to renounce his Polish, or Hungarian, or Spanish citizenship, and therefore, even though he speaks without an accent, and is educated, and has a first-class mind, he cannot even get a job teaching school. And Sabine, un-equipped as she is, is going to take care of him, and they are going to marry, and her mother will never accept him or forgive her. . . ."

His name was Frédéric. His father was a well-to-do banker in ——. In the fall of 1939, when the sky was full of German planes day after day, the house Frédéric grew up in, along with whole blocks of other houses, was destroyed by a bomb. The family was in the country when this happened. The caretaker was killed, but no one else. Then the Russians came, and they were allowed to keep one room in that enormous country place, and Frédéric's father arranged for him to escape in a Norwegian fishing vessel. Or perhaps it was on foot, across the border, with a handful of other frightened people. His father remained, to avoid the confiscations of his property, and his mother would not leave his father. For a year and a half, Frédéric lived in the Belleville quarter of Paris. Would you like to see him the way he was at that time? He is stretched out on a bed, in an ugly furnished room that he shares with a waiter in a café in the rue de Ménilmontant. He is fully dressed, except for his bare feet, which are thin and aristocratic. The bulb in the unshaded ceiling fixture is not strong enough to bother his eyes. The one window is open to the night. The soft rain fills the alleyway outside with small sounds, sounds that are all but musical, and he is quite happy, though the walls are mildewed and the bedclothes need airing and the sheets are not clean and shortly he will have to get up and spend the rest of the night on the stone floor. He turns on his back, and with his hands clasped under his head, he thinks: *She is hearing this rain. . . .*

The girl who hid out from the Gestapo in Mme Cestre's apartment had brought him to a party where Sabine was, and he saw her home from the party, but she could not, of course, ask him in. One of the ways by which Ferdinand and Miranda are to be distinguished from all commonplace lovers is that, along with Prospero, Ariel, and Caliban, they have no island.

It has sunk beneath the sea. Sometimes Frédéric and Sabine meet in an English tea room that is one flight up and rather exposed to the street, but there is one table that is private, behind a huge chart of the human hand showing the lines of the head and the heart, and the mountains of Venus, Jupiter, Saturn, the Sun, Mercury, and Mars. Also the swellings of the palmar faces of the five fingers, indicative of (beginning with the thumb) the logical faculty and the will; materialism, law and order, idealism; humanity, system, intelligence; truth, economy, energy; goodness, prudence, reflectiveness. When the weather permits, the lovers meet on the terrace in front of the Jeu de Paume.

This time, she arrives first. She goes up that little flight of marble steps and crosses the packed dirt to where there are two empty iron chairs. It is a beautiful evening. There are pink clouds against a nearly white sky. Shortly afterward he comes. There is a greenish pallor to his skin. His hands are beautiful and expressive. And he is just her height and just her age, and he speaks French without an accent. His suit is threadbare, but so are most people's suits in France at this time. The part of the terrace they are sitting in now is like the prow of a ship. They look down at the bicycles and motorcars and taxis that come over the bridge and disappear into the delta of wide and narrow streets that flows into the Place de la Concorde. He says: "You are looking at the hole in my shoe?"

"I was looking at your ankle," she says.

"You don't like it?" he says anxiously. "It is the wrong kind of ankle?"

"I was thinking I would like to draw it."

"I was afraid you thought it looked Polish," he says. (Or Hungarian. Or Spanish. I forget which he was.)

They see that the old woman who collects rent for the chairs is coming toward them. He digs down in his coat pocket and produces a five-franc note. Wrinkled and dirty and sad, the old woman gives him his change and moves on.

"You have never thought of committing suicide?" he asks after a time.

She shakes her head.

"I think I used to be in love with death," he says. "I sat in a cold room on an unmade bed with the barrel of a loaded revolver in my mouth, counting to . . . the number varied. Sometimes it was three, sometimes it was seven, and sometimes it was ten."

Farther along the balustrade, the old woman has got into an altercation with a middle-aged couple, and the altercation is being carried on in two languages.

"I was not in any particular trouble, and one is supposed to want to live. . . . What are they saying? They speak too fast for me."

"The man is saying that in America it does not cost anything to sit down in a public park."

"And is he indignant?"

"Very."

"Good," Frédéric says, nodding. "I have hated that old woman for a year and a half. And is she giving him as good as she is taking?"

"Yes, but he does not speak French, and she does not understand English."

"Too bad, too bad. Shall we go and translate for him? With a little help from us, it may become an international incident— the start of the war between the United States and the U.S.S.R." He starts to rise, and she puts a hand on his wrist, restraining him.

A few minutes later, he turns to her and says: "You are going to your aunt's?"

She nods. "You could come too. She has told me to bring you. And you would like them."

"I'm sure I would."

And then, after an interval, in a toneless voice, he says: "I must not keep you."

She gets up from her chair and walks with him to the head of the stairs. In the sky the two colors are now reversed. The clouds are white, and the sky they float in is pink. As they shake hands he does not say: "Will you marry me?" but this question hangs in the air between them, and is why she looks troubled and why he steps out into the traffic like a sleep-walker. Oblivious of the horns and shouts of angry drivers, he arrives safely at the other side. She stands watching him until he passes the Crillon and is hidden by a crowd of people who are waiting in a circle around the red carpet, hoping to see the King of Persia.

Would you like to know about the King of Persia?

Not particularly. What I would like to know is the name of that white château with the green lawn in front of it that Barbara Rhodes was always looking for.

One time when Eugène and Sabine were going down to the country together, there was a picture, behind glass, in their compartment. Eugène was furious at her because she had given her seat to an old woman who was sitting on her suitcase in the corridor, and so had made him sit next to a stranger. Or perhaps it was because the old woman was large and crowded him in his corner. Or it might not have been that at all, but something that had nothing to do with her that was making him cold and abstracted. Ultimately the cause of his black moods declared itself, but first you had the mood in its pure state, without any explanation. She stood in the corridor for a while, looking at the landscape that unreeled itself alongside the train, and when the old woman got off at Orléans, she went back into the compartment. She was eager for the trip to be over. The compartment was airless and cramped. With her head against the seat back she sat watching the sunset and noting the signs that meant she was nearing the country of her childhood. She found herself staring at the photograph opposite her. It was of a white château that looked like a castle in a fairy tale. Was it Sully, she wondered. Or Luynes? Or Chantilly? There was a metal tag on the frame, but it was tarnished and could not be read.

You don't know what château it was?

There is every reason to be grateful that these losses occur, that every once in a while something that is listed in the inventory turns up missing. Otherwise people couldn't move for the clutter that they make around themselves.

I do not take such a charitable view of Eugène's behavior as you seem to. Many people have had to live with disappointment and still not—

He was also capable of acts of renunciation and of generosity that were saintlike. We all have these contradictions in our natures. . . . In the family they were accustomed to his moods and did not take them seriously. There was a time when Alix thought that their life might go differently (though not necessarily better)—that he had reached a turning point of some kind. His dark mood had lasted longer than usual, and one morning she sat up in bed and looked at him, and was frightened. What he looked like was a drowned man.

It was a Saturday, so he did not go to his office. And suddenly, in the middle of the morning, she missed him. She went through the apartment, glancing in the baby's room, then in their bedroom, then in the dressing room. The bathroom door was open. She turned and went back down the hall. He must have gone out. But why did he go out without telling her where he was going? And how could he have done it so quietly, so that she didn't hear either the study door open or the front door close. Unless he didn't want her to know that he was going out. She had a sudden vision of him ill, having fainted in the toilet. She opened the door of that little room. It was empty.

"Eugène?" she said anxiously, and at that moment the front door closed. She turned around in surprise.

There was still time to stop him, to ask where he was going. When she opened the front door, she heard the sound of feet descending the stairs and, leaning far over the banister, caught a glimpse of his head and shoulders, which were hidden immediately afterward by a turn in the staircase.

"Eugène!" she called, and, loud and frightened though her voice sounded in her own ears, he still did not stop. The footsteps reiterated his firm intention never to stop until he had arrived at a place where she could not reach him. When they changed from the muffled sound made by the stair carpet to the harsh clatter of heels on a marble floor, she turned and hurried back into the apartment, through the hall, through the drawing room, and out onto the balcony, where she was just in time to see him emerge from the building and start up the sidewalk. She tried to pitch her voice so that only he would hear her calling him, and a man on the other side of the street looked up and Eugène did not. He went right on walking.

Step by step, with him, she hurried along the balcony to the corner of the building, where she could look down on the granite monument and the cobblestone square. Hidden by trees briefly, Eugène was now visible again, crossing a street. There was a taxi waiting, but he did not step into it. He kept on walking, past the café, past the entrance to the Métro, past the barbershop, past the trousered legs standing publicly in the midst of the odor that used to make her feel sick as a child. Again he was hidden by trees. Again she saw him, as he skirted a sidewalk meeting of two old friends. He crossed another ray of the star, and then changed his direction slightly, and she perceived that the church steps was his destination. There, in the gray morning light, one of the priests (Father Quinot, or Father Ferron?) stood with his hands behind his back, benevolently nodding and answering the parting remarks of a woman in black.

The image that Alix now saw before her eyes—of Eugène on his knees in the confessional—was only the beginning, she knew. More was required. Much more. The heart that was now ready to surrender itself was not simple. There would be intellectual doubts, arguments with Father Quinot, with Father Ferron, appointments with the bishop, a period of retreat from her and from the world, in some religious house, where no one could reach him, while he examined his faith for flaws. Proof would be submitted to him from the writings of St. Thomas, St. Gregory, St. Bonaventure. And when he returned to her, with the saints shielding him so that each time she put out her hand she touched the garment of a saint, his mind would be full of new knowledge of how men *know*, how the angels *know*, how God in his infinite being becomes all *knowledge* and all *knowledge* is a *knowledge* of Him.

This being true, clear, and obvious even to a slow mind like hers, a person given to looking apprehensively at mirrors and clocks, and there being also no way of joining him on his knees (though there were two stalls in the mahogony confessional, the most that was given to Father Quinot or Father Ferron to accomplish would be to listen to their alternating confession, not their joint one)—this being true, she would not go down and wait for him in the street, as she longed to do, even though it be hours from now, past midnight, or morning, before he reappeared. She would stay where she was, and when he came home she would try not to distract him, or to seem to lay the slightest claim upon his attention or his feelings, in order that . . .

Each of the woman's parting remarks seemed to give rise to another, and as Eugène drew closer, Alix thought: *What if she doesn't stop talking in time?* For Eugène would not wait. He was much too proud to stand publicly waiting, even to speak to the priest. "Oh, please," she said, under her breath. The woman turned her head, as if this supplication had been heard. But then she remembered something else that she wanted to say, and Eugène kept on going, and disappeared down the steps of the Métro.

Shortly after this, he went to see M. Carrère, who was exceedingly kind. Eugène outlined his situation to him, and M. Carrère asked if Eugène had any objection to working for an American firm that he was connected with through his son. "The job would be over there?" Eugène asked, and M. Carrère said: "No, here. I assume that Mme de Boisgaillard would not want to live so far from her mother. Suppose I arrange for an interview?"

The interview went well, and after an hour's talk, Eugène was asked to come back the next day, which he did. They made him an offer, and he accepted it.

A few nights later, when Mme Viénot went in to say good night to her mother, Mme Bonenfant said: "I wonder if Eugène will be happy working for an American firm. He doesn't speak any English."

"If it is like other foreign firms that have a branch in Paris, the personnel will be largely French," Mme Viénot said. "I have heard of this one, as it happens. In America they make frigidaires. Sewing machines. Typewriters. That sort of thing."

"It doesn't sound very intellectual," Mme Bonenfant said. "Are you sure that you understood correctly?"

"Quite sure, Maman. . . . In France, the firm manufactures only machine guns."

M. and Mme Carrère never came back to the château. They found another quiet country house that was more comfortable and closer to Paris. But from time to time, when Mme Viénot went into the post office, she was handed a letter that was addressed to him. The letters no doubt contained a request of some sort; for money, for advice, for the use of his name. And how it was answered might change the lives of she did not like to think how many people. In any case, the letter had to be forwarded, and it gave her acute pleasure to think that he would recognize her handwriting on the envelope.

Hector Gagny never came back either, with his new wife. But Mme Straus came at least once a year. Her summer was a round of visits. For a woman past seventy, without a place of her own in which to entertain, with neither wealth nor much social distinction, she received a great many invitations—many more than she could accept. And if the friends who were so eager to have her come and stay with them did not always invite her back, there were always new acquaintances who responded to her gaiety, opened their hearts to her, and—for a while at least—adjusted the salutation of their letters to conform with the rapidly increasing tenderness of hers.

A blank space in her calendar between the end of June and the middle of September meant a brief stay at Beaumesnil. She was at the château just after the affair of the robbers, and she brought two friends with her, a M. and Mme Mégille. Monsieur was a member of the permanent staff of the Institut Océanographique, and very distinguished. And since he had been brought up in the country he did not mind the fact that there was no electricity.

They never found that short circuit?

Oh yes. This was a piece of foolishness on Mme Viénot's part. You won't believe it, but she could not get that gold bullion out of her mind. She induced the priest at Coulanges to come and go all through the house with her, holding a forked stick. There was one place where it responded violently, and in opening up the wall the gardener sawed through the main electric-light cable.

But surely Mme Viénot was too intelligent to believe that—

Yes, she did. Mme Viénot is the Life Force, with dyed hair and too much rouge, and the Life Force always believes. Defeated, flat on her back, she waved her arms and legs like a beetle, and in a little while she was walking around again.

Every novel ought to have a heroine, and she is the heroine of this one. She is a wonderful woman—how wonderful probably no one knows, except an American woman she met only once, on a train journey—a woman who, curiously enough, knew Barbara and Harold Rhodes, though only slightly. The two women opened their hearts to each other, as women sometimes do on a train or sharing a table in the tea room of a department store, and they have continued to write to each other afterward, long letters full of things they do not tell anyone else.

What Mme Viénot did the summer Barbara and Harold were with her was miraculous. She had nothing whatever to work with, and bad servants, and somehow she kept up the tone of the establishment and provided meals that were admirable. Singlehanded, she saved the château. It would have gone for back taxes if she had not done what she did. No one else in the family could have saved it. As a person, Mme Cestre was more sympathetic, perhaps, but she was an invalid, and introspective. And the men . . .

What about the men?

Well, what about them?

I guess you're right. Go on with what you were saying.

Once more they dined by candlelight. When they went up to bed, they were handed kerosene lamps at the foot of the stairs. There was no writing desk in Mme Straus's room, and so, sitting up in bed, she used a book to write on. Her hair was in two braids and her reading glasses were resting far down on the bridge of her nose. She wrote rapidly, with no trace of a quaver:

. . . Maman Minou finds that she has been a long time without news of her dear American children. The last letter from Harold, written in English, was translated for me by a friend, but tonight I am not in Paris. I beg him not to be vexed with me. Can he not find, at his office, a good-natured comrade who knows how to read French and will translate this letter into English? But my dear friend, why this sudden change? Your old letters, and those of dear Barbara, were perfectly written. It makes me wonder whether you perhaps no longer wish to correspond with poor Minou in France.

The fountain pen stopped. The old eyes went on a voyage round the room, searching for something to say (one does not create an atmosphere of concert pitch out of accusations of neglect) and came to rest on a large stain in the wallpaper:

Your presence surrounds me here. I go looking for you, and find my friends occupying your room. I put flowers there for them but Oh miracle! the moment the flowers are in their vase, they fly off toward you. Take them, then, my dears, and may their perfume spread around you. Here it is gray, cheerless, cold. The surroundings are agreeable, even so. M. and Mme Mégille are charming. Sabine pleases me very much. The lady of the manor dolls herself up for each new arrival. So droll! Alix is adorable. She is going off to visit cousins in Toulon next week. I shall miss her. Have you pretty concerts and plays to see? In this moment when we are in summer, are you not in winter? And at the hour when I am writing to you—eleven o'clock at night—your hour of the omelette, the good odor of which I smell even here?

She thought the United States was in South America?

Apparently. Some people have no sense of geography.— The letter ended:

Life is rather difficult here, but I am so eager to obey our dear President Pinay, whom we admire so much, that all becomes easy. Your dear images still have a place in my little chamber, which you know. Pray for your old Maman Minou, who embraces you with all her loving heart.

Antoinette Straus-Muguet

Please put the date and the year of your letters. Thank you.

Why didn't they answer her letter? It isn't like them.

I'll get around to that in a minute. One thing at a time. She blew the lamp out—

We have to hear about the lamp?

Yes. And settled herself between the damp sheets. And it was at that moment that the odor of kerosene brought back to her something priceless, a house she had not seen for half a century.

The youngest of a large family, she had all through her childhood been the charming excitable plaything of older brothers and sisters. When evening came, so did Charles and Emma and Andrée and Edouard and Lucienne and Maurice and Marguerite and Anna. They gathered in the nursery to assist in putting Minou to bed, invented new games when her head hung like a heavy flower on its stalk, and, as they peeled her clothes off over her head, cried: "Skin the rabbit! Don't let the little white bunny get away." "Stop her!" "Catch her, somebody!" And when she escaped from them, they tracked her down with all the cruelty of love, and carried her on their shoulders around the nursery, a laughing overexcited child with too bright eyes and a flushed face and a nature that was too highstrung and delicate to be playing such games at the end of the day.

All dead, the pursuers; long dead; leaving her no choice but to pursue.

As for the Americans, it was much harder to think in French when they were not in France. They had to sit down with a French-English dictionary and a French grammar, and it took half a day to answer one of Mme Straus's letters, and they were leading a busy life. Also, he hated to write letters. He used to wait for days before he opened a letter from Mme Straus, because of his shame at not having answered the last one. But they did answer some of the letters. They did not altogether lose touch with her.

Quite apart from the effort it took, and the fact that year after year the friendship had nothing to feed on, her letters to them were really very strange. ("The monsieur who is at Fifth Avenue is not my relative, but my niece is flying over soon, on business for the house, of which she is administrator, director, in place of her dead husband. She will be, *alone*, in our confidence, but see you, become acquainted with you, speak to you of Maman Minou. You will see how nice she is. Answer her telephone calls above everything. She will give you news of me, and fresh news . . .") None of the people she said were coming to America and that Harold and Barbara could expect to hear from ever turned up. And there was one frantic, only half-legible letter, which they had to take to the friend who had lived in the Monceau quarter, to translate for them. She found it distrait, full of idioms that she had never seen and that she didn't believe existed. The letter was about money. Mme Straus' income, with inflation, was no longer adequate to meet her needs. Her daughter had refused to do anything for her, and Mme Straus was afraid that she would be put out of the convent. In the next letter it appeared that this crisis had passed: Mme Straus Muguet's children, to whom her notary had made a demand, had finally understood that it was their duty to help her. "Forgive me," she wrote, "for boring you with all my miseries, but you are all my consolation." Her letters were full of intimations of increasing frailty and age, and continually asked when they were coming back to France. At last they were able to write her that they were coming, in the spring of 1953, and she wrote back: "If Heaven wills it that I have not already departed for my great journey, it will be with arms wide open that I will receive you. . . ."

And was she there to receive them?

They went first to England, and had two weeks of flawless weather. The English countryside was like the Book of Hours, and they loved London. They arrived in Paris on May Day Eve, and by nightfall they were in the Forest of Fontainebleau, in a rented car, on their way south. They spent the night in Sens, and in the morning everyone they saw carried a little nosegay of muguets. After their other trip, they enrolled in the Berlitz, and spent one winter conscientiously studying French. Though that was years ago now, it did seem that their French had improved.

The boy learns to swim in winter, William James said, and to skate in summer.

From Provence, Barbara wrote to Mme Straus that they would be in Paris by the end of the second week in May. When they were settled in—someone had told them about a small hotel whose windows overlooked the gardens of the Palais-Royal—Harold telephoned, and the person who answered seemed uncertain of whether Mme Straus could come to the telephone. The stairs have become too much for her, he thought. There was another of those interminable waits, during which he had a chance to reflect. Five years is a long time, and to try and pick up the threads again, with people they hardly knew, and with the additional barrier of language . . . But they couldn't not call, either. . . .

Mme Straus's voice was just the same, and she seemed to be quite free of the doubts that troubled him. They settled it that she would come to their hotel at seven that evening.

At quarter after six, as they were crossing the Place du Palais-Royal, Barbara said: "Aren't we going to have an apéritif?"

They had only five weeks altogether, for England and France, and there was never a time, it seemed, when they could sit in front of a sidewalk café, as they used to do before, and watch the people. They were both tired from walking, and he very much wanted a bath before dinner, but he decided that with luck they could do it, in spite of the crowd of people occupying the tables of that particular café, and the overworked waiter. They did it, but without pleasure, because he kept looking at his watch. They hurried through the gardens, congratulating themselves on the fact that it was still only twenty minutes of seven—just time enough to get upstairs and bathe and dress and be ready for Mme Straus.

"You have company," Mme la Patronne said as they walked into the hotel. "A lady." There was a note of disapproval in her voice. "She has been waiting since six o'clock."

The Americans looked at each other with dismay. "You go on upstairs," he said, and hurried down the hall to the little parlor where Mme Straus was waiting, with two small parcels on the sofa beside her. His first impression was that she looked younger. Could he have misjudged her age? She kissed him on both cheeks, and told him how well he looked. They sat down and he began to tell her about Provence. Then there was an awkward pause in the conversation, and to dispell it they asked the questions people ask, meeting after years. When Barbara came in, he started to leave the room, intending to go upstairs and at least wash his face and hands, but Mme Straus stopped him. It was the moment for the presentation of the gifts, and again they were dismayed that they had not thought to bring anything for her. They were also dismayed at her gifts—a paper flower for Barbara, a white scarf for Harold that had either lain in a drawer too long or else was of so shoddy a quality that it bore no relation to any man's evening scarf he had ever seen. Mme Straus had learned to make paper flowers—as a game, she said, and to amuse herself. "Oeillet," she said, resuming her role of language professor, and Barbara pinned the pink carnation on her dark violet-colored coat, where it looked very pretty, if a trifle strange.

They left the hotel intending to have dinner at a restaurant in the rue de Montpensier, but it was closed that night, and so Mme Straus led them across the Place du Théâtre-Français, to a restaurant where, she assured them, she was well known and the food and wine were excellent. It was noisy and crowded; the maître d'hôtel received Mme Straus coldly, but at least the waiter knew her and was friendly. "He is like a son to me," she said, as they sat down.

There were a dozen restaurants in the neighborhood where the food was better, and Harold blamed himself for not insisting that they go to some place more suited to a long-delayed reunion, but Mme Straus seemed quite happy. Nobody had very much to say.

The Vienna Opera was paying a visit to Paris, and during dinner he explained that he had three tickets for *The Magic Flute*. She said: "Quelle joie!" and then: "Where are they?" He told her and she exclaimed: "But we won't be able to see the stage!"

The tickets had cost five times what tickets for the Opéra usually cost, and were the most he felt he could afford. He said: "They're in the center," and she seemed satisfied. And would they arrange for her to stay at their hotel that night, since the doors of her convent were closed at nine o'clock?

Arm in arm, they walked to the bus stop, and waving from the back of the bus, she was swept away.

"It isn't the same, is it?" he said, as they were walking back to their hotel.

"We're not the same," Barbara said. "She took one look at us and saw that the jig was up."

"Too bad."

"If you hadn't got tickets for the opera—"

"I know. Well, one more evening won't kill us."

Harold found that Mme Straus could stay at their hotel the night of the opera, and when she arrived—again an hour early —she was delighted with her room. "It's just right for a jeune fille," she said, laughing. And did Barbara have a coat she could wear? And wouldn't it be better if they had dinner in the same place, because the service was so prompt, and above all they didn't want to be late.

When they arrived at the Opéra, she introduced them to the tall man in evening clothes who was taking tickets, and they were introduced again on the stairs, to an ouvreuse or someone like that. They climbed and climbed and eventually arrived at their tier, which was above the "basket." Their seats were in the first row and they had a clear view of the stage and the stage was not too far away. Mme Straus arranged her coat and offered Harold and Barbara some candy. Stuffed with food and wine, they said no, and she took some herself and then seized their hands affectionately. She made them lean far forward so that she could point out to them, in the tier just below, the two center front-row seats that her father and mother had always occupied. She regretted that *Les Indes Galantes* was not being performed during their stay in Paris. A marvelous spectacle.

The Magic Flute was also something of a spectacle, and the soprano who sang the role of Pamina had a very beautiful voice.

Harold had failed to get a program and so they didn't know who it was. In the middle of the first act, he became aware of Mme Straus's restlessness. At last she leaned toward him and whispered that this opera was always sung at the Comique; that it did not belong on so large a stage. The Opéra was more suited to *Aida*. She found the singing acceptable but the opera itself did not greatly interest her. Did he know *Aida*? It was her favorite. Again she pressed the little bag of candy on him in the dark, and he suddenly remembered the strange behavior of Mme Marguerite Mailly, when they went backstage after her play. A few minutes later, hearing the rustle of the little bag again coming toward him, he was close to hating Mme Straus-Muguet himself. They left their seats between the acts, and as they walked through the marble corridors, he noticed a curious thing: because their French had improved, Mme Straus understood what they were saying, but not always what they meant, and when they explained, it only added to the misunderstanding. Wherever her quick intuitive mind was, it wasn't on them.

After the performance, she insisted that they go across the street, as her guests, and have something to eat. Harold and Barbara drank a bottle of Perrier water, and Mme Straus had a large ham sandwich.

"I am always hungry," she confessed.

Worn out with the effort of keeping up the form of an affectionate relationship that had lost its substance, they sat and looked at the people around them. Mme Straus borrowed the souvenir program of a young woman at the next table, and they learned the name of the soprano with the beautiful voice:

Irmgard Seefried. Then Mme Straus brought up the matter of
when they would see her next. Barbara said gently that they
were only going to be in Paris a few more days, and that this
was their last evening with her.

"Ah, but chérie, just one time! After five years!"

"Two times," Barbara said, and Mme Straus smiled. She was
not hurt, it seemed, but only pretending.

They said good night on the stairs of the little hotel, and the
Americans went off early the next morning, to Chartres; they
wanted to see the cathedral again. When they got back to the
hotel, Mme Straus had gone, leaving instructions about when
they were to telephone her. There were several telephone calls
during the next two days and in the end they found themselves
having lunch with her, in that same impossible restaurant. She
took from her purse a postcard she had just received from her
daughter, who was traveling in Switzerland. It was simple and
affectionate—just such a card as any daughter might have sent
her mother from a trip, and Mme Straus seemed to have forgotten that they knew anything about her daughter that wasn't
complimentary.

At the end of the meal, Mme Straus asked for the *addition*,
and Harold, partly out of concern for her but much more out
of a deep desire to get to the bottom of things, reached for his
wallet. In the short time that remained, perhaps it was possible
to discover the simple unsentimentalized truth. At the risk of
being crass and of hurting her feelings, he insisted on paying
for the luncheon she had invited them to, and, smiling indul-
gently, she let him. So I could have paid for all the other times,
he thought. And should have.

"Now what would you like to do?" she asked. "What would
you like to see? Do you like looking at paintings and old furniture?"

They got into a taxi and drove to the shop of a cousin of
Mme Straus's husband. It was a decorator's shop, and the taste
it reflected was not their taste, in furniture or in objets d'art.
Finding nothing else that she could admire, Barbara pretended
to an interest in a Chinese luster tea set. "You like it?" Mme
Straus said. "It is charming, I agree." She could not be prevented from calling a salesman and asking the price—three
hundred thousand francs. Mme Straus whispered, "I will speak

to them, and tell them you are my rich American friends." She
giggled. "Because of me, they will give you a prix d'ami."

Barbara said that the tea set was much too expensive. As she
turned away, her short violet-colored coat swept one of the
cups out of its saucer. With a lunge Harold caught it in
mid-air.

They went upstairs and looked at what they were told were
Raphaels. "Copies," Harold said, committed now to his disagreeable experiment. "And not necessarily copies of a painting
by Raphael."

The salesman did not disagree, or seem offended. Seeing
that they were not interested in what he showed them, he
asked what painters they did like.

"Vuillard and Bonnard," Harold said.

They were shown a small, uninteresting Bonnard and told
that there were more in the shop if they would like to see
them. Harold shook his head. It was tug of war, with Mme
Straus endeavoring to give her husband's cousin the impression that Harold and Barbara were rich American collectors
and might buy anything, and Harold and Barbara trying just as
hard to convey the truth.

Mme Straus started to leave the shop with them, and then
hesitated. "I have some business to discuss with monsieur upstairs," she said, and kissed them, and said good-by, and perhaps she would come to the airport.

In the taxi Harold said: "Is that the explanation? All this
elaborate scheming so she can get her commission?"

"No," Barbara said. "I don't really think it is that. . . . I
think it is more likely something she thought of on the spur of
the moment. A role she performed just for the pleasure of per-
forming it. But I kept thinking all the time we were with her,
there is something about her manner and her voice. I couldn't
place it until we were in that shop. She is like the women in
stores who try to sell you something. Whatever she is, or whoever she was, she knows that world. I think that's why Pierre
disapproved of our being with her. . . . But it is the young
she likes. Now that we are no longer young, it isn't worth her
while to enchant us."

The other reunions were not disappointing. They liked
Sabine's husband, and she was exactly as they remembered

her. It was as if they had bicycled home in the moonlight from the Allégrets' party the night before. She did not even look any older. The questions she asked were the right questions. They could convey to her in a phrase, a word, the thing that needed to be said. She is all eyes and forehead, Harold thought, looking at her. But what he was most aware of was how completely she took in what they said to her, so that talking to her was not like talking to anybody else. Walking to her door from the restaurant where they had had dinner, he heard their four voices, all proceeding happily like a quartet for strings. Allegro, andante, etc. While he was telling Frédéric about an experience with some gypsies outside the walls of Aigues-Mortes, she began to tell Barbara about the robbers. Harold stopped talking to listen. Then, turning to Frédéric, he asked: "She's not making this up?" and Frédéric said: "No, no, it all happened," and Harold said: "I guess when anything is that strange you can be sure it happened." Looking up at the lamplit underside of the leaves of the chestnut trees, he thought: We're in Paris, I am not dreaming that we are in Paris. . . .

The next day, they met Eugène and Alix for lunch, and that too was easy and pleasant. Eugène spoke English, which made a difference. And he was in a genial mood. Their eyes had no trouble meeting his. They did not have to make conversation out of passing the sugar back and forth. *We're not the same, are we?* they all three agreed silently, and after that he treated them and they treated him with simple courtesy. And unwittingly, Harold saw, they had pleased Eugène by inviting him to this restaurant. He informed them that Napoleon used to play chess here, and that the décor was unchanged since that time. With its red curtains, its red plush, it was exactly right, and what a classical restaurant should look like. . . . He enjoyed his lunch as well. And the wine was of his choosing. He was sardonic only once, with the waiter, who urged them a shade too insistently to have strawberries.

After lunch they strolled through the gardens of the Palais-Royal, and Barbara took a picture of the three others, standing in front of the spray of a fountain. When Eugène left to go back to his office, Alix said, somewhat to their surprise, that, yes, she would like to go and see the rose garden at Bagatelle

with them. In appearance she was totally changed. She was not
an unconfident young woman with a baby; she was a stylish
Parisian matron. Her hair was cut short, in a way that was
becoming to her. Her black suit had the tailoring of Paris, and
what made them instantly at ease and happy with her was that
she didn't pretend she wasn't pleased with it. "All my life I've
wanted a black suit," she said, when Barbara spoke of it. If she
understood the meaning of pretense, she did not understand
the need for it. It had no part in her nature. We thought all
these years that we remembered her, Harold said to himself—
her voice, her face, how nice she is, how much we liked being
with her. But all we had, actually, was a dim recollection of
those things. And it didn't even include the most important
fact about her—that she would never under any circumstances
turn away from the presence of love, happy or unhappy.

Because she was wearing a tight skirt, they stopped off first
at the apartment in the rue Malène, and Barbara and Harold
saw Alix's children, who were charming, and had a visit with
Mme Cestre while Alix was changing her clothes. At Bagatelle,
something awaited them—a red brick wall almost a hundred
feet long, and trained against it were climbing roses and white
and blue clematis, demonstrating their cousinship. Both flowers
were at the very perfection of their blooming period. It was
one more ecstatic experience, to put with the lavender-blue
searchlight, the rainy night in San Remo, the one-ring circus,
and the medieval city that was enclosed in itself like a rose. Sitting on a bench, with the wall in front of them, Alix talked
about her present life. All that Harold remembered afterward
was the one sentence: "I don't mind doing the washing and
ironing, or anything else, so long as I don't have to sit with
them in the park." It reduced the Atlantic Ocean to a puddle,
and he began to tell her about their efforts to adopt a child.
Then they looked at the roses some more. And then they
made their way to a bus stop, and back into the city. She got
off first, and they waved until they couldn't see her any longer.
They saw her once more after that. Sabine had a party for
them, an evening party, and invited Alix and Eugène and also
her sister and brother-in-law.

The man who looked like an acrobat but wasn't?

He was a performer. Their instinct about him was right. But

his performance was intellectual; he balanced budgets in the
air. He had changed so in five years that they didn't recognize
him. He didn't refer to the evening they had spent together,
and they didn't remember until afterward who he was.

And Sabine was different, Harold suddenly realized. In one
respect she had changed. That strange suggestion of an unpro-
voked or unrelated amusement was not there any longer. Was
this because it was now safe to be serious? In any case, she was
happy.

Feeling that the party was for them, they tried too hard, and
didn't really enjoy themselves, but it didn't matter; they had
already reached the people they wanted to reach. Including
that waiter, Joseph.

Pierre, you said his name was.

His name was Joseph, but they didn't know it. The patron's
name being Joseph also, he called himself Pierre, to avoid confusion. But his name was really Joseph. The simplest things are
often not what they seem. . . . The restaurant in the alley off
the Place St. Sulpice had gone downhill. The patron had taken
to drink, and their friend was now working in a brasserie on
the boulevard St. Germain. The first time they stopped in, he
was off duty. They left a message—that they would be back
two days later. They almost didn't go back. Though they had
exchanged Christmas cards with him faithfully, would they
have anything to say to him? It didn't seem at all likely. When
they walked in, there he was, and he saw them and smiled, and
they knew that they didn't have to have anything to say to
him. They loved him. They had always loved him.

He led them to a table and they asked him what to order
and he told them, just as he used to do; but when Harold
asked him to bring three glasses with the bottle of wine, he
shook his head and said warningly, as to a younger brother:
"This is a serious restaurant." He stood by their table, talking
to them while they ate, or left them to go look after another
table and then returned to pick up where they had left off. They
found they had too much to say to him. When they left, they
promised to meet him at noon on Sunday—for an apéritif,
they assumed. On Sunday, the four of them—Joseph's wife was
there beside him—sat for a while in front of the brasserie,
watching the people who passed, and talking quietly, and when

the Americans got up to go, they discovered that they had been invited to lunch, in Joseph's apartment, seven flights up, in the rue des Ciseaux. It was a tiny apartment, with two rooms, and only two windows. But out of each they could see a church tower, Joseph's wife showed them. And they could hear the bells. She confessed to Barbara that they greatly regretted not having children, and that all their affection should be heaped on a canary. It was wrong, but they could not help it. And Barbara explained that at home they had a gray cat to whom they gave too much affection also. The canary's name was Fifi, and all that love it had no right to poured back out of its throat, and remarks were frequently addressed to it from the lunch table. Lunch went on for hours. Joseph had cooked it himself, that morning and the day before, and they saw that there is, in France, a kind of hospitality that cannot be paid for and that is so lavish one can only bow one's head in the presence of it. They drank pernod, timidly, before they began to eat. They drank a great deal of wine during lunch. They drank brandy after they stopped eating. From time to time there were toasts. Raising his glass drunkenly, Harold exclaimed: "A Fifi!" and a few minutes later Joseph pushed his chair back and said: "A nos amis, à nos amours!" The Americans were just barely able to get down the stairs.

Side by side with what happens, the friendship that unexpectedly comes into full flower, there is always, of course, the one that could and does not. Among the clients of the little restaurant in the rue de Montpensier there was a tall interesting-looking man, in his late forties, and his two barely grown sons. The father usually arrived first, and the sons joined him, one at a time. In their greeting there was so much undisguised affection that the Americans found them a pleasure to watch. But who were they, and where was the boys' mother? Was she ill? Was she dead? And why, in France, did they eat in a restaurant instead of at home? Like a fruit hanging ripe on the bough, the acquaintance was ready to begin. All it needed was a word, a smile, a small accident, and they would all five have been eating together. If they had been on shipboard, for instance—but they were not on shipboard.

And who were they? Were they aware of the Americans?

Of course. How could they not be? The Americans went to

a movie that was on the other side of Paris, and when the lights came on, there sitting in the row ahead of them were the father and his two sons. It was all Harold could do not to speak to them. . . . Though their story is interesting, and offers some curious parallels, I don't think I'd better go into it here.

The Americans continued to see things, and to be moved by what they saw, and to love France. During the few days they were in Paris, there was an illumination of Gothic and Renaissance sculpture at the Louvre, and a beautiful exhibition of medieval stained-glass windows, at the Musée des Arts Décoratifs.

And Mme Viénot?

They didn't see her. And neither did they try to see Jean Allégret. They were afraid it would be pushing their luck too far, and also they were in Paris such a short time, and there were so many things they wanted to see and do. They saw a school children's matinee of *Phèdre* at the Comédie Française and a revival of *Ciboulette* at the Comique. Harold got up one morning at daybreak and wandered through the streets and markets of Les Halles. Coming home with his arms full of flowers, he stopped and stared at an old woman who was asleep with her cheek pressed against the pavement. His eyes, traveling upward, saw a street sign: rue des Bons Enfants. The scene remained intact in his mind afterward, like a vision; like something he had learned.

Did they adopt a child?

No. It is not easy, and before they had managed to do it, Barbara became pregnant. It was as if someone in authority had said Since you are now ready and willing to bring up anybody's child, you may as well bring up your own. . . . So strange, life is. Why people do not go around in a continual state of surprise is beyond me. In the foyer of the Musée Guimet, Barbara saw a Khmer head—very large it was, and one side of the face seemed to be considering closely, from the broadest possible point of view, all human experience; the expression of the other half was inward-looking, concerned with only one fact, one final mystery.

Those people whose windows look out on the gardens of the Palais-Royal know that though the palace is built of stone it is not gray but takes its color from the color of the sky, which varies according to the time of day. In the early morning, at daybreak, it is lavender-blue. In the evening it is sometimes flamingo-colored. If you walk along the rue La Feuillade shortly after five o'clock in the morning, you will come to a bakery that is below the street level, and the smell of freshly baked bread is enough to break your heart. And if you stand late at night on the Pont des Arts, you will find yourself in the eighteenth century. The lights in the houses along the Quai Malaquais and the Quai de Conti are reflected in the river, and the reflections elongate as if they were trying to turn into Japanese lanterns. The Louvre by moonlight is a palace, not an art gallery. And if you go there in the daytime you must search out the little stairway that leads up to a series of rooms where you can buy, for very little money, engravings of American flowers—the jack-in-the-pulpit, the May apple, the windflower —that were made from specimens collected by missionaries and voyageurs in the time of Louis XIV. At the flower market there is a moss rose that is pale pink with a deeper pink center, and you will walk between trenches of roses and peonies that are piled like cordwood. And though not every day is beautiful (sometimes it is cold, sometimes it is raining) there will be days when the light in the sky is such that you wonder if—

I know, I know. Everybody feels that way about Paris. London is beautiful too. So is Rome. So, for that matter, is New York. The world is full of beautiful cities. What interests me is Mme Viénot. It is a pity that they did not bother to see her.

She was in the country. But just because the Americans didn't see her is no sign we can't. . . . It is a Tuesday. The sky in Touraine is a beautiful, clear, morning-glory blue. She wheels her bicycle from the kitchen entryway, mounts it, and rides out of the courtyard. The gardener and his wife and boy are stacking the hay in the park in front of the house, and a M. Lundqvist is leaning out of the window of Sabine's room. He waves to her cheerfully, and she waves back.

She stops to talk to the gardener, who is optimistic about the hay but thinks it is time they had rain; otherwise there will be no fodder for the cows, and the price of butter will go sky-high, where everything else is already.

Halfway down the drive she turns and looks back over her

shoulder. The front of the house, with its steep gables, box hedge, raked gravel terrace, and stone balustrade, says: "If one can only sustain the conventions, one is in turn sustained by them . . ." Reassured, she rides on. She is going to haggle with the farmer, five miles away, who supplies her with cream and butter and the plain but admirable cheese of the locality. When she looks back a second time, the trees have closed in and the château is lost from sight. But it can be seen again from the public road, across the fields—a large, conspicuous white-stone house, the only house of this size for several miles around.

M. and Mme Bonenfant celebrated their son's coming of age here, and the marriages of their two daughters, and of one of their granddaughters. Like all well-loved, well-cared for, hospitable, happy houses, the Château Beaumesnil gives off a high polish, a mellowed sense of order, of the comfort that is felt by the eye and not the behind of the beholder. A stranger walking into the house for the first time is aware of the rich texture of sounds and silences. The rugs seem to have an affinity for the floor they lie on. The sofas and chairs announce: "We will never allow ourselves to be separated under any circumstances." "This is rightness," the house says. "This is what a house should be; and to have to live anywhere else is the worst of all possible misfortunes."

The village is just the same—or practically. M. Canourgue's stock is now on open shelves instead of under the counter or in the back room. There is a clock in the railway station, and the station itself is finished. Though the travel posters have been changed and the timetables are for the year 1953, the same four men are seated on the terrace of the Café de la Gare.

The village is proud of its first family, and also of the fact that the old lady chose to throw in her lot with theirs. Mme Bonenfant is eighty-eight now, and suffers from forgetfulness. Far too often she cannot find her handkerchief or the letter she had in her hand only a moment ago. On her good days she enjoys the quickness and clarity of mind that she has always had. She is witty, she charms everyone, she is like an ivory chess queen. On her bad days chère Maman sits with her twisted old hands in her lap, quiet and sad, and sometimes not really there; not anywhere. It bothers her that she cannot remember how many great-grandchildren she has, and she says to Sabine: "Was that before your dear father died?" and realizes from the look of horror that this question gives rise to that she has confused a son-in-law who is dead with one who is very much alive. She leaves the house only to go to Mass on Sunday, or to the potager with her wicker garden basket and shears. She is still beautiful, as a flower stalk with its seed pod open and empty or a tattered oak leaf is beautiful. The potager never ceases to trouble her, because ever since the war the fruit trees, flowers, and vegetables have been mingled in a way that is not traditional. And terrible things have happened to the scarecrow. "Look at me!" he cries. "Look what has happened to me!" Mme Bonenfant, snipping away at the sweet-pea stems, answers calmly: "To me also. All experience is impoverishing. A great deal is taken away, a little is given in return. Patience is obligatory—the patient acceptance of much that is unacceptable."

Now it is evening, but not evening of the same day. The house is damp, and it has been raining since early morning. There are no guests at the moment. With her poor circulation Mme Bonenfant feels the cold, and so sometimes even in summer a small fire is lit for her in the Franklin stove in the petit salon. Mme Viénot is sitting at the desk, going over her accounts. Alix is on the divan. And Mme Bonenfant is going through a box of old letters.

"This is what the world used to be like," she says suddenly. "It is a letter from my father to his sister in Paris. 'The two young people'—Suzanne and Philippe, he is referring to—'evinced a delicate fondness for each other that we ought to be informed of. . . .'"

"And were they informed of it?" Alix asks.

"Yes. Shortly afterward," Mme Bonenfant says, and goes on reading to herself. When she finishes the letter, she puts it back in its envelope and drops it into the fire. The paper bursts into flame, the pale-brown ink turns darker for a few seconds and then this particular link with the remote past is gray ashes, and even the ashes are consumed.

"But surely you aren't destroying old letters!" Mme Viénot exclaims.

"When I am gone, who will be interested in reading them?" Mme Bonenfant says.

"*I* am interested," Mme Viénot says indignantly. "We all are. I have implored you—I implore you now—not to burn family letters."

"You didn't know any of the people," Mme Bonenfant says with finality, as though Mme Viénot were still a child.

Though she is very old, and tired, and forgetful, she is still the head of the family.

Now suppose I pass my hand over the crystal ball twice. What do we see? The furniture is under dust covers, the shutters are closed, the grass is not cut in the park, the potager is a tangle of weeds and briers. Sometimes in the night there are footsteps on the gravel terrace in front of the house, but no one lies in bed with a wildly beating heart, hearing them. All the rooms of the house are quiet except the third-floor room at the head of the stairs. The shutters here have come loose; they must not have been fastened securely. At some time, the ornamental shield has been removed from the fireplace, and occasionally there is a downdraft that redistributes the dust. Wasps beat against the windowpanes. In the night the shutters creak, the black-out paper flaps softly, the room grows cold. The mirrors recall long-forgotten images: the Germans; the young American couple; M. Lundqvist; Mme Viénot as a girl, expectant and vulnerable. Moonlight comes and goes. The mirrors remember the poor frightened squirrel that got in and could not get out. And in the hall at the foot of the stairs—this is really very strange—the grandfather's clock chimes again and again, though there is nobody to wind it.

You are not asking me to believe that?

No. The wheels turn, revealing (but in the dark, and to nobody) the exact hour of the day or night when footsteps are heard on the gravel. The children on their teeter-totter on the clock face are not afraid. They go right on recording the procession of seconds. Time is their only concern: the relentless thieving that nobody pays any attention to; or if they have become aware of it, they try not to think about it.

If you are of a certain temperament, you do think about it, anyway. You think about it much too much, until the sense

of deprivation becomes intolerable and you resort to the
Lost-and-Found Office, where, by an espèce de miracle, everything has been turned in, everything is the way it used to be. It
requires only a second to throw open the shutters and remove
the dust covers and air out musty rooms. "Do, do, l'enfant,
do . . ." Alix sings, pushing the second-hand baby carriage
back and forth under the shade of the Lebanon cedar, until
Annette lets go of her thumb and falls fast asleep. The departure is as abrupt as if she had stepped into a little boat. The
baby carriage has become a familiar sight on the roads around
the château. Propped up on a fat pillow, the fat baby stares at
the barking dog, at M. Fleury when he drives past in his noisy
camion, at the little boy, Alix's friend, who has now fully
mastered the art of riding a bicycle and rides round and round
the baby carriage, sometimes not using his hands. Watching
Alix go off down the driveway, Mme Viénot is sometimes
tempted to say to her sister: "She does not look happy," but it
is not the kind of remark one shouts into a hearing aid, if one
can avoid it, and also, Mme Viénot reflects, it is quite possible
that Mathilde's daughters do not confide in her, either.

During the daytime, Sabine reads or draws. She makes
drawings of grasses and leaves and fruit from the garden. She
makes a drawing of the two rain-stained statues, with the
house in the background. Mme Viénot observes that no letters
come for her, and that she does not seem to expect any. There
is a note from a cousin, and Sabine leaves it unopened on the
table in her room for three days. The sound of her voice
coming from her grandmother's room is cheerful, but that is
perhaps nothing more than the effect chère Maman has on her,
on everybody. Mme Bonenfant arranges bouquets in the manner of Fantin-Latour, who is her favorite painter, in the hope
that Sabine will be tempted to paint them. Sabine draws the
children instead.

For the second week in a row, Eugène does not come down
from Paris. Neither does he write, though Alix writes to him.
In the evenings, Mme Viénot works at her desk in the petit salon. The two girls sit side by side on the ottoman, sharing the
same pool of lamplight. Alix is knitting a sweater for the baby,
Sabine is reading *Gone With the Wind* in French, Mme Bonenfant and Mme Cestre face each other across the little round

table, with the *diamonoes* spread out on the green baize cloth. If she plays with anyone else, Mme Bonenfant finds that the game tires her. But Mme Cestre, far from being impatient with her mother when it takes her so long to decide where to place her counter, does not even notice, and has to be reminded that it is now her turn. The evenings pass very much as they did during the war, except that everybody is a little older, trucks do not come and go in the courtyard all night, and the only male in the house is a little boy of four, who shows no signs of ever becoming a professional soldier.

When they have all gone up to bed, the grandfather's clock in the downstairs hall chimes eleven fifteen and eleven thirty and a quarter of twelve and midnight.

Hearing the clock strike, Mme Viénot gets up from her desk, where she is writing a letter, and goes into the room across the hall. Mme Bonenfant is sitting up in bed, and when Mme Viénot takes the book from her hands, she sees that her mother has been reading Bossuet's funeral oration on the Grand Condé. The white bedspread is lying on a chair, neatly folded. The room's slight odor of camphor and old age Mme Viénot has long since become accustomed to. Mme Bonenfant removes her spectacles, folds them, and puts them on the night table, beside the photograph of her dead son.

Mme Viénot takes away the pillows at her mother's back, and the old woman lies flat in the huge double bed, as she will lie before very long in her grave. Is she afraid, Mme Viénot wonders. Does she ever think about dying?

There is little or no point in asking. Her mother would not consider this a proper subject for conversation. Actually, there are a good many subjects that chère Maman, close as she is to the end of her life, does not care to speak of. To question her about the past, to try to get at her secrets, is merely to provoke a smile or an irrelevant remark.

As she opens the window a few inches, Mme Viénot suddenly remembers how when she was a child her mother, smelling of wood violets, used to come and say good night to her. If one only lives long enough, every situation is repeated. . . .

Back in her own room, she undresses and puts on her night-gown and the dark-red wrapper, which is worn at the cuffs, she notices. Seated at the dressing table, she digs her fingers into a jar of cleansing cream and, having wiped away powder and rouge, confronts the gray underface. She and it have arrived at a working agreement: the underface, tragic, sincere, irrevocably middle-aged, is not to show itself until late at night when everyone is in bed. And in return for this discreet forbearance, Mme Viénot on her part is ready to acknowledge that the face she now sees in the mirror is hers.

She goes over to the desk and takes up the letter where she left off. When it is finished, she puts it in its envelope, licks the flap, seals it, and puts it with several other letters, all written since she came upstairs. The pile of letters represents the future, which can no more be trusted to take care of itself than the present can (though experience has demonstrated that there is a limit, a point beyond which effort cannot go, and many things happen, good and bad, that are simply the work of chance).

She begins a new letter. After a moment her pen stops moving, and she listens to the still house. Again there is a creaking sound, but it is in the walls, not in the passage outside her door. The pen moves on again, like a machine. Mme Viénot is waiting for Sabine to come and say good night. The poor child must be disheartened at losing her job with *La Femme Elégante*, and it is indeed a pity, but such things happen, and she is prepared to offer comfort, reassurance, the indisputable truth that what seems like misfortune is often a blessing in disguise. She glances impatiently at her wrist watch, and sees that it is quarter of one. She writes two more letters, even so. Her acquaintance, now that she no longer lives in Paris, shows a tendency to forget her unless prodded regularly with letters and small attentions. Paying guests, when they leave, cannot be counted on to remember indefinitely what an agreeable time they have had, and so may fail to return or fail to send other clients. A note, covering one page and part of the next, serves to remind them, if it is a question of someone's searching out a pleasant, well-situated, wholly proper establishment, that they know just the place—a handsome country house about two hundred kilometers from Paris and not far from Blois.

Mme Viénot takes off the red dressing gown and puts it over the back of a chair, gets into bed, and opens the book on her bedside table. She reads a few lines and then turns out the light. It is time that Sabine learned to be more thoughtful of others.

Stretched out flat, she discovers how tired she is, and for a moment or two she passes directly into that stage of conscious dreaming that precedes sleep. Between dreams, she reflects that the younger generation has very little affection for Beaumesnil. It is important only to Eugène.

The telephone rings, and when Mme Viénot answers it, she hears the voice of Mme Carrère. Monsieur has had a slight relapse—nothing serious, but the doctors think it would be advisable for him to be in the country, where there is absolute quiet, in a place that did him so much good before. They arrive that afternoon by car, and find their old rooms waiting for them. "You will want to rest after your long drive," Mme Viénot says. "Thérèse will bring you a can of hot water immediately. Then you need not be disturbed until dinnertime." And closing the door behind her, she passes happily over the border into sleep, but the ratching, scratching sound draws her back into consciousness. The sound continues at irregular intervals. A squirrel or a fieldmouse, she tells herself. Or a rat.

After half an hour she sits up in bed, turns on the light, props the pillows behind her back. With a sigh at not being able to go to sleep when she so much needs a good night's rest, she reaches for the book. It is the memoirs of Father Robert, an early nineteenth-century Jesuit missionary, who lived among the Chinese, and was close to God. Mme Viénot puts what happened to him, his harsh but beautifully dedicated life, between her and all silences, all creaking noises, all failures, all searching for answers that cannot be found.

STORIES 1963–1976

Contents

A Final Report

*I*n the matter of the estate of Pearl M. Donald, deceased, who carried me on a pillow when I was a sickly baby, a little over fifty years ago, *Probate No. 2762*, for many years my mother's best friend and our next-door neighbor, a beautiful woman with a knife-edge to her voice and a grievance against her husband (What? What on earth could it have been? Everybody loved him): *Final report to the Honorable Frank Mattein, Judge of the County Court of Logan County, Illinois: The undersigned, Margaret Wilson, Executor of the Last Will of Pearl M. Donald, deceased, respectfully states: 1. That on or about the 17th day of June, 1961, Pearl M. Donald departed this life* . . . though it was far from easy. It took her almost twenty years of not wanting to live anymore. And if she had been left in her own house, in all that frightful squalor and filth and no air and the odor of cats' defecation, she might have needed still more time. But when she was carrying me on a pillow it was not a question of when she would die but of whether I would live.

It is safe to assume that she shared my mother's fears, comforted her, lied to her—comforting lies, about the way I looked today as compared with the way I looked yesterday; and that at some point she took my mother in her arms and let her cry. Though Aunty Donald lived to be so old, there was no question of her mental competence. She left a will, which was duly approved and admitted to probate. Letters testamentary were duly issued; the executor was duly qualified; an inventory of all estate assets, both real and personal, was filed and approved by the court; notices for the filing of claims were published, as provided by law; and proof of heirship was made, from which it appears *that the decedent left her surviving no husband* (there is nothing like the law for pointing out what everybody knows) *and the following named person as her only heir at law: Agnes Jones,* an adult cousin, whom I have never heard of.

I don't, of course, remember being carried on the pillow, but I remember the playhouse in Aunty Donald's back yard. It was made of two upright-piano boxes put together, in the fashion of that period, with windows and a door, and real shingles on the roof. It had belonged to a little girl named Mary King. The Donalds' house used to be the Kings'. And when I got to be five or six years old, my mother, seeing that I loved the playhouse, which was locked, which I never went in, and which I shouldn't have loved, since I was a little boy and playhouses are for little girls—my mother asked if she could buy the playhouse for me and Aunty Donald said no, she was keeping it for Bun. Bun was her dog—a bulldog. I don't know whether it was at that point that she stopped being my mother's best friend (my mother seldom took offense, but when she did it was usually permanent) or whether Aunty Donald said that because she had already stopped being my mother's best friend. There is so much that children are not told and that it never occurs to them to ask. Anyway, I went on peering through the windows of the locked playhouse at the things Mary King had left behind when the Kings moved away, and hoping that someday the playhouse would be unlocked and I could go inside. Once I heard my mother mention it to my Aunt Annette, and I realized from the tone of her voice that it was a mildly sore subject with her but not taken so seriously that—that what? That I didn't spend a great many hours in Aunty Donald's kitchen with the hired girl while my mother and Aunty Donald were talking in the front part of the house. I don't remember what they talked about. It didn't interest me, and so I went out to the kitchen, where I could do some of the talking. And in return I even listened. The hired girl's name was Mae, and she had a child in the state institution for the feeble-minded, on the outskirts of town. She was not feeble-minded herself, but neither was she terribly bright, I suppose. The men joked about her. My father had seen her leaving the Donalds' house all dressed up, on her afternoon off, and he had not recognized her. From the rear, the men agreed, she was some chicken. When you saw her face, it was a different story. She was about as homely as it is possible to be. Scraggly teeth, a complexion the color of putty, kinky hair, and a slight aura of silliness. What I talked to her about I don't know. Children never seem to suffer from a lack of things to say. What she talked to me about was the fact that Aunty Donald wouldn't let her have cream in her coffee. This was half a century ago, when hired girls got four or five dollars a week. At our house nobody ever told the hired girl she couldn't have what we had. So far as I know. And I seem to remember telling my mother that Aunty wouldn't let Mae have cream in her coffee, but whether I remember or only think I remember, I undoubtedly did tell my mother this, because I told her everything. It was my way of dealing with facts and with life. The act of telling her made them manageable. I don't suppose I told her anything about Aunty Donald that she didn't know already. And she was a very good and loving mother, and didn't tell me everything by way of making her facts and her life manageable. She just shone on me like the sun, and in spite of my uncertain beginning I grew. I was not as strong as other children, but I came along. I stayed out of the cemetery.

Of all those times next door during my childhood, there are only four distinct memories. Two of them take place on the Donalds' front porch, in the summertime. It is almost dark, and my father is smoking a cigar, and the women are fanning themselves, and suddenly all this serenity vanishes because of a change in the color of the sky. The sunset is long past, and yet the sky above the houses on the other side of the street is growing pink. There is only one thing it could be. Aunty goes indoors and finds out from the telephone operator where the fire is, but they do not jump in the car, because there is no car, and if you are in your right mind you don't drive to a fire in a horse and buggy. Instead, my mother and Aunty Donald sit taking the catastrophe in from the porch swing. The whole sky is a frightening red now, and in their voices I hear something I have never heard before. It occurs to me that we might be witnessing The End of the World, so often mentioned in the Presbyterian Sunday school. In simple fact, it is the Orphans' Home burning down.

No. 2: One of the things that Aunty Donald held against her husband was that he spoke with a Scottish accent. He had every right to. (He always referred to Scotland as "the old country," and I thought as a child that it was the only place so called.) In the dusk, sitting on the porch steps, he suddenly exclaimed, "Pe'll, Pe'll, there's a speeder on you!" And though she had been married to him for I don't know how long—ten or fifteen years, I would guess—she affected not to understand that a "speeder" was a spider. She was from a little town nearby—Dover, Illinois—and according to the executor's report owned property there at the time of her death, a house that was sold for $1,600, for which somebody had been paying $22 a month rent.

The two other set pieces both happen upstairs. We—my mother and I—are in Aunty's bedroom, and on the big brass double bed there are a great many Christmas presents, wrapped either in white paper with red ribbon or red paper with white ribbon. They are of all shapes and sizes, and interest me very much. Aunty is showing my mother something that still has to be wrapped—a bottle of cologne or some crocheted doilies, that sort of thing—and my mother is admiring whatever it is, and as I stand there, it is borne in on me, by intuition, that in all this collection of presents there is nothing for me.

The final memory is of a nightmare that I had when I was wide awake. I am in bed, in the Donalds' spare room, and the door is open, and I can see out into the hall. At the head of the stairs there is a large picture of a man in a nightshirt on a tumbled bed, by a brook, over which red-coated huntsmen are jumping their horses. The man is asleep and doesn't know the danger he is in. The horses' hoofs are going to come down on him and kill him, and there is nothing I can do to save him. Though it does not take very much to make me cry, this time I do not. I know that Aunty is just down the hall and would hear me and get up out of bed and come to me, and still I do not make a sound. I stare at the picture until I fall asleep and dream about it. What I was doing there I do not know. I had been left with Aunty for the night. My mother and father must have been away, and perhaps they took my brother with them.

Twenty-five or thirty years later, I spoke of the picture to Aunty Donald, and asked if I could see it. By that time, my mother was dead and we had moved away, like the Kings, and there was a layer of dust over everything. She was no longer the housekeeper that she used to be, but apart from this there was no change in her house, which pleased me, because there was nothing but change everywhere else. Our house, next door, had been sold to strangers and the furniture scattered.

The house is still standing, but I have never been inside it since the day the moving men emptied it room by room. To come to see Dr. and Aunty Donald was to walk straight into the past. Ninth Street was lined with handsome shade trees that kept the houses from seeming ordinary, which they were, Aunty Donald's house no less than the others. But the inside of her house was not ordinary, it was amazing. When she was a young woman nobody thought her taste peculiar, for the simple reason that everyone else's taste was peculiar, too. It was an age that admired individuality, and in most cases individuality was arrived at through the marriage of Grand Rapids and *art nouveau*. Accident and sentiment also played a part. The total effect was usually homelike and comfortable, once the eye got over the shock. But a whole generation after all the other beaded portieres in Lincoln had been taken down, Aunty Donald's continued to divide the sitting room from the dark, gloomy dining room, and when you pushed your way through, it made an agreeable rattle. Along with the porticre, all sorts of things survived their period. For example, two long peacock feathers in a hand-painted vase on the upright piano that was never tuned and never played on. In an old snapshot that I came upon recently, I saw, to my surprise and pleasure, that most of my mother's friends were, as young women, beautiful. Some of them went on being beautiful, but Aunty Donald did not. The Donalds had no children. She lost both her parents. And Dr. Donald lost a good deal of money in a business venture that I never understood. Add to this those grotesque but common deprivations that people don't like to talk about, such as false teeth and bifocals and the fear of falling. Aunty Donald was sufficiently aware of all that she had lost, and did not want to add to it by throwing things away—even such things as the evening paper and second-class mail. Also clothes that were worn out or long out of fashion. Cups that had lost their handle, saucers that had no cup. The wallpaper had not even been changed, but was allowed to go on fading. In the sitting room, up next to the ceiling, at repeated intervals the same three knights rode up to the same castle that they used to ride up to when I was a small child. So it was reasonable to assume that the picture of the man sprawled out on the tumbled bed by a brook was still hanging at the head of the stairs, but it turned out that the picture was not there. Dr. Donald had taken it to Chicago, and it was hanging in a club near the stockyards. He had loaned it to them, Aunty said, but she would get it back. From that time on, she nagged him to bring the picture home so I could have it, and he promised to. Each time I went to see them he would say, "Billie, I haven't forgotten about your picture." And one night the club burned down, and then she had something else to blame him for. One more thing. The truth is, he— The truth is I have no idea what the truth is. Perhaps he gave the picture to the club, and would have been embarrassed to ask for it back, and so pretended that he kept forgetting to ask for it. Anyway, it is preserved forever, the way all lost things are. It is quite safe, from mildew and from the burning pile (*Nov. 19 Virgil Edmonds, George Colby, Roy Miller, Clarence Sylvester, labor for cleaning decedent's residence, $12, $12, $16, $16,* and what a bonfire it must have been).

Whatever the picture was like, it wasn't the picture I remember; I know this much about pictures looked at in childhood. It was in color, perhaps hand-colored but more likely a lithograph. The man on the bed was not being trampled to death but dreaming of the hunt or steeplechase or whatever it was that was going on in the air above his bed. And I am glad I do not have it, because I cannot throw things away, either, and the attic is full of souvenirs of the past from which the magic has long since evaporated. The playhouse, strangely, I still regret. I find myself wondering if it is still there. The executor's report does not list it.

I assumed that Aunty loved me, because of the way her face would light up when she opened the front door and saw me standing there. I know she loved my mother and father. And everybody loved my brother Edward, who was called "Happy." They loved him with a special love because when he was five years old he got his left leg caught in the wheel of a buggy and it had to be cut off above the knee. But they loved him before that, because he was a beautiful little boy, and because he was a handful. Being good, being well-behaved, simply didn't interest him. He did what he felt like doing, and spankings had no effect. Anything you didn't want him to investigate you had to keep locked up or on a shelf too high for him to reach. He gave up cigars when he was five. In the space of five minutes one afternoon, he turned the hose on my mother and my Aunt Edith and my father. The women retired shrieking into the house but my father walked right through the stream of water to the outside faucet and cut it off at the source. My Aunt Annette and Dr. Donald both worshiped the ground my brother walked on. The look in their eyes when they spoke to him or about him, the pleasure they took in telling stories about things he did when he was little, the way they said his name made this quite plain. As it happened, they were also devoted to each other. From the beginning of Time all these friendships were; from before I was born. And they lasted out the lifetime of all the people involved, and most of them lived to be very old. Dr. Donald was a small, compact man, in appearance and in character totally unlike anyone else in Lincoln. He was a horse dealer as well as a veterinary, and at one time he had a livery stable on the east side of the courthouse square. During the First World War, he supplied horses to the American Expeditionary Force. There is a picture of my brother in a pony cart alone and holding the reins. My father was earning a modest salary, and he was not extravagant by nature, and I rather think that the pony cart and the succession of ponies must have come from Dr. Donald's stable and were eventually returned to it. I was under the impression that I, too, would have a pony, when I was old enough. Perhaps I would have, except for the fact that the world was changing. My father sold the carriage horse when I was six years old, and bought a seven-passenger Chalmers. Where the barn had stood there was now a garage. The change from horses to cars cannot have made Dr. Donald any happier than it made me. It didn't affect Aunty Donald one way or the other, because she never went anywhere except to our house, and she didn't come there often. If you wanted to see her, you had to go to her house. She went to my mother's funeral, I have no doubt. And then, just before her own, she went to the hospital and to a nursing home. In between, for forty-one years, she never went out of her front door except to sweep the leaves off the front porch or to open the mailbox, or to pick up the *Evening Courier*. The reason she gave for not going anywhere was that it was not suitable for the wife of a horse doctor to accept invitations. The horse doctor was universally loved and admired. People went to him for advice about financial matters and they also went to him when the time had come for them to open their hearts to somebody. In short, it was all in her head.

He lived to be almost ninety, and during his last illness, which went on for months, she took care of him herself. Often she was up all night with him. After he died, the change set in. She looked older, of course, but then she *was* old. In order to sit down, when you went to see her, you had to remove a pile of newspapers or a party hat with tired-looking cloth roses on it or a box of old letters or, sometimes, it was hard to say exactly what—an object. She would be pleased to see you, but you had the feeling as you were leaving that when the front door closed she would pick up the conversation with herself where it had left off and forget that you'd been there until she got a card from you at Christmastime. A cousin of mine who took care of her legal affairs for a time found that if he wanted to get her signature on a paper it was a good idea to telephone first, because she had stopped answering the door. She was deaf, but not that deaf; she just let the doorbell ring. I have tried this myself. In a little while, sometimes in a surprisingly little while, it stops ringing, leaving instead a silence that is full of obscure satisfaction. The same thing was true for the man who came to read the gas and electric-light meter, and for the salesman who was trying to interest her in a life-insurance policy, and for the minister who was concerned about her soul, and for the neighbors who wanted to bring some warm food over to her in a covered dish—they all took to telephoning first. Sometimes she let the telephone ring and ring.

A young woman turned up who had known Dr. Donald. I don't know her name or where she came from, but she was a businesswoman, energetic and capable, and with an understanding of financial affairs that most women did not have, and the patience to explain them. Her first visit was followed by others. It is easy to deduce from what happened what must have led up to it. The pleasure of finding a letter in the mailbox instead of the usual circulars, and of putting fresh sheets on the bed in the spare room because someone was coming on the six-fifteen train. What could it have been like except having the child, the affectionate daughter, that she had wanted and been denied? At last, someone was concerned about her. All sorts of people who actually were concerned about her—her husband's friends, the men at the bank, and the neighbors on Ninth Street—were satisfied that she was being taken care of and that they needn't worry about her anymore. So they weren't worried about her, until somebody gossiping over the back fence said that Mrs. Donald had said that the young woman wanted her to sign over to her everything she owned, with the understanding that she would take care of Mrs. Donald as long as she lived. In a small place, word always gets around—rather quickly, in fact. And small-town people are not in the habit of shrugging off responsibility. Two of Dr. Donald's friends—much younger men than he was, but he had a gift for friendship and it was not limited to his contemporaries —went to see Aunty Donald, and shortly afterward the young woman retired from the field.

Unfortunately, though they could protect her from being taken advantage of, they could not protect her from loneliness. She started feeding a stray cat, and then she let the cat into the house one cold night, and the cat had kittens. The dilemma is classical, and how you solve it depends on what kind of person you are. Between five-fifteen and five-thirty every morning, the back door opened and out came the cats. The smell of coffee drifted through the house, and another day was added to the long chain that went back, past the First World War and the Spanish-American War and the assassinations of Garfield and McKinley, to the eighteen-seventies, when things were so much pleasanter and quieter than they are now. The chain is not as strong as it seems: The beaded portiere fell down. All by itself. For no reason. In the middle of the night, she told me. It couldn't have been caused by a sudden stirring of air, because the windows were closed. When she came downstairs in the morning, the first thing she saw was the empty doorway, and then she saw the glass beads all over the sitting-room floor.

The rest I know only from hearsay. I never saw her again after this visit. She fell and broke her hip. Out of the kindness of her heart, the woman who lived next door put food out for the cats, but no one expected Aunty Donald to come home from the hospital. She did come home, looking a lot thinner and older, and she went on as before, except that the experience had taught her something. If an accident could befall her, it could befall her cats. She found it harder and harder to let them out into a world full of vicious dogs, poisoned meat, boys with slingshots and BB guns, and people who don't like cats. She put down some shredded newspaper in a roasting pan in the back hall and showed it to the cats, and they quickly got the idea, and after that she didn't have to let them out of the house at all. At her age one doesn't go around opening windows recklessly in all kinds of weather, and so the house— to put it bluntly—smelled. Since she never went out of it, she had no idea how strong the smell really was. Sometimes when she had neglected to put down fresh paper, the cats retired to a corner somewhere, and this added to the unpleasantness. For she was half blind and could not be expected to go around on her hands and knees searching for the source of the smell. And if she had someone in to clean, as people often urged her to do, what was to prevent the cleaning woman from lifting the piano scarf or the corner of the bedroom rug and finding who knows how much money and putting it quietly in her apron pocket? No thank you.

One day she heard the doorbell ring, and this time it didn't stop ringing. It went on and on until finally, against her better judgment, she opened the door. The caller was not Death, but it might just as well have been. My brother is a forceful, decisive man, with a big heart and a loud, cheerful voice and enough courage for three people, but he had to excuse himself after five minutes and go to the front door for a breath of fresh air. By nightfall she was in bed in a nursing home. She lived on a few weeks, expecting that this time, too, she would go home, and instead she died in her sleep.

The Donalds' house had too many trees around it, and so the grass was thin. The house was heated by hot-air registers, and had its own smell, as all houses did in those days. I don't remember ever having a meal in the dark dining room, though I must have, and don't remember any flowers, inside or out, unless possibly iris around the foundations. No, I'm sure there weren't any. The flowers were on our side of the fence. Flower beds around a birdbath in the backyard, flower beds all along one side of the house, and vines on trellises—a trumpet vine, clematis, a grape arbor. What I remember cannot be true, if only because the climate of Illinois is not right for it, but the effect is of a full-blown lushness that I associate with Lake Como, which I have never seen, and old-fashioned vaudeville curtains. What can my mother and Aunty Donald have seen in each other? Something; otherwise the names of my older and younger brothers and my name would not have appeared in her will as beneficiaries—one-seventeenth of the estate each: $1,182.55, less Illinois inheritance tax amounting to $108.72. Or about twice her annual income. How did she live in the nineteen-fifties on $55 a month? On air; she must have subsisted on air and old memories and fear—the fear of something happening to her cats.

She did not ever say that she preferred me to my older brother, but when I was a child and cared one way or the other, I used to think that she would not have said so often that she carried me on a pillow if she hadn't meant that my brother was Dr. Donald's favorite and I was hers. I understood the principle of equity, even though I had not yet encountered the word. I know now that she loved my brother the way everyone else did—because of the terrible thing that had happened to him, and because of his pride, which kept him from feeling sorry for himself. And because he was so wicked when he was little, and so bold. How their faces shone with amusement when someone told the story of the hose, or how, totally unafraid, he said to the gypsy, "Mr. Gypsy, what have you got in your *bag*?"

Aunty Donald would not have let anyone but my brother remove her from her house to that nursing home, or have believed anyone else who told her, as he did, that it was only for a week or so. She believed him because he had had his leg cut off when he was five years old and still did everything that other boys could do. To see Dr. Donald with him when my brother was a grown man was to see, unforgettably, the image of love. We—my brother and his wife and I—went to the races with him in Chicago. Dr. Donald didn't touch my brother, but his hands fluttered around him. The expression on the old man's face was of someone looking into the sun.

The balance transferred from the conservator's account to the executor's account was $2,073.04. In Aunty's bank account: $82.55. Half a year's interest on government bonds: $300. The rent from the house in Dover. On October 24th, the executor deposited the first collection of money found in the house: $293 in bills and $51.40 in coins. On November 3rd: $325 in gold pieces, which should have been turned in thirty years before. Thirty years before, Aunty was in her late fifties, and voted the straight Republican ticket, if she voted at all. She was, in any case, strong-minded. She did as she pleased, without regard for fiscal policies. On May 4th, these items: Proceeds from the sale of old car: $25, the standard price for junk. (I didn't know they had a car. I thought of Dr. Donald as loyal exclusively to horses.) A flower urn brought $15, which means that some woman in Lincoln had had her eye on it. $18 in gold, and $12.45 in cash. On June 29th, somebody made a down payment of $500 on the house on Ninth Street, the total sale price being $7,000. A big house for that, but it undoubtedly was run down. On August 7th: *liquidating dividend from German-American National Bank Stock owned by T. A. Donald*, but no mention of the stock, and the bank hasn't been called that since shortly after the sinking of the *Lusitania*. An uncashed dividend check turned up somewhere, in a book or in a box of old letters or God knows where. And then, oddly, jewelry not bequeathed in her will. A diamond ring: $175. An amethyst ring with a small pearl: $20. A small pocket watch: $5 (meaning it wouldn't run). A pearl and rhinestone (!) ring: $3. A small locket on a chain (which I have a feeling I remember, the only jewelry I remember her wearing, but perhaps this is imagination). A diamond ring: $150, and a dinner ring with small diamonds: $200. A down payment of $250 on the house in Dover. Proceeds from the sale of cufflinks, tiepins, collar buttons, etc.: $10. An imitation ruby ring: $7. All this in January and February. In March, a pin, another watch, and a ring: $25. They must have turned up in some hiding place, though the house had been cleaned, by four men, several months before. And probably these items were not mentioned in the will because Aunty had forgotten she had them.

The disbursements are less eccentric. It took $817.21 (the Abraham Lincoln Memorial Hospital, St. Joseph's Nursing Home) to help her out of this life. There is a charge for sewerage-system service—stopped-up drain or sink or toilet. And Ernest J. Gottlieb was paid $12 for opening a safe in the basement. Some of the money was probably there; or the jewelry. Or the safe could have been empty. Anything is possible. The spray of flowers for her own casket cost $34, and the funeral expenses were $1,470, so she was buried within the circumference of the middle class. She died in June, and the yard was mowed all through July, August, and September, and the water and gas were not turned off until the following February. The doctor bills were $150.50. In Lincoln, doctors still dispensed medicine. Apparently she had stopped taking the evening paper; there is no item for the paper boy. But from time to time during the settling of the estate, notices were run in the Lincoln *Evening Courier* and the Dover *Times*. Carl Simmons was paid $3 for painting a "For Sale" sign. There is no telephone bill. In April the yard was raked, the porch and the windows were repaired. There are two items for real-estate taxes. The First Presbyterian Church received $500, according to the fifteenth clause of the will, and various sums of money were paid out for the recording of affidavits and for appraisals, broker's and auctioneer's commissions, and court costs. The executor's commission was $1,500, the attorney's fee $2,500.

In June the yard was mowed again, and on August 8th the house passed into the hands of somebody else and was no longer Aunty Donald's. The three knights that for so long rode up to that faded castle have no doubt been covered over. There is no mention in the final report of the peacock feathers or the piano that was never tuned and never played on. My cousin told me that the contents of the house were sold intact to someone from out of town, for $2,000; that the buyer wanted the clothes for theatrical purposes, and also thought they might be of interest to museums and historical societies.

It was all carted off to a warehouse somewhere until he had a chance to go over everything and see what was there. It would have been a pleasure to go through Aunty Donald's things, up to a point, and after that probably nauseating. This is the past unillumined by memory or love. The sediment of days, what covered Troy and finally would have covered her if my brother hadn't come and taken her away.

The Value of Money

"M Y son Ned, from New York," Mr. Ferrers said.
Why, he's proud of me, Edward Ferrers thought; he
wouldn't be introducing me like this if he weren't.

He put his thin hand through the grilled window in the
waiting room of the railway station and shook hands with the
ticket agent, who said, "Glad to know you, Ned."

The ticket agent checked Edward's return ticket (the
sleeping-car reservation needed to be confirmed in Chicago)
and ignored the telegraph's urgent, lisping *click-click* . . .
click-click . . . *click-click-click* . . . *click* . . . *click*. . . .
The wall calendar, compliments of Orton Grain & Feed Co.,
was open to the month of June 1952.

Edward Ferrers came home to Draperville once every three
years, for three or four days, which wasn't quite long enough
for him to get used to the way the town looked, and so he was
continually noting the things that had changed and the things
that had not changed. He also had changed, of course, and
not changed. He had acquired the tense, alert air of a city man,
and his accent was no longer that of the Middle West but a
mixture, showing traces of all the places he had lived in. On
the other hand, people who had known him as a little boy on
his way to the Presbyterian Sunday school or marching with
the Boy Scouts on the Fourth of July had no trouble recognizing him, even though he was now forty-three years old and
the crown of his head was quite bald.

"I want to stop at the bank for a minute," he said, as they
were leaving the station.

"What for?" Mr. Ferrers demanded.

"I want to cash a check."

"How much do you need?"

"I just want to be sure I have enough for the diner and the
porters and the taxi home," Edward said. "Ten dollars ought
to do it, with what I have." His voice in speaking to his father
was gentle but careful, as if he were piloting a riverboat upstream with due regard for submerged sandbars and dangerous snags under the smoothly flowing surface of the water.

Mr. Ferrers took out his billfold, which was as orderly as his person, and extracted two new ten-dollar bills. "Your Aunt Alice is expecting us at one," he said. "You don't want to keep her waiting."

Edward took the money and put it in his billfold, which was coming unsewed and was stuffed with he had no idea what. "I'll give you a check when we get home," he said.

"All right," Mr. Ferrers said.

Neither as a child nor as an adult had Edward ever lied to his father, but he did hold back information that he had reason to think his father would be troubled by. For example, he didn't tell his father what his salary as an associate professor was, or how much money he had. If his father knew, it would upset him, certainly. And what would upset him even more was that Edward had failed to put anything by. One of the primary rules of Mr. Ferrers's life was that a certain percentage of what he made should be saved for a rainy day.

As a sullen adolescent Edward had accused his father—often in his mind and once to his face—of caring about nothing but money. This was not true, of course. Mr. Ferrers never confused the making of money with a man's concern for his family or his own self-respect. But he took money seriously (who doesn't?) and to this day carried about with him, in his inside coat pocket, a little memorandum book containing an up-to-the-minute detailed statement of his assets. He took it out and showed it to Edward the day before, while they were admiring the roses in the backyard. What would have happened if Edward had asked to see what was written in the little book he didn't dare think. His father would probably have said that it wasn't any of his business, and in fact it wasn't.

They got in the front seat of the car and Mr. Ferrers rolled the window up on his side, though it was a warm day. He was past seventy, and the gradual refining and shrinking process of old age had begun, and with it had come a susceptibility to drafts.

"I can raise my window, too," Edward said.

Mr. Ferrers shook his head. "I'll tell you if I feel it."

The car was a Cadillac, five years old but without a scratch. It had been washed in honor of Edward's visit and looked brand-new.

"We ought to leave Alice's around three, if you want to see Dr. McBride," Mr. Ferrers said.

"I thought he was dead."

"Not at all. Old Doc goes his merry way at eighty-eight, spending his capital and thinking he can cure his ills and pains, which at his age is impossible. And Ruth hasn't had a new dress in many years. But he knows you're here, and he'll be hurt if you don't come to see him. . . . I tried to head your Aunt Alice off, but she wanted to do something for you."

"I know," Edward said.

"You'd think that by having people at the house where they could see you that that ought to satisfy them, but it doesn't. They all want to have you for cocktails or something, and the result is that I don't get any time with you—which I don't like. But there's nothing I can do about it."

"This evening we'll have some time," Edward said.

"Three days is not enough."

"I know it isn't."

Once they had left the business district there was no traffic whatever. As Edward drove, he continued to look both at the quiet empty street ahead of them and in the little oblong, bluish rearview mirror, at his father. Mr. Ferrers was aware that he was being studied, but what reasonable man is afraid of the scrutiny of his own child? Before he retired and moved back to Draperville, Illinois, Mr. Ferrers had been the vice-president in charge of the Chicago office of a large public-utility company. He was accustomed to speak with authority, and with confidence that his opinion, which had been arrived at cautiously and with due regard for the opinions of others, was the right one. He also came from a long line of positive people. Introspection was as foreign to his nature as dishonesty. Right was right and wrong was wrong, and to tell one from the other you had only to examine your own conscience. In general, Mr. Ferrers was on the side of the golden mean, or, as he would have put it, the middle of the road. When it came to politics, he threw moderation to the winds and was a fanatical Republican. Though he could not swallow the Book of Genesis, he believed every word that was printed in the Chicago *Tribune*. Also that Franklin Roosevelt had committed suicide. Fishing and golf were his two great pleasures. At the bridge table he deliberated, strumming his fingers, without realizing that he was holding up the game, and drove his wife, Edward's step-mother, to make remarks that she had meant to keep to herself. Now that his eyesight had begun to fail, he had trouble recognizing people at any distance, and so he spoke courteously to everyone he met on the street. He had no enemies. The younger men, Edward's contemporaries, looked up to him and came to him for advice. The older men, Mr. Ferrers's lifelong friends, considered it a privilege to be allowed to fasten the fly on the end of his fishing line, and loved him for his forthrightness, and saw to it that he did not lack company at five o'clock in the afternoon, when he got out the ice trays and the glasses and a bottle of very good Scotch.

"This part of town hasn't changed at all," Edward remarked.

He meant the houses. The look of things had changed drastically. The trees were gone. In a nightmare of three or four years' duration, the elm blight had put an end to the shade—to all those long, graceful, leafy branches that used to hang down over roofs and porches and reach out over the brick pavement toward the branches on the other side. Now everything looked uncomfortably exposed, as if standing on the sidewalk you could tell how much people owed at the bank. Not that there had ever been much privacy in Draperville, Edward thought; but now there was not even the appearance of privacy. . . . In the dark, cold, hungry, anxious to get home to his supper, he used to ride over these very lawns on his bicycle, and when he was close enough to the front porch he would reach backward into his canvas bag, take out a folded copy of the Draperville *Evening Star*, and let fly with it. That dead self, the boy he used to be. *The one you used to have such trouble with*, he wanted to say to his father, but Mr. Ferrers did not like talking about the past. "That's all water over the dam," he said once when Edward asked him a question about his mother. On the other hand, he did sometimes like to talk about local history—what the business district was like when he was a boy, where some long defunct dry goods store or shoe store or law office or livery stable used to be, and who the old families were. And gossip said that when he went to see old Dr. McBride, he talked about Edward's mother. So perhaps it's only that he doesn't like to talk about the past with me,

Edward thought. Aloud, he said, "This car drives very easily, after our 1936 Ford."

"You ought to get a new car," Mr. Ferrers said.

"The old one runs. It runs very well."

"I know, but so does a new car. And Janet might enjoy having a car that isn't sixteen years old, did you ever stop to think of that?"

Edward smiled, without taking his eyes from the street, and did not commit himself. This was not the first time that his father had brought up the subject of their car, which had stopped being a joke and was now an affront to the whole family. Except possibly his Aunt Alice, who didn't have a car, because she had very little money—barely enough to live on. What she did have slipped through her fingers. This was equally true of Edward. When he was a little boy, his father made him lie stretched out on his hand in shallow water. "Don't be afraid, I won't take my hand away," he said, and when Edward stopped thrashing and looked back, his father was ten feet away from him and he had learned to swim. But learning the value of money was something else again.

On Edward's sixth birthday, Mr. Ferrers started his son off with a weekly allowance of ten cents—a sum so large in Edward's eyes that when Mrs. McBride gave him another dime for ice-cream cones, he wasn't sure whether it was morally right for him to take it. With advancing age, the ten cents became a quarter, all his own, to spend when and on what he pleased, and of course once it was spent there was no possibility of more until another week rolled around. In first-year high school, the quarter became fifty cents, and then, in Chicago, where he had lunch at school and carfare to consider, it jumped suddenly to three dollars. By walking to school, and a good deal of the time not eating any lunch, he could buy books, and did. Sometimes quite expensive ones. And in college he had sixty, then seventy-five, and then ninety dollars a month, with no questions asked, out of which he fed himself and paid for the roof over his head and bought still more books. If he ran short toward the end of the month, he lived on milk and graham crackers—which was not what his father had intended. And once when he ran out of money early in the month because he had shared what he had with a roommate whose check from home didn't come, he got a job waiting tables at a sorority house. What it amounted to was that he had learned when the money ran out not to ask for more.

When he finished college, he thought he wanted to teach English, but after three years of graduate work he threw up his part-time appointment with the university where he had been an undergraduate, took the hundred dollars that he had in a savings account, borrowed another hundred from his father, and went to New York on a Greyhound bus and got a job. After working three weeks, he paid his father back. A great load fell from Mr. Ferrers's shoulders with this act. He sat with Edward's letter and the check for a hundred dollars in his hand and wept. The only one of his three children who had ever given him cause for worry had demonstrated that he was responsible where money was concerned, and Mr. Ferrers felt that his work had been accomplished. It appeared to be so well accomplished that Edward, receiving raise after raise, in four years reached a point at which he must be making about as much income as his father. Since his father never revealed how much money he earned, this had to be concluded by inference, from his scale of living and his remarks about other people. Edward decided on ten thousand dollars a year as his mark, and when he reached it he rested there a few months, during the summer of 1939. His father and stepmother came East for the World's Fair in Flushing Meadow. Sitting in the Belgian Pavilion, with a clear view of the French Pavilion, where the food was better but notoriously expensive, Edward announced that he had resigned from his job in order to get a Ph.D. and go back to teaching. Mr. Ferrers took this decision calmly. Edward was a grown man now, he said, and he would not presume to tell him how to lead his life.

As Edward drove up in front of the place where his aunt lived, Mr. Ferrers said, "Don't get too close to the curbing—you'll scrape the whitewalls."

"How is that?" Edward asked.

Mr. Ferrers opened the door on his side and looked. "You're all right," he said.

Though now and then some old house would be divided into apartments, this was the only building in Draperville that had been originally designed for that purpose. It was two stories high, frame, with small porches both upstairs and down. It was painted a dreary shade of brown, and it backed on the railroad tracks. Mr. Ferrers's sister lived on the second floor, at the top of a rather steep flight of stairs.

"You go ahead, son," he said. "I have to take my time."

There were two doors at the top of the stairs. The one on the right opened and Edward's Aunt Alice said, "I've been watching for you. Come in, come in," and put her arms around him and gave him a hearty smack. Looking past her into the apartment, he saw that his stepmother had already come.

"What a pretty dress," he said.

"I put it on for you," his Aunt Alice said, and her face lit up with pleasure.

Edward loved her because his mother had loved her, and because she had been very good to him after his mother died—the one person who brought cheerfulness and jokes into a house where life had come to a standstill and people sat down to meals and went upstairs to bed and practiced the piano and read the evening paper and answered the telephone only because they didn't know what else to do. He always thought of her as she was then, and so it was a shock to find her with white hair, false teeth, wrinkles, rimless bifocals, and hands twisted out of shape by arthritis. And living alone for so many years had made her melancholy. Only her voice was not changed. Unlike most people of her generation, she could speak about her feelings. The night before, sitting off in a corner with him where nobody could hear what they were saying, she said, "I know I'm old, but my heart is young." During a long life, very little happiness had come her way and she had taken every bit of it, without a moment's fear or hesitation. And would again.

"Well, Alice," Mr. Ferrers said as he kissed her, "how are all your aches and pains today?"

"They're not imaginary, as you seem to think."

"Don't listen to him," Edward said.

"I know he just likes to get my goat," she said. "But even so."

"If you can't stand a little teasing," Mr. Ferrers said.

"I don't mind teasing, but sometimes your teasing hurts."

When they were children and he got into a fight on the way home from school, she dropped her books and sailed in and pulled his tormentors off him. Mr. Ferrers had had asthma as a boy and was not strong, but he outgrew it; the time came when he didn't need anybody to protect him. From the way she spoke his name, it was perfectly clear to Edward how much his aunt loved his father still.

The living room of the apartment was robbed of light by the porch. The deep shade that was lacking everywhere outside was here, softening the colors of Oriental rugs that were familiar to him from his childhood; like books that he had read over and over. His childhood was separated sharply from his adolescence by his mother's death, which occurred when he was ten. He was thirteen when his father remarried, and when he was fifteen they moved from Draperville to Chicago. He had known his stepmother since he was four years old. She had been his kindergarten teacher, and so it was not as if his father had married a stranger.

When Mr. and Mrs. Ferrers came East for a visit with Edward and his wife, the two couples played gin rummy with a good deal of gaiety and went for long drives. Edward's wife and his stepmother were comfortable together. If there was ever any strain, it was between father and son—because Edward had miscalculated the length of time it took to drive from the handsome street of old houses in Litchfield, Connecticut, to the inn where Mr. Ferrers could sit down to his evening drink; or because Mr. Ferrers could not keep off the subject of politics even though he knew what Edward thought of Senator McCarthy. But when Edward was going to high school in Chicago, it was different. He did not like to think of all that his stepmother had put up with—the sullenness; the refusal to admit her completely into his affections lest he be disloyal to his mother; the harsh judgments of adolescence; sand in the bathroom, tears at the dinner table, and implacable hostility toward his father. As if to make belated amends, he sat now holding her hand in his and reminding her of things that had happened when they were living in Chicago.

"Do you remember what a time you had teaching me to drive?" he said, and they both laughed. Streetcars had exerted a fatal attraction for him. He killed the engine on Sheridan

Road. Returning to the garage where the car was kept, he couldn't decide between the entrance and the exit and almost drove up on a concrete post.

"I used to hear you coming home," Helen Ferrers said, "when we lived on Greenleaf Avenue, and your walk sounded so like your dad's that I couldn't tell which of you it was."

Edward also had put up with something. For the first few years, she suffered from homesickness and she and his father went home to Draperville as often as they could, and they had a good deal of company—mostly Helen's friends, who came up to Chicago for a few days to do some shopping. There was no guest room in the apartment, and when they had company Edward slept in the dining room, on a daybed that opened out. In his room there were twin beds with satin spreads on them, and before he got into bed at night, he folded the one on his bed carefully and put it on the other, but sometimes forgot to pin back the glass curtains so they wouldn't be rained on during the night. He studied at a card table, and in his closet, in a muslin bag, were Helen's evening dresses. The two pictures on the wall were colored French prints, from a series entitled *Les Confiances d'Amour*. By the light switch there was a small framed motto:

> *Hello, guest, and Howdy-do.*
> *This small room belongs to you.*
> *And our house and all that's in it.*
> *Make yourself at home each minute.*

Helen let go of his hand in order to go out to the kitchen and help put lunch on the table. Edward heard his Aunt Alice say, "I'm all ready. As soon as the ice tea is poured, we can sit down. I know Ed likes to have his meals on time."

"You shouldn't have gone to so much trouble," Helen said —meaning sweet corn and garden tomatoes and fried chicken and a huge strawberry shortcake.

"It wasn't any trouble," his aunt said, which was of course untrue; at her age everything was hard for her, and usually she was perfectly willing to admit it. When they pushed their chairs back from the table, an hour later, she said, "No, you can't help me, any of you. I won't hear of it. I don't have Ned with me very often, and we're going to talk, we're not going to stand around in the kitchen doing dishes. I don't mind doing them if I can take my time."

What they talked about, sitting in a circle in her small, dark living room, was her health. The doctor was trying cortisone, and she thought it had helped her. She had more movement in her fingers, and could put her hair up without feeling so much pain in her shoulder.

They were late getting away—it was after three-thirty when they said good-bye and got in the car and drove off to call on Dr. McBride, whom they found sitting up in bed in the downstairs room that used to be his den. "Sit right here on the bed where I can see you," he said.

"He won't be comfortable," Mrs. McBride objected.

"How do you know?" Dr. McBride said. He was born in Scotland and spoke with a noticeable burr. "Sit down, my boy. Don't pay any attention to your auntie. I've been expecting you. You have your mother's eyes. You remember her?"

Edward nodded.

"And you like living in New York?"

"Yes."

"And you're teaching. That's a fine profession for a man to be in. Very fine. You'll never have to worry for fear your life is being wasted. And how old are you now?"

Edward told him.

"I can recall very well the day you were born. Would you like to hear about it?"

"Yes, I would," Edward said.

"It was an extremely hot day, in the middle of August. . . ."

Looking into the old man's faded blue eyes, Edward thought, This is the first real conversation that we have ever had.

While Mrs. McBride and his father talked about the new road to Peoria and what a difference it would make, Dr. McBride held Edward's hand and told him things he had done and said when he was a little boy, and then he began to tell Edward about his own boyhood in Scotland. "My father was very strict," he said, "and by the time I was eleven years old I'd had enough of his heavy hand and I made up my mind to run away to America. I told my mother, because I couldn't bear not to, and because I knew she'd feel worse if I'd kept it from her. She gave me all the money there was in the teapot, and told me I mustn't leave without saying good-bye to my father. So I did. I edged my way all around the room until I arrived at the door, and then I said, 'Good-bye, Father, I'm leaving home,' and started running as fast as my legs would carry me. . . ."

He got a job on a tramp schooner that landed him eventually on the coast of California. He was homesick and couldn't find work, slept in doorways, and was half starved when he met up with a man whose name was also McBride, a well-to-do rancher who had recently lost his only son.

Somewhere, possibly during that far-off boyhood in Scotland, Dr. McBride had been exposed to the storyteller's art. He understood the use of the surprising juxtaposition, the impact of things left unsaid. Again and again there was a detail that couldn't not be true. He never relapsed into the pointless, never said "to make a long story short," and seemed not even to be aware that he was telling stories, and yet there was not one unnecessary word.

"Oh, but did that really happen?" Edward exclaimed. "How marvellous."

"It *was* marvellous," Dr. McBride agreed.

And a minute later Edward said, "But weren't you afraid of him?" He said, "He was still waiting, after all that time?" And "It's so beautiful—that it worked out that way." Looking altogether a different person—as if the essential part of him, his true self that could never show its face in Draperville because no child after he grows up can ever be wholly natural with his parents, had come and joined them on the bed—he asked, "And then what happened?" The old man's eyes lit up. He had found the perfect audience.

Mr. Ferrers consulted his wristwatch and then said, "Much as I hate to do this, Ruth, we've got to be moving on. We're due at the Franklins' at five."

Dr. McBride winked at Edward and said, "Your father is the slave of time," and went on telling the story of his life.

Edward got up from the bed only because it was the third time his father had spoken to him about leaving, and even then it was very hard to do. The stories he did not hear now he never would, and he had the feeling that he was depriving himself of his birthright.

"I thought you'd decided to spend the rest of your life there," Mr. Ferrers said crossly when they were in the car. "Do you have any idea what time it is?"

"I know, Dad," Edward said, "but I couldn't bear to leave. He's the most wonderful storyteller I ever heard, and I didn't even know it."

"I've heard Doc's stories," Mr. Ferrers said dryly. "He's always the hero."

What made Mr. Ferrers's anger so impressive was that it was never unleashed. The change in him now was less than it was in Edward, whose voice rose in pitch, in spite of his efforts to control it. He stammered as he defended himself from his father's remarks. The effect of this skirmish was to move them both back in time, to Edward's fifteenth year and Mr. Ferrers's forty-fifth—the difference being that Edward regarded it as a personal failure in steering the riverboat upstream, whereas Mr. Ferrers five minutes later had dismissed the incident from his mind.

At the Franklins', Edward threw himself into one conversation after another, enjoying himself thoroughly, and trying, as always, to make sure that no one was skimped—as if the amount of attention he paid to each person who had known him since he came into the world was something that he must try to apportion justly and fairly. Why this should be, he had never asked himself.

From the Franklins' they drove downtown again, to join Helen's family in the cafeteria of the New Draperville Hotel. With several drinks under his belt, Edward looked around the noisy dining room. The faces he saw were full of character, as small-town faces tend to be, he thought, and lined with humor, and time had dealt gently with them. By virtue of having been born in this totally unremarkable place and of having lived out their lives here, they had something people elsewhere did not have. . . . This opinion every person in the room agreed with, he knew, and no doubt it had been put into his mind when he was a child. For it was something that he never failed to be struck by—those sweeping statements in praise of Draperville that were almost an article of religious faith. They spoke about each other in much the same way. "There isn't a finer man anywhere on this earth," they would say, in a tone of absolute conviction, sometimes about somebody who was indeed admirable, but just as often it would be some local skinflint, some banker or lawyer who made a specialty of robbing widows and orphans and was just barely a member of the human race. A moment later, opposed to this falsehood and in fact utterly contradicting it, there was a more realistic appraisal, which to his surprise they did not hesitate to express. But it would be wrong to say that the second statement represented their true opinion; it was just their other one.

He saw that somebody was smiling at him from a nearby table, a soft-faced woman with blond hair, and he put his napkin down and crossed the room to speak to her. He even knew her name. She lived down the street from him, and when he was six years old he was hopelessly in love with her and she liked Johnny Miller instead.

When they walked into the house at ten o'clock, he was talked out, dead-tired, and sleepy, and aware that the one person who had been skimped was the person he had come to see in the first place, his father, and that he couldn't leave without a little time with his father, and that his father had no intention of permitting him to.

As they put their coats away in the hall closet, Helen said, "Ned, dear, you must be dead. I know I am. What time do you want breakfast?"

"Eight-thirty or nine o'clock will be all right," Mr. Ferrers said. "His train doesn't leave till eleven. You go on up. Ned and I want to have a little visit."

"I think I will," Mrs. Ferrers said. But first she went around the room emptying ashtrays and puffing up satin pillows, until the room looked as if there had never been anybody in it. The two men walked through the sun parlor and out onto the screened porch. Mr. Ferrers sat down in the chair that was always referred to as his, and lit a cigar. Edward sat on a bamboo sofa. They did not turn the light on but sat in the dim light that came from the living room. Mr. Ferrers began by remarking upon the many changes he had seen in his lifetime —the telephone, electric light, the automobile, the airplane— and how these changes had totally changed the way people lived. "It's been a marvellous privilege," he said, drawing on his cigar, "to have lived in a time when all this was happening."

Edward managed not to say that he would gladly have dispensed with all of these inventions. He listened to his father's denunciation of the New Deal as he would have to some over-familiar piece of music—"Fingal's Cave" or the overture to *Rosamunde*—aware that it was a necessary prelude to the more substantial part of the conversation, something uppermost in his father's mind that had to be said in order to get around to things that were deeper and more personal.

So long as Edward did not argue with his father or attempt to present the other side of the political picture, Mr. Ferrers did not investigate his son's opinions. As for converting Mr. Ferrers to the liberal point of view, history—the Depression, in particular—had done more than Edward could possibly have hoped to accomplish with rational arguments. Mr. Ferrers was aware that there is such a thing as social responsibility, and he merely complained that it had now gone far enough and any further effort in that direction would weaken the financial structure of the country. So far as Edward could make out, his father's financial structure had weathered the storm very well.

When Edward put his feet up and arranged the pillows comfortably behind his head, Mr. Ferrers said, "If you're too tired, son, go to bed." But kindly. There was no impatience in his voice.

"Oh, no," Edward said. "I just felt like stretching out."

"It's too bad it has to be this way. When we lived in Chicago, there was no one to consider but ourselves, and we could talk to our hearts' content."

Actually, in those days it was Mr. Ferrers who talked. Edward was full of secrets and couldn't have opened his mouth without putting his foot in it.

"Very nice," he said, when his father asked what he thought of his Aunt Alice's apartment. "She seemed very comfortable."

"She keeps very peculiar hours. She likes to read till two in the morning. But you can't tell other people how to lead their lives, and I guess she's happy doing that. And she's got all her things around her—all those old drop-leaf tables and china doodads she sets such store by and that no secondhand dealer would give you more than two dollars for, if that."

"Aunt Alice's things are better than you think," Edward said.

"If you like antiques," Mr. Ferrers said. "I used to argue with her, but I don't anymore. I've given up. There's a first-floor apartment coming vacant in the same building that she wants to move into. It's more expensive, but she complains about the stairs, and at her age they are a consideration. I'll probably have to help her with the rent. . . . She could have been in a very different situation today. I know of three very fine men who were crazy to marry her. She wouldn't have them. They've all done well for themselves."

They probably bored her, Edward said to himself in the dark.

"Father begged her with tears in his eyes not to marry Gene Hamilton," Mr. Ferrers said. "But she wouldn't listen to him."

"She's had lots of pleasure from her life, even so," Edward remarked.

"Now she wants to sell all her securities—she hasn't got very much: some Quaker Oats and some U.S. Gypsum and a few shares of General Motors—and buy an annuity, which at her age is the silliest thing you ever heard of."

Silly or not, she had his father to fall back on, Edward reflected philosophically. And then, less philosophically, he wondered what would happen if his Aunt Alice outlived his father. Who would look after her? Her only son was dead and she had no grandchildren. The question contained its own answer: Edward and his brothers would take on the responsibility that until now his father had shouldered alone.

"What was he like?"

"What was who like?"

"Grandfather Ferrers."

"He was as fine a man as you would ever want to know," Mr. Ferrers said soberly, and then he added to a long finished picture a new detail that changed everything. He said, "Father never saw me until my brother Will died."

Edward opened his eyes. His father very seldom ever said anything as revealing as this, and also it was in flat contradiction to the usual version, which was that his father and his grandfather had been extremely close.

The earliest surviving photographs of his father showed him playing the mandolin, with his cap on the back of his head and a big chrysanthemum in his buttonhole. His brother Will died at the age of twenty-five, leaving a wife and a child, and Grandfather Ferrers's health was poor, and so Edward's father, who had wanted to study medicine, dropped out of school instead and began to help support the family.

From where he lay stretched out on the sofa, Edward could see into the lighted living room of the house next door. The son-in-law sat reading a copy of *Life* under a bridge lamp. The two Scotties, whose barking Mr. Ferrers complained of, were quiet. There had been a divorce that had rocked the house next door to the foundations, but that, too, had quieted down. The whole neighborhood was still. Not even a television set. Just the insects of the summer night. His father would have been a good doctor, Edward thought, staring at the outlines of the house next door and the trees in the backyard, silhouetted against the night sky. He felt his eyelids growing heavier and heavier.

"But all that changed," Mr. Ferrers said. "Toward the end of his life we got to know each other."

Edward heard his stepmother moving about upstairs, and then without warning his mind darkened. When he came to, after he had no idea how long, Mr. Ferrers was discussing his will. Though Edward could hardly believe that this conversation was taking place at all, what made it seem even stranger was the fact that his father spoke without excitement of any kind, as if all his life he had been in the habit of discussing his financial arrangements with his children. The will was what Edward had assumed it would be. There was nothing that he could object to, nothing that was not usual. Everything was to go to his stepmother during her lifetime, and then the estate would be divided among Mr. Ferrers's three sons.

"I wanted very much to be able to leave you boys something at the time of my death," Mr. Ferrers said. "About fifteen thousand dollars is what I had planned. I wanted you to have a little present to remember me by. But with the state and federal inheritance tax, I don't see how this can be managed."

"It doesn't matter," Edward said.

"It matters to me," Mr. Ferrers said, and there they were, right back where they started.

Mr. Ferrers drew on his cigar and the porch was illuminated by a soft red glow. "When I was a young man," he said, "and just trying to get my feet on the ground, my father said to me, 'If you can just manage to save a thousand dollars, you'll never be in want, the whole rest of your life. . . .'" Though Edward had never heard Dr. McBride's stories, this story he knew by heart. His father had done it, had managed to save a thousand dollars, and his grandfather's words had proved true. As a young man, having been told the same thing by his father, Edward had put this theory to the test; he also had saved a thousand dollars, and then, gradually, unlike his father and his grandfather, he had spent it. Little by little, it went. But strangely enough, so far at least, the theory still held. He had never been in actual want, though the balance in their—his and Janet's—joint checking account at this moment his father would not have considered cause for congratulations.

It was an amusing thought that the same reticence that prevented his father from telling him just how much money he had would prevent him also from inquiring into Edward's financial circumstances. But it would not prevent him from asking if Edward was saving money. The conversation was clearly heading for this point, and so Edward braced himself and was ready when it arrived.

Mr. Ferrers said, "I assume you have managed to put something aside?"

Edward neither confirmed nor denied this.

"If you haven't, you should have," Mr. Ferrers said sternly. Then a long circuitous return to the same subject, this time in the guise of whether or not Edward had enough insurance, so that if anything happened to him Janet was taken care of.

Janet was taken care of. But not through Edward's foresight. She had money of her own, left her by her grandmother. They did not touch the principal but used the income.

"If anything happens to me, Janet is taken care of," Edward said. And it was all he said.

"That's fine," Mr. Ferrers said. "I'm very glad to hear it."

He passed on to the subject of Edward's two brothers, who

were in business together, and, though very different, were adjusting to each other's personalities. His older brother had already done extremely well; his younger brother, just starting out after a two-year period in the Army, when his schooling was interrupted, had, of course, a long way to go, but he was showing such a determination to succeed that Mr. Ferrers could find nothing but satisfaction in contemplating his son's efforts.

"I know," Edward said, and "That's true," and "He certainly does," and his answers sounded so drowsy that at last Mr. Ferrers said with exasperation, "If you're so sleepy, why don't you go to bed?"

"Because I don't feel like it," Edward said. "I'm fine here on the sofa." Leaving the riverboat with nobody at the wheel, he began to talk about himself—a thing he did easily with other people but not with his father. He talked about his teaching—what he tried to put into it, and what he got from it. And about a very talented pupil, who showed signs of becoming a writer. And then about the book that he himself had been occupied with for the past five years—a study of changing social life in nineteenth-century England as reflected in the diaries of the Reverend John Skinner.

His older brother, it appeared, considered that Edward was a failure—not only financially but as a teacher. If he were a successful teacher he would be called to Harvard or Princeton or Yale.

"I don't know that I'd be happy teaching at Harvard or Princeton or Yale," Edward said. "And I am happy where I am. And valued."

"He doesn't understand," Mr. Ferrers said. "He lives very extravagantly—too much so, I think. They're flying very high these days. But he judges people by how much money they make. I explained to him when he was here that you care about money, too, but that you also care about other things, and that you are content to have a little less money and do the kind of work that interests you. . . . But, of course, you two boys have always been very different. And I don't interfere in your lives. I've given each of you a good education, the best I could manage, and from that time on you have been on your own. And you all made good. I'm proud of each of you. I have three fine boys."

Edward, floating, suspended, not quite anywhere, felt the safety in his father's voice, and a freedom in talking to him that he had never had before, not merely with his father but perhaps not even with anybody. In an unsafe world, he was safe only with one person. Which was so strange a thought—that his father, whom he had consistently opposed and resisted his whole life, and at one time even hated, should turn out to be the one person he felt utterly safe with—that he sat up and re-arranged the pillows.

He would have gone on talking, half awake, drowsy but happy, for hours, and when Mr. Ferrers said, "Well, son, it's almost midnight, you'd better get some sleep," he got up from the sofa reluctantly. They went back through the sun parlor into the living room, and Edward blinked his eyes at the light, having been accustomed to darkness. He sat down at his stepmother's desk, took her pen, and wrote out a check for twenty dollars, and handed it to his father, who, smiling, tore the check up and dropped it in the wastebasket and went on talking about how much it meant to him to have Edward home.

A Game of Chess

ON a mild evening in June, when the light in the sky, the softness of the air, the damp odors rising from the ground, and the roses everywhere all seemed to support the fiction that there is a natural harmony running through all natural things, Hugh and Laura Cahill came in from the country to have dinner with his older brother and sister-in-law, from Chicago. The train was crowded, and they had to sit across the aisle from each other. Hugh sat facing a little girl of two, who was dressed in white—starched white dress, white shoes and stockings, and a white piqué bonnet to show off her dark skin and immense dark Neapolitan eyes. She was restless. She bounced and jounced, she hung from her mother's neck, she got up and she got down, she flirted with the conductor, and from time to time, in spite of her mother's conscientious efforts to avoid this, the soles of her white kid shoes brushed against Hugh's light gabardine trousers. The smiles of apology that her mother and grandmother directed at him also asked him to tell them truthfully if there was ever since the beginning of time a more marvellously beautiful child. As the train plunged into the tunnel at Ninety-eighth Street, he leaned across the aisle and said, "I can hear Ellen saying to Amos, 'If we don't call them, they may find out we were in New York and be hurt.'"

"Would you have been hurt?" Laura asked.

He shook his head. "I'm not looking forward to the evening. Probably Ellen also had misgivings when she called us, but in the Middle West blood is thicker than water."

"Your trousers," Laura said.

"I know." He glanced down at the smudges. Ordinarily he wouldn't have cared, but it was the kind of thing Amos noticed, and Amos would much rather believe that Hugh had turned up at the Waldorf-Astoria with spots on his clothes than the truth, which was that his suit had just come back from the cleaner's. Aware that he would be made to feel the impassable gulf that exists between art and the automobile business, he had deliberately tried to avoid looking like a

398

painter—or rather, like the popular conception of a painter. He was wearing a sober foulard tie, with a white shirt. His shoes were shined. He had just had a haircut. But of course he had overlooked something; his grey felt hat had seen better days.

Sitting in front of a mirror in the ladies' room of the Biltmore, Laura Cahill pinned the gardenia among the dark-brown curls on top of her head, was dissatisfied with the effect, took the bobby pin out and tried again, sighed over the impossibility of doing anything with her hair—which had no body to it—and would have walked off and left the gardenia on the dressing table except that Hugh had given it to her and wanted her to wear it. They had been married a little over two years, and she was considerably younger than he, and even less confident, but whereas his face announced with an almost comic facility any uncertainty or self-doubt, any unmanageable feeling, she was perfectly able to keep her feelings to herself. She had never met Amos and Ellen.

When she rejoined Hugh, it was six-forty-five. He gave up looking for a vacant taxi and they took the Madison Avenue bus as far as Fiftieth Street, walked east to the Waldorf, went through the lobby, and found the house phones.

"He says to tell you he's shaving for Laura, not you," Ellen Cahill said cheerfully. "You know your brother."

"How are you?" Hugh asked.

"Fine. The Murphys are with us. They came along to keep us company."

"Yes?"

"We'll be down in a minute."

Rather than wait for what (since he did know his brother) was going to be more than a minute, he took Laura's arm and guided her into the tropical cocktail lounge. Sitting at a little table in this almost empty room, with their drinks in front of them, they killed a quarter of an hour.

"You'll like the Murphys," Hugh said. "Pete's a doctor, and very easygoing and unworried and kind. He and Amos are inseparable. And I think you'll like his wife. She's thin and melancholy and intelligent. I liked her best of any of their friends in Winnetka. I stopped in to see them once, on a Sunday morning, and Pete was out playing golf, and they'd had a party the night before, and she was tired and very funny. She kept finding pieces of spaghetti behind the sofa cushions and everywhere."

"Will Barbara be with them?" Laura asked.

"Probably. Unless she's tied up with commencement," he said, feeling a twinge of guilt. His niece had been here, in a convent school, since last fall, and they hadn't done anything about her. He worked at home, and the house was small, and company of any kind was a serious interruption. It affected his work. Ideas got away from him. Canvases that had started out well went bad or were only partly good. But they should have had her for a meal, or something. It was inexcusable. Tilting his glass this way and that, observing how the ice cubes remained serenely horizontal floating in Scotch and water, he said thoughtfully, "I love Amos, but I can't bear him. . . . Don't mind anything he says to you."

"I won't," Laura said.

"This time it's going to be different." He emptied his glass and picked up the check. "I have you. Always before, I've been outnumbered."

He didn't say, and was hardly aware that he thought, that it would *have* to be different, because whatever happened between Amos and him would take place in front of Laura.

They started through the lobby once more and discovered that, at the far end of a brown marble vista, they were being watched; they were the subject of a benign amusement. Even if Hugh hadn't stiffened, Laura would have known by the marked family resemblance that they were face-to-face with his older brother. Amos was broader in the shoulders, heavier, and older-looking, chiefly because he had less hair. His left arm, ending in a gloved hand, hung motionless at his side. He had lost his arm as the result of an accident with a shotgun; Amos and another boy were shooting at crows, and the gun (which they had been forbidden to touch) went off unexpectedly in the other boy's hands. The large woman with ash-blond hair and a black hat with pink roses on it—nothing to fear, nothing unfriendly in that direction.

Amos's greeting "Well, kid, it certainly is nice to see you," Hugh countered with a smile and an expression that was both alert and wary. *You're not going to fool me again?* he asked, with his eyes. *No monkey business like the last time we met? . . .*

Amos turned, his glance quickly took Laura in, and when his eyes met Hugh's again, he too was smiling. Amos approved. Amos had better approve, Hugh said to himself grimly.

An elevator took them all back upstairs to the fourteenth floor. They found the Murphys' room and knocked, and Pete came out carrying a bottle of whiskey. His hair was now partly grey, Hugh noticed, his face fuller than it had been thirty years ago when he wheeled his bicycle up the front walk and inquired, "Where's that Amos?" Aileen Murphy was still dressing, and so, instead of going in, they separated, the men taking the fire stairs, the two women the elevator, down to the thirteenth floor, to Barbara's room, which was much larger than her mother and father's and had a balcony and a view north over the city.

There was a profane squabble between Amos and Pete over whose liquor they were going to use, and Pete informed Amos that there was a men's bar in the hotel, very nice, where they put the whiskey bottle on the bar beside you.

"I've found it," Amos said.

Aileen Murphy came in and was introduced to Laura. Amos, offering Hugh a drink, said, "Hugh, do you count?" in the same stern tone of voice he had used long ago, checking up on whether Hugh had known enough to kiss the girl he took to the high-school fraternity dance when he said good night to her. He hadn't, but he did the next time, and she said, "Why did you do that?" and after that they didn't see each other except when they passed in the school corridors.

He stared at Amos now and said, "What do you mean?"

"One is not enough, two is plenty, three is you're drunk, and four there's no reason not to keep on going," Amos said, and burst out laughing.

Why make up jokes of your own was Amos's basic social principle, the idea that had always carried him along safely anywhere, in any company that he had ever wanted to find himself. Why avoid making the remarks that other people make, when the remarks are all there, ready to be used, and it's the surest way to make everybody like you? At thirteen, out of slavish admiration, Hugh had done his best to imitate Amos's jokes, his laugh, and never managed this successfully. On a raw November day, in the college stadium, he had humiliated

Amos by cheering when there was nothing to cheer at. He saw
Amos putting this new joke into his suitcase when he packed
to come East.

They had a conversation about their younger brother, who
had just finished college, after a period in the Army. "Rick
never tells me anything," Hugh said. "Does he tell you?"

Amos shook his head solemnly. "No, Hugh, he doesn't."

When they couldn't get together on their own grounds,
they could reach each other momentarily by talking about
their younger brother.

"He's too anxious to prove that he's capable," Amos said,
"and instead of asking for advice, he rushes in and announces
how everything is going to be, and then it's too late to do anything. But he'll learn. I took him horseback riding and I told
him off, right down the line, all the things that are wrong with
him. He took it and went straight to work on them."

There was a knock on the door and Pete Murphy's brother
Louis came in, with his wife. He and Pete met in the center of
the room, after not seeing each other for two years. They
shook hands, smiled, and turned away, leaving unfinished business (if there was any unfinished business between them) to be
settled at some other time. With a fresh drink in his hand
Hugh looked around the room and saw that there were no
empty chairs. Laura had settled herself on one of the twin
beds, with her back against the headboard, and was talking to
Barbara, who, nearly Laura's age, was stretched out, leaning
on her elbow, on the other bed, and telling her about her experiences as a practice teacher in a Puerto Rican neighborhood. "A friend of mine was teaching in the same school," she
said, "and she got a letter from a little boy. 'Dear Teacher,' it
said. 'You are very pretty, your friend is very pretty. I love you
but you do not love me. I do not like Miss Worthing.'" Hugh
sat down on the foot of Laura's bed, and then, aware that his
back was turned to her and that the evening would probably
seem interminable to her, among all these people she wasn't
related to and didn't know, he reached behind him and took
her high-heeled shoe in his hand.

They left the room finally, all nine of them. The Murphys went
on up in the elevator to the Starlight Roof while Hugh was

leaving his hat with the woman at the desk on the thirteenth floor. Amos, who had had four drinks, said, "Where did you get that hat? I'll give you five bucks so you can go and get yourself a good felt hat."

"That's a fine hat," Hugh said, his voice rising a little too sharp for banter—an effect that Amos never tired of producing. "It came from Tripler's. What more do you want?"

Amos was not impressed with Tripler's. His comment on Hugh's growing baldness, the circle on the crown of his head where the white scalp showed through his dark hair, Hugh was expecting. It was customary, both with Amos and with his father. He said, "I've got lots more hair than you had in 1960."

This counterattack Amos did not bother to understand, let alone guard against. It was too complicated to do any harm. It involved the recognition of the immutable difference between being six years old and being eleven, between being ten and being fifteen, between fourteen and nineteen, between thirty-eight and just arriving and forty-three arrived. Fairness compelled Hugh to compare not the present states of their respective baldnesses but his hair now with Amos's hair four years ago in Chicago. Fairness was a quality that Amos seemed to recognize and in general abide by, but somebody or something way back somewhere in the past had excused him from ever having to be fair with Hugh. As far as Hugh could make out, for Amos to be fair toward him would have been to say, *All right, I give up. I don't understand you and never will. If all you want is for me to treat you decently, I can easily enough. I can stop taking any interest in you—and will, from now on.*

Amos glanced at the light over the elevator doors, and then said to Laura, "Dad did the worst thing anybody can do."

Hugh waited for him to finish. Being older, Amos knew things—family history, old stories, old scandals—that he didn't. You never knew when something of this kind would burst out of him.

"He put water on his hair," Amos said. "And he still has some hair at seventy. I didn't used to have a stomach. I've put on twenty pounds since I stopped smoking. Hugh carries his weight well." And then Laura, whose brothers let each other alone, saw with astonishment that Amos was feeling Hugh's upper arm, the muscles of which Hugh obediently flexed. "Not bad," Amos said, and made Hugh feel how much bigger his own biceps were.

As they stepped into the elevator, Amos's attack shifted. "I was afraid you were going to marry a Jew," he said.

This was the fuse that had set off the fireworks the last time they saw each other, four years ago in Chicago. The argument, though bitter, got nowhere. Hugh grew red in the face, and then very pale. Amos dodged easily and expertly from one form of bigotry to the next, and brushed logic aside, cheerfully refusing to identify himself with anyone not in his rather pleasant economic circumstances.

"If he had," he said now, to Laura, "I'd never have had anything more to do with him."

Since childhood, Hugh reflected, looking at the floor of the ascending elevator, Amos had been threatening, continually threatening, to disown him.

Seated at a big round table under the blue artificial stars, Barbara Cahill asked her New York (and therefore cosmopolitan, worldly) uncle to translate the French words on the menu.

" '*Escargots*' is snails," he said.

"Oh, I know I wouldn't like snails!" she exclaimed.

As she grew older, she would look like her mother, Hugh thought. She was sweet and young and unspoiled, and beyond that he had no idea what she was like. In the last ten years he hadn't stayed long enough in Illinois to find out.

"You ought to try them. They're very good. They're cooked in white wine and parsley," he said, and was aware of an unreasonable surprise as he heard Amos and Laura, side by side across the table, both order roast beef well done. At home it had always been rare, and he had assumed that Amos would go on to the end of his life ordering roast beef and steak rare, as he himself did. "I'll have eels," he said, daring Amos to appropriate that, as he had so many other things that didn't belong to him. Amos ordered a salad and then said, "I don't know about the rest of you but I'm ready for another drink."

During the long wait, Hugh talked first to Barbara and then, while she was telling Laura about going to Mass at St. Patrick's with her mother, he turned to Louis Murphy's wife, who was on his left. Louis had held her chair out for her as she sat down, and Hugh had caught a certain protective concern in his manner. It was none of his business, but now, having had three drinks—one in the cocktail lounge and two very much stronger ones upstairs—and being slightly drunk (otherwise he would never have ordered eels), he leaned toward her and said, "Your husband is still in love with you."

"Why shouldn't he be?" she said, smiling. "You don't remember me, but I remember you."

"Did you grow up in Winnetka?"

"I was Ruth Hayes," she said, nodding.

"You know how it is when you're growing up," he said. "Somebody four years older is in another world." He hesitated, wondering if he had been impolite—if he should have said "one or two years older."

"I know," she said. "Louis was in love with various girls while I watched him from afar."

"Did you really?" he asked, in all seriousness.

"No." She smiled again at him, this time as if she were talking to a child. "I was in love with Bruce Coddington." Then, extricating them both from the past: "I saw one of your pictures at the Whitney Museum."

Hugh nodded. He was trying to follow the conversation between Amos and Laura, across the table. He heard Amos say, "You must come out to Chicago. We've got a housing project with niggers and white people living together."

This remark, intended to beat Laura out of the bushes and perhaps test the timbre of her rising voice, she allowed to pass unchallenged. She was there to defend Hugh, not to argue.

A moment later, Hugh heard Amos say, "You must see that Hugh makes a lot of money."

"I'd rather he painted better and made less," Laura said.

"You don't know what you're talking about," Amos told her indignantly. "Wait till you have children and the doctors' bills start coming in. If I hadn't had Pete for a friend, I'd have been ruined."

Louis Murphy's wife was searching through her purse for a blank piece of paper. In the end she gave Hugh a credit slip from Lord & Taylor, so that he could write down for her the name and address of the gallery that handled his paintings.

Ellen supplied him with a pencil, from her beaded evening purse.

"Deborah's more like you every day," she said, speaking of her youngest daughter. "She's even pigeon-toed—which is all right in a boy," she added hastily, lest this remark cause offense. "She even walks like you. I sometimes say to Amos, 'There goes Hughie across the lawn.'"

"Debbie's always the leader," Barbara said admiringly.

"She's in sixth grade," Ellen Cahill said, "believe it or not. They gave *Peter Pan* at school this year, and Debbie was Peter."

I was in a school play once, Hugh thought, and nobody came to see me. . . .

"Have you any children?" he asked, turning to Louis Murphy's wife.

"One. A girl seventeen."

Suddenly nervous lest she should ask him the same question, with Laura sitting directly across the table, he looked away and was grateful for the arrival of the waiter. Ellen Cahill offered her rare roast beef around the table to anyone who wanted it, just as an hour or two before she had offered Pete Murphy and his wife Barbara's spacious room. Her last anxious "Are you sure you wanted eels?" Hugh answered with "Yes. I've never had eels before," but he didn't want them and he wished he could put the queer white slices in his coat pocket. He looked up when Aileen Murphy was served a roast squab, and wondered, Should I have had that?

Amos passed his plate across to Ellen, so that she could cut his meat for him, and Hugh, noticing how quiet Barbara was, the only unmarried person at the table, said to her, "Just you wait. Your time is coming."

"But I'm enjoying myself, Uncle Hugh," she said earnestly.

And perhaps she is, he thought. Or perhaps she had not yet realized that she had a right to be bored in the company of older people.

The conversation took on an antiphonal quality. The remarks Amos made to Laura, a moment later Ellen made to Hugh. With his roast beef half eaten, Amos asked his wife to dance with him. At the age of ten, Hugh thought, he would not have done this. Nothing could have induced him to stop eating until his plate was empty, and then it would have been passed up the table for a second helping. Hugh looked at Ruth Murphy questioningly, and then they pushed their chairs back and went out on the dance floor, which was so crowded that dancing was impossible.

Standing in front of a urinal in the men's room half an hour later, Hugh was startled by a hearty slap on the back. "I'm going to buy you a drink," Amos said. "You've been refusing drinks all evening, and now I'm going to buy you a drink you can't refuse."

They found a cocktail room, around the corner from the elevators, and Amos wanted to stand at the bar, but the bartender wouldn't serve them until they sat down at one of the tables.

"I want to talk to you, Hugh," Amos said. "I want to talk to you about your work. The time has come for you to take the bull by the horns." Hugh sat stiffly, unable to answer. He and Laura had got up from the table together and parted in the foyer with the understanding that he would wait there for her. He stood up, with his eyes on the people passing the door, and said, "I want to talk to you, too," and went outside. Laura was not there, so he went on into the dining room, intending to bend down and say to Barbara, "Will you come with me? I want you to wait for Laura outside." But to his surprise Laura was at the table with the others. She had not waited for him.

When he went back to the cocktail room, he found Amos sitting just as he had left him, heavy and solemn and larger than life-size—an epic figure waiting to give advice that was not asked for.

"What bull by what horns?" Hugh said as he sat down.

"I mean you've got to decide once and for all whether you're going to hold down a job or be an artist."

"But I have decided. I quit my job with Blake & Seymour last fall. I'm devoting all my time to painting."

"You've got to make up your mind," Amos said solemnly. "You can't work both sides of the street, no matter how smart you are."

He expatiated at some length on this dilemma that no longer existed. He questioned the wisdom of Hugh's living in the country. He insisted that Hugh needed more experience of the world. "You're leading too sheltered a life. You've always been on the defensive. At least you are with me, so I figure you are with other people."

"I know," Hugh said. "But now I want to be friends."

Amos's face was contorted by a look of disgust. This wasn't at all what he had meant; it was another instance of cheering when the other side scored a gain, of the joke with the painfully wrong inflection. "No . . . None of that. I'm hard," he said, and allowed Hugh to see, from the look in his eyes, just how hard he was. But there was something histrionic about that look, something that suggested that it had been practiced before a bathroom mirror while Amos was shaving. "I don't care about anybody but my family. They can hurt me, but nobody else."

"*I* can hurt you," Hugh said.

Amos shook his head. "No. Neither you or Dad."

The knight takes the pawn.

Hugh's expression was a mixture of bewilderment, hurt feelings, and the sense of loss. His offer had been sincere; he had been ready—at least he hoped he was ready—to be friends with Amos, and he had not counted on the possibility that this offer would not be acceptable. So he's done it at last, he thought; he's washed his hands of me.

Though Amos had never supported him in a moment of need, there had always been some slight comfort in the idea that Amos was there, loyal to his friends, and powerful; that his help, never asked for, would even so have been forthcoming at a word from Hugh, the word he had so far been too proud to speak. "If you don't care about anybody," he said, accepting his casting out, "why are you telling me what to do? And what do you mean 'hard'?"

Before Amos could explain, Pete Murphy appeared, out of nowhere.

"Sit down," Amos said. And then to Hugh, "*Pete* is my friend."

Pete refused the offer of a drink. Amos didn't resume. The three of them sat, silent. Realizing that the conversation could not proceed in the presence of an interested observer, Pete got up and left. It turned out then that Hugh was not rejected after all; the word "friends" was rejected. They were to be "brothers."

"Downstairs," Amos said, "you said Rick never tells you anything. Well, you never tell me anything."

"I'm ready now," Hugh said. "What do you want to know?"

Amos did not commit himself. It was still Hugh's move. There was one thing he could say that would make all the rest clear, but something warned him not to say it. Instead, he asked, "Do you remember a letter you wrote me after I got in a fight with the Chi Psi's in my sophomore year and moved out of the fraternity house? It was a beautiful letter, and I'm sorry I never answered it."

The word "beautiful" made Amos wince. As for the letter, apparently he didn't remember ever having written it. Or *does* he remember, Hugh wondered. It was the only time that Amos had ever offered to help him or tried to understand him, and he could not imagine now why he hadn't answered it.

Amos wanted to know why Hugh didn't have a show every year, and Hugh explained that he worked slowly, that he didn't have that many canvases he was willing to have people see, that he had been, in effect, holding down two jobs.

"Don't give me that," Amos said. "I'm a salesman and a farmer." This meant that Amos managed Ellen's four hundred acres of farmland in central Illinois, not that he ever rode a tractor. "It's just as easy to fall in love with a girl with money," Amos used to say when he was twenty, but actually he had married for love, like everybody else.

Again Hugh felt the pull of the unsaid thing. To hold back something as important as that, he decided, was to be afraid. "A minute ago you were complaining that I never tell you anything. Do you understand the word 'neurotic'?"

"Yes."

"Well, I was."

"Are you still?" Amos demanded.

"I don't know," Hugh said, confused. This was not the question Amos should have asked. It was the last question he would have asked Amos, if the shoe had been on the other foot.

"What made you that way?"

"The usual reasons—what makes other people like that." Now that it was too late, he was cautious. "Their childhood, the past, something." His heart sank. All evening long he had been conscious of the approval of the figure in the chair at the head of the couch, the shadowy presence who listened, the patient, kind, supporting, encouraging, faceless father-substitute, whom he had found his way to when things finally came to a standstill and he was no longer able to work or to love any human being. . . . But he shouldn't have told Amos. In telling Amos he had behaved incorrectly; he had rejected the inner warning and failed to remember that confession can be a form of self-injury. And now he would have to go on without any encouragement and support.

"I have the same background as you," Amos was saying, "and I'm not neurotic."

What was so hard, Hugh thought, was just to believe it—to believe that anything as terrible as that could happen: that she had died and left them. "You may have been stronger," he said.

This explanation Amos was willing to accept, in the literal as well as in the psychological sense.

"Sometimes I think Mother's death had a good deal to do with it," Hugh said.

"It was hard on me, too," Amos said.

The house was like a shell, and the food tasted of tears. And he and Amos undressed in the same room and got into their beds, and he never spoke to Amos under the cover of the dark about the terror that gripped him, and Amos never spoke to him. Neither of them tried to comfort the other.

"But I was all right," Hugh continued, "until I was twenty-five."

"You were nineteen when you tried to commit suicide."

"That was part of it," Hugh admitted. Without realizing it, he jerked his head up. His eyes went all around the room searching for help.

"That was something you had no right to do," Amos said sternly.

"No right to cut my wrists?"

"No right to disgrace your family. You didn't think of anybody but yourself. You're selfish, Hugh."

Again Pete Murphy appeared, though he didn't sit down this time; and again they waited until he went away.

"Barbie and I have been feuding," Amos said. "She almost

flunked out of school last year. She didn't apply herself. That's why we sent her East to school."

"She thinks the world of you," Hugh said, by way of pouring oil on troubled waters. "I had such a nice conversation with her during dinner. . . . She says you never write to her; that she hasn't had a single letter from you since she's been here."

"I haven't written to her purposely. I don't want her to think she can get away with anything."

"She must have been pleased that you came to see her graduate."

Amos didn't answer. He was trying to get the attention of the bartender.

Hugh waited until Amos turned around, and then, leaning forward intently, with his elbows on the table, he said, "You said I was selfish. I want to know why."

"Also," Amos said, "she was running around with this guy twenty-eight years old. She's no judge of people, Hugh. She always picks out a lame duck. It's all right to be tenderhearted, but this guy had a nervous breakdown while he was in the Army—at least that's what *he* calls it. There's something creepy about him. I can't stay in the same room with him. I had to get out of the house when he was there. Ellen's forbidden her to see him or write to him, but she does anyway." His eyes filled with tears, which slowly overflowed the lids. "She wants to be a nun, Hugh, and I just don't know what to do."

There was nothing theatrical or rehearsed about this performance, and Hugh was moved by the tears, and by what Amos said, and by the fact that Amos was exposing his feelings to him. He waited while Amos unfolded a clean white handkerchief and blew his nose and regained his composure.

The bartender brought another round of drinks, and Amos took up finally the matter of Hugh's selfishness, which turned out to be nothing more (nor less) than the fact that they hadn't done anything about Barbara.

"Laura called her, but she—"

"You didn't ask her for Thanksgiving or Christmas," Amos said.

If they'd had Barbara for Thanksgiving and Christmas, they couldn't have had Laura's brother; the house was too small. But how to explain this to Amos, whose house was large, and whose hospitality was always being taken advantage of. They could have asked her out to the country some other time, and should have. But he'd been having difficulties with his work all through the fall and early winter. Lots of labor went into canvases which were eventually discarded. That seemed to have stopped, thank God.

"When I first came to New York," Hugh said. "I was always having to go someplace I didn't feel like going to, on holidays. Some family or business connection of Dad's trying to be kind. I used to dread it. From what Barbara told Laura over the phone, I gathered she had friends. In school, I mean. And some boy had been taking her to all the shows, she said. We just assumed she'd rather spend Christmas with Ellen's cousins on Long Island."

Amos was not interested in Hugh's excuses. Having made his accusation, though, he put it aside and began to talk about his younger daughter. "Debbie's got the same cockeyed brain you have," he said.

Hugh resented this at first, before he understood that it was half a criticism, half a grudging compliment. On the other hand, to have a brain at all, to be in any way brighter than or different from the average person was, so far as Amos was concerned, cockeyed. "You have a photographic mind," he said accusingly.

Hugh denied this.

"All you have to do is look at a book and get an A," Amos said. "I never could do that. . . . Don't look at me like that. I'm not running you down. I think you're quite a classy guy. I'm trying to build you up."

"I don't need building up," Hugh said. As evidence that he was doing all right, he offered the recognition that, during the past five years, his work had received from various critics and museum curators. "It's quite an honor," he said, "to be in the annual show at the Whitney Museum. They don't bother with anybody who isn't good."

"I'm a big duck in a little pond; you're a little duck in a big pond," Amos said serenely. "Ellen knows a woman who studied at the Art Institute. She knows a lot about art. I mentioned that I had a brother who is a painter, and drew a blank. . . . You've got to keep your name before the public, Hugh."

"I'm after bigger game," Hugh said. "I'm competing with Eakins."

"How much does he make a year?"

"He's dead."

"Well, then," Amos said agreeably, "maybe you've got to die to be great. But you have to turn out more paintings than you have been doing these last few years." He went on to tell Hugh about Grandma Moses: "She did what was expected of her; she raised her family and didn't even begin to paint till she was past seventy—with barn paint. Maybe you take it a little too seriously, Hugh."

"Maybe."

"Another instance of your selfishness," Amos said, "is your unwillingness to have children."

"But I'm not unwilling!" Hugh exclaimed.

Amos pounced. "Is there something wrong with you?"

Hugh shook his head.

Pete Murphy was standing in the doorway, with Laura and Barbara. He borrowed a chair from a nearby table, and they all three sat down.

The oblique approach, Hugh thought. Why was it he could never remember to protect himself against the double move, in which his castle took Amos's castle and Amos's bishop then took his queen.

"Doc," Amos said loudly, "I want you to give Hugh the name of a good gynecologist. You must know one."

When they were seated once more at the table in the dining room, Amos turned to Louis Murphy's wife and said belligerently, "What you need is a drink. You look too healthy."

"Oh, Amos!" Ellen Cahill exclaimed. "I hoped you'd criticize *me*!"

"There's nothing the matter with you," Amos said. "You're perfect." Then, to the table in general: "That's my wife. Beautiful woman."

I don't understand it, Hugh said to himself wearily. I don't understand why I didn't kill him. . . . And Laura had not blamed him with so much as a look for discussing the subject there was no reason or need to discuss, in such a place, and with Amos, of all people. Instead, she had turned to Pete, as if he were an old and trusted friend. No, he had told her, he didn't know any doctors in New York. But two years was not an extraordinary time to wait. He had friends who had waited seven years and then had three children in a row. Matter-of-factly, but with the most glowing kindness in his blue eyes, he had answered her questions and described his own treatment, while Amos and Hugh had an argument about the check and Amos won.

The waiter arrived with the dessert course. Hugh thought of asking Laura to dance with him, and then, seeing that she and Amos had met head-on in serious conversation, he decided that she would prefer not to be interrupted. He glanced around the table. No one was loud, no one was drunk, but Amos. Was he drunk because this evening was dedicated, whether the others enjoyed it or not, to his meeting with Hugh? Was Amos's loud voice a mark of his respect?

Louis Murphy and his wife got up to dance, and Hugh moved around the table and sat beside Aileen Murphy, his friend, whom he had had no chance to talk to. She touched his forehead with her fingers.

"Furrows," she said. "You're having a serious time."

"It *is* serious," Hugh admitted. "And when you get home, you'd better defend me, after the way I feel about you."

"Ellen defends you," Aileen Murphy said. "She takes your side against Amos—and besides, you don't need anybody to defend you."

Across the table, Amos said to Laura, "Take a look at him and decide what you want him to be. Hugh doesn't have much ability to get on with people. You have to be the one to do it—meet people and make contacts and smooth the way for him. I wouldn't be what I am if she"—his eyes found Ellen—"hadn't made me that."

"Amos is sensitive," Aileen Murphy said in a low voice to Hugh. "You get under his skin more than you realize."

"I don't mean to," Hugh said.

"Possibly not, but you do. You and Amos are both extremes. So is Rick. You're a family of individualists. I don't know anybody like you." She shook her head mournfully.

Hugh heard Amos say, "When are you coming out to the Middle West?"

"Our car is so old it would never stand the trip," Laura said.

"Get him to buy you a new one," Amos said.

Laura laughed.

"He can afford it," Amos said. "Or if he can't, he's a damn fool to have left his job."

Barbara leaned across her mother and said to Laura, "Dad isn't like this. You mustn't pay any attention to him. He's really very kind. And he and Uncle Hugh only seem different on the surface. Underneath, they're quite a lot alike."

"Tell me about your children," Hugh said, remembering suddenly a boy and a girl, three and four—somewhere about that age—tracking mud in and out of the Murphys' house in Winnetka. "Are they remarkable?"

"They're not handsome," Aileen Murphy said.

"I don't mean handsome. Are they intelligent?"

"No," she said, reflecting. "I wouldn't say they were."

"But I don't mean that kind of intelligent," Hugh persisted. He was dead tired, he realized, and his brain was befuddled. "I mean are they wise in a certain way, about the world?"

"You've got to come West and see us," she said.

"Do you have Russian blood in you?"

"A little Jewish." She pointed to her thin Roman nose. Actually, he knew, she was Irish on both sides of the family.

"I asked if you had Russian blood in you," he said, "because you like to talk about life. You have a feeling for— You're realistic about people." Then watching Pete and Laura leave the table and go toward the dance floor: "What about Pete? Is he realistic?"

"Doc loves everybody."

"You mean he has no shrewdness, where people are concerned."

"That's right."

"Does he lose by it?"

"Not a thing," Aileen Murphy said, smiling. And then, sadly: "He has fair-weather friends."

Dancing with Laura, Pete Murphy said, "Don't you pay any attention to Amos. Amos doesn't know anything about painting."

"I know that," Laura said.

"I wouldn't offer Hugh advice, any more than Hugh would

try to tell Amos how to sell automobiles. . . . The thing is not to worry."

"I don't," Laura said, "but we're living on very little money. And Hugh likes to be extravagant."

"My family is taken care of," Pete said, "if anything happens to me. So what I make I spend—and a little more. It's what I enjoy, and what makes *me* happy. And if I lose five hundred dollars on the races, I don't tell Amos."

The party broke up around a quarter of one. Hugh tried to pay for his share of the dinner check and Amos waved him aside indignantly. Barbara said good night and left them. There was talk of going on to someplace else—to the Copacabana. For Hugh the evening was finished; he was ready to go home. He invited Amos to come out to the country with Barbara and Ellen, any time during the remainder of their three-day visit. This invitation was left hanging. Amos wanted Pete to go with him to see the Mets play the Cardinals; Pete wanted to go to the races. They decided, while Amos was tipping the waiter, to go their own ways.

All eight of them crowded into one elevator, and the four Cahills got off at the thirteenth floor. Amos had decided that he was tired and wanted to go to bed. They wandered through the corridor, made a wrong turning, and retraced their steps. Amos, reverting to the age of eleven, began ringing the bells of all the doors that lined the corridor. Ellen tried to stop him. Loud, drunk, and not at all unpleasant, Amos was not to be stopped. "I'll tell them Hugh did it," he said.

They got Hugh's hat. The two brothers, the two sisters-in-law said good-bye, and five minutes later, as Laura and Hugh were trying to find their way out of the lobby to the Park Avenue entrance of the hotel, they ran into Amos and Ellen, on their way to join the others at the Copacabana. At this final parting, the handshake of Hugh and Amos was prolonged, the expression in Amos's eyes tender, misty, and only slightly histrionic.

"He's got a handshake like a gorilla," Amos said proudly, to Laura.

*

"I had a feeling he would notice," Laura said, going home on the train. "And sure enough, he did. He said, 'Where'd you get that ring?' and I said, 'Hugh gave it to me.'"

"That was smart of you," Hugh said. "To realize, I mean, before you met him, that he'd look to see whether I'd given you an engagement ring."

"I just had a feeling," she said, and settled into the seat contentedly, with her head on his shoulder. They were taking the last train. The coach was almost full. The passengers were tired, and many of them sat and dozed, with their heads drooping, their necks bent to one side. Hugh looked down at the ring on the fourth finger of Laura's left hand—the diamond between two smaller sapphires, in a gold setting. It had been her grandmother's. Next to the false engagement ring was the plain gold wedding band Hugh had given her.

"Do you wish I'd given you an engagement ring?" he asked suddenly.

"No."

"I don't like diamonds."

"Someday I'd like you to give me a ring."

"What kind of ring?"

"For a special reason," she said. "On a special occasion."

He waited, unable to imagine what she had in mind.

"I'd like you to give me an emerald ring when our first child is born."

"I don't know that I trust myself when it comes to choosing a ring," he said. "What if I got one and you don't like it?"

"We could go and pick it out together," she said. "When you reached out and took my shoe, Barbara was telling me that Amos never has eyes for any other woman but Ellen, and she thought you had overheard."

"No. I didn't."

"She said, 'I'd just love to have a husband who'd reach out and take my foot, to say that he was following the conversation and loved me.'"

The train drew to a stop at 125th Street. When it started up again, Laura said, "It must be terrifying to be an older brother and have a younger brother who shows a kind of early promise, and then nothing seems to come of it for a while, and then the predictions begin to come true. . . . And being help-less," she added.

Amos *helpless?* Hugh wondered. He was exhausted. He felt battered and bruised. The encounter had not come off as well as he had hoped, but at least Amos had not got through (and he always had in the past) his inmost defenses. The fight had been a draw.

"I thought you'd never come back to the table," Laura said. "When you and Amos weren't there, it left a vacuum. Nobody had anything to say."

"I was caught," Hugh said. "Very nice of him, wasn't it, to ask Pete to recommend a doctor. And in front of Barbara. How *can* he do things like that?"

"It didn't matter," Laura said.

"It mattered to me," Hugh said. "I don't understand it. I don't understand why I didn't pick up a chair and brain him with it. There was the chair, and there I was, and he deserved to be killed, and I couldn't lift my arms to do it. I couldn't move. You had to do everything."

"It wasn't important," Laura said. And then, slowly: "I have only one complaint against you." (She had several, as it turned out, all handed to her, all expertly put in her mind by Amos.) "You don't love me the way Amos loves Ellen."

Oh my God, he thought, he's got through to *her*!

"You didn't ask me to dance with you," Laura said.

He sat up in the seat indignantly. "I was dancing with you all evening," he said. "Everything I said and did was for you and on account of you."

Neither of them said anything more. He knew that, having said this, she would forgive him, she would never refer to it again. She didn't hold grudges or put things aside in order to bring them up against him later. He sat back in the seat and drew her head over against his shoulder once more. Looking down at her soft brown hair, at the gardenia now edged with ivory, a chilling idea occurred to him: What if she defended me from Amos cleverly and successfully but at the expense of her faith that *I* can defend *her*? Was that Amos's triumph for this evening?

He couldn't bear to go on thinking about this, and put it out of his mind, but Amos continued to occupy his thoughts.

What had he ever done to Amos that Amos should want to destroy him or to destroy his marriage?

As he sat pondering this unsolvable question, he noticed his own hands, and then thoughtfully, as if he had never seen them before, moved the fingers of one hand back and forth, surprised at what a thing the human hand is, how many ways, and how marvellously, the fingers moved. And then, with no shudder or feeling of any kind, he had a momentary image of the immovable sleeve, the gloved facsimile of a hand that he had so long ago become accustomed to that when he was with Amos he never gave it a thought.

The Poor Orphan Girl

THE poor orphan girl had no mother and no father and was raised by her grandmother on one of the wind-swept islands of the Outer Hebrides. When she began running after the boys, her grandmother shipped her off to a cousin in Glasgow. At first the girl was well behaved and lent a hand wherever it was needed, and the cousin thought the grandmother just didn't understand the younger generation. But then she started staying out late at night and keeping bad company, and the cousin saw what the grandmother was up against. So she had a serious talk with the girl, and the girl made all sorts of promises, which she didn't keep, and the cousin didn't want to be blamed if the girl got in the family way, so she took her to an employment agency that specialized in sending servants to America.

"Mercy!" exclaimed the head of the most dependable domestic employment agency in New York City, when she looked at the girl's folder. "An unspoiled country girl, willing and strong, and with a heart of gold!" The folder was shown to a Class A client with a Fifth Avenue address, who snapped her up. The immigration papers were filled out, and the deposit paid, and the girl found herself on a boat going to America. What she was expecting was, naturally, what she had seen in the flicks. What she got was a six-by-eleven bedroom looking out on the back of another building, with a closet six inches deep, and the customary dwarf's bathtub that you find in servants' bathrooms in old apartment buildings. On the other hand, the girl had never before had a bed all to herself and a toilet that wasn't either outdoors or on the landing and shared by several large families. She wrote home to her grandmother that she was in luck.

She got on all right with the cook, and there was no heavy work, because a cleaning woman came in twice a week and a laundress two days, and the windows were done by a window-washing company, and all the girl had to do was remember what she was told. Unfortunately, this was more than she could manage. During dinner parties she couldn't decide whether you serve from the right and clear from the left or serve from the left and clear from the right, so she did both, and when she made the beds the top sheet was not securely fastened, and she used the master's washcloth to clean the tub, and what with one thing and another, including the state of her room, she received notice after two weeks and returned to the employment office looking only a little less fresh than when she arrived from Scotland. The head of the agency said, "This time suppose we don't aim quite so high. You don't mind children?" The girl said no, she liked children—which was true, she did—and off she went to an address on Park Avenue. The interview was successful, and she found herself in the exact same bedroom with the shallow closet and the little bath, only the room looked out on a blank wall instead of the back of another building. The work was harder than before and the hours much longer, but at least there were no dinner parties. She was supposed to have breakfast ready by quarter of eight, which was impossible, but she tried. Then she walked the children to the corner where they took the school bus, and made the children's beds, and picked up the toys, and ran the vacuum, and stuffed the clothes into the washing machine and the dryer, and so on.

In the afternoon she walked the dog and went to the supermarket, where she soon knew everybody, and Joe, who weighed the vegetables and was old enough to be her father, said, "Here comes my sweetheart," and Arthur the butcher said, "Tell me—where'd you get those beautyful eyes?" Then she took the children to the Park, and got their supper, and so on. She was supposed to baby-sit when the master and mistress went out, but they didn't very often go out. Once in a blue moon, to an early movie, was about the extent of it. If she had been in Glasgow, she would have known what to do with her evenings. Here she didn't know anybody, so she went to bed.

One day when she was with the children in the Park, she met a girl named Cathleen, who asked her to go with her to a dance hall on Eighty-sixth Street. This turned out to be very different from the Outer Hebrides, and just like the flicks. The next morning, her head was full of impressions, mostly of a sad young man who said he was in love with her and almost persuaded her to go home with him, and she was simultaneously pleased with herself for resisting temptation and sorry she hadn't done it. She burned the bacon, and the master wrinkled his nose over the coffee, but by that time she was stretched out on her bed getting forty winks. As the day wore on, a number of things went wrong; the dishwasher foamed all over the kitchen floor, because she had used the washing-machine detergent, and she broke a cup, and put a pair of red corduroy overalls in the washing machine in the same load with some pillowcases and the mistress's blouses and the children's underwear. They all were stained a permanent pink, but the mistress forgave her, because anyone can make a mistake now and then, and the cup was too small a matter to make a thing of. During dinner, the telephone rang, and it was for her. Though she had intended to fall into bed as soon as she finished the dinner dishes, she got dressed instead and met Cathleen at a bar on Second Avenue where they fed dimes into a jukebox, and another boy wanted her to go home with him, and she was so tired she almost did, but instead she left before Cathleen was ready, and was home in bed by two o'clock. She overslept, and there wasn't even time to comb her hair. She managed to stay out of sight until the master had left for his office, but then she forgot, so the mistress did catch her looking like I don't know what. A queer expression passed over her face, but she didn't say anything, and the girl realized that the mistress wasn't ever going to say anything *no matter what happened*.

The telephone always seemed to ring during dinner, and though there was an extension in the kitchen, the girl didn't think it was polite for her to answer it, so she let the master get up from the table and go to the phone in the bedroom. Sometimes, after the third or fourth call, she thought she could detect a note of irritation in his voice when he said, "It's for you." But she had the tray ready with the whiskey and the ice cubes and the jigger and all when he got home at night, and that he liked. As for the children, at first they didn't want to have anything to do with her. The mistress explained that they were very attached to the previous mother's helper—a German girl who had left to get married—and she was not to mind. She didn't. That is, she didn't mind anything but the fact they were being brought up as heathens. So she told them about how the Jews crucified Our Lord, and about the Blessed Saints, and Mary and Joseph, and promised to take them to Mass, and in no time they were eating out of her hand.

She found out there were more bars and dance halls than you could shake a stick at, and she was in one or another of them five nights out of seven. The other two nights she went straight to bed as soon as she had pressed the button on the dishwashing machine. In a hamburger bar she met a boy with blond wavy hair who was an orphan like her, only he had been raised in a Home. Though he didn't say he was in love with her, still and all she liked him. He was interesting to talk to, because so many things seemed to have happened to him, and he didn't ask her to go home with him, so she had no chance to refuse. She didn't really expect to hear from him again, but he called the very next night. She met him in front of the movie house, and during the movie she could feel his arm resting lightly on the back of her seat, and once or twice he gave her shoulder a squeeze, but she didn't have to move her leg away or say "Don't." Afterward, they went to a bar on First Avenue. She told him all about her cousin's family in Glasgow, and about coming over on the boat, and the things she liked about Cathleen and the things she didn't like, and about the way it used to be at home before her mother died and she went to live with her grandmother. Finally she was all talked out, and she just sat there, feeling happy and peaceful. He said, "Another beer?" and she said no, and he had one last one, which he didn't spend any time over, and then he put his hand on the back of her neck and said, "Come on, baby, I'll walk you to your domicile." And that was what she thought they were doing, only when she looked up they were standing in front of the building where *he* lived. He said, "I just want to get a coat, I'm chilly," and she said, "I'll wait here," and he said, "At this time of night, in this neighborhood? Are you out of your mind?" So she followed him up six flights of stairs, and the first thing she knew she was having her clothes torn off her, and the rest she didn't remember. It was daylight when she got home, and she had to wake the night elevator man, who was married and cranky, and he made a fresh remark, which she ignored.

*

She went to church but she was afraid to go to confession, for
fear the priest would find out she was an orphan and put her in
a Home. If she had only saved her money, she could have got
on the boat and gone back to Scotland, but she had bought
clothes instead. Lots of clothes. The children's closets were
full of them. She could hear her grandmother's voice saying,
"You're going to the dogs," and it was true, she was. She also
had a stomach-ache, and it didn't go away. For three days she
went around doubled up with the pain, and then the mistress
noticed it and made her go to a doctor. They paid her wages
while she was in the hospital having her appendix out, and for
two weeks afterward, but they didn't want her to come back,
because they had this colored woman, so she went to see the
lady at the employment agency who had been so nice to her,
only this time she was busy and somebody else gave her an address on Lexington Avenue, and on the way there she passed a
bar-and-grill she liked the looks of. It was called Home on the
Range, and it was pitch dark even in the daytime. Maybe I
ought to start a New Life, the girl thought, and it turned out
they did need a waitress, so that was that. Except that she
wasn't forgotten. The children remembered her. Of all the
maids, they liked her the best, and never forgot what she told
them. And one night about a year after she left, the master was
awakened out of a sound sleep by the ringing of the telephone,
and a sad-voiced young man asked to speak to her. "No, you
can't speak to her!" the master said indignantly. "Do you realize what time it is?" The sad voice seemed surprised to learn
that it was the middle of the night, and unable to understand
why anybody should mind being called at that hour, and unwilling to believe that the girl wasn't there.

The Gardens of Mont-Saint-Michel

THE elephantine Volkswagen bus didn't belong to the French landscape. Compared to the Peugeots and Renaults and Citroëns that overtook it so casually, it seemed an oddity. So was the family riding in it. When they went through towns people turned and stared, but nothing smaller would have held the five of them and their luggage, and the middle-aged American who was driving was not happy at the wheel of any automobile. This particular automobile he loathed. There was no room beyond the clutch pedal. To push it down to the floor he had to turn his foot sideways, and his knee ached all day long from this unnatural position. "Have I got enough room on my right?" he asked continually, though he had been driving the Volkswagen for two weeks now. "Oh God!" he would exclaim. "There's a man on a bicycle." For he was suffering from a recurring premonition: *In the narrow street of some village, though he was taking every human precaution, suddenly he heard a hideous crunch under the right rear wheel. He stopped the car and with a sinking heart got out and made himself look at the twisted bicycle frame and the body lying on the cobblestones. . . .* A dozen times a day John Reynolds could feel his face responding to the emotions of this disaster, which he was convinced was actually going to happen. It was only a matter of when. And where. Sometimes the gendarmes came and took him away, and at other times he managed to extricate himself by thinking of something else. At odds with all this, making his life bearable, was another scene—the moment in the airport at Dinard when he would turn the keys over to the man from the car-rental agency and be free of this particular nightmare forever.

Dorothy Reynolds, sitting on the front seat beside her husband, loved the car because she could see out of it in all directions. Right this minute she asked for nothing more than to be driving through the French countryside. Her worries, which were real and not, like his, imaginary, had been left behind, on the other side of the Atlantic Ocean. She could only vaguely remember what they were.

"In France," she said, "nothing is really ugly, because every-thing is so bare."

"In some ways I like England better," he said.

"It's more picturesque, but it isn't as beautiful. Look at that grey hill town with those dark clouds towering above it," she said, turning around to the two older girls in the seat directly behind her. And then silently scolded herself, because she was resolved not to say "Look!" all the time but to let the children use their own eyes to find what pleased them. The trouble was, their eyes did not see what hers did, or, it often seemed, any-thing at all.

This was not, strictly speaking, true. Reynolds's niece, Linda Porter, had 20/20 vision, but instead of scattering her atten-tion on the landscape she saved it for what she had heard about —the Eiffel Tower, for example—and for the mirror when she was dressing. She was not vain, and neither was she interested in arousing the interest of any actual boy, though boys and men looked at her wherever she went. Her ash-blond hair had been washed and set the night before, her cuticles were flaw-less, her rose-pink nail polish was without a scratch, her skirt was arranged under her delightful young bottom in such a way that it would not wrinkle, her hand satchel was crammed with indispensable cosmetics, her charm bracelet was the equal of that of any of her contemporaries, but she was feeling forlorn. She had not wanted to leave the hotel in Concarneau, which was right on the water, and she could swim and then lie in the sun, when there was any, and she had considered the possibil-ity of getting a job as a waitress so she could spend the rest of her life there, only her father would never let her do it. She had also considered whether or not she was in love with the waiter in charge of their table in the dining room, who was young and good-looking and from Marseilles; when a leaf of lettuce leaped out of the salad bowl, he said "*Zut!*" and kicked it under the table. He asked her to play tennis with him, but un-fortunately she hadn't brought her own racquet and he didn't have an extra one. Also, it turned out he was married.

How strange that she should be sitting side by side with someone for whom mirrors did not reflect anything whatever. Alison Reynolds, who was eleven and a half, considered the hours when she was not reading largely wasted. "If Dantès has had lunch," she once confided to her father, "then I have had lunch. Otherwise I don't know whether I've eaten or not." With a note of sadness in her voice, because no matter how vivid and all-consuming the book was, or how long, sooner or later she finished it, and was stranded once more in ordinariness until she had started another. She couldn't read in the car because it made her feel queer. She was very nearsighted, and by the time she had found her glasses and put them on, the blur her mother and father wanted her to look at had been left behind. All châteaux interested her, and anything that had anything to do with Jeanne d'Arc, or with Marie Antoinette. Or Marguerite de Valois. Or Louise de La Vallière.

Because her mind and her cousin's were so differently occupied, they were able to let one another alone, except for some mild offensive and defensive belittling now and then, but Alison and her younger sister had to ride in separate seats or they quarreled. Trip was lying stretched out, unable to see anything but the car roof and hating every minute of the drive from Fougères, where they had spent the night. It didn't take much to make her happy—a stray dog or a cat, or a monkey chained to a post in a farmyard, or an old white horse in a pasture—but while they were driving she existed in a vacuum and exerted a monumental patience. At any moment she might have to sit up and put her head out of the car window and be sick.

They passed through Antrain without running over anybody on a bicycle, and shortly afterward something happened that made them all more cheerful. Another salmon-and-cream-colored Volkswagen bus, the first they had seen, drew up behind them and started to pass. In it were a man and a woman and two children and a great deal of luggage. The children waved to them from the rear window as the other Volkswagen sped on.

"Americans," Dorothy Reynolds said.

"And probably on their way to Mont-Saint-Michel," Reynolds said. "Wouldn't you know." They were no longer unique.

He saw a sign on their side of the road. She also noticed it, and they smiled at each other with their eyes, in the rearview mirror.

Eighteen years ago, they had arrived in Pontorson from

Cherbourg, by train, by a series of trains, at five o'clock in the afternoon. They had a reservation at a hotel in Mont-Saint-Michel, but they had got up at daybreak and were too tired to go on, so they spent the night here in what the *Michelin* described as an "*hôtel simple, mais confortable*," with "*une bonne table dans la localité.*" It was simple and bare and rather dark inside, and it smelled of roasting coffee beans. It was also very old; their guidebook said it had been the manor of the counts of Montgomery, though there was nothing about it now to indicate this. Their room was on the second floor and it was enormous. So was the bathroom. There was hot water. They had a bath, and then they came downstairs and had an apéritif sitting under a striped umbrella in front of the hotel. He remembered that there was a freshly painted wooden fence with flower boxes on it that separated the table from the street. What was in the flower boxes? Striped petunias? Geraniums? He did not remember, but there were heavenly blue morning glories climbing on strings beside the front door. Their dinner was too good to be true, and they drank a bottle of wine with it, and stumbled up the stairs to their room, and in the profound quiet got into the big double bed and slept like children. So long ago. And so uncritical they were. All open to delight.

In the morning they both woke at the same instant and sat up and looked out of the window. It was market day and the street in front of the hotel was full of people. The women wore long shapeless black cotton dresses and no makeup on their plain country faces. The men wore blue smocks, like the illustrations of Boutet de Monvel. And everybody was carrying long thin loaves of fresh bread. A man with a vegetable stand was yelling at the top of his lungs about his green beans. They saw an old woman leading a cow. And chickens and geese, and little black-and-white goats, and lots of bicycles, but no cars. It was right after the war, and gasoline was rationed, but it seemed more as if the automobile hadn't yet been heard of in this part of France.

They were the only guests at the hotel, the only tourists as far as the eye could see. It was the earthly paradise, and they had it all to themselves. When they came in from cashing a traveler's check or reading the inscriptions on the tombstones in the cemetery, a sliding panel opened in the wall at the foot of the stairs and the cook asked how they enjoyed their walk. The waitress helped them make up their minds what they wanted to eat, and if they had any other problems they went to the concierge with them. The happier they became the happier he was for them, so how could they not love him, or he them? The same with the waitress and the chambermaid and the cook. They went right on drinking too much wine and eating seven-course meals for two more days, and if it hadn't been that they had not seen anything whatever of the rest of France, they might have stayed there, deep in the nineteenth century, forever.

Reynolds thought he remembered Pontorson perfectly, but something peculiar goes on in the memory. This experience is lovingly remembered and that one is, to one's everlasting shame, forgotten. Of the remembered experience a very great deal drops out, drops away, leaving only what is convenient, or what is emotionally useful, and this simplified version takes up much more room than it has any right to. The village of Pontorson in 1948 was larger than John Reynolds remembered it as being, but after eighteen years it was not even a village any longer; it was now a small town, thriving and prosperous, and one street looked so much like another that he had to stop in the middle of a busy intersection and ask a traffic policeman the way to the hotel they had been so happy in.

It was still there, but he wouldn't have recognized it without the sign. The fence was gone, and so were the morning glories twisting around their white strings, and the striped umbrellas. The sidewalk came right up to the door of the hotel, and it would not have been safe to drive a cow down the street it was situated on.

"It's all so changed," he said. "But flourishing, wouldn't you say? Would you like to go in and have a look around?"

"No," Dorothy said.

"They might remember us."

"It isn't likely the staff would be the same after all this time."

Somewhere deep inside he was surprised. He had expected

everybody in France to stand right where they were (one, two, three, four, five, six, seven, eight, nine, *stillpost*) until he got back.

"I never thought about it before," he said, "but except for the cook there was nobody who was much older than we were. . . . So kind they all were. But there was also something sad about them. The war, I guess. Also, there's no place to park. Too bad." He drove on slowly, still looking.

"What's too bad?" Alison asked.

"Nothing," Dorothy said. "Your father doesn't like change."

"Do you?"

"Not particularly. But if you are going to live in the modern world—"

Alison stopped listening. Her mother could live in the modern world if she wanted to, but she had no intention of joining her there.

They circled around, and found the sign that said MONT-SAINT-MICHEL, and headed due north. In 1948 their friend the concierge, having found an aged taxi for them, stood in the doorway waving good-bye. Nine kilometers and not another car on the road the whole ride. Ancient farmhouses such as they had seen from the train window they could observe from close up: the weathered tile roofs, the pink rose cascading from its trellis, the stone watering trough for the animals; the beautiful man-made, almost mathematical orderliness of the woodpile, the vegetable garden, and the orchard. Suddenly they saw, glimmering in the distance, the abbey on its rock, with the pointed spire indicating the precise direction of a heaven nobody believed in anymore. The taxi driver said, "Le Mont-Saint-Michel," and they looked at each other and shook their heads. For reading about it was one thing and seeing it with their own eyes was another. The airiness, the visionary quality, the way it kept changing right in front of their eyes, as if it were some kind of heavenly vaudeville act.

After the fifth brand-new house, Reynolds said, massaging his knee, "Where are all the old farmhouses?"

"We must have come by a different road," Dorothy said.

"It has to be the same road," he said, and seeing how intently he peered ahead through the windshield she didn't argue. But surely if there were new houses there could be new roads.

Once more the abbey took them by surprise. This time the surprise was due to the fact they were already close upon it. There had been no distant view. New buildings, taller trees, something, had prevented their seeing it until now. The light was of the seacoast, dazzling and severe. Clouds funneled the radiance upward. It seemed that flocks of angels might be released into the sky at any moment.

"There it is!" Dorothy cried. "Look, children!"

Linda added the name Mont-Saint-Michel to the list of places she could tell people she had seen when she got home. Alison put her glasses on and dutifully looked. Mont-Saint-Michel was enough like a castle to strike her as interesting, but what she remembered afterward was not the thing itself but the excitement in her father's and mother's voices. Trip sat up, looked, and sank back again without a word and without the slightest change in her expression.

The abbey was immediately obscured by a big new hotel. Boys in white jackets stood in a line on the left-hand side of the road, and indicated with a gesture of the thumb that the Volkswagen was to swing in here.

"What an insane idea," Reynolds murmured. He had made a reservation at the hotel where they had stayed before, right in the shadow of the abbey.

At the beginning of the causeway, three or four cars were stopped and their occupants had got out with their cameras. He got out too, with the children's Hawkeye, and had to wait several minutes for an unobstructed view. Then he got back in the car and drove the rest of the way.

At the last turn in the road, he exclaimed, "Oh, *no!*" In a huge parking lot to the right of the causeway there were roughly a thousand cars shining in the sunlight. "It's just like the World's Fair," he said. "We'll probably have to stand in line an hour and forty minutes to see the tide come in."

A traffic policeman indicated with a movement of his arm that they were to swing off to the right and down into the parking lot. Reynolds stopped and explained that they were spending the night here and had been told they were to leave the car next to the outer gate. The policeman's arm made exactly the same gesture it had made before.

"He's a big help," Reynolds said as he drove on, and Trip said, "There's a car just like ours."

"Why, so it is," Dorothy said. "It must be the people who passed us."

"And there's another," Trip said.

"Where?" Alison said, and put on her glasses.

They left the luggage in the locked Volkswagen and joined the stream of pilgrims. Reynolds stopped and paid for the parking ticket. Looking back over his shoulder, he saw the sand flats extending out into the bay as far as the eye could see, wet, shining, and with long, thin, bright ribbons of water running through them, just as he remembered. The time before, there were nine sightseeing buses lined up on the causeway, from which he knew before he ever set foot in it, that Mont-Saint-Michel was not going to be the earthly paradise. This time he didn't even bother to count them. Thirty, forty, fifty, what difference did it make. But the little stream that flowed right past the outer gate? *Gone.* . . . Was it perhaps not a stream at all but a ditch with tidal water in it? Anyway, it had been just too wide to jump over, and a big man in a porter's uniform had picked Dorothy up in his arms and, wading through the water, set her down on the other side. Then he came back for Reynolds. There was no indication now that there had ever been a stream here that you had to be carried across as if you were living in the time of Chaucer.

The hotels, restaurants, cafés, Quimper shops, and souvenir shops (the abbey on glass ashtrays, on cheap china, on armbands, on felt pennants; the abbey in the form of lead paperweights three or four inches high) had survived. The winding street of stairs was noisier, perhaps, and more crowded, but not really any different. The hotel was expecting them. Reynolds left Dorothy and the children in the lobby and went back to the car with a porter, who was five foot three or four at the most and probably not old enough to vote. Sitting on the front seat of the Volkswagen, he indicated the road they were to take out of the big parking lot, up over the causeway and down into the smaller parking lot by the outer gate, where Reynolds had tried to go in the first place. The same policeman waved them on, consistency being not one of the things the French are nervous about. With the help of leather straps the porter draped the big suitcases and then the smaller ones here and there around his person, and would have added the hand luggage if Reynolds had let him. Together they staggered up the cobblestone street, and Reynolds saw to his surprise that Dorothy and the children were sitting at a café table across from the entrance to the hotel.

"It was too hot in there," she said, "and there was no place to sit down. I ordered an apéritif. Do you want one?"

And the luggage? What do I do with that? his eyebrows asked, for she was descended from the girl in the fairy tale who said, "Just bring me a rose, dear Father," and he was born in the dead center of the middle class, and they did not always immediately agree about what came before what. He followed the porter inside and up a flight of stairs. The second floor was just as he remembered it, and their room was right down there —where he started to go, until he saw that the porter was continuing up the stairs. On the floor above he went out through a door, with Reynolds following, to a wing of the hotel that didn't exist eighteen years before. It was three stories high and built in the style of an American motel, and the rooms that had been reserved for them were on the third floor—making four stories in all that they had climbed. The porter never paused for breath, possibly because any loss of momentum would have stopped him in his tracks. Reynolds went to a window and opened it. The view from this much higher position was of rooftops and the main parking lot and, like a line drawn with a ruler, the canal that divides Brittany and Normandy. He felt one of the twin beds (no sag in the middle) and then inspected the children's room and the bathroom. It was all very modern and comfortable. It was, in fact, a good deal more comfortable than their old room had been, though he had remembered that room with pleasure all these years. The flowered wallpaper and the flowered curtains had been simply god-awful together, and leaning out of the window they had looked straight down on the heads of the tourists coming and going in the Grande Rue—tourists from all over Europe, by their appearance, their clothes, and by the variety of languages they were speaking. There were even tourists from Brittany, in their *pardon* costumes. And they all seemed to have the same expression on their faces, as if it were an effect of the afternoon light. They looked as if they were soberly aware that they had come to a dividing place in their lives and nothing would be quite the same for them after this. And all afternoon and all evening there was the sound of the omelette whisk. In a room between the foyer of the hotel and the dining room, directly underneath them, a very tall man in a chef's cap and white apron stood beating eggs with a whisk and then cooking them in a long-handled skillet over a wood fire in an enormous open fireplace.

Reynolds listened. There was no *whisk, whisk, whisk* now. Too far away. A car came down the causeway and turned in to the parking lot. When night came, the buses would all be gone and the parking lot would be empty.

In this he was arguing from what had happened before. The tourists got back on the sightseeing buses, and the buses drove away. By the end of the afternoon he and Dorothy were the only ones left. After dinner they walked up to the abbey, again, drawn there by some invisible force. It was closed for the night, but they noticed a gate and pushed it open a few inches and looked in. It was a walled garden from a fifteenth-century Book of Hours. There was nobody around, so they went in and closed the gate carefully behind them and started down the gravel path. The garden beds were outlined with bilateral dwarf fruit trees, their branches tied to a low wire and heavy with picture-book apples and pears. There was no snobbish distinction between flowers and vegetables. The weed was unknown. At the far end of this Eden there was a gate that led to another, and after that there were still others—a whole series of exquisite walled gardens hidden away behind the street of restaurants and hotels and souvenir shops. They visited them all. Lingering in the deep twilight, they stood looking up at the cliffs of masonry and were awed by the actual living presence of Time; for it must have been just like this for the last five or six hundred years and maybe longer. The swallows were slicing the air into convex curves, the tide had receded far out into the bay, leaving everywhere behind it the channels by which it would return at three in the morning, and the air was so pure it made them lightheaded.

Before Reynolds turned away from the window, three more cars came down the causeway. Here and there in the parking lot a car was starting up and leaving. Though he did not know it, it was what they should have been doing; he should have rounded up Dorothy and the children and driven on to Dinan, where there was a nice well-run hotel with a good restaurant and no memories and a castle right down the street. But his clairvoyance was limited. He foresaw the accident that would never take place but not the disorderly reception that lay in wait for them downstairs.

On the way into the dining room, half an hour later, they stopped to show the children how the omelettes were made. The very tall man in the white apron had been replaced by two young women in uniforms, but there was still a fire in the fireplace, Reynolds was glad to see; they weren't making the omelettes on a gas stove. The fire was quite a small one, though, and not the huge yellow flames he remembered.

"*Cinq*," he said to the maître d'hôtel, who replied in English, "Will you come this way?" and led them to a table in the center of the dining room. When he had passed out enormous printed menus, he said, "I think the little lady had better put her knitting away. One of the waiters might get jabbed by a needle." This request was accompanied by the smile of a man who knows what children are like, and whom children always find irresistible. Trip ignored the smile and looked at her mother inquiringly.

"I don't see how you could jab anybody, but put it away. I want an omelette *fines herbes*," Dorothy said.

The maître d'hôtel indicated the top of the menu with his gold pencil and said, "We have the famous omelette of Mont-Saint-Michel."

"But with herbs," Dorothy said.

"There is no omelette with herbs," the maître d'hôtel said.

"Why not?" Reynolds asked. "We had it here before."

The question went unanswered.

The two younger children did not care for omelette, famous or otherwise, and took an unconscionably long time making up their minds what they did want to eat for lunch. The maître d'hôtel came back twice before Reynolds was ready to give him their order. After he had left the table, Dorothy said, "I don't see why you can't have it *fines herbes*."

"Perhaps they don't have any herbs," Reynolds said.

"In *France*?"

"Here, I mean. It's an island, practically."

"All you need is parsley and chives. Surely they have that."

"Well maybe it's too much bother, then."

"It's no more trouble than a plain omelette. I don't like him."

"Yes? What's the matter with him?"

"He looks like a Yale man."

This was not intended as a funny remark, but Reynolds laughed anyway.

"And he's not a good headwaiter," she said.

The maître d'hôtel did not, in fact, get their order straight. Things came that they hadn't ordered, and Trip's sole didn't come with the omelettes, or at all. Since she had already filled up on bread, it was not serious. The service was elaborate but very slow.

"No dessert, thank you," Reynolds said when the waiter brought the enormous menus back.

"Just coffee," Dorothy said.

Reynolds looked at his watch. "It says in the green *Michelin* there's a tour of the abbey with an English-speaking guide at two o'clock. We just barely have time to make it. If we have coffee we'll be too late."

"Oh, let's have coffee," Dorothy said. "They won't start on time."

As they raced up the Grande Rue at five minutes after two, he noticed that it was different in one respect: The shops had been enlarged; they went back much deeper than they had before. The objects offered for sale were the same, and since he had examined them carefully eighteen years before, there was no need to do anything but avert his eyes from them now.

The English-speaking tour had already left the vaulted room it started from, and they ran up a long flight of stone steps and caught up with their party on the battlements. A young Frenchman with heavy black-rimmed glasses and a greenish complexion was lecturing to them about the part Mont-Saint-Michel played in the Hundred Years' War. There was a group

just ahead of them, and another just behind. The guides ma-
nipulated their parties in and out of the same rooms and up
and down the same stairs with military precision.

"There were dungeons," Alison Reynolds afterward wrote
in her diary, "where you could not sit, lie, or stand and were
not allowed to move. Some prisoners were eaten by rats! There
were beautiful cloisters where the monks walked and watered
their gardens. There was the knights' hall, where guests stayed.
The monks ate and worked in the refectory. . . ."

"It's better managed than it used to be," Dorothy said. "I
mean, when you think how many people have to be taken
through."

The tour was also much shorter than Reynolds remembered
it as being, but that could have been because this time they
had an English-speaking guide. Or it could just be that what
he suspected was true and they were being hurried through.
He could not feel the same passionate interest in either the history or the architectural details of the abbey that he had the
first time, but that was not the guide's fault. It was obvious
that he cared very much about the evolution of the Gothic
style and the various uses to which this immensely beautiful
but now lifeless monument had been put, through the centuries. His accent made the children smile, but it was no farther from the mark than Reynolds's French, which the French
did not smile at only because it didn't amuse them to hear
their language badly spoken.

When the tour was over, the guide gathered the party
around him and, standing in a doorway through which they
would have to pass, informed them that he was a student in a
university and that this was his only means of paying for his
education. The intellectual tradition of France sat gracefully
on his frail shoulders, Reynolds thought, and short or not his
tour had been a model of clarity. And was ten francs enough
for the five of them?

Traveling in France right after the war, when everybody was
so poor, he had been struck by the way the French always
tipped the guide generously and thanked him in a way that was
never perfunctory. It seemed partly good manners and partly a
universal respect for the details of French history. A considerable number of tourists slipped through the doorway now

without putting anything in the waiting hand. Before, the guide stood out in the open, quite confident that no one would try to escape without giving him something.

At the sight of the ten-franc note, the young man's features underwent a slight change, by which Reynolds knew that it was sufficient, but money was not all the occasion called for, and there was a word he had been waiting for a chance to use. "*Votre tour est très sensible,*" he said, and the guide's face lit up with pleasure.

Only connect, Mr. E. M. Forster said, but he was not talking about John Reynolds, whose life's blood went into making incessant and vivid connections with all sorts of people he would never see again, and never forgot.

The wine at lunch had made him sleepy. He waited impatiently while Dorothy and the children bought slides and postcards in the room where the tour ended. Outside, at the foot of the staircase, his plans for taking a nap were threatened when Dorothy was attracted to a museum of horrors having to do with the period when Mont-Saint-Michel was a state prison. But by applying delicate pressures at the right moment he got her to give up the museum, and they walked on down to their hotel. When he had undressed and pulled the covers back, he went to the window in his dressing gown. Some cars were just arriving. American cars. He looked at his watch. It was after four, and the parking lot was still more than half full. On the top floor of the hotel just below, and right next to an open window, he could see a girl of nineteen or twenty with long straight straw-blond hair, sitting on the side of a bed in an attitude of despondency. During the whole time he stood at the window, she didn't raise her head or move. He got into his own bed and was just falling asleep when somebody came into the courtyard with a transistor radio playing rock and roll. He got up and rummaged through his suitcase until he found the wax earplugs. When he woke an hour later, the courtyard was quiet. The girl was still there. He went to the window several times while he was running a bath and afterward while he was dressing. Though the girl left the bed and came back to it, there was no change in her dejection.

"That girl," he said finally.

"I've been watching her too," Dorothy said.

"She's in love. And something's gone wrong."

"They aren't married and she's having a baby," Dorothy said.

"And the man has left her."

"No, he's in the room," Dorothy said. "I saw him a minute ago, drinking out of a wine bottle."

The next time Reynolds looked he couldn't see anyone. The room looked empty, though you couldn't see all the way into it. Had the man and the girl left? Or were they down below somewhere? He looked one last time before they started down to the dining room. The shutters in the room across the court were closed. That was that.

At dinner Reynolds got into a row with their waiter. For ten days in Paris and ten more days at a little seaside resort on the south coast of Brittany they had met with nothing but politeness and the desire to please. All the familiar complaints about France and the French were refuted, until this evening, when one thing after another went wrong. They were seated at a table that had been wedged into a far corner of the room, between a grotto for trout and goldfish and the foot of a stairway leading to the upper floors of the hotel. Reynolds started to protest and Dorothy stopped him.

"Trip wants to stay here so she can watch the fish," she explained.

"I know," he said as he unfolded his napkin, "but if anybody comes down those stairs they'll have to climb over my lap to get into the dining room."

"They won't," she said. "I'm sure it isn't used." Then to the children, "You pick out the one you want to eat and they take it out with a net and carry it to the kitchen."

"I have a feeling those trout are just for decoration," Reynolds said.

"No," Dorothy said. "I've seen it done. I forget where."

Nobody came down the stairs, and the trout, also undisturbed, circled round and round among the rocks and ferns. Though the room was only half full, the service was dreadfully slow. When they had finished the first course, the waiter, rather than go all the way around the table to where he could pick up Reynolds's plate, said curtly, "Hand me your plate," and

Reynolds did. It would never have occurred to him to throw the plate at the waiter's head. His first reaction was always to be obliging. Anger came more slowly, usually with prodding.

The service got worse and worse.

"I think we ought to complain to the headwaiter," Dorothy said. Reynolds looked around. The maître d'hôtel was nowhere in sight. They went on eating their dinner.

"The food is just plain bad,'" Dorothy announced. "And he forgot to give us any cheese. I don't see how they can give this place a star in the *Michelin*."

When reminded of the fact that he had forgotten to give them any cheese, the waiter, instead of putting the cheese board on the table, cut off thin slices himself at the serving table and passed them. His manner was openly contemptuous. He also created a disturbance in the vicinity of their table by scolding his assistant, who had been courteous and friendly. In mounting anger Reynolds composed a speech to be delivered when the waiter brought the check. Of this withering eloquence all he actually got out was one sentence, ending with the words "*n'est plus un restaurant sérieux.*" The waiter pretended not to understand Reynolds's French. Like a fool Reynolds fell into the trap and repeated what he had said. It sounded much more feeble the second time. Smirking, the waiter asked if there was something wrong with their dinner, and Reynolds said that he was referring to the way it was served, whereupon the waiter went over to the assistant and said, in English, "They don't like the way you served them." It was his round, definitely.

Reynolds glanced at his wristwatch and then pushed his chair back and hurried Dorothy and the three children out of the dining room and through the lobby and down the street to the outer gate, and then along a path to higher ground. They were in plenty of time. The sunset colors lingered in the sky and in the ribbons of water. The children, happy to have escaped from the atmosphere of eating, climbed over the rocks, risking their lives. Dorothy sat with the sea wind blowing her hair back from her face. He saw that she had entirely forgotten the unpleasantness in the dining room. She responded to

Nature the way he responded to human beings. Presently he let go of his anger, too, and responded to the evening instead.

"What if they fall?" she said. "It could be quicksand."

"If it's quicksand, I'll jump in after them. Isn't it lovely and quiet here?"

For in spite of all those cars in the parking lot they had the evening to themselves. Nobody had come down here to see the tide sweep in. At first it was silent. They saw that the channels through the sandbars were growing wider, but there was no visible movement of water. Then suddenly it began to move, everywhere, with a rushing sound that no river ever makes on its way to the sea. It was less like a force of Nature than like an emotion—like the disastrous happiness of a man who has fallen in love at the wrong season of life.

When it was over, they walked up to the abbey in the dusk, by a back way that was all stairs, and down again along the outer ramparts, looking into the rear windows of houses and restaurants, and were just in time to be startled by a blood-curdling scream. It came from a brightly lighted room in a house that was across a courtyard and one story down from where they were. It could have been a woman's scream, or a child's. There was an outbreak of angry voices.

"What *is* it, Daddy?" the children asked. "What are they saying?"

"It's just a family argument," Reynolds said, making his voice sound casual. His knees were shaking. Listening to the excited voices, he made out only one word— "*idiot.*" Either the scream had come from a mental defective or somebody was being insulted. The voices subsided. The Americans walked on until they came to a flight of steps leading down to the street in front of their hotel.

When the children were in bed, Reynolds and Dorothy sat at the window of their room, looking out at the night. "The air is so soft," she said, and he said, "Ummm," not wanting to spoil her pleasure by saying what was really on his mind, which was that they should never have come here and that nothing on earth would make him come here again. In a place where things could easily have been kept as they were—where, one would have thought, it was to everybody's advantage to keep them that way—something had gone fatally wrong. Something had been allowed to happen that shouldn't have happened.

And it was not only here. The evening they arrived in Paris, the taxi driver who took them from the boat train to their hotel on the Left Bank said, "*Paris n'est plus Paris.*" And in the morning Madame said when she gave them their mail, "Paris is changed. It's so noisy now." "New York too," he said, to comfort her. But the truth was that nowhere in New York was the traffic like the Boulevard Saint-Germain. The cars drove at twice the speed of the cars at home, and when the lights changed there was always some side street from which cars kept on coming, and pedestrians ran for their lives. Like insects. The patrons who sat at the tables on the sidewalk in front of Lipp could no longer see their counterparts at the Deux Magots because of the river of cars that flowed between them. The soft summer air reeked of gasoline. And there was something he saw that he could not get out of his mind afterward: an old woman who had tried to cross against the light and was stranded in the middle of the street, her eyes wide with terror, like a living monument.

Reynolds was quite aware that to complain because things were not as agreeable as they used to be was one of the recognizable signs of growing old. And whether you accepted change or not, there was really no preventing it. But why, without exception, did something bad drive out something good? Why was the change always for the worse?

He had once asked his father-in-law, a man in his seventies, if there was a time—he didn't say whether he meant in history or a time that his father-in-law remembered, and, actually, he meant both—when the world seemed to be becoming a better place, little by little. And life everywhere more agreeable, more the way it ought to be. And then suddenly, after that, was there a noticeable shift in the pattern of events? Some sort of dividing line that people were aware of, when everything started to go downhill? His father-in-law didn't answer, making Reynolds feel he had said something foolish or tactless. But his father-in-law didn't like to talk about his feelings, and it was just possible that he felt the same way Reynolds did.

Once in a while, some small detail represented an improvement on the past, and you could not be happy in the intellectual climate of any time but your own. But in general, so far as the way people lived, it was one loss after another, something hideous replacing something beautiful, the decay of manners, the lapse of pleasant customs, as by a blind increase in numbers the human race went about making the earth more and more unfit to live on.

In the morning, Reynolds woke ready to pay the bill and leave as soon as possible, but it was only a short drive to Dinard, and their plane didn't leave until five o'clock in the afternoon, so after breakfast they climbed the steps of the Grande Rue once more, for a last look at the outside of the abbey, and found something they had overlooked before—an exhibition marking the thousandth year of the Abbey of Mont-Saint-Michel. There were illuminated manuscripts: St. Michael appearing to Aubert, Bishop of Avranches, in a dream and telling him to build a chapel on the Mount; St. Michael weighing souls, slaying dragons, vanquishing demons, separating the blessed from the damned; St. Michael between St. Benoît and the archbishop St. William; St. Michael presenting his arms to the Virgin; St. Michael the guardian of Paradise. There was a list of the Benedictine monks living and dead at the time of the abbot Mainard II, and an inventory of the relics of the monastery at the end of the fifteenth century. There was the royal seal of William the Conqueror, of Philip the Fair, of Philip the Bold, of Louis VIII, of Philip Augustus. There was an octagonal reliquary containing a fragment of the cranium of St. Suzanne the Virgin Martyr. There was a drawing, cut by some vandal from an illuminated manuscript, of Jeanne d'Arc, Alison's friend, with her banner and sword, corresponding exactly to a description given at her trial, and a letter from Charles VII reaffirming that Mont-Saint-Michel was part of the royal domain. There were maquettes of the abbey in the year 1000, in 1100, in 1701, and as it was now. There was an aquarelle by Viollet-le-Duc of the flying buttresses. There were suits of armor, harquebuses, a pistolet, and some cannonballs. There was far more than they could take in or do justice to. When they emerged from the exhibition rooms, dazed by all they had looked at, Reynolds remembered the little gardens. It would never do to go away without seeing them. He couldn't find the gate that opened into the first one, and he wasn't sure, after eighteen years, on which side of the Mount they were, but Dorothy had noticed a sign, down a flight of steps from the abbey, that said THE BISHOP'S GARDEN. They bought tickets from an old woman sitting at a table under a vaulted archway and passed into what was hardly more than a strip of grass with a few flowers and flowering shrubs, and could have been the terrace of a public park in some small provincial French town. Reynolds began to look for the medieval gardens in earnest, and in the end they found themselves in what must once have been the place they were looking for. It was overrun with weeds, and hardly recognizable as a garden, and there was only that one.

Later, after he had closed and locked his suitcase, he went to the window for the last time. The shutters of the room that had contained so much drama were still closed. Looking down on the courtyard between the new wing of their hotel and the hotel in front of it, he knew suddenly what had happened. The medieval gardens didn't exist any more. To accommodate an ever-increasing number of tourists, the hotels had been added on to. So that they could hold thousands of souvenirs instead of hundreds, the souvenir shops had been deepened, taking the only available land, which happened to be those enchanting walled gardens. The very building he was in at that moment, with its comfortable if anonymous rooms with adjoining bath, had obliterated some garden that had been here for perhaps five hundred years. One of the miracles of the modern world, and they did just what people everywhere else would have done—they cashed in on a good thing. And never mind about the past. The past is what filled the gigantic parking lot with cars all summer, but so long as you have the appearance you can sell that; you don't need the real thing. What's a garden that has come down intact through five hundred years compared to money in the bank? *This is something I will never get over*, he thought, feeling the anger go deeper and deeper. *I will never stop hating the people who did this. And I will never forgive them—or France for letting them do it. What's here now is no longer worth seeing or saving. If this could happen here, then there is no limit to what can happen everywhere else. It's all going down, and down. There's no stopping it. . . .*

In order to pay the bill, he had to go to the cashier's desk, which was at the far end of the dining room. As he started there, walking between the empty tables, he saw that the only maître d'hôtel in the whole of France who looked like a Yale man was avoiding his eyes—not because he felt any remorse for putting them next to the fish tank with a clown for a waiter, or because he was afraid of anything Reynolds might say or do. He didn't care if Reynolds dropped dead on the spot, so long as he didn't have to dispose of the body. He was a man without any feeling for his métier, *tout simplement*, and so the food and the service had gone to hell in a basket.

While Reynolds was at the concierge's desk in the foyer, confirming their reservations at the airport by telephone, a gentle feminine voice said behind him, in English, "Monsieur, you left your traveler's checks," and he turned and thanked the cashier profusely.

He started up the stairs to see about the luggage and the concierge called after him, "Monsieur, your airplane tickets!"

They had banded together and were looking after him.

The same boy who carried the luggage up four flights of stairs now carried it down again and out through the medieval gate to the Volkswagen. "We were here eighteen years ago," Reynolds said to him as he took out his wallet. "You have no idea how different it was."

This was quite true. Eighteen years ago, the porter was not anywhere. Or if he was, he was only a babe in arms. But he was a Frenchman, and knew that a polite man doesn't sneer at emotions he doesn't feel or memories he cannot share. He insisted on packing the luggage for Reynolds, and tucked Dorothy and the children in, and closed the car doors, and then gave them a beautiful smile.

It's true that I overtipped him, Reynolds thought. But then, looking into the porter's alert, intelligent, doglike eyes, he knew that he was being unjust. The tip had nothing to do with it. It was because he was a harmless maniac and they all felt obliged to take care of him and see him on his way.

Over by the River

THE sun rose somewhere in the middle of Queens, the exact moment of its appearance shrouded in uncertainty because of a cloud bank. The lights on the bridges went off, and so did the red light in the lantern of the lighthouse at the north end of Welfare Island. Seagulls settled on the water. A newspaper truck went from building to building dropping off heavy bundles of, for the most part, bad news, which little boys carried inside on their shoulders. Doormen smoking a pipe and dressed for a walk in the country came to work after a long subway ride and disappeared into the service entrances. When they reappeared, by way of the front elevator, they had put on with their uniforms a false amiability and were prepared for eight solid hours to make conversation about the weather. With the morning sun on them, the apartment buildings far to the west, on Lexington Avenue, looked like an orange mesa. The pigeons made bubbling noises in their throats as they strutted on windowsills high above the street.

All night long, there had been plenty of time. Now suddenly there wasn't, and this touched off a chain explosion of alarm clocks, though in some instances the point was driven home without a sound: Time is interior to animals as well as exterior. A bare arm with a wristwatch on it emerged from under the covers and turned until the dial was toward the light from the windows.

"What time is it?"

"Ten after."

"It's always ten after," Iris Carrington said despairingly, and turned over in bed and shut her eyes against the light. Also against the clamor of her desk calendar: *Tuesday 11, L. 3:30 Dr. de Santillo . . . 5:30–7:30? . . . Wednesday 1:45, Mrs. McIntosh speaks on the changing status of women. 3:30 Dr. F. . . . Friday 11 C. Get Andrea . . . Saturday, call Mrs. Stokes. Ordering pads. L ballet 10:30. 2 Laurie to Sasha's. Remaining books due at library. Explore dentists. Supper at 5. Call Margot . . .*

Several minutes passed.

"Oh my God, I don't think I can make it," George Carrington said, and put his feet over the side of the bed, and found he could make it, after all. He could bend over and pick up his bathrobe from the floor, and put it on, and find his slippers, and close the window, and turn on the radiator valve. Each act was easier than the one before. He went back to the bed and drew the covers closer around his wife's shoulders.

Yawning, stretching, any number of people got up and started the business of the day. Turning on the shower. Dressing. Putting their hair up in plastic curlers. Squeezing toothpaste out of tubes that were all but empty. Squeezing orange juice. Separating strips of bacon.

The park keepers unlocked the big iron gates that closed the river walk off between Eighty-third and Eighty-fourth Streets. A taxi coming from Doctors Hospital was snagged by a doorman's whistle. The wind picked up the dry filth under the wheels of parked cars and blew it now this way, now that. A child got into an orange minibus and started on the long, devious ride to nursery school and social adjustment.

"Have you been a good girl?" George inquired lovingly, through the closed door of the unused extra maid's room, where the dog slept on a square of carpet. Puppy had not been a good girl. There was a puddle of urine—not on the open newspaper he had left for her, just in case, but two feet away from it, on the black-and-white plastic-tile floor. Her tail quivering with apology, she watched while he mopped the puddle up and disposed of the wet newspaper in the garbage can in the back hall. Then she followed him through the apartment to the foyer, and into the elevator when it came.

There were signs all along the river walk:

NO DOGS
NO BICYCLES
NO THIS
NO THAT

He ignored them with a clear conscience. If he curbed the dog beforehand, there was no reason not to turn her loose and let her run—except that sometimes she stopped and arched her back a second time. When shouting and waving his hands didn't discourage her from moving her bowels, he took some newspaper from a trash container and cleaned up after her.

At the flagpole, he stood looking out across the river. The lights went off all the way up the airplane beacon, producing an effect of silence—as if somebody had started to say something and then decided not to. The tidal current was flowing south. He raised his head and sniffed, hoping for a breath of the sea, and smelled gasoline fumes instead.

Coming back, the dog stopped to sniff at trash baskets, at cement copings, and had to be restrained from greeting the only other person on the river walk—a grey-haired man who jogged there every morning in a gym suit and was afraid of dogs. He smiled pleasantly at George, and watched Puppy out of the corner of his eyes, so as to be ready when she leapt at his throat.

A tanker, freshly painted, all yellow and white, and flying the flag of George had no idea what country until he read the lettering on the stern, overtook him, close in to shore—so close he could see the captain talking to a sailor in the wheelhouse. To be sailing down the East River on a ship that was headed for open water . . . He waved to them and they waved back, but they didn't call out to him *Come on, if you want to*, and it was too far to jump. It came to him with the seriousness of a discovery that there was no place in the world he would not like to see. Concealed in this statement was another that he had admitted to himself for the first time only recently. There were places he would never see, experiences of the first importance that he would never have. He might die without ever having heard a nightingale.

When they stepped out of the elevator, the dog hurried off to the kitchen to see if there was something in her dish she didn't know about, and George settled down in the living room with the *Times* on his lap and waited for a glass of orange juice to appear at his place at the dining-room table. The rushing sound inside the walls, as of an underground river, was Iris running her bath. The orange juice was in no hurry to get to the dining-room table. Iris had been on the phone daily with the employment agency and for the moment this was the best they could offer: twenty-seven years old, pale, with dirty blond hair, unmarried, overattached to her mother, and given to burning herself on the antiquated gas stove. She lived on tea and cigarettes. Breakfast was all the cooking she was entrusted

with; Iris did the rest. Morning after morning his boiled egg
was hard enough to take on a picnic. A blind man could not
have made a greater hash of half a grapefruit. The coffee was
indescribable. After six weeks there was a film of grease over
everything in the kitchen. Round, jolly, neat, professionally
trained, a marvellous cook, the mother was everything that is
desirable in a servant except that, alas, she worked for somebody else. She drifted in and out of the apartment at odd
hours, deluding Iris with the hope that some of her accom-
plishments would, if one were only patient, rub off on her
daughter.

"Read," a voice said, bringing him all the way back from
Outer Mongolia.

"Tonight, Cindy."

"Read! Read!"

He put the paper down and picked her up, and when she
had settled comfortably in his lap he began: " 'Emily was a
guinea pig who loved to travel. Generally she stayed home and
looked after her brother Arthur. But every so often she grew
tired of cooking and mending and washing and ironing; the
day would seem too dark, and the house too small, and she
would have a great longing to set out into the distance. . . .' "

Looking down at the top of her head as he was reading, he
felt an impulse to put his nose down and smell her hair. Born
in a hurry she was. Born in one hell of a hurry, half an hour
after her mother got to the hospital.

Laurie Carrington said, "What is the difference, what is the
difference between a barber and a woman with several children?" Nobody answered, so she asked the question again.

"I give up," Iris said.

"Do you know, Daddy?"

"I give up too, we all give up."

"A barber . . . has razors to shave. And the woman has
shavers to raise."

He looked at her over the top of his half-glasses, wondering
what ancestor was responsible for that reddish blond hair.

"That's a terribly funny one, Laurie," he said. "That's the
best one yet," and his eyes reverted to the editorial page. A
nagging voice inside his head informed him that a good father

would be conversing intelligently with his children at the breakfast table. But about what? No intelligent subject of conversation occurred to him, perhaps because it was Iris's idea in the first place, not his.

He said, "Cindy, would you like a bacon sandwich?"

She thought, long enough for him to become immersed in the *Times* again, and then she said, "I would like a piece of bacon and a piece of toast. But not a bacon sandwich."

He dropped a slice of bread in the toaster and said, "Pyrozz-quozz-gill"—a magic word, from one of the Oz books. With a grinding noise the bread disappeared.

"Stupid Cindy," Laurie remarked, tossing her head. But Cindy wasn't fooled. Laurie used to be the baby and now she wasn't anymore. She was the oldest. And what she would have liked to be was the oldest *and* the baby. About lots of things she was very piggy. But she couldn't whistle. Try though she might, *whhih, whhih, whhih*, she couldn't. And Cindy could.

The toast emerged from the toaster and Iris said, "Not at the breakfast table, Cindy." The morning was difficult for her, clouded with amnesia, with the absence of energy, with the reluctance of her body to take on any action whatever. Straight lines curved unpleasantly, hard surfaces presented the look of softness. She saw George and the children and the dog lying at her feet under the table the way one sees rocks and trees and cottages at the seashore through the early morning fog; just barely recognizable they were.

"Why is a church steeple—"

"My gloves," he said, standing in the front hall, with his coat on.

"They're in the drawer in the lowboy," Iris said.

"Why is a church steeple—"

"Not those," he said.

"Why is a—"

"Laurie, Daddy is talking. Look in the pocket of your chesterfield."

"I did."

"Yes, dear, why is a church steeple."

"Why is a church steeple like a maiden aunt?"

"I give up."

"Do you know, Daddy?"

"No. I've looked in every single one of my coats. They must be in my raincoat, because I can't find that either."

"Look in your closet."

"I did look there." But he went into the bedroom and looked again anyway. Then he looked all through the front-hall closet, including the mess on the top shelf.

Iris passed through the hall with her arms full of clothes for the washing machine. "Did you find your raincoat?" she asked.

"I must have left it somewhere," he said. "But where?"

He went back to the bedroom and looked in the engagement calendar on her desk, to see where they had been, and it appeared that they hadn't been anywhere.

"Where did we go when we had Andrea to baby-sit?"

"I don't remember."

"We had her two nights."

"Did we? I thought we only went out one night last week."

She began to make the bed. Beds—for it was not one large bed, as it appeared to be in the daytime, but twin beds placed against each other with a king-sized cotton spread covering them both. When they were first married they slept in a three-quarter bed from his bachelor apartment. In time this became a double bed, hard as a rock because of the horsehair mattress. Then it also proved to be too small. For he developed twitches. While he was falling asleep his body beside her would suddenly flail out, shaking the bed and waking her completely. Six or seven times this would happen. After which he would descend at last into a deep sleep and she would be left with insomnia. So now there were twin beds, and even then her bed registered the seismic disturbances in his, though nothing like so much.

"We went to that benefit. With Francis," she said.

"Oh . . . I think I did wear my raincoat that night. No, I wore the coat with the velvet collar."

"The cleaner's?"

"No."

"I don't see how you could have left your raincoat somewhere," she said. "I never see you in just a suit. Other men, yes, but never you."

He went into the hall and pulled open a drawer of the lowboy and took out a pair of grey gloves and drew them on.

They had been his father's and they were good gloves but too small for him. His fingers had burst open the seams at the end of the fingers. Iris had mended them, but they would not stay sewed, and so he went to Brooks and bought a new pair—the pair he couldn't find.

"The Howards' dinner party?" he said.

"That was the week before. Don't worry about it," Iris said. "Cindy, what have you been doing?"—meaning hair full of snarls, teeth unbrushed, at twenty-five minutes past eight.

"It makes me feel queer not knowing where I've been," George said, and went out into the foyer and pressed the elevator button. From that moment, he was some other man. Their pictures were under his nose all day but he had stopped seeing them. He did not even remember that he had a family, until five o'clock, when he pushed his chair back from his desk, reached for his hat and coat, and came home, cheerfully unrepentant. She forgave him now because she did not want to deal with any failure, including his, until she had had her second cup of coffee. The coffee sat on the living-room mantelpiece, growing cold, while she brushed and braided Cindy's hair.

"Stand still! I'm not hurting you."

"You are too."

The arm would not go into the sweater, the leggings proved to be on backwards, one mitten was missing. And Laurie wild because she was going to be late for school.

The girls let the front door bang in spite of all that had been said on the subject, and in a moment the elevator doors opened to receive them. The quiet then was unbelievable. With the *Times* spread out on the coffee table in the living room, and holes in the Woman's Page where she had cut out recipes, she waited for her soul, which left her during the night, to return and take its place in her body. When this happened she got up suddenly and went into the bedroom and started telephoning: Bloomingdale's, Saks, the Maid-to-Order service, the children's school, the electrician, the pediatrician, the upholsterer—half the population of New York City.

Over the side of the bed Cindy went, eyes open, wide awake. In her woolly pajamas with feet in them. Even though it was dark outside—the middle of the night—it was only half dark in the bedroom. There was a blue night-light in the wall plug by the doll's house, and a green night-light in the bathroom, beside the washbasin, and the door to the bathroom was partly open. The door to the hall was wide open and the hall light was on, but high up where it wasn't much comfort, and she had to pass the closed door of Laurie's room and the closed door to the front hall. Behind both these doors the dark was very dark, unfriendly, ready to spring out and grab her, and she would much rather have been back in her bed except it was not safe there either, so she was going for help.

When she got to the door at the end of the hall, she stood still, afraid to knock and afraid not to knock. Afraid to look behind her. Hoping the door would open by itself and it did. Her father—huge, in his pajamas, with his hair sticking up and his face puffy with sleep. "Bad dream?" he asked.

Behind him the room was all dark except for a little light from the hall. She could see the big windows—just barely—and the great big bed, and her mother asleep under a mound of covers. And if she ran past him and got into the bed she would be safe, but it was not allowed. Only when she was sick. She turned and went back down the hall, without speaking but knowing that he would pick up his bathrobe and follow her and she didn't have to be brave anymore.

"What's Teddy doing on the floor?" he said, and pulled the covers up around her chin, and put his warm hand on her cheek. So nice to have him do this—to have him there, sitting on the edge of her bed.

"Can you tell me what you were dreaming about?"

"Tiger."

"Yes? Well, that's too bad. Were you very frightened?"

"Yes."

"Was it a big tiger?"

"Yes."

"You know it was only a dream? It wasn't a real tiger. There aren't any tigers in New York City."

"In the zoo there are."

"Oh yes, but they're in cages and can't get out. Was this tiger out?"

"Yes."

"Then it couldn't have been a real tiger. Turn over and let me rub your back."

"If you rub my back I'll go to sleep."

"Good idea."

"If I go to sleep I'll dream about the tiger."

"I see. What do you want me to do?"

"Get in bed with me."

What with Teddy and Raggedy Ann and Baby Dear, and books to look at in the morning, and the big pillow and the little pillow, things were a bit crowded. He put his hand over his eyes to shut out the hall light and said, "Go to sleep," but she didn't, even though she was beginning to feel drowsy. She was afraid he was going to leave her—if not right this minute then pretty soon. He would sit up in bed and say *Are you all right now?* and she would have to say *Yes*, because that was what he wanted her to say. Sometimes she said no and they stayed a little longer, but they always went away in the end.

After a while, her eyes closed. After still another while, she felt the bed heave under her as he sat up. He got out of bed slowly and carefully and fixed the covers and put the little red chair by the bed so she wouldn't fall out. She tried to say *Don't go*, but nothing happened. The floorboards creaked under the carpeting as he crossed the room. In the doorway he turned and looked at her, one last look, and she opened her eyes wide so he would know she wasn't asleep, and he waved her a kiss, and that was the last of him, but it wasn't the last of her. Pretty soon, even though there wasn't a sound, she knew something was in the room. Hiding. It was either hiding behind the curtains or it was hiding in the toy closet or it was hiding behind the doll's house or it was behind the bathroom door or it was under the bed. But wherever it was it was being absolutely still, waiting for her to close her eyes and go to sleep. So she kept them open, even though her eyelids got heavier and heavier. She made them stay open. And when they closed she opened them again right afterward. She kept opening them as long as she could, and once she cried out *Laurie!* very loud, but in her mind only. There was no sound in the room.

The thing that was hiding didn't make any sound either, which made her think maybe it wasn't a tiger after all, because tigers have a terrible roar that they roar, but it couldn't have been anything else, for it had stripes and a tail and terrible teeth and eyes that were looking at her through the back of the little red chair. And her heart was pounding and the tiger knew this, and the only friend she had in the world was Teddy, and Teddy couldn't move, and neither could Raggy, and neither could she. But the tiger could move. He could do anything he wanted to except roar his terrible roar, because then the bedroom door would fly open and they would come running.

She looked at the tiger through the back of the little red chair, and the tiger looked at her, and finally it thrashed its tail once or twice and then went and put its head in the air conditioner.

That isn't possible. . . . But it was. More and more of his body disappeared into the air conditioner, and finally there was only his tail, and then only the tip of his tail, and when that was gone so was she.

The young policeman who stood all night on the corner of East End Avenue and Gracie Square, eight stories below, was at the phone box, having a conversation with the sergeant on the desk. This did not prevent him from keeping his eyes on an emaciated junkie who stood peering through the window of the drugstore, past the ice-cream bin, the revolving display of paperbacks, the plastic toys, hair sprays, hand creams, cleansing lotions, etc., at the prescription counter. The door had a grating over it but the plate-glass window did not. One good kick would do it. It would also bring the policeman running.

The policeman would have been happy to turn the junkie in, but he didn't have anything on him. Vagrancy? But suppose he had a home? And suppose it brought the Civil Liberties Union running? The policeman turned his back for a minute and when he looked again the junkie was gone, vanished, nowhere.

Though it was between three and four in the morning, people were walking their dogs in Carl Schurz Park. Amazing. Dreamlike. And the sign on the farther shore of the river that changed back and forth continually was enough to unhinge the mind: PEARLWICK HAMPERS, became BATHROOM HAMPERS, which in turn became PEARLWICK HAMPERS, and sometimes for a fraction of a second BATHWICK HAMPERS.

In the metal trash containers scattered here and there along the winding paths of the park were pieces of waxed paper that had been around food but nothing you could actually eat. The junkie didn't go into the playground because the gates were locked and it had a high iron fence around it. He could have managed this easily by climbing a tree and dropping to the cement on the other side. Small boys did it all the time. And maybe in there he would have found something—a half-eaten Milky Way or Mounds bar that a nursemaid had taken from a child with a finicky appetite—but then he would have been locked in instead of out, and he knew all there was to know about that: Rikers Island, Sing Sing, Auburn, Dannemora. His name is James Jackson, and he is a figure out of a nightmare— unless you happen to know what happened to him, the steady rain of blows about his unprotected head ever since he was born, in which case it is human life that seems like a nightmare. The dog walkers, supposing—correctly—that he had a switch-blade in his pocket and a certain amount of experience in using it, chose a path that detoured around him. The wind was out of the southeast and smelled of the sea, fifteen miles away on the other side of Long Beach and Far Rockaway. The Hell Gate section of the Triborough Bridge was a necklace of sickly-green incandescent pearls. When the policeman left his post and took a turn through the south end of the park, the junkie was sitting innocently on a bench on the river walk. He was keeping the river company.

And when the policeman got back to his post a woman in a long red coat was going through the trash basket directly across the street from him. She was harmless. He saw her night after night. And in a minute she would cross over and tell him about the doctor at Bellevue who said she probably dreamed that somebody picked the lock of her door while she was out buying coffee and stole her mother's gold thimble.

The threads that bound the woman in the long red coat to a particular address, to the family she had been born into, her husband's grave in the Brooklyn cemetery, and the children who never wrote except to ask for money, had broken, and she was now free to wander along the street, scavenging from trash containers. She did not mind if people saw her, or feel that what she was doing was in any way exceptional. When she

found something useful or valuable, she stuffed it in her
dirty canvas bag, the richer by a pair of sandals with a broken
strap or a perfectly clean copy of *Sartor Resartus*. What in the
beginning was only an uncertainty, an uneasiness, a sense of
the falsity of appearances, a suspicion that the completely
friendly world she lived in was in fact secretly mocking and
hostile, had proved to be true. Or rather, had become true—for
it wasn't always. And meanwhile, in her mind, she was perpetually composing a statement for her own use and understanding, that would cover this situation.

Three colored lights passed overhead, very high up and in a
cluster, blinking. There were also lights strung through the
park at intervals, and on East End Avenue, where taxicabs
cruised up and down with their roof-lights on. Nobody wanted
them. As if they had never in their life shot through a red light,
the taxis stopped at Eighty-third Street, and again at Eighty-
fourth, and went on when the light turned green. East End
Avenue was as quiet as the grave. So were the side streets.

With the first hint of morning, this beautiful quiet came to
an end. Stopping and starting, making a noise like an electric
toaster, a Department of Sanitation truck made its way down
Eighty-fourth Street, murdering sleep. Crash. Tinkle. More
grinding. Bump. Thump. Voices. A brief silence and then the
whole thing started up again farther down the street. This was
followed by other noises—a parked car being warmed up, a
maniac in a sports car with no muffler. And then suddenly it
was the policeman's turn to be gone. A squad car drove by,
with the car radio playing an old Bing Crosby song, and picked
him up.

Biding his time, the junkie managed to slip past the service
entrance of one of the apartment buildings on East End Avenue without being seen. Around in back he saw an open
window on the ground floor with no bars over it. On the other
hand he didn't know who or what he would find when he
climbed through it, and he shouldn't have waited till morning.
He stood flattened against a brick wall while a handyman took
in the empty garbage cans. The sound of retreating footsteps
died away. The door to the service entrance was wide open. In
a matter of seconds James Jackson was in and out again,

wheeling a new ten-speed Peugeot. He straddled the bicycle as if he and not the overweight insurance broker in 7E had paid good money for it, and rode off down the street.

"'Cloudy with rain or showers . . .' Cindy, did you know you dreamt about a tiger last night?"

"Cindy dreamt about a tiger?" Iris said.

"Yes. What happened after I left?"

"Nothing."

"Congratulations. I dreamt the air conditioner in our room broke and we couldn't get anybody to come and fix it."

"Is it broken?" Iris asked.

"I don't know. We'll have to wait till next summer to find out."

"Good morning, Laurie. Good morning, Cindy," Jimmy the daytime elevator man said cheerfully. No answer. But no rudeness intended either. They did not know they were in the elevator.

The red-haired doorman at No. 7 Gracie Square stretched out his arms and pretended he was going to capture Cindy. This happened morning after morning, and she put up with it patiently.

"Taxi!" people wailed. "*Taxi!*" But there were no taxis. Or if one came along there was somebody in it. The doorman of No. 10 stood in the middle of East End Avenue and blew his whistle at nothing. On a balcony five stories above the street, a man lying on his back with his hips in the air was being put through his morning exercises by a Swedish masseur. The tired middle-aged legs went up and down like pistons. Like pistons, the elevators rose and fell in all the buildings overlooking the park, bringing the maids and laundresses up, taking men with briefcases down. The stationery store and the cleaners were now open. So was the luncheonette.

The two little girls stopped, took each other by the hand, and looked carefully both ways before they crossed the car tunnel at No. 10. On the river walk Laurie saw an acquaintance and ran on ahead. Poor Cindy! At her back was the park—very agreeable to play in when she went there with her mother or the kindergarten class, but also frequented by rough boys with water pistols and full of bushes it could be hiding in—and on her right was the deep pit alongside No. 10; it could be down there, below the sidewalk and waiting to spring out when she came along. She did not look to see if it was there but kept well over to the other side, next to the outer railing and the river. A tug with four empty barges was nosing its way upstream. The Simpsons' cook waved to Cindy from their kitchen window, which looked out on the river walk, and Cindy waved back.

In the days when George used to take Laurie to kindergarten because she was too small to walk to school by herself, he had noticed her—a big woman with blond braids in a crown around her head. And one day he said, "Shall we wave to her and see what happens?" Sometimes her back was turned to the window and she didn't know that Cindy and Laurie were there. They did not ever think of her except when they saw her, and if they had met her face to face she would have had to do all the talking.

Laurie was waiting at the Eighty-third Street gate. "Come on," she said.

"Stupid-head," Cindy said.

They went into the school building together, ignoring the big girls in camel's-hair coats who held the door open for them. But it wasn't like Jimmy the elevator man; they knew the big girls were there.

Sitting on the floor of her cubby, with her gym sneakers under her bottom and her cheek against her green plaid coat, Cindy felt safe. But Miss Nichols kept trying to get her to come out. The sandbox, the blocks, the crayons—Cindy said no to them all, and sucked her thumb. So Miss Nichols sat down on a little chair and took Cindy on her lap.

"If there was a (   )?" Cindy asked finally.

In a soft coaxing voice Miss Nichols said, "If there was a what?"

Cindy wouldn't say what.

The fire engines raced down Eighty-sixth Street, sirens shrieking and horns blowing, swung south through a red light, and came to a stop by the alarm box on the corner of East End Avenue and Gracie Square. The firemen jumped down and stood talking in the middle of the street. The hoses remained neatly folded and the ladders horizontal. It was the second false alarm that night from this same box. A county fair wouldn't have made more commotion under their windows but it had happened too often and George and Iris Carrington went on sleeping peacefully, flat on their backs, like stone figures on a medieval tomb.

In the trash basket on the corner by the park gates there was a copy of the *Daily News* which said, in big letters, "TIGER ESCAPES," but that was a different tiger; that tiger escaped from a circus in Jamestown, Rhode Island.

"What *is* it?" Iris asked, in the flower shop. "Why are you pulling at my skirt?"

The flower-shop woman (pink-blond hair, Viennese accent) offered Cindy a green carnation, and she refused to take it. "You don't like flowers?" the woman asked, coyly, and the tiger kept on looking at Cindy from behind some big, wide rubbery green leaves. "She's shy," the flower-shop woman said.

"Not usually," Iris said. "I don't know what's got into her today."

She gave the woman some money, and the woman gave her some money and some flowers, and then she and Cindy went outside, but Cindy was afraid to look behind her. If the tiger was following them, it was better not to know. For half a block she had a tingling sensation in the center of her back, between her shoulder blades. But then, looking across the street, she saw that the tiger was not back there in the flower shop. It must have left when they did, and now it was looking at her from the round hole in a cement mixer.

The lights changed from red to green, and Iris took her hand and started to cross over.

"I want to go that way," Cindy said, holding back, until the light changed again. Since she was never allowed on the street alone, she was not really afraid of meeting the tiger all by herself. But what if some day it should walk into the elevator when Jimmy wasn't looking, and get off at their floor, and hide behind Laurie's bicycle and the scooters. And what if the front door opened and somebody came out and pressed the

elevator button and the tiger got inside when they weren't
looking. And what if—

"Oh, please don't hold back, Cindy! I'm late as anything!"

So, dangerous as it was, she allowed herself to be hurried
along home.

Tap, tap, tap . . .

In the night this was, just after Iris and George had got to
sleep.

"Oh, no!" Iris moaned.

But it was. When he opened the door, there she stood.

Tap, tap . . .

That same night, two hours later. Sound asleep but able to
walk and talk, he put on his bathrobe and followed her down
the hall. Stretched out beside her, he tried to go on sleeping
but he couldn't. He said, "What were you dreaming about this
time?"

"Sea-things."

"What kind of seethings?"

"Sea-things under the sea."

"Things that wiggled?"

"Yes."

"Something was after you?"

"Yes."

"Too bad. Go to sleep."

Tap, tap . . .

This time as he heaved himself up, Iris said to him, "*You* lie
still."

She got up and opened the door to the hall and said,
"Cindy, we're tired and we need our sleep. I want you to go
back to your bed and stay there."

Then they both lay awake, listening to the silence at the
other end of the hall.

"I came out of the building," Iris said, "and I had three letters
that Jimmy had given me, and it was raining hard, and the
wind whipped them right out of my hand."

He took a sip of his drink and then said, "Did you get them?"

"I got two of them. One was from the Richards children, thanking me for the toys I sent when Lonnie was in the hospital. And one was a note from Mrs. Mills. I never did find the third. It was a small envelope, and the handwriting was Society."

"A birthday party for Cindy."

"No. It was addressed to Mr. and Mrs. George Carrington. Cocktail party, probably."

He glanced at the windows. It was already dark. Then, the eternal optimist (also remembering the time he found the button that flew off her coat and rolled under a parked car on Eighty-fifth Street): "Which way did it blow? I'll look for it tomorrow."

"Oh, there's no use. You can see by the others. They were reduced to pulp by the rain, in just that minute. And anyway, I did look, this afternoon."

In the morning, he took the Seventy-ninth Street crosstown bus instead of the Eighty-sixth, so that he could look for the invitation that blew away. No luck. The invitation had already passed through a furnace in the Department of Sanitation building on Ninety-first Street and now, in the form of ashes, was floating down the East River on a garbage scow, on its way out to sea.

The sender, rebuffed in this first tentative effort to get to know the Carringtons better, did not try again. She had met them at a dinner party, and liked them both. She was old enough to be Iris's mother, and it puzzled her that a young woman who seemed to be well bred and was quite lovely looking and adored *Middlemarch* should turn out to have no manners, but she didn't brood about it. New York is full of pleasant young couples, and if one chooses to ignore your invitation the chances are another won't.

"Did you hear Laurie in the night?" Iris said.

"No. Did Laurie have a nightmare?"

"Yes. I thought you were awake."

"I don't think so."

He got up out of bed and went into the children's rooms

and turned on the radiators so they wouldn't catch cold. Laurie was sitting up in bed reading.

"Mommy says you had a bad dream last night."

"There were three dreams," she said, in an overdistinct voice, as if she were a grown woman at a committee meeting. "The first dream was about Miss Stevenson. I dreamed she wasn't nice to me. She was like the wicked witch."

"Miss Stevenson loves you."

"And the second dream was about snakes. They were all over the floor. It was like a rug made up of snakes, and very icky, and there was a giant, and Cathy and I were against him, and he was trying to shut me in the room where the snakes were, and one of the snakes bit me, but he wasn't the kind of snake that kills you, he was just a mean snake, and so it didn't hurt. And the third dream was a happy dream. I was with Cathy and we were skating together and pulling our mommies by strings."

With his safety razor ready to begin a downward sweep, George Carrington studied the lathered face in the mirror of the medicine cabinet. He shook his head. There was a fatal flaw in his character: Nobody was ever as real to him as he was to himself. If people knew how little he cared whether they lived or died, they wouldn't want to have anything to do with him.

The dog moved back and forth between the two ends of the apartment, on good terms with everybody. She was in the dining room at mealtimes, and in the kitchen when Iris was getting dinner (when quite often something tasty fell off the edge of the kitchen table), and she was there again just after dinner, in case the plates were put on the floor for her to lick before they went into the dishwasher. In the late afternoon, for an hour before it was time for her can of beef-and-beef-byproducts, she sat with her front paws crossed, facing the kitchen clock, a reminding statue. After she had been fed, she went to the living room and lay down before the unlit log fire in the fireplace and slept until bedtime. In the morning, she followed Iris back and forth through room after room, until Iris was dressed and ready to take her out. "Must you nag me so?"

Iris cried, but the dog was not intimidated. There was something they were in agreement about, though only one of them could have put it in words: It is a crime against Nature to keep a hunting dog in the city. George sometimes gave her a slap on her haunches when she picked up food in the gutter or lunged at another dog. And if she jerked on her leash he jerked back, harder. But with Iris she could do anything—she could even stand under the canopy and refuse to go anywhere because it was raining.

Walking by the river, below Eightieth Street, it wasn't necessary to keep her on a leash, and while Iris went on ahead Puppy sniffed at the godforsaken grass and weeds that grew between the cement walk and the East River Drive. Then she overtook Iris, at full speed, overshot the mark, and came charging back, showing her teeth in a grin. Three or four times she did this, as a rule—with Iris applauding and congratulating her and cheering her on. It may be a crime against Nature to keep a hunting dog in the city, but this one was happy anyway.

After a series of dreams in which people started out as one person and ended up another and he found that there was no provision for getting from where he was to where he wanted to go and it grew later and later and even after the boat had left he still went on packing his clothes and what he thought was his topcoat turned out to belong to a friend he had not seen for seventeen years and naked strangers came and went, he woke and thought he heard a soft tapping on the bedroom door. But when he got up and opened it there was no one there.

"Was that Cindy?" Iris asked as he got back into bed.

"No. I thought I heard her, but I must have imagined it."

"I thought I heard her too," Iris said, and turned over.

At breakfast he said, "Did you have any bad dreams last night?" but Cindy was making a lake in the middle of her oatmeal and didn't answer.

"I thought I heard you tapping on our door," he said. "You didn't dream about a wolf, or a tiger, or a big black dog?"

"I don't remember," she said.

"You'll never guess what I just saw from the bedroom window," Iris said.

He put down his book.

"A police wagon drove down Eighty-fourth Street and stopped, and two policemen with guns got out and went into a building and didn't come out. And after a long while two more policemen came and *they* went into the building and pretty soon they all came out with a big man with black hair, handcuffed. Right there on Eighty-fourth Street, two doors from the corner."

"Nice neighborhood we live in," he said.

"Daddy, Daddy, Daddy, Daddy!" came into his dreams without waking him, and what did wake him was the heaving of the other bed as Iris got up and hurried toward the bedroom door.

"It was Cindy," she said when she came back.

"Dream?" he asked.

"Yes."

"I heard her but went on dreaming myself."

"She doesn't usually cry out like that."

"Laurie used to."

Why all these dreams, he wondered, and drifted gently back to sleep, as if he already knew the answer. She turned and turned, and finally, after three-quarters of an hour, got up and filled the hot-water bottle. What for days had been merely a half-formed thought in the back of her mind was now suddenly, in the middle of the night, making her rigid with anxiety. She needed to talk, and couldn't bring herself to wake him. What she wanted to say was they were making a mistake in bringing the children up in New York City. Or even in America. There was too much that there was no way to protect them from, and the only sensible thing would be to pull up stakes now, before Laurie reached adolescence. They could sublet the apartment until the lease ran out, and take a house somewhere in the South of France, near Aix perhaps, and the children could go to a French school, and they could all go skiing in Switzerland in the winter, and Cindy could have her own horse, and they both would acquire a good French accent, and be allowed to grow up slowly, in the ordinary way, and not be jaded by one premature experience after another, before they were old enough to understand any of it.

With the warmth at her back, and the comforting feeling that she had found the hole in the net, gradually she fell asleep too.

But when she brought the matter up two days later he looked at her blankly. He did not oppose her idea but neither did he accept it, and so her hands were tied.

As usual, the fathers' part in the Christmas program had to be rehearsed beforehand. In the small practice room on the sixth floor of the school, their masculinity—their grey flannel or dark-blue pin-striped suits, their size 9, 10, 11, 11½, and 12 shoes, their gold cufflinks, the odor that emanated from their bodies and from their freshly shaved cheeks, their simple assurance, based on, among other things, the *Social Register* and the size of their income—was incongruous. They were handed sheets of music as they came in, and the room was crammed with folding chairs, all facing the ancient grand piano. With the two tall windows at their backs they were missing the snow, which was a pity. It went up, down, diagonally, and in centrifugal motion—all at once. The fact that no two of the star-shaped crystals were the same was a miracle, of course, but it was a miracle that everybody has long since grown accustomed to. The light outside the windows was cold and grey.

"Since there aren't very many of you," the music teacher said, "you'll have to make up for it by singing enthusiastically." She was young, in her late twenties, and had difficulty keeping discipline in the classroom; the girls took advantage of her good nature, and never stopped talking and gave her their complete attention. She sat down at the piano now and played the opening bars of "O come, O come, Emmanuel / And ransom captive I-i-i-zrah-el . . ."

Somebody in the second row exclaimed, "Oh God!" under his breath. The music was set too high for men's voices.

"The girls will sing the first stanza, you fathers the second—"

The door opened and two more fathers came in.

"—and all will sing the third."

With help from the piano (which they would not have downstairs in the school auditorium) they achieved an approximation of the tune, and the emphasis sometimes fell in the right place. They did their best, but the nineteenth-century words and the ninth-century plainsong did not go well together. Also, one of the fathers had a good strong clear voice, which only made the others more self-conscious and apologetic. They would have been happier without him.

The music teacher made a flip remark. They all laughed and began again. Their number was added to continually as the door opened and let in the sounds from the hall. Soon there were no more vacant chairs; the latecomers had to stand. The snow was now noticeably heavier, and the singing had more volume. Though they were at some pains to convey, by their remarks to one another and their easy laughter, that this was not an occasion to be taken seriously, nevertheless the fact that they were here was proof of the contrary; they all had offices where they should have been and salaries they were not at this moment doing anything to earn. Twenty-seven men with, at first glance, a look of sameness about them, a round, composite, youngish, unrevealing, New York face. Under closer inspection, this broke down. Not all the eyes were blue, nor were the fathers all in their middle and late thirties. The thin-faced man at the end of the second row could not have been a broker or a lawyer or in advertising. The man next to him had survived incarceration in a Nazi prison camp. There was one Negro. Here and there a head that was not thickly covered with hair. Their speaking voices varied, but not so much as they conceivably might have—no Texas drawl, for instance. And all the fingernails were clean, all the shoes were shined, all the linen was fresh.

Each time they went over the hymn it was better. They clearly needed more rehearsing, but the music teacher glanced nervously at the clock and said, "And now 'In Dulci Jubilo.'"

Those who had forgotten their Latin, or never had any, eavesdropped on those who knew how the words should be pronounced. The tune was powerful and swept everything before it, and in a flush of pleasure they finished together, on the beat, loudly, making the room echo. They had forgotten about the telephone messages piling up on their desks beside the unopened mail. They were enjoying themselves. They could have gone on singing for another hour. Instead, they had to get up and file out of the room and crowd into the elevators.

In spite of new costumes, new scenery, different music,

and—naturally—a different cast, the Christmas play was always the same. Mary and Joseph proceeded to Bethlehem, where the inns were full, and found shelter in the merest suggestion of a stable. An immature angel announced to very unlikely shepherds the appearance of the Star. Wise Men came and knelt before the plastic Babe in Mary's arms. And then the finale: the Threes singing and dancing with heavenly joy.

"How did it sound?" George asked, in the crowd on the stairs.

"Fine," Iris said.

"Really? It didn't seem to me—maybe because we were under the balcony—it didn't seem as if we were making any sound at all."

"No, it was plenty loud enough. What was so nice was the two kinds of voices."

"High and low, you mean?"

"The fathers sounded like bears. Adorable."

In theory, since it was the middle of the night, it was dark, but not the total suffocating darkness of a cloudy night in the country. The city, as usual, gave off light—enough so that you could see the island in the middle of the river, and the three bridges, and the outlines of the little houses on East End Avenue and the big apartment buildings on Eighty-sixth Street, and the trees and shrubs and lampposts and comfort station in the park. Also a woman standing by the railing of the river walk.

There was no wind. The river was flowing north and the air smelled of snow, which melted the moment it touched any solid object, and became the shine on iron balustrades and on the bark of trees.

The woman had been standing there a long time, looking out over the water, when she began awkwardly to pull herself up and over the curved iron spikes that were designed, by their size and shape, to prevent people from throwing themselves into the river. In this instance they were not enough. But it took some doing. There was a long tear in the woman's coat and she was gasping for breath as she let herself go backward into space.

*

The sun enters Aquarius January 20th and remains until February 18th. *"An extremely good friend can today put into motion some operation that will be most helpful to your best interest, or else introduce you to some influential person. Go out socially in the evening on a grand scale. Be charming."*

The cocktail party was in a penthouse. The elevator opened into the foyer of the apartment. And the woman he was talking to—or rather, who was talking to him—was dressed all in shades of brown.

"I tried to get you last summer," she said, "but your wife said you were busy that day."

"Yes," he said.

"I'll try you again."

"Please do," somebody said for him, using his mouth and tongue and vocal cords—because it was the last thing in the world he wanted, to drive halfway across Long Island to a lunch party. "We hardly ever go anywhere," he himself said, but too late, after the damage had been done.

His mind wandered for an instant as he took in—not the room, for he was facing the wrong way, but a small corner of it. And in that instant he lost the thread of the story she was telling him. She had taken her shoe off in a movie theater and put her purse down beside it, and the next thing he knew they refused to do anything, even after she had explained what happened and that she must get in. Who "they" were, get in where, he patiently waited to find out, while politely sharing her indignation.

"But imagine!" she exclaimed. "They said, 'How valuable was the ring?'"

He shook his head, commiserating with her.

"I suppose if it hadn't been worth a certain amount," she went on, "they wouldn't have done a thing about it."

The police, surely, he thought. Having thought at first it was the manager of the movie theater she was talking about.

"And while they were jimmying the door open, people were walking by, and nobody showed the slightest concern. Or interest."

So it wasn't the police. But who was it, then? He never found out, because they were joined by another woman, who smiled at him in such a way as to suggest that they knew each other. But though he searched his mind and her face—the plucked eyebrows, the reserved expression in the middle-aged eyes—and considered her tweed suit and her diamond pin and her square figure, he could not imagine who she was. Suppose somebody—suppose Iris came up and he had to introduce her?

The purse was recovered, with the valuable ring still in it, and he found himself talking about something that had occupied his thoughts lately. And in his effort to say what he meant, he failed to notice what happened to the first woman. Suddenly she was not there. Somebody must have carried her off, right in front of his unseeing eyes.

". . . but it isn't really distinguishable from what goes on in dreams," he said to the woman who seemed to know him and to assume that he knew her. "People you have known for twenty or thirty years, you suddenly discover you didn't really know how they felt about you, and in fact you don't know how anybody feels about anything—only what they *say* they feel. And suppose that isn't true at all? You decide that it is better to act as if it is true. And so does everybody else. But it is a kind of myth you are living in, wide awake, with your eyes open, in broad daylight."

He realized that the conversation had become not only personal but intimate. But it was too late to back out now.

To his surprise she seemed to understand, to have felt what he had felt. "And one chooses," she said, "between this myth and that."

"Exactly! If you live in the city and are bringing up children, you decide that this thing is not safe—and so you don't let them do it—and that thing *is* safe. When, actually, neither one is safe and everything is equally dangerous. But for the sake of convenience—"

"And also so that you won't go out of your mind," she said.

"And so you won't go out of your mind," he agreed. "Well," he said after a moment, "that makes two of us who are thinking about it."

"In one way or another, people live by myths," she said.

He racked his brain for something further to say on this or any other subject.

Glancing around at the windows which went from floor to ceiling, the woman in the tweed suit said, "These vistas you have here."

He then looked and saw black night, with lighted buildings far below and many blocks away. "From our living room," he said, "you can see all the way to the North Pole."

"We live close to the ground," she said.

But where? Cambridge? Princeton? Philadelphia?

"In the human scale," he said. "Like London and Paris. Once, on a beautiful spring day, four of us—we'd been having lunch with a visiting Englishman who was interested in architecture—went searching for the sky. Up one street and down the next."

She smiled.

"We had to look for it, the sky is so far away in New York."

They stood nursing their drinks, and a woman came up to them who seemed to know her intimately, and the two women started talking and he turned away.

On her way into the school building, Laurie joined the flood from the school bus, and cried, "Hi, Janet . . . Hi, Connie . . . Hi, Elizabeth . . ." and seemed to be enveloped by her schoolmates, until suddenly, each girl having turned to some other girl, Laurie is left standing alone, her expression unchanged, still welcoming, but nobody having responded. If you collect reasons, this is the reason she behaved so badly at lunch, was impertinent to her mother, and hit her little sister.

He woke with a mild pain in his stomach. It was high up, like an ulcer pain, and he lay there worrying about it. When he heard the sound of shattered glass, his half-awake, oversensible mind supplied both the explanation and the details: Two men, putting a large framed picture into the trunk compartment of a parked car, had dropped it, breaking the glass. Too bad . . . And with that thought he drifted gently off to sleep.

In the morning he looked out of the bedroom window and saw three squad cars in front of the drugstore. The window of the drugstore had a big star-shaped hole in it, and several policemen were standing around looking at the broken glass on the sidewalk.

*

The sneeze was perfectly audible through two closed doors. He turned to Iris with a look of inquiry.

"Who sneezed? Was that you, Laurie?" she called.

"That was Cindy," Laurie said.

In principle, Iris would have liked to bring them up in a Spartan fashion, but both children caught cold easily and their colds were prolonged, and recurring, and overlapping, and endless. Whether they should or shouldn't be kept home from school took on the unsolvability of a moral dilemma—which George's worrying disposition did nothing to alleviate. The sound of a child coughing deep in the chest in the middle of the night would make him leap up out of a sound sleep.

She blamed herself when the children came down with a cold, and she blamed them. Possibly, also, the school was to blame, since the children played on the roof, twelve stories above the street, and up there the winds were often much rawer, and teachers cannot, of course, spend all their time going around buttoning up the coats of little girls who have got too hot from running.

She went and stood in the doorway of Cindy's room. "No sneezing," she said.

Sneeze, sneeze, sneeze.

"Cindy, if you are catching another cold, I'm going to shoot myself," Iris said, and gave her two baby-aspirin tablets to chew, and some Vitamin C drops, and put an extra blanket on her bed, and didn't open the window, and in the morning Cindy's nose was running.

"Shall I keep her home from school?" Iris asked, at the breakfast table.

Instead of answering, George got up and looked at the weather thermometer outside the west window of their bedroom. "Twenty-seven," he said, when he came back. But he still didn't answer her question. He was afraid to answer it, lest it be the wrong answer, and she blame him. Actually, there was no answer that was the right answer: They had tried sending Cindy to school and they had tried not sending her. This time, Iris kept her home from school—not because she thought it was going to make any difference but so the pediatrician, Dr.

de Santillo, wouldn't blame her. Not that he ever said anything. And Cindy got to play with Laurie's things all morning.
She played with Laurie's paper dolls until she was tired, and
left them all over the floor, and then she colored in Laurie's
coloring book, and Puppy chewed up one of the crayons but
not one of Laurie's favorites—not the pink or the blue—and
then Cindy rearranged the furniture in Laurie's doll house so
it was much nicer, and then she lined up all Laurie's dolls in a
row on her bed and played school. And when it was time for
Laurie to come home from school she went out to the kitchen
and played with the eggbeater. Laurie came in, letting the
front door slam behind her, and dropped her mittens in the
hall and her coat on the living-room rug and her knitted cap
on top of her coat, and started for her room, and it sounded as
if she had hurt herself. Iris came running. What a noise Laurie
made. And stamping her foot, Cindy noted disapprovingly.
And tears.

"Stop screaming and tell me what's the matter!" Iris said.
"Cindy, I hate you!" Laurie said. "I hate you, I hate you!"
Horrible old Laurie . . .

But in the morning when they first woke up it was different.
She heard Laurie in the bathroom, and then she heard Laurie
go back to her room. Lying in bed, Cindy couldn't suck her
thumb because she couldn't breathe through her nose, so she
got up and went into Laurie's room (entirely forgetting that
her mother had said that in the morning she was to stay out of
Laurie's room because she had a cold) and got in Laurie's bed
and said, "Read, read." Laurie read her the story of "The
Tinder Box," which has three dogs in it—a dog with eyes as
big as saucers, and a dog with eyes as big as millwheels, and a
third dog with eyes as big as the Round Tower of Copenhagen.

Tap, tap, tap on the bedroom door brought him entirely
awake. "What's Laurie been reading to her?" he asked, turning
over in bed. That meant it was Iris's turn to get up. While she
was pulling herself together, they heard *Tap, tap, tap* again.
The bed heaved.

"What's Laurie been reading to you?" she asked as she and
Cindy went off down the hall together. When she came back

into the bedroom, the light was on and he was standing in front of his dresser, with the top drawer open, searching for Gelusil tablets.

"Trouble?" she said.

Standing in the doorway of Cindy's room, in her blue dressing gown, with her hairbrush in her hand, Iris said, "Who sneezed? Was that you, Cindy?"

"That was Laurie," Cindy said.

So after that Laurie got to stay home from school too.

"I saw Phyllis Simpson in Gristede's supermarket," Iris said. "Their cook committed suicide."

"How?"

"She threw herself in the river."

"No!"

"They think she must have done it sometime during the night, but they don't know exactly when. They just came down to breakfast and she wasn't there. They're still upset about it."

"When did it happen?"

"About a month ago. Her body was found way down the river."

"What a pity. She was a nice woman."

"You remember her?"

"Certainly. She always waved to the children when I used to walk them to school. She waved to me too, sometimes. From the kitchen window. What made her do such a thing?"

"They have no idea."

"She was a big woman," he said. "It must have been hard for her to pull herself up over that railing. It's quite high. No note or anything?"

"No."

"Terrible."

On St. Valentine's Day, the young woman who lived on tea and cigarettes and was given to burning herself on the gas stove eloped to California with her mother, and now there was no one in the kitchen. From time to time, the employment agency went through the formality of sending someone for Iris to interview—though actually it was the other way round. And either the apartment was too large or they didn't care to work for a family with children or they were not accustomed to doing the cooking as well as the other housework. Sometimes they didn't give any reason at all.

A young woman from Haiti, who didn't speak English, was willing to give the job a try. It turned out that she had never seen a carpet sweeper before, and she asked for her money at the end of the day.

Walking the dog at seven-fifteen on a winter morning, he suddenly stopped and said to himself, "Oh God, somebody's been murdered!" On the high stone stoop of one of the little houses on East End Avenue facing the park. Somebody in a long red coat. By the curve of the hip he could tell it was a woman, and with his heart racing he considered what he ought to do. From where he stood on the sidewalk he couldn't see the upper part of her body. One foot—the bare heel and the strap of her shoe—was sticking out from under the hem of the coat. If she'd been murdered, wouldn't she be sprawled out in an awkward position instead of curled up and lying on her side as though she was in bed asleep? He looked up at the house. Had they locked her out? After a scene? Or she could have come home in the middle of the night and discovered that she'd forgotten to take her key. But in that case she'd have spent the night in a hotel or with a friend. Or called an all-night locksmith.

He went up three steps without managing to see any more than he had already. The parapet offered some shelter from the wind, but even so, how could she sleep on the cold stone, with nothing over her?

"Can I help you?"

His voice sounded strange and hollow. There was no answer. The red coat did not stir. Then he saw the canvas bag crammed with the fruit of her night's scavenging, and backed down the steps.

Now it was his turn. The sore throat was gone in the morning, but it came back during the day, and when he sat down to dinner he pulled the extension out at his end and moved his mat, silver, and glass farther away from the rest of them.

"If you aren't sneezing, I don't think you need to be in Iso-lation Corner," Iris said, but he stayed there anyway. His colds were prolonged and made worse by his efforts to treat them; made worse still by his trying occasionally to disregard them, as he saw other people doing. In the end he went through box after box of Kleenex, his nose white with Noxzema, his eyelids inflamed, like a man in a subway poster advertising a cold rem-edy that, as it turned out, did not work for him. And finally he took to his bed, with a transistor radio for amusement and company. In his childhood, being sick resulted in agreeable pampering, and now that he was grown he preferred to be both parties to this pleasure. No one could make him as com-fortable as he could make himself, and Iris had all but given up trying.

On a rainy Sunday afternoon in March, with every door in the school building locked and the corridor braced for the shock of Monday morning, the ancient piano demonstrated for the benefit of the empty practice room that it is one thing to fum-ble through the vocal line, guided by the chords that accom-pany it, and something else again to be genuinely musical, to know what the composer intended—the resolution of what cannot be left uncertain, the amorous flirtation of the treble and the bass, notes taking to the air like a flock of startled birds.

The faint clicking sounds given off by the telephone in the pantry meant that Iris was dialing on the extension in the mas-ter bedroom. And at last there was somebody in the Carring-tons' kitchen again—a black woman in her fifties. They were low on milk, and totally out of oatmeal, canned dog food, and coffee, but the memo pad that was magnetically attached to the side of the Frigidaire was blank. Writing down things they were out of was not something she considered part of her job. When an emergency arose, she put on her coat and went to the store, just as if she were still in North Carolina.

The sheet of paper that was attached to the clipboard hanging from a nail on the side of the kitchen cupboard had the menus for lunch and dinner all written out, but they were for yesterday's lunch and dinner. And though it was only nine-thirty, Bessie already felt a mounting indignation at being kept in ignorance about what most deeply concerned her. It was an old-fashioned apartment, with big rooms and high ceilings, and the kitchen was a considerable distance from the master bedroom; nevertheless, it was just barely possible for the two women to live there. Nature had designed them for mutual tormenting, the one with an exaggerated sense of time, always hurrying to meet a deadline that did not exist anywhere but in her own fancy, and calling upon the angels or whoever is in charge of amazing grace to take notice that she had put the food on the hot tray in the dining room at precisely one minute before the moment she had been told to have dinner ready; the other with not only a hatred of planning meals but also a childish reluctance to come to the table. When the minute hand of the electric clock in the kitchen arrived at seven or seven-fifteen or whatever, Bessie went into the dining room and announced in an inaudible voice that dinner was ready. Two rooms away, George heard her by extrasensory perception and leapt to his feet, and Iris, holding out her glass to him, said, "Am I not going to have a second vermouth?"

To his amazement, on Bessie's day off, having cooked dinner and put it on the hot plate, Iris drifted away to the front of the apartment and read a magazine, fixed her hair, God knows what, until he discovered the food sitting there and begged her to come to the table.

"They said they lived in Boys Town, and I thought Jimmy let them in because he's Irish and Catholic," Iris said. "There was nothing on the list I wanted, so I subscribed to *Vogue*, to help them out. When I spoke to Jimmy about it, he said he had no idea they were selling subscriptions, and he never lets solicitors get by him—not even nuns and priests. Much as he might want to. So I don't suppose it will come."

"It might," George said. "Maybe they were honest."

"He thought they were workmen because they asked for the eleventh floor. The tenants on the eleventh floor have moved out and Jimmy says the people who are moving in have a five years' lease and are spending fifty thousand dollars on the place, which they don't even *own*. But anyway, what they did was walk through the apartment and then down one floor and start ringing doorbells. The super took them down in the back elevator without asking what they were doing there, and off they went. They tried the same thing at No. 7 and the doorman threw them out."

Walking the dog before breakfast, if he went by the river walk he saw in the Simpsons' window a black-haired woman who did not wave to him or even look up when he passed. That particular section of the river walk was haunted by an act of despair that nobody had been given a chance to understand. Nothing that he could think of—cancer, thwarted love, melancholia—seemed to fit. He had only spoken to her once, when he and Iris went to a dinner party at the Simpsons' and she smiled at him as she was helping the maid clear the table between courses. If she didn't look up when he passed under her window it was as though he had been overtaken by a cloud shadow—until he forgot all about it, a few seconds later. But he could have stopped just once, and he hadn't. When the window was open he could have called out to her, even if it was only "Good morning," or "Isn't it a beautiful day?"

He could have said, *Don't do it. . . .*

Sometimes he came back by the little house on East End Avenue where he had seen the woman in the red coat. He invariably glanced up, half expecting her to be lying there on the stoop. If she wasn't there, where was she?

In the psychiatric ward of Bellevue Hospital was the answer. But not for long. She and the doctor got it straightened out about her mother's gold thimble, and he gave her a prescription and told her where to go in the building to have it filled, and hoped for the best—which, after all, is all that anybody has to hope for.

The weather thermometer blew away one stormy night and after a week or two George brought home a new one. It was round and encased in white plastic, and not meant to be screwed to the window frame but to be kept inside. It registered the temperature outside by means of a wire with what looked like a small bullet attached to the end of it. The directions said to drill a hole through the window frame, but George backed away from all that and, instead, hung the wire across the sill and closed the window on it. What the new thermometer said bore no relation to the actual temperature, and drilling the hole had a high priority on the list of things he meant to do.

There was also a racial barometer in the apartment that registered *Fair* or *Stormy*, according to whether Bessie had spent several days running in the apartment or had just come back from a weekend in her room in Harlem.

The laundress, so enormously fat that she had to maneuver her body around, as if she were the captain of an ocean liner, was a Muslim and hated all white people and most black people as well. She was never satisfied with the lunch Bessie cooked for her, and Bessie objected to having to get lunch for her, and the problem was solved temporarily by having her eat in the luncheonette across the street.

She quit. The new laundress was half the size of the old one, and sang alto in her church choir, and was good-tempered, and fussy about what she had for lunch. Bessie sometimes considered her a friend and sometimes an object of derision, because she believed in spirits.

So did Bessie, but not to the same extent or in the same way. Bessie's mother had appeared to her and her sister and brother, shortly after her death. They were quarreling together, and her mother's head and shoulders appeared up near the ceiling, and she said they were to love one another. And sometimes when Bessie was walking along the street she felt a coolness and knew that a spirit was beside her. But the laundress said, "All right, go ahead, then, if you want to," to the empty air and, since there wasn't room for both of them, let the spirit precede her through the pantry. She even knew who the spirit was.

It was now spring on the river, and the river walk was a Chinese scroll which could be unrolled, by people who like to do things in the usual way, from right to left—starting at Gracie Square and walking north. Depicted were:

A hockey game between Loyola and St. Francis de Sales
Five boys shooting baskets on the basketball court
A seagull

An old man sitting on a bench doing columns of figures

A child drawing a track for his toy trains on the pavement with a piece of chalk

A paper drinking cup floating on the troubled surface of the water

A child in pink rompers pushing his own stroller

A woman sitting on a bench alone, with her face lifted to the sun

A Puerto Rican boy with a transistor radio

Two middle-aged women speaking German

A bored and fretful baby, too hot in his perambulator, with nothing to look at or play with, while his nurse reads

The tugboat *Chicago* pulling a long string of empty barges upstream

A little girl feeding her mother an apple

A helicopter

A kindergarten class, in two sections

Clouds in a blue sky

A flowering cherry tree

Seven freight cars moving imperceptibly, against the tidal current, in the wake of the *Herbert E. Smith*

A man with a pipe in his mouth and a can of Prince Albert smoking tobacco on the bench beside him

A man sorting his possessions into two canvas bags, one of which contains a concertina

Six very small children playing in the sandpile, under the watchful eyes of their mothers or nursemaids

An oil tanker

A red-haired priest reading a pocket-size New Testament

A man scattering bread crumbs for the pigeons

The Coast Guard cutter *CG 40435* turning around just north of the lighthouse and heading back toward Hell Gate Bridge

A sweeper with his bag and a ferruled stick

A little boy pointing a red plastic pistol at his father's head

A pleasure yacht

An airplane

A man and a woman speaking French

A child on a tricycle

A boy on roller skates

A reception under a striped tent on the lawn of the mayor's house

The fireboat station

The Franklin Delano Roosevelt Drive, a cinder path, a warehouse, seagulls, and so on

Who said *Happiness is the light shining on the water. The water is cold and dark and deep. . . .*

"It's perfectly insane," George said when he met Iris coming from Gristede's with a big brown-paper bag heavy as lead under each arm and relieved her of them. "Don't we still have that cart?"

"Nobody in the building uses them."

"But couldn't you?"

"No," Iris said.

"All children," Cindy said wisely, leaning against him, with her head in the hollow of his neck, "all children think their mommy and daddy are the nicest."

"And what about you? Are you satisfied?"

She gave him a hug and a kiss and said, "I think you and Mommy are the nicest mommy and daddy in the whole world."

"And I think you are the nicest Cindy," he said, his eyes moist with tears.

They sat and rocked each other gently.

After Bessie had taken the breakfast dishes out of the dishwasher, she went into the front, dragging the vacuum cleaner, to do the children's rooms. She stood sometimes for five or ten minutes, looking down at East End Avenue—at the drugstore, the luncheonette, the rival cleaning establishments (side by side and, according to rumor, both owned by the same person), the hairstyling salon, and the branch office of the Chase Manhattan Bank. Together they made a canvas backdrop for a procession of people Bessie had never seen before, or would not recognize if she had, and so she couldn't say to herself, "There goes old Mrs. Maltby," but she looked anyway, she took it all in. The sight of other human beings nourished her mind. She read them as people read books. Pieces of toys, pieces of puzzles that she found on the floor she put on one shelf or another of the toy closet in Cindy's room, gradually introducing a disorder that Iris dealt with periodically, taking a whole day out of her life. But nobody told Bessie she was supposed to find the box the piece came out of, and it is questionable whether she could have anyway. The thickness of the lenses in her eyeglasses suggested that her eyesight was poorer than she let on.

She was an exile, far from home, among people who were not like the white people she knew and understood. She was here because down home she was getting forty dollars a week and she had her old age to think of. She and Iris alternated between irritation at one another and sudden acts of kindness. It was the situation that was at fault. Given halfway decent circumstances, men can work cheerfully and happily for other men, in offices, stores, and even factories. And so can women. But if Iris opened the cupboard or the icebox to see what they did or didn't contain, Bessie popped out of her room and said, "Did you want something?" And Iris withdrew, angry because she had been driven out of her own kitchen. In her mind, Bessie always thought of the Carringtons as "my people," but until she had taught them to think of themselves as her people her profound capacity for devotion would go unused; would not even be suspected.

You can say that life is a fountain if you want to, but what it more nearly resembles is a jack-in-the-box.

Half awake, he heard the soft whimpering that meant Iris was having a nightmare, and he shook her. "I dreamt you were having a heart attack," she said.

"Should you be dreaming that?" he said. But the dream was still too real to be joked about. They were in a public place. And he couldn't be moved. He didn't die, and she consulted with doctors. Though the dream did not progress, she could not extricate herself from it but went on and on, feeling the appropriate emotions but in a circular way. Till finally the sounds she made in her sleep brought about her deliverance.

*

The conversation at the other end of the hall continued steadily—not loud but enough to keep them from sleeping, and he had already spoken to the children once. So he got up and went down the hall. Laurie and Cindy were both in their bathroom, and Cindy was sitting on the toilet. "I have a stomach ache," she said.

He started to say, "You need to do bizz," and then remembered that the time before she had been sitting on the toilet doing just that.

"And I feel dizzy," Laurie said.

"I heard it," Iris said as he got back into bed.

"That's why she was so pale yesterday."

And half an hour later, when he got up again, Iris did too. To his surprise. Looking as if she had lost her last friend. So he took her in his arms.

"I hate everything," she said.

On the top shelf of his clothes closet he keeps all sorts of things—the overflow of phonograph records, and the photograph albums, which are too large for the bookcases in the living room. The snapshots show nothing but joy. Year after year of it.

On the stage of the school auditorium, girls from Class Eight, in pastel-colored costumes and holding arches of crepe-paper flowers, made a tunnel from the front of the stage to the rear right-hand corner. The pianist took her hands from the keys, and the headmistress, in sensible navy blue, with her hair cut short like a man's, announced, "Class B becomes Class One."

Twenty very little girls in white dresses marched up on the stage two by two, holding hands.

George and Iris Carrington turned to each other and smiled, for Cindy was among them, looking proud and happy as she hurried through the tunnel of flowers and out of sight.

"Class One becomes Class Two." Another wave of little girls left their place in the audience and went up on the stage and disappeared into the wings.

"Class Two becomes Class Three."

Laurie Carrington, her red hair shining from the hairbrush, rose from her seat with the others and started up on the stage.

"It's too much!" George said, under his breath.

Class Three became Class Four, Class Four became Class Five, Class Five became Class Six, and George Carrington took a handkerchief out of his right hip pocket and wiped his eyes. It was their eagerness that undid him. Their absolute trust in the Arrangements. Class Six became Class Seven, Class Seven became Class Eight. The generations of man, growing up, growing old, dying in order to make room for more.

"Class Eight becomes Class Nine, and is now in the Upper School," the headmistress said, triumphantly. The two girls at the front ducked and went under the arches, taking their crepe-paper flowers with them. And then the next two, and the next, and finally the audience was left applauding an empty stage.

"Come here and sit on my lap," he said, by no means sure Laurie would think it worth the trouble. But she came. Folding her onto his lap, he was aware of the length of her legs, and the difference of her body; the babyness had departed forever, and when he was affectionate with her it was always as if the moment were slightly out of focus; he felt a restraint. He worried lest it be too close to making love to her. The difference was not great, and he was not sure whether it existed at all.

"Would you like to hear a riddle?" she asked.

"All right."

"Who was the fastest runner in history?"

"I don't know," he said, smiling at her. "Who was?"

"Adam. He was the first in the human race. . . . Teehee-heeheehee, wasn't that a good one?"

Waking in the night, Cindy heard her mother and father laughing behind the closed door of their room. It was a sound she liked to hear, and she turned over and went right back to sleep.

"What was that?"

He raised his head from the pillow and listened.

"Somebody crying 'Help!'" Iris said.

He got up and went to the window. There was no one in the

street except a taxi driver brushing out the back seat of his hack. Again he heard it. Somebody being robbed. Or raped. Or murdered.

"Help . . ." Faintly this time. And not from the direction of the park. The taxi driver did not look up at the sound, which must be coming from inside a building somewhere. With his face to the window, George waited for the sound to come again and it didn't. Nothing but silence. If he called the police, what could he say? He got back into bed and lay there, sick with horror, his knees shaking. In the morning maybe the *Daily News* would have what happened.

But he forgot to buy a *News* on his way to work, and days passed, and he no longer was sure what night it was that they heard the voice crying "Help!" and felt that he ought to go through weeks of the *News* until he found out what happened. If it was in the *News*. And if something happened.

The Thistles in Sweden

THE brownstone is on Murray Hill, facing south. The year is 1950. We have the top floor-through, and our windows are not as tall as the windows on the lower floors. They are deeply recessed, and almost square, and have divided panes. I know that beauty is in the eye of the beholder and all that, but even so, these windows are romantic. The apartment could be in Leningrad or Innsbruck or Dresden (before the bombs fell on it) or Parma or any place we have never been to. When I come home at night, I look forward to the moment when I turn the corner and raise my eyes to those three lighted windows. Since I was a child, no place has been quite so much home to me. The front windows look out on Thirty-sixth Street, the back windows on an unpainted brick wall (the side of a house on Lexington Avenue) with no break in it on our floor, but on the floor below there is a single window with a potted plant, and when we raise our eyes we see the sky, so the room is neither dark nor prisonlike.

Since we are bothered by street noises, the sensible thing would be to use this room to sleep in, but it seems to want to be our living room, and offers two irresistible arguments: (1) a Victorian white marble fireplace and (2) a stairway. If we have a fireplace it should be in the living room, even though the chimney is blocked up, so we can't have a fire in it. (I spend a good deal of time unblocking it, in my mind.) The stairs are the only access to the roof for the whole building. There is, of course, nothing up there, but it looks as if we are in a house and you can go upstairs to bed, and this is very cozy: a house on the top floor of a brownstone walk-up. I draw the bolt and push the trapdoor up with my shoulder, and Margaret and I stand together, holding the cat, Floribunda, in our arms so she will not escape, and see the stars (when there are any) or the winking lights of an airplane, or sometimes a hallucinatory effect brought about by fog or very fine rain and mist—the lighted windows of midtown skyscrapers set in space, without any surrounding masonry. The living room and the bedroom both have a door opening onto the outer hall, which, since we are on the top floor and nobody else in the building uses it, we regard as part of the apartment. We leave these doors open when we are at home, and the stair railing and the head of the stairs are blocked off with huge pieces of cardboard. The landlord says that this is a violation of the fire laws, but we cannot think of any other way to keep Floribunda from escaping down the stairs, and neither can he.

The living-room curtains are of heavy Swedish linen: life-sized thistles, printed in light blue and charcoal grey, on a white background. They are very beautiful (and so must the thistles in Sweden be) and they also have an emotional context; Margaret made them, and, when they did not hang properly, wept, and ripped them apart and remade them, and now they do hang properly. The bedroom curtains are of a soft ivory material, with seashells—cowries, scallops, sea urchins and sand dollars, turbinates, auriculae—drawn on them in brown indelible ink, with a flowpen. The bedroom floor is black, the walls are sandalwood, the woodwork is white. On the wall above the double bed is a mural in two sections—a hexagonal tower in an imaginary kingdom that resembles Persia. Children are flying kites from the roof. Inside the tower, another child is playing on a musical instrument that is cousin to the lute. The paperhanger hung the panels the wrong way, so the tower is even stranger architecturally than the artist intended. The parapet encloses outer instead of inner space—like a man talking to somebody who is standing behind him, facing the other way. And the fish-shaped kite, where is that being flown from? And by whom? Some other children are flying kites from the roof of the tower next to this one, perhaps, only there wasn't room to show it. (Lying in bed I often, in my mind, correct the paperhanger's mistake.) Next to the mural there is a projection made by a chimney that conducts sounds from the house next door. Or rather, a single sound: a baby crying in the night. The brownstone next door is not divided into apartments, and so much money has been spent on the outside (blue shutters, fresh paint, stucco, polished brass, etc.) that, for this neighborhood, the effect of chic is overdone. We assume there is a nurse, but nobody ever does anything when the baby cries, and the sound that comes through the wall is unbearably sad. (Unable to stand it any longer,

Margaret gets up and goes through the brick chimney and picks the baby up and brings it back into our bedroom and rocks it.)

The double chest of drawers came from Macy's unfinished-furniture department, and Margaret gave it nine coats of enamel before she was satisfied with the way it looked. The black lacquered dining table (we have two dining tables and no dining room) is used as a desk. Over it hangs a large engraving of the Spanish Steps, which, two years ago, in the summer of 1948, for a brief time belonged to us—flower stands, big umbrellas, Bernini fountain, English Tea Room, Keats museum, children with no conception of bedtime, everything. At night we drape our clothes over two cheap rush-bottom chairs, from Italy. The mahogany dressing table, with an oval mirror in a lyre-shaped frame and turned legs such as one sees in English furniture of the late seventeenth century, came by express from the West Coast. The express company delivered it to the sidewalk in front of the building, and, notified by telephone that this was about to happen, I rushed home from the office to supervise the uncrating. As I stepped from the taxi, I saw the expressman with the mirror and half the lyre in his huge hands. He was looking at it thoughtfully. The rest of the dressing table was ten feet away, by the entrance to the building. The break does not show unless you look closely. And most old furniture has been mended at one time or another.

When we were shown the apartment for the first time, the outgoing tenant let us in and stood by pleasantly while we tried to imagine what the place would look like if it were not so crowded with his furniture. It was hardly possible to take a step for oak tables and chests and sofas and armoires and armchairs. Those ancestral portraits and Italian landscapes in heavy gilt frames that there was no room for on the walls were leaning against the furniture. To get from one room to the next we had to step over pyramids of books and scientific journals. An inventory of the miscellaneous objects and musical instruments in the living room would have taken days and been full of surprises. (Why did he keep that large soup tureen on the floor?) We thought at first he was packing, but he was not; this was the way he lived. If we had asked him to make a place in his life for us too, he would have. He was a very nice man. The disorder was dignified and somehow enviable, and the over-furnished apartment so remote from what went on down below in the street that it was like a cave deep in the forest.

Now it is underfurnished (we have just barely enough money to manage a small one-story house in the country and this apartment in town), instead, and all light and air. The living-room walls are a pale blue that changes according to the light and the time of day and the season of the year and the color of the sky. The walls are hardly there. The furniture is half old and half new, and there isn't much of it, considering the size of the room: a box couch, a cabinet with sliding doors, a small painted bookcase, an easy chair with its ottoman, a round fruitwood side table with long, thin, spidery legs and a glass tray that fits over the top, the table and chairs we eat on, a lowboy that serves as a sideboard, another chair, a wobbly tea cart, and a canvas stool. The couch has a high wooden back, L-shaped, painted black, with a thin gold line. It was made for an old house in Dover, New Hampshire, and after I don't know how many generations found itself in Minneapolis. I first saw it in Margaret's mother's bedroom in Seattle, and now it is here. It took two big men and a lot of patient maneuvering to get it four times past the turning of the stairs. The shawl that is draped over the back and the large tin tray that serves as a cof-fee table both came from Mexico—a country I do not regard as romantic, even though we have never been there. The low-boy made the trip from the West Coast with the dressing table, and one of its Chippendale legs got broken in transit, or by that same impetuous expressman. I suppose it is a hundred and fifty or two hundred years old. The man in the furniture-repair shop, after considering the broken leg, asked if we wanted the lowboy refinished. I asked why, and he said, "Because it's been painted." We looked, and sure enough it had. "They did that sometimes," he said. "It's painted to sim-ulate mahogany." I asked what was under the paint, and he picked up a chisel and took a delicate gouge out of the under-side. This time it was his turn to be surprised. "It's mahog-any," he announced. The lowboy was painted to simulate what it actually was, it looks like what it is, so we let it be.

The gateleg table we eat on has four legs instead of the usual six. When the sides are extended, it looks as if the cabinet-maker had been studying Euclid's geometry. Margaret found it in an antique shop in Putnam Valley, and asked me to come look at it. I got out of the car and went in and saw the table and knew I could not live without it. The antique dealer said the table had an interesting history that she wasn't free to tell us. (Was it a real Hepplewhite and not just in the style of? Was it stolen?) She was a very old woman and lived alone. The shop was lined with bookshelves, and the books on the shelves and lying around on the tables were so uncommon I had trouble keeping my hands off them. They were not for sale, the old woman said. They had belonged to her husband, and she was keeping them for her grandchildren; she herself read nothing but murder mysteries.

Margaret wanted the table, but she wanted also to talk about whether or not we could afford it. I can always afford what I dearly want—or rather, when I want something very much I would rather not think about whether or not we can afford it. As we drove away without the table, I said coldly, "We won't talk about it." As if she were the kind of wife she isn't. And we did talk about it, all the way home. The next day we were back, nobody had bought the table in the meantime, I wrote out a check for two hundred dollars, and the old woman gave us a big rag rug to wrap around the marvel so it wouldn't be damaged on the drive home. Also heavy twine to tie it with. But then I asked for a knife, and this upset her, to my astonishment. I looked carefully and saw that the expression in her faded blue eyes was terror: She thought I wanted a knife so I could murder her and make off with the table *and* the check. It is disquieting to have one's intentions so misjudged. (Am I a murderer? And is it usual for the murderer to ask for his weapon?) "A pair of scissors will do just as well," I said, and the color came back into her face.

The rug the table now stands on is only slightly larger than the tabletop. It is threadbare, but we cannot find another like it. For some reason, it is the last yellowish beige rug ever made. People with no children have perfectionism to fall back on.

The space between the fireplace and the door to the kitchen is filled by shelves and a shallow cupboard. The tea cart is kept under the stairs. Then comes the door to the coat closet, the inside of which is painted a particularly beautiful shade of Chinese red, and the door to the hall. On the sliding-door cabinet (we have turned the corner now and are moving toward the windows) there is a pottery lamp with a wide perforated grey paper shade and such a long thin neck that it seems to be trying to turn into a crane. Also a record player that plays only 78s and has to be wound after every record. The oil painting over the couch is of a rock quarry in Maine, and we have discovered that it changes according to the time of day and the color of the sky. It is particularly alive after a snowfall.

Here we live, in our modest perfectionism, with two black cats. The one on the mantelpiece is Bastet, the Egyptian goddess of love and joy. The other is under the impression that she is our child. This is our fault, of course, not hers. Around her neck she wears a scarlet ribbon, or sometimes a turquoise ribbon, or a collar with little bells. Her toys dangle from the tea cart, her kitty litter is in a pan beside the bathtub, and she sleeps on the foot of our bed or curled against the back of Margaret's knees. When she is bored she asks us to remove a piece of the cardboard barricade so she can go tippeting down the stairs and pay a call on the landlord and his wife, Mr. and Mrs. Holmes, who live in the garden apartment and have the rear half of the second floor, with an inside stairs, so they really do go upstairs to bed. The front part of the second floor is the pied-à-terre of the artist who designed the wallpaper mural of the children flying kites from a hexagonal tower in an imaginary kingdom that resembles Persia. It is through the artist's influence (Mr. Holmes is intimidated by her) that we managed to get our rent-controlled apartment, for which we pay a hundred and thirteen dollars and some odd cents. The landlord wishes we paid more, and Mr. and Mrs. Venable, who live under us, wish we'd get a larger rug for the living room. Their bedroom is on the back, and Margaret's heels crossing the ceiling at night keep them awake. Also, in the early morning the Egyptian goddess leaves our bed and chases wooden spools and glass marbles from one end of the living room to the other. The Venables have mentioned this subject of the larger rug to the landlord and he has mentioned it to us. We do nothing about it, except that Margaret puts the spools and marbles out of Floribunda's reach when we go to bed at night, and walks around in her stocking feet after ten o'clock. Some day, when we are kept awake by footsteps crossing our bedroom ceiling, hammering, furniture being moved, and other idiot noises, we will remember the Venables and wish we had been more considerate.

The Venables leave their door open too, and on our way up the stairs I look back over my shoulder and see chintz-covered chairs and Oriental rugs and the lamplight falling discreetly on an Early American this and an Old English that. (No children here, either; Mrs. Venable works in a decorator's shop.) Mrs. Pickering, third floor, keeps her door closed. She is a sweetfaced woman who smiles when we meet her on the stairs. She has a grown son and daughter who come to see her regularly, but her life isn't the same as when they were growing up and Mr. Pickering was alive. (Did she tell us this or have I invented it?) If we met her anywhere but on the stairs we would have racked our brains to find something to say to her. The Holmeses' furniture is nondescript but comfortable. Mrs. Holmes has lovely brown eyes and the voice that goes with them, and it is no wonder that Floribunda likes to sit on her lap. *He* wants everybody to be happy, which is not exactly the way to be happy yourself, and he isn't. If we all paid a little more rent, it would make him happier, but we don't feel like it, any of us.

I am happy because we are in town: I don't have to commute in bad weather. I can walk to the office. And after the theater we jump in a cab and are home in five minutes. I stand at the front window listening to the weather report. It is snowing in Westchester, and the driving conditions are very bad. In Thirty-sixth Street it is raining. The middle-aged man who lives on the top floor of the brownstone directly across from us is in the habit of posing at the window with a curtain partly wrapped around his naked body. He keeps guppies or goldfish in a lighted tank, spends the whole day in a kimono ironing, and at odd moments goes to the front window and acts out somebody's sexual dream. If I could only marry him off to the old woman who goes through the trash baskets on Lexington Avenue, talking to herself. What pleasure she would have in showing him the things she has brought home in her string bag—treasures whose value nobody else realizes. And what satisfaction to him it would be to wrap himself in a curtain just for her.

The view to the south is cut off by a big apartment building on Thirty-fifth Street. The only one. If it were not there (I spend a good deal of time demolishing it, with my bare hands) we would have the whole of the sky to look at. Because I have not looked carefully enough at the expression in Margaret's eyes, I go on thinking that she is happy too. When I met her she was working in a publishing house. Shortly after we decided to get married she was offered a job with the *Partisan Review*. If she had taken it, it would have meant commuting with me or even commuting at different hours from when I did. When I was a little boy and came home from school and called out, "Is anybody home?" somebody nearly always was. I took it for granted that the same thing would be true when I married. We didn't talk about it, and should have. I didn't understand that in her mind it was the chance of a fulfilling experience. Because she saw that I could not even imagine her saying yes, she said no, and turned her attention to learning how to cook and keep house. If we had had children right away it would have been different; but then if we had had children we wouldn't have been living on the top floor of a brownstone on Thirty-sixth Street.

The days in town are long and empty for her. The telephone doesn't ring anything like as often as it does when we are in the country. There Hester Gale comes across the road to see how Margaret is, or because she is out of cake flour, and they have coffee together. Margaret sews with Olivia Bingham. There are conversations in the supermarket. And miles of woods to walk in. Old Mrs. Delano, whose front door on Thirty-sixth Street is ten feet west of ours, is no help whatever. Though she knows Margaret's Aunt Caroline, she doesn't know that Margaret is her niece, or even that she exists, probably, and Margaret has no intention of telling her. Any more than she has any intention of telling me that in this place where I am so happy she feels like a prisoner much of the time.

She is accustomed to space, to a part of the country where there is more room than people and buildings to occupy it. In her childhood she woke up in the morning in a big house set on a wide lawn, with towering pine trees behind it, and a copper beech as big as two brownstones, and a snow-capped mountain that mysteriously comes and goes, like an idea in the mind. Every afternoon after school she went cantering through the trees on horseback. Now she is confined to two rooms—the kitchen cannot be called a room; it is hardly bigger than a handkerchief—and these two rooms are not enough. This is a secret she manages to keep from me so I can go on being happy.

There is another secret that cannot be kept from me because, with her head in a frame made by my head, arms, and shoulder, I know when she weeps. She weeps because her period was five days late and she thought something had happened that she now knows is not going to happen. The child is there, and could just as well as not decide to come to us, and doesn't, month after month. Instead, we consult one gynecologist after another, and take embarrassing tests (only they don't really embarrass me, they just seem unreal). And what the doctors do not tell us is why, when there is nothing wrong with either of us, nothing happens. Before we can have a child we must solve a riddle, like Oedipus and the Sphinx. On my forty-second birthday I go to the Spence-Chapin adoption service and explain our situation to a woman who listens attentively. I like her and feel that she understands how terribly much we want a child, and she shocks me by reaching across the desk and taking the application blank out of my hands: Forty-two is the age past which the agency will not consider giving out a child for adoption.

Meanwhile, Margaret herself has been adopted, by the Italian market under the El at Third Avenue and Thirty-fourth Street. Four or five whistling boys with white aprons wrapped around their skinny hips run it. They also appear to own it, but what could be more unlikely? Their faces light up when Margaret walks into the store. They drop what they are doing and come to greet her as if she were their older sister. And whatever she asks for, it turns out they have. Their meat is never tough, their vegetables are not tarnished and limp, their sole is just as good as the fish market's and nothing like as expensive. Now one boy, now another arrives at our door with a carton of groceries balanced on his head, having taken the stairs two steps at a

time. Four flights are nothing to them. They are in business
for the pure pleasure of it. They don't think or talk about love,
they just do it. Or perhaps it isn't love but joy. But over what?
Over the fact that they are alive and so are we?

It occurs to the landlord that the tenants could carry their
garbage down to the street and then he wouldn't have to. I
prepare for a scene, compose angry speeches in the bath.
Everybody knows what landlords are like—only he isn't like
that. He isn't even a landlord, strictly speaking. He has a good
job with an actuarial firm. The building is a hobby. It was very
run down when he bought it, and he has had the pleasure of
fixing it up. We meet on the front sidewalk as I am on my way
to work. Looking up at him—he is a very tall man—I announce that I will not carry our garbage down. Looking down
at me, he says that if we don't feel like carrying our garbage
down he will go on doing it. What an unsatisfactory man to
quarrel with.

I come home from the office and find that Margaret has
spent the afternoon drawing: a pewter coffeepot (Nantucket),
a Venetian-glass goblet, a white china serving dish with a
handle and a cover, two eggs, a lemon, apples, a rumpled napkin with a blue border. Or the view from the living room all
the way into the bedroom, through three doorways, involving
the kind of foreshortened perspective Italian Renaissance artists
were so fond of. Or the view from the bedroom windows (the
apartment house on Thirty-fifth Street that I have so often
taken down I now see is all right; it belongs there) in sepia wash.
Or her own head and shoulders reflected in the dressing table
mirror. Or the goblet, the coffeepot, the lemon, a green pepper, and a brown luster bowl. The luster bowl has a chip in it,
and so the old woman in the antique shop in Putnam Valley
gave it to us for a dollar, after the table was safely stowed away
in the backseat of the car. And some years later, her daughter,
sitting next to me at a formal dinner party, said, "You're mistaken. Mother was absolutely fearless." She said it again, perceiving that I did not believe her. Somebody is mistaken, and it
could just as well as not be me. Even though I looked quite
carefully at the old woman's expression. In any case, there is
something I didn't see. Her husband—the man whose books
the old woman was unwilling to sell—committed suicide. "I

was their only child, and had to deal with sadness all my life—
sadness from within as well as from without." If the expression
in the old woman's eyes was not terror, what was it?

Floribunda misses the country, and sits at the top of the living-
room stairs, clawing at the trapdoor. She refuses to eat, is
shedding. Her hairs are on everything. One night we take her
across Park Avenue to the Morgan Library and push the big
iron gate open like conspirators about to steal the forty-two-
line Gutenberg Bible or the three folios of Redouté's roses.
Floribunda leaps from Margaret's arms and runs across the
sickly grass and climbs a small tree. Ecstatically she sharpens
her claws on the bark. I know that we will be arrested, but it is
worth it.

Neither the landlord and his wife, nor the artist and her husband, who is Dutch, nor Mrs. Pickering, nor the Venables ever
entertain in their apartments, but we have a season of being
sociable. We have the Fitzgeralds and Eileen Fitzgerald's
father from Dublin for dinner. We celebrate Bastille Day with
the Potters. We have Elinor Hinkley's mother to tea. She arrives at the head of the stairs, where she can see into the living
room, and exclaims—before she has even caught her breath—
"What beautiful horizontal surfaces!" She is incapable of small
talk. Instead, she describes the spiritual emanations of a row
of huge granite boulders lining the driveway of her house on
Martha's Vineyard. And other phenomena that cannot be described very easily, or that, when described, cannot be appreciated by someone who isn't half mad or a Theosophist.
    Dean Wilson brings one intelligent, pretty girl after another
to meet us. Like the woman in Isak Dinesen's story who sailed
the seas looking for the perfect blue, he is looking for a flawless
girl. Flawless in whose eyes is the question. And isn't flawless-
ness itself a serious flaw? "What a charming girl," we say
afterward, and he looks in our faces and is not satisfied, and
brings still another girl, including, finally, Ivy Sérurier, who is
half English and half French. When she was seven years old her
nurse took her every day to the Jardin du Luxembourg and
there she ran after a hoop. She is attracted to all forms of oc-
cult knowledge, and things happen to her that do not happen

to anyone who does not have a destiny. The light bulbs respond to her amazing stories by giving off a higher voltage. The expression on our faces is satisfactory. Dean brings her again, and again. He asks Margaret if she thinks they should get married, but he cannot quite bring himself to ask Ivy this question.

On a night when we are expecting Henry Coddington to dinner, Hester and Nick Gale come up the stairs blithely at seven o'clock, having got the invitation wrong. Or perhaps it is our fault. There is plenty of food, and it turns out to be a pleasant evening. The guests get on well, but Henry must have thought we did not want to know why Louise left him and took their little girl, whom he idolizes—that we have insulated ourselves from his catastrophe by asking this couple from the country. Anyway, he never comes or calls again. But other people come. Melissa Lovejoy, from Montgomery, Alabama, comes for Sunday lunch, and her hilarious account of her skirmishes with her mother-in-law make the tears run down my cheeks. Melissa, who loves beautiful china, looks around the living room and sees what no one else has ever seen or commented on—a Meissen plate on the other end of the mantelpiece from the Egyptian cat. It is white, with very small green grape leaves and a wide filigree border. Margaret's brother John had it in his rucksack when he made his way from Geneva to Bordeaux in May 1940. As easily as the plate could have got broken, so he could have ended up in a detention camp and then what? But they are both safe, intact, here in New York. He has his own place, on Lexington Avenue in the Fifties. On Christmas Eve he bends down and selects a present for Margaret and another for me from the pile under the tree at the foot of the stair.

On New Year's Eve, John and Dean and Ivy and Margaret and I sit down to dinner. The champagne cork hits the ceiling. Between courses we take turns getting up and going into the bedroom and waiting behind a closed door until a voice calls "Ready!" If you were a school of Italian painting or a color of the spectrum or a character from fiction, what school of Italian painting or color or character would you be? John is Dostoevski's Idiot, Margaret is lavender blue. Elinor Hinkley joins us for dessert. Just before midnight a couple from the U.N., whom Dean has invited, come up the stairs and an hour later on the dot they leave for another party. It is daylight when we push our chairs back. We have not left the table (except to go into the front room while the questions are being framed) all night long. With our heads out of the window, Margaret and I wait for them to emerge from the building and then we call down to them, "Happy New Year!" But softly, so as not to wake up the neighbors.

Margaret's Uncle James, who is not her uncle but her mother's first cousin, comes to dinner, bringing long-stemmed red roses. He confesses that he has been waiting for this invitation ever since we were married—eight or nine years—and he thoroughly enjoys himself, though he is dying of cancer of the throat. Faced with extinction, you can't just stand and scream; it isn't good manners. And men and women of that generation do not discuss their feelings. Anyway he doesn't. Instead he says, "I like your curtains, Margaret," and we are filled with remorse that we didn't ask him sooner. But still, he did come to dinner. And satisfied his curiosity about the way we live. And we were surprised to discover that we were fond of him— as the rabbit is surprised to discover that he is what was concealed in the magician's hat. *I am not the person you thought I was*, Uncle James as much as says, sitting back in the easy chair but not using the ottoman lest he look ill.

I realize that the air is full of cigarette smoke, and prop the trapdoor open with a couple of books—but only a crack. At eleven-thirty Uncle James rises and puts his coat on and says good night, and tromps down the stairs, waking the Venables, and Mrs. Pickering, and the artist and her husband, and Mr. and Mrs. Holmes. And we lock the doors and say what a nice evening it was, and empty the ashtrays, and carry the liquor glasses out to the kitchen, and suddenly perceive an emptiness, an absence. "Floribunda? . . . Pussy?" She is nowhere. She has slipped through the crack that I thought was too small for her to get through. Fur is deceptive, her bone structure is not what I thought it was, and perhaps cats have something in common with cigarette smoke. I have often seen her attenuate herself alarmingly. Outside, on the roof, I call softly, but no little black cat comes. In the night we both wake and talk about her. The bottom of the bed feels strange when we put our feet out and there is nothing there, no weight. When morning comes I dress and go up to the roof again, and make my way toward Park Avenue, stepping over two-foot-high tile walls and making my way around projections and feeling giddy when I peer down into back gardens.

Margaret, meanwhile, has dressed and gone down the stairs. She rings the Delanos' bell, and the Irish maid opens the door. "A little cat came in through my bedroom window last night and the mistress said to put her on the street, so I did." *On the street* . . . when she could so easily have put her back on the roof she came from! "Here, Puss, Puss, Puss . . . here, Puss!" Up Thirty-sixth Street and down Thirty-fifth. All her life she has known nothing but love, and she is so timid. How will she survive with no home? What will the poor creature do? We meet Rose Bernstein, who has just moved into town from our country road, and just as I am saying "On the street. Did you ever hear of anything so heartless?" there is a faint miaow. Floribunda heard us calling and was too frightened to answer. I find her hiding in an areaway. Margaret gathers her up in her arms and we say good-bye to Rose Bernstein, and, unable to believe our good fortune, take her home. Our love and joy.

In Chicago there is an adoption agency whose policy with respect to age is not so rigid as Spence-Chapin's. We pull strings. (Dean Wilson has a friend whose wife's mother is on the board.) Letters pass back and forth, and finally there we are, in Chicago, nervously waiting in the reception room. Miss Mattie Gessner is susceptible (or so I feel) to the masculine approach. It turns out that she voted for Truman too; and she doesn't reach across the desk and take the application from my hands. Instead she promises to help us. But it isn't as simple as the old song my mother used to sing: Today is not the day they give babies away with a half a pound of tay. The baby that is given to us for adoption must be the child of a couple reasonably like us—that is to say, a man and woman who, in the year 1952, would have a record player that plays only 78s and that you wind by hand; who draw seashells on their bedroom curtains and are made happy by a blocked-up fireplace and a stairway that leads nowhere. And this means we must wait God knows how long.

So we do wait, sometimes in rather odd places for a couple with no children. For example, by the carousel in Central Park. The plunging horses slowly come to a halt with their hoofs in midair. The children get off and more children climb up, take a firm grip on the pole, and look around for their mother or their nurse or their father, in the crowd standing in the open doorway. Slowly the cavalcade begins to move again, and I take the little boy in the plaid snowsuit, with half a pound of English Breakfast, and Margaret takes half a pound of Lipton's and the little girl with blue ribbons in her hair.

We start going to the country weekends. And then we go for the summer, taking suitcases full of clothes, boxes of unread books, drawing materials, the sewing machine, the typewriter. And in September all this is carried up four flights of stairs. And more: flowers, vegetables from the garden, plants we could not bear to have the frost put an end to, even though we know they will not live long in town. And one by one we take up our winter habits. When Saturday night comes around we put on our coats at ten o'clock and go out to buy the Sunday *Times* at the newspaper stand under the El. We rattle the door of the antique shop on Third Avenue that always has something interesting in the window but has never been known to be open at any hour of any day of the week. On three successive nights we go to *Ring Round the Moon*, *King Lear*, and *An Enemy of the People*, after which it seems strange to sit home reading a book. I am so in love with Adlai Stevenson's speeches that, though I am afraid of driving in ordinary traffic in New York City, I get the car out of the garage and we drive right down the center of 125th Street, in a torchlight parade, hemmed in by a flowing river of people, all of whom feel the way we do.

How many years did we live in that apartment on Thirty-sixth Street? From 1950 to— The mere dates are misleading, even if I could get them right, because time was not progressive or in sequence, it was one of Mrs. Hinkley's horizontal surfaces divided into squares. On one square an old woman waters a houseplant in the window of an otherwise blank wall. On another, Albertha, who is black, comes to clean. When she leaves, the apartment looks as if an angel had walked through it. She is the oldest of eleven children. And what she and Margaret say, over a cup of coffee, makes Margaret more able to deal with her solitary life. On another square, we go to the Huguenot Church on Sunday morning, expecting something new and strange, and instead the hymns are perfectly familiar to us from our Presbyterian childhoods: In French they have become more elegant and rhetorical, and it occurs to me that they may not reach all the way to the ear of Heaven. But the old man who then mounts the stairs to the pulpit addresses Seigneur Dieu in a confident voice, as if they are extremely well acquainted, the two of them. On another square we go to Berlitz, and the instructor, a White Russian named Mikhael Miloradovitch, sits by blandly while Margaret and I say things to each other in French that we have managed not to say in English. I am upset when I discover that she prefers the country to the city. The discussion becomes heated, but because it is in French nothing comes of it. We go on living in the city. Until another summer comes and we fill the car, which is now nearly twenty years old, to the canvas top with our possessions; then, locking the doors of the apartment, we drive off to our other life. At which point the shine goes out of this one. The slipcovers fade and so do the seashells and thistles that are exposed to the direct light of the summer sun. Dust gathers on the books, the lampshades, the record player. In the middle of the night, a hand pries at the trapdoor and, finding it securely locked, tries somewhere else. The man out of Krafft-Ebing shows himself seductively to our blank windows. And the intense heat builds up to a violent thunderstorm. After which there is a spell of cooler weather. And a tragedy. For two days there has been no garbage outside Mrs. Pickering's door in the morning. She does not answer her telephone or the landlord's knocking, and she has not said she was going away. The first floor extends farther back than the rest of the house, and he is able to place a ladder on the roof of this extension. From the top of the ladder he stares into the third-floor bedroom at a terrible sight: Mrs. Pickering, sitting in a wing chair, naked. He thinks it is death he is staring at, but he is mistaken; she has had a stroke. He breaks the door down, and she is taken to the hospital in an ambulance. She does not die, but neither does she ever come back to this apartment. Passing her door on our way up the stairs, we are aware of the silence inside, and think uneasily of those two days and nights of helpless waiting. Along with the silence there is the sense of something malign, of trouble of a very serious kind that could spread all through the house. To ward it off, we draw closer to the other tenants, linger talking on the stairs, and speak to them in a more intimate tone of voice. We have the Holmeses and the Venables and the artist and her husband up for a drink. It doesn't do the trick. There *was* something behind Mrs. Pickering's door. My sister's only son turns up and, since we are in the country, we offer him the apartment to live in until he finds a job. He leads a life there that the books and furniture do not approve of. He brings girls home and makes love to them in our bed, under the very eyes of the children flying kites. He borrows fifty bucks from me, to eat on, and to get some shirts, so he won't look like a bum when he goes job hunting. He has a check coming from his previous job, in Florida, and will pay me back next week. The check doesn't come, and he borrows some more money, and then some more, and it begins to mount up. Jobs that were as good as promised to him vanish into thin air, and meanwhile we are his sole means of support. I listen attentively to what I more and more suspect are inventions, but his footwork is fast, and what he says could be true; it just isn't what he said before, quite. My bones inform me that I am not the first person these excuses and appeals have been tried out on. He comes to my office to tell me that he has given up the idea of staying in New York and can I let him have the fare home, and I dial my sister's number in Evansville, Indiana, and hand the receiver to him and leave the room.

I give up smoking on one square, and on another I go through all the variant pages of a book I have been writing for four and a half years and reduce it to a single pile of manuscript. This I put in a blue canvas duffel bag that can absentmindedly be left behind on the curbing when we drive off to the country at eleven o'clock of a spring night. At midnight, driving up the Taconic Parkway, I suddenly see in my mind's eye the backseat of the car: The blue duffel bag is not there. Nor, when we come to a stop in front of our house on Thirty-sixth Street at one o'clock in the morning, is it on the sidewalk where I left it. With a dry mouth I describe it to the desk sergeant in the police station, and he gets up and goes into the back room. "No, nothing," he calls. And then, as we are almost at the door, "Wait a minute."

On another square Margaret starts behaving in a way that is not at all like her. Sleepy at ten o'clock in the evening, and when I open my eyes in the morning she is already awake and looking at me. Her face is somehow different. Can it be that she is . . . that we are going to . . . that . . . I study her when she is not aware that I am looking at her, and find in her behavior the answer to that riddle: If we are so longing for a child that we are willing to bring up somebody else's child— anybody's child whatever—then we may as well be allowed to have our own. Margaret comes home from the doctor bringing the news to me that I have not dared break to her.

After boning up on the subject, in a book, she shows me, on her finger, just how long the child in her womb now is. And it is growing larger, very slowly. And so is she. The child is safe inside her, and she is safe so long as she remains a prisoner in this top-floor apartment. The doctor has forbidden her to use the stairs. Everybody comes to see her, instead—including an emanation from the silent apartment two floors below. A black man, a stranger, suddenly appears at the top of the stairs. His intention, unclear but frightening, shows in his face, in his eyes. But the goddess Bastet is at work again, and the man comes on Albertha's day, and she, with a stream of such foul-mouthed cursing as Margaret has never heard in her life, sends him running down the stairs. If he had come on a day that was not Albertha's day, when Margaret was there alone— But this holds true for everything, good or bad.

Margaret's face grows rounder, and she no longer has a secret that must be kept from me. The days while I am at the office are not lonely, and time is an unbroken landscape of day-dreaming. When I get home at six o'clock, I creep in under the roof of the spell she is under, and am allowed into the day-dream. But what shall we tell Miss Mattie Gessner when she comes to investigate the way we live?

The apartment, feeling our inattention, begins to withdraw from us sadly. And then something else unexpected happens. The landlord, having achieved perfection, having created the

Peaceable Kingdom on Thirty-sixth Street, is restless and wants to begin all over again. "You'll be sorry," his wife tells him, stroking Floribunda's ear, and he is. But by that time they are living uptown, in a much less handsome house in the Nineties —a house that needs fixing from top to bottom. But it will never have any style, and it is filled with disagreeable tenants who do not pay their rent on time. On Thirty-sixth Street we have a new landlord, and in no time his hand is on everything. He hangs a cheap print of van Gogh's *The Drawbridge* in the downstairs foyer. We are obliged to take down the cardboard barricade and keep our doors closed. Hardly a day passes without some maddening new improvement. The artist is the first to go. Then we give notice; how is Margaret to carry the baby, the stroller, the package from the drugstore, etc., up four flights of stairs? *What better place can there be to bring up a child in?* the marble fireplace asks, remembering the eighteen-eighties, when this was a one-family house and our top-floor living room was the nursery. The stairway to the roof was devoted to the previous tenant (the man who lived in the midst of a monumental clutter) and says bitterly, in the night, when we are not awake to hear, *They seem as much a part of your life as the doors and windows, and then it turns out that they are not a part of your life at all. The moving men come and cart all the furniture away, and the people go down to the street, and that's the last you see of them. . . .*

What will the fireplace and the stairway to the roof say when they discover that they are about to be shut off forever from the front room? The landlord is planning to divide our apartment into two apartments and charge the same for each that he is now getting for the floor-through. For every evil under the sun there is a remedy or there is none. I soak the mural of the children flying kites, hoping to remove it intact and put it up somewhere in the house in the country. The paper tears no matter how gently I pull it loose from the wall, and comes off in little pieces, which end up in the wastebasket.

Now when I walk past that house I look up at the windows that could be in Leningrad or Innsbruck or Dresden or Parma, and I think of the stairway that led only to the trapdoor in the roof, and of the marble fireplace, the bathroom skylight, and the tiny kitchen, and of what school of Italian painting we would have been if we had been a school of Italian painting, and poor Mrs. Pickering sitting in her bedroom chair with her eyes wide open, waiting for help, and the rainy nights on Thirty-sixth Street, and the grey-and-blue thistles, the brown seashells, the Mills Brothers singing *Shine, little glowworm, glimmer, glimmer*, and the guests who came the wrong night, the guest who was going to die and knew it, the sound of my typewriter, and of a paintbrush clinking in a glass of cloudy water, and Floribunda's adventure, and Margaret's empty days, and how it was settled that, although I wanted to put my head on her breast as I was falling asleep, she needed even more (at that point) to put her head on mine. And of our child's coming, at last, and the black cat who thought *she* was our child, and of the two friends who didn't after all get married, and the old woman who found one treasure after another in the trash baskets all up and down Lexington Avenue, and that other old woman, now dead, who was so driven by the need to describe the inner life of very large granite boulders. I think of how Miss Mattie Gessner's face fell and how she closed her notebook and became a stranger to us, who had been so deeply our friend. I think of the oversexed ironer, and the Holmeses, and the Venables, and the stranger who meant no-body good and was frightened away by Albertha's cursing, and the hissing of the air brakes of the Lexington Avenue bus, and the curtains moving at the open window, and the baby crying on the other side of the wall. I think of that happy grocery store run by boys, and the horse-drawn flower cart that some-times waited on the corner, and the sound of footsteps in the night, and the sudden no-sound that meant it was snowing, and I think of the unknown man or woman who found the blue duffel bag with the manuscript of my novel in it and took it to the police station, and the musical instrument (not a lute, but that's what the artist must have had in mind, only she no longer bothers to look at objects and draws what she remem-bers them as being like) played in the dark, over our sleeping bodies, while the children flew their kites, and I think if it is true that we are all in the hand of God, what a capacious hand it must be.

SO LONG,
SEE YOU TOMORROW

For Robert Fitzgerald

I
A Pistol Shot

THE gravel pit was about a mile east of town, and the size of a small lake, and so deep that boys under sixteen were forbidden by their parents to swim there. I knew it only by hearsay. It had no bottom, people said, and because I was very much interested in the idea that if you dug a hole straight down anywhere and kept on digging it would come out in China, I took this to be a literal statement of fact.

One winter morning shortly before daybreak, three men loading gravel there heard what sounded like a pistol shot. Or, they agreed, it could have been a car backfiring. Within a few seconds it had grown light. No one came to the pit through the field that lay alongside it, and they didn't see anyone walking on the road. The sound was not a car backfiring; a tenant farmer named Lloyd Wilson had just been shot and killed, and what they heard was the gun that killed him.

At the coroner's inquest, Wilson's uncle, who had lived with him for a number of years and was a man in his late sixties, testified that while he was feeding the horses he saw his nephew's lantern as he passed on his way to the cow barn. The horse barn and the cow barn were about five hundred feet apart. He did not hear the shot and he was not aware that there was anybody on the farm that morning who did not belong there. The household at that time consisted of Wilson, his two little boys, aged six and nine, his elderly housekeeper, and the uncle, Fred Wilson.

The housekeeper then took the stand and testified that on the last morning of his life Lloyd Wilson got up at five-thirty as usual, dressed, and built two fires. While he was waiting for the one in the kitchen range to catch, he stood talking and joking with her. He was in a cheerful mood and left the house whistling. Usually he was through milking and back in the kitchen before she had breakfast ready. At seven o'clock, knowing that he had to go to town and pick up a man he had engaged to do some belated corn shucking for him, she told the younger of the two little boys to go see what was keeping his father so long. He asked for a flashlight, and she peered out into the darkness and then said he didn't need a flashlight, he could see the lantern shining from the open door of the barn. In a very short while she heard him coming back to the house. He was crying. When she opened the storm door and called out to him, he said, "Papa is dead! He is sitting there with his eyes open but he is dead. . . ."

Who believes children. Brushing him and his story aside she ran to the barn. Wilson was sitting on a milking stool in the middle stall, his body sunk over against the partition. She caught him by the hand and cried, "Lloyd, what on earth is the matter with you?"—thinking he had been stricken with heart failure or possibly apoplexy. As the child had said, he was sitting there with his eyes open but he was dead.

The housekeeper and Fred Wilson did the necessary things —that is to say, she went back to the house and made a number of telephone calls, and he finished milking the cows and turned them out into the pasture and then sat beside the body until the undertaker and his assistant came and took it back to town. Rigor mortis had set in, and they had to cut the sleeve of his jacket in order to take off his clothes. They removed the jacket, coat, corduroy vest, and flannel shirt, before they saw a small red stain on the undershirt, over the heart.

In those days—I am talking about the early nineteen-twenties—people in Lincoln mostly didn't lock their doors at night, and if they did it was against the idea of a burglar. One sometimes read in the evening paper that some man had been arrested for disorderly conduct, but that meant drunkenness. Without thinking I would have said that acts of violence could hardly be expected to flourish in a place where the houses were not widely separated and never enclosed by a high wall and where it would have been hard to do anything out of the way that somebody by one accident or another or from simple curiosity would not happen to see. But consider the following sentence, from a history of Logan County published in 1911: "While there have been in the neighborhood of about fifty fatal shooting affrays . . . very few have occurred where the parties were well known or of considerable standing in the community." As a rule the shooting, or the knifing, or the clubbing, was in a coal miner's shack or a back alley or a lonely farmhouse, but one of the crimes mentioned in that book took place in a house on Tenth Street, one street over from the house we lived in when I was a child. What distinguished the murder of Lloyd Wilson from all the others was a fact so shocking that the Lincoln *Courier-Herald* hesitated several days before printing it: The murderer had cut off the dead man's ear with a razor and carried it away with him. In that pre-Freudian era people did not ask themselves what the ear might be a substitution for, but merely shuddered.

2

The Period of Mourning

I VERY much doubt that I would have remembered for more than fifty years the murder of a tenant farmer I never laid eyes on if (1) the murderer hadn't been the father of somebody I knew, and (2) I hadn't later on done something I was ashamed of afterward. This memoir—if that's the right name for it—is a roundabout, futile way of making amends.

Before I can go into all that, I have to take up another subject. When my father was getting along in years and the past began to figure more in his conversation, I asked him one day what my mother was like. I knew what she was like as my mother but I thought it was time somebody told me what she was like as a person. To my surprise he said, "That's water over the dam," shutting me up but also leaving me in doubt, because of his abrupt tone of voice, whether he didn't after all this time have any feeling about her much, or did have but didn't think he ought to. In any case he didn't feel like talking about her to me.

Very few families escape disasters of one kind or another, but in the years between 1909 and 1919 my mother's family had more than its share of them. My grandfather, spending the night in a farmhouse, was bitten on the ear by a rat or a ferret and died three months later of blood poisoning. My mother's only brother was in an automobile accident and lost his right arm. My mother's younger sister poured kerosene on a grate fire that wouldn't burn and set fire to her clothing and bore the scars of this all the rest of her life. My older brother, when he was five years old, got his foot caught in a turning carriage wheel.

I was so small when these things happened that either I did not know about them or else I didn't feel them because they took place at one remove, so to speak. When my brother undressed at night he left his artificial leg leaning against a chair. It was as familiar to me, since we slept in the same room, as his cap or his baseball glove. He was not given to feeling sorry for himself, and older people were always careful not to show their sorrow over what had happened to him. What I felt about his "affliction" was tucked away in my unconscious mind (assuming there is such a thing) where I couldn't get at it.

My younger brother was born on New Year's Day, at the height of the influenza epidemic of 1918. My mother died two days later of double pneumonia. After that, there were no more disasters. The worst that could happen had happened, and the shine went out of everything. Disbelieving, we endured the wreath on the door, and the undertaker coming and going, the influx of food, the overpowering odor of white flowers, and all the rest of it, including the first of a series of house-keepers, who took care of the baby and sat in my mother's place at mealtime. Looking back I think it more than likely that long before she ever laid eyes on us that sallow-faced, flat-chested woman had got the short end of the stick. She came from a world we knew nothing about, and I don't remember that she ever had any days off. She may have made a stab at being a mother to my older brother and me, but it would have taken a good deal more than that to break through our resistance. We knew what we had had, and were not going to be taken in by any form of counterfeit affection.

My mother's sisters and my father's sisters and my grand-mother all watched over us. If they hadn't, I don't know what would have become of us, in that sad house, where nothing ever changed, where life had come to a standstill. My father was all but undone by my mother's death. In the evening after supper he walked the floor and I walked with him, with my arm around his waist. I was ten years old. He would walk from the living room into the front hall, then, turning, past the grandfather's clock and on into the library, and from the library into the living room. Or he would walk from the library into the dining room and then into the living room by another doorway, and back to the front hall. Because he didn't say any-thing, I didn't either. I only tried to sense, as he was about to turn, which room he was going to next so we wouldn't bump into each other. His eyes were focused on things not in those rooms, and his face was the color of ashes. From conversations that had taken place in front of me I knew he was tormented by the belief that he was responsible for what had happened. If he had only taken this or that precaution . . . It wasn't true, any of it. At a time when the epidemic was raging and people were told to avoid crowds, he and my mother got on a crowded train in order to go to Bloomington, thirty miles away, where the hospital facilities were better than in Lincoln. But even if she had had the baby at home, she still would have caught the flu. My older brother or my father or I would have given it to her. We all came down with it.

I had to guess what my older brother was thinking. It was not something he cared to share with me. I studied the look in his hazel eyes and was startled: If I hadn't known, I would have thought that he'd had his feelings hurt by something he was too proud to talk about. It was the most he could manage in the way of concealment. At night we undressed and got into bed and fell asleep without taking advantage of the dark to un-burden our hearts to each other. It strikes me as strange now. It didn't then. Though we were very different, he knew me in-side out—that is to say, he knew my weaknesses and how to play on them, and this had made me leery about exposing my feelings to him. I also suspect that I had told on him once too often. I have no way of knowing what he might have said. What I didn't say, across the few feet that separated our two beds, was that I couldn't understand how it had happened to us. It seemed like a mistake. And mistakes ought to be recti-fied, only this one couldn't be. Between the way things used to be and the way they were now was a void that couldn't be crossed. I had to find an explanation other than the real one, which was that we were no more immune to misfortune than anybody else, and the idea that kept recurring to me, perhaps because of that pacing the floor with my father, was that I had inadvertently walked through a door that I shouldn't have gone through and couldn't get back to the place I hadn't meant to leave. Actually, it was the other way round: I hadn't gone anywhere and nothing was changed, so far as the roof over our heads was concerned, it was just that she was in the cemetery.

When I got home from school I did what I had always done, which was to read, curled up in the window seat in the library or lying flat on my back on the floor with my feet in a chair, in the darkest corner I could find. The house was full of places to read that fitted me like a glove, and I read the same books over and over. Children tend to derive comfort and support from the totally familiar—an umbrella stand, a glass ashtray backed with brightly colored cigar bands, the fire tongs, anything. With the help of these and other commonplace objects—with the help also of the two big elm trees that shaded the house from the heat of the sun, and the trumpet vine by the back door, and the white lilac bush by the dining-room window, and the comfortable wicker porch furniture and the porch swing that contributed its *creak . . . creak . . .* to the sounds of the summer night—I got from one day to the next.

My father got from one day to the next by attending faithfully to his job. He was the state agent for a small fire insurance company and traveled from one end of Illinois to the other, inspecting risks and cultivating the friendship of local agents so they would give more business to his company. On Saturday morning, sitting in the library, he would put a check on each inspection slip as he finished glancing over it, and when he had a pile of them he would hand them to me and I would sit on the floor and arrange them around me alphabetically, by towns, proud that I could be of use to him. He left on Tuesday morning, carrying a grip that was heavy with printed forms, and came home Friday afternoon to a household that was seething with problems he was not accustomed to dealing with. His sadness was of the kind that is patient and without hope. He continued to sleep in the bed he and my mother had shared, and tried to act in a way she would have wanted him to, and I suspect that as time passed he was less and less sure what that was. He gave away her jewelry, and more important to me, her clothes, so I could no longer open her closet door and look at them.

I overheard one family friend after another assuring him that there was no cure but time, and though he said, "Yes, I know," I could tell he didn't believe them. Once a week he would wind all the clocks in the house, beginning with the grandfather's clock in the front hall. Their minute and hour hands went round dependably and the light outside corroborated what they said: it was breakfast time, it was late afternoon, it was night, with the darkness pressing against the windowpanes. What the family friends said is true. For some people. For others the hands of the clock can go round till kingdom come and not cure anything. I don't know by what means my father came to terms with his grief. All I know is that it was more than a year before the color came back into his face and he could smile when somebody said something funny.

When people spoke about my mother it was always in generalities—her wonderful qualities, her gift for making those around her happy, and so on—that didn't tell me anything I didn't know before. It was as if they couldn't see her clearly for what had happened to her. And to us. She didn't like having her picture taken and all we had was a few snapshots and one formal photograph, taken when she was in her early twenties, with her hair piled on top of her head and a black velvet ribbon around her throat. She was only thirty-eight when she died, but she had grown heavy, as women of that period tended to do. There was no question about the mouth or the soft brown eyes. The rest I did not recognize, though I was willing to believe that she had once looked like that. This picture didn't satisfy my father either, and he got the photographer who had taken it to touch it up so she would look more like a mature woman. The result was something I was quite sure my mother had never looked like—vague and idealized and as if she might not even remember who we were. My mother sometimes got excited and flew off the handle, but not this woman, who died before her time, leaving a grief-stricken husband and three motherless children. The retouched photograph came between me and the face I remembered, and it got harder and harder to recall my mother as she really was. After I couldn't remember any more except in a general way what she looked like, I could still remember the sound of her voice, and I clung to that. I also clung to the idea that if things remained exactly the way they were, if we were careful not to take a step in any direction from the place where we were now, we would somehow get back to the way it was before she died. I knew that this was not a rational belief, but the alternative—that when people die they are really gone and I would never see her again—was more than I could manage then or for a long time afterward.

When my father was an old man, he surprised me by remarking that he understood what my mother's death meant to me but had no idea what to do about it. I think it would have been something if he had just said this. If he didn't, it was possibly because he thought there was nothing he or anybody else could do. Or he may have thought I would reject any help he tried to give me. As a small child I sometimes had the earache, and I would go to him and ask him to blow cigar smoke in my ear. He would stop talking and draw me toward him and with his lips almost touching my ear breathe warm smoke into it. It was as good a remedy as any, and it was physically intimate. One night—I don't know how old I was, five or six, maybe— bedtime came and I kissed my mother good night as usual and then went over to my father and as I leaned toward him he said I was too old for that any more. By the standards of that time and that place I expect I was, but I had wanted to anyway. And how was I to express the feeling I had for him? He didn't say, then or ever. In that moment my feeling for him changed and became wary and unconfident.

All up and down Ninth Street there were children I could play with, and sometimes I did, but I preferred to play by myself. On the most beautiful spring day of the year I stayed in the house, reading *Tik-Tok of Oz*. And when I grew tired of reading I shut myself up in a darkened room and played with my postcard projector or with a toy theater I had made out of shirt cardboards. All this worried my father, both from the standpoint of my not being outdoors enough and because if I continued to be interested in such things, how on earth would I support myself when I grew up? There was nothing comical or odd in his thinking this. We are what we are, and he was a businessman, and in his mind there was no better thing that one could be. From time to time his hand came down on some elaborate fancy and I had to pick up the pieces and go somewhere where he wasn't in order to feel cheerful again. If he spoke impatiently to me or with what seemed to me to be harshness, I could not keep back the tears, which added to his annoyance. As he turned away I had the feeling he had washed his hands of me. Was I not the kind of little boy he wanted to have? He didn't say that either. It is hard enough for adults to keep their emotional reactions in something like balance. Children simply feel what they feel, and I knew I was not the apple of my father's eye.

We were both creatures of the period. I doubt if the heavy-businessman-father-and-the-oversensitive-artistic-son syndrome exists any more. Fathers have become sympathetic and kiss their grown sons when they feel like it, and who knows what oversensitive is, considering all there is to be sensitive to.

When a sufficient number of months had been torn off the calendar so that my mother's friends felt they could invite my father to their dinner parties, they did. And he got dressed up and went. They were matchmaking, of course, and like all matchmakers had mixed motives. I doubt if he needed their help. He was still only in his early forties, and he had always been handsome, and liked women, and it would have been strange if he hadn't found somebody who was willing to love him. I had no comprehension whatever of the sexual and emotional needs of a man of his age. He was simply my father, and I assumed that for the rest of his life he would be—"faithful to my mother's memory" is how I had heard grown people express it.

While he was having his social life, I was having mine. Our room at school decided to have a Halloween party and it was a question of where to have it. I offered our house and the offer was accepted. When I told my father he shook his head doubtfully and asked what I planned to do. I said I was going to carve a pumpkin and put some cornstalks around in the living room. He didn't think the party was at all a good idea, it would mean extra work for the housekeeper, and next time I'd better ask before I did something like that. Since I had committed myself, I could go ahead with it, provided it was confined to an empty maid's room and they used the back stairs. My mother wasn't there to tell him that this was unthinkable and so that's what happened. Deeply embarrassed, I led the teacher and my classmates through rooms that were brightly lit and had always been so hospitable, through the dining room to the pantry and up the narrow uninviting back stairs. Nobody seemed to find this in any way strange. I don't think it was much of a Halloween party. What has stayed in my mind all these years is a scene that occurred by the laundry basket in the back hall. The teacher had been chosen to be the "victim" and sat down on a chair and allowed herself to be blindfolded. At that point, ideas of propriety made me hesitate. I motioned to one of the girls, who took my place. When the teacher re-moved the blindfold she was smiling with pleasure because a young boy—because she *thought* a young boy had kissed her.

In telling me that he was going to be married my father was as gentle as he knew how to be. He didn't expect me to offer any objection, and wouldn't have been deflected from his purpose if I had.

A year or two before this, at the Country Club on a summer day, wandering idly near the caddie house I came upon a sight I didn't understand. I thought at first it was some new kind of animal. Then I retreated in horror. What I was looking at was a snake in the act of swallowing a frog that was too large and wouldn't go down. Neither would the idea that another woman was not only going to sit in my mother's place at the dinner table but also take her place in my father's heart.

Where a hardier boy would have run away from home or got in trouble with the police, I sat with my nose in a book so I wouldn't have to think about things I didn't like and couldn't prevent happening. It wasn't enough for me, or for my older brother and my younger brother and me, to slip through that door to the way things used to be, when the time came; my mother would expect us to bring my father with us. And if he was married to another woman, how could we?

We had moved from our fixed position and there was now no possibility of getting back to the way things were before she died. I could not tell whether the heavy feeling in my chest had to do with what might happen or with what had already happened and was irremediable.

The kindergarten run by Miss Lena Moose and Miss Lucy Sheffield was on the second floor of a building just off the courthouse square, and the young woman who became my stepmother used to go from house to house at nine o'clock in the morning, collecting the children. When we were all assem-bled, she walked us downtown. She must have been in her early twenties then. As a child she had lived on Ninth Street, though she didn't any more. At noon, on the day of my mother's funeral, when we went into the dining room she was there. I sat down at the table but I could not eat. My throat was blocked from crying. She came and stood behind my chair and talked to me, and urged me to eat some of the baked potato on my plate. For her sake, because she was young and pretty and because I had always liked her, I managed to do it. The taste of that baked potato has remained with me all the rest of my life.

In fairy tales the coming of a stepmother is never regarded as anything but a misfortune. Presumably this is not because of the great number of second wives who were unkind to the children of their husband's first marriage, though examples of this could be found, but because of the universal resentment on the children's part of an outsider. So that for the father to remarry is an act of betrayal not only of the dead mother but of them, no matter what the stepmother is like.

What strange and unlikely things are washed up on the shore of time. I have in my possession a tattered photograph album full of snapshots of my stepmother as a young woman. Very pretty and sweet she was, with a fur muff and a picture hat and her skirts almost to the floor. There are pictures of her with friends, with her mother and sister, with one or another of her four brothers, with elderly relatives on the front stoop of a turn-of-the-century house in, I think, Boston. There are two group pictures, taken by a local photographer, of a masquerade party—one with masks and one without, so that you can see who the pirate, the clown, the Columbine, etc., were. Half the people there I knew when I was growing up. And then more pictures of my stepmother: in Washington, D.C., during the First World War, with a thin-faced man in army uniform whom she was in love with at the time but did not marry; back in Lincoln, holding her sister's baby, and so on. What beautiful clothes. What glorious automobiles. What good times.

At the beginning and end of the album, pasted in what must have been blank places, since they run counter to the sequence, are a dozen pictures of my father. Except for the one where he is standing with a string of fish spread out on a rock beside him, he is always in a group of people. He has a golf stick in his hand. Or he is smoking a pipe. Or he is wearing a bathing suit and has one arm around my stepmother's waist and the other around a woman I don't recognize. And looking at these faded snapshots I see, the child that survives in me sees with a pang that—I am old enough to be that man's father, and he has been dead for nearly twenty years, and yet it troubles me that he was happy. Why? In some way his happiness was at that time (and forever after, it would seem) a threat to me. It was not the kind of happiness that children are included in, but why should that trouble me now? I do not even begin to understand it.

If I had by some supernatural sleight of hand managed to pull off that trick and brought my mother back from the cemetery and if we had continued to live the way we did before, we would have found ourselves on an island in a river of change, for it was the year 1921, and women had begun to cut off their hair and wear their skirts above their knees and drink gin out of silver flasks in public. Now and then one of them drank too much and had to be taken home. The gossips had a great deal to shake their heads over. In the light of what followed, the twenties seem on the whole a charming, carefree period. So far as good manners are concerned, it was the beginning of the end. When my mother went riding with my father on Sunday morning she rode sidesaddle (think of it!) and came out of the house and down the steps of the front porch in a divided skirt that swept the cement walk. I try to imagine her with bobbed hair and her skirts above her knees and I fail utterly.

It was still possible to think, as my father did, that the present was in every way an improvement over the past, and that the future was bound to be even more satisfactory. He also believed in keeping up with the times. When Prohibition came in, he announced that he was ready to obey the Law and give up drinking—by which he meant a glass of beer or a shot of bourbon, in masculine company. When it turned out that other people were not going to do this, he made his own gin and bought rotgut whiskey from a bootlegger named Coonhound Johnny, like his friends.

On one occasion he even overshot the mark. Friday afternoons I went to dancing school and pushed girls around in the one-step, the fox trot, and the waltz. They held themselves at arm's length, their backs as stiff as a ramrod, their manner remote. The dancing teacher was young and animated and something under five feet tall, which meant that she was my

522   SO LONG, SEE YOU TOMORROW

height even though she wore very high heels. There was also a class for adults on Thursday evenings, to which my father and stepmother went before they were married. One night they put their cheeks together and did a new dance that they had been practising in private. It was called the Toddle, and everybody stopped to look at them, and the dancing teacher, very red in the face, asked them to leave the floor.

It is characteristic of my father that though he was angry at her and never went back, he did not remove me from the children's class. On Friday afternoon the dancing teacher kept me after the other boys and girls had gone. She was in trouble, though she didn't quite manage to say what it was. Did she sense that I was half on her side and nobody else much was? She had done the right thing, without stopping to think that the two people involved were of good family and she was a grass widow with two small children to support and from out of town. She may not, in fact, even have known who was and who wasn't of good family. I felt sorry for her, as I would have for anybody in tears. And disloyal to my father as I stood there listening to the things she said about him. And embarrassed that he was the object of scandal.

One of the things my mother loved about my father was that he was a natural musician. Hoping that this talent might have been inherited, she arranged for my older brother to take piano lessons from a nun who taught music in the Catholic school. When I was six I accompanied him to the house where the nuns lived, for my first music lesson. Sister Mary Anise showed me where to put my hands on the keyboard and I looked up at her teeth, which were frightfully crooked, and burst into tears. She told my brother to bring me back when I was seven—by which time she was wearing false teeth that were not crooked and I could look at her with equanimity. I was not musical and I didn't like to practise. What I did like was the lives of the composers, doled out to me one at a time in the form of unbound sheets of printed matter that had to be folded and sewed together at the spine, and a perforated sheet of illustrations to be pasted in at the appropriate places. In the first of these books I read how Johann Sebastian Bach's wicked elder brother was jealous of his talent and wouldn't let him have access to the music he wanted, so he got up in the night and copied it by moonlight, ruining his eyesight. I formed an attachment to the young put-upon Johann Sebastian Bach, and after him to Handel and his Water Music, and Haydn and Mozart and Beethoven and Schubert and Schumann and Mendelssohn and Wagner's operas and classical music in general. It didn't improve my playing. "Flat," my mother would call out from the next room, when I was practising at home. "E-flat, not E-natural." And I would get up from the piano stool and go look at the clock in the front hall.

My father kept a small victrola on top of the upright piano in the living room and after dinner, having played a new record through two or three times while he figured out the chords, he was off, he had it. He played ragtime and songs from the musicals of the period. He had a beautiful touch and people loved to hear him. One day he sat down at the piano with me and tried to teach me how to play by ear. I didn't understand one word he was saying.

It gave him no pleasure to hear me stumble through "The Shepherd Boy's Prayer," and also he wanted me to like his kind of music, so, when I was twelve, without inquiring how I felt about it, he took me away from Sister Mary Anise and Bach and Handel and Haydn, and arranged for me to take lessons from a young married woman who played the organ in the Catholic church and was my stepmother's closest friend. The piece she gave me to learn, at my father's suggestion, was "Alice Blue Gown." I liked her but I came to have a deep dislike for that inane song as, week after week, I played it and nothing else. I also made no progress. I had found a small plot of ground on which I could oppose my father without being actively disobedient.

Because he was finishing out a period of mourning, which in those days had to be three years, roughly, or there was talk, he and my stepmother waited. She was in California for a while and when I went for my music lesson I would be given a fat envelope that had come in the mail inside another envelope addressed to my music teacher. Nobody explained that this was so the housekeeper couldn't steam the envelope open and read what was inside; instead, they acted as though it was the most natural thing in the world for a twelve-year-old boy to be bringing a love letter home to his father.

The reason life is so strange is that so often people have no choice, but in this case I think convenience entered into it: I mean, my father could have rented a box at the post office. He may have been deterred by the fact that if he was seen entering and leaving the post office and taking mail out of a box, people would very soon have guessed why. So in short he had no choice either, about that or about selling the house, which was so full of associations with my mother. In a matter of two or three weeks after he put it on the market, it was bought by a man who had had enough of farming and wanted to live in town. One day while I was in school the moving men came and what furniture my father hadn't managed to sell or give away ended up in a much smaller house that he had rented on an unpaved street out near the edge of town.

I went straight home from school to the new house. Though as a grown man I have often stood and looked at the old house, I have never been inside it since that day, when a great many objects that I remember and would like to be re-united with disappeared without a trace: Victorian walnut sofas and chairs that my fingers had absently traced every knob and scroll of, mahogany tables, worn Oriental rugs, gilt mirrors, pictures, big square books full of photographs that I knew by heart. If they hadn't disappeared then, they would have on some other occasion, life being, as Ortega y Gasset somewhere remarks, in itself and forever shipwreck.

The rented house had no yard to speak of, the porch steps were ten feet from the front sidewalk, and our house and the house next door were identical. The bites that woke me in the night proved to be bedbugs, concealed under a loose corner of the wallpaper, and the exterminator took care of them. My father probably thought that since we were not going to stay there it didn't matter too much what the house was like. Or there may not, at that moment, have been anything better. I used to stand and compare the two identical houses, detail by detail, the way you compare repeats in wallpaper hoping to find some small difference. I did not so much miss the old house as blot it completely out of my mind. We had gone down in the world and there didn't seem to be anything to do but make the best of it. Ninth Street had the air of having been there since the beginning of time. Generations of children had grown up there, leaving their bicycles where people could fall over them, making leaf houses, climbing trees, playing run-sheep-run on summer evenings. The unpaved street we were now living on had no past and no future but only a wan present in which it was hard to think of anything to do.

One evening in October my father and Grace McGrath came down the stairs in her sister's house and were married on the landing, by the Catholic priest, who couldn't marry them in a church because my father was a Protestant. I was the only person present under the age of thirty. My older brother was away at college, my younger brother asleep in his crib. Now was the moment to forget about that door I had walked through without thinking, and about the void that could sometimes be bridged in dreams, and about the way things used to be when my mother was alive. Instead, I clung to them more tightly than ever, even as I was being drawn willy-nilly into my father's new life.

3

The New House

THE small towns in central Illinois nearly all owe their existence to the coming of the railroads in the decade before the Civil War. I have always had the impression that Lincoln is in some way different from the others but perhaps that is only because I lived there. It is the county seat and has two coal mines, now worked out. It has never had any sizable factories, and owes its modest prosperity to the surrounding farmland. In the year 1921 the shade trees that everywhere lined the residential streets had had time to come full size and made the town seem older than it actually was. It was not easy to tell when the houses were built, because their age was so frequently disguised by subsequent additions, and so they seemed timeless and as inseparably a part of the people who lived in them as their voices or their names or the way they combed their hair.

My father found most old things oppressive, but especially old houses with high ceilings and odd-shaped rooms that opened one out of another, offering a pleasant vista that required a great deal of coal to heat in the harsh Illinois winters. Intending to escape all this by building, he bought a double lot in Park Place, a subdivision so recently laid out that the trees were only five feet tall and had to be staked against the north wind. All but two of the existing houses were on the right-hand side of the street, facing a cow pasture that I think has not been built on to this day. The building lots were narrow and the houses much closer together than they were in the old part of town, but there was an ornamental brick gateway leading into the street and a grass plot down the center, and it was fashionable. In present-day Lincoln it is fashionable to live clear out in the country, surrounded by cornfields.

My father and my stepmother had seen a stucco house in Bloomington that they liked, and they got an architect to copy the exterior and then the three of them fiddled with the interior plans until they were satisfactory. I was shown on the blue-

prints where my room was going to be. In a short time the cement foundation was poured and the framing was up and you
could see the actual size and shape of the rooms. I used to go
there after school and watch the carpenters hammering: *pung,
pung, pung, kapung, kapung, kapung, kapung*. . . . They
may have guessed that I was waiting for them to pick up their
tools and go home so I could climb around on the scaffolding
but they didn't tell me I couldn't do this, or in fact pay any attention to me at all. And I had the agreeable feeling, as I went
from one room to the next by walking through the wall instead of a doorway, or looked up and saw blue sky through the
rafters, that I had found a way to get around the way things
were.

When, wandering through the Museum of Modern Art, I
come upon the piece of sculpture by Alberto Giacometti with
the title "Palace at 4 A.M.," I always stand and look at it—
partly because it reminds me of my father's new house in its
unfinished state and partly because it is so beautiful. It is about
thirty inches high and sufficiently well known that I probably
don't need to describe it. But anyway, it is made of wood, and
there are no solid walls, only thin uprights and horizontal
beams. There is the suggestion of a classic pediment and of a
tower. Flying around in a room at the top of the palace there is
a queer-looking creature with the head of a monkey wrench. A
bird? a cross between a male ballet dancer and a pterodactyl?
Below it, in a kind of freestanding closet, the backbone of
some animal. To the left, backed by three off-white parallelo-
grams, what could be an imposing female figure or one of the
more important pieces of a chess set. And, in about the position a basketball ring would occupy, a vertical, hollowed-out
spatulate shape with a ball in front of it.

It is all terribly spare and strange, but no stranger than the
artist's account of how it came into being: "This object took
shape little by little in the late summer of 1932; it revealed itself
to me slowly, the various parts taking their exact form and
their precise place within the whole. By autumn it had attained
such reality that its actual execution in space took no more
than one day. It is related without any doubt to a period in my
life that had come to an end a year before, when for six whole
months hour after hour was passed in the company of a

woman who, concentrating all life in herself, magically transformed my every moment. We used to construct a fantastic
palace at night—days and nights had the same color, as if everything happened just before daybreak; throughout the whole
time I never saw the sun—a very fragile palace of matchsticks.
At the slightest false move a whole section of this tiny construction would collapse. We would always begin it over again.
I don't know why it came to be inhabited by a spinal column
in a cage—the spinal column this woman sold me one of
the very first nights I met her on the street—and by one of the
skeleton birds that she saw the very night before the morning
in which our life together collapsed—the skeleton birds that
flutter with cries of joy at four o'clock in the morning very
high above the pool of clear, green water where the extremely
fine, white skeletons of fish float in the great unroofed hall. In
the middle there rises the scaffolding of a tower, perhaps unfinished or, since its top has collapsed, perhaps also broken.
On the other side there appeared the statue of a woman, in
which I recognize my mother, just as she appears in my earliest
memories. The mystery of her long black dress touching the
floor troubled me; it seemed to me like a part of her body, and
aroused in me a feeling of fear and confusion. . . ."

I seem to remember that I went to the new house one winter day and saw snow descending through the attic to the upstairs bedrooms. It could also be that I never did any such
thing, for I am fairly certain that in a snapshot album I have
lost track of there was a picture of the house taken in the circumstances I have just described, and it is possible that I am
remembering that rather than an actual experience. What we, or
at any rate what I, refer to confidently as memory—meaning a
moment, a scene, a fact that has been subjected to a fixative
and thereby rescued from oblivion—is really a form of storytelling that goes on continually in the mind and often changes
with the telling. Too many conflicting emotional interests are
involved for life ever to be wholly acceptable, and possibly it is
the work of the storyteller to rearrange things so that they
conform to this end. In any case, in talking about the past we
lie with every breath we draw.

Before the stairway was in, there was a gaping hole in the
center of the house and you had to use the carpenters' rickety

ladder to get to the second floor. One day I looked down through this hole and saw Cletus Smith standing on a pile of lumber looking at me. I suppose I said, "Come on up." Anyway, he did. We stood looking out at the unlit streetlamp, through a square opening that was some day going to be a window, and then we climbed up another ladder and walked along horizontal two-by-sixes with our arms outstretched, teetering like circus acrobats on the high wire. We could have fallen all the way through to the basement and broken an arm or a leg but we didn't.

Boys don't need much of an excuse to get on well together, if they get on at all. I was glad for his company, and pleased when he turned up the next day. If I saw him now the way he was then, I don't know that I would recognize him. I seem to remember his smile, and that he had large hands and feet for a boy of thirteen. And Cletus Smith isn't his real name.

Did I know him because he was in my room at school? I try to picture him standing at the blackboard and can't. It is so long ago. Were we in the same Boy Scout troop, which would have meant that at some time during that fall we had studied the Scout manual together and practised tying reef knots and clove hitches and running bowlines, and considered what merit badges we would try for next? I don't know the answer. I only know that I knew him. From somewhere. And that we played together in that unfinished house day after day, risking our necks and breathing in the rancid odor of sawdust and shavings and fresh-cut lumber.

Ninth Street was an extension of home, and perfectly safe. Nobody ever picked on me there. When I passed beyond Ninth Street, it could be rough going. The boys in the eighth grade dominated the school yard before school and at recess time. They were, by turns, good-natured in a patronizing way, or mean, or foulmouthed about girls, or single-mindedly bent on improving their proficiency in some sport. Sometimes they would go to the trouble of twisting a younger boy's arm behind his back or put a foot out and trip him as he ran past, and if he fell and hurt himself they were happy for a whole quarter of an hour afterward, but their attention seldom settled on any one boy for very long.

Looking back, it seems clear enough that I brought my

difficulties on myself. To begin with, I was as thin as a stick. In any kind of competitive game, my mind froze and I became half paralyzed. The baseball could be counted on to slip through my overanxious fingers. Nobody wanted me on their team. I was a character. I also had the unfortunate habit, when called on in class, of coming up with the right answer. It won me a smile of approval from the teacher, and it was nice to see my name on the Honor Roll. It was not nice to be chased home from school by two coal miners' sons who were in the same room with me but only because they could not escape from the truant officer. Nowhere was I safe against them—neither in the classroom, where their eyes were always on me, or in the school yard, where they danced around me, pushing me off balance and trying to get me to fight back so they could clean up on me.

All this took place in plain sight of everybody, all the boys I had grown up with, and no hand was ever raised in my defense, nobody ever came to my rescue—I expect partly because they had their own vulnerabilities and did not want to be singled out for attack, but obviously there was something about me that invited it. Since I did not know what it was, I couldn't do anything to change it, and any emotion I felt—physical inadequacy, fear, humiliation, the whole repertoire of the adolescent—showed in my face. I was such easy game that I wonder that their pleasure in tormenting me lasted as long as it did. When they were fourteen they dropped out of school and I never saw them again. Where else could they have gone but down in the mine with their fathers? If somebody told me they had contracted black lung I don't know that I could manage to be sorry.

The gap between my older brother and me was too great for me to emulate his pleasures or contribute to them, and I would have been glad for a brother nearer my own age, to defend me when I got in trouble, and to do things with. At about this time, one of my mother's friends, a woman I knew but not very well, invited me to come to her house after school on Friday and stay until Sunday afternoon. She had a son who was a year or two older than I was and everything a boy that age ought to be—open and easy with adults, bright in school, and beyond being pushed around by his contemporaries. I slept in the same room with him and I was with him all day Saturday and Sunday. Without any experience to go on, I tried to be a good guest. Most of the time he was friendly, and then suddenly he would mutter something under his breath that I could not quite hear and that I knew from a heaviness in my heart was the word "sissy." I ignored it, not knowing what else to do; not having enough experience of the world to take my toothbrush and pyjamas and go home, leaving him to explain to his mother why I wasn't there. At bedtime, standing by the wide-open window of his room, he had me do setting-up exercises with him. He was patient when I didn't do them right, and also funny, and it was so nice to be doing something with another boy for a change. But then he muttered that word under his breath that I wasn't supposed to be able to say that he had actually said. He was exactly the kind of boy I would have liked to be, and I was ready to imitate him in any way I could. One minute I was encouraged to do this and the next I felt—I was made to feel—that he despised me. Probably all it amounted to was that his mother had decided on this act of kindness without consulting him, and he was angry because my being there had spoiled his Saturday. In any case, the point I am trying to make is that it was a new experience for me to have the companionship of another boy day after day. Whatever I suggested doing we did. I never asked Cletus if there wasn't something he'd rather be doing, because he was always ready to do what I wanted to do. It occurs to me now that he was not very different from an imaginary playmate. When I was with him, if I said something the boys in the school yard would have jeered at, he let the opportunity pass and went on carefully teetering with one foot in front of the other, or at most, without glancing in my direction, which would have endangered his balance, nodded.

I supposed he must have liked me somewhat or he wouldn't have been there. And that he was glad for my companionship. He didn't act as if there was some other boy waiting for him to turn up. He must have understood that I was going to live in this house when it was finished, but it didn't occur to me to wonder where he lived.

When I was a child I told my mother everything. After she died I learned that it was better to keep some things to myself.

My father represented authority, which meant—to me—that he could not also represent understanding. And because there was an element of cruelty in my older brother's teasing (as, of course, there is in all teasing) I didn't trust him, though I perfectly well could have, about larger matters. Anyway, I didn't tell Cletus about my shipwreck, as we sat looking down on the whole neighborhood, and he didn't tell me about his. When the look of the sky informed us that it was getting along toward suppertime, we climbed down and said "So long" and "See you tomorrow," and went our separate ways in the dusk. And one evening this casual parting turned out to be for the last time. We were separated by that pistol shot.

There was never any real doubt about who had killed Lloyd Wilson. The only person who had any reason to do it was Clarence Smith, Cletus's father. Among the things that Cletus failed to tell me was the fact that he had grown up in the country. He had only been living in town a few months. His mother had sued his father for a divorce, the grounds being extreme and repeated cruelty. His father then filed a cross bill charging her with infidelity and naming Lloyd Wilson, who lived on the adjoining farm, as corespondent.

The Lincoln *Courier-Herald* was, and is, a self-respecting small-town newspaper and it did not feel called upon to provide the salacious details, which are safely buried in the court records. I think it highly unlikely that Cletus was present at the divorce trial. How much did he know? Enough, probably. Enough so that it was preferable to play with a boy he hardly knew than with somebody he might be tempted to confide in—if there was any such person.

When the divorce proceedings went against him, Cletus's father sold his lease and gave up farming and moved in with Cletus's grandparents in town. He was depressed and given to fits of weeping. And he could not keep from talking about his troubles. Men who had known him for many years took to crossing over to the other side of the street when they saw him coming.

Lloyd Wilson confessed to his two brothers that he lived in fear of an attack on his life, and they told him he ought to leave town immediately. Like a figure in a dream, he took all the steps he should have taken, but in slow motion. He went to see the woman whose land he farmed and asked to be released from his contract, which did not expire until March. He consulted a lawyer.

On the morning that he was killed he left the barn door open wide so as to catch the morning light when it came. The light from his lantern must have fallen just short of the toe of the murderer's boot.

I assume that I knew all this once, since it was published in the evening paper and I was old enough to read. In the course of time the details of the murder passed from my mind, and what I thought happened was so different from what actually did happen that it might almost have been something I made up out of whole cloth. And I might have gone right on thinking that Cletus's father had come home unexpectedly and found Cletus's mother in bed with a man and killed them both, but one day, as if I had suddenly broken through a brick wall, I realized that there are always sources of information about the past other than one's own recollection, and that I didn't need to remain in total ignorance about something that interested me so deeply. I wrote to my stepcousin Tom Perry and asked him if he could dig up for me those issues of the *Courier-Herald* that had anything in them about the murder of Lloyd Wilson. He reported back to me that the *Courier*'s file (the *Herald* was dropped a long time ago) did not go back to the year 1922 and that the public library had destroyed its file six months before and what I'd better do was apply to the Illinois State Historical Society in Springfield. It was as if I was inquiring into the funeral of Abraham Lincoln. But anyway, I did as he said, and the Historical Society sent me, from its microfilm library, photostatic copies, not always entirely legible, of eight issues of a newspaper once as familiar to me as the back of my hand. It was, of course, much more than I had asked for, a small segment of the past, remote and yet in perfect focus, like something seen through the wrong end of a pair of binoculars: ads for movies starring Norma Talmadge and Wallace Reid, good quality of men's suits at Griesheim's clothing store at $7, and many other things equally hard to believe.

I don't know where the office and printing plant of the Lincoln *Courier* is now; only that it isn't where it used to be, on

North Kickapoo Street, half a block from the courthouse square.

Several of the pieces about the murder were written by the editor, whom I remember as a high-strung, dark-haired man with a green eyeshade and a cigarette in the corner of his mouth. His stories give the impression of being dashed off in the last minutes before the paper went to press; that is to say, they are repetitious and disordered and full of not very acute speculation. Also of clichés and reticences which the ideas of the period no doubt required. People are quoted as saying things I have trouble believing that they actually said, at least in those words. I am reasonably sure, for example, that Cletus's father did not say to a man he met on the street the day before the murder, "I am broken and a failure and I have nothing for which to live." Nobody I know in the Middle West has ever gone out of his way to avoid ending a sentence with a preposition. But it isn't fair, in any case, to blame that overworked small-town newspaper editor for not writing as well as Roughead. Especially since I am indebted to him for any knowledge I have of what happened.

The sheriff was on the point of taking some prisoners to the courthouse for trial when the undertaker called him. The deputy sheriff and the coroner went out to the Wilson farm and Fred Wilson showed them the stall Lloyd Wilson was in, the pail that had only a little milk in it, the milking stool, the gloves that he always wore when he was milking and that were still on his hands when they found him. Near the door of the cow barn the two men from town saw some footprints, which they covered with boards so they would stay fresh. All morning, search parties beat over the muddy fields and along the banks of a creek that ran through both farms. The bloodhounds arrived from Springfield, by train, and were taken to the scene of the crime. Two hundred people were there waiting for them. The footprints were uncovered and the dogs were led to the cow barn and unleashed. Sniffing, they circled an implement shed and a haystack and returned to the barn and then they jumped a barbed-wire fence and took off, with a pack of excited men running after them. Just before the dogs got to the farmhouse Clarence Smith had recently moved out of, they turned aside, at a gate, and followed the lane out to the public road. After pausing at the mailbox they crossed over to the other side of the road and lost the scent. Twice they were led back to the cow barn and let loose. The first time, they went into the yard of the Smith farm and up onto the porch. The second time, they turned aside again, into a cornfield, and followed a trail of footprints until they ended up on the hard road, a quarter of a mile west of the lane.

Clarence Smith had sold his lease to a younger man named James Walker. After the bloodhounds were taken back to town, Walker came out of the farmhouse and walked out to the public road. A handful of men lingered by the entrance to the lane and, moved by a floating curiosity, they gathered around him while he pulled down the flap of the mailbox. What were they expecting? At most a letter or two that they would not be allowed to read and yesterday's *Courier-Herald*. In the mailbox was an object so startling that they all stepped back and waited. James Walker took the gold watch out of the mailbox and opened the case and found the initials "C.S." It could only be Clarence Smith's watch, but when was it left there and for what reason? James Walker drove in to town and turned it over to the sheriff, who considered the possibility that it was a plant, put there by someone other than Clarence Smith to make it appear that he was the murderer.

That evening, the sheriff went to the house of Clarence Smith's parents and learned that they had no idea where their son was. Neither had anyone else. He was last seen leaving the Grand Theater at 10:45 on the night before Lloyd Wilson was killed. The State's attorney didn't issue a warrant charging Cletus's father with the murder. He was merely wanted for questioning. The description sent to the police throughout the state reads: "Age 40 years, height 5 feet 7 inches, weight 165 pounds, light brown hair slightly bald."

Neighbors reported that they had seen a strange automobile waiting near the Wilson farm on the night before the murder. One of them said that the automobile waited in the lane just off the hard road for at least two hours. He saw it for the last time at about nine o'clock, just before he went to bed. Another neighbor said that the automobile was not in the lane but at the edge of the hard road, and that it was standing with the lights turned off. Since Clarence Smith did not own a car, this raised the question of whether he might have had an accomplice.

There was a rumor that he was seen boarding the trolley car that ran between Peoria, Lincoln, and Springfield, on the day of the murder. Also that he had registered at a hotel in Springfield and that same night had received a long-distance telephone call there. Given the chance to believe something so interesting, people did, though the hotel denied that he had been there, and the person who saw him board the trolley never came forward. The rumor that he had a large sum of money on his person when he disappeared couldn't have been true either, since the money from the sale of his lease could all be accounted for.

There was another angle to the case that the *Courier* felt obliged to consider. In the spring of the year before he was killed, Lloyd Wilson's wife left him, taking their four girls, the youngest of whom was a baby eleven months old, and moved to town. She did not divorce him but got a legal separation. By the terms of this agreement he had to pay her $9,000, which in 1921 was a lot of money. My father's new house only cost $12,000, including the land it was built on. The settlement Lloyd Wilson made on his wife may have represented all the money he had.

I don't know what she looked like. Most farm women of her age were reduced by hard work and frequent child-bearing to a common denominator of plainness. I fancy, as people used to say when I was a child—I fancy that this was true of Lloyd Wilson's wife and that it was not true of Cletus's mother, but there is no warrant for my thinking this, and the simple truth is that though so much is made of the woman's beauty in love stories, passion does not require it. Plato's idea that lovers were originally one person, the two parts having become separated and desiring to be joined, is as good an explanation as any for what cannot in the mind of an outsider ever be convincingly accounted for.

The names and ages of the Wilson children were printed in the paper. Probably through happenstance, the names and ages of Clarence Smith's were not.

Cletus's mother had been an orphan and was brought up by

an aunt and uncle, who lived in town. When she left Cletus's father she moved back to the house she grew up in. The *Courier-Herald* gives the address, and I asked my cousin to see if there was a house at that address now. He reported back that there was and that it was one of a row of frame houses opposite the fairgrounds. Somewhat down at the heels, he said, and painted white, and like a lot of other small houses in town.

What the newspaper refers to as "the estrangement" occurred during the summer after Wilson's wife left him. "A year ago," the *Courier-Herald* goes on to say, "there were no better friends than Wilson and Smith. They were often in town together. If Smith bought a cigar for himself he also bought one for Wilson, who did the same. In an argument they stuck up for each other against all comers, and people often spoke about what bosom friends they were. Smith is considered, by people who knew him, to be a quiet, reserved man."

The only photograph I have ever seen of him, or of Lloyd Wilson, was printed on the front page of the *Courier-Herald*. Since it is a photostatic copy, black and white—or rather, brown and white—are reversed. Even so, they look enough alike to be taken for brothers. No doubt Cain and Abel loved each other, in their way, quite as much as, or even more than, David and Jonathan.

There are many questions I did not find the answer to by reading those old newspapers. For example, from whom did Cletus's mother learn about the murder? And how soon? And what happened then—hysterics, in front of her two sons? And what about the six-year-old child who was sent to the barn to see what was keeping his father so long? Were he and his brother peering out through a lace curtain when the bloodhounds went baying across the fields in pursuit of the man who had killed their father? Or did the housekeeper draw them away from the window? She was a countrywoman, and you don't see such sights every day. Chances are that all three of them were peering out of the window, unless the little boys' mother had already come for them.

For several days new details kept turning up: "It is said on high authority that Wilson and Mrs. Smith corresponded frequently since the Smith divorce last fall, and during the time that Smith was paying alimony to his former wife. It is believed that Smith knew of this alleged fact and brooded over the situation. Mrs. Smith is said to have been afraid of her former husband, and this fear is believed to have been communicated to Wilson. . . . Sheriff Ahrens called in a former farm hand of Smith's who had testified for him during the trial. This man had been working in the Coonsburg vicinity, had been regularly employed there, and had not seen Smith since a week ago Saturday night when he came out of the bathroom of the local barber shop and saw Smith waiting for a shave." And so on.

James Walker told the reporter from the *Courier-Herald* that one day shortly after Clarence Smith left the farm and he took possession, he came out of the woodshed and saw Smith standing on the porch. Walker said he was all by himself at the time, and glad to have somebody to talk to. When Smith said, "Do you mind if I have a look around?" he said, "Go ahead, help yourself"—as anybody would under the circumstances. But when Smith came back again a few days later and spent a long time in the barn and then went into one shed after another, Walker grew uneasy. If Smith had lost something why didn't he say what it was? It turned out that Walker himself had lost something instead, a small anvil. He was positive he had brought it with him when he moved, and so far as he knew there was no way Clarence Smith could have carried it off with him, but neither could the anvil have walked off by itself.

James Walker wrote to his wife and asked her to join him immediately, and after that Clarence Smith didn't come any more.

The day after Walker found the watch he found Clarence Smith's overcoat, in a storm buggy. The deputy sheriff, searching the barns and outbuildings with a flashlight, had seen it and thought it belonged to the new tenant. Kept warm by the coat and some lap robes, Clarence Smith had spent the night before the murder on his own farm and in the morning concealed himself behind a haystack and waited for Lloyd Wilson's lantern to come bobbing across the pasture.

Cletus's grandfather, when he was interviewed by that same reporter, said that if his son had committed the murder while mentally unbalanced from jealousy he wouldn't be found alive; he wouldn't want to live.

Cletus's mother, perhaps too distraught to be charitable, said, "I do not believe he killed himself. I think he carried out plans for his escape." What plans? There is no evidence that he had made any.

Partly out of fear and partly to get away from curiosity-seekers, Walker and his wife moved into temporary quarters in town. The sheriff's office was kept busy answering calls from people who wanted to know if Clarence Smith had been found. Most of them had heard that he had drowned himself in the gravel pit. The *Courier-Herald* was at some pains to scotch this rumor also: "Deputy William Duffy, who conducted a thorough examination of the gravel pit the morning of the murder, does not believe that Smith or any other person drowned himself in the pit. The earth around it was soft, due to the thaw. On two sides the bank was steep and tracks would have shown clearly. At the point where it would have been possible to dive from a springboard, the water was shallow and a person would have had to wade out in the shallows before reaching deep water. Encircling the entire pit, looking for tracks in the soft earth, Mr. Duffy found absolutely nothing."

On Friday, the third of February, fifteen days after Lloyd Wilson's body was found leaning against a partition in his barn, another body was fished up from the bottom of Deer Creek gravel pit, where the deputy sheriff said it couldn't be. It was lying face down across the dredging bucket. Cletus's father, not wanting to live, had shot himself through the head. Dangling from his right wrist, at the end of a shoestring, was a .38 revolver with two empty chambers. A flashlight protruded from his coat pocket. A strand of baling wire was wound around his neck and waist. Until it was severed by the dredging bucket it had attached the body to whatever the heavy weight was that was holding it down. In going through the other pockets the undertaker found a razor still deeply stained with red, a bloody handkerchief, a watch chain, and several shotgun shells.

At the coroner's inquest, the only witnesses were the sheriff and the three men who worked at the gravel pit. The jury returned the following verdict: "We, the undersigned jurors, do find that Clarence C. Smith came to his death by a gunshot wound inflicted by his own hand, with suicidal intent." There was no effort to establish a motive for the suicide and no mention of the murder of Lloyd Wilson. At the final hearing in the murder case, the verdict was "Death from a gunshot wound inflicted by an unknown hand."

Several hundred people tried to get a look at Clarence Smith's body while it was at the undertaker's and were turned away. The funeral was in his father's house. "Reverend A. S. Hubbard, pastor of the First Baptist Church, was in charge of the services. A male quartet, standing on the stair landing, gave a number of selections. Pallbearers were Joseph McElhiney, John Holmes, Frank Mitchell, and Roy Anderson. Numerous floral tokens of sympathy were received by the family and the funeral was one of the largest held in Lincoln in some time."

Cletus's father was not buried at the crossroads with a stake through his heart but in the cemetery along with everybody else. The day after the funeral a gunstock was found floating on the surface of the gravel pit. The following afternoon the dredging bucket brought up the rest of the gun. In the barrel was a defective shell. When the shotgun failed to go off, the shell jammed, and the ejector didn't remove it. And so Lloyd Wilson was killed with a revolver instead.

Cletus's grandfather was summoned to the sheriff's office to identify the gun and said he knew his son had a shotgun but he didn't know what it looked like or remember having seen the gun among the things his son brought with him when he moved from the farm. The sheriff then asked if Clarence Smith's sons hunted with him. "Identification of the gun"—I am quoting from the *Courier-Herald*—"was made this afternoon by the oldest son of Clarence C. Smith, who recognized the manufacturer's mark. The boy has a bicycle of the same make." Between the time that Cletus and I climbed down from the scaffolding and went our separate ways and the moment when he was confronted with the broken gun in the sheriff's office, he must have crossed over the line into maturity, and though he is referred to as a boy, wasn't one any longer.

Shortly after this his mother wrote to Lloyd Wilson's housekeeper asking that a photograph she had given him be returned to her. The *Courier-Herald* got hold of this letter and published one sentence from it: "I am the most miserable woman in the world."

4

In the School Corridor

I HAVE a hazy half-recollection, which I do not trust, of sitting and staring at Cletus's empty desk at school. Somebody —I think it was my grandmother—said his grandmother came and took him away. It cannot have been true; he had only one grandmother and she was living right there in town. What probably happened is that his mother kept him out of school, and when she left Lincoln he went with her.

I didn't wonder what the evening paper meant precisely when it said that Cletus's father had accused his mother of having been intimate with the murdered man. I wouldn't at that age have been so innocent as to think it meant they were on friendly terms with each other. When I thought about the matter at all I thought about the ear, which was never found. I knew it was a most terrible thing that had happened to Cletus and that he would forever be singled out by it, but I didn't try to put myself in his place or even think that maybe I ought to find out where he lived and get on my bicycle and go see him. It was as if his father had shot and killed him too.

The carpenters and plumbers and electricians finally stopped getting in each other's way and left the new house entirely to the painters. I came home with white paint on my clothes and my father suggested that I stay away from Park Place until the paint on the woodwork was dry. He was exasperated at the architect and at himself; if the concrete foundation had been sunk two or three feet lower into the ground, it wouldn't have required a great many loads of expensive topsoil to bring the lawn up to the necessary level. The day we moved in, Grace, overtired, dropped a bottle of iodine she was putting in the medicine cabinet of the upstairs bathroom and it fell into the washstand and broke. She and I spent our first evening in the new house scrubbing at what looked like bloodstains on the shining white wall.

The house was too new to be comfortable. It was like having to spend a lot of time with a person you didn't know very well. And I missed the way it used to be when there was no roof yet and the underflooring was littered with shavings and bent nails and pieces of wood I could almost but not quite think what to do with. Now there was nothing on the floor but rugs and you couldn't do daring things because if you did you might leave a mark on the wallpaper.

My father was always away during the middle of the week, my little brother spent two or three days at a time with my grandmother, who idolized him, and so Grace and I were often alone together. The people who lived in the houses all up and down the street were either related to her or her close friends. They were in and out of one another's houses all day long, and several afternoons a week they sat down to bridge tables. Expertly shuffling and reshuffling cards, they went to work. Auction, this was. Contract bridge hadn't yet supplanted it. Once, looking over Grace's shoulder, I saw her make a grand slam in clubs when the highest trump card in her hand was the nine. The women serenely doubled and redoubled each other's bids without ever losing their way in the intricacies of some piece of gossip, and the one who was adding up the score was still able to deplore, with the others, the shockingness of some new novel that they had all put their names down for at the library.

Fourteen was when boys graduated into long trousers and since I hadn't yet arrived at that age I was still wearing corduroy knickerbockers. When I couldn't stop reading *A Tale of Two Cities*, I put my long black cotton stockings across the bottom of the bedroom door so my father wouldn't see the crack of light and come in and tell me to go to sleep. I had a one-tube radio set in my room, on the desk where I studied. Above it, on the wall, was a map of North America, with colored pins for all the radio stations I had picked up. The pin that gave me the most pleasure was stuck at Havana, Cuba, which I got only once. My ears hurt from the headphones and my feet were cold all winter long. My room was on the northwest corner of the house and the hot-air registers didn't do what was expected of them. And once something happened that was so strange I couldn't get over it. I heard Eggy Rinehart, two blocks away, call his mother to the telephone. The radio set had picked up his voice out of the air, but *how?* From the telephone wires? Nobody could tell me.

When I came home from Scout meeting, the aerial on the roof showed faintly against the stars. Before I walked into the house I left the front walk and went and peered through the crack of light between the drawn shade and the sill of the living-room window. I wanted to make sure that my father and Grace weren't having a "party." The word had undergone a sinister metamorphosis. Originally it meant ice cream in molds and other children arriving with presents for me, or if it was a grown-up party then the best linen tablecloth and place cards and little paper cups full of nuts and a centerpiece of cut flowers from the greenhouse. And more spoons and forks than usual. During Prohibition it came to mean people getting together for the purpose of drinking. Gossip made it sound worse than it was; there were limits. But I didn't know what they were and therefore assumed that there weren't any, and that if "parties" were not orgies exactly they were in that general area. Among Grace's friends were a handsome raven-haired woman who had a year or two before lost her husband and a humorous unmarried woman who worked at the bank. They were both at our house a good deal and my father referred to them jocosely as his harem. I knew that they weren't really, but what was I to think when I heard them laughing about how Lois went upstairs and took off all her clothes (at my mother's parties people didn't do such things) and came down wrapped in a bath towel and did the hootchie-kootchie dance? Anyway, I didn't want to blunder into something like that, so I looked before I walked into the house.

After a short while, all this I now think rather jolly behavior had stopped. It was merely a manifestation of the times and did not reflect their true personalities. They settled down into something like the ordinary quiet life of most married couples.

Grace could whistle like nobody's business, and I have a vivid memory of her rendition of "Here's to the heart that beats for me, true as the stars above. / Here's to the day when mine she'll be. Here's to the girl I love," as she made her way backwards down the stairs with a dust mop. It is like a still from an old movie. She never gets to the bottom of the stairs. In the remaining ten years before I took off for good, she was never impatient with me and I don't think I was ever rude to her. There was enough self-control in that household for six families. Unlike the wicked stepmother in the fairy tales, she had a gentle nature and could not bear any kind of altercation. And it was not in her to wrestle, like Jacob with the angel, until I stopped being faithful to a dead woman and accepted her as my mother. Instead she chose the role of the go-between. When my older brother had a Saturday-night date and wanted my father to let him have the car, he enlisted her aid and went off with the car keys in his pocket.

Grace's mother lived directly across the street from us with her son Ted, who was at that time a bachelor. Mrs. McGrath was a stately, warm-hearted old woman, much looked up to by her children. Grace's brothers were jovial, exceedingly kind men who, together, on next to nothing, had started a sand and gravel business and been successful. They loved to tell funny stories and whenever they were gathered together there was the sound of laughter. They also confused me by treating me as if I were a genuine relation. I didn't so much hold out against them as proceed with caution.

In that insufficiently heated bedroom on the northwest corner of the house in Park Place I was taken by surprise by the first intimations of a pleasure that I did not at first know how to elicit from or return to the body that gave rise to it, which was my own. It had no images connected with it, and no object but pure physical sensation. It was as if I had found a way of singing that did not come from the throat. I stumbled upon it by accident and it did not cross my mind that anybody might ever have had this experience except me. Therefore I did not connect these piercing exquisite sensations with the act of murder that removed Cletus Smith from Lincoln, or with what other men and women did that was all right for them to do provided they were married. Or even with what older boys talked about in the locker room at school. It was an all but passive, wholly private passion that turned me into two boys, one of whom went to high school and was conscientious about handing in his homework and tried out for the glee club and the debating society and lingered after school talking to his algebra teacher. The other boy was moody and guilt-ridden and desired nothing from other people but their absence.

When I was in bed, with the light out, the two boys became one, and I thought about the aerial on the roof, and how the cold air above our house was full of unknown voices and dance music, from a radio station downtown and from stations in Springfield and Peoria and Bloomington and Danville and Chicago and Kansas City. In college I read Shakespeare's *The Tempest* for the first time and was reminded immediately of what went on over the house in Park Place.

My father was offered a promotion that meant he would work in the Chicago office of the fire insurance company and be home every night like other men. At his age he didn't want to travel from one small town to another and be at the mercy of railroad timetables any more. Also, he was ambitious and gratified that they wanted him. My stepmother could not bear the thought of leaving Lincoln and her family and her friends. Night after night she wept while she and my father talked behind the closed door of their room. After a few years she could say that she preferred living in Chicago, but she was never again as lighthearted as she was before they left Lincoln.

The move to Chicago came in March but I stayed behind to finish the school year. I was taken in by old Mrs. McGrath. Her house had only two bedrooms, and for three months Grace's brother Ted and I slept in his room, in twin four-poster beds. One would have thought that having the company of a schoolboy was the one thing hitherto lacking in his very agreeable life. At night he took off his toupee and hung it on a bedpost, and as we were undressing he imparted his favorite words of wisdom to me, such as "Marriage is what takes the giggles out of the girls," or "You can't make a man mad by giving him money," or "All little things are nice." In the morning before school we all three crowded into the breakfast nook off the kitchen and ate buckwheat cakes and maple syrup. I persisted in feeling that I was putting them to a great deal of trouble when I don't suppose I was, actually.

When it was time for me to go to Chicago, Ted and another of Grace's brothers drove me there, stopping on the way to inspect a gravel pit in Joliet. They checked in at the La Salle

Hotel, in Chicago, and we had dinner. As I stood gaping at the coffered ceiling, the like of which I had never seen before, they stuffed ten-dollar bills in my pockets. I didn't know whether it was right for me to take the money or not, and tried not to, but they assured me that it was perfectly all right, my father wouldn't mind, and in the end I took half of it. Instead of using the elevated railway, as I expected, we drove all the way from the Loop to Rogers Park in a taxi so I could see the city. As I looked out of the window at Sheridan Road they looked at me, and were so full of delight in the pleasure they were giving me that some final thread of resistance gave way and I understood not only how entirely generous they were but also that generosity might be the greatest pleasure there is.

Home was now an apartment on the second floor of a three-story brick building. The apartment house was a block west of Sheridan Road, in a quiet neighborhood, and Lake Michigan was only a short walk from where we lived. There were still lots of big old-fashioned single-family houses with front porches and trees and some sort of lawn and a homelike look to them. My father found a job for me in his office as a filing clerk, and he and I went to work together on the El. In the evening the boys used to cluster on the sidewalk with their bicycles and I would walk by them with a dry mouth and my eyes focused on something farther down the street. I usually ended up at the Lake, where I sat on a rock pile looking out over the water. This went on for most of the summer, until one evening I found my way blocked by a bicycle wheel. The boy who was astride the bicycle asked if I was Jewish. It was not anti-Semitism, he was just curious. The circle opened and took me in. I mean, I could stand around with them and nobody objected to my being there.

After Labor Day I started to school. In a city high school of three thousand students, where there was so much going on after school—band practice, fencing, the Stamp Collectors Club, the History Club, the French Club, the Players, the Orchestra, the Camera Club, the Chess and Chequer Club, the Architectural Society, and so on—the failure to do well in sports didn't make you an object of derision. Once in an outdoor gym class a football came through the air and I managed to hang on to it. This was long after the class had stopped expecting me to catch anything and there was general rejoicing and disbelief. But they never rode me. I was accepted for what I was. It was, after all, not a small town but a big city, and in that school there was no one who was not accepted.

The school building was of grey stone and enormous. It was ten times as big as the old, overcrowded, yellow-brick high school in Lincoln, and the classrooms I had to go to were sometimes far apart. One day during the first week or so of school as I was hurrying along a corridor that was lined with metal lockers I saw Cletus Smith coming toward me. It was as if he had risen from the dead. He didn't speak. I didn't speak. We just kept on walking until we had passed each other. And after that, there was no way that I could not have done it.

Why didn't I speak to him? I guess because I was so surprised. And because I didn't know what to say. I didn't know what was polite in the circumstances. I couldn't say *I'm sorry about the murder and all that*, could I? In Greek tragedies, the Chorus never attempts to console the innocent bystander but instead, sticking to broad generalities, grieves over the fate of mankind, whose mistake was to have been born in the first place.

If I had been the elderly man I am now I might have simply said his name. Or shaken my head sadly and said, "I know, I know. . . ." But would that have been any better? I wasn't an elderly man, the bloodhounds had never been after my father, and I didn't know (how could anybody know, how many times has such a thing happened to a thirteen-year-old boy?) what he had been through. Any more than a person who hasn't had a car door slammed on his fingers knows what that is like.

Boys are, from time to time, found hanging from a rafter or killed by a shotgun believed to have gone off accidentally. The wonder is it happens so seldom.

I think now—I think if I had turned and walked along beside him and not said anything, it might have been the right thing to do. But that's what I think *now*. It has taken me all these years even to imagine doing that, and I had a math class on the second floor, clear at the other end of the building, and there was just barely time to get there before the bell rang.

5

The Emotion of Ownership

UNTIL I was six years old, my father kept a carriage horse, and on hot July evenings we would leave the house on Ninth Street and go driving to cool off. Sometimes the couple who lived next door would be invited to go with us. My brother sat in the front seat, between my father and Dr. Donald, and I sat in back, between Mrs. Donald and my mother. The dog—though we all shouted "Go *home!*" at him—went too, trotting between the wheels of the carriage with his tongue lolling out.

No matter what street my father chose to drive out of town by, the landscape was much the same once we got out in the country. Plowed fields or pasture, all the way to the horizon. There were trees for the cattle to stand under in the heat of the day, and the fields were separated from each other by Osage-orange hedgerows that were full of nesting birds.

The conversation in the front seat of the carriage was about what was growing on both sides of the road: corn, wheat, rye, oats, alfalfa. The women, blind to this green wealth, talked about sewing and "receipts"—the word they used for recipes. I was of an age to appreciate anything that looked like something it wasn't, and when we passed a cluster of mailboxes I would turn and look back. Long-legged wading birds is what they put me in the mind of, though we were a considerable distance from anything that could be called a body of water.

Dr. Donald owned land near Mason City. The eighty-acre farm that my father might have inherited had, to his undying regret, been sold by my grandparents. Living carefully and putting aside half his salary, he had managed to buy a farm, but it was a little too far away to drive to in a horse and carriage, and since he couldn't look at his own land, as he would undoubtedly have liked to do, he enjoyed looking at other people's. With a gesture of the whip he would direct Dr. Donald's attention to a large and well-built barn and they would be moved to admiration. By nature home-loving, I looked at the houses instead. How bleak they were, compared to our house in town. No big shade trees, no wide front porch to sit on, no neighbors all up and down the street. If there were flowers they didn't amount to more than a few dusty hollyhocks or some nasturtiums growing in a tin basin on a stump.

Suppose Cletus had come to spend the day with me when we were small children. There would have been a dog following us around. And in the barn a horse, a high carriage with red wheels, hay, bags of oats, etc. But then he would have discovered that I had never harnessed the horse to the carriage, and that we couldn't ride him bareback to round up the cows because there weren't any. The house was a lot larger and more comfortable than his, and there was a sandpile in the back yard, but what was a sandpile compared to the horse barn, the cow barn, sheds, corncribs, the chicken house, the root cellar, the well, the windmill, the horse trough, and a swimming hole? In town there were cardinals and bluebirds and tanagers and Baltimore orioles, but he had the mourning dove, the forever inquiring bob-*white?*, the hoot owl, and the whippoorwill.

My father sold the horse and carriage and tore down the barn and built a garage to put the new seven-passenger Chalmers in, and after that we could drive to Mt. Pulaski, where his farm was. Tagging around after him then, I became aware of a richness that wasn't visual but came from the way the smells were laid on: dried-out wood, rusting farm machinery, the manure pile, the pigpen, yarrow, and onion grass, quicklime from the outhouse, in spring the frost leaving the ground, in summer the hay lying cut in the fields. All things considered, I doubt very much if Cletus would have been eager to change places with me.

The black fertile soil of Logan County was, and so far as I know still is, owned by people whose ancestors came from Kentucky or Indiana or Ohio, bringing with them no more than they could fit into a lurching covered wagon. They staked out as much land as they had a fancy to and cleared it slowly, putting a few more acres under cultivation each year. Their children and grandchildren, born on this land, felt they belonged there. Their great-grandchildren either sold their patrimony or got someone else to farm it for them. Living in town quite comfortably in big old houses set well back from the street, they kept an eye on what was going on out in the country, and when the crops were delivered at the grain elevator they took, as was customary, half the profits. They did not consider a tenant farmer their social equal, any more than a carpenter or a stonemason or a bricklayer. The farmer who owned the land he farmed they could and did accept. When Cletus and I were playing together the question of social position didn't come up. And neither did it come up on the school playground. It was something that descended upon people when they were older. The names on the mailboxes that claimed my attention when I was a small child were proof enough that the tenant farmers were of the same stock as the townspeople who looked down on them socially. Their forebears had perhaps come on a later wave of European migration and found that land was no longer plentiful at a dollar and a quarter an acre. Or they could have been hamstrung by some family misfortune. Or simply lacked the talent for rising in the world.

Roaming the courthouse square on a Saturday night, the tenant farmers and their families were unmistakable. You could see that they were not at ease in town and that they clung together for support. The women's clothes were not meant to be becoming but to wear well, to last them out. The back of the men's necks was a mahogany color, and deeply wrinkled. Their hands were large and looked swollen or misshapen and sometimes they were short a finger or two. The discontented hang of their shoulders is possibly something I imagined because I would not have liked not owning the land I farmed. Very likely they didn't either, but farming was in their blood and they wouldn't have cared to be selling real estate or adding up columns of figures in a bank.

On the seventh day they rested; that is to say, they put on their good clothes and hitched up the horse again and drove to some country church, where, sitting in straight-backed cushionless pews, they stared passively at the preacher, who paced up and down in front of them, thinking up new ways to convince them that they were steeped in sin.

*

If I knew where Cletus Smith is right this minute, I would go and explain. Or try to. It is not only possible but more than likely that I would also have to explain who I am. And that he would have no recollection of the moment that has troubled me all these years. He lived through things that were a good deal worse. It might turn out that I had made the effort for my sake, not his.

I don't know where he is. It isn't at all likely that we will run into each other somewhere or that we would recognize each other if we did. He could even be dead.

Except through the intervention of chance, the one possibility of my making some connection with him seems to lie not in the present but in the past—in my trying to reconstruct the testimony that he was never called upon to give. The unsupported word of a witness who was not present except in imagination would not be acceptable in a court of law, but, as it has been demonstrated over and over, the sworn testimony of the witness who was present is not trustworthy either. If any part of the following mixture of truth and fiction strikes the reader as unconvincing, he has my permission to disregard it. I would be content to stick to the facts if there were any.

The reader will also have to do a certain amount of imagining. He must imagine a deck of cards spread out face down on a table, and then he must turn one over, only it is not the eight of hearts or the jack of diamonds but a perfectly ordinary quarter of an hour out of Cletus's past life. But first I need to invent a dog, which doesn't take very much in the way of prestidigitation; if there were cattle there had to be a dog to help round them up. In that period—I don't know how it is now—farm dogs were usually a mixture of collie and English shepherd. The attraction between dogs and adolescent boys can, I think, be taken for granted. There is no outward sign of trouble in the family. The two farms are both on the right-hand side of the new hard road and have a common boundary line. The Wilson house, with its barns and sheds, is next to the road and an eighth of a mile closer to town. To get to where Cletus lives you have to drive up a narrow lane that has a gate at either end of it. When it is almost time for Cletus to come home from school the dog squeezes herself under the gates and trots off up the road to the mailboxes, where she settles down in a place that she has made for herself in the high grass with her chin resting on her four paws. These mailboxes too are on posts and look like wading birds.

In the very few years since my father disposed of the horse and carriage, there has been a change in the landscape. It is now like a tabletop, the trees mostly gone, the hedges uprooted in favor of barbed wire—resulting in more land under cultivation, more money in the bank, but also in a total exposure. Anyone can see what used to be reserved for the eye of the hawk as it wheeled in slow circles.

If a farm wagon or a Model T Ford goes by, the dog follows it with her eyes but she does not raise her head. She is expecting a boy on a bicycle.

The tenant farmers whose names are on those mailboxes where the dog lies waiting for Cletus to come home from school apply the words of the Scriptures to their own lives, insofar as they are able. Including the commandment to do unto others as you would have them do unto you. And they cling together when they are in town largely because they cannot imagine a situation in which the people they see in the stores or on the sidewalk (and who do not appear to see them) could possibly need their help. It is different in the country.

The bicycle is painted a bright blue, and Cletus has only had it for three months. When he first saw it, beside the Christmas tree, his heart almost stopped beating. On rainy days he walks to school rather than have it get old and rusty like the other bikes in the wooden rack at the side of the one-room schoolhouse. With the dog loping along beside him he pedals for dear life over the final stretch of road. The dog waits each time until he has closed the gate and then she trots on ahead importantly, as if by himself the boy wouldn't know the way home. Scratching hens have destroyed the grass in the farmyard, and the house could do with a coat of paint, but the roof doesn't leak and the barns are not about to fall down. The dog follows Cletus up onto the porch, leaving her neat footprints wherever she has been. With her head cocked she watches while he puts his schoolbooks beside the door and bends down to untie his shoelaces. His head is now on a level with hers. The plumed tail wags seductively. He leans forward so that she can smell his breath and, smelling hers, wrinkles his nose with distaste.

"Whew! What have you been eating? Dead fish?" Dead something.

There is no telling how long she would let him go on looking into her agate-colored eyes. Forever, possibly. She has made him a present of herself and nothing he does or doesn't do will make her take it back. "Good dog," he says, and steps out of his shoes. The dog knows better than to try and sneak into the house with him, but that doesn't mean she likes being kept out. She withdraws her long, pointed, sensitive nose an inch at a time, allowing the door to close. Then she whines softly, inviting him to relent.

Let us consider the kitchen the dog is not allowed into. Steam on the windows. Zinc surfaces that have lost their shine. Wooden surfaces that have been scrubbed to the texture of velvet. The range, with two buckets of water beside it ready to be poured into the reservoir when it is empty. The teakettle. The white enamel coffeepot. The tin matchbox on the wall. The woodbox, the sink, the comb hanging by a string, the roller towel. The kerosene lamp with a white glass shade. The embossed calendar. The kitchen chairs, some with a crack in the seat. The cracked oilcloth on the kitchen table. The smell of Octagon soap. To the indifferent eye it is like every farm kitchen for a hundred miles around, but none of those others would have been waiting in absolute stillness for Cletus to come home from school, or have seemed like all his heart desired when he walks in out of the cold.

When Cletus stands by the pasture fence, an old white work-horse comes, expecting a lump of sugar and possibly hoping to be loved. Anyway, Cletus loves him. And, rounding up the cows, rides him in preference to any of the other horses. And when he has tears to shed he does it with his forehead against the horse's silky neck.

In the daytime the sky is an inverted bowl over the prairie. On a clear night it is sometimes powdered with stars.

Coming home from school Cletus often sees Mrs. Wilson and the two little boys out by the clothesline. Risking a fall he takes both hands off the handlebars and waves, and they wave back.

It is not by accident that Cletus is often in the Wilsons' buggy when the two families drive off to church together or to town to see the fireworks on the Fourth of July. They are his second family. If his mother sends him to the Wilsons' because she has suddenly discovered that she is out of vanilla or allspice, there is a good chance that Mrs. Wilson will cut a slice off a loaf of bread that has just come out of the oven and spread butter and jam on it and give it to him. He likes her apart from that, though; he likes her because she is always the same.

When it was time for him to go to school the Wilson girls showed him the shortcut through the fields to the other road and the one-room schoolhouse, and Hazel had to tell the teacher his name. With all those strange boys and girls staring at him he lost the power of speech. The teacher was young and pretty and showed him how to hold the colored crayon.

If Cletus wants to know something and his father isn't there to show him, he goes looking for Mr. Wilson. Who doesn't lose patience with him if he fails to get it right on the first try. When Mr. Wilson says to Cletus's father, "I saw a cock pheasant crossing the road this morning, I don't suppose you feel like taking the afternoon off to go hunting," it is understood that, providing it isn't a school day, Cletus will go with them. His mother was afraid and wanted him to wait until he was older but Mr. Wilson said, "Better for him to learn now, while he hasn't got a lot of other things in his mind. . . . Here, boy. You hold it like this. With the stock against your right shoulder. And you keep both eyes open and sight along the barrel to that bead. If you obey the rules that your father tells you and don't go out with some fool who's never had a shotgun in his hand before, you can't get into trouble."

Sometimes he rests his hand on Cletus's shoulder while he is talking. At such moments Cletus feels that no matter what he might do, even if it was something quite bad that he had to go to jail for, Mr. Wilson would see a reason for it. And stand by him. Not that his father wouldn't also, but Mr. Wilson is somebody Cletus isn't even related to.

In that flat landscape a man cursing at his horses somewhere off in the fields can be heard a long way. All sounds carry: the dinner bell, wheels crossing a cattle guard, the clatter of farm machinery. When the gasoline engine sputters and dies or the blades of the mowing machine jam, Cletus knows that Mr. Wilson, a quarter of a mile away, has heard it and is waiting for the sound of the engine or the mowing machine to start up again. If it doesn't, he leaves his own work and comes across the pasture to see what the trouble is. With their heads almost touching, his father and Mr. Wilson study the difficulty. Wrenches and pliers pass back and forth between them with as much familiarity as if they owned their four hands in common.

In midsummer, with thunderheads blotting out more and more of the blue sky, it could be his father's hay that they are tossing up onto the wain or it could be Mr. Wilson's. They know, of course, but it is beside the point. When the hay-makers no longer cast a shadow it means that the sun has gone under a huge, ominous, dark grey cloud. A breeze springs up and they work faster. They don't even so much as glance at the sky. They don't need to. The precariously balanced load grows higher and higher. When the wagon won't hold any more they climb up onto it and race for the barn, and with the first rain-drops pattering on the oak leaves they congratulate themselves on getting the hay under cover in time. This happens not just once but year after year.

So far as Clarence Smith was concerned, no other man had ever shown a concern so genuine or so dependable, and he did his best to pay it back in kind. When Lloyd Wilson had a sick calf, instead of calling the vet he got Clarence to come and look at it, and Clarence stayed up all night doctoring the animal and keeping it warm with blankets. In the morning Cletus woke up early and threw the covers off and dressed and ran all the way to the barn where they were, and got there in time to see the calf struggle to his feet. His father said, "I guess that's that," and brushed Mr. Wilson's thanks aside, and they went home.

And when his father gets behind in his spring plowing because of the rains, Mr. Wilson joins him after supper with his horse and plow and together they turn over the soil in the lower forty by moonlight.

Cletus thinks of it as their lower forty; actually, it is someone else's. Land, barns, sheds, farmhouse—everything but livestock and machinery—belong to Colonel Dowling, whose snub-nosed Franklin is often parked by the entrance to the lane. The

crops that are planted and the price at which they are sold
await his decision. The lightning rods on the roof of the house
and both barns are his idea. It is right, of course, to put your
trust in the Lord. But in moderation. Things that people can
manage without His help He shouldn't be asked to take care
of. After the time the Franklin got so badly mired in the lane
that his tenant had to come with a team and pull him out,
Colonel Dowling doesn't put his entire trust in the Franklin
either, but tells himself it is just as easy to leave the car by the
side of the road and walk in.

He is a self-made man. His father was a hod carrier who
drank more than was good for him, and fell off a scaffolding
and broke his neck, leaving his widow with six children to bring
up. She did it by taking in washing. As Ed Dowling fought his
way up in the world, he married a woman with money and
made himself into a gentleman. It was no small accomplishment, but it cut him off somewhat from his brothers and
sisters, who are not above making fun of him behind his back.

A gentleman doesn't have one set of manners for the house
of a poor man and another for the house of someone with an
income comparable to his own. He never enters the farmhouse
without knocking. Even though it is legally his. And he remembers to wipe the spring mud off his shoes. He also makes
a point of asking Cletus's mother if she is satisfied with the
present arrangements, and this could lead to, if she thinks the
kitchen needs repainting, his offering to supply the paint. He is
always courteous to her and he knows the boys' names. If that
is all he knows about them, it is not greatly to be wondered at.
One farm boy is very much like another. The cat has invariably
got their tongue.

Satisfied that his tenant's wife is a good housekeeper, he
shows no interest in the second floor, and therefore doesn't
know about the broken-backed copy of *Tom Swift and His
Flying Machine* that is lying open, with the pages to the floor,
in the fluff under the bed in the small room on the right at the
head of the stairs.

Colonel Dowling is older than Cletus's father, and has snow-
white hair, and Cletus finds it natural that when they stand
talking by the pump or when they walk over the fields together
his father calls the older man "Colonel" and Colonel Dowling

calls his father "Clarence." But sometimes the Colonel brings a friend with him, somebody from town who doesn't know the first thing about farming, and with Cletus's father standing right there he will say "my corn" or "my oats" or "my drainage ditch." If he says it often enough, Cletus drops behind out of earshot. Even if his father, after working these acres for twelve years, doesn't feel the emotion of ownership, Cletus does.

Another card, from that same pack: his brother Wayne, who is eight years younger than he is. Wayne and Cletus are as different as day and night, people say. Or, to put it differently, as different as the oldest child and the second one often are.

Watching his mother as she holds Wayne's chin in her hand and parts his hair with a wet comb, Cletus remembers that she used to do this to him.

All the way home from school there are clouds racing across the sky and the air is warm and humid. Wayne is sitting on the porch steps when Cletus rides into the yard. He has pulled a strawberry box apart and is making an airplane with the pieces of thin wood. As Cletus steps over him he bends down and tries to take it from him in order to make an improvement, but Wayne jerks it back.

"Aunt Jenny is here," he says. "Somebody gave her a ride out from town. And we're having strawberry shortcake for supper."

Except for Jenny Evans, who is her mother's sister, Fern Smith has no living relatives. Her mother died when she was three and her father gave her to Aunt Jenny to bring up and went out West, where he found a job on a cattle ranch in Wyoming. From time to time he sent money, never very much. Now he is dead too. So is Tom Evans, Jenny's husband.

As people get older they get more alike in character and appearance and could all be leading the same life. Or almost. Shut up in the little house opposite the fairgrounds, Aunt Jenny talks to the hot-water faucet that drips, and the kitchen drawer that has a tendency to stick. She also sings, hymns mostly, in a high quavering voice: "That Old Rugged Cross" and "Art Thou Weary, Art Thou Sad" and "How glorious must the mansions be / Where thy redeemed shall dwell with thee. . . ." Without meaning to, she has grown heavy but she eats so little that short of starving to death there doesn't seem much she can do about it. Sometimes she goes out to work as a practical nurse, and comes home and sits by the kitchen table soaking her feet in a pan of hot water and Epsom salts. When she gets into bed and the springs creak under her weight, she groans with the pleasure of lying stretched out on an object that understands her so well.

The face that passes in and out of the small unframed mirror over the kitchen sink is that of an old woman whose chin has hairs on it, whose teeth spent the night in a glass of water, whose glasses are bifocal, causing her to step down into space if she isn't careful. She is full of fears, which are nursed by the catastrophes she reads about in the paper. The front and back doors are locked day and night against bad boys, a man with a mask over the lower part of his face, pneumonia, a fall. There is, even so, something buoyant in her nature that makes people pleased to see her coming toward them on the street, and usually they stop to talk to her and hear about the catastrophes. She winds up the conversation by saying cheerfully, "Life is no joke." What sensible person wouldn't agree with her.

The house is her one great accomplishment. Against all odds she has managed to hang on to it. "It's a poor man's house," she loves to say, "and not much to look at." It doesn't do to brag about your possessions, especially to people who have less. The mortgage is paid off and she doesn't have to take in roomers. It is all hers—meaning the pollarded catalpa tree by the front sidewalk, the woodshed around in back, the outside sloping cellar door, and the porch light that doesn't turn on. Meaning also the white net curtains that have turned grey and are about ready for the ragbag, the nine-by-twelve linoleum rug in the front room, with the design worn completely away in places, the ugly golden-oak furniture that could be duplicated in any secondhand store, "Sir Galahad" and "The Dickey Bird," and the smell of the kerosene heater. The two upstairs rooms are hot in summer and expensive to heat in winter, and so she doesn't use them. The big double bed all but blocking the front door makes the front room look queer, but she has stopped caring what people think. She means to die here, in her own house, in this very bed.

Meanwhile, she is not alone in the world. From the fairgrounds to the first fence post of the farm is a little over a mile, and when Aunt Jenny is feeling blue she puts on her hat and coat and, armed with grape jelly or a jar of pickles, pays them a visit. She tries not to come too often and she is careful never to take sides between husband and wife. Blessed is the peacemaker for he shall—inherit the kingdom of heaven? . . . see God? She can't remember, offhand, and keeps meaning to open the Bible to Matthew 5, and see which it is. Clarence is kind to her and brings her fruit and vegetables that she cans and lives on all winter. Fern is in the habit of leaving Wayne with her when she goes to the stores. And used to do the same thing with Cletus when he was small.

"Come and give your old auntie a kiss," she says now when Cletus appears in the doorway. "I know you don't like to kiss people but it won't kill you, not this once."

"It's going to rain," he says, and either his mother doesn't hear him or else she failed to connect what he has just said with the washing on the line. He goes on upstairs and takes off his school clothes and hangs them on an already overcrowded hook. The room gets progressively darker as the rainstorm that is moving across the prairie approaches.

Even in the dead of winter, the only heat there ever is in this room comes through the ventilator in the floor. Voices also are carried by it. Though he can hear the conversation in the room below, he manages not to understand it. What sounds like somebody moving furniture around is the first thunder, faint and far away.

The water in the china pitcher comes from the cistern and is rainwater and rust-colored. He fills the bowl and the water immediately turns cloudy from the soap and dirt on his hands. From the room below he hears "Fortunately I have witnesses."

Him, among others. She has—his mother has fits of weeping in the night. The walls are thin. Lying awake, he hears threats he tries not to believe and accusations he doesn't understand. And envies the dog, who can put her head on her paws and go to sleep when she doesn't like the way things are.

Raindrops spatter against the windowpane and he turns and looks out. The tops of the trees are swaying in the wind. The sky behind the windmill is a greenish almost-black, and his mother and Aunt Jenny, with their coats over their heads, are yanking the sheets from the line. There is a flash of lightning that makes everything in sight turn pale, and then deep rolling thunder.

He goes on soaping his hands slowly, lost in a daydream about a motorcycle he has seen in the Sears, Roebuck catalogue.

As Aunt Jenny is drawn toward the farm, so the hired man, Victor Jensen, feels the pull of town. Bright and early on the morning of Decoration Day he gets dressed up fit to kill and starts off down the highway. The same thing happens on the Fourth of July and Labor Day. Though they know what he is heading for, they do not make any effort to stop him. It is his reward for not belonging to anybody and not having anybody who belongs to him. He isn't home by milking time, and they know then that he won't come home at all. In the morning when they go to his room in the barn his bed has not been slept in. Various neighbors report that they have seen him in town—during the parade, or on the courthouse square, or at the band concert, reeling. Two days later, a buggy drives up the lane and stops. Cletus comes to the door and Lloyd Wilson says, "I passed Victor on the road just now. He was headed in this direction and I tried to get him to climb in with me but he wouldn't. I thought you'd like to know." Cletus and his father go out looking for the hired man and find him lying in a ditch a quarter of a mile from home, and put him to bed in his room in the barn. Except for the stench of alcohol on his breath and the dried vomit on his clothes, it is like undressing a child. The next day he is up in time to help with the chores. He is deathly pale and his hands shake. Nobody mentions his absence and he is not apologetic—just withdrawn. As if he had answered a summons and is in no way responsible for what followed.

Another card: the cats run to greet Cletus when he walks into the barn. His father is already there, milking Flossie, and Victor is milking the new cow. "Sorry I'm late," Cletus says and picks up a milk bucket and a stool and sits down beside Old Bess, and then there are three of them going squirt-squirt, in approximately the same rhythm. He isn't as good a milker as his father, but nobody is. When his father was Cletus's age he was milking fifteen cows morning and night. The level of the milk rises slowly in the pails, and Old Bess manages to hit him in the eye with her tail, as usual.

"I thought I told you to come straight home from school."

"Teacher kept me."

"You been causing trouble?"

"I had to stay and make up an arithmetic test. I flunked it the first time."

"Not what I send you to school for."

"I know."

If Cletus didn't go to school at all he wouldn't care. It is the way things are here that matters. He can't grow up fast enough. When he is grown, there won't be anything his father can do that he can't do.

He is sitting at the kitchen table with his head bent over his arithmetic. He puts the end of his lead pencil in his mouth frequently so the numbers will be black instead of grey. The darkness outside presses against the windowpanes here also, but they are too accustomed to this to notice it.

"I must go home," Mr. Wilson says, and doesn't.

Except for the chores, all farming is at a standstill. Snow lies deep on the ground and in much deeper drifts wherever it met with an obstruction. The wooden fence posts and the well roof are capped, and icicles hang from the gutters.

His father and Mr. Wilson are talking about the relative merits of clover and alfalfa as a cover crop. Cletus would like to follow this conversation but there are twelve problems and he has only done half of them. "What's nine times seven?" he asks his mother, who tells him and then rests her chin on Wayne's curls and utters the single word "Bedtime." Wayne wants Cletus to go upstairs with him.

"Why does he have to be such a baby? There's nothing upstairs that is going to hurt him."

"Oh, be nice and go with him. You were afraid of the dark once. You just don't remember."

So he closes his book and gets up from the table, though he hasn't finished the assignment and Teacher will probably be sore at him.

Teacher wasn't sore at him, as it turned out. She knows he is a gentle boy and tries hard.

*

The rain is drumming on the tin roof of the shed off the kitchen where the separator is, and where Cletus's mother makes them keep their work shoes so they won't track the barnyard mud and manure into the house. He ties his shoelaces and makes a dash for it, with the dog bounding at his heels. When they arrive at the horse barn his hair is plastered to his head and his shirt is sticking to his back. The dog gets as close to him as she can and then shakes herself.

"Thanks. How'd you like it if I did that to you?"

He doesn't really hold it against her and she doesn't look guilty. They both know it is just something she has to do because she is a dog. It is warm and dry in the barn and he soon stops shivering. He cleans out the stalls and puts down fresh hay for the horses and fills the water buckets, all the while enjoying the sight of the rain coming down on the plowed field beyond the open door.

In the night he gives Wayne a poke and says, "Move over, you're crowding me out of bed." Sometimes Cletus jabbers in his sleep. Mostly they lie curled together in what is not a very large bed sleeping the sleep of stones. The north wind howling around the corner of the house only serves to deepen this unknowing.

Dressing for church Clarence Smith puts on a clean white shirt and discovers that Fern hasn't washed his collars. And is angry with her. He has his duties to perform and she has hers, one of which is to see that he has clean clothes to put on.

The small country church is packed with his neighbors, all of whom are wearing clean collars. The giving out of the hymn number causes them to rise and add the droning of their country voices to the wheezing of the little organ. Since the preacher said that the point of the parables is mysterious and needs explaining, they have no choice but to believe him. The details— the great supper, the lost lamb, the unproductive vineyard, the unjust steward, the sower, and the seed sown secretly—they are familiar with and understand. Above the transparent dome they live and work under there is another even grander where they will reside in mansions waiting to receive them when they are done with farming forever.

What Clarence Smith sees as he helps his wife into the front seat of the buggy after church is a woman who in the sight of God is his lawfully wedded wife and owes him love, honor, and obedience. Other people, with nothing at stake, see that there is a look of sadness about her, as if she lives too much in the past or perhaps expects more of life than is reasonable.

6

Lloyd Wilson's Story

THOUGH he had brothers he was on good terms with, the person he turned to for companionship or when he had something weighing on his mind was the overserious man on the neighboring farm. After twelve years he found it hard to believe there had ever been a time when he and Clarence weren't friends. At night, in the immense darkness, the only light he could see came from the Smiths' house.

He remembered the day they came. A raw, wet, windy day in March. He was plowing next to the road when he saw an unfamiliar wagon piled high with stuff drive up the lane at Colonel Dowling's, and he threw the reins over the horse's neck and started across the fields. When he got to the house, the front door was unlocked and standing open but the new neighbors were still outside, looking around to see where they were—the man a little under average height, and a young woman with a baby. They'd been on the road since daybreak. They couldn't have been thirty yet, either of them, but already there were wrinkles in the man's forehead and at the corners of his eyes. His voice was low, and if he could indicate something by a gesture instead of speech, he did. And what crossed Lloyd Wilson's mind was how defenseless he seemed.

Saying "Easy . . . easy . . . now your side . . . a little more . . . more . . . a little more," the two men maneuvered a heavy wardrobe up the stairs and through a narrow doorway. You didn't have to be much of a judge of character to see that the woman had been hoping for something better and the man was being patient with her. She didn't seem to know what to do first. Brought up in town, he said to himself. And then, noticing how small her wrists were: "Here, ma'am, let me have that. It's too heavy for a woman to carry." As he handled their furniture and their crockery, and box after box of possessions they hadn't been able to part with, he found out things about them, that first day, that it would have taken him years to discover under ordinary circumstances. Poking the baby's stomach gently with his forefinger, he produced a smile. "Two of my own," he said as he turned away. He came upon the woman standing forlornly in the midst of a kitchen that had been stripped of everything, including the stove, and said, "My wife is expecting you folks for supper." She wasn't, but no matter. And anyways, they knew she couldn't be expecting them because nobody knew they were coming. When the others sat down to eat, Fern nursed her baby in the rocking chair in the parlor. Afterward, he walked the new neighbors back to their house and waited till they had lit the lamps.

In the county clerk's platbook the hundred and sixty acres that Lloyd Wilson farmed were listed as belonging to Mrs. Mildred Stroud. It did not trouble him, or at least it did not trouble him very much, that the cows were his and the grass they cropped was not. The rent he had to pay on the pasture acreage was not unreasonable. His father had had the place before him and had saved up enough money over the years so that when his health failed and he had to give up farming he could live out his days in town.

Mrs. Stroud was a woman in her early fifties with two unmarried daughters who lived at home and were kept in the dark about her financial affairs, as she had been kept in the dark about her husband's—until he died suddenly and the president of the bank began to explain things to her. He started in as though speaking to a child and then had to pull himself up short. It had been his fixed opinion that all women are ignorant about money matters, but this woman didn't happen to be, and the questions she put to him were just the questions he would have preferred not to answer. It was quite impossible to take advantage of her. Inadvertent mistakes didn't escape her notice either. Like most extremely clever people, she underestimated the intelligence of others. She could have remarried and chose not to because it would have meant discussing what she did with her money.

She appeared at her farm frequently and without giving her tenant any warning. If she did that, what would have been the point in her coming? When she pitched into Lloyd Wilson for some piece of slackness, he cleared his throat and moistened his lips, as if he was about to argue with her, but instead he turned away, pretending that something a few feet to the right or left of them had engaged his attention at that moment. At other times, cap in hand, he was overly polite, in a way that could be taken for rudeness, but this she simply ignored. She knew, because she had made it her business to know everything about him, that if he hadn't got his corn in by the time he should have it was probably because he was off planting somebody else's corn—some neighbor who, because of sickness or whatever, wasn't able to do it himself. She could have made an issue of this and didn't. In the end her corn got planted and she was never actually out of pocket. It was the principle of the thing that she objected to. As her tenant his first responsibility ought to be to her. If she didn't like the way he farmed she could ask him to leave and put some other tenant on the place instead, but they both knew that this wasn't about to happen.

The secret that Mildred Stroud managed to keep from him, though not from herself, was that she found him physically attractive. But she was fifteen years older than he was, and, knowing the cruelty of Lincoln gossip, didn't choose to be the subject of it. And anyway it was out of the question.

Chewing on a grass blade, he remarked—this was in the days when he and Clarence were still friends and he could say whatever came into his head, knowing it wouldn't be repeated or misunderstood—"A good wife is a woman who is always tired, suffers from backache and headaches, and moves away from her husband in bed because she doesn't want any more children." And Clarence supposed that it wasn't just any good wife he was speaking of.

What Lloyd Wilson didn't say (because there was nothing anybody could do about it anyway and why should he burden Clarence with his trouble, if you could call it that) was that he didn't seem capable any more of the kind of feelings he used to have. He was perfectly aware of his wife's good qualities. She worked like a slave, from morning till night, holding up her end of things. She was a good mother. There was no question about any of this. Sometimes he thought it was just that they were so used to each other. He knew how she felt about almost everything, and, most of the time, what she was going to say before she said it. If they had been brother and sister it wouldn't have been very different—except that she was jealous. If he so much as looked at another woman she acted as if he'd done something unforgivable. Once or twice she worked herself up to such a pitch that she went upstairs and started packing. He knew that such persuasion as he could muster was half-hearted and wouldn't convince her to change her mind. If she was bent on leaving him there was nothing he could do about it. She didn't leave him, she only threatened to. None of those women meant anything to him, he said. And with her face averted she said, "The trouble is, I don't mean anything to you either."

Whether he himself would have come to this conclusion if she hadn't embarrassed him by putting it into words, he couldn't say. All he knew was that he wished she hadn't said it. He was ready to provide for her and to treat her with respect, but he couldn't work up a semblance of the emotion that would have made her happy.

Between these crises they lived like any other married couple. You could not have told from her voice as she said, "I'm about to put things on the table, Lloyd," or his voice as he said, "Pass the salt and pepper, please," that there was anything wrong.

He wondered if other men felt the same way about their wives or if it was just him. He was almost forty years old and lately it had seemed to him that he had lived a long time and that just about everything that could happen to him had happened.

When his evening chores were done he walked over the hill and, leaning against a post in the cow barn, directed a steady stream of conversation at the back of Clarence's head. When Clarence and Victor carried the milk to the shed off the kitchen where the separator was, he followed them. And from there into the house. Anything to keep from going home. Sometimes he told himself he ought not to go to the Smiths' so often. He was afraid of becoming a nuisance, and still not quite able to stay away. One night, sitting in their kitchen, he tried to tell them how much their friendship meant to him, and then broke off in embarrassment, because anything he might say seemed so much less than he felt.

"You don't have to tell us," Fern said, smiling at him. "And anyway, it isn't as one-sided as you appear to think." Then she changed the subject.

He sat back, glad that he had spoken and glad she had stopped him from going on. He also recognized that what she said wasn't just politeness. They were themselves in front of him, as if he had assured them (he hadn't, but it was nevertheless true) that he didn't expect them to be anything they weren't. All this was altered irrevocably by a change in him so unexpected that it was as if it had happened without his knowing a thing about it. And after that he could not go on being natural in front of them.

He said silently (but nevertheless wanting to be heard) *Clarence, you ought not to trust me . . .* half expecting Clarence to answer *Why not?* If Clarence had, then he would have said *Because all my life I've been a stranger to myself.*

He hated himself for being weak, for having no will, but it wasn't that he didn't try to overcome the feelings he knew he shouldn't have. Time after time he thought he had overcome them, and it always turned out that he hadn't. Excuses to pay a visit to the barns (where she wouldn't be, so there was no harm in it) or to the house (where she would be) occurred to him constantly. He would reject four in a row and find himself hurriedly acting on the fifth. His feet took him there, without his consent. He might as well have given in in the first place.

Searching for a clue to her feelings, he was alert to the quality of her voice when she spoke to her children or Clarence. He knew when she was depressed. He knew also that like most married people she and Clarence quarreled sometimes. Did he imagine it or was it true that they got on better with each other and were more cheerful when he was around?

If he did what he knew he ought to do, which was not go there any more, Clarence would wonder why. So would she. The idea that she would think of him at all pleased him. All day long he thought about her. The cows sensed that he hardly knew what he was doing and turned their heads as far as their stanchions would permit and looked at him gravely.

He sighed, and then a moment later sighed again—deep sighs that seemed to come from as far down as they could come. To have escaped from that deadness, from the feeling that all he had to look forward to was more of the same . . .

But he was careful. He didn't make a simple remark without rehearsing it beforehand. And he continually removed the expression from his face lest it be the wrong one, and give him away. He also avoided any strong light, such as the lamp on the kitchen table. Sometimes a weakness overcame him, his legs were unstrung, and he had to find some place to sit down, but this was easy enough to disguise. It was his voice that gave him the most trouble. It sounded false to him and not like his voice at all.

His wife yawned and then yawned again a minute later, and put the cover on her workbasket and gathered up her mending. "I declare, it's snowing," she said. She got up and went into the bedroom, and he sat looking at the snow, which was coming down in big cottony flakes.

"Aren't you coming, Lloyd?"

He turned the wick down until the lamp sputtered and went out. Then he went into the next room and, sitting on the edge of the bed, began to undress. *As long as she doesn't know how I feel about her* . . .

He kissed her eyelids.

"Now, why would you want to do a thing like that?" Clarence asked.

"Well, land is cheap, for one thing. I could own my own farm and raise what I pleased on it, and not have to share the profits."

"Or the losses, in a bad year. You've been on the Stroud place all your life. It's home to you. You know everybody for miles around and they know you. If you get into trouble, you can expect help."

"True enough," Lloyd Wilson said soberly. He knew that if Clarence did not say "help from me" it was because he didn't want to remind him how beholden he was.

"Who knows what it is like in Iowa. You may find that people are friendly out there and then again they may not be."

What Fern felt, he could not make out. Nothing, maybe.

Maybe she resented his friendship with Clarence and would be glad if he moved away.

She was standing at the stove, with an apron on, rinsing the supper dishes in a pan of hot water. She had moved the lamp to a shelf higher than her head and the light fell on the nape of her neck, the place that in women and small children always seemed to express their vulnerability. Looking at the soft blond hairs that had escaped from the comb, he thought of all those people who, because of their religion, had knelt down in great perturbation of mind and had their heads chopped off. His heart was flooded with love for her and he lost the thread of what Clarence was saying.

Riding into town with him, Clarence said, "Fern's as cross as a bear this morning."

"Yes," he said, trying to seem no more interested than if Clarence had said he had to replace some part in the manure spreader.

"I wish I knew what's eating her."

"Maybe nothing. Maybe she's just tired or doesn't feel well."

"Maybe."

"In any case, I doubt if she's the only woman in Logan County that's as cross as a bear this morning."

"There's no pleasing her sometimes," Clarence said, and there the conversation ended. But it had opened up vistas of hope, where before there had been none.

Parting the slit in the front of his underwear, he sent his urine in an arch out onto the frozen ground. It glittered in the moonlight. He was in the shadow of the porch roof, where he could not be seen by anybody driving past—though who would be, before daylight? With one knee bent and his foot braced against the porch railing he stood staring off into the darkness where she was. A minute passed, and then another. The first cock crowed, even though the light in the east hadn't changed. At his back a woman's voice said, "Lloyd, what on earth are you doing out there?" and he turned and went into the house.

He thought his secret was safe until one day when he walked into the kitchen and asked, "Where's Clarence?" and she said coldly, "Why do you keep up this pretense of friendship any longer when you don't like us the way you used to?"

He was dumfounded, and started to defend himself, and then broke off. If he didn't say what was on his heart now he might as well crawl into a hole somewhere and die. His life wouldn't be worth living. . . .

Out it came. Everything. Pouring out of him. He expected to be driven from the house and instead she looked at him the way she looked at her children when they were upset over something—as if, as a human being, he had a right to his feelings, whatever they were. When he took her in his arms she neither accepted his kiss nor resisted it.

Instinct told him that it would end badly.

For a week they avoided each other and accident kept bringing them face to face when there was nobody else around. Each time, they turned away without saying a word, without even touching each other. And got in deeper and deeper. He knew he should be sorry but he was not. Which didn't keep him from grieving for the best friend he had ever had. As if Clarence had met with an accident.

The flood of feeling that informed his heart was like nothing he had ever experienced. If his wife, lying with her back to him on the far side of the bed, knew he was awake she did not show it. Reassured by the sound of her breathing, he lit a match and looked to see what time it was. He had never before not been able to fall asleep the minute his head hit the pillow. Now hour after hour went by and he felt no need for sleep. He felt as if he had just been born.

He lay on his side for a while and then turned, trying not to produce an upheaval in the bed. If things had been different, if they'd met when they were young, before Clarence had come along and . . . He turned again. He was in the habit of going to his father when he had a problem to deal with that was totally beyond his experience. He went to his father now and said *What am I going to do?* And his father said *Stay on this side of the boundary line till you get over it.* Good enough advice but if he didn't get over it? This question his father did not seem to want to answer. But he knew also that if his father had come up with a solution he wouldn't have been interested. He turned again so that he was lying on his back, and tears of gratitude ran down his face, past his ears, through the stubble on his jaw, and were soaked up by the pillowcase, which smelled of sunshine. . . .

The alarm clock went off and ran all the way down and he didn't move. Sleep, when it finally came, had felled him. His wife shook him awake and he was under the impression that he answered her, but all he did was sit up in bed and reach for the matches and light the lamp to dress by. Shaking the grates in the kitchen stove he was aware, suddenly, of how cut off they now were from everybody. And committed to lying.

There was nothing to be done about it. He didn't want to not love her. It was as simple as that. And with the lantern swinging from his hand he went off into the darkness as on any other morning—as he did on the last morning of his life.

Clarence and the hired man started to carry the full milk pails into the shed where the separator was, and when he didn't follow them Clarence turned and said, "Aren't you coming?"

"Not tonight," he said, only to have his excuses brushed aside.

The memory of making love lay like a bandage across the front of his mind, day and night.

He waited for her to tell him where they would meet, and when. And marveled at the excuses she thought up to get to him. No matter what the excuse was, it always worked. No excuse at all worked equally well. He thought, *If Clarence comes in from the fields unexpectedly and she isn't there, and he doesn't wonder where she is or go out looking for us* . . . which didn't prevent him from thinking, also, *We can't go on doing this to him. He doesn't deserve it.*

Pulling the bridle over the horse's nose he wondered if they were already the talk of the neighborhood.

"I caught Cletus looking at us."

"What do you mean?"

"As if we'd turned into strangers."

"You imagine it," she said, and kissed him.

*

He found notes in his pocket that she had put there without his knowing it, and that Marie might have found when she went through his clothes on washday. Were there others that he didn't discover in time?

He waited for his wife to say something and she didn't.

He meant to warn Fern about the notes and forgot.

There was no limit to the falsehood and deception, the smiles he made himself smile, and even so he was caught off guard. Walking from the barn to the house he felt Clarence's arm draped over his shoulder and before he could stop himself he moved away to avoid the physical contact. Also to escape responding to it, which would have been to tell Clarence and get it over with. When it was too late, he wished he had.

7

Innocent (more or less) Creatures

"Lloyd is preoccupied."

It was the first time Cletus had ever heard the word and apparently it didn't mean what you might think.

"About what?" his mother asked.

"I have no idea," his father said.

She didn't for a minute believe him; his manner and his voice and the look in his eyes all betrayed him. He suspected them. Of how much there was no telling. Of something. Another man would have come out with it. As long as he went on pretending not to know, her hands were tied. Maybe that was his game.

She watched him for two days. On the morning of the third, he asked if there was any more coffee and she said accusingly, "You're not fooling me! I know that you know."

When it turned out that she was mistaken and he didn't know, there was no way she could take the words back. It was as if a hole opened suddenly at their feet and they fell into it.

Over the mirror in the barbershop there is a colored poster, framed, of a woman with a pompadour. Her ample bust emerges from a water lily. She is holding an eyedropper elegantly and advocating Murine for the eyes. On the opposite wall, a whole row of calendars for the year 1921. On the linoleum floor, swatches of straight light brown hair. A minute before, they were part of Cletus Smith. Now they are waiting for the broom. The wall clock says seventeen minutes after two (tick/tock tick/tock) and the odor of bay rum lingers on the air. Sitting in the barber chair, with his head pushed down so that his chin is resting on his collarbone, Cletus can only look sidewise. He sees a shadow fall on the plate-glass window and then withdraw abruptly.

With a wave of his clippers the barber indicates the sidewalk, empty now. "Wasn't that your friend?"

The question is not directed at Cletus but at his father, waiting his turn under the row of calendars. When there is no answer the barber is not offended. People either answered prying questions, in which case you found out something you didn't know before, or they ignored them and if you bided your time you found out the answer anyway. Friend no longer, he remarked to himself. And then his eyebrows rose because of what he saw in the mirror: the boy was blushing.

Riding on the seat of the cultivator in the field that lay next to the road, Lloyd Wilson did not raise his head when Clarence drove by in the buckboard wagon, with Cletus on the seat beside him.

The two men met once, by accident, at the mailboxes, and after that they saw to it that they didn't meet anywhere. Though they were no longer on speaking terms they couldn't avoid seeing each other at a distance in the fields. And at night the lighted windows of one another's houses, once a comfort, only made them uneasy, since it was a reminder of all the things that were not the way they used to be.

Fred Wilson finished reading the evening paper and took off his glasses in order to rub his eyes. The family resemblance was apparent for a moment. "Well, tomorrow's another day," he said, and stood up.

"Sleep well, Uncle Fred," Marie Wilson said.

"If I don't, I don't know whose fault it will be but mine," he said cheerfully, and went off to his room back of the kitchen. The children said good night to their mother, and then to their father, and went upstairs to bed. The clock ticked, loudly at times. A piece of wood collapsed in the stove. Lloyd Wilson was aware that the silence in the room was not of the ordinary kind, and braced himself. His wife rolled the sock she had just finished darning into a ball and said, "Has something happened between you and Clarence?"

"No."

"You haven't quarreled?"

"No."

"Then what *is* the matter?"

"I don't know."

"You mean you don't know how to tell me?"

He didn't know how to lie. To other people, yes, but not to her. He said slowly, "I guess that's what I do mean." He saw that her face was flushed and her eyes bright with tears. "We—"

"If it's what I think it is, I don't want to hear about it."

"What happened was that we—"

"I told you, I don't want to hear about it."

"—couldn't prevent it."

"And that makes it more comfortable for both of you, I'm sure. But don't ask me to believe it too. From now on you go your way and I'll go mine."

What she meant by this statement he didn't know and it didn't seem like a good time to ask. Their eyes met and with an effort he kept his glance from faltering. The accusing look and the missing front tooth were things he had not bargained for when he stood up before the minister. Or she either, he thought sadly.

Days went by and he had almost come to the conclusion she didn't mean anything by that statement, and that things had settled back into the way they were before, when she announced that she was going to take the children and move in with her sister in town.

He said the first thing that came into his head, which was "But you don't get on with her."

"I know. But she says she'll take us in. Blood being thicker than water."

He sat back and listened while she talked their whole married life out of existence. At no time did he argue with her or deny any statement she made. Finally, when there was nothing more to say, she picked up the lamp and went into the next room, and he followed her, and they undressed and got into bed as if nothing whatever had happened. After a while he said, in the dark, "You can take the girls but not the boys."

There was no answer from the far side of the bed.

He knew that even now he could persuade her to change her mind, but if he did—

"I have never before in my life been happy," he said, "and I will not give it up."

*

Because there wasn't room for everything in the buggy, they took with them only the baby's paraphernalia and what the rest of them needed for the night, and left the battered suitcases and an old leather trunk for him to bring the next day. Nobody spoke all the way in to town. When he pulled on the reins the little girls were ready and one by one jumped from the metal step of the buggy. Hazel stood waiting for her mother to hand the baby down to her. "Be good girls," he called after them but they were too frightened by what was happening to turn and smile at him. He waited until they had all disappeared into the house and then gave the whip a flick. He hadn't meant for things to go this far, and neither had he thought ahead to what might happen next. Coming back to the farm, his spirits lifted for no reason. Or perhaps because a thing hanging over them for so long had at last happened, clearing the air.

Fred never asked questions. The little boys couldn't understand why their mother wasn't there, and he didn't know what she might have said to them, so he told them to be quiet and eat their supper. In the night he heard Orville crying and got up and brought him into his own bed, where he dropped off instantly. But after that he let them cry themselves to sleep, hoping they'd get over it sooner.

He tried to be both mother and father to them, which wasn't easy. When Saturday night came round, he placed the washtub in the middle of the kitchen floor and filled it with warm water from the stove and they stood in it. He poured soapy water over their thin shoulders, as he had seen their mother do, and examined their ears for dirt, but his hands were not as gentle or as practised as hers and Dean looked at him accusingly and said, "You hurt me!"

"Do it yourself, then," he said. But he was damned if he was going to let them grow up in town, not knowing how to handle an axe or plow a straight furrow.

He heard about a widow woman over toward Harmon Springs who was living with relatives and dependent on them for her keep. She might be a little too old for the work but if he got somebody younger, people would talk. "I'll have to think about it," she said when he told her why he had come.

She didn't have to think about it very long. As he was getting back into the buggy the front door flew open and she called out to him to wait while she gathered together a few garments. Settling herself on the seat beside him she said, "Just call me 'Mrs. B'—everybody does." She meant everybody in Harmon Springs.

What with cataracts in both eyes and dizzy spells that came over her if she got down on her knees and poked with the broom in dark corners, the widow didn't do a great deal about the dust that blew into the house from the plowed fields or notice that the pots and pans had acquired a coating of grease. She loved to stand and talk, and one listener was as good as another. "Stop me if I've told you this before, I don't want to repeat myself," she said, but there was no stopping her, or even getting a word in edgewise.

Though she was grateful not to be living on the charity of cousins once removed who raised their eyebrows if she asked for a second helping of chicken and gravy, still the days were long and she wished that people would drop in more. To some she might appear just an ordinary farm woman, but her family had supplied the State of Tennessee with a congressman and a judge. "Well, ma'am, I know you must be right proud of them," Lloyd Wilson said on his way out the door.

It was more than she could do to keep track of his coming and going. Just when she thought he was going to settle down at last and she could dispose of the things she'd been saving up to tell him, he put his jacket on and left the house—to do what, since it was dark outside and the chores were done, she couldn't imagine.

"Pshaw," she said to the little boys as she went after them with a washrag. "If you expect to grow up a big strong man like your father, you can't object to a little soap."

It is not a crime to ask questions, especially indirect ones, and from Fred Wilson's reluctant answers the widow had no difficulty in putting two and two together. She also questioned the little boys about their mother, and said primly, "I hope I shall have the pleasure of meeting her some day."

They did not like her very much but at least she was a woman, she wore skirts, and so they leaned against her some-times out of habit or when they missed their mother. They were very good about coming when she called, and the rest of the time they wandered around together as if they were afraid of being separated.

Riding past on his bicycle, Cletus was conscious of the fact that Mrs. Wilson wasn't there—only that old woman. No more slices of bread that was still warm from the oven. If he saw the little boys or Mr. Wilson he stopped to talk to them. Mr. Wilson acted as though everything was just the same. "Cletus," he said, "you're looking very spry this morning. Do you think we're in for some more rain?" But it wasn't the same, if he never came to their house any more the way he used to. And the Wilson girls weren't going to be at school to see him graduate from seventh grade.

Wayne had a basket of toys that he kept at Aunt Jenny's house, but instead of playing with them he followed her around all morning, talking her leg off—about what she had only a vague idea, for she was only half listening. Finally her patience gave way and she said, "Wayne, honey, be quiet a moment, I can't hear myself think!" And from the way he stood there, looking at her, she realized that he understood perfectly that she was half sick about what was happening out in the country and why his mother was unable to give him her undivided attention, the way she used to. "Not that it matters whether I do or don't hear myself think. You must forgive me, dear heart. I'm not responsible this morning. Now then," and she sat down in a rocking chair and gathered him on her lap and he put his head on her shoulder and they rocked.

After a while he said, "Aunt Jenny, what happens if—what happens if people wake up after they're buried and can't get out?"

"That couldn't happen. They're already in Heaven. And on the Resurrection Day their bodies and their souls are joined and they live happy ever after." Looking at him she could tell that he partly believed what she said and partly didn't believe it, having seen the crows picking at the carcasses of dead animals.

When his mother came to get him he gathered up his things and stood there waiting, but she said, "Run outside and play. Aunt Jenny and I have things to talk about."

The fairgrounds were deserted. The circus had gone ten days before, and it was too soon for the county fair. There was nothing to look at and nobody to talk to. When he got tired of waiting on the front steps he went back into the house and his mother made him go outdoors again.

It will wear itself out, Clarence said to himself, provided he was patient and didn't drive Fern to do something foolish. He was patient, up to a point. For him, he was very patient. But she knew just where he drew the line, and, daring him, stepped over it. When he lost his temper he did things he could hardly believe afterward. Once when they were having an argument she screamed and Victor picked up a bucket of water and threw it over him. The shock brought him to his senses. He looked down and saw he had the poker in his hand.

What *she* did she did deliberately, and she never said she was sorry.

Somebody turned the wick of the lamp up too high and it made a fine layer of soot over everything. He expected her to burst into tears and start taking down the front-room curtains. Instead she laughed.

He asked her to go with him to see his parents and she refused. "But if you don't come they'll think we aren't getting along."

"Which is only the truth."

"They've had enough trouble in their lives. I don't want to add to it."

"You won't be," she said. "They know. Everybody knows. That's all people have to think about."

Since there was work to be done outside, he gave up and reached for his jacket.

All his socks had holes in them. The strawberry bed was loaded with fruit and she didn't bother to pick it. She left the beans on the vines until they were too big to eat. He no longer had a wife—only a prisoner.

Unwatered too long, the Christmas cactus in the front window died and ended up on the rubbish pile. When it was time for her plate of scraps the dog came and wolfed them down and then withdrew into her house. The cats followed

Fern Smith around, purring as usual, and with their tails straight up in the air. Since they were neither faithful nor obedient themselves they saw no reason why women should be.

The widow knew that if she talked long enough at Fred Wilson he would have to lower the newspaper that hid his face and listen to her. Whether he wanted to or not. He heard about the habits of her late husband, and the hard life they had had—so much sickness, and losing the farm because they couldn't keep up payments on the mortgage, the younger son, her favorite, dead of a ruptured appendix, the older one who seldom came to see her because his wife made trouble if he did, and the daughter who lived too far away and never wrote except once in a great while, to say that things were not going well with them. In exchange for all this information which he did not particularly want, Fred Wilson felt obliged to tell her something, so he told her about his wife's lingering illness. "Poor thing," she said sympathetically. "But she's better off now. She's out of it at last."

When he said how grateful he was to his nephew for taking him in after she died, the widow said, "But wouldn't you be happier in your own home?"

"I loved my wife too much ever to remarry," he said firmly. He might not be able to read everybody's mind but he had no trouble reading hers.

The widow had other strings to her bow. One day she met Colonel Dowling in the Smiths' lane and he bowed to her and she never got over it. The social life that went on in her mind was vivid and kept her from being lonely. When Colonel Dowling said *Mrs. B., would you care to take a spin in my car?* she said *No, thank you,* or *Well, since you insist,* depending on her mood.

At Aunt Jenny's house, in a dresser drawer crammed with odds and ends of female clutter, there is an oval picture of her at the age of twenty-three. Every other picture of herself she has destroyed. She was never a beautiful woman but neither was she as plain as she imagined. When this picture was taken she was head over heels in love with Tom Evans, but for some reason love, even of the most ardent and soul-destroying kind, is never caught by the lens of the camera. One would almost think it didn't exist.

Downstairs, on a bracket shelf next to a vase with hand-painted pink roses on it, there is a matching picture of him, taken at the same time. His hair is roached and he is wearing a high stiff collar, and hardly anything shows in his face but his Welsh ancestry. His father and mother were rabid Methodists, but the rigid attitudes that they tried to hand down to him did not stand the test of experience and he ended up not believing in God. "I believe in paying your bills on time," he said, when he wanted to excite the pious. "And in common politeness."

He worked hard, because he liked to work, and was thrifty because he enjoyed that also. He worked for somebody else not because he had an ordinary mind but because the town wouldn't support a second plumbing business. Occasionally he treated himself to a glass of beer but the swinging doors of a saloon did not have an irresistible attraction for him. His fastidiousness could be explained easily enough by assuming that a nobleman's child and a commoner's had been switched in their cradles. But in Logan County there are no castles for the baby to be carried from in the middle of the night, and in fact no noblemen. So there must have been some other explanation.

He died in agony, of a gall-bladder attack, when he was in his early fifties, and the oval photograph, adapting itself to circumstances, is now clearly the photograph of a dead man.

He could not have loved Fern more if she had been his own daughter. To an outsider it seemed that Aunt Jenny was relegated to the position of waiting on them. Waiting on them was her whole pleasure, and she did not ask herself whether they valued her sufficiently. Or at all. Innocence is defined in dictionaries as freedom from guilt or sin, especially through lack of knowledge; purity of heart; blamelessness; guilelessness; artlessness; simplicity, etc. There is no aspect of the word that does not apply to her.

Without the heavyset aristocratic man snoring away on his side of the bed, without the fresh-eyed child whose hair ribbon needs retying; without the conversation at meals and the hearty appetites and getting dressed for church on time; without the tears of laughter and the worry about making both

ends meet, the unpaid bills, the layoffs, both seasonal and unexpected; without the toys that have to be picked up lest
somebody trip over them, and the seven shirts that have to be
washed and ironed, one for every day in the week; without the
scraped knee and the hurt feelings, the misunderstandings that
need to be cleared up, the voices calling for her so that she is
perpetually having to stop what she is doing and go see what
they want—without all this, what have you? A mystery: How is
it that she didn't realize it was going to last such a short time?

When Lloyd Wilson got upset at the thought of the money
that used to be in his savings account in the Lincoln National
Bank and wasn't there any longer, he reminded himself that he
had a chance to object to the amount of the settlement and
just said, "Where do I sign?" She had cleaned him out, but he
owed her something, and he couldn't let his children starve. It
didn't occur to him, though, that she would turn the little girls
against him. They sat with their mother in church, all in a row,
and if he tried to catch their eye or smiled at them they looked
straight ahead at nothing.

When they were older they would feel different, maybe, but
all the same, it hurt his feelings. He changed his life insurance
policies so that the boys were the sole beneficiaries.

Mrs. Stroud drove out to her farm earlier in the day to avoid
the heat. While they were inspecting the corncribs she said
crossly, "Your marital difficulties do not interest me but I don't
like to see this place going to wrack and ruin because of them.
The woman you have hired to keep house for you is old and
half blind, and the house is by no means the way your wife
kept it."

"I know," he said, for once neither evasive nor verging on
insolence.

"My house in town is always clean and I see no reason why
this house, which, after all, is mine too, shouldn't be the same
way."

"I'll speak to her," he said soberly, but he didn't. As though
he were gifted with second sight, he regarded the arrangement
as temporary.

*

As Cletus walked into the cool shade of the house he heard voices. His mother's voice. And then Aunt Jenny's. He knew the cookie jar was empty but he put his hand in it anyway, hoping to be surprised, and as he felt around inside, his mother said, "That was last Saturday. Naturally I was nervous but it turned out there was no cause to be." She waited until he had gone upstairs to his room before she continued: "When I got home I said to you know who, I said, 'It may interest you to know that I've consulted a lawyer.' I decided the time had come to tell him."

"I don't know as I'd have done that," Aunt Jenny said. "That is, not if you're meaning to avoid trouble."

Fern Smith wasn't meaning to avoid trouble; she was bent on making it. It was her only hope.

"It set him back on his heels. I knew it would."

Aunt Jenny raised her eyes to indicate the ventilator in the ceiling.

"If we don't mention any names, how can Cletus tell who we're talking about? And I haven't mentioned any."

"What did he say?"

"Clarence?"

"No, the man in town."

"He listened, and asked questions, and finally he said, 'Mrs. Smith, I think we can safely say we have a case.'"

A case of what, Cletus wondered.

With Lloyd Wilson's wife gone, what prevented her from throwing a shawl over her shoulders and running across the fields to his house? The whole community. It was one thing to behave in such a way as to provoke gossip and quite another for them to live in open immorality. They had talked about it often. She didn't care if every woman she knew stopped speaking to her, but they wouldn't let their husbands have anything to do with him, and that might make it very difficult. There wasn't a man for miles around who wasn't indebted to him for something, but the only one who ever seemed to feel this was Clarence.

And Mrs. Stroud?

He didn't know. With her, anything was possible. When she came out to the farm these days she had a cat-and-mouse expression on her face that was new—as if she was enjoying the situation he had got himself into and was watching with amusement to see what he would do next.

People will stand only so much. And there is a line that you can't cross over, no matter how much you would like to. If he did cross over it and he got a letter informing him that after the first of March Mrs. Stroud had no further need for his services, where would they go then? Who would take him on as a tenant when they found out that he was living with a woman who was not his wife? Their courage failed them.

Clarence believed Fern when she said that she had neither seen Lloyd nor talked to him, but he knew in his bones that they communicated with each other somehow. He questioned the boys and searched in odd corners about the farm—a hollow tree, an abandoned chicken house, a shed that was far enough from the house so that Lloyd could have gone there at night without the risk of being seen. But the dog would have barked, and the boys clearly knew nothing. About that, anyway. How much else they knew he didn't like to think. One minute she was careful and talked in a low voice, or she would get up and shut the door. And then suddenly it didn't matter to her any more what she said or who heard her. Standing at the head of the stairs in her nightgown, she shouted down at him, "You treat the horses better than you treat me!" It wasn't true, and she knew it.

She said she had been in love with somebody else when she married him. He didn't know whether to believe her or not; it might be something she made up on the spur of the moment, to knock the wind out of him.

He drove in to town and got drunk and came home and climbed on top of her. It didn't work. She fought like a wildcat, and he fell off the bed and lay tangled up in the bedclothes. In a sudden weariness of soul he dropped off to sleep and woke in broad daylight, with a hangover and a foul taste in his mouth. The bed was empty.

He went to see the Baptist minister and they had a long talk. In the minister's study, with the door closed. Some things he could hardly bring himself to say, but he felt better after he had said them. And the expression on the minister's face was sympathetic when he said, "Why don't we kneel down right now and ask for God's help." So they did. And he wasn't embarrassed. At that point he would have done anything.

Standing by the front door, with the rain blowing in their faces, the minister said, "Tell her to come and see me. It may be that I can show her where the path of duty lies."

Fern Smith didn't go to see him. Instead she went to town, to the little house across from the fairgrounds. When Aunt Jenny's opinion didn't conform to hers it could be brushed aside.

The widow could not let a farm wagon pass by without running to the front window to see who was *in* the wagon. It wasn't likely, therefore, that she would fail to notice that her employer had something on his mind. Poor man, he missed his family and was regretting the way he had behaved. She intended to try and make him understand—she was just waiting for the auspicious moment—that he mustn't be afraid his wife wouldn't forgive him. If he went to her in the right spirit and told her how sorry he was, things were bound to work out the way he wanted them to. And when his wife did forgive him and came home, then she might be glad of a little help with the housework.

And if not? . . .

Bravely, Mrs. B. decided she was not going to let selfish considerations stand in the way of Lloyd's happiness.

When Cletus walked into the cow barn the cats ran to greet him. His father was already there, milking Flossie. Victor should have been milking the cow on the other side of him but he had gone off on a bender, even though it wasn't a national holiday. Cletus picked up a milk bucket and stool and sat down. He tried to adjust the rhythm of his squirt-squirt to his father's. Old Bess moved her feet restlessly and he said, "So, boss." The cats rubbed against his ankles, purring, but he didn't feel them. The night before, the terrible voice had given him something new to worry about: *I can walk out of this house any time I feel like it, taking the boys with me.* He fell back into the same deep sleep as if nothing had happened, but this morning, while he was mooning over his cereal, there it was.

He saw that Blackie was sitting with his pink mouth

stretched wide open and he squirted a stream of milk into it. Sixteen years old that cat was, and his ears all cut up from fighting, and hardly a tooth in his head.

She won't do it, Cletus thought. But why shouldn't she? What was there to stop her, except fear of his father, and she wasn't afraid, of anything or anybody.

The level of milk rose in the two pails. His father whistled the same sad tune he whistled all day long. When he stood up, Cletus said, "Last night I heard something."

"Outside?"

"No."

"Shouldn't listen to conversations that don't concern you."

"I wasn't trying to listen."

"I see. Well, what did you hear?"

"Mama said, *she* said she might move into town and take me and Wayne with her."

"We'll cross that bridge when we come to it."

"Pa . . ."

"Yes, son."

"Promise me you won't get sore if I say something?" He waited and there was no answer from the next stall. "Please don't argue with her about it, Pa."

"Why not? Do you want to move into town with her?"

"You know I don't. But you shouldn't have said you wouldn't let her do it. If you tell her she can't do something, then she has to do it."

"Why, you little fucker!"

The heavy hand shot out and sent him sprawling. What the boy had said was true, but a lot of difference that made. The bucket was overturned, a pool of milk began to spread along the barn floor. With his right ear roaring with pain and one whole side of his face gone numb, he picked himself up and drew the stool out from between the cow's legs and put the bucket under her. He managed not to cry, but his hands shook, and the milk squirted unevenly into the pail.

"The next time you try to tell me how to run my affairs it won't be just a clout on the head, I'll break your God damn back," Clarence Smith said. He picked up his stool and moved on to the adjoining stall and sat down and, with his head pressed against the cow's side, resumed his sad whistling.

*

The conversation didn't turn out the way the widow expected. She thought Lloyd Wilson would open his heart to her and instead he said, "Yes, well, I'll think about it," and picked up the *Farmer's Almanac*.

She paused in her crocheting and pushed the lamp closer to him. Either he didn't want to talk about it or he had something else on his mind that he couldn't bring himself to discuss with her. Maybe money troubles. Or it could be that Mrs. Stroud was making difficulty. She was not a very nice woman and had her nose into everything.

8

The Machinery of Justice

CLARENCE was fastening the pasture gate with a loop of wire when it came over him that she was gone. He broke into a run. In his mind he saw the note propped against the sugar bowl on the kitchen table. When he flung the door open she was standing at the stove, her hair damp with steam, stirring the clothes in the big copper boiler. They stared at each other a moment and then she said, "No, I'm still here."

When she did leave, six weeks later, he had no premonition of it.

He was informed, through the mail, by her lawyer, that any attempt to get in touch with her or with their children except through him could be considered as constituting harassment, and that whatever steps were necessary to protect her from it would be taken.

The next thing that happened was a notice from the county clerk's office: she was suing him for a divorce.

Shortly thereafter, Fern Smith sat in her lawyer's office discussing a notice she had received from Clarence's lawyer. It was out of their hands now. They had stopped shouting at each other and put their faith in legal counsel. With the result that how things could be made to look was what counted, not how they actually were.

The divorce proceedings and the cross bill were tried as a single case in the fall term of court. In the jury box and in the visitors' part of the courtroom were men Clarence Smith knew, and, averting his eyes from them, he had to sit and hear his most intimate life laid bare. He did not recognize the description of himself, and he wondered how Fern's lawyer could utter with such a ring of sincerity statements he must know had no foundation in truth. Or how she could sit there looking like a victim when it was she who had made it all come about. Her lawyer had found half a dozen witnesses who were pleased to testify to his bad temper—which surprised him. He had not known that he had any enemies. He had only one witness for his side, but he was counting on that one witness to establish the falsehood of everything that was said.

All but unrecognizable in a new suit and shaved by the barber, the hired man testified to "intimacies." He used other words that had been put in his mouth by Clarence's lawyer. On various occasions, he said, he had come upon the plaintiff and Wilson in an embrace or kissing, or with his hand inside her blouse. When his employer was off the property, Wilson would come to the house and the shade in the upstairs bedroom would be drawn and it would be an hour or more sometimes before he reappeared.

Pacing back and forth in front of the jury box, Fern Smith's lawyer spoke eloquently of the close ties that bound the two households together, and in particular of the friendship of the two men. Was it not a fact, was it not an incontrovertible fact that over a period of many years before the present discord arose, and with Clarence Smith's full knowledge and approval, Lloyd Wilson had frequently gone to the Smiths' house when Smith was off the premises? Before proceeding with the cross-examination, he would like to offer, as evidence bearing on the reliability of the witness's testimony, the fact that he was seldom without the smell of liquor on his breath, and that he had spent the night of July 4th in jail in an inebriated condition.

Clarence's lawyer leapt to his feet and exclaimed, "Your Honor, I object," and the judge said sourly, "Objection overruled."

Victor was easily trapped into saying things he did not mean, and that could not be true, and his confusion was such that the courtroom was moved to laughter again and again. After that, Clarence was called to the witness stand and placed under oath, and heard acts of his described that he could not truthfully deny. What Fern's lawyer did not tell the gentlemen of the jury was the provocation that led up to this violent behavior. And when Clarence tried to, he was instructed by the judge to confine his remarks to answering the questions put to him by counsel.

Nobody said, in court, that Clarence Smith was pierced to the heart by his wife's failure to love him, and it wouldn't have made any difference if they had.

The evening paper reported that Mrs. Fern Smith was granted a decree of divorce against her husband, on the grounds of extreme and repeated cruelty, the charges in his cross bill not being substantiated in the eyes of the jury. He was ordered to pay fifty dollars a month alimony, and she was granted custody of the children.

The ringing of the locusts wore itself out and stopped, only to start up again in the treetops. With Aunt Jenny standing over him telling him what to do next, Cletus carried load after load of junk up the outside cellar stairs and on out to the alley. Cans of long-dried paint and varnish. Jars of preserve that had gone bad or were too old to be trusted. Empty medicine bottles. Bundles of old magazines and newspapers. An iron bedstead. A chair with a cane seat that had given way. A sheet-iron stove with one leg missing. A ten-gallon milk can with a hole in the bottom. Screens so eaten with rust that you could put your finger through them. Occasionally she would decide that something—a bamboo picture frame with its glass broken or a silk dress that was stained under the arms—was too good to throw away, and it was put aside until she could recollect somebody who would be glad to have it. Going through a box of old letters, she came upon a canceled bankbook and turned the pages thoughtfully. "I have a little money," she remarked. (*Why did she say that? It was the one thing she meant to tell nobody.* . . .) "Tom had a life insurance policy that was all paid up when he died. I may not be in the same class with John D. Rockefeller, but you'd find that five thousand dollars was a lot of money if you tried to save it. . . . It'll go to your mother when I die. I just wanted you to know how things are." Which wasn't exactly the truth; what she really wanted was for him to say something—to be surprised by this cat she had inadvertently let out of the bag. "I mean you won't starve," she said.

It took both of them to carry the horsehair mattress spotted with mildew. As they were coming back from the alley, she said, "That's enough for today. There's a storeroom that needs cleaning out but it can wait." He closed the cellar door, she gave him the padlock, which had been in her apron pocket, and they went into the house by way of the back porch. She wanted to say *I don't like the way things have turned out any better than you do*, and was afraid to say it lest Cletus think she wasn't glad to have them under her roof.

She made him wash his hands at the kitchen sink and gave him a glass of cold milk and a large piece of gooseberry pie.

Leaning against the sink, he took a swallow of milk and then said, "When Victor and Pa come in from the fields, who gets their meals?"

"Nobody, so far as I know. It isn't easy for them, I'm sure, but any man knows how to fry bacon and eggs and make coffee."

"They're used to eating more than that."

"He may have to get somebody to keep house for him, like Mr. Wilson," she said, and could have bit her tongue out.

"You'll have Sunday dinner with us, won't you?" his mother said. "Come right from church, so we can have a good visit."

There was no way Clarence could say no or he would have. He didn't tell her that he had stopped going to church.

When they sat down to the table, he saw that his mother had cooked all his favorite dishes, and he tried to eat, though he had no appetite. From his father's uneasiness and from the careful absence of any expression on her face, he knew that her feelings were hurt. She had expected him to tell them everything he couldn't tell the judge and the jury, and when he didn't she thought it was because he didn't trust them.

"We've been expecting the boys to pay us a visit," she said, "but so far they haven't. I dare say Fern won't allow it."

"I don't imagine she would do that," he said, avoiding her glance.

His mother and father were the only two people on earth he trusted at this point, but where to begin? With the fact that he was having trouble scraping together the money to pay his ex-wife's alimony? There wasn't anything he could tell them that wouldn't make them grieve, and anyway, he couldn't bear to talk about it.

He knew what had been done to him but not what he had done to deserve it.

It would have been a help if at some time some Baptist preacher, resting his forearms on the pulpit and hunching his shoulders, had said *People neither get what they deserve nor deserve what they get. The gentle and the trusting are trampled on. The rich man usually forces his way through the eye of the needle, and there is little or no point in putting your faith in Divine Providence. . . .* On the other hand, how could any preacher, Baptist or otherwise, say this?

Fern was advised by her attorney that it would be better if she and Lloyd Wilson didn't see each other for a time. When they wrote to each other, they were careful to post the letters themselves. Her letters were very long, his short. It was not natural to him to put his feelings on paper. But as she read and reread his letters, the words that were not there were put there by her imagination, until she was satisfied that he really did love her as much as she loved him.

The dog waited every afternoon by the mailbox. She knew when it was time to round up the cows, but the boy might come and not find her there. So she went on waiting, and when she saw the man coming toward her she ran off into a cornfield, but only a little ways. She didn't really try to escape the beating she knew he was going to give her.

Cletus started to ride out to the farm on his bicycle and his mother said, "Where are you going?" and he told her and she said, "I'd rather you didn't." When he asked why not, she looked unhappy and said, "Please don't argue with me, Cletus. If your father wants to see you, he'll say so."

It was only a hairline hesitation that kept her from telling him everything. Eventually, when he was grown, she would sit down with him some day and tell him the whole story from the beginning, and he would appreciate all she had been through, and forgive her. *Your father wouldn't give me my freedom,* she would say, *and so I had to go to court and get it that way. . . .* In these imaginary conversations it did not occur to her that he might not forgive her. *If Lloyd hadn't been in love with me,* she imagined herself saying. *Or if he had loved his wife, I guess I would have gone on being married to your father, ill-suited to each other though we were. . . .*

At the memory of Lloyd Wilson's hands resting on her

shoulders as he bent down and kissed her, she shuddered with happiness.

By staring at her fixedly, Wayne made the acquaintance of a little girl named Patsy, who lived four or five houses down the street from Aunt Jenny's house. She had a tricycle, which they rode up and down the cement sidewalk, and only now and then did they quarrel about whose turn it was. He went to Patsy's house early in the morning, and when lunchtime came and Patsy's mother asked him if he would like to stay and eat with them, he always said yes. When she said, "Don't you think it would be a good idea if you ran home and told your mother?" he said, "She won't mind."

Patsy's mother thought it would be nice if Wayne's mother said, "Thank you for being so nice to my little boy," or something of that kind, instead of not even bothering to look up when she was passing the house. And her name in the paper and all.

In a town the size of Lincoln there are no well-kept secrets. Somebody told somebody who told somebody who told somebody who told Clarence about the fat letters with no return address that Fern dropped in the big green box in front of the post office after dark. It didn't even take very long for this to happen. Or for Fern to find out that Clarence knew.

Only now, after the long battle had been won, did she become frightened. She found herself thinking, for the first time, about Clarence. About what she had done to him. And what he might be capable of. She hadn't wanted to take the fifty dollars a month alimony. It was the lawyer's idea. She found herself reliving the moment when Clarence picked up the poker and started for her. And other moments like it.

The dog came racing down the lane and threw herself upon Cletus, and he let the bicycle fall and buried his face in her fur. But after that, nothing was the way he thought it would be. He had expected to follow his father around, helping him with whatever he was doing, and instead they sat in the house all afternoon, trying to think of things to say.

"Thou shalt not bear false witness," the Bible said—but why

not, if the jury couldn't tell the difference between the truth and a pack of lies and neither could the judge? Dressed in black and wearing a veil as if she was in mourning for him, dabbing her eyes with her handkerchief, she fooled them all. The Bible also said, "Thou shalt not covet thy neighbor's wife," and he was ordered to pay them fifty dollars a month. That was their reward, for breaking the Ten Commandments.

How was he to explain this to a half-grown boy? Also he was ashamed—ashamed and embarrassed at all his son had been put through. He knew that Cletus would have preferred to stay out here with him and he couldn't even manage that.

As a result of that humiliating day in court Clarence Smith's sense of cause and effect suffered a permanent distortion. His mind was filled with thoughts that, taken one by one, were perfectly reasonable but in sequence did not quite make sense.

He had no idea how long some of his silences were.

At last the hands of the clock allowed him to say, "It's time you were starting back to town."

"Can't I stay and help with the milking?"

"You don't want to be on the road on a bicycle after dark."

"I could get out of the way if a car comes."

"You better go now. Your mother will worry about you."

He waved goodbye to his father, who was standing on the porch steps, and kicked the standard of his bicycle up into the catch on the rear mudguard and said, "No, Trixie. Don't look at me like that. You can't go with me. . . . No . . . No, do you hear? *No!*"

On the following Saturday he asked his mother if he could ride out to the farm and again she said, "I'd rather you didn't."

She couldn't bear to tell him that his father had sent word by a neighbor that she was not to let him come any more.

Whether they are part of home or home is part of them is not a question children are prepared to answer. Having taken away the dog, take away the kitchen—the smell of something good in the oven for dinner. Also the smell of washday, of wool drying on the wooden rack. Of ashes. Of soup simmering on the stove. Take away the patient old horse waiting by the pasture fence. Take away the chores that kept him busy from the time he got home from school until they sat down to supper. Take away the early-morning mist, the sound of crows quarreling in the treetops.

His work clothes are still hanging on a nail beside the door of his room, but nobody puts them on or takes them off. Nobody sleeps in his bed. Or reads the broken-backed copy of *Tom Swift and His Flying Machine*. Take that away too, while you are at it.

Take away the pitcher and bowl, both of them dry and dusty. Take away the cow barn where the cats, sitting all in a row, wait with their mouths wide open for somebody to squirt milk down their throats. Take away the horse barn too—the smell of hay and dust and horse piss and old sweat-stained leather, and the rain beating down on the plowed field beyond the open door. Take all this away and what have you done to him? In the face of a deprivation so great, what is the use of asking him to go on being the boy he was. He might as well start life over again as some other boy instead.

Just when she had about given up hoping, the widow met Lloyd Wilson's wife and was much taken with her.

Fingering a list of things that only she knew where to put her hands on, in chests and dresser drawers and cardboard boxes pushed back under the eaves in the attic, Marie Wilson made polite conversation. She could hardly believe the disorder and filth that met her eyes everywhere she looked. The windows were so thickly coated with dust and cobwebs you could hardly see out of them. The table runner on the parlor table had ink stains on it, and somebody had burned a hole in the big rag rug that it had taken her all one winter to make. She knew without having to look that no broom ever went searching for lint under the beds. The place hadn't been aired for weeks, and the whole house but especially the downstairs bedroom stank of kerosene and sweaty clothing and stale human breath. Clapping her hands together she caught a clothes moth.

What the widow was waiting for as she talked on and on was a sign that the approval was reciprocated. Sitting on the edge of her chair, Marie Wilson said, "That's quite true," and "I know what you mean," and "I'm sure you're right," and finally, reaching the end of her patience, she said, "I'm afraid you'll have to excuse me, I have things to do." Still talking, the widow followed her up the attic stairs.

But it was the little boys that upset her most. They were thin and pale and answered her questions listlessly, as if they were addressing a stranger. She said, "You know that your father wouldn't let me take you with me?" and they nodded. She brushed the hair out of their eyes, and kissed them, and touched them on the cheek and on the shoulder as she talked to them, and the strangeness wore off eventually. After that they wouldn't let her out of their sight. As she bent down to say goodbye to them they both started to cry.

Lloyd had driven in to town to get her and when she had gathered up what she wanted he drove her back. She did not criticize the widow's housekeeping. It was his business who he got to look after him. They had sat in an uncomfortable silence all the way out to the farm, but now he began to talk about the possibility of his finding a place somewhere in Iowa —which would mean that she would never see the boys at all. She asked him to bring them in to town now and then to spend the night with her and he answered, "It would only make it worse for them." After which they both relapsed into silence. He could feel that there was something on the tip of her tongue which for some reason she kept deciding not to say. When he stopped in front of the boarding house where she was now living she started to get out of the buggy and then turned to him and said, "I know you don't care in the least about me, or your daughters, but I don't see how you could do that to Clarence."

He looked down at his hands, with the reins looped through his fingers, and didn't answer.

It rained and rained, and when the sky cleared there was a light frost. The leaves started falling, and the dog could see stars shining in the tops of the trees. Having run away and been whipped for it until she could hardly stand, she stayed on the property. If she went looking for the boy it was never farther than the foot of the lane. Sometimes Clarence forgot to feed her and she had to remind him. What he put in her pan was not at all like the scraps the woman used to give her.

The lawyer who had presented Clarence's case in court so

badly sent him a much larger bill than he had expected. Though there was plenty of work that needed doing outside, he sat in the house brooding. The dog came and stood looking in at him through the screen door, and he burst out at her in a rage and she crept away.

Lloyd Wilson went to see his wife and asked her once more to divorce him so that he and Fern could marry. She listened to what he had to say and then replied that she would think about it. From her tone of voice he knew what her answer would be. She was not going to divorce him, and he had no grounds for divorcing her.

Her eyelids were closed but Fern wasn't asleep. She knew that she slept sometimes, because she passed in and out of dreaming. Daybreak was a comfort. The birds. A rooster crowing. It meant that time existed. At night everything stood still.

The milkman, clinking his bottles. People went about their rounds, things happened that had nothing to do with her divorce—this she needed to be reminded of. It would have been a further comfort to get up and go downstairs and make a pot of coffee, but then she would wake Aunt Jenny in the front room. Sometimes she dozed. When she let go completely it was always with a jerk that shook the bed and brought her wide awake.

As if she were watching a play she relived the time Tom locked her in her room. How old was she? Eighteen? Nineteen? "You're too young to know your own mind," he said. On the other hand she wasn't too young to have fallen in love with a man with a wife and two children. "I won't have you breaking up somebody's home!" he shouted. And she said— even as the words came out of her mouth she regretted them —she said, "You're not my father and I won't have you or anybody else telling me what I can or can't do." So he locked her in her room, and she climbed out the window onto the roof of the back porch and slid down the drainpipe. He knew what was happening but didn't stir from his chair. When she got home, he was still sitting there and they had it out, at two o'clock in the morning.

Whether she would have accepted Clarence if she hadn't

been sick with love for a man she couldn't have was a question she had never until now tried to answer. At all events, when Clarence turned up and began courting her there wasn't any shouting. Tom was polite to him but distant. And he said nothing whatever to her. He didn't need to. She knew that he prided himself on his ability to maneuver people around to the position he wanted them to take and usually he was successful, but not this time. Not with her. She came to the table with her face set, and the two of them ate in silence, unless Aunt Jenny said something, and even then they didn't always bother to answer. When she burst out, "What is it you have against him?" he wiped his mouth with his napkin and leaned back in his chair and looked at her. Then he said "Are you sure you want to hear it?" and she said "Yes."

Perhaps at another time in her life she might have listened to him and have considered the fact that nobody had ever understood her the way he did. But in the reckless mood she was in, it was his very understanding that drove her to act. She had to prove to him that he could be wrong too; that things were not necessarily always the way he thought.

At one point she interrupted him and he said, "Just let me finish. When you are picking a husband there are only two things that count—good blood and a good disposition. One day, on the courthouse square, before ever he turned up here, I saw him taking something out on his horses. I didn't enjoy it. And you wouldn't have, either." He sat looking at her for a moment and then he said, "I see I might as well have been addressing a fence post. Try to understand that other people are real and have feelings too. And some things, once they are done, can't be undone." And he got up and left the table.

When she announced that she and Clarence were going to be married and live on a farm in McLean County he said, "Very well, but don't expect me to give you my blessing or come to the wedding."

The wild geese were flying south.

The nights turned cold. They finished shucking the corn. And one day Victor and Clarence came out of the house and stood together talking. Victor was wearing the new suit, and he had an old leather satchel with him. Since Clarence had been

cleaned out by the lawsuit and couldn't afford to pay him anything, he had offered to work for his keep. The offer was not
accepted.

"I hope everything goes all right with you," he said now,
shading his eyes from the direct light of the sun.

"I'll manage somehow, I guess," Clarence said, and they
shook hands.

"You can always reach me through my sister in New Holland."

Victor picked up the satchel and started off down the lane,
and that was the last the dog ever saw of him.

It turned warm again and there was a week of fine weather.
Except for the oak trees, all the leaves had fallen. Otherwise it
was like summer. With her paws resting on her nose, the dog
followed the circling of a big horsefly, and when it zoomed off
she closed her eyes and went to sleep, and dreamed that she
was chasing a rabbit.

Instead of getting on a train and going to Iowa to look for
good land, Lloyd Wilson temporized. He told himself he
couldn't leave before the first of November, and then it was
November and the days went by and there was always something that needed doing, and with one excuse and another he
kept himself from facing the fact that what he was proposing
to do was impossible. He had spent his whole life on this place
and leave it he could not. Even though the things people were
saying about Clarence made it sound like he was more than
half crazy and capable of anything.

"You haven't given me much notice," Colonel Dowling said.
"And I don't know that I can find somebody overnight."

He noticed that Clarence put his finger inside his collar, as if
it were choking him, and that his hands were restless, and he
stuttered. None of this was at all like him. But he was prepared
to give his tenant a satisfactory character, as far as it went. An
unqualified recommendation wouldn't have been right, in the
circumstances. He just wasn't the man he used to be, before
he dragged his wife into court and all that. But it ought to be
possible to say something sufficiently commendatory so that
Clarence could still manage to find a place. The praise shouldn't

be of so specific a kind that, if there was trouble later on, the people that took him on as their tenant would feel that he, the Colonel, had been less than candid. One way or another, he would work it out. He was at his best with ambiguities of this kind.

To his surprise, Clarence didn't ask for any recommendation. Instead he shook hands and walked down the rickety wooden stairs and out onto the sidewalk, where he stood blinking in the harsh sunlight. He now had no wife, no family, and no farm, all through Lloyd Wilson's doing.

It snowed and then there were three or four days of soft weather, leaving the ground bare again. After that, the nights were very cold.

It was the time of year when the man usually sawed up fallen trees and split the logs and filled the woodshed with firewood. The dog took note of the fact that he didn't do any of these things. The woods were alive with quail and pheasant and he didn't go hunting.

The new tenant turned up with an acquaintance, a bald-headed older man whom he kept turning to for his opinion. They went through the house with Clarence, and then they walked around outside, inspecting the barns and the outbuildings, and asking a great many questions about yield and acreage. At one point all three men turned to look at the dog, and it didn't take any great intelligence on her part to know who it was they were discussing.

Cletus didn't feel like hanging around the schoolyard after school, watching boys he didn't know (and who showed no signs of wanting to know him) shoot baskets. So he came straight home, if you could call it that, even though there was nothing to do when he got there. He opened the door of the icebox and a female voice called from the front room, "Cletus, you'll spoil your supper," so he closed the door again—there wasn't anything he wanted anyway—and went outdoors and sat on the back steps, in the bleak sunshine.

The teacher, who was not young or pretty, had given each of them a map of South America and told them to fill in the names of the countries and rivers, but Cletus didn't feel like it. With a stick he drew crosses in the dirt, making life difficult for an ant who had business in that patch of bare ground. Though it had been going on for days, he was only now aware of a distant hammering: *Pung, pung, pung, kapung, kapung, kapung, kapung* . . . Somebody must be building a new house.

Twisting the heel of his shoe he erased the lines he had drawn in the dirt and, with them, the ant. Then he got up and went toward the hole in the back fence.

When the man and the old man started bringing things out of the house, the dog couldn't imagine what had got into them. Bedsteads, mattresses, chairs. Tables, kitchen utensils, tools. Boxes of this and that. All out on the grass where they would get rained on.

The old man said, "Are you sure you want to get rid of this nice set of encyclopedia?"

"If you want it, put it in the car, Dad," Clarence said.

The farmyard began to fill up with people and he shut her up in the woodshed, though she wasn't meaning to do anything unless called upon. All she could see was the light that came through the cracks between the boards, but she could hear perfectly. More and more buggies and wagons kept arriving, and a person with a very loud voice kept shouting, "Wullabulla, wullabulla," and pounding on a table with a wooden mallet in such a way that it hurt her ears, *and the animals seemed to be leaving!* First the cows, that she had the privilege of rounding up every evening of her life. And then the sheep. She could hear them baaing with fright. Then the hogs. Then the chickens and turkeys. And finally the horses, which was too much. How was the man going to plow without them? It must be the work of the loud voice, and if the man had only opened the door of the woodshed the dog would have helped him drive that person clean off the property. To remind him that she was there, able and willing, she barked and barked.

When he finally did let her out, the shouting had stopped and all the things that had been standing about on the grass were either gone or in somebody's buggy or wagon, and the few people who were left were going, and the sun was already down behind the hill.

Clarence got a length of rope and tied the dog to a tree, which she didn't understand any more than she understood why he felt it was necessary to shut her up in the shed. Then he brought some more things out of the house—a suitcase, fishing poles, a flashlight, an axe, an umbrella—and put them in the car. The old man pointed to the doghouse, and Clarence said, "That stays here."

While his father waited in the car, Clarence walked through all the empty rooms one last time. Then he locked the kitchen door and put the key under the mat. "I'm glad this day is over," he said and, taking a firm stance in front of the car radiator, he gave the crank half a dozen quick heaves and then ran around and climbed into the driver's seat. The roar of the engine diminished as he adjusted the spark.

The old man saw the dog looking at them expectantly and said, "What if that fella doesn't come?"

"He'll come," Clarence said. "He told me it might be dark before he got here, but he promised me he'd come today."

The borrowed Model T drove off down the lane and the dog was tied up, with night coming on, and no lights in the house, and no smoke going up the chimney.

She waited a long long time, trying not to worry. Trying to be good—trying to be especially good. And telling herself that they had only gone in to town and were coming right back, even though it was perfectly obvious that this wasn't true. Not the way they acted. Eventually, in spite of her, the howls broke out. Sitting on her haunches, with her muzzle raised to the night sky, she howled and howled. And it wasn't just the dog howling, it was all the dogs she was descended from, clear back to some wolf or other.

She heard footsteps and was sure it was the boy: *He had heard her howling and come from wherever it was he had been all this time and was going to rescue her. . . .*

It turned out to be the man's friend from over the way. He put his lantern on the ground and untied her and talked to her and stroked her ears, and for a minute or two everything was all right. But then she remembered how they didn't tell her to get in the car with them but drove off without even a backward look, and she let out another despairing howl.

Lloyd Wilson tried to get her to go home with him but she

couldn't. If she did that, who would be on hand here to guard the property?

In a little while he was back with some scraps for her, which she swallowed so fast that she didn't know afterward what it was she'd eaten. He filled the bowl with water from the pump and left it by the door of her house. Then he called to her and whistled, but she wouldn't budge. "Have it your own way, but I doubt if anybody's going to get a wink of sleep," he said cheerfully, and went off into the darkness.

She howled at intervals all night, and set the other dogs in the neighborhood to barking. The next day when the man's friend came to see how she was getting on, she went halfway to meet him, wagging her behind.

The widow fed her, and the little boys put their arms around her and kissed her on the top of her head, and she felt some better.

That night at supper, with the dog sitting beside his chair and listening as if the story was about her, Lloyd Wilson said, "You never had to tell him anything. When he died, I swore I'd never have another. . . ."

The dog raised her head suddenly. Then she got up and went to the door: a wagon or a cart had turned into the lane at her place. She whined softly, but nobody paid any attention until there were footsteps outside and she started barking. "Be quiet, Trixie," Lloyd Wilson said and pushed his chair back from the table. In the light from the open door he saw a young man who looked as if he were about ready to start running.

"Name's Walker," he said. "I'm your new neighbor. I told Mr. Smith I'd be here two days ago but my wife took sick and we had to put off coming. She's still in Mechanicsburg, where I left her. . . . No thanks, that's very nice of you. On my way through town I stopped and got something to eat at the café. You haven't seen anything of my dog, have you?"

Seeing the rope dangling from the tree, James Walker kept the dog tied up for the next two days, though he had been assured it wasn't necessary. But he also fed her and saw that her pan had water in it and talked to her sometimes. And when night came there was a light in the kitchen window, and the dog smelled wood smoke. Things could have been worse. From time to time she wanted to howl, and managed not to.

The day after that, trucks came, bringing cattle and hogs and farm machinery and furniture. And that evening the young man untied the rope and said, "Come on, old girl, I need you to help me round up the cows." She understood what he said all right, but she wasn't his old girl, and she lit off down the road as fast as lightning.

Clarence spent much of the time in his room with the door closed. He had dark circles under his eyes. His clothes hung on him. When his mother called him he came to the table, but throughout the meal he looked at his plate rather than at them, and they had to ask him two or three times before he understood that they wanted him to pass something.

His mother tried to get him to see a doctor, but he wouldn't. "There's nothing wrong with my health," he said, in such a way that she was afraid to pursue the matter.

Cletus was sure that his father would come to see them on Christmas morning, bringing presents. Ice skates was what he wanted. A rifle would be even better but you couldn't use it in town, and anyway it would be too expensive. Wayne still believed in Santa Claus. On Christmas Eve, when they undressed, their empty stockings were hanging from the foot of the bed, and they saw by the streetlamp that it was snowing. When they woke up in the morning their stockings were full, and there were more presents waiting for them downstairs. Aunt Jenny had got out her best tablecloth and roasted a capon, and there was a small artificial Christmas tree in the center of the table. They ate till they were stuffed. When they pushed their chairs back, his mother started to clear the table and Aunt Jenny said, "Leave all that till we've had a chance to digest our dinner."

Cletus still wasn't worried. His father had never not given them anything for Christmas.

Wayne wanted to play Old Maid. As Cletus sorted out his cards he listened for the sound of footsteps on the porch. After a while Aunt Jenny got up and began to stir around in the kitchen.

"I find it very strange of your father not to make any effort about your Christmas," Fern Smith said. What she found even stranger was that Cletus didn't seem to care. Maybe it was a stage he was going through, but he seemed so indifferent these days. About everything.

The decorated tree on the courthouse lawn was much too large to go in any house. On Christmas Eve people had sung carols around it, but now the square was deserted, except for two men standing in front of the drugstore. One of them was a traveling salesman who hated Christmas. The other was Clarence. Though he was looking straight at the big Christmas tree, he didn't know it was there. Or what day it was. Or why the courthouse square was so deserted.

"I thought the world of him," he said to the traveling salesman, "till he broke up my home. . . ."

Once the dog thought she saw Wayne from a distance, but it turned out to be only another little boy who looked like him. People tried to catch her but she didn't let them get that near. Her coat was dry and her eyes were lackluster and she was skin and bones. She lived on rabbits and other small animals and an occasional chicken that got loose from the run. Finally she ended up in town, where some children chased her and threw sticks at her but she managed to get away from them. At night she foraged in garbage cans.

In the end she found them. Clarence Smith's mother looked out of the window at the side yard and exclaimed, "I declare, it looks like we've got company."

From the way the man made over her, the dog thought she was going to be allowed to stay. And that he would take her to where the boy was. She smiled ingratiatingly at the old woman, who said, "It's all right with me if you want to keep her here," but that wasn't what happened.

In the condition she was in, Clarence couldn't bring himself to give her a beating. He took her back to the farm and said, "I guess you'll have to keep her tied up for a little while. I don't know what's got into her. She's always been a good dog, and never given me any trouble."

Then he went around the place, looking in all the sheds and in the cow barn and the horse barn, for something he'd forgotten or lost somewhere. And a few days later he came back and did the same thing.

The new man's woman came, and more snow fell, and the ground was white, and the snow turned to ice, and the dog slipped and slid when she tried to go anywhere, so she stayed in her house and slept. Sometimes she dreamed she was waiting at the mailbox for the boy to come riding up the road on his bicycle.

Awake she wasn't anybody's dog. When she felt like wandering she waited until the new man wasn't looking and then slipped away.

"The new tenant couldn't get Trixie to stay on the place," Fern said to Cletus. "So your father took her to the vet's and had her put out. With chloroform. You must forgive him. He isn't himself."

She wasn't herself either, or she would have kept this information from him, or at least broken it to him more gently.

Her letters to Lloyd Wilson were now almost entirely taken up with her fears about Clarence.

The lawyer who had successfully steered Fern through the divorce proceedings twiddled his thumbs thoughtfully. Then, leaning back in his chair, he said, "Did Smith actually say in so many words that he was going to shoot you?"

"No," Lloyd Wilson said. "But I know that he has a gun. And from the way he is acting—"

The lawyer glanced at his desk calendar to see what his next appointment was. "I dare say you have every reason to be alarmed, but unless you can provide a witness who is ready to swear that Smith threatened to take your life, I doubt if the sheriff's office will consider that there are sufficient grounds to issue a warrant for his arrest. Suppose you keep in touch with me, and if there is any change in the situation . . ."

9

The Graduating Class

W HEN I go home, usually because of a funeral, I always
end up walking down Ninth Street. I give way to it as if
it was a sexual temptation. The house we lived in has changed
hands several times, and some fairly recent owner sheared off
the whole back part—the pantry, the back stairs, the kitchen,
the laundry where the cookstove was, and that upstairs bedroom where the Halloween party took place. Why? To save
fuel? The porch railings and the trellises are gone, and so is the
low iron fence that separated the front yard from the sidewalk.
The high curbing and the two cement hitching posts are still
there, having outlived their purpose by half a century. The elm
blight killed off the two big trees I played under, and in their
place are some storm-damaged maples, so oddly placed that
they must have been planted by the birds. In the back yard,
where the flower garden used to be, there is a structure about
the size and shape of a garage, but with a curtained picture
window. Somebody must live in it.

The house next door went up in smoke and flames one
night ten or fifteen years ago—defective wiring—and where it
stood there is a two-story apartment house that covers half of
what used to be our side yard. Here and there all over town
big old houses are missing, or between two old houses that
have survived somebody has inserted a new house, spoiling my
recollection of things. When I come upon the new hospital I
totally lose my bearings. Where exactly was the little grocery
store my mother used to send me to when she discovered she
was out of rice or butter or baking soda? And which wing of
the hospital has obliterated the huge bed of violets in the back
yard of the house where old Mrs. Harts lived with her son
Dave, who never married? And was the bed of violets huge
only because the child who once a year knocked on the back
door and asked for permission to pick them was so small?

When I dream about Lincoln it is always the way it was in

my childhood. Or rather, I dream that it is that way—for the geography has been tampered with and is half real, half a rearrangement of my sleeping mind. For example, the small red-brick house where Miss Lena Moose and Miss Lucy Sheffield lived. It was probably built during the administration of General Ulysses S. Grant, and must have had dark woodwork and heavy curtains shutting out the light. When I dream about it, the proportions are so satisfying to the eye and the rooms so bright, so charming and full of character that I feel I must somehow give up my present life and go live in that house: that nothing else will make me happy. Or I dream that I am standing in front of a house on Eighth Street—a big white house with a corner bay window and carpenter's lace and scalloped siding. I have been brought to a stop there on the sidewalk by the realization that my mother is inside. If I ring the doorbell, she will come and let me in. Or somebody will. And I will go through the house until I find her. But what is she doing there when it is not our house? It doesn't even look like our house. It was built in the eighteen-nineties, and our house is much older than that, and anyway, it's on Ninth Street. In order to deal with this riddle I let my mind wander up Eighth Street, beginning at the corner where the streetcars turn and go downtown, and before I get to the house I was dreaming about I realize there is no such house, and I am, abruptly, awake.

After six months of lying on an analyst's couch—this, too, was a long time ago—I relived that nightly pacing, with my arm around my father's waist. From the living room into the front hall, then, turning, past the grandfather's clock and on into the library, and from the library into the living room. From the library into the dining room, where my mother lay in her coffin. Together we stood looking down at her. I meant to say to the fatherly man who was not my father, the elderly Viennese, another exile, with thick glasses and a Germanic accent, I meant to say *I couldn't bear it*, but what came out of my mouth was "I can't bear it." This statement was followed by a flood of tears such as I hadn't ever known before, not even in my childhood. I got up from the leather couch and, I somehow knew,

with his permission left his office and the building and walked
down Sixth Avenue to my office. New York City is a place
where one can weep on the sidewalk in perfect privacy.

Other children could have borne it, have borne it. My older
brother did, somehow. *I* couldn't.

In the Palace at 4 A.M. you walk from one room to the next by
going through the walls. You don't need to use the doorways.
There is a door, but it is standing open, permanently. If you
were to walk through it and didn't like what was on the other
side you could turn and come back to the place you started
from. What is done can be undone. It is there that I find Cletus Smith.

The little house opposite the fairgrounds looks as if there is
nobody there. As if they have gone away on a trip somewhere.
Aunt Jenny has pulled the shades to the sill. That way, people
won't peer in and see what she sees whenever she closes her
eyes, and sometimes when they are wide open. The double
bed in the front room is made up and Cletus is lying on it,
with his shoes extending over the side so they won't dirty the
spread. He is lying on his left side, in the fetal position, as if he
is trying to get out of this world by the way he came into it.

The house smells of coffee percolating and then of bacon
frying. He does not answer when she tells him breakfast is
ready. And neither does he come. Sitting at the kitchen table
she blows on her coffee but it is still too hot to drink, so she
pours some of it into her saucer. . . . (It is time to let go of all
these people and yet I find it difficult. It almost seems that the
witness cannot be excused until they are through testifying.)

Aunt Jenny gets up suddenly and goes into the next room
and puts her hand on Cletus's forehead. He has no fever but
his skin feels clammy and he is very pale. His eyes are open but
he doesn't look at her. As she takes her hand away he says,
"Would you be afraid if he came here?"

"If who came here?"

He doesn't enlighten her and after a moment she says yes,
she would.

"Where do you think he is?"

"I haven't the least iota."

Her hand is not steady enough to drink from the saucer and so she pours the coffee back into the cup and forgets to drink it. The clock ticks louder at some times than at others. She stops hearing it entirely and hears, instead, the sound of her own heavy breathing. Quarter of nine comes and she clears her throat and says, "Time you left for school. You'll be late." He is already late. The clock is five minutes slow, which she knows but has for the moment forgotten. His books are on a chair by the door, but he knows, even if she doesn't, that he can never go to that school again. He walks in the Palace at 4 A.M. In that strange blue light. With his arms outstretched, like an acrobat on the high wire. And with no net to catch him if he falls.

The meeting in the school corridor, a year and a half later, I keep reliving in my mind, as if I were going through a series of reincarnations that end up each time in the same failure. I saw that he recognized me, and there was no use in my hoping that I would seem not to have recognized him, because I could feel the expression of surprise on my face. He didn't speak. I didn't speak. We just kept on walking.

I remember thinking afterward, *When enough time has passed he will know that I haven't told anybody.* . . . But I still went on worrying for fear he would think that the reason I didn't speak to him was that I didn't want to know him, after what happened. Which is, I'm afraid, what he did think. What else?

Did he go home and tell his mother? And did they then pack up and move to another part of Chicago to get away from me?

If I'd had the presence of mind to say, "You don't have to worry, I won't tell anybody," would they have been able to stay where they were? Would his mother have trusted a fifteen-year-old boy to keep such a promise, even if I had made it?

Sometimes I almost remember passing him in the school corridors afterward. And I think, though I am not at all sure of this, that I can remember being happy that I was keeping his secret. Which must mean that he was there, that we continued to pass each other in the halls, that he didn't move away. But if he had stayed on at that school, sooner or later we would have been in the same classroom, and I know that we weren't.

Five or ten years have gone by without my thinking of Cletus at all, and then something reminds me of him—of how we played together on the scaffolding of that half-finished house. And suddenly there he is, coming toward me in the corridor of that enormous high school, and I wince at the memory of how I didn't speak to him. And try to put it out of my mind.

One day last winter, plagued by guilt, I brought down from the attic a grocery carton stuffed with old papers, diplomas, newspaper clippings, letters from college friends I haven't seen for thirty or forty years, and so on, and went through it until I found my high-school yearbook. The photographs of the graduating class are arranged in vertical panels, fifteen oval likenesses to a page. Cletus ought to have been between Beulah Grace Smith and Sophie Sopkin and he isn't. If he had been, I would, I think, have been able to put him out of my mind forever. I went through the yearbook carefully from cover to cover looking for him. He isn't in any group picture or on any list of names.

There is a limit, surely, to what one can demand of one's adolescent self. And to go on feeling guilty about something that happened so long ago is hardly reasonable. I do feel guilty, even so. A little. And always will, perhaps, whenever I think about him. But it isn't only my failure that I think about. I also wonder about him, about what happened to him. Whether he was spared the sight of his father's drowned body. Whether after a while he and his mother were able to look at each other without embarrassment. Whether he had as lonely a time as I did when he first moved to Chicago. And whether the series of events that started with the murder of Lloyd Wilson—whether all that finally began to seem less real, more like something he dreamed, so that instead of being stuck there he could go on and by the grace of God lead his own life, undestroyed by what was not his doing.

BILLIE DYER
AND OTHER STORIES

Contents

Billie Dyer

I

IF you were to draw a diagonal line down the state of Illinois from Chicago to St. Louis, the halfway point would be somewhere in Logan County. The county seat is Lincoln, which prides itself on being the only place named for the Great Emancipator before he became President. Until the elm blight reduced it in a few months to nakedness, it was a pretty late-Victorian and turn-of-the-century town of twelve thousand inhabitants. It had coal mines but no factories of any size. "Downtown" was, and still is, the courthouse square and stores that after a block or two in every direction give way to grass and houses. Which in turn give way to dark-green or yellowing fields that stretch all the way to the edge of the sky.

When Illinois was admitted into the Union there was not a single white man living within the confines of what is now the county line. That flat farmland was prairie grass, the hunting ground of the Kickapoo Indians. By 1833, under coercion, the chiefs of all the Illinois Indians had signed treaties ceding their territories to the United States. The treaties stipulated that they were to move their people west of the Mississippi River. In my childhood—that is to say, shortly before the First World War—arrowheads were turned up occasionally during spring plowing.

The town of Lincoln was laid out in 1853, and for more than a decade only white people lived there. The first Negroes were brought from the South by soldiers returning from the Civil War. They were carried into town rolled in a blanket so they would not be seen. They stayed indoors during the daytime and waited until dark for a breath of fresh air.

Muddy water doesn't always clear overnight. In the running conversation that went on above my head, from time to time a voice no longer identifiable would say, "So long as they know their place." A colored man who tried to attend the service at one of the Protestant churches was politely turned away at the door.

The men cleaned out stables and chicken houses, kept furnaces going in the wintertime, mowed lawns and raked leaves and did odd jobs. The women took in washing or cooked for some white family and now and then carried home a bundle of clothes that had become shabby from wear or that the children of the family had outgrown. I have been told by someone of the older generation that on summer evenings they would sit on their porches and sing, and that the white people would drive their carriages down the street where these houses were in order to hear them.

I am aware that "blacks" is now the acceptable form, but when I was a little boy the polite form was "colored people"; it was how they spoke of themselves. In speaking of things that happened long ago, to be insensitive to the language of the period is to be, in effect, an unreliable witness.

In 1953, Lincoln celebrated the hundredth anniversary of its founding with a pageant and a parade that outdid all other parades within living memory. The *Evening Courier* brought out a special edition largely devoted to old photographs and sketches of local figures, past and present, and the recollections of elderly people. A committee came up with a list of the ten most distinguished men that the town had produced. One was a Negro, William Holmes Dyer. He was then sixty-seven years old and living in Kansas City, and the head surgeon for all the Negro employees of the Santa Fe line. He was invited to attend the celebration, and did. There was a grand historical pageant with a cast of four hundred, and the Ten Most Distinguished Men figured in it. Nine of them were stand-ins with false chin whiskers, stovepipe hats, frock coats, and trousers that fastened under the instep. Dr. Dyer stood among them dressed in a dark-blue business suit, and four nights running accepted the honor that was due him.

Two years later, he was invited back again for a banquet of the Lincoln College Alumni Association, where he was given a citation for outstanding accomplishment in the field of medicine. While he was in town he called on the president of the college, who was a childhood friend of mine. "What did you talk about?" I asked, many years later, regretting the fact that so far as I knew I had never laid eyes on William Dyer. My friend couldn't remember. It was too long ago. "What was he like?" I persisted, and my friend, thinking carefully, said, "Except for the color of his skin he could have been your uncle. Or mine."

I have been looking at an old photograph of six boys playing soldier. They are somewhere between ten and twelve years old. There are trees behind them and grass; it is somebody's backyard. Judging by their clothes (high-buttoned double-breasted jackets, trousers cut off at the knee, long black stockings, high-button shoes), the photograph was taken around 1900. One soldier has little flowers in his buttonhole. He and four of the others are standing at attention with their swords resting on their right shoulders. They can't have been real swords, but neither are they made of wood. The sixth soldier is partly turned but still facing the camera. As soon as the bulb is pressed he will lead the attack on Missionary Ridge. I assume they are soldiers in the Union Army, but who knows? Boys have a romantic love of lost causes. They must have had to stand unblinking for several minutes while the photographer busied himself under his black cloth. One of them, though I do not know which one, is Hugh Davis, whose mother was my Grandmother Blinn's sister. And one is Billie Dyer. His paternal grandmother was the child of a Cherokee Indian and a white woman who came from North Carolina in the covered-wagon days.

Billie Dyer's grandfather, Aaron Dyer, was born a slave in Richmond, Virginia, and given his freedom when he turned twenty-one. He made his way north to Springfield, Illinois, because it was a station of the Underground Railroad. It is thirty miles to the southwest of Lincoln, and the state capital. In Springfield, the feeling against slavery was strong; a runaway slave would be hidden sometimes for weeks until the owner who had traced him that far gave up and went home. Then Aaron Dyer would hitch up the horse and wagon he had been provided with, and at night the fugitive, covered with gunnysacks or an old horse blanket, would be driven along some winding wagon trail that led through the prairie. Clop, clop, clopty clop. Past farm buildings that were all dark and ominous. Fording shallow streams and crossing bridges with loose wooden floorboards that rumbled. Arousing the comment of owls. Sometimes Aaron Dyer sang softly to himself.

Uppermost in his mind, who can doubt, was the thought of a hand pulling back those gunnysacks to see what was under them.

As for the fugitive concealed under the gunnysacks in the back of Aaron Dyer's wagon, whose heart beat wildly at the sound of a dog barking half a mile away, what he (or she) was escaping from couldn't have been better conveyed than in these complacent paragraphs from the Vicksburg, Mississippi, *Sun* of May 21, 1856:

> Any person, by visiting the slave depot on Mulberry Street, in this city, can get a sight of some of the latest importations of Congo negroes.
>
> We visited them yesterday and were surprised to see them looking so well, and possessing such intelligent countenances. They were very much like the common plantation negro—the only difference observable being the hair not kinking after the manner of the Southern darkey, while their feet, comparatively speaking, being very small, having a higher instep, and well-shaped in every respect.
>
> Some of the younger of these negroes are very large of their age, and are destined to attain a large growth. They all will make first-rate field hands, being easily taught to perform any kind of manual service. Their docility is remarkable, and their aptitude in imitating the manners and customs of those among whom they are thrown, is equally so.

On Decoration Day I saw, marching at the head of the parade, two or three frail old men who had fought in the war that freed them.

Two families lived in our house before my father bought it, in the early nineteen-hundreds. It had been there long enough for shade trees to grow around and over it. The ceilings were high, after the fashion of late-Victorian houses, and the downstairs rooms could not be closed off. My father complained, with feeling, about the coal bill. Like all old houses, it gave off sounds. The stairs creaked when there was no one on them, the fireplace chimneys sighed when the wind was from the east, and the sound, coming through the living-room floor, of coal being shoveled meant that Alfred Dyer was minding the furnace. Sometimes I went into the pantry and opened the cellar door and listened. The cellar stairs had no railing and the half-light was filtered through cobwebs and asbestos-covered heating pipes, and I never went down there. Sitting in the window seat in the library I would look out and see Mr. Dyer coming up the driveway to the cellar door. If he saw me playing outside he would say "Evening," in a voice much lower than any white man's. His walk was slow, as if he were dragging an invisible heaviness after him. It did not occur to me that the heaviness was simply that he was old and tired. Or even that he might have other, more presentable clothes than the shapeless sweater and baggy trousers I saw him in. I was not much better informed about the grown people around me than a dog or a cat would have been. I know now that he was born in Springfield, and could remember soldiers tramping the streets there with orders to shoot anybody who appeared to rejoice in the assassination of Abraham Lincoln. I have been told that for many years he took care of my Grandfather Blinn's horses and drove the family carriage. The horses and carriage were sold when my Uncle Ted persuaded my grandfather to buy a motorcar, and Mr. Dyer went to work for the lumber company.

Whoever it was that tried to worship where he wasn't wanted, it was not Alfred Dyer. He was for decades the superintendent of the African Methodist Episcopal Sunday school and led the choir. He knew the Bible so well, his daughter said, that on hearing any scriptural quotation he could instantly tell where it came from. As he was shaking the grates and setting the damper of our furnace, it seems likely that the Three Holy Children, Shadrach, Meshach, and Abednego, were more present to the eye of his mind than the little boy listening at the head of the cellar stairs.

After our house there were two more, and then Ninth Street dipped downhill, and at the intersection with Elm Street the brick pavement ended and the neighborhood took on an altogether different character. The houses after the intersection were not shacks, but they were not a great deal more. Grass did not grow in their yards, only weeds. There was usually a certain amount of flotsam and jetsam, whatever somebody more well-to-do didn't want and had found a way to get rid of. The Dyers' house was just around the corner on Elm Street. It was shaped like a shoebox and covered with green roofing paper. Elm Street was the dividing line between the two worlds. On either side of this line there were families who had trouble making both ends meet, but those who lived below the intersection didn't bother to conceal it.

As I sorted out the conversation of the grown people in my effort to get a clearer idea of the way things were, I could not help picking up how they felt, along with how they said they felt. While they agreed it was quite remarkable that Alfred Dyer's son William had got through medical school, at the same time they appeared to feel that in becoming a doctor he had imitated the ways of white people, as darkies were inclined to do, and done something that was not really necessary or called for, since there were, after all, plenty of white doctors. Apart from the doctors, the only things I can think of that the white people of Lincoln were at that time willing to share with the colored people were the drinking water and the cemetery.

Billie Dyer's mother was born in Sedalia, Missouri, the legal property of the wife of a general in the Union Army. Her father and mother ran away and were caught and returned, and the general put her father on the block and he was sold to someone in the South and never heard of again. When her children asked what the place where she was born was like, she told them she couldn't remember. And that nobody could come and take her away because the slaves were freed, all of them, a long time ago, and there would never be slaves again.

For things that are not known—at least not anymore—and that there is now no way of finding out about, one has to fall back on imagination. This is not the same thing as the truth, but neither is it necessarily a falsehood. Why not begin with the white lady? When he took the clean washing in his express wagon and knocked on her back door, she called him by his brother's name. She couldn't tell them apart. He didn't let on he wasn't Clarence.

The smell of laundry soap was the smell of home. With steam on the inside of the windows you couldn't always see out.

It was raining hard when school let out. Some children had raincoats and rubbers they put on. He ran all the way home, to keep from getting wet. He threw open the front door and fought his way through drying laundry to get to the kitchen, where his mother was, and said, "Mama, I'm starving," and she gave him a piece of bread and butter to tide him over.

With his hands folded and resting on the edge of the kitchen table, he waited for his father to say, "O Lord, we thank Thee for this bountiful sustenance. . . ." Pork chops. Bacon and greens. Sausages. Fried cornmeal mush. In summer coleslaw, and sweet corn and beets from the garden.

Saturday night his mother took the washtub down from its nail in the kitchen and made him stand in it while she poured soapy water over his head and scrubbed his back and arms. When she said, "Now that's what I call one clean boy!" he stepped out of the tub, his eyes still shut tight, and she threw a towel around him, and then it was Clarence's turn to have the inside of his ears dug at with a washrag.

In Sunday school, making the announcements and leading the singing, his father seemed twice as big as he did at home. Preacher told them about the hand: "Think of it, brothers and sisters and all you children, a hand—just a hand all by itself, no arm—*writing on the wall!*" For Sunday dinner they had chicken and dumplings, and sometimes there were little round egg yolks in the gravy.

He said, "Mama, I don't feel good," and her hand flew to his forehead. Then she went and got the bottle of castor oil and a big spoon, and said, "Don't argue with me, just open your mouth." Lying in bed with a fever, he listened to the old mahogany wall clock. Tick . . . and then tock . . . and then tick . . . and then tock . . . If he told his mother a lie she looked into his eyes and knew. Nothing bad could happen to them, because his father wouldn't let it happen. But if any of them talked back to him he got a switch from outside and whupped them. It wasn't even safe to say "Do I have to?"

His sister Mary didn't want to go to school, because the teacher made fun of her and said mean things. The teacher didn't like colored children. "Why can't I stay here and help you with the washing and ironing?" Mary said, and his mother said, "You'll be bending over a washtub soon enough. Go to school and show that white woman you aren't the stupid person she takes you for." After he finished his homework he helped Mary with hers. It was hard to get her to stop thinking about the teacher and listen to what he was telling her. "Nine and seven is not eighteen," he said patiently.

He fell asleep to the sound of his father's voice in the next room reading from the Bible. The patchwork quilts were old and thin, and in the middle of the night, when the fire in the kitchen stove died down, it was very cold in the house. One night when he went to bed it was December 31, 1899, and when he woke up he was living in a new century.

When he brought his monthly report card home from school his mother went and got her glasses and held it out in front of her and said, "Is that the best you can do?" Then she put the report card where they could all see it and follow his example.

If my Great-Aunt Ev's name was mentioned, my mother or my Aunt Annette would usually tell, with an affectionate smile, how she cooked with a book in her hand. They didn't mean a cookbook, and the implication was that her cooking suffered from it. She had graduated from the Cincinnati Conservatory of Music, and spoke several languages—which people in the Middle West at that time did not commonly do. The question "What will people think?" hardly ever crossed her mind. I have been told that my grandmother was jealous of her sister because my grandfather found her conversation so interesting. When her son Hugh Davis brought Billie Dyer home to play and they sat with their heads over the checkerboard until it was dark outside, she set an extra place at the table and sent one of the other children to ask Billie Dyer's mother if it was all right for him to stay for supper. Before long he was just one more child underfoot.

When he was alone with Hugh he thought only about what they were making or doing, but he never became so accustomed to the others that he failed to be alert to what they said. The eternal outsider, he watched how they ate and imitated it, and was aware of their moods. He learned to eat oysters and kohlrabi.

The first time they played hearts he left the hand that was dealt him face-down on the table. "Pick up your cards," Hugh said. "You're holding up the game." The cards remained on the table. Mr. Davis said, "When your father told you you must never play cards, this isn't the kind of card-playing he meant. He meant playing for money. Gambling." Hugh, looking over his shoulder, helped him to arrange them in the proper suits. The hand that held the cards was small and thin and bluish brown on the outer side, pink on the inner.

At home, at the supper table, he said, "At the Davises' they—" and his sister Sadie said, "You like it so much at them white folks' house, why don't you go and live with them?"

He and Hugh Davis were friends all through grade school and high school. On Saturdays they went fishing together, and when they were old enough to be allowed to handle a gun they went hunting. Rabbits, mostly.

With a dry throat and weak knees and a whole row of Davises looking up at him solemnly, Hugh embarked upon the opening paragraphs of the high-school commencement address: "The Negro is here through no fault of his own. He came to us unwilling and in chains. He remains through necessity. He inhabits our shores today a test of our moral civilization . . ." This must have been in the spring of 1904. I imagine there was a certain amount of shifting of feet on the part of the audience.

On his way to school, Billie Dyer had to pass an old house on Eighth Street that I remember mostly because there was a huge bed of violets by the kitchen door. I was never inside it but Billie Dyer was, and in that house his fate was decided. The house belonged to a man named David H. Harts, who was of my grandfather's generation. He had fought in the Civil War on the Union side, and been mustered out of the Army with the rank of captain. Though he had no further military service, he was always spoken of as Captain Harts. He was a member of the local bar association but applied himself energetically to many other things besides the practice of law. He was elected to the State Assembly, served a term as mayor of Lincoln, and ran for governor on the Prohibition ticket. His investments in coal mines, real estate, proprietary medicine, and interurban railroads had made him a wealthy man, but he was not satisfied to go on accumulating money; he wanted the men who worked for him to prosper also. Because coal mining was a seasonal occupation, he started a brick factory, so that the miners would have work during the summer months.

Everybody knew that Billie Dyer got very good grades in school, and Captain Harts's son John, who was four years older, would sometimes stop him on his way home from school. After a visit to the icebox they would sit on the back steps or under the grape arbor or in his room and talk. At some point in his growing up, John Harts had eye trouble sufficiently serious that the family doctor suggested he stop studying for a while and lead a wholly outdoor life. For months he lived all alone in a cabin in the woods. Every three or four days his father would drive out there with provisions. Occasionally he stayed the night. John Harts tried not to count the days between his father's visits or to wonder what time it was. Denied books, his hearing became more acute. He recognized the *swoosh* that meant a squirrel had passed from one tree to another. He heard, or didn't hear, the insects' rising and falling lament. The birds soon stopped paying any attention to him. He made friends with a toad. As he and his father sat looking into the fire his father told one story after another about his boyhood on a farm in Pennsylvania; about the siege of Vicksburg; about how when they were floating past what looked like an uninhabited island in the Mississippi they were fired on by Confederate infantry; about how when they were defending a trestle bridge some fifteen miles south of Jackson, Tennessee, Henry Fox, a sergeant in Company H, ran across the bridge in full view of the enemy and brought relief at the end of the day; how when they were stationed between the White and Arkansas rivers, a large number died of the malaria from the cypress swamp; how he was captured and used the year he spent in a military prison to study mathematics and science. Even though John Harts had heard some of these stories before, he never tired of hearing them. Lying awake, listening to the sound of his father's breathing, he knew there was no one in the world he loved so much. Sometimes his father brought his older brother and came again early the next morning, so that his brother would be in time for school. One Saturday he brought Billie Dyer. With their trousers rolled above the knee, they cleaned out the spring together. When it got dark, John

Harts saw that Billie Dyer wished he was home. He talked him out of his fear of the night noises by naming them. There was a thunderstorm toward morning, with huge flashes of lightning, so that for an instant, inside the cabin, they saw each other as in broad daylight.

There is no record of any of this. It is merely what I think happened. I cannot, in fact, imagine it not happening. At any rate, it is known that when John Harts went away to college he wrote to Billie Dyer every week—letters of advice and encouragement that had a lasting effect on his life. At twenty-one, John Harts went to work as an engineer for the Chicago & Alton Railroad, and while he was operating a handcar somewhere on the line an unscheduled fast train sent the handcar flying into the air. People surmised that he didn't hear or see the locomotive until it was suddenly upon him, but in any case the flower of that family was laid to rest in Section A, Block 4, Lot 7 of the Lincoln Cemetery.

From time to time after that, Billie Dyer would put on his best clothes and pay a call on Captain Harts and his wife. When he graduated from high school, Captain Harts said to him, "And what have you decided to do with your life?" At that time, in Lincoln, it was not a question often asked of a Negro. Billie Dyer said, "I would like to become a doctor. But of course it is impossible." Captain Harts spoke to my grandfather and to several other men in Lincoln. How much they contributed toward Billie Dyer's education I have no way of knowing, but it does not appear to have been enough to pay all his expenses. It was thirteen years from the time he finished high school until he completed his internship at the Kansas City General Hospital. This could mean, I think, that he had to drop out of school again and again to earn the money he needed to go on with his studies. On the other hand, given the period, is it wholly beyond the realm of possibility that he should have come up against instructors who felt they were serving the best interests of the medical profession when they gave him failing marks for work that was in fact satisfactory, and forced him to take courses over again? In July 1917 he came home ready to begin the practice of medicine, but America had declared war on Germany, the country was flooded with recruiting posters ("Uncle Sam Wants YOU!"), and they got to him. He was the first Negro from Lincoln to be taken into the Army.

2

In 1975, a Dallas real-estate agent named Jim Wood, wandering through a flea market in Canton, Texas, bought an Army-issue shaving kit, a Bible, and a manuscript. He collected shaving memorabilia and they were a single lot. Nothing is more improbable or subject to chance than the fate of objects. On the flyleaf of the Bible was written, in an old-fashioned hand, "To Dr. William H. Dyer from his father and mother." The manuscript appeared to be a diary kept by Dr. Dyer during the First World War. Months passed before Wood bothered to look at it. When he did, he became so interested that he read it three times in one sitting. He was convinced that Dr. Dyer must have made a significant contribution to the community he lived in, wherever that might be, and to the medical profession. So, for several years, with no other information than the diary contained, he tried to find Dr. Dyer or his heirs. Finally it occurred to him to write to the Lincoln public library.

The diary is a lined eight-by-twelve-inch copybook with snapshots and portrait photographs and postcards pasted in wherever they were appropriate. That it escaped the bonfire is remarkable; that it fell into the hands of so conscientious a man is also to be wondered at.

What seems most likely is that Dr. Dyer's wife was ill and that someone not a member of the family broke up the household. But then how did the diary get to Texas from Kansas City? It is eerie, in any case, and as if Dr. Dyer had gone on talking after his death, but about a much earlier part of his life. When the odds are so against something happening, it is tempting to look around for a supernatural explanation, such as that William Dyer's spirit, dissatisfied with the life he had led (the unremitting hard work, the selfless dedication to the sick and to the betterment of his race), longed for a second chance. Or, if not that, then perhaps wished to have remembered the eight months he spent in a half-destroyed country, where the French girls walked arm in arm with the colored soldiers and ate out of their mess pans with them, and death was everywhere.

On the first page of the diary he wrote, "With thousands of others I decided to offer my life upon our Nation's altar as a sacrifice that Democracy might reign and Autocracy be forever crushed." In 1917, the age of public eloquence was not quite over, and when people sat down on a momentous occasion and wrote something it tended to be a foot or two above the ground.

Three hundred friends and neighbors were at the railroad station to see him off, on a Sunday afternoon, and he was kept busy shaking hands with those who promised to remember him in their prayers. Somebody took a snapshot of him standing beside his father and mother. Alfred Dyer's rolled-brim hat and three-piece suit do not look as if they had been bought for someone else to wear and handed on to him when they became shabby. He is a couple of inches taller than his son. Both are fine-looking men.

From the diary: "Mother and Father standing there with tears in their eyes . . . when I kissed them and bade them farewell. . . . My eyes too filled with tears, my throat became full, and for miles as the train sped on I was unable to speak or to fix my mind upon a single thought."

His orders were to proceed to Fort Des Moines, a beautiful old Army post, at that time partly used as a boot camp for medical officers. He was disappointed with his quarters (a cold room in a stable) and did not at first see the need for a medical officer to spend four hours a day on the drill field.

After two months he was moved to Camp Funston, in Kansas. It was the headquarters of the 92nd Division, which was made up exclusively of Negro troops—the Army was not integrated until thirty-one years later, by executive order of Harry Truman. The barracks at Camp Funston were still being constructed, and thousands of civilian workmen poured into the camp every day, along with the draftees arriving by train from Kansas, Missouri, Colorado, Arizona, and Texas. He was assigned to the infirmary of the 317th Ammunition Train, and when he was not treating the sick he weeded out recruits who were physically unfit for military service. The year before, he had fallen in love with a young woman named Bessie Bradley, who was teaching in a night school. His free weekends were spent in Kansas City, courting her. In January and February, an epidemic of cerebrospinal meningitis swept through the camp and kept him on his feet night and day until it subsided. In March, he got a ten-day furlough and took Bessie Bradley to Illinois and they were married.

At Camp Funston a bulletin was read to all the soldiers of the 92nd Division: "The Division Commander has repeatedly urged that all colored members of his commands, and especially the officers and noncommissioned officers, should refrain from going where their presence will be resented. In spite of this injunction, one of the Sergeants of the Medical Department has recently . . . entered a theater, as he undoubtedly had a legal right to do, and precipitated trouble by making it possible to allege race discrimination in the seat he was given. . . . Don't go where your presence is not desired."

This bulletin so stuck in his craw that he managed to get his hands on a copy of it, and it is written out in his diary in full, against some ultimate day of judging.

Early in June, the order came for the division to proceed to Camp Upton for embarkment overseas. Lieutenant Dyer tried to call his wife, but the troops were denied access to telegraph and telephone lines. The next day, the trains began pulling out of the camp. When his section drew into the railway station in Kansas City, he saw that there was an immense crowd. Without any hope whatever that his wife would be among them or that he would find her if she were, he put his head out of the train window and heard her calling to him.

The division was hurried from Camp Upton to the embarkation port at Hoboken and onto a magnificent old steamship that until the war had been carrying passengers back and forth across the Atlantic for the Hamburg-American line. It put out to sea with five thousand men on board, and when Lieutenant Dyer went on deck the next morning he saw that they had joined a great convoy of nine transport ships, two battle cruisers, and half a dozen destroyers. His ship was under the command of a colonel of a unit of the National Guard.

From the diary: "From the very start there was that feeling of prejudice brought up between the white and colored officers, for among the first orders issued were those barring colored officers from the same toilets as the whites, also barring them from the barber shop and denying colored officers

the use of the ship's gymnasium." The sea was calm. The enlisted men were continually on the lookout for periscopes but
saw instead flying fishes and porpoises and a whale that spouted.
Lieutenant Dyer was assigned the daily sanitary inspection of
certain compartments in the fore part of the ship, and the
physical examination of six hundred men. Twice a day he
submitted written reports to the ship's surgeon. On June
21st, shots were fired from all the surrounding ships at what
proved to be a floating beer keg. A convoy of British destroyers
brought them safely into the harbor at Brest. At nine-fifteen in
the evening, when the men of his unit began to go ashore, the
sun was still above the horizon. He was struck by the fact that
the houses were all of stone and closely jammed together and
very old, and by the expression of sadness on the faces of the
French people. The women young and old all were in black
and seemed to be in the deepest mourning. Four little tykes
standing by the roadside sang, "Hail, hail, the gang's all here!
What the hell do we care now," in perfect English. His unit
marched three miles through the gathering darkness to a barracks that had been a prison camp during the time of Napoleon ("a terrible and dirty old place"), and stayed there four
days awaiting orders. Twice he got a pass into the city. The
French people were friendly when he went into a shop or attempted to converse with them. He sat down on a park bench
and children congregated around him. Soon they were sitting
on his knees and, pointing, told him the French words for his
eyes, nose, ears, and neat mustache.

After three days and nights on a train and a nine-mile hike,
his unit ended up in a camp outside a village forty-eight kilometers southeast of Poitiers. It was a beautiful region, untouched by the war. The men pitched their shelter tents in a
level field, the officers were billeted in nearby manor houses.
They were the first American troops in this region, and the natives fell in love with them and came visiting every day. ("With
them there was *No Color Line.*") On Bastille Day, before a great
crowd, the troops gave a demonstration of American sports—
footraces, three-legged races, boxing, wrestling, and baseball.

On July 22nd, Companies B and C, with Lieutenant Dyer
as their medical officer, had orders to proceed to Marseilles,
where they were to procure trucks for the 317th Ammunition

Train and drive them to the front. The officers rode first class, the enlisted men were crowded in boxcars but happy to be making the trip. It was the height of summer, and everywhere women and old men and children were working in the fields. He saw ox teams but no horses. And no young men. Along the tracks, leaning on their pickaxes and shovels as they waited for the train to pass by, were hundreds of German soldiers with "PG" printed in large white letters on the backs of their green coats. In the railway station of every city they came to he saw trainload after trainload of French soldiers headed for the front, where the last great German offensive was being beaten back in the second Battle of the Marne. His own train went east, through vineyards. At Montluçon there was a stopover of several hours, and an elderly English professor showed Lieutenant Dyer and another officer about the city and then took them to the home of an aristocratic French family to meet a pupil of his, a young lady who was very anxious to hear the English spoken by Americans. After Lyons they turned south, following the Rhône Valley. Every time the train emerged from a tunnel, the men in the boxcars cheered. On the fourth day, after emerging from a tunnel three miles long, he saw the blue water of the Mediterranean.

The population of Marseilles was so mixed that it seemed as if God had transplanted here a sample of His people from all the kingdoms of the earth. Most of the men were in uniform of some sort. The Algerian soldiers (many of them "black as tar") with their little red skullcaps and the Hindus in their turbans and loose garments were the strangest. How in such garments could they fight in the trenches? As the men of his company walked through the streets, people exclaimed, "Ah, Americans!" They were welcome in the best hotels, the best theaters, everywhere. But it was a wicked city. Sitting at a table in a sidewalk café, he saw many beautiful women who were clearly prostitutes.

No ammunition trucks were available, and so they traveled back through the same picturesque scenery until gradually it became less picturesque and the farms less well tended. At Is-sur-Tille, where there was a huge American advance-supply base, they spent the greater part of the day on a siding. That night, no lights were allowed in the railroad cars, and from this they knew they were approaching the front. The 92nd Division headquarters was now at Bourbonne-les-Bains, three hundred kilometers southeast of Paris. As Lieutenant Dyer stepped down onto the station platform, the first officers he saw were from his old Camp Funston unit. He reported to the division surgeon and was put on duty in a camp just outside the city.

During the week that his unit remained here, their lockers were taken from them, their equipment was reduced to fifty pounds, and they were issued pistols and ammunition. On the twelfth of August they left the camp in a long convoy of motortrucks, which traveled all afternoon and night and stopped the next morning in the pretty little village of Bruyères. Here they were quartered in an old barracks that turned out to be comfortable enough when put in sanitary condition. Bruyères was a railroad terminal where American and French divisions and supplies were unloaded for the front. Aside from some humiliating divisional orders, which the diary does not go into, his stay there was pleasant. In the evening he walked out on the hills beyond the town and watched the anti-aircraft guns firing at German bombers. The distant flashes of cannons were like sheet lightning on the horizon.

Toward the end of August, on a night of the full moon—though it was almost totally obscured by clouds—he sat in a crowded truck with a rifle between his knees and his eyes focused on the dim road ahead. The convoy drove without lights, and they kept passing Army vehicles that had broken down or had slid off the road into a ditch, and infantrymen who, because of fatigue and the weight of their packs, had fallen out of the line to rest. He gave up counting the houses with their roofs gone or that were completely destroyed. The whole countryside had a look of desolation. At three o'clock in the morning, the convoy arrived at a silent and largely destroyed town. The truck he was riding in drove up an alley and stopped. He and two other officers lay down in front of a building that appeared to be intact and, using the stone doorstep for a pillow, fell asleep from exhaustion. In the morning, the occupants of the building, leaving for work, stepped over them. He got up and asked where they were and was told that it was Raon-l'Étape, in the Vosges.

For two days the American troops bivouacked in a wood,

with German planes lingering high in the air above them in spite of the anti-aircraft guns. Then they were moved back to the town, and that night an enemy bomber dropped four bombs on the place where they had camped, creating terrific explosions. He was billeted at the house of a Mme. Crouvésier, whose two sons were in a prison camp in Germany. Working chiefly at night, because the Germans had occupied this area for three weeks in 1914 and knew the roads perfectly, the 317th moved ammunition of all calibers from the woods where it was hidden to four regiments of American infantry and a French artillery unit that was operating with them. The town was full of graves—in backyards, in gardens, everywhere. While he stood looking at an enemy observation balloon it suddenly went up in a fiery cloud. A German plane was brought down at Raon-l'Étape and the dead aviators were given a military funeral, which he attended.

After nearly a month here, he again found himself in a convoy, which drove all day and at 11 p.m. stopped along the roadside for the night. The truck he was riding in was so crowded that he got out and slept on the ground, wrapped in his blankets, and was awakened two hours later by a downpour. He moved under the truck, but his blankets became so wet that he gave up and moved back into the truck, and with the rain trickling down the back of his neck finished out the night.

Two days later, they reached their destination—the Argonne Forest. There were no accommodations for them, not even water to drink, or to cook with, and the mud everywhere was over their shoe tops. They pitched their tents under bushes and trees to keep from being observed by the enemy airplanes constantly flying over. The companies of the 317th were detailed to handle supplies at a nearby railhead and deliver hundreds of horses to units at the front. ("While camped in this wet, filthy woods, many of our boys became ill from the dampness, cold, and exposure, thereby causing me much work and worry, caring for them.") Division headquarters issued a bulletin that Negro soldiers would be used to handle mustard-gas cases, because they were less susceptible than whites. ("Why is the Negro less susceptible to mustard gas than the whites? *No one can answer.*") On September 25th, a very heavy bombardment began, and it kept up for thirty-six hours without a stop.

("The old woods . . . trembled as if by earthquake, the flashes of the cannon lighted up the inside of our tents, and our ears were deafened.") Lieutenant Dyer went several times to the American evacuation hospital, a quarter of a mile away, and saw a continuous stream of ambulances bringing wounded soldiers to it from the front. The dead were also being brought back, on trucks, piled like cordwood and dripping blood.

They moved on, to Sainte-Menehould, forty-seven kilometers west of Verdun, and were billeted on the top floor of a French barracks. From their windows they could see the lines. The area was full of American soldiers plodding along under their heavy packs. Standing on the top of a hill, he could make out the Argonne Forest, with smoke hanging over it. Big guns were belching from all the surrounding hills. The 317th worked round the clock. With no tall trees and only one other building near it, the barracks made a fine target. ("All through the night the fighting kept up and though scared stiff and expecting to be blown to atoms at any moment I finally fell asleep.")

On the seventh of October, Companies B and C left Sainte-Menehould. The trucks drove south and east all day, in a driving rain, with a cold wind. In many places the road was camouflaged with green burlap supported on wire fences sometimes fifteen feet high and thickly interwoven with bushes and small trees. They passed through towns where not one house was standing whole and there was no longer any civilian population. A ruin next to a graveyard meant that there had been a church on this spot. Even the grass was burned up. ("At 5 p.m. we reached the city of Commercy, where we had orders to spend the night. We were taken to a French barracks where there were fairly good quarters for officers and men. We had just gotten comfortably located in the building, quite glad to get out of the inclement weather, and were preparing to eat, when another order came for the ammunition train to move on. . . . The rain fell and the wind blew and I sat on an open truck helping the driver watch the road to prevent running over an embankment, which would probably have meant our death. . . . All night long we traveled on, wondering what our destination would be and why we should be ordered to move on such a night.") At four in the morning, the convoy stopped in the village of Belleville. Cold, wet, and hungry, he got down and stomped on the ground, hoping to generate a little body heat. At daybreak a feed cart came by and the driver pitched them a few steaks left over from the breakfast of a labor battalion.

Belleville was so protected by the surrounding hills that the shells from the enemy guns at Metz almost never reached it. Lieutenant Dyer and another lieutenant were billeted in the ancient, dilapidated house of an elderly French couple. The officers' second-floor room had one small window. On the walls and rafters were a few traces of whitewash. There was a fireplace and two immense wardrobes. Over their heads was a loft full of straw, in which rats, mice, and birds nested. Sometimes their frisking sent chaff down on the faces of the two men. The beds were good. Lying in his, Lieutenant Dyer listened to the sound of the German planes overhead and tried to gauge, by the whine of a falling shell, whether the explosion would be a safe distance away.

He set up his infirmary in a small electrical plant. Because of the constant cold and rainy weather, there was a great deal of sickness among the colored troops. (Not once does he speak of what in America was called "the Spanish flu," but it was that, undoubtedly, that the men in his company were coming down with.)

Companies A, D, E, F, and G and their artillery, in training in the South of France since July, arrived in Belleville. ("Major Howard, my commanding officer from whom I had been separated about four months, called to see me . . . and complimented me on my good work, saying he had seen the Division Surgeon and not one complaint was made against me. During the whole month of October we labored on, hearing much talk of peace and were very anxious for the final drive, which would end forever Autocracy and give Democracy the right to reign. On the morning of November 8th, however, while we were in the midst of our activities, a terrible thing occurred at Belleville. . . . A colored boy who had been convicted of rape in August was hanged or lynched in an open field not far from my infirmary. The execution was a military order, but so openly and poorly carried out that it was rightly termed a lynching.")

The next day, the drive against Metz began, and two days later, while tremendous barrages were being laid down by the artillery in support of the infantry's advances, the news reached them that Germany had signed an armistice. As everywhere else in the Western world, bells rang, whistles blew, people shouted for joy.

On December 6th, he and another officer climbed into a truck and after a two-hour ride through no-man's-land arrived in Metz. He found it untouched by the fighting and the most beautiful city he had seen in France. The buildings were modern; the streets were wide and well paved and lighted with gas or electricity; there were streetcars riding up and down. But the people were cold and unfriendly to them, and spoke German mostly, and it was clear from the way a pack of children followed them in the street that they had never seen a Negro before.

On the night of December 15th, he was awakened by the orderly boy. In a heavy fog, a passenger train from Metz had plowed into a troop train full of happy French soldiers returning home from the front. It was a dreadful sight. The cars were telescoped and splintered, and the bodies of the dead and dying were pinned under the wreckage. The rest of the night he dressed wounds and put splints on broken arms and legs.

Three days later, the 317th began to leave Belleville. Now on foot, now in trucks or trains, they moved westward toward their port of embarkation. Sometimes he slept on straw, in dirty makeshift buildings that had been occupied by other soldiers before them and were infested with lice. For two days and nights he rode in a crowded railway coach with the rain dripping down on him from a leak in the ceiling. On Christmas Eve, in the ancient village of Domfront, in Normandy, the medical unit stood about in the rain and snow until 3 a.m., waiting to be billeted by a captain who, it turned out, had forgotten about them. Shivering in the cold, he remembered the Biblical text: *Foxes have holes and the fowls of the air have nests, but the Son of Man hath not where to lay his head.*

The people of Domfront were extremely hospitable, and the colored troops reciprocated by being on their best behavior. He was kept busy inspecting them daily for vermin and acute infections, but he found time to visit the places of historical interest and had his picture taken at the foot of the castle wall. Then he himself came down with influenza and had to be looked after by the men of his medical corps.

Late in January, his unit was ordered to proceed to the delousing station at Le Mans. The weather was cold, and there was a light snow on the ground. They reached Le Mans at eleven o'clock at night, after a twelve-hour ride. When he climbed down out of the truck, he had difficulty walking. He took off his boots and discovered that his feet were frozen. ("For a week thereafter, my feet were so swollen and blistered that I was unable to wear a shoe or leave my quarters.") During the two weeks he spent at the delousing camp he ran into several boys from Springfield that he knew. They had seen hard service with the 8th Illinois Infantry and showed it.

The unit made its final train journey from Le Mans to Brest, where thousands of soldiers were now crowded into the area around the port. The barracks were long wooden shacks with a hall running through the middle and small rooms opening off it. The only heat came from two stoves, one at either end of the hall. ("The weather was extremely damp and chilly at Brest, the raw wind off the ocean penetrating to the marrow.") There was more sickness.

On the morning of February 22nd, the 317th marched to the port. They had been informed by a bulletin from headquarters that if there was any disorder in the ranks they would be sent back to camp and detained indefinitely. Their packs uniformly rolled, their guns and shoes polished, they moved in utter silence like a funeral procession. The *Aquitania* rode at anchor in the harbor, and they were loaded onto small barges and ferried out to it. Lieutenant Dyer's cabin had mahogany fittings and a private bathroom. There were taps for fresh water and salt water, and the soap did not smell of disinfectant. While he was in the tub soaking, the room began to rock, and he realized that they had put out to sea. There is more, but why not leave him there, as lighthearted as he was probably ever going to be.

3

Of Dr. Dyer's roughly forty years of medical practice in Kansas City there is no record that I know of. The pattern of his days must have been regular and consistent. I picture him with a stethoscope in the pocket of his white coat and a covey of interns crowding around him.

In 1946, Hugh Davis, who was then living in California and an architect, came with his wife to Lincoln for a family visit. While he was there, he got Dr. Dyer's address and wrote to him to say that they would be going through Kansas City with a stopover of several hours and would like to see him. The answer was an invitation to dinner. There had been no communication between them for a good many years. The walls of the Dyers' Kansas City apartment were covered with Bessie Dyer's paintings, which the Davises liked very much. She was self-taught, with the help of a book that she got from the public library. They all sat down to a full Thanksgiving dinner, though actually Thanksgiving was about ten days away. And the friendship simply picked up where it had left off.

Two years later, when the Dyers went out to California, they were entertained at Hugh and Esther Davis's house in Palo Alto, along with a medical acquaintance the Dyers were staying with. My younger brother was also invited. He had just come out of the Army after a tour of duty in Germany, and was enrolled in law school at Stanford. He remembers Dr. Dyer as soft-spoken and very friendly, if a trifle guarded. He seemed to want, and need, to talk about the situation of educated Negroes in America—how they are not always comfortable with members of their own race, with whom they often have little or nothing in common, and are not accepted by white people whose tastes and interests they share. He was neither accusing nor bitter about this, my brother said. My brother mentioned the fact that Dr. Dyer's mother had helped take care of him when he was a baby, and Dr. Dyer was pleased that my brother remembered her. Three or four times he interrupted the conversation to say "I never expected to sit down to dinner with a grandson of Judge Blinn."

Hugh Davis's widow let me see a few of Dr. Dyer's letters to him written between 1955 and 1957. They are about politics (he was an ardent Republican), the hydrogen bomb, various international crises, a projected high-school reunion that never took place, his wife's delicate health, and—as one would expect of any regular correspondence—the weather. They are signed "Your friend, Billie Dyer." In each letter there is some mention of his professional activity—never more than a sentence, as a rule; taken together they give a very good picture of a man working himself to death.

In January 1956, at which time he was seventy years old, he wrote, "I suppose I should apologize for not having written you sooner but believe it or not, I am now working harder and with longer hours than ever before. Silly, you say, well I quite agree but the occasion is this. In the last four months I have been put on the staffs of three of the major hospitals in our city. I thought at first it was an honor but with the increase in activities which such appointments entail, my work has increased twofold. Since it is the first time that one of my race has had such appointments, I have been working diligently to make good, thereby keeping those doors open." He was still acting as a surgeon for the Santa Fe Railroad, and also for the Kansas City, Kansas, police department.

Three months later he wrote, "Since I have taken on new hospital assignments I have been working much too hard. I was in Chicago this week three days attending the Convention of American Association of Railway Surgeons and derived great benefit from the lectures and demonstations on recent advances in medicine and surgery."

In June he spent a couple of weeks in the wilds of Minnesota fishing and had a glorious time, though the fishing was poor. In August he wrote, "I am still working as hard as ever altho my physical resistance is not what it used to be & I find I must resort to more frequent short periods of rest."

The letter he wrote in November is largely about the suppression of the Hungarian uprising: "My heart goes out to those people. I was in France in the First World War & I saw refugees going down the roads with a little cart pulled by a donkey & all of their earthly possessions piled high on it. They had been driven from their homes by the advancing German Armies & it was a pitiful sight to behold." He also mentions the fact that the vision in his right eye is somewhat impaired because of a small cataract, and adds, "I am still working at a tremendous pace but realize that I must soon slow down."

In March of the following year he wrote, "I hardly have time to breathe. Indeed I know that at my age I should not be trying such a pace but having broken thru a barrier which was denied me so many years . . ."

In July he wrote, "I too am having my troubles with a nervous dermatitis which all of the skin specialists tell me is due to overwork. . . . I am planning on spending a couple of weeks on the lakes in northern Minnesota for I am very tired and need a rest."

And in August: "I will be 71 years old the 29th of this month and am in fairly good health for an old man of my years. I therefore thank the good Lord for His blessings. . . . I thought I would get out to California this summer but I had to buy a new car, so will have to defer my visit another year. . . . I agree with you that Ike has been a little wishy washy since he has been in the White House. It seems that he speaks softly but does not carry the big stick like Teddy Roosevelt once did. Hugh I shall never forget the political rallies and torchlight processions they had in Lincoln when we were boys. We don't see anything like that any more, and when the circuses came to town with their big parades. How I pity the generations of kids today, who are denied such thrills. Remember the old swimming hole in Kickapoo Creek where we used to swim naked and have so much fun. Hugh those were the days."

In January there was a notice in the Lincoln *Evening Courier*: "Dr. William Dyer, a native of Lincoln, was found dead in his car after an automobile accident at Kansas City, Kan., Tuesday morning. He apparently suffered a heart attack while driving."

There have been at least three histories of Logan County. The first was published in 1878 by a firm that went through the state doing one county after another. It has portrait engravings and brief biographies of the leading citizens, for which they must have paid something. The style is a little like First and Second Chronicles: "Michael and Abram Mann, John Jessee and Thomas Sr., Lucas and Samuel Myers were from Ohio and are now in their graves." Many natural wonders that the early settlers remembered found their way into this book—prairie fires so numerous that at night they lighted up the whole circuit of the horizon. And mirages. Also extreme hardships—the ague, caused by hunting their horses in the wet grass, and a drop in the temperature so great and so sudden, on a rainy December afternoon in 1836, that men on horseback were frozen to the saddle. And primitive artifacts, such as a door with wooden hinges, a wooden lock, and a buckskin drawstring.

Another history, published in 1911, was the work of a local man and is overburdened with statistics. The most recent is a large book—nine by twelve—heavy to hold in the hand and bound in red Leatherette. The likeness of Abraham Lincoln is on the cover, embossed in gold, as if somewhere in the afterlife his tall shade had encountered King Midas. There are hundreds of photographs of people I don't know and never heard of, which is not to be wondered at since we moved away from Lincoln in 1923, when I was fourteen years old.

Someone who had never lived there might conclude from this book that the town had no Negroes now or ever. Except for the group pictures of the Lincoln College athletic teams, in which here and there a dark face appears among the lighter ones, there are no photographs of black men and women. And though there are many pictures of white churches of one denomination or another, there is no picture of the African Methodist Episcopal Church—only a column of text, in which the buildings it occupied and the ministers who served it are listed. And these sentences: "Mr. Arian [surely Aaron misremembered?] Dyer and wife Harriet moved here from Springfield, Illinois, in 1874. . . . The sinners in Lincoln found the hope in Christ and joined the church. Among them were Alfred Dyer and wife Laura. . . ."

I go through the book looking for the names that figured so prominently in the conversation of my elders and find almost none. And realize that the place to look for them is the cemetery. The past is always being plowed under. There is a page of pictures of the centennial parade, but nowhere are the names of the Ten Most Distinguished Men called to mind. What is

one to think if not that the town, after celebrating its hundredth birthday, was done with history and its past, and ready
to live, like the rest of America, in a perpetual present?

In the index I found "Dyer, William, 90, 202." Both references turned out to be concerned with a white man of that
name.

Love

M iss Vera Brown, she wrote on the blackboard, letter by letter in flawlessly oval Palmer method. Our teacher for the fifth grade. The name might as well have been graven in stone.

As she called the roll, her voice was as gentle as the expression in her beautiful dark-brown eyes. She reminded me of pansies. When she called on Alvin Ahrens to recite and he said, "I know but I can't say," the class snickered but she said, "Try," encouragingly, and waited, to be sure that he didn't know the answer, and then said, to one of the hands waving in the air, "Tell Alvin what one-fifth of three-eighths is." If we arrived late to school, red-faced and out of breath and bursting with the excuse we had thought up on the way, before we could speak she said, "I'm sure you couldn't help it. Close the door, please, and take your seat." If she kept us after school it was not to scold us but to help us past the hard part.

Somebody left a big red apple on her desk for her to find when she came into the classroom, and she smiled and put it in her desk, out of sight. Somebody else left some purple asters, which she put in her drinking glass. After that the presents kept coming. She was the only pretty teacher in the school. She never had to ask us to be quiet or to stop throwing erasers. We would not have dreamed of doing anything that would displease her.

Somebody wormed it out of her when her birthday was. While she was out of the room the class voted to present her with flowers from the greenhouse. Then they took another vote and sweet peas won. When she saw the florist's box waiting on her desk, she said, "Oh?"

"Look inside," we all said.

Her delicate fingers seemed to take forever to remove the ribbon. In the end, she raised the lid of the box and exclaimed.

"Read the card!" we shouted.

Many Happy Returns to Miss Vera Brown, from the Fifth Grade, it said.

She put her nose in the flowers and said, "Thank you all very, very much," and then turned our minds to the spelling lesson for the day.

After school we escorted her downtown in a body to a special matinee of D. W. Griffith's *Hearts of the World*. She was not allowed to buy her ticket. We paid for everything.

We meant to have her for our teacher forever. We intended to pass right up through sixth, seventh, and eighth grades and on into high school taking her with us. But that isn't what happened. One day there was a substitute teacher. We expected our real teacher to be back the next day but she wasn't. Week after week passed and the substitute continued to sit at Miss Brown's desk, calling on us to recite and giving out tests and handing them back with grades on them, and we went on acting the way we had when Miss Brown was there because we didn't want her to come back and find we hadn't been nice to the substitute. One Monday morning she cleared her throat and said that Miss Brown was sick and not coming back for the rest of the term.

In the fall we had passed on into the sixth grade and she was still not back. Benny Irish's mother found out that she was living with an aunt and uncle on a farm a mile or so beyond the edge of town. One afternoon after school Benny and I got on our bikes and rode out to see her. At the place where the road turned off to go to the cemetery and the Chautauqua grounds, there was a red barn with a huge circus poster on it, showing the entire inside of the Sells-Floto Circus tent and everything that was going on in all three rings. In the summertime, riding in the backseat of my father's open Chalmers, I used to crane my neck as we passed that turn, hoping to see every last tiger and flying-trapeze artist, but it was never possible. The poster was weather-beaten now, with loose strips of paper hanging down.

It was getting dark when we wheeled our bikes up the lane of the farmhouse where Miss Brown lived.

"You knock," Benny said as we started up on the porch.

"No, you do it," I said.

We hadn't thought ahead to what it would be like to see her. We wouldn't have been surprised if she had come to the door herself and thrown up her hands in astonishment when she saw who it was, but instead a much older woman opened the door and said, "What do you want?"

"We came to see Miss Brown," I said.

"We're in her class at school," Benny explained.

I could see that the woman was trying to decide whether she should tell us to go away, but she said, "I'll find out if she wants to see you," and left us standing on the porch for what seemed like a long time. Then she appeared again and said, "You can come in now."

As we followed her through the front parlor I could make out in the dim light that there was an old-fashioned organ like the kind you used to see in country churches, and linoleum on the floor, and stiff uncomfortable chairs, and family portraits behind curved glass in big oval frames.

The room beyond it was lighted by a coal-oil lamp but seemed ever so much darker than the unlighted room we had just passed through. Propped up on pillows in a big double bed was our teacher, but so changed. Her arms were like sticks, and all the life in her seemed concentrated in her eyes, which had dark circles around them and were enormous. She managed a flicker of recognition but I was struck dumb by the fact that she didn't seem glad to see us. She didn't belong to us anymore. She belonged to her illness.

Benny said, "I hope you get well soon."

The angel who watches over little boys who know but they can't say it saw to it that we didn't touch anything. And in a minute we were outside, on our bicycles, riding through the dusk toward the turn in the road and town.

A few weeks later I read in the Lincoln *Evening Courier* that Miss Vera Brown, who taught the fifth grade in Central School, had died of tuberculosis, aged twenty-three years and seven months.

Sometimes I went with my mother when she put flowers on the graves of my grandparents. The cinder roads wound through the cemetery in ways she understood and I didn't, and I would read the names on the monuments: Brower, Cadwallader, Andrews, Bates, Mitchell. In loving memory of. Infant daughter of. Beloved wife of. The cemetery was so large and so many people were buried there, it would have taken a long time to locate a particular grave if you didn't know where it was already. But I know, the way I sometimes know what is in wrapped packages, that the elderly woman who let us in and who took care of Miss Brown during her last illness went to the cemetery regularly and poured the rancid water out of the tin receptacle that was sunk below the level of the grass at the foot of her grave, and filled it with fresh water from a nearby faucet and arranged the flowers she had brought in such a way as to please the eye of the living and the closed eyes of the dead.

The Man in the Moon

IN the library of the house I grew up in there was a box of photographs that I used to look through when other forms of entertainment failed me. In this jumble there was a postcard of my mother's brother, my Uncle Ted, and a young woman cozying up together in the curve of a crescent moon. I would have liked to believe that it was the real moon they were sitting in, but you could see that the picture was taken in a photographer's studio. Who she was it never occurred to me to ask. Thirty or forty years later, if his name came up in conversation, women who were young at the same time he was would remark how attractive he was. He was thin-faced and slender, and carried himself well, and he had inherited the soft brown eyes of the Kentucky side of the family.

In the small towns of the Middle West at that time—I am speaking of, roughly, the year 1900—it was unusual for boys to be sent away to school. My uncle was enrolled in a military academy in Gambier, Ohio, and flunked out. How much education he had of a kind that would prepare him for doing well in one occupation or another I have no idea. I would think not much. Like many young men born into a family in comfortable circumstances, he felt that the advantages he enjoyed were part of the natural order of things. What the older generation admired and aspired to was dignity, resting on a firm basis of accomplishment. I think what my uncle had in mind for himself was the life of a classy gent, a spender—someone who gives off the glitter of privilege. And he behaved as if this kind of life was within his reach. Which it wasn't. There was a period—I don't know how long it was, perhaps a few months, perhaps a year or so—when if he was strapped and couldn't think of anybody to put the bite on, he would write out a check to himself and sign it with the name of one of his sisters or of a friend.

I don't think anything on earth would have induced my father to pass a bad check, but then his family was poor when he was a child, and lived on the street directly behind the jail. Under everything he did, and his opinions about human behavior, was the pride of the self-made man. He blamed my uncle's shameless dodges on his upbringing. When my Grandfather Blinn would try to be strict with his son, my father said, my grandmother would go behind his back and give Teddy the money. My grandmother's indulgence, though it may have contributed to my uncle's lapses from financial probity, surely wasn't the only cause of them. In any case, the check forging didn't begin until both my grandparents were dead.

My grandfather was brought up on a cattle farm in Vermont not far from the Canadian border. He left home at sixteen to work as a bookkeeper in a pump factory in Cincinnati. Then he began to read law in a law office there. More often than not, he read on an empty stomach, but he mastered Blackstone's *Commentaries* and Chitty's *Pleadings*, and shortly before his twenty-first birthday (nobody thinking to inquire into his age, which would have prevented it) he was admitted to the bar. What made him decide to move farther west to Illinois I don't know. Probably there were already too many lawyers in Ohio. When he was still in his early thirties he tried to run for Congress on the Republican ticket and was nosed out by another candidate. Some years later the nomination was offered to my grandfather at a moment when there was no serious Democratic opposition, and he chose not to run because it would have taken him away from the practice of law. By the time he was forty he had a considerable reputation as a trial lawyer, and eventually he argued cases before the Supreme Court. Lawyers admired him for his ability in the courtroom, and for his powers of close reasoning. People in general saw in him a certain largeness of mind that other men didn't have. From the way my mother spoke of him, it was clear that—to her—there never had been and never could be again a man quite so worthy of veneration. My uncle must often have felt that there was no way for him to stand clear of his father's shadow.

Because my grandfather had served a term on the bench of the Court of Claims, he was mostly spoken of as Judge Blinn. His fees were large but he was not interested in accumulating money and did not own any land except the lot his house stood on. He was not at all pompous, but when he left his office and came home to his family he did not entirely divest himself of the majesty of the law, about which he felt so deeply. From a large tinted photograph that used to hang over the mantel-piece in my Aunt Annette's living room, I know that he had a fine forehead, calm grey eyes, and a drooping mustache that partly concealed the shape of his mouth.

There were half a dozen imposing houses in Lincoln but my grandfather's house wasn't one of them. It stood on a quiet elm-shaded street, and was a two-story flat-roofed house with a wide porch extending all across the front and around the sides. It was built in the eighteen-seventies and is still there, if I were to drive down Ninth Street. It is well over a hundred years old—what passes for an old house in the Middle West. My father worked for a fire-insurance company and was gone three days out of the middle of the week, drumming up business in small-town agencies all over the state. We lived across the street from my grandfather's house. Though I haven't been in it for sixty years, I can still move around in it in my mind. Sliding doors—which I liked to ease in and out of their recesses—separated the back parlor, where the family tended to congregate around my grandmother's chair, from the front parlor, where nobody ever sat. There it was always twilight because the velvet curtains shut out the sun. If I stood looking into the pier glass between the two front windows I saw the same heavy walnut and mahogany furniture in an even dimmer light. Whether this is an actual memory or an attempt on the part of my mind to adjust the past to my feelings about it I am not altogether sure. The very words "the past" suggest lowered window shades and a withdrawal from brightness of any kind. Orpheus in the Underworld. The end of my grandfather's life —he died horribly, of blood poisoning, from a ferret bite— cast a shadow backward over what had gone before, but in point of fact it was not a gloomy house, and the life that went on in it was not withdrawn or melancholy.

My Aunt Edith was the oldest. Then came my mother. Then Annette. Between Annette and my uncle there was another child, who didn't live very long. My grandmother was mor-bidly concerned for my uncle's safety when he was little, and Annette was told that she must never let him out of her sight when they were playing together. She was not much older than he was, and used to have nightmares in which something happened to him. They remained more or less in this relationship to each other during the whole of their lives.

My mother and her sisters had a certain pride of family, but it had nothing to do with a feeling of social superiority, and was, actually, so unexamined and metaphysical that I never understood the grounds for it. It may have been something my grandmother brought with her from Kentucky and passed on to her children. That branch of the family didn't go in for genealogy, and the stories that have come down are vague and improbable.

When I try the name Youtsey on a Southerner, all the response I ever get is a blank look. There appear to have been no statesmen in my grandmother's family, no colonial governors, no men or women of even modest distinction. That leaves money and property. My grandmother's father, John Youtsey, owned a hundred acres of land on the Licking River, where he raised strawberries for the markets of Cincinnati. He was also a United States marshal—that is to say, he had been appointed to carry out the wishes of the judicial district in which he lived, and had duties similar to those of a sheriff. Three of his sons fought in the Civil War, on the side of the North. Shortly before the war broke out, he began to build a new house with bricks fired on the place. I saw it once. I was taken there by one of my mother's cousins. The farm had passed out of the family and was now owned by a German couple. My grandmother used to take her children to Kentucky every summer and when the July term of court was over, my grandfather joined them. My mother told me that the happiest days of her childhood were spent here, playing in the attic and the hayloft and the water meadows, with a multitude of her Kentucky cousins. But as I looked around I saw nothing that I could accept as a possible backdrop for all that excitement and mirth and teasing and tears. There wasn't even a child's swing. The farmer's wife told us to look around as much as we liked, and went back to her canning. We paused in the doorway of a long empty room. I concluded from the parquet floors that it must have been the drawing room. Since my mother's cousin had gone to some trouble to bring me here, I felt that I ought to say something polite, and remarked, "In my great-grandfather's time this must have been a beautiful room," and he said with a smile, "Grandfather kept his wheat in it." My uncle may have inherited his *folie des grandeurs* from some improvident ancestor but it wasn't, in any event, the bewhiskered old gentleman farmer who built and lived in this house.

The lessons that hardship had taught my Grandfather Blinn he was unable to pass on to his son. He must have had many talks with Ted about his future, and the need to apply himself, and what would happen to him if he didn't. Hunger that is only heard about is not very real. My uncle had a perfect understanding of how one should conduct oneself after one has arrived; it was the getting there that didn't much interest him. The most plausible explanation is that he was a changeling.

From history of Logan County published in 1911 I learned that Edward D. Blinn, Jr.—that is, my Uncle Ted—was the superintendent of the Lincoln Electric Street Railway. My grandfather must have put him there, since he was a director and one of the incorporators of this enterprise. One spur of the streetcar tracks went from the courthouse square to the Illinois Central Railroad depot, another to a new subdivision in the northwest part of town, and still another to the cemeteries. In the summertime the cars were open on the sides, and in warm weather pleasanter than walking. Except during the Chautauqua season, they were never crowded. The conductor stomped on a bell in the floor beside him to make pedestrians and farm wagons get out of the way, and from time to time showers of sparks would be emitted by the overhead wires. What did the superintendent have to do? Keep records, make bank deposits, be there if something went wrong, and in an emergency run one of the cars himself (with his mind on the things he would do and the way he would live when he had money). The job was only a stopgap, until something more appropriate offered itself. *But what if nothing ever did?*

When my grandfather's back was turned, Ted went to Chicago and made some arrangements that he hoped would change the course of his life; for a thousand dollars (which, of course, he did not have), a firm in Chicago agreed to supply him with an airplane and, in case my uncle didn't choose to fly it, a pilot. It was to be part of the Fourth of July celebration.

The town agreed to pay him two thousand dollars if the plane went up.

Several years ago the contract was found tucked between the pages of a book that had been withdrawn from the Lincoln College library—God knows how it got there. It is dated June 27, 1911—to my surprise; for it proves that I was a few weeks less than three years old at the time, and I had assumed that to be able to remember the occasion as vividly as I do I must have been at least a year older than that.

The plane stood in a wheat field out beyond the edge of town. The wheat had been harvested and the stubble pricked my bare legs. My father held me by the hand so I would not get lost in the crowd. Very few people there had ever seen an airplane before, and all they asked was to see this one leave the ground and go up into the air like a bird. Several men in mechanic's overalls were clustered around the plane. Now and then my uncle climbed into the cockpit and the place grew still with expectation. The afternoon wore on slowly. The sun beat down out of a brassy sky. Word must have passed through the crowd that the plane was not going to go up, for my father said suddenly, "We're going home now." Looking back over my shoulder I saw the men still tinkering with the airplane engine. My father told me a long time later that while all this was going on my grandfather was pacing the floor in his law office, thinking about the thousand dollars he would have to raise somehow if the plane failed to go up, and that if it did go up there was a very good chance his only son might be killed.

Using what arguments I find it hard to imagine (except that a courtroom is one thing and home is another, and drops of water wear away stone), Ted persuaded my grandfather to buy a motorcar. The distance from my grandfather's house to his law office was less than a mile, and the roads around Lincoln were unpaved, with deep ruts. Even four or five years later, when motorcars were beginning to be more common, an automobile could sink and sink into a mudhole until it was resting on its rear axle. But anyway, there it was, a Rambler, with leather straps holding the top down, brass carriage lamps, and the emergency brake, the gearshift, and the horn all on the outside above the right-hand running board. It stood in front of my grandfather's house more like a monument than a means of locomotion. It is unlikely that anyone but Ted ever drove it, and it must have given a certain dash to his courtship of a charming red-headed girl named Alma Haller. I have pursued her and her family through three county histories and come up with nothing of any substance. Her father served several terms as a city alderman, he was a director of the streetcar company, and he owned a farm west of Lincoln, but there is no biography, presumably because he was not cooperative. Anyway, the soft brown eyes, the understanding of what is pleasing to women, assiduousness, persistence, something, did the trick. They were engaged to be married. And if either family was displeased by the engagement I never heard of it.

My uncle had the reputation in Lincoln of being knowledgeable about motors, and a friend who had arranged to buy an automobile in Chicago asked Ted to go with him when he picked it up. On the way down to Lincoln the car skidded and went out of control and turned over. My uncle was in the seat beside the driver. His left arm was crushed and had to be amputated. My grandmother's premonitions were at last accounted for. What I was kept from knowing about and seeing because I was a small child it does not take very much imagination to reconstruct. He is lying in a hospital bed with his upper chest heavily bandaged. There are bruises on his face. He is drowsy from morphine. Sometimes he complains to the nurse or to Annette, sitting in a chair beside his bed, about the pain he feels in the arm that he has lost. Sometimes he lies there rearranging the circumstances that led up to the accident so that he is at the wheel of the car. Or better still, not in the car at all. When the morphine wore off and his mind was clearer, what can he have thought except that it was somebody else's misfortune that came to him by mistake?

When he left the hospital, and forever afterward, he carried himself stiffly, as if he were corseted. He did not let anyone help him if he could forestall it, and was skillful at slipping his overcoat on in such a way that it did not call attention to the fact that his left arm was immovable and ended in a grey suède glove.

A few years ago, one of Alma Haller's contemporaries told me that she had realized she was not in love with Ted and was on the point of breaking off the engagement but after the accident felt she had to go through with it. They went through with it with style. All church weddings that I have attended since have seemed to me a pale imitation of this one. In a white corduroy suit that my mother had made for me, I walked down the aisle of the Episcopal church beside my Cousin Peg, who was a flower girl. I assume that I didn't drop the ring and that the groom put it on the fourth finger of the bride's left hand, but that part I have no memory of; though the movie camera kept on whirring there was no film in it. What was he thinking about as he watched the bridal procession coming toward him? That there would be no more sitting in the moon with girls who had no reason to expect anything more of him than a good time? That there, in satin and lace, was his heart's desire? That people were surreptitiously deciding which was the real arm and which the artificial one? All these things, perhaps, or none of them. The next thing I remember (the camera now having film in it again) is my mother depositing me on a gilt chair, at the wedding reception, and saying that she would be right back. Her idea of time and mine were quite different. The bride's mother, in a flame-colored velvet dress, interested me briefly; my grandmother always wore black. I had never before seen footmen in knee breeches and powdered wigs passing trays of champagne glasses. Or so many people in one house. And I was afraid I would never see my mother again. Just when I had given up all hope, my Aunt Edith appeared with a plate of ice cream for me.

In the next reel, it is broad daylight and I am standing—again with my father holding my hand—on a curb on College Avenue. But this time it is so I will not step into the street and be run over by the fire engines. As before, there is a crowd. It is several months after the wedding. There is a crackling sound and yellow flames flow out of the upstairs windows and lick the air above the burning roof of the house where the wedding reception took place. The gilt furniture is all over the lawn, and there is talk about defective wiring. The big three-story house is as inflammable as a box of kitchen matches.

In the hit-or-miss way of children's memories, I recall being in a horse and buggy with my aunt and uncle, on a snowy night, as they drove around town delivering Christmas presents. And on my sixth birthday our yard is full of children. All the

children I know have come bringing presents, and when London Bridge falls I am caught in the arms of my red-haired
aunt, and pleased that this has happened. Then suddenly she
was not there anymore. She divorced my uncle and I never saw
her again. After a couple of years she remarried and moved
away, and she didn't return to Lincoln to live until she was an
old woman.

As often happened with elderly couples during that period, my
grandmother's funeral followed my grandfather's within the
year. In his will he named all four of his children as executors,
and Ted quit his job with the streetcar company in order to
devote himself to settling the estate. My grandfather did not
leave anything like as much as people thought he would. He
was in the habit of going on notes with young men who needed
to borrow money and had no collateral. When the notes came
due, more often than not my grandfather had to make good
on them, the co-signer being unable to. He also made personal loans, which his family knew about but which he didn't
bother to keep any record of since they were to men he considered his friends, and after his death they denied that there
was any such debt. Meanwhile, it became clear to anyone with
eyes in his head that my uncle was spending a lot of money
that could only have come from the estate. My mother and my
aunts grew alarmed, and asked my father to step in and represent their interests. He found that Ted had already spent more
than half of the money my grandfather left. Probably he didn't
mean to take more than his share. It just slipped through his
fingers. He would no doubt have run through everything, and
with nothing to show for it, if my father hadn't stopped him.
My father was capable of the sort of bluntness that makes
people see themselves and their conduct in a light unsoftened
by excuses of any kind. I would not have wanted to be my
uncle when my father was inquiring into the details of my
grandfather's estate, or have had to face his contempt. There
was nothing more coming to Ted when the estate was finally
settled, and, finding himself backed into a corner, he began
forging checks. The fact that it didn't lead to his being arrested
and sent to prison suggests that the sums involved were not
large. I once heard my mother say to my Aunt Edith (who had

stopped having anything to do with him) that when she wrote to Ted she was always careful not to sign her full name. The friends whose names he forged were young, in their twenties like my uncle, and poor as Job's turkey. How he justified doing that to them it would be interesting to know. When it comes to self-deception we are all vaudeville magicians. In any case, forging checks for small amounts of money relieved his immediate embarrassment but did not alter his circumstances.

Children as they pass through one stage of growth after another are a kind of anthology of family faces. At the age of four I looked very much like one of my mother's Kentucky cousins. Holding my chin in her hand, she used to call me by his name. Then for a while I looked like her. At the age of eleven or twelve I suddenly began to look like my Uncle Ted. When people remarked on this, I saw that it made my father uneasy. The idea that if I continued to look like him I would end up forging checks amused me, but faulty logic is not necessarily incompatible with the truth, which in this case was that when, because of Christmas or my birthday, I had ten or fifteen dollars, I could always think of something to spend it on. All my life I have tended to feel that money descends from heaven like raindrops. I also understood that it doesn't rain a good deal of the time, and when I couldn't afford to buy something I wanted I have been fairly content to do without it. My uncle was not willing, is what it amounted to.

When my mother died during the influenza epidemic of 1918–19, I turned to the person who was closest to her, for comfort and understanding. I am not sure whether this made things harder for my Aunt Annette or not. Her marriage was rocky, and more than once appeared to be on the point of breaking up but never did. When my Uncle Will came home he would pass through the living room, leaving behind him a sense of strain between my aunt and him, but as far as I could make out it had nothing to do with my being there. Sometimes I found my Uncle Ted there, too. I didn't know, and didn't ask, where he was living and what he was doing to support himself. I think it was probably the low point of his life. There was no color in his face. His eyes never lit up or looked inquiringly or with affection at any of the people seated around the dining-room table. If he spoke, it was to answer yes or no to a question from my aunt. That when he and Annette were alone he opened his heart to her as freely as I did I have no doubt.

Defeat is a good teacher, Hazlitt said. What it teaches some people is to stop trying.

Except for the very old, nothing, good or bad, remains the same very long. My father remarried, and was promoted, and we had to move to Chicago. I went to high school there, and my older brother went off to college, at the University of Illinois, in Champaign-Urbana. On the strength of his experience with the streetcar company, my uncle had managed to get a job in Champaign, working for a trolley line that meandered through various counties in central and southern Illinois. Nobody knew him there, or anything about him. He was simply Ed Blinn, the one-armed man at the ticket counter. He kept this job for many years, from which I think it can be inferred that he didn't help himself to the petty cash or falsify the bookkeeping. During the five years that my brother was in college and law school they would occasionally have dinner together. He tried to borrow money from my brother, whose monthly allowance was adequate but not lavish, and my brother stopped seeing him. Once, when Ted came up to Chicago, he invited me to have dinner with him at the Palmer House. Probably he felt that it was something my mother would have wanted him to do, but this idea didn't occur to me; adolescents seldom have any idea why older people are being nice to them. He was about forty and I was fifteen or sixteen, and priggishly aware that, in taking me to a restaurant that was so expensive, he was again doing things in a way he couldn't afford. He had an easier time chatting with the headwaiter than he did in getting any conversation out of me. After we got up from the table he gave me a conducted tour of a long corridor in the hotel that was known as Peacock Alley. I could see that he was in his natural element. I would have enjoyed it more if there had been peacocks. When I followed my brother down to the university I didn't look my uncle up, and he may not even have known I was there.

Some years later, from a thousand miles away, I learned that he had married again. He married a Lincoln woman, the letter from home said. Edna Skinner. He and his wife were running a rental library in Chicago, and she was expecting a baby. Then I heard that the baby died, and they had moved back to Lincoln, and she was working at the library, and somebody had found him a job running the elevator in the courthouse—where (as people observed with a due sense of the irony of it) his father had practiced law.

By that time my father had retired from business and he and my stepmother were living in Lincoln again. When I went back to Illinois on a visit, I saw my Aunt Annette. She was angry at Ted for marrying. Though she did not say so, what she felt, I am sure, was that there were now two children she couldn't let out of her sight. And she disliked his new wife. She said, "Edna only married him because she was impressed with his family." All this, however, didn't prevent my aunt from doing what she could for them. The grocer was given to understand that they could charge things to her account. She did this knowing that my Uncle Will was bound to notice that the grocery bills were padded, and would be angry with her. As he was. She refused to tell the grocer that her brother and his wife were not to charge things anymore, and my Uncle Will, not being sure what the consequences would be if he put a stop to it, allowed it to continue. Also, living in a small town, there is always the question of what people will think. One would not want to have it said that, with the income off several farms and a substantial balance at the bank, one had let one's brother-in-law and his wife go hungry.

I did not meet Edna until I brought my own wife home to Lincoln for the first time. We had only been married three or four months. When we were making the round of family visits, it struck me as not quite decent not to take her to meet Ted and the aunt I had never seen. My father didn't think that this was necessary. Though they all lived in the same small town, my father never had any reason to be in the courthouse or the library, and he hadn't had anything to do with Ted since the days, thirty years before, when he had to step in and straighten out the handling of my grandfather's estate. But I saw no reason I shouldn't follow my own instincts, which were not to leave anybody out. I was thirty-six and so grateful to have escaped from the bachelor's solitary existence that all my feelings were close to the surface. I couldn't call Ted, because they had no telephone, but somebody told me where they were living and we went there on a Sunday morning and knocked on the screen door. As my uncle let us in, I saw that he was pleased we had come. The house looked out across the college grounds and was very small, hardly big enough for two people. Overhanging trees filtered out the sunlight. I found that I had things I wanted to say to him. It was as if we had been under a spell and now it was broken. There was a kind of easy understanding between us that I was not prepared for. I felt the stirring of affection, and I think he may have as well.

Edna I took to on sight. She had dark eyes and a gentle voice. She was simple and open with my wife, and acted as if meeting me was something she had been hoping would happen. Looking around, I could see that they didn't have much money, but neither did we.

I wrote to them when we got home, and heard from her. After my uncle died, she continued to write, and she sent us a small painting that she had done.

Not long ago, by some slippage of the mind, I was presented with a few moments out of my early childhood. My grandfather's house, so long lived in by strangers, is ours again. The dining-room table must have several leaves in it, for there are six or eight people sitting around it. My mother is not in the cemetery but right beside me. She is talking to Granny Blinn about . . . about . . . I don't know what about. If I turn my head I will see my grandfather at the head of the table. The windows are there, and look out on the side yard. The goldfish are swimming through their castle at the bottom of the fishbowl. The door to the back parlor is there. Over the sideboard there is a painting of a watermelon and grapes. No one stops me when I get down from my chair and go out to the kitchen and ask the hired girl for a slice of raw potato. I like the greenish taste. When I come back into the dining room I go and stand beside my uncle. He finishes what he is saying and then notices that I am looking with curiosity at his glass of beer. He holds it out to me, and I take a sip and when I make a face he laughs. His left hand is resting on the white damask tablecloth. He can move his fingers. The catastrophe hasn't happened. I would have liked to linger there with them, but it was like trying to breathe underwater. I came up for air, and lost them.

The view after seventy is breathtaking. What is lacking is someone, *anyone*, of the older generation to whom you can turn when you want to satisfy your curiosity about some detail of the landscape of the past. There is no longer any older generation. You have become it, while your mind was mostly on other matters.

I wouldn't know anything more about my uncle's life except for a fluke. A boy I used to hang around with when I was a freshman in Lincoln High School—John Deal—had a slightly older sister named Margaret. Many years later I caught up with her again. My wife and I were on Nantucket, and wandered into a shop full of very plain old furniture and beautiful china, and there she was. She was married to a Russian émigré, a bearlike man with one blind eye and huge hands. He was given to patting her affectionately on the behind, and perfectly ready to be fond of anyone who turned up from her past. I learned afterward that he had been wounded in the First World War and had twice been decorated for bravery. Big though his hands were, he made ship's models—the finest I have ever seen. That afternoon, as we were leaving, she invited us to their house for supper. The Russian had made a huge crock of vodka punch, which he warned us against, and as we sat around drinking it, what came out, in the course of catching up on the past, was that Margaret and Edna Blinn were friends.

Remembering this recently, I looked up Margaret's telephone number in my address book. The last letter I had had from her was years ago, and I wasn't sure who would answer. When she did, I said, "I want to know about my Uncle Ted Blinn and Edna. How did you happen to know her?"

"We were both teaching in the public schools," the voice at the other end of the line said. "And we used to go painting together."

"Who was she? I mean, where was she from?"

"I don't know."

"Was she born in Lincoln?"

"I kind of think not," the voice said. "I do know where they met. At your grandfather's farm, Grassmere."

"My grandfather didn't have a farm."

"Well, that's where they met."

"My grandfather had a client, one of the Gilletts, who owned a farm near Elkhart—I think it was near Elkhart. Anyway, she moved East and he managed the farm for her. It was called Gracelands. Could it have been there that they met?"

"No. Grassmere."

Oral history is a tangle of the truth and alterations on it.

"They had a love affair," Margaret said. "And Edna got pregnant and lost her job because of it."

"Even though they got married?"

"Yes. It was more than the school board could countenance, and she was fired. He quit his job in Champaign and they went to Chicago and opened a rental library."

"I know. . . . What did the baby die of?"

"It was born dead."

Looking back on my uncle's life, it seems to me to have been a mixture of having to lie in the bed he had made and the most terrible, undeserved, outrageous misfortune. The baby was born dead. He lost his arm in that automobile accident and no one else was even hurt. They put whatever money they had into that little rental library in Chicago just in time to have it go under in the Depression.

The oldest county history mentions an early pioneer, Thomas R. Skinner, who came to that part of Illinois in 1827, cleared some land near the town of Mt. Pulaski, and was the first county surveyor and the first county judge. Edna was probably a direct or a collateral descendant. She may also have been the daughter of W. T. Skinner, who was superintendent and principal of the Mt. Pulaski High School. Whatever her background may have been, she was better educated and more cultivated than any of the women in my family, and if she had had money would, I think, have been treated quite differently.

From that telephone call and the letter that followed I learned a good deal that I hadn't known before. Edna worshipped my uncle, Margaret said. She couldn't get over how wonderful, how distinguished, he was. He was under no illusions whatever about himself but loved her. He called her "Baby."

She never spoke about things they lacked, and never seemed to realize how poor they were. She lived in a world of art and music and great literature. He had a drinking problem.

They lived in many different houses—in whatever was vacant at the moment, and cheap. For a while they lived in what had been a one-room Lutheran schoolhouse. They even lived in the country, and Ted drove them into town to work in a beat-up Ford roadster. Whatever house they were living in was always clean and neat. Annette gave them some of my Grandmother Blinn's English bone china, and Edna had some good furniture that had come down in her family—two Victorian chairs and a walnut sofa upholstered in mustard-colored velvet.

Annette and my Uncle Will Bates went to Florida for several months every winter, and while they were away Ted and Edna lived in their house. She loved my Aunt Annette, and was grateful to her for all she had done for them, and didn't know that the affection was not returned.

Margaret found Ted interesting to talk to and kind, but aloof. She had no idea what he was paid for running the elevator in the courthouse. Edna's salary at the library was seventy-five dollars a month. He made a little extra money by selling cigarettes out of the elevator cage, until some town official put a stop to it because he didn't have a license.

My uncle always dressed well. (Clothes of the kind he would have thought fit to put on his back do not wear out, if treated carefully.) Edna had one decent dress, which she washed when she got home from the library, and ironed, and wore the next day. She loved clothes. When she wanted to give herself a treat she would buy a copy of *Harper's Bazaar* and thumb through the pages with intense interest, as if she were dealing with the problem of her spring wardrobe.

She was a Christian Scientist and tended to look on the bright side even of things that didn't have any bright side. She would be taken with sudden enthusiasms for people. When she started in on the remarkable qualities of someone who wasn't in any way remarkable, Ted would poke fun at her. The grade-school and high-school students who came to the library looking for facts for their essays on compulsory arbitration or whales or whatever found her helpful. She encouraged them to develop the habit of reading, and to make something of their lives. Some of them came to think of her as a friend, and remained in touch with her after they left school. At the end of the day, Ted came to the library to pick her up and walk home with her. Margaret didn't think that he had any men friends.

They had a dog, a mutt that had attached himself to them. Whatever Ted asked the dog to do he would try to do, even if it was, for a dog, impossible. Or when he had, in fact, no clear idea of what was wanted of him. He made my uncle laugh. Not much else did.

He must have been in his early sixties when he got pneumonia. He didn't put up much of a fight against it. Edna believed that he willed himself to die.

"Sometimes she would invite me for lunch on Sunday," Margaret said. "Your uncle ate by himself in the other room—probably because there weren't enough knives and forks for three. Having fed him, Edna would get out the card table and spread a clean piece of canvas on it or an old painting, and set two places with the Blinn china. The forks were salad forks, so small that they tended to get lost on the plates. And odd knives and spoons, jelly glasses, and coffee cups from the ten-cent store. Then she would bring on, in an oval silver serving dish, an eggplant casserole, or something she had invented. She was a superb cook, and she did it all on a two-burner electric plate. After the lunch dishes were washed and put away we would go off painting together. There was nothing unusual about her watercolors but her oils were odd in an interesting way. She couldn't afford proper canvas and used unsized canvas or cardboard, and instead of a tube of white lead she had a small can of house paint. She had studied at the Art Institute when they lived in Chicago. I think now that she saw her life as being like that of Modigliani or some other bohemian starving in a garret on the Left Bank. Ted was ashamed of the way they lived. . . . Only once did she ask me for help. She had seen a coat that she longed for, and it was nine dollars. Or it may have been that she needed nine dollars to make up the difference, with what she had. At that time you could buy a Sears, Roebuck coat for that. Anyway, she asked if I would take two paintings in exchange for the money. . . . When I saw her after her heart attack she was lovely and slender—much as she must have looked when she and Ted first knew each other. She spent the last year or so of her life living in what had been a doctor's office. . . . That nine-dollar coat continues to haunt me."

She was buried beside Ted, in the Blinn family plot. My grandfather's headstone is no higher than the sod it is embedded in, and therefore casts no shadow over the grave of his son.

With Reference to
an Incident at a Bridge

(For Eudora Welty)

WHEN I see ten-year-old boys, walking along the street in New York City or on the crosstown bus, I am struck by how tiny they are. But at the time I am speaking of, I wasn't very big myself. So far as I was concerned, the town of Lincoln was the Earthly Paradise, the apple that Eve prevailed upon Adam to eat being as yet an abstraction, and therefore to all intents and purposes still on the tree. I had an aunt and uncle living in Bloomington, thirty miles away, and for a time I went to Peoria with my mother to have my teeth straightened. Those two towns, and Springfield, the state capital, constituted the outer limits of the known world. The unknown world, the infinitude of unconscious emotions and impulses, didn't come up in ordinary conversation, though I daresay there were some people who were aware of it.

At twelve I was considered old enough to join the Presbyterian church, and did. In Sunday school and church I recited, along with the rest of the congregation, "I believe in the Holy Ghost, the holy catholic church, the communion of saints, the forgiveness of sins, the resurrection of the body, and the life everlasting." That any part of this formal confession was not self-evident did not cross my mind, nor, I think, anyone else's. We said it because it was true, and vice versa.

Twelve was also the age at which I could join the Boy Scouts and I did that, too. There was only one Scout troop in town, and the scoutmaster, Professor C. S. Oglevee, was a man in his early fifties, who taught biology at Lincoln College, and was the official weather observer. He was, as well, an unordained minister and an Elder in the Presbyterian church. The Scouts were all drawn from the Presbyterian Sunday school.

At Scout meeting I said, "A Scout is trustworthy, loyal, helpful, courteous, kind," and so on, with the same fervor that I recited the Apostles' Creed, and downtown I went out of my way to help elderly people across the street who could have managed perfectly well on their own, for the traffic was negligible. A Model A or a Model T Ford proceeding at the speed of fifteen miles an hour or a farm wagon was what it generally amounted to.

In a short while I passed from second-class to first-class Scout, and kept the silver fleur-de-lys on my hat polished, and looked forward to becoming an Eagle Scout, beyond which there were no further pinnacles to climb. In my imagination the right sleeve of my uniform was covered with merit badges from the cuff to the shoulder, and I did accumulate quite a few.

One day, in quest of specialized information of some sort, I went to see Professor Oglevee at home. He lived in a beautiful old mansion out at the edge of town. It had been built by a pillar of the church, whose widow Professor Oglevee was in the position of a son to. The house was set well back from the street, and painted white, and had a porte cochere, and was shaded by full-grown elm trees. The architect who designed it must have had the antebellum mansions of Georgia and Mississippi in mind. There was no other house in town like it. The white columns along the front had formerly graced the façade of the Lincoln National Bank. In that house I heard the word "whom" for the first time. A woman answering the telephone while a church social was going on outside in the garden said, "To whom do you wish to speak? . . . To *whom?*"—stopping me in my tracks.

On one side of the lawn there was an apple orchard and on the other a pasture with a little stream running through it: Brainerd's Branch. It says something about old Mrs. Brainerd that children could go there without a sense that they were trespassing. In the early spring I used to walk along the stream listening to the musical sound it made, and sometimes stopping to build a dam. Tucked away in a remote corner of the pasture was a one-room clubhouse with a fireplace, which my brother's generation of Boy Scouts had built under Professor Oglevee's direction. Scout meetings were held there, and after the formal business was out of the way we sat around on the floor roasting wienies over the coals and studying the *Scout Manual.*

Professor Oglevee's room was on the ground level of the house, where the floor was paved with uncemented tiles that clanked as you walked over them. To get to his desk by the window we had to thread our way between piles of scientific and nature publications. Afterward he took me outside and explained the mysteries of his rain gauges. He was a walking encyclopedia. With a dozen boys at his heels, all clamoring for his undivided attention, he moved through the woods identifying trees and plants and mosses. He was immensely patient, good-natured, and kind. So clearly so that I felt there was not room in his nature for the unpredictable crankiness and unreasonable severity other grown-ups exhibited from time to time. If anybody said one word against him, even today, I would get excited. Which means, of course, that I didn't allow for the fact that he was a fallible human being. The flaws that as a fallible human being he must have had nobody ever knew about, in any case. But on one occasion he shocked me. Somebody said "Professor? . . . Professor? . . . Professor, what kind of a tree is this the leaf of?" and he glanced at it and said, "A piss-elm." Though he then apologized for his language, the fact remained that he had said it.

Whose idea it was to organize the Cub Scouts I don't remember, if I ever knew. A great many things seemingly happened in the air over my head. Cub Scouts had to be between ten and twelve years old, and they did not all go to the Presbyterian Sunday school. It was left to the Boy Scouts to lead them. Among the six or eight little boys who turned up for the first meeting was Max Rabinowitz, whose father had a clothing store on a rather dingy side street facing the interurban tracks and the Chicago & Alton depot, and was a Russian Jew. This distinction would not have meant anything to me if it also had not represented a prejudice of some kind on the part of my elders. I suppose it is why I remember Maxie and not any of the others.

There were a dozen or more old families in town who were German Jewish. The most conspicuous were the Landauers and the Jacobses. Nate Landauer ran a ladies' ready-to-wear shop on the north side of the courthouse square, and his brother-in-law, Julius Jacobs, a men's clothing store on the west side of the square. Once a year my father or my mother took my brother and me downtown and we were fitted out by

Mr. Jacobs with a new dark-blue suit to wear to church on Easter Sunday.

The school yard had various forms of unpleasantness, but anti-Semitism was not one of them. In the Presbyterian church, the doctrine of Original Sin was held over our heads, with no easy or certain way to get off the hook. It was hardly to be expected that the Crucifixion was something the Jews could live down. But on the other hand, it was a very long time ago, and the Landauers and the Jacobses were not present. Mrs. Landauer and Mrs. Jacobs both belonged to my mother's bridge club.

At that age, if I thought about social acceptance at all it was as one of the facts of nature. Looking back, I can see that manners entered into it, but so did money. The people my parents considered to be of good families all had, or had had, land, income from property, something beside wages from a job.

The Russian-Jewish family was quite different. They were immigrants, spoke imperfect English, and had only recently passed through Ellis Island. So far as the Lincoln *Evening Courier* was concerned, news that was not local tended to be about a threatened coal strike or calling out the National Guard to quell some disturbance. Very seldom was there any mention of what went on in Europe. I was a grown man before I learned about the pogroms that drove the Rabinowitzes from their homeland. When I try to recall what the inside of Mr. Rabinowitz's store was like, what emerges through the mists of time is an impression of thick-soled shoes, heavy denim, corduroy, and flannel—work clothes of the cheapest kind. The bank held a mortgage on the stock or I don't know Arkansas. The chances are that he held out until the Depression and then went under, along with a great many other people whose financial underpinnings were more substantial.

What made Maxie want to be a Cub Scout? Had he been reading Ernest Thompson Seton and contracted a longing for the wilderness? Or did he, a newcomer, in his loneliness just want to belong to a group, any group, of boys his own age? We taught the Cub Scouts how to tie a clove hitch and a running bowline and how (if you were lucky) to build a fire without any matches and other skills appropriate to the outdoor life. Somebody, after a few weeks, decided that there ought to

670   BILLIE DYER AND OTHER STORIES

be an initiation. Into what I don't think we bothered to figure
out.

On a Monday night we walked the little boys clear out of
town in the moonlight and halted when we came to a bridge.
Somebody suggested a footrace with blindfolds on. A handkerchief was included in the official Cub Scout uniform and
they all had one. If they had been sent running up the road
until we called to them to stop, they might have tripped or
bumped into each other and fallen down, but probably
nothing worse. I noticed that the bridge we were standing on
had low sides that came up about to the little boys' belly buttons. I cannot pretend that I didn't know what was going to
happen, but a part of me that I was not sufficiently acquainted
with had taken over suddenly, and he/I lined the blindfolded
boys up with their backs to one side of the bridge, facing the
other, and said, "On your marks, get set, *go!* . . ." and they
charged bravely across the bridge and into the opposite railing
and knocked the wind out of themselves.

I believe in the forgiveness of sins. Some sins. I also believe
that what is done is done and cannot be undone. The reason I
didn't throw myself on my knees in the dust and beg them
(and God) to forgive me is that I knew He wouldn't, and that
even if He did, I wouldn't forgive myself. Sick with shame at
the pain I had inflicted, I tore Max Rabinowitz's blindfold off
and held him by the shoulders until his gasping subsided.

Considering the multitude of things that happen in any one
person's life, it seems fairly unlikely that those little boys remembered the incident for very long. It was an introduction
to what was to come. And cruelty could never again take them
totally by surprise. But I have remembered it. I have remembered it because it was the moment I learned that I was not to
be trusted.

My Father's Friends

M Y father died in 1958, a few months after his eightieth—
and my fiftieth—birthday. The day after he was buried,
my stepmother brought out two heavy winter overcoats for
me to try on, and then she and my older brother and I went to
the storeroom above the garage, and she showed me a brown
leather suitcase of my father's, a much more expensive piece of
luggage than I had ever owned. None of this was my idea, but
I nevertheless could feel on my face an expression of embarrassment, as if I had been caught out in something. My stepmother was not given to thinking ill of people but when my
brother and I were children he had assumed the role of the
prosecuting attorney. I glanced at his face now; nothing unkind there. The coats wouldn't have fitted him, or my younger
brother, and since I was named after my father, the initials on
the suitcase were mine, and who would want a suitcase with
somebody else's initials on it? So why did I feel that I had appeared to be showing a too avid interest in the spoils?

Later on that afternoon I started out on foot to call on two
of my father's friends who were not well enough to come to
the funeral. The first, Dean Hill, was a man my father went
fishing with. He was also a cousin of my stepmother. He had
inherited a great many acres of Illinois farmland, and he had a
beautiful wife. Apart from a trip to Biloxi in the dead of winter,
they lived very much as other Lincoln people of moderate
means did. I had known him since I was a young boy, and
never had a conversation with him. When I go home to Lincoln I tend to put aside whatever in my life I suspect would be
of no interest to people there, and sometimes this results in my
feeling that I am going around with my head in a brown paper
bag. But on this occasion I felt I could be my true self. To my
surprise I found that he read books. In Lincoln the women put
their names down for best-sellers at the desk of the public
library, and the men read the evening newspaper. "What the
book is about is a matter of indifference to me," Dean Hill
said. "I am interested in the writer—in what he is carefully not

saying, or saying and doesn't know that he is. What his real position is, as distinct from the stated one. It keeps me amused. All forms of deception are entertaining to contemplate, don't you find? Particularly self-deception, which is what life is largely made up of."

I found myself telling him about my guilty feelings at accepting my father's things, and he nodded and said, "Once when I was sitting in a jury box the judge said, 'Will the defendant rise,' and I caught myself just in time. If one isn't guilty of one thing one is certainly guilty of another is perhaps the only explanation for this kind of irrational behavior. . . . I'm glad you have the coats and the suitcase, and I'm sure your father would be too. Enjoy them." He then went on to speak affectionately of my father. "I have no other friend like him," he said. "I am already beginning to feel the loss. Most people have a hidden side. Your father was exactly what he appeared to be. It is very rare."

I left the house with a feeling of exhilaration. I couldn't help feeling that my father's part in this old friendship had somehow been handed on to me, like the overcoats and the suitcase. And in fact it had. When Dean Hill and his wife came to New York six months later, he invited me to lunch at the Plaza, and the conversation was easy and intimate. Everything that he had to say interested me because of its originality and wisdom. While living all his life in a very small Middle Western town and keeping his eye on his farms, he had managed to be aware of the world outside in a way that no one else there was. Or at least no one I knew. He was worried about my stepmother. It was a case of the oak and the ivy, he said, and he didn't think she would manage very well without my father. (He was quite right. She was ten years younger than my father, and when he was alive she was perky and energetic and always talking about taking off for somewhere—except that they couldn't, because of his emphysema. After he was gone, the tears she wiped away with her handkerchief were simply followed by more tears. She spent the remaining fifteen years of her life in nursing homes, unable to cope with her sadness.)

I wrote to Dean Hill, and he answered my letters. The last time I saw him, in Lincoln, twenty-eight years ago, I could talk to him but he couldn't talk to me. He had had a stroke. His speech was garbled and unintelligible. He appeared to feel that it was his fault.

My second call, the day after the funeral, was on Aaron McIvor, who for ten years was a golfing companion of my father's. They also occasionally did some business together. Mr. McIvor dabbled in a number of things, including local politics, and he must have made a living out of all this or he would have gone to work for somebody else. Now and then my father would be asked to handle an insurance policy personally, and in doing so he used the name of Maxwell, McIvor & Company as agent.

Though it would be accurate to say that Aaron McIvor was not like anybody else in Lincoln, it would also, in a way, be meaningless, since small-town people of that period were so differentiated that the same thing could have been said of nearly everybody. He had sad eyes and a sallow complexion and two deep furrows running down his cheeks. The tips of his fingers were stained with nicotine and the whites of his eyes were yellowish also, in a way more often found in dogs than in human beings. Nothing that he said was ever calculated to make people feel better about themselves, but he could be very funny.

As I zigzagged the five or six blocks between Dean Hill's house and the McIvor's that afternoon, I was struck by how little the older residential part of Lincoln had changed. A house here or there where no house was before. A huge old mansion gone.

Aaron McIvor's daughter in-law directed me up the stairs to his bedroom. The ashtray on a chair beside his bed was full of cigarette butts. He looked the same, only old. I didn't stay long and I wished I hadn't gone to see him, because he had things to say against my father that, the day after his funeral, I didn't feel like listening to.

"McIvor is eccentric," my father would say, when his name came up in conversation. It was not something my father would have wanted anybody to say about him. But he did not expect people to be perfect, and Mr. McIvor's eccentricities in no way interfered with the friendship. Because he said so many unflattering things, it was assumed that he was a truthful man. I don't think this necessarily follows. But if you wanted him you had to take him as he was. The caustic remarks were brushed aside or forgiven. And people loved to tell how, when he was courting his wife, he never brought her candy or flowers but simply appeared, in the evening after supper, and stretched out in the porch swing with his head in her lap and went to sleep.

His wife, whom I called "Aunt" Beth, was my mother's closest friend. When I shut my eyes now, I see her affectionate smile, and the way her brown eyes lighted up. People loved her because she was so radiant. It cannot have been true that she was never tired or that there was nothing in her life to make her unhappy or depressed or complaining, but that is how I remember her.

When I was a little boy of six I met her on a cinder path at the Chautauqua grounds one day and she opened her purse and took out a dime and gave it to me. "I don't think my father would want me to take it," I said. My father knew a spendthrift when he saw one, and, hoping to teach me the value of money, he had put me on an allowance of ten cents a week, with the understanding that when the ten cents was gone I was not to ask for more. Also, if possible, I was to save part of the ten cents. "It's perfectly all right," Aunt Beth said. "Don't you worry. I'll explain it to him." I took off for the place where they sold Cracker Jack. And she stands forever, on the cinder path at the Chautauqua grounds, smiling at the happiness she has just set free. I long to compare her with something appropriate, and nothing is, quite, except the goodness of being alive.

The thing about my mother and Aunt Beth was that they were always so lighthearted when they were together. Sometimes I understood what they were laughing about, sometimes it would be over my head. My father and mother were both mad about golf. I used to caddie for my father, and if he made a bad approach shot he was inconsolable. He would pick his ball out of the cup and walk toward the next tee still analyzing what he had done that made the ball end up in a bunker instead of on the green near the flag. You felt he felt that if he could only have lived that moment over again and kept his shoulder down and followed through properly, the whole rest of his life might have been different. And that Aaron McIvor mournfully agreed with him. The two women were unfazed by such disasters. My mother would send a fountain of sand into the air and go right on describing a dress pattern or some china she had seen in a house in Kentucky. When she and Aunt Beth had talked their way around nine holes—usually my father and Mr. McIvor played in a foursome of men—they would add up their scores and sit down on the balcony of the clubhouse until their husbands joined them. Then, more often than not, they would come back to our house for Sunday-night supper. When my mother went out to the kitchen, Mr. McIvor would get up from his chair and follow her with the intent to ruffle her feathers. My mother had no use for the family her younger sister had married into. Perched on the kitchen stool, Mr. McIvor said admiring things about them. How well educated they were. How good they were at hanging on to their money. How one of them found a mistake of twenty-seven cents in his monthly bank statement and raised such Cain about it that the president of the bank, came to him finally in tears. How no tenant farmer of theirs ever drew a simple breath that they didn't know about. And so on. My mother would emerge from the pantry with a plate of hot baking-powder biscuits in her hand and her face flushed with outrage, and we would sit down to scrambled eggs and bacon.

In my Aunt Annette's sun parlor there was a wicker porch swing that hung on chains from the ceiling. *Creak . . . creak . . .* Just as if you were outdoors, only you weren't. It was a good place from which to survey what went on in Lincoln Avenue. Sitting with her arm resting on the back of the swing, my aunt was alternately there and not there, like cloud shadows. Now her attention would be focused on me (for I was twelve years old and I had lost my mother a couple of years before and my father had sold our house and was on the point of remarrying and I needed her), now on a past that stretched well beyond the confines of my remembering. I didn't mind when she withdrew into her own thoughts; her physical presence was enough. One day I saw, on the sidewalk in front of the house, a very small woman in a big black hat. Not just the brim, the whole hat was big, an elaborate structure of ribbon and straw and jet hatpins that she moved under without disturbing.

"Who is *that?*" I asked.

Turning her head, my aunt said, "Old Mrs. McIvor. Aaron's mother. She was born in England."

"Some hat," I said.

"She's been going by the house for many years and I have never seen her without it."

The things I am curious about now I was not curious about then. Where, in that small town of twelve thousand people, did Aaron McIvor's mother live? Did she live by herself? And if so, on what? And what brought her all the way across the Atlantic? And what happened to his father? And how on earth did she come by that hat? None of these questions will I ever know the answer to.

Pre-adolescent boys, at a certain point, become limp, pale, undemanding, unable to think of anything to do, so saturated with protective coloration that they are hardly distinguishable from the furniture, and not much more aware of what is going on around them. I'm not quite sure when Aunt Beth and Mr. McIvor adopted a baby, but it didn't occur to me that any disappointment or heartache had preceded this decision. If I ever saw the baby, lack of interest prevented me from remembering it.

I must have been thirteen or fourteen when I heard that Aunt Beth had cancer and was in the hospital. I felt I ought to go see her. I thought my mother would want me to. My Aunt Annette was in Florida and there was no one to enlighten me about what to expect. I went from room to room of the hospital, reading the cards on the doors and peering past the white cloth screens, and on the second floor, in the corridor, I ran into her. She was wearing a hospital gown and her hair was in two braids down her back. Her color was ashen. She saw me, but it was as if she were looking at somebody she had never seen before. Since then, I have watched beloved animals dying. The withdrawal, into some part of themselves that only they know about. It is, I think, not unknown to any kind of living creature. A doctor passed, in a white coat, and she turned and called after him urgently. I skittered down the stairs and got on my bicycle and rode away from the hospital feeling I had made a mistake. I had and I hadn't. She was in no condition to receive visitors, but I had acquired an important item of knowledge—dying is something people have to live through, and while they are doing it, unless you are much closer to them than I was to her, you have little or no claim on them.

After she was gone, when I rode past her house, I always thought of her. The house had a flat roof and the living-room windows came almost to the floor of the front porch. The fact that there were so few lights burning on winter evenings may have accounted for the look of sadness. Or it could have been my imagination.

For years after we moved to Chicago my stepmother was homesick, and we always went down to Lincoln for the holidays so that she could be with her family. One evening, a couple of days after Christmas, I happened to be walking down Keokuk Street, and when I came to the McIvors' house I turned in at the front walk. I don't know what made me do it. Recollection of those Sunday-night suppers when my mother was alive, perhaps, or of my father and Mr. McIvor retiring to my father's den, where he kept the whiskey bottle, for a nightcap. The housekeeper let me in. The little boy—I had almost forgotten about him—who peered at me from behind her skirt must have been six or seven. Mr. McIvor hadn't come home from his office yet, she said, and retired to the kitchen.

I couldn't remember ever having been inside the house before, and I looked around the living room: dark varnished woodwork, Mission furniture, brown wallpaper, brown lampshades. It didn't seem at all likely that after Aunt Beth died Mr. McIvor destroyed all traces of her, but neither did it seem possible that she would have chosen to live with this disheartening furniture. There were brass andirons in the fireplace but no logs on them and no indication that the fireplace was ever used. No books or magazines lying around, not even the *Saturday Evening Post*. The little boy wanted to show me the Christmas tree, in the front window. The tree lights were not on, and he explained that they were broken. The opened presents under the tree—a cowboy suit, a puzzle, a Parcheesi board, and so on—were still in the boxes they had come in. With a screwdriver that the housekeeper produced for me I located the defective bulb, and the colored lights shone on the child's pleased face. The stillness I heard as I stood looking at the lighted tree was beyond my power to do anything about. I said good-bye to the little boy and picked up my hat and coat and left, without waiting for Mr. McIvor to come home.

When I married I took my wife to Lincoln. She was introduced to all the friends of the family, including Aaron McIvor, whom she was charmed by. She told me afterward that at one point in their conversation he turned and looked at me and then said, "He's a nice boy but queer—very queer."

When I went to see Mr. McIvor on the day after my father's funeral, his criticism boiled down to the fact that my father liked women too much, and let them twist him around their little finger.

My father was an indulgent husband, but he hated change and was devoted to his habits, and it took a prolonged campaign and all sorts of stratagems on my stepmother's part to get him to agree to enclose the screened porch or buy a new car. In any case, he was not a skirt chaser. So what did all this mean?

I think even more than by what he said I was upset by his matter-of-fact tone of voice—as if my father's death had aroused no feelings in him whatever. There was no question that my father considered Aaron McIvor his friend. Could it be that he disliked my father, and perhaps always had? Or did he dislike everybody, pretty much?

As I listened to him, I wondered if he had been envious of my father—of his success in business, and of the fact that he was, many people would have said, as fortunate in his second marriage as he was in his first. Because Aaron McIvor had made a decision and stuck to it didn't mean that he never considered the alternative. And even a so-so marriage might have been better than the unshared bed and the unending solitude he came home to day after day for something like forty years.

"I don't agree with you," I said, and "I don't think that's right." And he said with a sniff, "I knew him better than you did."

It crossed my mind, after I had left the house, that he might have been playing with me the game he used to play with my mother. But on those far-off Sunday evenings he had a look of glee in his eyes, where now there was simply animosity. From which it did not appear that I was excluded.

I always assumed he was fond of my mother or he wouldn't have enjoyed teasing her. Was it on her account that he resented the fact that my father had remarried—if he did resent it? If I had had my wits about me, I would have retraced my steps and asked Dean Hill what he thought. He and Aaron McIvor were not, so far as I know, friends, but they had spent a lifetime in the same small town, where everything is known, about everybody. Also, they were direct opposites—the one so even-tempered and observant and responsive to any kind of cordiality, the other so abrasive. And opposites often instinctively understand each other. Whether Dean Hill came up with a believable explanation or not, ambiguity was meat and drink to him, and he would probably have considered the conversation in that bleak upstairs bedroom from angles I hadn't thought of. He might even have suggested, tactfully, that in my being so hot under the collar there just could be something worth looking into. My father and I were of very different temperaments, and he didn't know anything about the kind of life I was blindly feeling my way toward. He had only my best interests at heart, but as an adolescent and in my early twenties I had resented his advice and sometimes taken pleasure in doing the opposite of what he urged me to do.

Instead, I stopped off at my Aunt Annette's. She listened to my account of the visit to Aaron McIvor and did not attempt to explain his behavior, beyond saying he had always been that way. She then told me something I didn't know: "As Beth lay dying, she said to Aaron, 'You are the dearest husband any woman ever had.'"

In the face of that, nothing I had been thinking seemed worth giving serious consideration to. She was his life. There wasn't the faintest chance of his finding another woman like her, and it was not in his nature to make concessions. So he made do with housekeepers, and brought up his son. When he was stumped by something he went to see the old woman with the big black hat, who knew a thing or two about bringing up children (or so I like to think) and who was not put off by anything he said, being of the opinion that his bark was worse than his bite.

The Front and the Back Parts
of the House

THOUGH it took me a while to realize it, I had a good father. He left the house early Tuesday morning carrying his leather grip, which was heavy with printed forms, and walked downtown to the railroad station. As the Illinois state agent for a small fire and windstorm insurance company he was expected to make his underwriting experience available to local agents in Freeport, Carbondale, Alton, Carthage, Dixon, Quincy, and so on, and to cultivate their friendship in the hope that they would give more business to his company. I believe he was well liked. Three nights out of every week he slept in godforsaken commercial hotels that overlooked the railroad tracks and when he turned over in the dark he heard the sound of the ceiling fan and railway cars being shunted. He knew the state of Illinois the way I knew our house and yard.

He could have had a much better job in the Chicago office but my mother said Chicago was no place to raise children. When the offer came a second time, ten years later, my father accepted it. He was forty-four and ready to give up the hard life of a traveling man. My stepmother wept at the thought of leaving her family and Lincoln but came to like living in Chicago. They lived there for twenty years. With my future in mind—he wasn't just talking—my father assured me solemnly that you get out of life exactly what you put into it. I took this with a grain of salt; a teacher in my high school in Chicago, a woman given to reading Mencken and *The American Mercury*, had explained to me that there are people who have always drawn the short end of the stick and will continue to. But for my father the maxim was true. He reserved a reasonable part of his life for his responsibilities to his family and his golf game, and everything else he put into the fire-insurance business. He ended up Vice-President in Charge of the Western Department, which satisfied his aspirations. When the presidency was offered to him he turned it down. It would have meant moving East, and he foresaw that in the New York office he would be confronted with problems he might not be able to deal with confidently.

A detached retina brought his career to a premature end. They moved back to Lincoln, to the same street, Park Place, but a different house. I was in my early forties and living in the country, just beyond the northern suburbs of New York City, and trying to make a living by writing fiction, when my father wrote me that it was about time I paid them a visit. He met me at the station, and as we drove into Park Place I saw that time is more than an abstract idea: Maple and elm saplings that were staked against the wind when we moved away had become shade trees. I spent the first evening with my father and my stepmother, and next morning after breakfast I walked over to my Aunt Annette's. She was my mother's younger sister, and they were very close. I loved going to her house because nothing ever changed there. When she sold it many years later because the stairs got to be too much for her, I felt the loss, I think, more than she did.

In that house the present had very little resonance. The things my aunt really cared about had all happened in the early years of her life. My Great-Grandfather Youtsey's farm on the Licking River in Kentucky, where she spent every summer of her childhood, had passed out of the family. The Kentucky aunts and uncles she was so fond of she was not free to visit anymore. Her father and mother and my mother were all lying side by side in the cemetery.

In the front hall, under the stairs, there was a large framed engraving of the Colosseum, bought in Rome the year I was born. In the living room there were further reminders: Michelangelo's *Holy Family*, the Bridge of Sighs, and a Louis XV glass cabinet full of curios. Lots of Lincoln people had been to Chicago, and some even to New York, but very few had any firsthand knowledge of what Europe was like—except the coal miners, and they didn't count. The sublime souvenirs kept their importance down through time.

Over the high living-room mantelpiece was a portrait-size tinted photograph of my Grandfather Blinn. I could almost but not quite remember him. When I stood and contemplated it I was defeated by the unseeing look that likenesses of dead people always seem to have. My Aunt Annette was his favorite child. To his boyhood on his father's cattle farm near St. Johnsbury, Vermont, and to the obstacles he surmounted in order to become a lawyer, the photograph offered no clue whatever. Nor did it convey what a warmhearted man he was. What it did suggest, if anybody wanted to look at it that way, was that in my uncle's house a dead man was held in greater esteem than he was.

My aunt had made what other members of the family considered a mistaken marriage, which she had long ago stopped discussing with anyone. If she had really wanted to she could have extricated herself from it. It was as if she believed in the irrevocability of choices, and was simply living with the one she had made as a young woman.

My Uncle Will had graduated from Yale with an engineering degree, and held a license to practice surveying, but he also had inherited several farms, and he was gone from six-thirty in the morning until late afternoon, making sure that his tenant farmers didn't do something that might be to their advantage but not his. I guess he was an intelligent man, but if one of the main elements in your character is suspicion, intelligence is more often than not misused. My aunt was a very beautiful woman and he loved her but her beauty was a torment to him. He did not want her to accept invitations of any kind and they never entertained. It upset him if she even went to the Friday-afternoon bridge club, because what if the hostess's husband were to leave his office early and come home?

Annette was alone in the house all day, with no one to talk to but the colored woman in the kitchen. Lula had a great many children and from time to time she quit in order to have another. Sometimes she just quit. Or my aunt fired her because she had failed to show up for too many mornings in a row. She was always eventually asked to come back, because my aunt needed her in the skirmishing that took place with my Uncle Will. The indignant things Annette didn't feel it was safe to say to him Lula, looking him straight in the eye, said. My uncle seldom took offense, perhaps because she was colored and his servant and not to be taken seriously, or perhaps because she was not afraid of him and so had his grudging respect. When my aunt couldn't find her glasses she borrowed Lula's, which, even though there was only one lens and that had a crack in it, worked well enough. And when she felt like crying, Lula let her cry.

Like the house, my aunt changed very little over the years. Her hair turned grey, and she was heavier than she was when I was a child, but her clear blue eyes were still the eyes of a young woman.

I opened the front door and called out and she answered from the sun porch. My feelings poured out of me, as always when I was with her. Suddenly she interrupted what I was telling her to say, "I have a surprise for you. Hattie Dyer is in the kitchen."

I got up from my chair and for the length of time it took me to go through the house blindly like a sleepwalker I had the beautiful past in my hand. When I walked into the kitchen I saw a grey-haired colored woman standing at the sink and I said "Hattie!" and went and put my arms around her.

I don't know what I expected. I hadn't thought that far. Or imagined what her response might be.

There was no response. Any more than if I had hugged a wooden post. She did not even look at me. As I backed away from her in embarrassment at my mistake, she did not do or say anything that would make it easier for me to get from the kitchen to the front part of the house where I belonged.

If I had acted differently, I asked myself later—if I had been less concerned with my own feelings and allowed room for hers, if I had put out my hand instead of trying to embrace her, would the truce between the front and the back parts of the house have held? Would she have wiped her hand on her apron and taken my hand? And said (whether it was true or not) that she remembered me? And listened politely to my recollections of the time when she worked in our kitchen? And then perhaps I would have perceived that her memories of that time were vague or nonexistent, so that we very soon ran out of things to say?

I didn't tell my aunt what had happened. I was afraid she would say "Why did you put your arms around her?" and I didn't know why. Also, I thought she might be provoked at Hattie, and I didn't want to have to consider her feelings as well as my own.

The next time I was in Lincoln, a year or two later, Lula was back and saw me coming up the walk and opened the front door to me.

Twice a day, with dragging footsteps—for he was an old man —Alfred Dyer came up the brick driveway of our house on Ninth Street to clean out the horse's stall and feed and curry him, and shovel coal into the furnace. His daughter Hattie kept house for my Grandmother Blinn at the end of her life when, immobilized by dropsy, she sat beside the cannel-coal fire in the back parlor, unable to arrive at the name of one of her children or grandchildren without running through the entire list of them. I don't remember ever being alone with her, though I expect I was. Or anything she ever said to me. I was five years old when she died. The day after her funeral my mother sat down at the kitchen table with Hattie and when they had finished talking about the situation in that house my mother asked her if she would like to come across the street and work in ours.

Hattie was a good cook when she came to us and she learned effortlessly anything my mother chose to teach her. She was paid five dollars a week—two hundred and sixty dollars a year, the prevailing wage for domestic servants in the second decade of this century. If you take into consideration the fact that it was one-twelfth of my father's annual salary, it doesn't seem so shocking.

The week took its shape from my father's going away and returning, but otherwise every day was a repetition of other days, with, occasionally, an event intruding upon the serenity of the expected. My older brother came down with chicken pox and I caught it from him. Or we had company. Or the sewing woman settled down in an empty bedroom and, with her mouth full of pins, arranged tissue-paper patterns and scraps of dress material on the headless dress form. Sometimes my mother's friends came of an afternoon and the tea cart was wheeled into the living room and they sat drinking tea and talking as if their lives depended on it, and I would go off upstairs to play and come down an hour later to find them gone and Hattie washing the teacups.

Monday mornings two shy children that I knew were hers

came to the back door with an express wagon and Hattie gave them our washing, tied up in a sheet, for her mother to do. I knew that old Mrs. Dyer's house was on Elm Street, near the intersection at the foot of Ninth Street hill, and I assumed that when Hattie finished the supper dishes and closed the outside kitchen door behind her, that was where she went. It may or may not have been true. After three or four days Mrs. Dyer sent the washing back, white as snow and folded in such a way that it gave my mother pleasure as she put it away in the upstairs linen closet.

There were places in that house that I went to habitually, the way animals repeat their rounds: the window seat in the library, the triangular space behind a walnut Victorian sofa in the living room, the unfurnished bedroom over the kitchen. And if I was suddenly at loose ends because the life had gone out of the toys I was playing with, I would find my mother and be gathered onto her lap and consoled. If she was not home I would wander out onto the back porch and listen to the upward-spiraling sound of the locusts.

The dog went to my mother when he wasn't sure we all liked him as much as it is possible for a dog to be liked, and felt better after she had talked to him. My brother, who was four years older than I, had a running argument with her about whether he was eleven or, as he insisted, twelve. If in the dead of winter my father opened his three-tiered metal fishing box and sorted through the flies, he chose the room where she was to do it in. When summer came she packed a picnic hamper, and my father brought the horse and carriage around to the high curbing in front of the house, and against a disapproving background of church bells we drove out into the country to a walnut grove with a stream running through it. My mother sat on a plaid lap rug and pulled in one sunfish after another, while my father tramped upstream casting for bass. We could have been the only people on earth. I think my mother enjoyed those long drowsy fishing expeditions but in any case she did whatever it made him happy to do. How much he loved her I heard in his voice whenever he called to her. And how much she loved him I saw in her face when he arrived on the front porch on Friday afternoon and we all came out of the house to greet him. As my father stood with his arms around us, the dog wormed his way past my legs so that his presence too would be recognized.

The Christmas holly that the first grade had cut out of red and green paper and pasted on the schoolroom windows was replaced by George Washington's hatchet, which turned up again on the scorecard that my mother brought home to me from her bridge club. When we looked at the teacher we also saw the calendar on the wall behind her desk: April 1, 1915: April Fool's Day.

I have learned to read. I can read sentences out of the evening paper. The big black headlines are often about the war between Germany and the Allies. From the window seat in the library I watch as my father stands and holds an opened-out page of the Lincoln *Evening Courier* across the upper part of the fireplace so the chimney won't smoke. (The war between *us* broke out when I was three or four years old. I woke up in the night with a parched throat and called out—it was by no means the first time this had happened—for a drink. And waited for my mother's footsteps and the bathroom glass against my dry lips. Instead, his voice, from across the hall, said, "*Oh*, get it yourself!") The newspaper catches fire and floats up the chimney, and I pull the curtain behind me in order to peer out at the darkness and the piles of snow. In May, where the piles of dirty snow were, the flowering almond is in bloom. It has suckered and spread through the wire fence into the Kiests' yard. Do the flowers on that side belong to them or to us?

D. W. Griffith's *Birth of a Nation* is showing at the movie theater downtown and there are scenes in it that have made all the colored people in Lincoln angry. I am told to stay out of the kitchen.

The sentences we are called on to read out loud in class are longer and more complicated. We have to memorize the forty-eight states and their capitals, and the countries of South America. With a pencil behind his ear, my father goes through an accumulation of inspection slips, making a check mark now and then, and hands them to me to alphabetize. (Spreading them around me on the rug, I am proud to be of help to him.)

Slumped down in her chair, my mother feels with the toe of her shoe for the buzzer that is concealed under the dining-room rug. My brother and I find her searching hilarious. My father wonders why she just doesn't buy a little bell she can ring. In the end she has to give up, and calls out to the kitchen. The pantry door swings open and Hattie appears to clear away the plates and bring the dessert. She too thinks it is funny that the buzzer is never where it is supposed to be.

How many years was she with us? Five, by my calculations. One day I went out to the kitchen for a drink of water and saw her daughter Thelma at the kitchen sink with an apron on. She said she had come to work for us. She was twelve years old but tall for her age. I asked my mother where Hattie was and my mother said, "She's been having trouble with her husband and moved to Chicago." My mother didn't say what the trouble was and I assumed it was one of the things that are not explained to children. But I felt the trouble was serious if Hattie had to go away. And her absence made me aware of an unpleasant possibility: Things could change.

To everything that my mother said to Thelma she answered "Yes, ma'am" and "No, ma'am," but as though she were hearing it from a great distance, and she moved with the slowness of a person whose heart is somewhere else. My mother detected a film of grease on all the dishes and spoke to her about it. When there was no improvement, she decided that Thelma wasn't ever going to be like Hattie, and let her go.

The good-natured farm girl who was in our kitchen after that was taking classes at night so she could pass an examination and work in the post office. My mother was satisfied with her but spoke regretfully of Hattie, who knew what she wanted done without having to be told.

The school calendar has marched straight on to the fall half of the year 1918. We have learned how to do long division. The women who come to our house in the afternoon put their teacups aside and hem diapers as they sit gossiping. They all know what my mother has told me in confidence, that I am going to have a baby brother or a baby sister. They also know —in a small town there was no way for such a thing not to be known—that my mother had a difficult time when my brother was born, and again with me. Only my Aunt Annette knew that at this time she had premonitions of dying.

My mother hopes that the baby will be a girl, and I am sure

that what my mother wants to have happen will happen. Nothing turned out the way anybody hoped or expected it to. My younger brother was born in a hospital in Bloomington during the height of the epidemic of Spanish influenza. Toward the end of the first week in January, Alfred Dyer, coming up the driveway to tend the furnace, cannot have failed to see the funeral wreath on the door.

There is no cure but time. One of my mother's friends said that, putting her hand on my father's shoulder as he sat, hardly recognizable, in his chair. I thought about my mother in the cemetery and wondered if she would wake up and try to get out of her coffin and not be able to. But children have to go to school no matter what happens at home. I learned that the square root of sixty-four is eight, and that π is 3.14159 approximately, and represents the ratio of the circumference to the diameter of a circle.

Years passed without my thinking about Hattie Dyer at all, and then suddenly there I was backing away from her in confusion. When I told my wife about it she said, "It wasn't Hattie you embraced but the idea of her." Which was clearly true, but didn't explain Hattie's behavior.

Because my mother was fond of her it doesn't necessarily follow that Hattie was fond of my mother. My mother may have been only the white woman she worked for. But if this were true I think I would have sensed it as a child. Perhaps—it was so long ago—she neither remembered nor cared what my mother was like by the time I put my arms around her in my aunt's kitchen.

If I had had the courage to stand my ground and say to her, "Why do you refuse to admit that you knew me when I was a little boy?" I don't think she would have given me any answer. However, people do communicate their feelings helplessly. Jealousy can be felt even in the dark. Lovers charge the surrounding air with their delirium. What I felt as I backed away from that unresponsive figure was anger.

My Aunt Edith was married to a doctor and lived in Bloomington. They had no children and she wanted to take the baby when my mother died, but my father clung to the belief that my mother would have wanted him to keep the family together and not let my brothers and me grow up in separate households, no matter how loving. We were too young to shift for ourselves while he was away, and what he needed was a woman who knew how to run a house and take care of a baby. Hattie could have managed it with one hand tied behind her. So could Annette's Lula. And they would have brought life into the house with them. I cannot believe that there were no more colored women like them in Lincoln. But he thought (and so did everybody else) that he had to have a white woman. The first housekeeper was hired because she had been a nurse. She had nothing whatever to say, not even about the weather. She had never been around children before, and I felt no inclination to lean against her.

My brother and I struggled against the iron fact that my mother wasn't there anymore. Or ever going to be. Tears did not help. The house was like a person in a state of coma. If Annette had not turned up sometime during every day I think we would all have stopped breathing. Any domestic crisis that arose remained undealt with until my father came home. He never knew when he left the house on Tuesday morning what brand-new trouble he would find when he returned on Friday afternoon. My mother's clothes closet was empty. Her silver-backed comb and brush and hand mirror were still on her dressing table, but without the slight disorder of hairpins, powder, powder puff, cologne, smelling salts, and so on, they were reduced to being merely objects. How endless the nights must have been for him, in the double bed where, when he put out his hand, it encountered only the cold sheets.

The first housekeeper lasted three months. The second took offense no matter which way the wind blew, and it would have been better to have no one. She made mischief between the two sides of the family and was dismissed when she developed erysipelas. The farm girl passed her examination and gave notice. And so it went. Each time my father's arrangements collapsed he turned in desperation to old Mrs. Dyer, and though she was crippled with rheumatism she came and fed us until he found someone to take over from her.

During this period he made an appointment with the local photographer. The result is a very strange picture. My father sits holding the baby on his lap. The baby looks uncomfortable but not about to cry. My father is wearing a starched collar and a dark-blue suit, and looks like what he was, a sad self-made man. My older brother has a fierce expression on his face, as if he means to stare the camera out of countenance. I am standing beside him, a thin little boy of ten, in a Norfolk jacket, knee pants, and long black stockings. The photographer was a man with a good deal of manner, and as he ducked his head under the black cloth and then out again to rearrange the details of our bodies I was threatened with an attack of the giggles, which would not have been appropriate, because my father meant the picture to be a memorial of our bereavement.

Annette and her husband were in the habit of spending the winter in Florida. The first Christmas after my mother's death she sent him and my Cousin Peg down South without her so she could be with us. Shortly after that I became aware of conversations behind closed doors and then somebody forgot to close the door. Out of fury because she had been dismissed, the second housekeeper had written several unsigned poison-pen letters to my Grandmother Maxwell, in which she said that my father was carrying on with my Aunt Annette. My Uncle Will Bates received similar letters. His response was to put a stop to Annette's coming to our house at all.

My brother felt that it would be disloyal to my father if he set foot in my uncle's house. Nothing on earth (and certainly not the awkwardness) could have kept me from being where Annette was. What I didn't tell her about my feelings she seemed to know anyway. She told Lula to put an extra place at the table for me, and made me feel loved. She also got me to accept (as far as I was able at that age to do this) the succession of changes that came about, a year later, when my father's grief wore itself out and he put his life with my mother behind him. Children, with no conception of how life goes on and on, expect a faithfulness that comes at too high a price. Now that I am old enough to be his father I have no trouble saying yes, of course he should have remarried. He had always liked women, and without feminine companionship, without someone sitting at the opposite end of the table whom he could feel tenderly about, he would have turned sour and become a different man. He began to accept invitations, and the matchmakers put their heads together.

There used to be, and probably still is somewhere, a group picture of the guests at my father's wedding, which took place in the house of my stepmother's sister, in 1921. The photographer set up his tripod and camera on the lawn in front of the house, and as the guests assembled in front of him there was a good deal of joking and laughter. I had already passed over the line into puberty but not yet reached the stage of hypercritical judgments when I would find the loud laughter of a room full of grown people enjoying themselves unbearable.

During the years that my father lived in Chicago his heavy leather grip, that my mother had hated the sight of, remained on a closet shelf unless we took the train down to Lincoln. There were several people he felt obliged to call on whenever he went home, and one of them was Mrs. Dyer, who still lived in the little house at the foot of Ninth Street hill. He expected his sons to go with him. The visits went on as long as she lived. Mr. Dyer was never there, and I think must have died. I was not expected to take part in the conversation; only to be there. And so my eyes were free to roam around the front room we sat in. The iron potbellied stove, the threadbare carpet, the darkened wallpaper. The calendar, courtesy of the local lumber company. The hard wooden chairs we sat on. Mrs. Dyer and my father talked about her health, about changes in Lincoln, about how fast time goes. And then he made some excuse that got us on our feet. As we were saying good-bye he took out his billfold and extracted a new ten-dollar bill. But not one word did either of them say about the thing that had brought him there, which was that in the time of his greatest trouble, when there was no one else he could have turned to, she didn't fail him.

In a box of old papers, not long ago, I found an eighty-page history of the town of Lincoln, published by Feldman's Print Shop, in 1953, when Lincoln was celebrating the hundredth anniversary of its founding. Thumbing through it I came upon a picture of Mrs. Dyer, looking just the way I remembered her. She was beautiful as an old woman, and probably always was.

In the photograph she is wearing a black silk dress with a lace collar. Her mouth is sunken in with age, but her eyes are as bright as a child's, and from her smile you'd think it had been a privilege to stand over a tub of soapy water doing other people's washing year in and year out. Surrounding the picture there is an interview with Hattie, who had been chosen as "a respected citizen of the community" to give "something of the history of one of our distinguished colored families." The interview is only five hundred words long, and I assume that much of what she said never got into print. For example, what about her brother Dr. William Dyer? Was the interviewer aware that he had succeeded in becoming a doctor when this was exceedingly rare for a Negro and that he was on the surgical staffs of the best hospitals in Kansas City? Or that he was also among those citizens of Lincoln who were especially honored at the centennial celebration? Perhaps the history went to press before this fact was known. In any case, while Dr. Dyer was in town for the honoring he stayed with her. He had managed to put himself in a position where no white man could summon him with the word "Boy!" She must have been immensely proud of him. The interview does quote Hattie as saying that in Alfred Dyer's house "there were no intoxicants allowed, no dancing, no card playing, but how we loved to dance! And we did dance when they were away from home." As long as her father was able to work, Hattie said, he was employed by the B. P. Andrews Lumber Company in town. I suspect he had many jobs, some of them overlapping. It is hard to believe how little people were paid for their labor in those days, but the Dyers managed. They didn't have to walk along the railroad right-of-way picking up pieces of coal. In the interview, Hattie said she was a year old when she was brought to the house on Elm Street.

When her mother first came to Lincoln from Missouri, she worked in a boardinghouse run by a Mrs. Jones, Hattie said. It was on the site of the high school—which, in the twenties, when I went there, was an old building with deep grooves in the stairs worn by generations of adolescent feet. Mrs. Jones's establishment must have ceased to exist a very long time ago. If you have ever eaten in a boardinghouse you know every last one of them. The big oak dining-room table with all the leaves in it, and barely enough room for the thin young colored woman to squeeze between the chair backs and the sideboard. No sooner were the dishes from the midday meal washed and put back on the table and the pots and pans drying upside down in a pyramid on the kitchen range than it was time to start peeling potatoes for supper. Jesus loved her and that got her back on her feet when she was too tired to move. And before long, Alfred Dyer was waiting at the kitchen door to take her to prayer meeting.

"In looking back over the years," Hattie said to the interviewer, "I am proud of my father and mother, who were highly regarded by all who knew them, white as well as black. Their deep religious faith has been my help and strength throughout my life."

During one of those times when my father was searching for a housekeeper and Mrs. Dyer was in our kitchen, she stopped me as we got up from the table at the end of dinner and asked if I'd like to go to church with her to hear a choir from the South. It was a very cold night and there was a white full moon, and walking along beside Mrs. Dyer I saw the shadows of the bare branches laid out on the snow. Our footsteps made a squeaking sound and it hurt to breathe. The church was way downtown on the other side of the courthouse square. As we made our way indoors I saw that it was crammed with people, and overheated, and I was conscious of the fact that I was the only white person there. Nobody made anything of it. The men and women in the choir were of all ages, and dressed in white. For the first time in my life I heard "Swing Low, Sweet Chariot," and "Pharaoh's Army Got Drownded," and "Were You There When They Crucified My Lord?" and "Joshua Fit de Battle of Jericho." Singing "Don't let nobody turn you round," the choir yanked one another around and stamped their feet (in church!). I looked at Mrs. Dyer out of the corner of my eye. She was smiling. "Not my brother, not my sister, but it's me, *O Lord!*" the white-robed singers shouted. The people around me sat listening politely with their hands folded in their laps, and I thought, perhaps mistakenly, that they too were hearing these spirituals for the first time.

*

I could have asked my aunt about Hattie and she would have told me all that a white person would be likely to know, but I didn't. More years passed. I found that I had a nagging curiosity about Hattie—about what her life had been like. Finally it occurred to me that my Cousin Tom Perry, who lives in Lincoln, might be able to learn about her. He wrote back that I had waited too long. Among white people there was nobody left who knew her, and he couldn't get much information from the black people he talked to. He did find out that when she moved back to Lincoln, she lived in the little house on Elm Street. Tom was in high school with her son, who was an athlete, a track star. He became an undertaker and died in middle age, of cancer of the throat. Hattie spent the last years of her life in Springfield with one of her daughters. Her son was born after Hattie came back to Lincoln to live, and his last name was Brummel, so whatever the trouble with her husband was, they stayed together.

In his letter my cousin said that at the time of his death Alfred Dyer owned his own house and the houses on either side of it. This surprised me. He did not look like a property owner. All three houses were torn down recently, Tom said, and the site had not been built on.

I have not been inside our house on Ninth Street since I was twelve years old. It was built in the eighteen-eighties, possibly even earlier. The last time I drove past it, five years ago, I saw that the present owners had put shutters on the front windows. Nothing looks right to me that is not the way I remember it, but it is the work of a moment, of less time than that, to do away with the shutters and bring back into existence the lavender-blue clematis on the side porch and the trellis that supported it, the big tree in the side yard that was killed by the elm blight, the house next door that burned down one night twenty-five or thirty years ago.

Though I know better, I half believe that if the front door to our house were opened to me I would find the umbrella stand by the window in the front hall and the living-room carpet would be moss green. Sometimes I put myself to sleep by going from room to room of that house, taking note of my father's upright piano with the little hand-wound Victrola on it, Guido Reni's *Aurora* over the living-room mantelpiece, the Victorian sofas and chairs. I make my way up the front stairs by the light of the gas night-light in the upstairs hall, and count the four bedroom doors. Or I go through the dining room into the pantry, where, as the door swings shut behind me and before I can push open the door to the brightly lit kitchen, I experience once more the full terror of the dark. Beyond the kitchen is the laundry, where the big iron cookstove is. Opening off this room are two smaller rooms, hardly bigger than closets. One contains jars of preserved fruit and vegetables and a grocery carton full of letters to my mother from my father. The other room is dark and has a musty odor. The dog sleeps here, on a square of old dirty carpet, and there is a toilet of an antiquated kind. Hattie is expected to use this toilet and not the one in the upstairs bathroom that we use. You could argue, I suppose, that some such arrangement would have been found in other old houses in Lincoln, and because it was usual may not have given offense—a proposition I do not find very convincing.

My mother was thirty-seven when she died. When I try to recall what she was like, I remember what a child would remember. How she bent over the bed and kissed me good night and drew the covers around my chin. How she made me hold still while she cut my bangs. If I try to see her as one adult looking at another, I realize how much there is that I don't know. One day I heard her exclaim into the telephone "It won't do!" and wondering what wouldn't do I listened. After a minute or two it became clear that a colored family was on the point of buying a house on the other side of the street from ours, and that my mother was talking to somebody at the bank. This in itself was odd. If my father had been home, she would have got him to do it. She must have believed that the matter wouldn't wait until he got home. "It won't do!" she kept repeating into the telephone. "It just won't do." A few weeks later, when a moving van drew up before the house in question, it was to unload the furniture of a white family.

One of the things I didn't understand when I was a child was the fact that grown people—not my father and mother but people who came to our house or that they stopped to talk to on the street—seemed to think they were excused from taking the feelings of colored people into consideration. When they said something derogatory about Negroes, they didn't bother to lower their voices even though fully aware that there was a colored person within hearing distance. Quite apart from what Hattie may have overheard in Lincoln, what she saw and lived through in Chicago, including race riots, might easily have been enough to make her fear and hate all white men without exception. And so in that case it was the color of my skin—the color of my skin and the physical contact—that accounted for what happened in my Aunt Annette's kitchen. Having arrived at this conclusion I found that I didn't entirely believe it, because at the time I had the feeling that Hattie's anger was not a generalized anger; it had something to do with who I was. Did somebody in our family do something unforgivable to her? My Grandmother Blinn? Not likely. My father always leaned over backward to be fair and just toward anybody who worked for him. Though I cannot bring back the words, I can hear, in a kind of replay, the sound of my mother and Hattie talking. We are in the throes of spring housecleaning. Her black hair bound up in a dish towel, my mother stands in the double doorway between the front hall and the living room and directs Hattie's attention to a corner of the ceiling where a spider has taken refuge. With a dust mop on the end of a very long pole, Hattie dislodges it. There is no sullenness in Hattie's voice and no strain in my mother's. They are simply easy with one another.

In the end I decided that I must be barking up the wrong tree, and that what happened in my aunt's kitchen was simply the collision of two experiences. And I stopped thinking about it until I had a second letter from my cousin. "I don't understand it," he wrote. "The colored people in Lincoln have always been very open. If you asked one of them a question you got the answer. This is different. They don't seem to want to talk about Hattie Dyer." In a P.S. he added that the elderly black man who took care of his yard was reading one of my books. Miss Lucy Jane Purrington, whose yard he also looked after, had lent it to him. And in a flash I realized what the unforgivable thing was and who had done it.

*

From time to time I have published fiction that had as a background a small town very much like Lincoln, or even Lincoln itself. The fact that I had not lived there since I was fourteen years old sealed off my memories of it, and made of it a world I knew no longer existed, that seemed always available for storytelling. Once, I began to write a novel without knowing what was going to happen in it. As the details unfolded before my mind, I went on putting them down, trusting that there was a story and that I would eventually find it. The novel began with an evening party in the year 1912. I didn't bother to make up the house where the party took place because there at hand was our house on Ninth Street and it gave me pleasure to write about it. The two main characters were an overly conscientious young lawyer named Austin King and his wife, Martha, who was pregnant. He had not been able to bring himself to say no to a letter from Mississippi relatives proposing to visit. At the beginning of the novel the relatives have arrived, the party is about to begin, and Martha King is not making things any easier for her husband by lying face down across her bed and refusing to speak to him.

Characters in fiction are seldom made out of whole cloth. A little of this person and something of that one and whatever else the novelist's imagination suggests is how they come into being. The novelist hopes that by avoiding actual appearances and actual names (which are so much more convincing than the names he invents for them), by making tall people short and red-headed people blond, that sort of thing, the sources of the composite character will not be apparent.

We did in fact have a visit of some duration from my Grandmother Maxwell's younger sister, who lived in Greenville, Mississippi, and her husband, their two grown sons, married daughter, son-in-law, and grandchild, a little girl of four. Remembering how their Southern sociability transformed our house, I tried to bring into existence a family with the same ability to charm, but whose ambiguous or destructive natures were partly imagined and partly derived from people not even born at the time of this visit. The little girl crossed over and became the daughter of Austin and Martha King. The young woman of the invented family was unmarried, and an early feminist, and without meaning to she whittled away at the marriage of her Northern cousin, whom she had fallen in love with. Though I did my best to change my Mississippi relatives beyond recognition, many years later my father told me that in one instance I had managed to pin the donkey's tail on the part of the animal where it belonged. But it was wholly by accident. If you turn the imagination loose like a hunting dog, it will often return with the bird in its mouth.

About fifty pages into the writing of the novel I had a dream that revealed to me the direction the story was trying to take and who the characters were stand-ins for. My father was musical, and could play by ear almost any instrument he picked up, and once had the idea of putting on a musical comedy with local talent. The rehearsals took place in our living room. He sat at the piano and played the vocal score for the singers. My mother sat on the davenport listening and I sat beside her. Things did not go well. The cast was erratic about coming to rehearsals, the tenor flagrantly so. One rainy evening only one member of the cast showed up, the pretty young woman who had the soprano lead. She and my father agreed that there was not much point in going on with it. Two and a half years after my mother's death she became my stepmother. It is not the sort of thing that is subject to proof, but I nevertheless believe, on the strength of the dream and of the novel I had blindly embarked on, that I caught something out of the air—a whiff of physical attraction between the young woman and my father. And since it was more than I could deal with I managed not to think about it for the next twenty-seven years.

Austin King's house was clearly our house, to anyone who had ever been in it. In 1912 Hattie was across the street at my Grandmother Blinn's. But during the visit of my Great-Aunt Ina and her family Hattie was working in our kitchen. However, I never had it in mind to write about her. Rachel, the colored woman who worked in the Kings' kitchen, was imaginary. Insofar as she was modeled on anyone, it was the West Indian maid of a family in New York I came to know years later. They lived in a big old-fashioned sunless but cheerful apartment off upper Madison Avenue. The front door was never locked, and I used to open it often when I was a solitary young man. I forget whether Renée came from Haiti or Guadeloupe.

About her private life I knew nothing whatever and I don't think the family she worked for did either.

In a run-down part of Lincoln I once saw a railroad caboose that had come to rest on concrete blocks, in a yard littered with cast-off objects that were picturesque but of no value: a funeral basket, a slab of marble, a broken-down glider, etc. Rachel had to live somewhere, and so why not here? Her five children were not all by the same father but they were all equally beautiful to her. She was easygoing, and perfectly able to be a member of the family one minute and a servant the next, but nobody owned her or ever would. None of this corresponds in any way with the little I know about Hattie Dyer's life and character, but I am afraid that is beside the point. In an earlier, quasi-autobiographical novel, thinking that my father and stepmother would probably not be comfortable reading about themselves, I made the protagonist's father a racetrack tout living far out on the rim of things, and an elderly friend of the family said disapprovingly, "Why did you make your father like that?" So perhaps there is no way to avoid or forestall identifications by a reader bent on making them.

When I was working on the novel about the Kings, it did not occur to me that Hattie would read it or even know it existed. A few women who had known me as a child would put their names on the waiting list at the Lincoln Public Library, one or two at the most might buy it, is what I thought. Men didn't read books. The *Evening Courier* and the Chicago *Tribune* supplied them with all the reading matter they required.

Early on in the writing of the novel the characters took over, and had so much to say to one another that mostly what I did was record their conversation. The difference between this and hallucination is not all that much. One day a new character appeared, and inserted himself retroactively into the novel. He came on a slow freight train from Indianapolis. "Riding in the same boxcar with him, since noon, were an old man and a fifteen-year-old boy, and neither of them ever wanted to see him again. His eyes were bloodshot, his face and hands were gritty, his hair was matted with cinders. His huge, pink-palmed hands hung down out of the sleeves of a corduroy mackinaw that was too small for him and filthy and torn. He had thrown away his only pair of socks two days before. There was a hole in the sole of his right shoe, his belly was empty, and the police were on the lookout for him in St. Louis and Cincinnati."

On the night of the party, while Rachel was still at the Kings', he appeared at her house and frightened all the children, one of whom was his. Rachel was not totally surprised when she walked in on him. She had dreamt about him two nights before. When she realized he was not just after money but meant to settle down with them she took her children and fled. I was frightened of him, too, even as he took life on the page. For a week he stayed blind drunk, and as I described how he lay half undressed on a dirty unmade bed, barely able to lift the bottle to his mouth, I thought *Why not?* and let the fire in the stove go out, and the outside door blew open, and in a little while he died of the cold he had stopped feeling.

I have no reason to think that Hattie's husband, Fred Brummel, was anything but a decent man. My mother's statement that Hattie was having trouble with him possibly amounted to no more than that they were of two minds about moving to Chicago. If Hattie did indeed read my book then what could she think but that I had portrayed her as a loose woman and her husband as a monster of evil? And people in Lincoln, colored people and white, would wonder if I knew things about Fred Brummel that they didn't, and if he was not the person they took him for. I had exposed their married life and blackened his character in order to make a fortune from my writing. I was a thousand miles away, where she couldn't confront me with what I had done. And if she accused me to other people it would only call attention to the book and make more people read it than had already. If all this is true (and my bones tell me that it *is* true) then why, when I walked into my aunt's kitchen, should she be pleased to see me?

I do not feel that it is a light matter.

Any regret for what I may have made Hattie feel is nowhere near enough to have appeased her anger. She was perfectly right not to look at me, not to respond at all, when I put my arms around her. I must have seen Fred Brummel at one time or another or else why does his name conjure up a slight, handsome man whose skin was lighter than Hattie's? If, now, I were to go out to the cemetery in Lincoln and find his grave (which would take some doing) and sit beside it patiently for a good long time, would I learn anything more than that dust does not speak, to anyone, let alone to a stranger? He was once alive. He married Hattie and they had several children. That much is a fact. It does not seem too much to assume that he was happy on the day she told him she would marry him. And again when he held his first child in his arms. And that he was proud of Hattie, as proud as my father was of my mother. Who are now dust also.

The Holy Terror

M Y older brother and I shared a room when we were children, and he was so good at reading my mind that it left
me defenseless against his teasing. When I learned something
that the family was holding back from him and hadn't considered it safe to tell me, either, my first thought was *He will
see it in my face!* But by that time he and I were living in different parts of the country and seldom saw each other, and
from necessity I had acquired, like any other adult, an ability
to mask my thoughts and feelings. His life was hard enough as
it was, and there was no question but that this piece of information would have made it more so. The older generation are
all dead now, and what they didn't want my brother to know
would still be locked up inside me if my brother's heart hadn't
stopped beating, one day in the summer of 1985.

The firm mouth, the clear ringing voice, the direct gaze. In
a family of brown-eyed or blue-eyed people his eyes were hazel.

As a small child—that is to say, when he was five years old—
he was strong and healthy and a holy terror. Threats and pun-
ishments slid off him like water off a duck's back. My father,
with the ideas of his period, believed that children should learn
obedience above everything else, but he was new at being a
father, and besides, three days a week he wasn't there. My
mother was young and pleasure-loving and couldn't say no to
an invitation to a card party, and often left my brother with the
hired girl, who was no match for him. He was named Edward,
after my Grandfather Blinn. My father's sister christened him
"Happy Hooligan," after a character in the funny papers, and
part of the name stuck. "Look out, Happy, don't do that!"
people shrieked, but he had already done it. One afternoon as
my mother emerged from the house dressed fit to kill, he
turned the garden hose on her. My Aunt Edith, hearing the
commotion, opened the screen door and came out to see what
was going on, and she too got a soaking. My brother continued to hold the two women at bay until the stream of water
abruptly failed: My father had crept around the side of the
house to the outdoor faucet. My brother dropped the hose

and ran. At that time, my Aunt Annette lived farther down the street and if he got to her he was safe. She was not afraid of anybody and would simply wrap her skirts around him and there he'd be. She was upstairs dressing and heard him calling her, but by the time she got to the front door my father was holding him by the arm, and possession is nine-tenths of the law.

Down through the years, when family stories were being brought out for company, someone was bound to tell the incident of the garden hose, and about how my father's cigars had to be kept under lock and key.

All such outrageous behavior came to an end before Hap had reached his sixth birthday. The year was 1909. My Aunt Annette, driving a horse and buggy, stopped in front of our house. There was something she wanted to tell my mother. As they were talking my brother said, "Take me with you." Annette explained that she couldn't but he seldom took no for an answer, and started climbing up the back wheel of the buggy in order to get in beside her. She finished what she had to say and flicked the horse's rump with her whip. I was a baby at the time and there is no way I could remember my mother's screams, but even so I am haunted by them.

My brother's left leg was amputated well above the knee. At some point in my growing up I was told, probably by my father, that if the surgeon had been able to leave three or four more inches of stump it would have made a considerable difference in my brother's walking.

By the time I was old enough to observe what was going on around me, my brother had an artificial leg—of cork, I believe, painted an unconvincing pink. When I opened my eyes in the morning there it was, leaning against a chair. I had no conscious feelings about it. It was just something my brother had to have so he could walk. Over his stump he wore a sort of sock, of wool, and the weight of the leg was carried by a cloth harness that went around his shoulders. In the evening after supper my father would give him lessons in walking properly: "If you will only lead with your wooden leg instead of dragging it behind you as you walk, it won't be noticeable." This was *almost* true. But when Hap was tired he forgot. It has been more than seventy years since we were boys together in that house, but my shoulder remembers the weight of his hand as we walked home through the dusk. If he saw someone coming toward us, the hand was instantly withdrawn.

In the earliest picture of my brother that I have ever seen, taken when he was a year old, he is sitting astride Granny Blinn's shoulders. He was her first grandchild and the apple of everybody's eye. As soon as he was old enough to walk he wanted to be with the men, where the air was blue with cigar or pipe smoke and the talk was about horses and hunting dogs, guns and fishing tackle. Between my Grandfather Blinn and my brother there was a deep natural sympathy—the old bear with the cub he liked the smell of. In my mind I see my brother sitting in the front seat of a carriage, studying now the details of the harness on the horse's back and now my grandfather's face for a response to what he is telling my grandfather. And being allowed to hold the reins when they came to a place where the horse was not likely to be startled by any sudden movement from the side of the road. At a very early age he resolved to follow my Grandfather Blinn into the profession of law, and he never deviated from this.

He was nine years old when my grandfather died. My grandmother died that same year, and the house was sold to a family named Irish, from out in the country. They had three boys and a girl, and Mrs. Irish's mother lived with them. I think it is more than likely that before the moving men had finished carrying the Irishes' furniture up the front walk and into the house Hap and Harold Irish had sized each other up and decided it was safe to make the first move. As it turned out, they were friends for life. Harold was a sleepy-eyed boy who noticed things that other people missed. My brother preferred his company to that of any other boy he knew. Harold understood, without having to be told, that my brother could not bear any expression of pity or any offer of help. With intelligence and skill he circumvented his physical handicap. My father and mother never made anything of this, but they cannot have failed to notice that there was very little other boys could do that Hap couldn't do also.

On October afternoons while the maple leaves came floating down from the trees, the boys of the neighborhood played football in a vacant lot on Eleventh Street. The game broke up when they couldn't see the ball anymore. With a smudged face and pieces of dry grass sticking to his clothes, Hap would place himself on the crossbar of Harold's bicycle, which was always waiting for him. He had a bicycle, and could ride it, but to do this with security and élan you need two good legs. Hashing over plays that had miscarried, they rode home to Ninth Street. If other offers of a ride were made, my brother declined them.

In winter when it was still dark I would be wakened by the sound of gravel striking against the window, and Hap would get up from his warm bed and dress and go off with Harold to see if they had caught anything in the traps they had set at intervals along Brainerd's Branch. They had learned from an ad in a boys' magazine that you could get a quarter for a properly stretched and dried muskrat skin, and they meant to become rich. If they waited till daylight they would find their traps sprung and empty. Other boys—coal miners' sons from the north end of town, they believed—also knew about that ad. More often than not it was bitterly cold, and to reach the pasture where the traps were they had to cope with a number of barbed-wire fences half buried in snowdrifts. I am sure, because I used to see it happen on other occasions, that Harold climbed through the barbed wire and walked on, leaving Hap to bend down and hold the wires apart and pull his artificial leg through after him. My mother was forever mending rips in his trousers.

The summer he was fifteen he and I were sent to a Boy Scout camp in Taylorville, Illinois. With the whole camp watching him he climbed up the ladder to the high-diving platform, his cotton bathing suit imperfectly concealing his stump, and hopped out to the end of the board and took off into a jack-knife. His life was one long exercise in gallantry. He wanted to make people forget he was crippled—if possible to keep them from even knowing that he was. He wanted to be treated like anyone else but behaved in such a way as to arouse universal admiration. Not leading with his artificial leg but dragging it after him across the clay court, he won the camp tennis singles. It is no wonder so many people loved him.

*

Before I was old enough to have any recollection of it, my Aunt Edith worked for a time as a nurse in a state asylum for the feeble-minded, out past the edge of town. She met there and eventually married a resident physician named William Young, who soon struck out on his own. As a child I loved to sit on one of his size 12 shoes while he walked back and forth talking to my mother about grown-up matters. A deep attachment existed between our whole family and this big, easygoing, humorous man, whose hands smelled of carbolic acid and who never said "Not now" to anything any child wanted him to do.

It was he who told me the truth about Hap's accident. I was in my late twenties when this happened. One day when we were alone together he spoke in passing of my brother's "affliction"—of what a pity it was. Out of a desire to make the unacceptable appear less so, I mentioned something I had been given to understand—that the leg had been broken in so many places they had no choice but to cut if off. My uncle looked at me a moment and then said, "It was a simple fracture, of a kind that not once in a hundred times would have required an amputation." After which, he went on to tell me what Hap didn't, and mustn't ever, know.

In those days, their fees being small, doctors commonly eked out their income by dispensing medicine themselves instead of writing out prescriptions. The family doctor in Lincoln, with easy access to morphine, had become addicted to it and should have been prevented from practicing. Uncle Doc, not liking the sound of what he was told over the telephone day after day about Hap's condition, got on a train and came to Lincoln. He saw immediately that the broken bone was not set. He also saw the unmistakable signs of gangrene. And taking my father aside, he told him that the leg would have to be cut off to save my brother's life.

"Your Grandfather Blinn called that doctor in and cursed him all the way back to the day he was born," Uncle Doc said to me. "In my whole life I have never witnessed anything like it."

This may have a little relieved my grandfather's feelings but it did not undo what had happened. My Aunt Edith, more sensibly, went to Chicago and came home with the finest set of lead soldiers money could buy. Cavalry officers wearing bearskin busbies and scarlet jackets. On black or white horses. For

many years my brother played with them with passionate pleasure. Nothing could really make up for the fact that he was
doomed to spend the rest of his life putting on and taking off
that artificial limb, and could never again run when he felt like
it, as fast as his two legs would carry him.

Since I was not a natural athlete like my brother, or an athlete
at all, it crossed my mind more than once that having an artificial leg would not have been such a great inconvenience to me,
because what I liked to do best was to retire to some out-of-
the-way corner of the house and read. I even entertained the
fantasy of an exchange with Hap. Along with this idea and
rather at odds with it was a superstitious fear that came over
me from time to time when I remembered that my mother's
only brother lost an arm in an automobile accident when he
was in his early twenties. Was there a kind of family destiny
that would one day overtake me as well?

There was a period in my life when I lay down on a psychoanalyst's couch four times a week and relived the past. Eventually we arrived at my brother's lead soldiers. I begged to be
allowed to play with them and my brother invariably said no.
He kept them out of my reach, on top of a high bookcase.
One day when Hap was out of the house I put a stool on the
seat of a straight chair and climbed up on it. I had just got my
hands on the box when I heard the front door burst open and
my brother called out, "Anybody home?" In my guilty fright I
tried to put the box back, lost my balance, and fell. If my
mother had not appeared from the back part of the house at
that moment, I don't know what my brother would have done
to me. Not one horseman survived intact. I see Hap now, sitting on the floor in the living room, gluing a head back on one
of them. The horse already had a matchstick for one of its hind
legs, so it would stand up. He never forgave me for what I had
done. I didn't expect him to.

The Germanic voice coming from a few feet beyond the
crown of my head suggested that my brother's accident had
been a great misfortune not only for him but for me also;
because I saw what happens to little boys who are incorrigible,
I became a more tractable, more even-tempered, milder person
than it was my true nature to be. About these thoughts that

one is told on good authority one thinks without their ever crossing the threshold of consciousness, what is there to say except "Possibly"? In support of the psychoanalytic conjecture, a submerged memory rose to the surface of my mind. At that Scout camp where Hap won the singles tennis championship I was awarded a baseball glove for Good Conduct.

Who has that picture of Hap sitting on Granny Blinn's shoulders, I wonder. Or the one of him driving a pony cart. It was a postcard—which means that it was taken by a professional photographer. On the reverse someone had written "Edward, aged seven, at the Asylum." It was an odd choice. Uncle Doc was practicing in Bloomington by that time. Did the family, even so, regard the asylum grounds as home territory? The road to the Lincoln Chautauqua ran alongside them, and driving by with my father and mother I used to stare at the inmates standing with their hands and faces pressed against the high wire netting, their mouths permanently slack and sometimes drooling. Perhaps the photographer wanted the institutional flower beds as a background. In the photograph my brother is wearing a small round cap. The pony and cart were not borrowed for the occasion but his own. He is holding the reins, and the pony is, of course, standing still. My brother's chin is raised and he is facing the camera, and the expression on his face is of a heartbreaking uncertainty.

Most children appear to be born with a feeling that life is fair, that it must be. And only with difficulty accommodate themselves to the fact that it isn't. That look on my brother's face—was it because of his sense of the disproportion between the offenses he had committed and the terrible punishment for them? Was he perhaps bracing himself for a second blow, worse than the first one? Or was it because of what happened to him when he left our front yard to play with other children? A little boy who couldn't run away from his tormentors or use his fists to defend himself because they were needed for his crutches, and who could easily be tripped and toppled, was irresistible. Since Hap refused, even so, to give up playing with them, my father paid a colored boy named Dewey Cecil to be his bodyguard.

*

I assumed, irrationally, that Hap would die before I did; he was older and when we were growing up together he always did everything first, while I came along after him and tried to imitate him when it was at all possible. During the past few years I have often thought, When he is gone there will be no one who remembers the things I remember. Meaning the conversations that took place in the morning when he and I were dressing for school. The time we had chicken pox together. The way the light from the low-hanging red-and-green glass shade fell on all our faces as we sat around the dining-room table. The grape arbor by the kitchen door. The closet under the stairs. The hole in the living-room carpet made by the rifle he said wasn't loaded. The time I tried to murder him with a golf club.

We were waiting for my father to finish his foursome, and for lack of anything better to do Hap threw my cap up in a tree, higher than I could reach. I picked up a midiron and started after him. With a double hop, a quick swing with his bum leg, and another double hop he could cover the ground quite fast, but not as fast as I could. I meant to lay him out flat, as he so richly deserved. Walter Kennett, the golf coach, grabbed me and held me until I cooled down.

My brother didn't mind that I had tried to kill him. He always liked it when I showed signs of life.

STORIES 1986–1999

STORIES 1960-1990

Contents

Grape Bay (1941)

A T low tide in Grape Bay, islands with sea grass on them appear and small striped fish are left stranded in the rocks.
It is possible to walk quite far out before you are in water up to
your knees. For hours it is that way. At high tide the islands go
down again and you can swim within six feet of the shore.
There are always a few people on the beach and those few—
Americans, for the most part—know each other intimately.
They sit in a tight circle and make jokes about Bermudians and
rub suntan oil on one another's backs and then stretch out
passively in the sun. Their children in tiny sunsuits go back and
forth with shovels and sand buckets, pouring water into the
sand and sand into the water. Occasionally their dogs go wild
and chase each other through the circle. Everybody sits up
then and complains mildly and brushes the sand off. But after
cigarettes have gone round they relax into positions that are
practically the same as before, except that different people have
assumed them.

A stranger coming to Grape Bay for the first time can open
the circle with a single friendly remark. Sweaters and beach
towels are moved and there is a place for him from then on.
There would have been a place for Hunt if he had spoken to
anybody, but he could never make the first move. It was not
merely shyness. When he was six years old his parents died,
one immediately after the other, and he went to live with his
paternal grandfather, who did not like children. It did not take
him long to learn what it means not to be wanted. Now that
he was grown, his first impulse was always to withdraw before
it became necessary, before someone asked him to.

The first time he appeared at Grape Bay he was ready any
moment to pick up his book and his beach towel and go away.
No one snubbed him or questioned in any way his right to be
on the beach, but no one spoke to him either. It was the same
the next time he came and each time after that. Apparently so
far as the other people on the beach were concerned, he didn't
exist. He could be in the water ten feet from three or four or
five of them and he could duck into wave after wave with them

and come up laughing and they would never know he was there.

When the children tripped and fell crying in front of him he stood them on their feet and told them there, there, they were all right, and they seemed to be grateful. The fact that they did not remember him afterward he attributed to some influence of the place, an influence to be found perhaps on any semitropical island. But it troubled him. He swam or dived into the waves until he was tired and then he went back to that part of the beach he had staked out for himself with his blue bath towel.

If he grew restless from lying too long in the sand he wandered up or down the beach with his shoes under his arm. Up the beach there were arches and caves that at high tide were accessible only from the water. Sand had accumulated inside them and enough light came in for Hunt to be able to read names and dates cut in the damp rock. Down the beach was a limestone cliff with cypress trees growing along the edge. When he had climbed to the top he was hidden from the beach by the trees. He took off his swimming trunks and sunned himself on a big rock, lying now on his back with his eyes closed, now on his stomach with his face resting on his hands. After a while he would crawl to the edge of the cliff and look down. In the clear water directly below he could nearly always find angelfish, poised or darting fiercely at each other. A wave would come in at regular intervals and erase them but when the sea stopped churning they were there again, vermillion and bright blue and sometimes ultramarine.

Hunt was staying at a guesthouse in Paget a mile or two from the shore. As a rule he came down to the beach after breakfast, left his bicycle in the trees, and stayed until lunchtime. In the afternoon he came again. One night after dinner he went outside and got his towel from the line. Nothing extraordinary had prompted him. He hadn't had enough, that was all.

At night everything along the road was unfamiliar. What surprised him most was the bay, which was not luminous as he had imagined but dark all the way out. He got off his bicycle at the top of Strawberry Hill and looked down, as though at a known face that had suddenly become unfriendly. Halfway down the hill was a house with its white roof bare to the sky.

Then the road curved slightly and the grape trees rose up, a region of dense formless shadow. Anything could be down there, he said to himself; and it was that which finally decided him.

At the bottom of the hill it was not so dark but that he found the path and managed to stay on it. When he had made his way through the trees to the beach he saw a light far down, almost at the foot of the cliff. Someone was moving about there with a flashlight. It would stay steady for a moment and then it would dance over the rocks and out toward the water. Hunt spread his towel and sat down.

The fact that he might not have the beach to himself hadn't occurred to him. He waited with a quickening of his heartbeat while the circle of light drew nearer and nearer until there was no question, finally, that the person with the flashlight, whoever it was, had seen him and was coming toward him across the sand. The circle reached Hunt and swung upward past his face. A voice behind the light, a young man's voice, said, "Oh, I'm sorry. I thought you were somebody else."

"That's all right," Hunt said quietly. No one could have told in the dark how disappointed he was. What he had expected was somebody who was looking for him. It had seemed quite possible for a moment. The flashlight turned toward the water. A wave broke across its path and then foam washed in.

"I thought you were Jerry Longtemple," the voice said. "He comes down here sometimes at night. I've seen you on the beach, though. My name is Dick Compton." The flashlight went off.

Hunt stood up and put out his hand in the darkness. "Mine's Hunt," he said.

He could see better without the light. The moment he shook hands with Compton he recognized him. He was younger than Hunt, about twenty-three or four, and he was staying somewhere down the beach. At least he always came from that way. Every day along about noon he would appear in a long white beach robe and make his way down the limestone cliff. It was worth watching. The robe blew out around him like a sail, and he came up the beach without hurrying and took his place in the circle.

"Cigarette?" Compton asked.

"Thanks," Hunt said.

The first two matches went out in the wind but they put their heads and their hands together over the third and it did the trick. The business of lighting cigarettes also formed a bridge that made it possible for them to go on talking. They both sat down on the towel.

"Nice night," Compton said.

"Beautiful!"

"Two or three times when you were down here on the beach I started to come over and talk to you," Compton said. "I like talking to people, but you looked as if you wanted to be by yourself and so I didn't."

Hunt leaned forward until his face was on his knees. "As a matter of fact," he said, "I've had enough of being by myself. If somebody doesn't talk to me pretty soon I'm going to swim out three or four miles and stay."

Compton laughed. "Nobody would talk to you out there," he said.

"How do you know?" Hunt asked, straightening up. "The bottom of the ocean may be a place where people talk and talk, to their heart's content."

"You can do that without drowning," Compton said.

"On dry land," Hunt said, "there's never anybody to talk to. Or if there is, they don't listen, they don't hear half of what you say."

Compton's cigarette flew into the darkness in a wide arc and disappeared twenty feet away.

"I'm listening," he said.

When Hunt came down to the beach next day the wind was blowing off the ocean. He left his bicycle leaning against the same tree and spread his beach towel on the same place in the sand. Anyone watching him would not have noticed the slightest change. Yet the day before was so different to him, so far away that he could hardly remember it.

There were low, swift-moving clouds, and from as far out as he could see, green waves were rolling in and spilling on top of each other. The children had withdrawn to the safety of the beach and were building a sand fortress there. Ordinarily they were scattered up and down the length of Grape Bay, and though two or three would sometimes settle in one spot it was never for long. Something always compelled them to drop what they were doing and go somewhere else. But this morning they were working together with concentration and a single purpose, as if they had decided to anticipate some future development in the race.

By comparison the grownups seemed to have retrogressed. They rode in on waves face down, like drowned people, and the moment they found themselves in shallow water jumped up and ran back for more. Hunt watched them for a while without any desire to become a part of their excitement. Then he made a hollow place for himself in the sand and closed his eyes. An hour passed and he got up suddenly and started running along the strip of hard wet sand. Occasionally he turned and trotted backward with his eyes on the limestone cliff.

The night before, he and Compton had sat side by side for over an hour, talking quietly and steadily, their faces turned toward each other or raised now and then to the sky. They talked about seasons and places, about books, about the war and the draft, about money, about sex, about love. Eventually they talked about death and what chances there were of something coming afterward. Now in broad light, with clouds travelling overhead where the stars had stood in their places, Hunt tried to remember each thing as it had been said, the whole conversation intact. Nothing like it had ever happened to him before. The astonishment of saying what you deeply believe and finding that everybody, or at least one other person, has gone down the same road; that nothing you think or feel is an isolated experience but always belongs to many people at the same time. Even his not knowing that, Hunt decided, was probably as much a part of the pattern as all the rest.

He felt drawn to Compton and curious about him—about where he lived, whether he was married or single, what he did for a living. At the time, their conversation had seemed intimate, but he realized now that it had been limited entirely to generalities, and that the first interruption had been sufficient to bring it to an end. While he was explaining why there could be no such thing as the immortality of the soul, Compton's flashlight went on with no warning and he rolled over on his side to look at a sand crab. It waved its claws at them irritably and, with both Compton and Hunt following, retreated across the sand. When it couldn't get away from the flashlight it suddenly dug down out of sight and left the two of them standing there.

There were so many arches and caves to explore that Hunt had never gone beyond the point where they ended. This morning he kept on until he came to sheer rock, which drove him back from the water and onto higher ground. There the trees closed in around him. When they opened again he found himself looking down on a huge pink hotel with acres of windows all shuttered tight, a casualty of the war. In Hamilton and on St. David's, where the American bases were being constructed, there were constant reminders of what was going on in Europe. But only when planes flew low over the beach or when the wind carried the sound of remote rifle practice did the war's shadow fall on this side of the island.

At this season of the year the windows of the hotel should have been wide open and looking out to sea. The grass should have been cut, the hibiscus hedges neatly trimmed. There ought to have been flowers. Shouts ought to have been coming from the tennis courts—"Deuce" . . . "Yours, partner" . . . "Deuce again." People ought to have been sitting around on deck chairs or at little tables under striped umbrellas. They ought to have been drinking long summer drinks and enjoying the fact that it was winter. Actually, though, there wasn't a living person in sight. Around the walks the grass was nearly knee high. Wild morning glories had taken possession of the tennis courts. The outdoor swimming pool was beginning to fill up with leaves.

The strange thing was that Hunt was not surprised by any of it. He had a curious feeling, as he turned and made his way back into the trees, that he had known about this place all along; that he had known exactly how it would be.

It was late in the morning when he got back to Grape Bay. He stumbled over the ruins of the sand fortress. The grown people, with the exception of a colored nurse, were huddled in their usual group. Compton was with them and sat with his back to the direction from which Hunt had come. His white beach robe was wrapped around his shoulders as a protection against the wind.

Hunt settled down in his own place and put half his mind
on a week-old copy of *Time* magazine, which he had found
lying on the beach. National and foreign affairs were damp
and stuck together. He was experimenting with various ways
of pulling pages apart when there was a violent upheaval
nearby. People rose to their knees, shouted, threw sand and
shells at one of the dogs, and finally drove him away. In that
interval Compton saw Hunt and came over.

"Hello," he said. "I looked for you when I first came down."

"I've been up the beach," Hunt said. He kept out of his
voice his pleasure in the fact that someone had at last been
looking for him, but when he smiled it broke out all over his
face. "What's the matter over there?" he asked. The circle was
quieter, though murmurs and exclamations of annoyance continued to go around.

"Oh, it's just Bert," Compton said.

"That woolly black-and-white dog?"

"Yes," Compton said. "He lifts his leg on people's clothes
wherever he finds them, and then five minutes later he comes
back expecting to be loved."

They both laughed, and Compton sat down tailor fashion
and began sifting handfuls of sand. He seemed to have little to
say this morning.

One topic of conversation after another died of its own
weight until he suggested that they go join the circle. Hunt
found himself then, as he had so often imagined, being introduced to Mrs. Rawson, to Mr. Hardy, to Jerry Longtemple,
Miss Clark, Mr. Draper, Mrs. Longtemple, Mrs. Clark, Mr.
Fearing, Madame Miramova, Mr. Hall. Seen from close up,
however, they were neither so charming nor so young as Hunt
had thought they were. It was like sitting in the front row at
the theatre and being conscious of greasepaint.

From the other side of the circle Mrs. Longtemple smiled at
Hunt and said, "Do you mind telling me how old you are?"

"He's twenty-eight," Jerry Longtemple said.

Hunt nodded.

"My son has no manners," Mrs. Longtemple said. "You
mustn't pay any attention to him. I have an older son who is in
the Navy. He looks quite like you. I think that must be the reason why I hanker for you."

"My mother also has a niece who is about your age," Jerry Longtemple said. "Lovely girl. Wears her hair parted in the middle, with little ribbons, and she's very anxious to marry again."

For a moment Hunt was embarrassed and colored deeply, but no one seemed to be paying any attention. The others were all talking about an American millionaire who owned most of Grape Bay and had built a large house overlooking it, on the top of the hill. Mrs. Clark had been there for tea, four years ago.

"He told me he bought it—all of it—in 1931 for fifty thousand dollars, his idea being that if worst came to worst he could always retire to this place and keep a cow and raise potatoes." Mrs. Clark looked around to see if her audience was amused. "Then he spent another hundred thousand dollars on the house," she continued, "and lived in it one winter from December to the middle of February." A small boy in a red sunsuit, with yellow curls under his straw hat, came and stood beside her, waiting for her to finish her story. "That was the winter it rained all the time," she said, "and so he hasn't been back since. . . . What is it, darling?"

What Mrs. Clark's little boy wanted was to be allowed to eat lunch with her, and after some discussion it was arranged. She took his hat off and brushed the hair out of his eyes, and he wandered off, stubbing his toe and getting up again.

The woman next to Hunt, Mrs. Rawson, asked him where he was staying. He started to describe the guesthouse and her attention wandered. He kept on doggedly, and when he had finished she said she thought she knew where it was. Then she leaned over his knees and spoke to Compton. "When's your sister coming, Dick?"

"Saturday morning," Compton said. He was stretched out flat, his face shielded by one arm.

"I must give a cocktail party for her," Mrs. Rawson said.

"I doubt if she'll let you," Compton said. He took his arm away and smiled at her, a smile that was disarming and satisfied Mrs. Rawson but not Hunt, who excused himself politely and went toward the water. He understood now why Compton had seemed so restless and uncommunicative, and he told himself, as the first wave broke over him, that there was no reason why Compton should have mentioned his sister or the fact that she was coming. The second wave caught him off balance, rolled him over and over along the bottom, and flung him gasping on the wet sand.

At quarter to seven on boat days a line of carriages formed in front of the customs house. The sound they made going through the streets, the trotting sound, sank in upon Hunt's half-awakened mind. Two separate stages of his life stirred in him. He was in the uncertain present and also in that far-off beginning when people were just changing over from horses to automobiles and his childhood existence was still ringed round with security and love. It took him a moment after he had opened his eyes to adjust himself to his loss.

An hour later during breakfast two deep blasts announced the anchoring of the boat. The quiet was so full of anticipation that Hunt took his coffee outside on the upper veranda and waited for the carriages. At first the traffic was all toward Hamilton, toward the waterfront; but suddenly there was a turning and everything seemed to come from the opposite direction, all the carriages returning now with tourists in them, with the fringed carriage tops bobbing and the drivers talking loudly and pointing with their whips. Though Hunt watched each one, peering at the people in it until the carriage had gone by, there was no face he recognized. Finally the traffic subsided to its ordinary level: a Negro on his way to work, a man driving a team of mules.

Hunt continued to sit there, watching the Portuguese gardener work his way along the flower beds and keeping track of two small lizards who were sunning themselves in a nearby flowering tree. When he could not sit still any longer he walked back and forth on the veranda, talking to himself, disposing of something now which would never have to be disposed of again. He had always gone everywhere and done everything by himself. He always would. The conversation on the beach that night had been an accident and hadn't changed anything, but only made it necessary for him to understand once and for all what kind of person he was. No matter where he was he would never belong, he would always stay on the sidelines, hungry-eyed. That was his nature. There were people of another kind, who never actually saw anything but whose very existence was wonderful because without any effort on their part you were continually aware of them. Such an attraction was not human necessarily. It belonged as much to the order of animals and things. And since it was everywhere there was no point in trying to possess it. That was what it meant to be grown up, to be mature. You could look at a bronze tiger in a hotel lobby and instantly it was yours. Having had it for that length of time (which would be plenty long enough) you could go on about your business. You did not have to find the hotel manager and make him an offer. Even if you wanted to, you could not carry around with you the intolerable burden of all the things and all the people in the world. It was enough that you yourself were alive and perceptive to their quality, whatever it was.

Before the boat sailed that afternoon Hunt rode into Hamilton to cash a check. When he came out of Trimingham's he had to wait, the street being full of carriages and bicycles, and he saw Compton with a girl who looked exactly like him, even to the excitement and the color of her eyes. The girl was having a terrible time to keep from falling off her bicycle, and Compton was laughing at her. Hunt swallowed hard. The old unvarying negative impulse rose to take possession of him, but he continued to stand there looking at Compton and that girl, who were somehow in themselves everything he had ever wanted to be or have. They were so close he could have stepped in front of them. He didn't move, though, or make a sound until they had passed. Then he turned suddenly and ran after them with his heart beating wildly and a feeling inside him like hundreds of windows being opened, like sunlight shining on the sea.

The Lily-White Boys

THE Follansbees' Christmas party was at teatime on Christmas Day, and it was for all ages. Ignoring the fire laws, the big Christmas tree standing between the two front windows in the living room of the Park Avenue apartment had candles on it. When the last one was lit, somebody flipped a light switch, and in the hush that fell over the room the soft yellow candlelight fell on the upturned faces of the children sitting on the floor in a ring around the base of the tree, bringing tears to the eyes of the susceptible. The tree was strung with loops of gold and silver tinsel and popcorn and colored paper, and some of the glass ornaments—the hardy tin soldier, the drum, the nutmeg, and the Man in the Moon—went all the way back to Beth Follansbee's childhood. While the presents were being distributed, Mark Follansbee stood by with a bucket of water and a broom. The room smelled of warm wax and balsam.

The big red candles on the mantelpiece burned down slowly in their nest of holly. In the dining room, presiding over the cut-glass punch bowl, Beth Follansbee said, "You let the peaches sit all day in a quart of vodka, and then you add two bottles of white wine and a bottle of champagne—be a little careful, it isn't as innocuous as you might think," and with her eyebrows she signaled to the maid that the plate of watercress sandwiches needed refilling. Those that liked to sing had gathered around the piano in the living room and, having done justice to all the familiar carols, were singing with gusto, "Seven for the seven stars in the sky and six for the six proud walkers. Five for the symbols at your door and four for the Gospel makers, Three, three, the rivals, Two, two, the lily-white boys, clothèd all in green-ho. One is one and all alone and evermore shall *be* so." And an overexcited little boy with a plastic spaceship was running up and down the hall and shouting "Blast off!"

The farewells at the elevator door were followed by a second round down below on the sidewalk while the doorman was blowing his whistle for cabs.

"Can we drop you?" Ellen Hunter called.

"No. You're going downtown, and it would be out of your way," Celia Coleman said.

The Colemans walked two blocks north on Park and then east. The sidewalks of Manhattan were bare, the snow the weatherman promised having failed to come. There were no stars, and the night sky had a brownish cast. From a speaker placed over the doorway of a darkened storefront human voices sang "O Little Town of Bethlehem." The drugstore on the corner was brightly lighted but locked, with the iron grating pulled down and no customers inquiring about cosmetics at the cash register or standing in front of the revolving Timex display unable to make up their minds.

The Venetian-red door of the Colemans' house was level with the sidewalk and had a Christmas wreath on it. In an eerie fashion it swung open when Dan Coleman tried to fit his key in the lock.

"Did we forget to close it?" Celia said and he shook his head. The lock had been jimmied.

"I guess it's our turn," he said grimly as they walked in. At the foot of the stairs they stood still and listened. Nothing on the first floor was disturbed. There was even a silver spoon and a small silver tray on the dining-room sideboard. Looking at each other they half managed to believe that everything was all right; the burglars had been frightened by somebody coming down the street, or a squad car perhaps, and had cleared out without taking anything. But the house felt queer, not right somehow, not the way it usually felt, and they saw why when they got to the top of the first flight of stairs.

"Sweet Jesus!" he exclaimed softly, and she thought of her jewelry.

The shades were drawn to the sills, so that people on the sidewalk or in the apartments across the way could not see in the windows. One small detail caught his eye in the midst of the general destruction. A Limoges jar that held potpourri lay in fragments on the hearth and a faint odor of rose petals hung on the air.

With her heart beating faster than usual and her mouth as dry as cotton she said, "I can understand why they might want to look behind the pictures, but why walk on them?"

"Saves time," he said.

"And why break the lamps?"

"I don't know," he said. "I have never gone in for house-breaking."

A cigarette had been placed at the edge of a tabletop, right next to an ashtray, and allowed to burn all the way down. The liquor cupboard was untouched. In the study, on that same floor at the back of the house, where the hi-fi, the tape deck, and the TV should have been there was a blank space. Rather than bother to unscrew the cable, the burglars had snipped it with wire cutters. All the books had been pulled from the shelves and lay in mounds on the floor.

"Evidently they are not readers," he said, and picked up volume seven of *Hakluyt's Voyages* and stood it on an empty shelf.

She tried to think of a reason for not going up the next flight to the bedrooms, to make the uncertainty last a little longer. Rather than leave her jewelry in the bank and never have the pleasure of wearing it, she had hidden it in a place that seemed to her very clever.

It was not clever enough. The star ruby ring, the cabochon emeralds, the gold bracelets, the moonstones, the garnet necklace that had been her father's wedding present to her mother, the peridot-and-tourmaline pin that she found in an antique shop on a back street in Toulon, the diamond earrings—gone. All gone. Except for the things Dan had given her they were all inherited and irreplaceable, and so what would be the point of insuring them.

"In a way it's a relief," she said, in what sounded to her, though not to him, like her normal voice.

"Meaning?"

"Meaning that you can't worry about possessions you no longer have."

She opened the top right-hand drawer of her dressing table and saw that the junk jewelry was still there. As she pushed the drawer shut he said, "The standard procedure," and took her in his arms.

The rest was also pretty much the standard procedure. Mattresses were pulled half off the beds and ripped open with a razor blade, drawers turned upside down, and his clothes closet completely empty, which meant his wardrobe now consisted of the dark-blue suit he had put on earlier this evening to go to the Follansbees' Christmas party. Her dresses lay in a colored confusion that spilled out into the room from the floor of her walk-in closet. Boxes from the upper shelves had been pulled down and ransacked—boxes containing hats, evening purses, evening dresses she no longer had occasion to wear, since they seldom went out at night except to go to the theater or dine with friends.

When the police came she let him do the talking. Christmas Eve, Christmas Day were the prime moments for break-ins, they said. The house had probably been watched. They made a list of the more important things and suggested that Dan send them an inventory. They were pleasant and held out no hope. There were places they could watch, they said, to see if anything belonging to the Colemans turned up, but chances were that . . . When they left he put the back of a chair against the doorknob of the street door and started up the stairs.

From the stairs he could see into their bedroom. To his astonishment Celia had on an evening dress he hadn't seen for twenty years. Turning this way and that, she studied her reflection in the full-length mirror on the back of a closet door. Off the dress came, over her head, and she worked her way into a scarlet chiffon sheath that had a sooty footprint on it. Her hair had turned from dark brown to grey and when she woke up in the morning her back was as stiff as a board, but the dress fit her perfectly. While he stood there, watching, and unseen, she tried them on, one after another—the black taffeta with the bouffant skirt, the pale sea-green silk with bands of matching silk fringe—all her favorite dresses that she had been too fond of to take to a thrift shop, and that had been languishing on the top shelf of her closet. As she stepped back to consider critically the effect of a white silk evening suit, her high heels ground splinters of glass into the bedroom rug.

Its load lightened by a brief stop in the Bronx at a two-story warehouse that was filled from floor to ceiling with hi-fi sets and color TVs, the Chrysler sedan proceeded along the Bruckner Elevated Expressway to Route 95. When the car slowed down for the tollgate at the Connecticut state line, the sandy-haired recidivist, slouched down in the right-hand front seat, opened his eyes. The false license plates aroused no interest whatever as the car came to a stop and then drove on.

In the middle of the night, the material witnesses to the breaking and entering communicated with one another, a remark at a time. A small spotlight up near the ceiling that was trained on an area over the living-room sofa said, *When I saw the pictures being ripped from the walls I was afraid. I thought I was going to go the same way.*

So fortunate, they were, the red stair-carpet said, and the stair-rail said, *Fortunate? How?*

The intruders were gone when they came home.

I had a good look at them, said the mirror over the lowboy in the downstairs hall. *They were not at all like the Colemans' friends or the delivery boys from Gristede's and the fish market.*

The Colemans' friends don't break in the front door, the Sheraton sideboard said. *They ring and then wait for somebody to come and open it.*

She will have my top refinished, said the table with the cigarette scar. *The number is in the telephone turnaround. She knows about that sort of thing and he doesn't. But it will take a while. And the room will look odd without me.*

It took a long time to make that star ruby, said a small seashell on the mantelpiece.

Precious stones you can buy, said the classified directory. *Van Cleef & Arpels. Harry Winston. And auctions at Christie's and Sotheby Parke Bernet. It is the Victorian and Edwardian settings that were unusual. I don't suppose the thieves will know enough to value them.*

They will be melted down, said the brass fire irons, *into unidentifiability. It happens every day.*

Antique jewelry too can be picked up at auction places. Still, it is disagreeable to lose things that have come down in the family. It isn't something one would choose to have happen.

There are lots of things one would not choose to have happen that do happen, said the fire irons.

With any unpleasantness, said the orange plastic Design Research kitchen wall clock, *it is better to take the long view.*

Very sensible of them to fall asleep the minute their heads hit the pillow, said the full-length mirror in the master bedroom. *Instead of turning and tossing and going over in their minds the things they have lost, that are gone forever.*

They have each other, a small bottle of Elizabeth Arden perfume spray said. *They will forget about what happened this evening. Or, if they remember, it will be something they have ceased to have much feeling about, a story they tell sometimes at dinner parties, when the subject of robberies comes up. He will tell how they walked home from the Follansbees' on Christmas night and found the front door ajar, and she will tell about the spoon and the silver tray the thieves didn't take, and he will tell how he stood on the stairs watching while she tried on all her favorite evening dresses.*

What He Was Like

HE kept a diary, for his own pleasure. Because the days passed by so rapidly, and he found it interesting to go back and see how he had occupied his time, and with whom. He was aware that his remarks were sometimes far from kind, but the person they were about was never going to read them, so what difference did it make? The current diary was usually on his desk, the previous ones on a shelf in his clothes closet, where they were beginning to take up room.

His wife's uncle, in the bar of the Yale Club, said, "I am at the age of funerals." Now, thirty-five years later, it was his turn. In his address book the names of his three oldest friends had lines drawn through them. "Jack is dead," he wrote in his diary. "I didn't think that would happen. I thought he was immortal. . . . Louise is dead. In her sleep. . . . Richard has been dead for over a year and I still do not believe it. So impoverishing."

He himself got older. His wife got older. They advanced deeper into their seventies without any sense of large changes but only of one day's following another, and of the days being full, and pleasant, and worth recording. So he went on doing it. They all got put down in his diary, along with his feelings about old age, his fear of dying, his declining sexual powers, his envy of the children that he saw running down the street. To be able to run like that! He had to restrain himself from saying to young men in their thirties and forties, "You do appreciate, don't you, what you have?" In his diary he wrote, "If I had my life to live over again—but one doesn't. One goes forward instead, dragging a cart piled high with lost opportunities."

Though his wife had never felt the slightest desire to read his diary, she knew when he stopped leaving it around as carelessly as he did his opened mail. Moving the papers on his desk in order to dust it she saw where he had hidden the current volume, was tempted to open it and see what it was he didn't want her to know, and then thought better of it and replaced the papers, exactly as they were before.

"To be able to do in your mind," he wrote, "what it is

731

probably not a good idea to do in actuality is a convenience not always sufficiently appreciated." Though in his daily life he was as cheerful as a cricket, the diaries were more and more given over to dark thoughts, anger, resentment, indecencies, regrets, remorse. And now and then the simple joy in being alive. "If I stopped recognizing that I want things that it is not appropriate for me to want," he wrote, "wouldn't this inevitably lead to my not wanting anything at all—which as people get older is a risk that must be avoided at all costs?" He wrote, "Human beings are not like a clock that is wound up at birth and runs until the mainspring is fully unwound. They live because they want to. And when they stop wanting to, the first thing they know they are in a doctor's office being shown an X ray that puts a different face on everything."

After he died, when the funeral had been got through, and after the number of telephone calls had diminished to a point where it was possible to attend to other things, his wife and and daughter together disposed of the clothes in his closet. His daughter folded and put in a suit box an old, worn corduroy coat that she remembered the feel of when her father had rocked her as a child. His wife kept a blue-green sweater that she was used to seeing him in. As for the rest, he was a common size, and so his shirts and suits were easily disposed of to people who were in straitened circumstances and grateful for a warm overcoat, a dark suit, a pair of pigskin gloves. His shoes were something else again, and his wife dropped them into the Goodwill box, hoping that somebody would turn up who wore size-9A shoes, though it didn't seem very likely. Then the two women were faced with the locked filing cabinet in his study, which contained business papers that they turned over to the executor, and most of the twenty-seven volumes of his diary.

"Those I don't know what to do with, exactly," his wife said. "They're private and he didn't mean anybody to read them."

"Did he say so?" his daughter said.

"No."

"Then how do you know he didn't want anybody to read them?"

"I just know."

"You're not curious?"

"I was married to your father for forty-six years and I know what he was like."

Which could only mean, the younger woman decided, that her mother had, at some time or other, looked into them. But she loved her father, and felt a very real desire to know what he was like as a person and not just as a father. So she put one of the diaries aside and took it home with her.

When her husband got home from his office that night, her eyes were red from weeping. First he made her tell him what the trouble was, and then he went out to the kitchen and made a drink for each of them, and then he sat down beside her on the sofa. Holding his free hand, she began to tell him about the shock of reading the diary.

"He wasn't the person I thought he was. He had all sorts of secret desires. A lot of it is very dirty. And some of it is more unkind than I would have believed possible. And just not like him—except that it *was* him. It makes me feel I can never trust anybody ever again."

"Not even me?" her husband said soberly.

"Least of all, you."

They sat in silence for a while. And then he said, "I was more comfortable with him than I was with my own father. And I think, though I could be mistaken, that he liked me."

"Of course he liked you. He often said so."

"So far as his life is concerned, if you were looking for a model to—"

"I don't see how you can say that."

"I do, actually. In his place, though, I think I would have left instructions that the diaries were to be disposed of unread. . . . We could burn it. Burn all twenty-seven volumes."

"No."

"Then put it back in the locked file where your mother found it," he said.

"And leave it there forever?"

"For a good long while. He may have been looking past our shoulders. It would be like him. If we have a son who doesn't seem to be very much like you or me, or like anybody in your family or mine, we can give him the key to the file—"

"If I had a son the *last* thing in the world I'd want would be for him to read this filth!"

"—and tell him he can read them if he wants to. And if he doesn't want to, he can decide what should be done with them. It might be a help to him to know that there was somebody two generations back who wasn't in every respect what he seemed to be."

"Who was, in fact—"

"Since he didn't know your father, he won't be shocked and upset. You stay right where you are while I make us another of these."

But she didn't. She didn't want to be separated from him, even for the length of time it would take him to go out to the kitchen and come back with a margarita suspended from the fingers of each hand, lest in that brief interval he turn into a stranger.

The Room Outside

THE house on Ninth Street, where I lived as a child, had eleven-foot ceilings, and the downstairs rooms opened out of each other and were hard to heat. In late October, with the coal bill much on his mind, my father went from room to room downstairs stuffing toilet paper in the cracks between the windows and the window frames. Storm windows would have been better but they were unknown in our part of the country in the early decades of this century. There was a fireplace in the living room and another in the room we called the library, and when anyone tried to start a fire in either of them puffs of smoke would blow out into the room. The chimneys do not draw well when they are cold, and from the window seat in the library I watch as my father arranges paper and kindling properly between the andirons, and then the logs, and puts a match to the paper and stands holding an opened-out page of the Lincoln *Evening Courier* across the upper part of the opening and waits patiently for the air to start going up the chimney instead of out into the room. If I pull the curtain around me and look out into the winter night, I see the house next door, the fence that divides our yard from the neighbors', a tree trunk, sometimes the moon. If I let the curtain fall back what I see is a reflection of the room I am in, superimposed on what is really out there. When the newspaper catches on fire and vanishes up the flue (because it has now begun to draw properly), I see that, too, reflected in the windowpane.

In the winter of 1931 I have taken the train from Boston to Providence to spend the day with Cletus Oakley and his wife. I am a graduate student at Harvard and he is teaching at Brown. When I was a freshman at the University of Illinois he made it impossible for me not to understand differential and integral calculus. Now, in his car, we drive to some place near Pomfret, Connecticut, where the snow lies across the countryside in deep drifts. He has brought snowshoes for the three of us. I have never had snowshoes on before and find it difficult to keep from stepping on my own feet. We talk as we walk and sometimes I trip and fall and Cletus helps me up. The sun is shining out of a cobalt-blue sky and the air is so dry that breathing is a pleasure. (Why did I never see them again when I liked them so much? How could I have been so stupid as to leave everything, including friendships, to chance?) When the light begins to fail, Cletus drives us to an eighteenth-century house, and there an old woman gives us tea and hot biscuits and honey. We are happy because of the fresh air and exercise, and she is happy because the spring garden catalogues have come.

When I was in my middle twenties I spent a winter on a farm in southern Wisconsin. There it was much colder than it was in Illinois, where, with the wind coming down off Lake Michigan, God knows it is cold enough. Bales of hay were banked all around the foundations of the farmhouse, which was heated by two sheet-iron wood-burning stoves, one upstairs and one downstairs in the room next to my small bedroom. And, of course, the cookstove in the kitchen. In the morning when I woke I sometimes saw a broad band of yellow light in the sky that I have never seen anywhere else, and before I could wash my face I often had to break a thin glaze of ice in the water pitcher on my dresser. The window had to be propped open, by a wooden spool in ordinary weather, a smaller spool if the temperature was twenty below, and if it was colder than that I didn't open the window at all. It was up to me to see that the woodbox in the kitchen was never empty and fill the reservoir on the side of the stove. The air was usually so dry you could run out of the house in your shirtsleeves and fill a bucket of water at the pump but you couldn't touch the pump handle with your bare hands. I also had to keep a patch of ground bare and sprinkled with corn for the quail. If it rained when the temperature was hovering around thirty-two degrees their feathers froze and they couldn't fly into the shelter of the woods.

Eventually there was so much snow on the roads that the snowplow couldn't get through and we were snowbound. One evening after supper the telephone rang and it was a neighbor saying that the mailman had got as far as the Four Corners, where our mailbox was. I put on extra-heavy underwear and, bundled to the eyes in sweaters and woollen scarves, I started to ski to the Four Corners. The snowdrifts were higher than the horse-and-rider fences, obliterating the divisions between the fields, and I saw what nobody in the family and none of the neighboring farmers had ever seen: a pack of wild dogs running in a circle in the bright moonlight.

My wife and I are planning to spend the first Christmas of our married life in Oregon with her mother and father. We have been living in a small, one-story house in northern Westchester County. It started to snow at dusk the evening before our departure and it has snowed all night. The view from the kitchen window is cribbed from John Greenleaf Whittier. The town snowplows have kept our road open and a taxi delivers us at Harmon station in plenty of time, but for the last hour no trains have come into or left the station. The ticket agent is noncommittal. We wait and wait, consult the station clock, count our luggage. Privately I entertain the possibility that we will spend this Christmas at home. At that moment, far down the tracks to the south, there is a light. "The Twentieth Century Limited to Chicago arriving on Track Four!" the ticket agent announces over the public-address system, and in no time at all we are in our snug compartment looking out at the snow falling in the Hudson River. We are off. We have got away. Upstate New York, Pennsylvania, Ohio, and Indiana are like a long, uninterrupted, white thought. In Chicago the slush is ankle deep. Then we pick up the thought where we left off. It is winter all the way across the Great Plains and the Rocky Mountains, but in Portland there is no snow on the ground and the camellias are in bloom.

Several families have lived in the house on Ninth Street since my father sold it and some of them loved it as much as I did. They also made changes. Out of kindness, people—sometimes acquaintances, sometimes strangers—send me snapshots of the exterior from the front or the side. Our trees have died of old age or the elm blight and been replaced by others, but why the shutters, and what in Heaven's name happened to the porch railing? Nothing is right that isn't the way I remember it, and

I drop the snapshots in the wastebasket. That room outside, superimposed on the snow: the reflection of the lamp, the table and the chair where my mother likes to sit when she sews, the white bookcase, the Oriental rugs, the man standing at the fireplace and the little boy peering out at the night—that image that was nothing more than a trick of the window glass—is indestructible.

A SET OF TWENTY-ONE
IMPROVISATIONS

Contents

1. *A love story*

"MADAME MOLE," everyone said, out of respect. For what she was and how she did things. The thick fur and the usually cold eye that saw immediately the disadvantages of a poorly located and badly laid out tunnel. Her own tunnel had never been equaled and indeed the full extent of it, taking both the upper and the lower level into consideration, was only guessed at, for visitors had seen only the first hundred ante-rooms. She was descended on her mother's side from the Moles of Longview, whose enormous spreading family tree had for its trunk a mole brought over in a cage by one of William the Conqueror's body servants. It escaped during the Battle of Hastings, into a land that had hitherto been happily free of them, and before that fatal moment when Harold glanced up at the sun and received an arrow in his eye, the mole had already established a temporary home under the battle-field. The family was ennobled under William Rufus, for the harassment they had caused the Saxons, and Charles II made the ninetieth baronet an earl in gratitude for the number of Cromwell's horses that had stepped in a tunnel and—but it is better not to go into all that, especially if you like horses. In a time of war, disasters are to be expected, unless you are a mole and can go below into the silence of old roots, and sleeping grubs, and ant chambers, flints, and fossils.

Madame Mole's husband was never called anything but Mole, for she had married beneath her. His family didn't bear thinking of, but he was a large good-natured willing creature, and, though not very many of her acquaintances realized this, she would have been nowhere without him. For she designed the new shafts of her great masterwork and he went to work with the hard end of his socially undistinguished nose and by nightfall there the new shaft was, ready for her to explore, and having reached the end of it, they would settle down cozily to-gether and she would chew his ears by way of showing her love and appreciation. Then she would go about arranging the fur-niture and putting out pieces of bone china where they would show to advantage. What is the natural life of a mole? I don't actually know, but a good long time, I should think. Mole traps rust immediately and are notoriously inefficient, and what exasperated gardener is willing to stand waiting at twenty minutes after 10 a.m. and twenty minutes after 4 p.m. for the barely perceptible heaving at the end of a run, and start furiously digging with a spade when it begins. Not one mole in a hundred thousand meets with an accident of any kind, and when it does happen you can be sure it was because they had grown careless. What happened to Madame Mole and her husband was something so much larger than a mere accident that they were at a loss to describe it. They were lying in bed one morning and she was comfortably chewing on his ear, when he saw that the bedroom chandelier was swinging. "Stop jiggling the bed," she said, and he said, "I'm not. *It's* doing it." At which point all the fine china plates fell off the wall and broke into smithereens and dirt began raining down on the bedsheets. While he was taking in what was happening, she leapt out of bed and rushed to each of the seven doors in turn. What should have been a shaft, and *was* a shaft when they went to sleep the night before, was blocked with stones, timbers, and rubbish. In places she could see the sky, and it would not have been too difficult to tunnel up into the open, at this stage, but think what would meet them if they did! She took hold of his ear with her teeth and dragged him out of the bed and under it, and while she lay huddled next to him in fright, he put his hard nose to the ground and started tunneling. Straight down, hour after hour, without any plan to guide him or any consideration for how it would look when the furniture was arranged and the china plates hung where they would show to best advantage: The Longview Willow and Spode that had come down to her from the Shaftsburys, and the hand-painted Limoges chocolate set that was a wedding present from Cousin Emma Noseby and I forget what all, but *she* never forgot. An earthquake was what they assumed it must be, and it did bear certain resemblances to an earthquake, for after a period of very difficult going suddenly they would find themselves in a fissure leading straight down toward the center of the earth, and then it was possible to make very good progress with no effort what-

soever. Machines is what it was. Huge yellow machines rented
out by an Italian contractor at two, three, and four hundred
dollars a day. Weighing many tons. Big enough to lift great
trees and fling them aside, with their roots exposed to the
shocked gaze of the sky. The arrangements of thousands and
thousands of years—roots, stones, fossilized ferns, and fossilized fish from the earliest years of the planet were crushed,
scraped up in huge mechanical shovels, poured into trucks,
and hauled away to desecrate some other part of the landscape.
And if Madame Mole and Mole had emerged from their
ruined mansion to see what was happening, they would have
been scooped up with the Longview Willow, and the sweet-
smelling leaf mold of centuries, the dear green grass, and the
murdered trees. There had been nothing to equal it in the way
of pure destruction since the Battle of Hastings. If it had been
for a housing development Madame Mole would have perhaps
accepted it with some degree of philosophic resignation. She
could understand homemaking even when it was aboveground
and so not very practical. But this was to make an eight-lane
highway for cars, a means for more people to get away from
their homes faster, because of all the things that had made home
unbearable—the polluted air, the noise of jet airplanes and so
on. It is just as well they never knew the nature of the disaster
that sent them down, down, down to the center of the earth.
When they reached it they had no idea. It was dark there, of
course, and he had left his wristwatch on the table beside their
bed, and so they simply kept on going. When he grew tired or
discouraged she chewed on his ear until he felt better. And
when she wept thinking of all of her treasures left behind, he
curled his fur tightly around her fur and in the shared warmth
they fell asleep. And when they woke he commenced digging.
Eventually the soil began to be looser, and the grubs more frequent, and finally there were root hairs and then big roots and
suddenly without any warning they emerged into broad daylight. They were in a terraced field, on a mountainside, in a
country that Madame Mole recognized instantly because there
was the blue leaning willow tree, and there was the lake, and
the bluebird in the sky, and the blue curlicue clouds, and the
houses with eaves that curled up at the corners. It was a view

she had seen ever since she could remember, because it was on every single piece of the Longview Willow china. "Oh you clever Mole, how glad I am I married you!" she cried, and they withdrew into the tunnel so that, chewing on his ear, she could plan the layout of their new home.

2. The industrious tailor

O NCE upon a time, in the west of England, there was an industrious tailor who was always sitting cross-legged, plying his needle, when the sun came up over the hill, and all day long he drove himself, as if he were beating a donkey with a stick. "I am almost through cutting out this velvet waistcoat," he would tell himself, "and when I am through cutting the velvet, I will cut the yellow satin lining. And then there is the buckram, and the collar and cuffs. The cuffs are to be thirteen inches wide, tapering to ten and a half—his lordship was very particular about that detail—and faced with satin. The basting should take me into the afternoon, and if all goes well, and I don't see why it shouldn't, I ought to be able to do all twenty-seven buttonholes before the light gives out."

When snow lay deep on the ground and the sheep stayed in their pens, the shepherd came down to the tavern and in the conviviality he found there made up for the months of solitude on the moors. During the early part of the summer, when it was not yet time for anybody to be bringing wheat, barley, and rye to the mill to be ground into flour, the miller got out his hook and line and went fishing. In one way or another, everyone had some time that he called his own. On the first of May, lads and lasses went into the wood just before daybreak and came back wearing garlands of flowers and with their arms around each other. From his window the tailor saw them setting up the Maypole, but he did not lay aside his needle and thread to go join in the dancing. It is true that he was no longer young and, with his bald head and his bent back and his solemn manner, would have looked odd dancing around a Maypole, but that did not deter the miller's wife, who weighed seventeen stone and was as light on her feet as a fairy and didn't care who laughed at her as long as she was enjoying herself.

When the industrious tailor came to the end of all the work that he could expect for a while and his worktable was quite bare, he looked around for some lily that needed gilding. Sorting his pins, sharpening his scissors, and rearranging his

747

patterns, he congratulated himself on keeping busy, though he might just as well have been sitting in his doorway enjoying the sun, for his scissors didn't need sharpening, and his patterns were not in disorder, and a pin is a pin, no matter what tray you put it in.

As with all of us, the tailor's upbringing had a good deal to do with the way he behaved. At the age of eight, he was apprenticed to his father, who was a master tailor and not only knew all there is to know about making clothes but also was full of native wisdom. While the boy was learning to sew a straight seam and how to cut cloth on the diagonal and that sort of thing, the father would from time to time raise his right hand, with the needle and thread in it, and, looking at the boy over the top of his spectacles, say "A stitch in time saves nine," or "Waste makes want," or some other bit of advice, which the boy took to his bosom and cherished. And he had never forgotten a wonderful story his father told about an ant and a grasshopper. Of all his father's sayings, the one that made the deepest impression on him was "Never put off till tomorrow what you can do today," though as a rule the industrious tailor had already done it yesterday and was hard at work on something that did not need to be done until the day after.

What is true of the day after tomorrow is equally true of the day after that, and the day after that, and the day after that, and so on, and in time a very curious thing happened. There was the past—there is always the past—and it was full of accomplishment, of things done well before they needed to be done, and the tailor regarded it with satisfaction. And there was the future, when things would have to be done, and bills would have to be made out and respectfully submitted and paid or not paid, as the case might be, and new work would be ordered, and so on. But it was never right now. The present had ceased to exist. When the industrious tailor looked out of the window and saw that it was raining, it was not raining today but on a day in the middle of next week, or the week after that, if he was that far ahead of himself, and he often was. You would have thought that he would sooner or later have realized that the time he was spending so freely was next month's, and that if he had already lived through the days of this month before it was well begun he was living beyond his means. But what is "already"? What is "now"? The words had lost their meaning. And this was not as serious as it sounds, because words are, after all, only words. "I could kill you for doing that," a man says to his wife and then they both cheerfully sit down to dinner. And many people live entirely in the past, without even noticing it. One day the tailor pushed his glasses up on his forehead and saw that he was in the middle of a lonely wood. He rubbed his poor tired eyes, but the trees didn't go away. He looked all around. No scissors and pins, no bolts of material, no patterns, no worktable, no shop. Only the needle and thread he had been sewing with. He listened anxiously. He had never been in a wood before. "Wife?" he called out, but there was no answer.

He knew that it was late afternoon, and that he ought to get out of the wood before dark, so he stuck the needle in his vest and started walking along a path that constantly threatened to disappear, the way paths do in the wood. Sometimes the path divided, and he had to choose between the right and the left fork, without knowing which was the way that led out of the wood. The light began to fail even sooner than he had expected. When it was still daytime in the sky overhead, it was already so dark where he was that he could find the path only by the feel of the ground under his feet.

"I don't see why this should happen to me," he said, and from the depths of the wood a voice said "To *who*?" disconcertingly, but it was only an owl. So he kept on until he saw a light through the trees, and he made his way to it, through the underbrush and around fallen logs, until he came to a house in a clearing. At this time of night they'll be easily frightened, he thought. I must speak carefully or they'll close the door in my face. When the door opened in answer to his knock and a woman stood looking out at him from the lighted doorway, he said politely, "It's all right, ma'am, I'm not a robber."

"No," the woman said, "you're an industrious tailor."

"Now, how did you know that?" he asked in amazement.

The woman did not seem to feel that this question needed answering, and there was something about her that made him uneasy, and so, though he would much rather that she invited him in and gave him a place by the fire and a bit of supper, he said, "If you would be kind enough to show me the way out of the wood—"

"I don't know that I can," the woman said.

"Isn't there a road of some kind?"

"There's a road," the woman said doubtfully, "but it wasn't built in your lifetime."

"I beg pardon?"

"And anyway, you'd soon lose it in the dark. You'll have to wait until morning. How did you happen to—"

At that point a baby began to cry, and the woman said, "I can't stand here talking. Come in."

"Thank you," he said. "That's very kind of you, ma'am," and as he stepped across the threshold there was suddenly no house, no lighted room, no woman. Nothing but a clearing in the wood.

In disappointment so acute that it brought tears to his eyes, he sat down on the ground and tucked his legs under him and tried to get used to the idea that he wasn't going to sit by a warm fire, under a snug roof, with a bit of supper by and by, and a place to lay his head at bedtime.

I will catch my death of pneumonia, he thought. He put his hand to his vest; the needle was still there. He felt his forehead, and then took his glasses off, folded them carefully, and put them in his vest pocket. Then he stretched out on the bare ground and, looking up through the trees, thought about his tailor shop, and about a greatcoat that he was working on. It was of French blue, part true cashmere and part Lincoln wool, with a three-tiered cape, and it wasn't promised until a fortnight, but he would have finished it and have given it to his wife to press if he hadn't suddenly found himself in this lonely wood. Then he thought about his wife, who would be wondering why he didn't come upstairs for his supper. And then about his father, who had a stroke and never recovered the use of his limbs or his speech. In the evening, after the day was over, the industrious tailor used to come and sit by his father's bed, and he would bring whatever he was working on—a waistcoat or a pair of knee breeches, or an embroidered vest— and spread it out on the counterpane, to show his father that the lessons had been well learned and that he needn't worry about the quality of work being turned out by the shop. And instead of being pleased with him, his father would push the work aside impatiently. There seemed to be something on his mind that he very much wanted to say, some final piece of wisdom, but when he tried to speak he could only utter meaningless sounds.

Now, through the tops of the bare trees, the tailor could see the stars, so bright and so far away . . . But how did it get to be autumn, he wondered. And why am I not cold? Why am I not hungry? He fell asleep and dreamed that he had more work to do than he could possibly manage, and woke up with the sun shining in his face.

"Wife?" he called out, before he remembered where he was or what had happened to him.

He sat up and looked around. There was no house in the clearing, and no sign that there ever had been, but there was a path leading off through the woods, and he followed it. At this time, more than half of England was forests, and so he knew that it might be days before he found his way out of the wood. "I must be careful not to walk in a circle," he told himself. "That's what people always do when they are lost." But one fallen tree, one sapling, one patch of dried fern, one bed of moss looked just like another, and he could not tell whether he was walking in a circle or not. Now and then, not far from the path, there would be a sudden dry rustle that made his heart race. Was it a poisonous viper? What was it? The rustle did not explain itself. Oddly enough, he himself, stepping on dry leaves and twigs, did not make a sound.

"I ought to be living on roots and berries," he said to himself, and though there were plenty of both, he did not know which were edible and which were not, and he did not feel inclined to experiment. But when he came to a spring, he thought, I will drink, because this far from any house or pasture it cannot be contaminated. . . . He knelt down and put his face to the water and nothing happened. His throat was as dry as before. The water remained just out of reach. He leaned farther forward and again nothing happened. The water kept receding until his face touched dry gravel. He raised his head in surprise and there was the beautiful spring, glittering, jewellike in the sunlight, pushing its way under logs and between boulders, murmuring as it went, but not to be drunk from.

"Can it be that I am dead?" the tailor asked himself. And then, "If I am dead, why has nobody told me where to go, or what's expected of me?"

As he walked on, he tried to remember if in the old days, before he suddenly found himself in this wood, he had ever got down on his hands and knees to drink from a spring. All he remembered was that when the other boys were roaming the woods and bathing in the river, he was in his father's shop learning to be a master tailor.

"It is possible that I am dreaming," he said to himself. But it did not seem like a dream. In dreams it is always—not twilight exactly, but the light is peculiar, comes from nowhere, and is never very bright. This was a blindingly beautiful sunny day.

"At all events," he said to himself, "I am a much better walker than I had any idea. I have been walking for hours and I don't feel in the least tired. And even if it should turn out that I have been walking in a circle—"

At that moment he saw, ahead of him, what seemed like a thinning out of trees, as if he was coming to the edge of the wood. It proved to be a small clearing with a house in it. Smoke was rising from the chimney, and as the tailor came nearer an unpleasant suspicion crossed his mind.

"Oh, it's you," the woman said, when she opened the door and saw him standing there. She had a baby in her arms, and she didn't look particularly pleased to see him, or concerned that he had passed the whole night on the bare ground and the whole day walking in a circle.

"I'm sorry to trouble you, ma'am," he said, "but if you will be so kind as to show me that road you were speaking of—"

The baby began to fret, and the woman jounced it lightly on her shoulder. "As you can see, I'm busy," she said. "And I don't see how you got here in the first place."

"Neither do I," he said.

"Did you come on a spring anywhere in the wood?"

He nodded.

"And did you drink from it?"

"I couldn't," he said. "When I put my face to the water, there wasn't any."

"I'm afraid there's nothing I can do," the woman said, and he saw that she was about to close the door in his face.

"Please, ma'am," he said, "if you'll just show me where that road begins I won't trouble you any further, I promise you."

"Why you had to come today of all days, when the baby's cutting a tooth, and the fire in the stove has gone out, and I still have to do the churning. . . . You haven't murdered somebody? No, I can see you haven't. If the police are after you—"

"The police are not after me," the tailor said with dignity, "and I haven't committed any crime that I know of."

"Well, that doesn't mean anything," the woman said. "Come, let me show you the road."

He followed her across the clearing, and when she stopped they were standing in front of a clump of white birch trees. Beyond it the tangled underbrush began, and the big trees.

"I don't see any road," the tailor said.

"That's what I mean," the woman said. She stood looking at him and frowning thoughtfully.

"Even if there was only a path—" the tailor began, and the woman said, "Oh, be quiet. If I let you go off into the woods again, you'll only end up here the way you did before. And I can't ask you into the house, because— Have you ever held a baby?"

"Oh, yes," the tailor said. "My children are grown now, but when they were little I often held them while my wife was busy doing something."

As he was speaking, the woman put the baby in his arms. The baby turned its head on its weak neck and looked at him. Though the woman made him uneasy, the baby did not. The baby's face contorted, and he saw that it was about to cry. "Hush-a," he said, and jounced it gently against his shoulder, and felt the head wobble against his neck, and the down on the baby's head, softer than any material in his shop.

"This may not work," the woman said, and started back across the clearing, and he followed her, still holding the baby.

At the door of the house she took a firm grip on the hem of the baby's garment and then she said, "Go in, go in," and after a last look over his shoulder at the clearing in the wood he stepped across the threshold, expecting to find himself outside again, and instead he was in his own shop, sitting cross-legged on his worktable.

*

He listened and heard the twittering of birds as they flitted from branch to branch in the elm tree outside, and then the miller's wife, laughing at some joke she had just made. He saw by the quality of the light outside that it was only the middle of the afternoon. A wagon came by, and the miller's wife called to whoever was in the wagon, and a man's voice said, "Whoa, there . . . Whoa . . . Whoa." The tailor listened with rapt attention to the conversation that followed, though he had heard it a hundred times. Or conversations just like it. All around him on the worktable were scraps of French-blue material, and he could see at a glance what was waiting to be stitched to what. Finally the man said, "That's rich! That's a good one. Gee-up . . ." and the wheels turned again, and the slow plodding was resumed and grew fainter and was replaced by the sound of a child beating on a tin pan. The miller's wife went home, but there were other sounds—a dog, a door slamming, a child being scolded. Then it was quiet for a time, and without thinking the tailor put his hand to his vest and found the needle. Two boys went by, saying, "I dare you to do it, I dare you, I double-dare you!" Do what, the tailor wondered, and went on sewing.

The quiet and the outbreaks of sound alternated in a way that was so regular that it almost seemed planned. A loud noise, such as a crow going caw, caw, caw, seemed to produce a deeper silence afterward. He studied the beautiful sound of footsteps approaching and receding, so like a piece of music.

The light began to fail and he hardly noticed it, because as the light went it was accompanied by all the sounds that mean the end of the day: men coming home from the fields, shops being closed, children being called in before dark.

When the tailor could not see any longer, he put his work aside and sat, listening and smiling to himself at what he heard, until his wife called him to supper.

3. *The country where nobody ever grew old and died*

THERE used to be, until roughly a hundred and fifty years ago, a country where nobody ever grew old and died. The gravestone with its weathered inscription, the wreath on the door, the black arm band, and the friendly reassuring smile of the undertaker were unknown there. This is not as strange as it at first seems. You do not have to look very far to find a woman who does not show her age or a man who intends to live forever. In this country, people did live forever, and nobody thought anything about it, but at some time or other somebody had thought about it, because there were certain restrictions on the freedom of the inhabitants. The country was not large, and there would soon not have been enough land to go around. So, instead of choosing an agreeable site and building a house on it, married couples chose an agreeable house and bought the right to add a story onto it. In this way, gradually, the houses, which were of stone, and square, and without superfluous ornamentation, became towers. The prevailing style of architecture was very much like that of the Italian hill towns. Arriving at the place where you lived, you rang the concierge's bell and sat down in a wicker swing, with your parcels on your lap, and were lifted to your own floor by ropes and pulleys.

A country where there were no children would be sadness incarnate. People didn't stop having them, but they were placed in such a way that the smallest number of children could be enjoyed by the greatest number of adults. If you wanted to raise a family, you applied for a permit and waited your turn. Very often by the time the permit came, the woman was too old to have a child and received instead a permit to help bring up somebody else's child.

Young women who were a pleasure to look at were enjoyed the way flowers are enjoyed, but leaving one's youth behind was not considered to be a catastrophe, and the attitudes and opinions of the young were not anxiously subscribed to. There is, in fact, some question whether the young of that country really were young, as we understand the word. Most people appeared to be on the borderline between maturity and early middle age, as in England in the late eighteenth century, when the bald pate and the head of thick brown hair were both concealed by a powdered wig, and physical deterioration was minimized by the fashions in dress and by what constituted good manners.

All the arts flourished except history. If you wanted to know what things were like in the period of Erasmus or Joan of Arc or Ethelred the Unready, you asked somebody who was alive at the time. People tended to wear the clothes of the period in which they came of age, and so walking down the street was like thumbing through a book on the history of costume. The soldiers, in every conceivable kind of armor and uniform, were a little boy's dream.

As one would expect, that indefatigable traveler Lady Mary Wortley Montagu spent a considerable time in this interesting country before she settled down in Venice, and so did William Beckford. Lady Mary's letters about it were destroyed by her daughter after her death, because they happened to contain assertions of a shocking nature, for which proof was lacking, about a contemporary figure who would have relished a prosecution for libel. For Beckford's experiences, see his *Dreams, Waking Thoughts, and Incidents* (Leipzig, 1832).

One might have supposed that in a country where death was out of the question, morbidity would be unknown. This was true for I have no idea how many centuries and then something very strange happened. The young, until this moment entirely docile and unimaginative, began having scandalous parties at which they pretended that they were holding a funeral. They even went so far as to put together a makeshift pine coffin, and took turns lying in it, with their eyes closed and their hands crossed, and a lighted candle at the head and foot. This occurred during Beckford's stay, and it is just possible that he had something to do with it. Though he could be very amusing, he was a natural mischief-maker and an extremely morbid man.

The mock funerals were the first thing that happened. The second was the trial, *in absentia*, of a gypsy woman who was accused of taking money with intent to defraud. This was not an instance of a poor foolish widow's being persuaded to bring her husband's savings to a fortune-teller in order to have the money doubled. In the first place, there were no widows, and the victim was a young man.

The plaintiff—just turned twenty-one, Beckford says, and exceedingly handsome—stated under oath that he had consulted the gypsy woman in the hope of learning from her the secret of how to commit suicide. For it seems that in this country as everywhere else gypsies were a race apart and a law unto themselves. They did not choose to live forever, so they didn't. When one of them decided that life had no further interest for him, he did something. What, nobody knew. It was assumed that the gypsy bent on terminating his existence sat down under a tree or by a riverbank, some nice quiet place where he wouldn't be disturbed, and in a little while the other gypsies came and disposed of the body.

The plaintiff testified that the gypsy woman studied his hand, and then she looked in her crystal ball, and then she excused herself in order to get something on the other side of a curtain. That was the last anybody had seen of her or of the satchel full of money which the plaintiff had brought with him.

The idea that a personable young man, on the very threshold of life, had actually wanted to die caused a tremendous stir. The public was barred from the trial, but Beckford was on excellent terms with the wife of the Lord Chief Justice and managed to attend the hearing in the guise of a court stenographer. The story is to be found in the Leipzig edition of his book and no other, which suggests that he perhaps did have something to do with the events he describes, and that from feelings of remorse, or shame, wrote about them and then afterward wished to suppress what he had written. At all events we have his very interesting account. The jury found for the plaintiff and against the gypsy woman. After the verdict was read aloud in the court, the attorney for the defense made an impassioned and—in the light of what happened afterward—heartbreaking speech. If only it had been taken seriously! He asked that the verdict stand, but that no effort be made to find his client, and that no other gypsy be questioned or molested in any way by the police. The court saw the matter in a different light, and during the next few days the police set about rounding up every single gypsy in the country. The particular gypsy woman who had victimized the young man with a bent for self-destruction was never found. The others were subjected to the most detailed questioning. When that produced no information, the rack and the thumbscrew were applied, to no purpose. You might as well try to squeeze kindness out of a stone as torture a secret out of a gypsy. But there was living with the gypsies at that time a middle-aged man who had been stolen by them as a child and who had spent his life among them. When he was brought into the courtroom between two bailiffs, the attorney for the defense lowered his head and covered his eyes with his hand. The man was put on the witness stand and, pale and drawn after a night of torture, gave his testimony. Shortly after this, the gravestone, the wreath, the arm band, and the smiling undertaker, so familiar everywhere else in the world, made their appearance here also, and the country was no longer unique.

4. The fisherman who had nobody to go out in his boat with him

ONCE upon a time there was a poor fisherman who had no one to go out in his boat with him. The man he started going out with when he was still a boy was now crippled with rheumatism and sat all day by the fire. The other fishermen were all paired off, and there was nobody for him. Out on the water, without a soul to talk to, the hours between daybreak and late afternoon were very long, and to pass the time he sang. He sang the songs that other people sang, whatever he had heard, and this was of course a good deal in the way of music, because in the olden times people sang more than they do now. But eventually he came to the end of all the songs he knew or had ever heard and wanted to learn some new songs. He knew that they were written down and published, but this was no help to him because he had never been to school and didn't know how to read words, let alone the musical staff. You might as well have presented him with a clay tablet of Egyptian hieroglyphics. But there were ways, and he took advantage of them. At a certain time, on certain days of the week, the children in the schoolhouse had singing, and he managed to be in the vicinity. He brought his boat in earlier those days, on one pretext or another, and stood outside the school building. At first the teacher was mystified, but he saw that the poor fisherman always went away as soon as the singing lesson was over, and putting two and two together he realized why the man was there. So, one day, he went to the door and invited the fisherman in. The fisherman backed away, and then he turned and hurried off down the road to the beach. But the next time they had singing, there he was. The schoolteacher opened a window so the fisherman could hear better and went on with the lesson. While the children were singing "There were three sisters fair and bright," the door opened slowly. The teacher pointed to a desk in the back row, and the fisherman squeezed himself into it, though it was a child's desk and much too small for him. The children waved their hands in the air and asked silly questions and giggled, but, never having been to school, the fisherman thought this was customary and did not realize that he was creating a disturbance. He came again and again.

People manage to believe in magic—of one kind or another. And ghosts. And the influence of the stars. And reincarnation. And a life everlasting. But not enough room is allowed for strangeness: that birds and animals know the way home; that a blind man, having sensed the presence of a wall, knows as well where to walk as you or I; that there have been many recorded instances of conversations between two persons who did not speak the same language but, each speaking his own, nevertheless understood each other perfectly. When the teacher passed out the songbooks, he gave one to the fisherman, well aware that his only contact with the printed page was through his huge, calloused hands. And time after time the fisherman knew, before the children opened their mouths and began to sing, what the first phrase would be, and where the song would go from there.

Naturally, he did not catch as many fish as he had when he was attending to his proper work, and sometimes there was nothing in the house to eat. His wife could not complain, because she was a deaf-mute. She was not ugly, but no one else would have her. Though she had never heard the sound of her own voice, or indeed any sound whatever, she could have made him feel her dissatisfaction, but she saw that what he was doing was important to him, and did not interfere. What the fisherman would have liked would have been to sing with the children when they sang, but his voice was so deep there was no possibility of its blending unnoticeably with theirs, so he sat in silence, and only when he was out in his boat did the songs burst forth from his throat. What with the wind and the sea-birds' crying, he had to sing openly or he would not have known he was singing at all. If he had been on shore, in a quiet room, the sound would have seemed tremendous. Out under the sky, it merely seemed like a man singing.

He often thought that if there had only been a child in the house he could have sung the child to sleep, and that would have been pleasant. He would have sung to his wife if she could have heard him, and he did try, on his fingers, to convey the sound of music—the way the sounds fell together, the rising and descending, the sudden changes in tempo, and the plea-sure of expecting to hear this note and hearing, instead, a dif-ferent one, but she only smiled at him uncomprehendingly.

The schoolteacher knew that if it had been curiosity alone that drew the fisherman to the schoolhouse at the time of singing lessons, he would have stopped coming as soon as his curiosity was satisfied, and he didn't stop coming, which must mean that there was a possibility that he was innately musical. So he stopped the fisherman one day when they met by acci-dent, and asked him to sing the scale. The fisherman opened his mouth and no sound came. He and the schoolteacher looked at each other, and then the fisherman colored, and hung his head. The schoolteacher clapped him on the shoulder and walked on, satisfied that what there was here was the love of music rather than a talent for it, and even that seemed to him something hardly short of a miracle.

In those islands, storms were not uncommon and they were full of peril. Even large sailing ships were washed on the rocks and broken to pieces. As for the little boats the fishermen went out in, one moment they would be bobbing on the waves like a cork, now on the crest and now out of sight in a trough, and then suddenly there wasn't any boat. The sea would have swal-lowed it, and the men in it, in the blinking of an eye. It was a terrible fact that the islanders had learned to live with. If they had not been fishermen, they would have starved, so they continued to go out in their boats, and to read the sky for warnings, which were usually dependable, but every now and then a storm—and usually the very worst kind—would come up without any warning, or with only a short time between the first alarming change in the odor of the air, the first wisps of storm clouds, and the sudden lashing of the waters. When this happened, the women gathered on the shore and prayed. Sometimes they waited all night, and sometimes they waited in vain.

One evening, the fisherman didn't come home at the usual time. His wife could not hear the wind or the shutters banging, but when the wind blew puffs of smoke down the chimney, she knew that a storm had come up. She put on her cloak, and wrapped a heavy scarf around her head, and started for the strand, to see if the boats were drawn up there. Instead, she found the other women waiting with their faces all stamped with the same frightened look. Usually the seabirds circled above the beach, waiting for the fishing boats to come in and the fishermen to cut open their fish and throw them the guts, but this evening there were no gulls or cormorants. The air was empty. The wind had blown them all inland, just as, by a freak, it had blown the boats all together, out on the water, so close that it took great skill to keep them from knocking against each other and capsizing in the dark. The fishermen called back and forth for a time, and then they fell silent. The wind had grown higher and higher, and the words were blown right out of their mouths, and they could not even hear themselves what they were saying. The wind was so high and the sound so loud that it was like a silence, and out of this silence, suddenly, came the sound of singing. Being poor ignorant fishermen, they did the first thing that occurred to them—they fell on their knees and prayed. The singing went on and on, in a voice that none of them had ever heard, and so powerful and rich and deep it seemed to come from the same place that the storm came from. A flash of lightning revealed that it was not an angel, as they thought, but the fisherman who was married to the deaf-mute. He was standing in his boat, with his head bared, singing, and in their minds this was no stranger or less miraculous than an angel would have been. They crossed themselves and went on praying, and the fisherman went on singing, and in a little while the waves began to grow smaller and the wind to abate, and the storm, which should have taken days to blow itself out, suddenly turned into an intense calm. As suddenly as it had begun, the singing stopped. The boats drew apart as in one boat after another the men took up their oars again, and in a silvery brightness, all in a cluster, the fishing fleet came safely in to shore.

5. *The two women friends*

THE two women were well along in years, and one lived in a castle and one lived in the largest house in the village that was at the foot of the castle rock. Though picturesque, the castle had bathrooms and central heating, and it would not for very long have withstood a siege, no matter how antiquated the weapons employed. The village was also picturesque, being made up of a single street of thatched Elizabethan cottages. The two women were friends, and if one had weekend guests it was understood that the other would stand by, ready to entertain them. When the conversation threatened to run out, guests at Cleeve Castle were taken to Cleeve House and offered tea and hot buttered scones, under a canopy of apple blossoms or in front of a roaring fire, according to the season. The largest house in the village had been made by joining three of the oldest cottages together, and the catalogue of its inconveniences often made visitors wipe tears of amusement from their eyes. The inconveniences were mostly felt by the servants, who had to carry cans of hot water and breakfast trays up the treacherous stairs, and who, when they were in a hurry, tripped over the uneven doorsills and bumped their heads on low beams. Guests at Cleeve House were taken to the castle and plied with gin and ghost stories.

One would have expected this arrangement, so useful to both women, to be lasting, but the friendship of women seems often to have embedded in it somewhere a fishhook, and as it happened the mistress of Cleeve House was born with a heavier silver spoon in her mouth, and baptized in a longer christening gown, and in numerous other ways was socially more enviable. On the other hand, the money that had originally gone with the social advantages was, alas, rather run out, and it was without the slightest trace of anxiety that the woman in the castle sat down to balance her checkbook. Weekend guests at the castle tended to be more important politically or in the world of the arts—flashy, in short. And the weekend guests at Cleeve House more important to know if it was a question of getting your children into the right schools or yourself into the right clubs. In a word, nobby. But how the woman who lived in the castle could have dreamed for one minute that she could entertain a member of the royal family and not bring him to tea at Cleeve House, to be amused by the catalogue of its inconveniences and the story of how it came to be thrown together out of three dark, cramped little cottages by an architect who was a disciple of William Morris, it is hard to say. Perhaps the friendship had begun to seem burdensome and the duties one-sided. Or perhaps it was the gradual accumulation of tactful silences, which avoided saying that the woman who lived in the village was top drawer and the woman who lived in the castle was not, and careless remarks, such as anybody might be guilty of with a close friend, which frankly admitted it. In any event, one does not go running here, there, and everywhere with a member of the royal family in tow. There is protocol to be observed, secretaries and chauffeurs and valets have to be consulted, and the conversation doesn't threaten to run out because what you have, in these circumstances, isn't conversation in the usual sense of the word. But anyway, the mistress of Cleeve House sat waiting for the telephone to ring, with the wrinkles ironed out of her best tablecloth, and her Spode tea set brought down from the highest shelf of the china closet, and the teaspoons polished till you could see your face in them, and her Fortuny gown taken out of its plastic bag and left to hang from the bedroom chandelier. And, unbelievably, the telephone did not ring. In the middle of the afternoon she had the operator check her phone to see if it was out of order. This was a mistake, because in a village people are very apt to put two and two together. By nightfall it was known all up and down the High Street that her in the castle was entertaining royalty and had left her in the big house to sit and twiddle her thumbs.

Not that the mistress of Cleeve House cared one way or the other about the royal family. No, it was merely the slight to a friendship of very long standing that disturbed her. And for the sake of that friendship, though it cost her a struggle, she was prepared to act as if nothing unusual had happened when the telephone rang on Sunday morning, and to suggest that the mistress of Cleeve Castle bring her guests to tea. The telephone rang on Monday morning instead. To anyone listening in, and several people were, it was clear that she was speaking a little too much as if nothing unusual had happened. However, the invitation—to drive, just the two of them, in the little car, over to the market town and have lunch at the Star and Garter —was accepted. And because one does not entertain royalty and then not mention it, the subject came up finally, in the most natural way, and the mistress of Cleeve House was able to achieve the tone she wanted, which was a mixture of rea-sonable curiosity and amused indifference. But it was all over between them, and they both knew it.

They continued to see each other, less often and less inti-mately, for another three or four months, and then the woman who lived in the largest house in the village finished it off in a way that made it possible for her to carry her head high. The husband of the woman who lived in the castle had, unwisely, allowed his name to be put up for a London club that was rather too grand for a man who had made a fortune in whole-sale poultry. Even so, with a great deal of help from various quarters or a little help from the right quarter, he might have made it. There were two or three men who could have pulled this off single-handed, and when one of them came down to Cleeve House for the weekend, it was the turn of the mistress of the castle to sit and wait for the telephone to ring. On Mon-day morning, the nanny of the children of Cleeve House (who were really the woman's grandchildren) took them to play with the children of the castle, as she had been doing every Monday morning all summer, and was told at the castle gate that the children of the castle were otherwise occupied. Though they had not been in any way involved and did not even know the cause of the falling out, the children of the castle and the chil-dren of Cleeve House were enemies from that day forth, and so were their nannies. The two husbands, being more worldly, still exchanged curt nods when they met in the High Street or on the railway platform. As for the two women, they very clev-erly managed never even to set eyes on one another.

Weekend guests at Cleeve House were taken for a walk, nat-urally, because it was one of the oldest villages in England, and when they saw the castle, with rooks roosting in the apertures of the keep, they cried out with pleasure at finding a place so picturesque that near London. When the mistress of Cleeve

House explained that she was no longer on friendly terms with the castle, their faces betrayed their disappointment. And with a consistency that was really extraordinary, people who were staying at Cleeve Castle sooner or later came back from a walk saying, "The village is charming, I must say. But who is that fascinating grey-haired woman who walks with a stick and lives in that largish house on the High Street? We're dying to meet her."

City people get over their anger, as a rule, but it is different if you live in a village. For one thing, everybody knows that you are angry, and why, and the slightest shift in position is publicly commented on, and this stiffens the antagonism and makes it permanent. Something very large indeed—a fire, a flood, a war, a catastrophe of some sort—is required to bring about a reconciliation and push the injured parties into one another's outstretched arms.

One winter morning, the village learned, via the wireless, that it was in the direct path of a new eight-lane expressway connecting London and the seacoast. The money for it had been appropriated and it was too late to prevent the road from being built, but the political connections of Cleeve Castle working hand in glove with the social connections of Cleeve House could perhaps divert it so that some other village was obliterated. After deliberating for days, the woman who lived in the castle picked up the telephone and called Cleeve House, but while the telephone was still ringing she hung up. The injury to her husband (what a way to repay a thousand kindnesses!) was still too fresh in her mind. There must be some other way of dealing with the problem, she told herself, and sitting down at her desk she wrote a long and affectionate letter to a school friend who was married to a Member of Parliament, imploring his help.

After considering the situation from every angle, the woman who lived in the largest house in the village came to the only sensible conclusion, which was that some things are worth swallowing your pride for, and she put on her hat and coat and walked up to the castle. But when she came to the castle gate, the memory of how her grandchildren had been turned away (the smallness of it!) filled her with anger, and she paid a call on the vicar instead.

In due time the surveyors appeared, with their tripods, sighting instruments, chains, stakes, and red flags, and the path of doom was made clear. The government, moved by humane considerations, did, however, build a new village. The cottages of Upper Cleeve, as it was called, were all exactly alike and as ugly as sin. There was no way on earth that you could join three of them together and produce a house that William Morris would have felt at home in. The castle was saved by its rocky situation, but its owners did not choose to look out on an eight-lane expressway and breathe exhaust fumes and be kept awake all night long by trucks and trailers. So the rooks fell heir to it.

6. The carpenter

O NCE upon a time there was a man of no particular age, a carpenter, whom all kinds of people entrusted with their secrets. Perhaps the smell of glue and sawdust and fresh-cut boards had something to do with it, but in any case he was not a troublemaker, and a secret is nearly always something that, if it became known, would make trouble for somebody. So they came to his shop, closed the door softly behind them, sat down on a pile of lumber, and pretended that they had come because they enjoyed watching him work. Actually, they did enjoy it. Some of them. His big square hands knew what they were doing, and all his movements were relaxed and skillful. The shavings curled up out of his plane as if the idea was to make long, beautiful shavings. He used his carpenter's rule and stubby pencil as if he were applying a moral principle. When he sawed, it seemed to have the even rhythm of his heartbeat. Though the caller might forget for five minutes what brought him here, in the end he stopped being interested in carpentry and said, "I know I can trust you, because you never repeat anything . . ." and there it was, one more secret added to the collection, a piece of information that, if it had got out, would have broken up a friendship or caused a son to be disinherited or ruined a half-happy marriage or cost some man his job or made trouble for somebody.

The carpenter had discovered that the best way to deal with this information that must not be repeated was to forget it as quickly as possible, though sometimes the secret was so strange he could not forget it immediately, and that evening his wife would ask, "Who was in the shop today?" For people with no children have only each other to spy on, and he was an open book to her.

Sometimes the person who had confided in him seemed afterward to have no recollection of having done this, and more than once the carpenter found himself wondering if he had imagined or misremembered something that he knew perfectly well he had not imagined and would remember to his dying day. In the middle of the night, if he had a wakeful period, instead of thrashing around in the bed and disturbing his wife's sleep, he lay quietly with his eyes open in the dark and was a spectator to plays in which honorable men were obliged to tell lies, the kind and good were a prey to lechery, the old acted not merely without wisdom but without common sense, debts were repaid not in kind but in hatred, and the young rode roughshod over everybody. When he had had enough of human nature, he put all these puppets back in their box and fell into a dreamless sleep.

For many years his life was like this, but it is a mistake to assume that people never change. They don't and they do change. Without his being able to say just when it happened and whether the change was sudden or gradual, the carpenter knew that he was no longer trustworthy—that is to say, he no longer cared whether people made trouble for one another or not. His wife saw that he looked tired, that he did not always bother to stand up straight, that he was beginning to show his age. And she tried to make his life easier for him, but he was a man firmly fixed in his habits, and there was not much she could do for him except feed him well and keep small irritations from him.

Out of habit, the carpenter continued not to repeat the things people told him, but while the secret was being handed over to him he marvelled that the other person had no suspicion he was making a mistake. And since the carpenter had not asked, after all, to be the repository of everybody's secret burden, it made him mildly resentful.

One day he tried an experiment. He betrayed a secret that was not very serious—partly to prove to himself that he could do such a thing and partly in the hope that word would get around that he was not to be trusted with secrets. It made a certain amount of trouble, as he knew it would, but it also had the effect of clearing the air for all concerned, and the blame never got back to him because no one could imagine his behaving in so uncharacteristic a fashion. So, after this experiment, he tried another. The butcher came in, closed the door softly, looked around for a pile of lumber to sit on, and then said, "There's something I've got to tell somebody."

"Don't tell me," the carpenter said quickly, "unless you want every Tom, Dick, and Harry to know."

The butcher paused, looked down at his terrible hands, cleared his throat, glanced around the shop, and then suddenly leaned forward and out it came.

"In short, he wanted every Tom, Dick, and Harry to know," the carpenter said to his wife afterward, when he was telling her about the butcher's visit.

"People need to make trouble the way they need to breathe," she said calmly.

"I don't need to make trouble," the carpenter said indignantly.

"I know," she said. "But you mustn't expect everyone to be like you."

The next time somebody closed the door softly and sat down and opened his mouth to speak, the carpenter beat him to it. "I know it isn't fair to tell you this," he said, "but I had to tell somebody . . ." This time he made quite a lot of trouble, but not so much that his wife couldn't deal with it, and he saw that the fear of making trouble can be worse than trouble itself.

After that, he didn't try any more experiments. What happened just happened. The candlemaker was sitting on a pile of lumber watching him saw a chestnut plank, and the carpenter said, "Yesterday the one-eyed fiddler was in here."

"Was he?" the candlemaker said; he wasn't really interested in the fiddler at the moment. There was something on his mind that he had to tell somebody, and he was waiting for the carpenter to stop sawing so he wouldn't have to raise his voice and run the risk of being overheard in the street.

"You know the blacksmith's little boy?" the carpenter said. "The second one? The one he keeps in the shop with him?"

"The apple of his eye," said the candlemaker. "Had him sorting nails when he was no bigger than a flea. Now he tends the bellows."

"That's right," said the carpenter. "Well, you know what the fiddler told me?"

"When it comes to setting everybody's feet a-dancing, there's no one like the one-eyed fiddler," the candlemaker

said. "But I don't know what he'd of done without the blacksmith. Always taking him in when he didn't have a roof over
his head or a penny in his pocket. Drunk or sober."

"You know what the fiddler told me? He said the blacksmith's little boy isn't his child."

"Whose is he?"

"Who does he look like?"

"Why, come to think of it, he looks like the one-eyed fiddler."

"Spitting image," the carpenter said. And not until that moment did he realize what was happening. It was the change in
the candlemaker's face that made him aware of it. First the
light of an impending confidence, which had been so clear in
his eyes, was dimmed. The candlemaker looked down at his
hands, which were as white and soft as a woman's. Then he
cleared his throat and said, "Strange nobody noticed it."

"You won't tell anybody what I told you?" the carpenter
found himself saying.

"No, of course not," the candlemaker said. "I always enjoy
watching you work. Is that a new plane you've got there?"

For the rest of the visit he was more friendly than usual, as if
some lingering doubt had been disposed of and he could now
be wholly at ease with the carpenter. After he had gone, the
carpenter started to use his new plane and it jammed. He
cleaned the slot and adjusted the screw and blew on it, but it
still jammed, so he put it aside, thinking the blade needed to
be honed, and picked up a crosscut saw. Halfway through the
plank he stopped. The saw was not following the pencil line.
He gave up and sat down on a pile of lumber. The fiddler had
better clear out now and never show his face in the village
again, because if the blacksmith ever found out, he'd kill him.
And what about the blacksmith's wife? She had no business
doing what she did, but neither did the blacksmith have any
business marrying someone young enough to be his daughter.
She was a slight woman with a cough, and she wouldn't last a
year if she had to follow the fiddler in and out of taverns and
sleep under hedgerows. And what about the little boy who so
proudly tended the bellows? Each question the carpenter asked
himself was worse than the one before. His head felt heavy
with shame. He sighed and then sighed again, deep heavy

sighs forced out of him by the weight on his heart. How could he tell his wife what he had done? And what would make her want to go on living with him when she knew? And how could he live with himself? At last he got up and untied the strings of his apron and locked the door of his shop behind him and went off down the street, looking everywhere for the one-eyed fiddler.

7. The man who had no friends and didn't want any

THERE was a man who had no enemies—only friends. He had a gift for friendship. When he met someone for the first time, he would look into the man or the woman or the child's eyes, and he never afterward mistook them for someone else. He was as kind as the day is long, and no one imposed on his kindness. He had a beautiful wife, who loved him. He had a comfortable, quiet apartment in town and a beautiful little house by the sea. He had enough money. All summer he taught children to sail boats on the salt water and on winter afternoons he sat in his club and helped old men with one foot in the grave to remember names, so they could get on with their recollecting. If necessary, he even helped them to remember the point of the recollection, which he had usually heard before. In the club he was never alone for a minute. If he sat down by the magazine table, the other members gathered around him like fruit flies—the young, uneasy new members as well as his bald-headed contemporaries. The places he had lived in stretched halfway around the world, and he was a natural-born storyteller. His conversation went to the head, like wine. At the same time, it went straight to the heart. He was a lovely man, and there aren't any more like him.

But there was also in the same club a man who had no friends—and, of course, not a single enemy either. He was always alone. He had never married. Though he had too much money, no one had ever successfully put the finger on him. He did not drink, and if someone who had been drinking maybe a little too much nodded to him on the way upstairs to the dining room, he did not respond, lest it turn out that he had been mistaken for somebody else. He tried sitting at the common table, in the hope that it would broaden his mind, but it was not the way he had been given to understand it would be, so he moved to a table by the window, a table for two, and for company he had an empty plate that did not contradict itself, a clean napkin that lived wholly in the present, a glittering glass tumbler that had its facts and figures straight, an unprejudiced knife, an unsentimental fork, and two logical spoons. Actually, his belonging to this particular club at all was due to a mistake on the part of the secretary of the committee on admissions, who had been instructed to notify another man of the same name that he had been elected to membership.

The man who had no friends did not want any, but he was observant, and from his table by the window he saw something no one else saw: The man who had no enemies, only friends, did not look well. It could be nothing more than one of those sudden jerks by which people grow older, but there was a late-afternoon light in his eye, and also his color was not good. Joking, he made use of the elevator when the others moved toward the stairs. And more and more he seemed like a man who is listening to two conversations at once. Sometimes for a week or ten days he would not appear at the club at all, and then he would be there again, moving through the stately, high-ceilinged rooms like a ship under full sail—but a ship whose rigging is frayed and whose oak timbers have grown lighter and lighter with time, and whose seaworthiness is now entirely a matter of the excellence of the builder's design.

The first stroke was slight. The doctor kept him in bed for a while, but he was able to spend the summer in his house by the sea, as usual. During the period of his convalescence, his wife informed the doorman at the club that he would be happy to see his friends. Naturally, they came—came often, came in droves, and found the invalid sitting up in bed, in good spirits, though not quite his old self yet. They were concerned lest they stay too long, and at the same time found it difficult to leave until they had blurted out, while it was still possible, how much he meant to them. These statements he was somehow able to dispose of with humor, so that they didn't hang heavy in the air afterward.

The man who had no friends also inquired about him, and the doorman, after some hesitation, gave him the message too, thinking that since this was the first time in fourteen years that he had ever asked about anybody, he must be a friend. But he didn't pay a call on the sick man. He had asked only out of curiosity. When he returned to town in September, he saw on the club bulletin board an announcement of a memorial service for the man who had a gift for friendship. He had died about a month before, in his sleep, in the house by the sea. The man who had no friends had reached the age where it is not unusual to spend a considerable part of one's time going to funerals, but no one had died whose obsequies required his presence, and again he was curious. He marked the date in the little memorandum book he always carried with him, and when the day came he got in a taxi and went to the service.

The small stone chapel filled up quickly, for of course they all came, all the friends of the man who had no enemies. They came bringing their entire stock of memories of him, which in one or two instances went back to their early youth. And in many cases there was something about their dress, some small mark of color—the degree of red or bright blue that is permitted in the ties of elderly men, the *Légion d'honneur* in a lapel—because it had seemed to them that the occasion ought not to be wholly solemn, since the man himself had been so impatient of solemnity. The exception was the man who had no friends. He wore a dark-grey business suit and a black-and-white striped tie, and sat alone in the back of the chapel. To his surprise, the funeral service was completely impersonal. Far from eulogizing the dead man or explaining his character to people who already knew all there was to know about it, the officiating clergyman did not even mention his name. There was a longish prayer, and then quotations from the Scriptures —mostly from the Psalms. The chapel had a bad echo, but the idea of the finality of death came through the garbled phrases, even so. The idea of farewell. The idea of a funeral on the water, and mourners peering, through torchlight, at a barque that is fast disappearing from sight. The man who had no friends sat observing, with his inward eye, his own funeral, in an empty undertaking parlor. The church was cold. He felt a draft on his ankles.

The young minister raised his voice to that pitch that is customary when the prayers of clergymen are meant to carry not only to the congregation but also to the ear of Heaven. There was a last brief exhortation to the Deity, and then the service was over. But during the emptying of the chapel something odd happened. The people there had not expected to derive such comfort from the presence of one another, and when their eyes met, their faces lit up, and they kept reaching out their hands to each other, over the pews. The man who had no friends saw what was happening and hurriedly put on his overcoat, but before he could slip out of the church, he felt his arm being taken in a friendly manner, and a man he knew only by sight said, "Ah yes, he belonged to you too, didn't he? Yes, of course." And no sooner had he extricated himself from this person than someone else said, "You're not going off by yourself? Come with us. Come on, come on, stop making a fuss!" And though he could hardly believe it, he found himself sitting on the jump seat of a taxi, with four other men, who took out their handkerchiefs and unashamedly wiped the tears away, blew their noses, and then sat back and began to tell funny stories about the dead man. When he got out of the cab, he tried to pay for his share, but they wouldn't hear of it, so he thanked them stiffly, and they called good-bye to him as if they were all his friends, which was too absurd—except that it didn't end there. The next day at the club they went right on acting as if they had a right to consider themselves his friends, and nothing he said or didn't say made any difference. They had got it into their heads he was a friend of the man who died, and so one of them. Shortly after the beginning of the new year, what should he find but a letter, on club stationery, informing him that he had been elected to the Board of Governors. He sat right down and wrote a letter explaining why he could not serve, but he saw at once that the letter was too revealing, so he tore it up. For the next three years he went faithfully, but with no pleasure, to the monthly dinners, and cast his vote with the others during the business meeting that followed the dinner. At the very last meeting of his term, just when he thought he was escaping, the secretary read off the names of the members who were to serve on the House Committee, and his name was among them. It seemed neither the time nor the place to protest, and afterward, when he did protest, he was told that it was customary for the members of the Board of Governors to serve on one committee or another after their term was finished. If he refused, the matter would be placed before the Board of Governors at their next meeting. He didn't want to call that much attention to himself, so he gave in. He served on the House Committee for two years, and at these meetings found that he was in sympathy with the prevailing atmosphere, which was of sharp candor and common sense. Inevitably he became better acquainted with his fellow committee members, and when they spoke to him on the stairs he couldn't very well not respond. For a while he continued to sit at his table by the window, but someone almost always came and joined him, so in the end he decided he might as well move over to the common table with the others. Later he served on the Rules Committee, the Archives Committee, the Art Committee, the Library Committee, the Music Committee, and the Committee on Admissions. Finally, when there were no more committees for him to serve on, someone dropped a remark in his presence and he saw the pit yawning before him. He took a solemn vow that he would never permit his name to be put up for president of the club, but it was put up; they did it without asking his permission, for it was an honor that had never been refused and they couldn't imagine anyone's wanting to refuse it.

He made an ideal president. He understood facts and figures, being a man of means, and since he had no family life, he was free to give all his time to the affairs of the club. A curmudgeon with a heart of gold is what they all said about him. Sometimes they even said it to his face. Fuming, he was made to sit for his portrait, shortly before he died, at the age of eighty-four, of pneumonia. As so often happens, the portrait was a failure. There was a bleak look in the eyes that wasn't at all like him, the members said, shaking their heads, and the one man who really understood him—who had never once tried to be his friend—was not there to contradict them.

8. A fable begotten of an echo of a line of verse by W. B. Yeats

ONCE upon a time there was an old man who made his living telling stories. In the middle of the afternoon he took his position on the steps of the monument to Unaging Intellect, in a somewhat out-of-the-way corner of the marketplace. And people who were not in a hurry would stop, and sometimes those who were in a hurry would hear a phrase that caught their attention, such as "in the moonlight" or "covered with blood," and would pause for a second and then be spellbound. It was generally agreed that he was better than some storytellers and not as good as others. And his wife would wait for him to come home, because what they had for supper depended on what he brought home in his pockets. She couldn't ask him to stop at this or that stall in the marketplace and buy what they needed. Being old, he was forgetful and would bring part of what she needed but not all. Standing on the marble steps of the monument, with his voice pitched so that it would carry over the shoulders of those who made a ring around him, he never forgot and he never repeated himself. That is to say, if it was a familiar story he was telling, he added new embellishments, new twists, and again it would be something he had never told before and didn't himself know until the words came out of his mouth, so that he was as astonished as his listeners, but didn't show it. He wanted them to believe what was in fact true, that the stories didn't come from him but through him, were not memorized, and would never be told quite that same way again.

Forgetfulness is the shadow that lies across the path of all old men. The statesman delivering an oration from the steps of the Temple of Zeus at times hesitated because he didn't know what came next. And the storyteller's wife worried for fear that this would happen to him, and of course one day it did. Kneeling in front of the executioner's block, the innocent prince traveling incognito waited for the charioteer who was going to force his way through the crowd and save him from

778

the axe, and nothing happened. That is to say, there was a pause that grew longer and longer until the listeners shifted their feet, and the storyteller took up in a different part of the story, and then suddenly swooped back to the prince and saved him, but leaving the audience with the impression that something was not right, that there was something they had not been told. There was. But could the storyteller simply have said at that point, "I don't remember what happened next"? They would have lost all faith in him and in his stories.

"I think you were just tired," his wife said when he told her what had happened. "It could happen to anybody." But in her heart she foresaw that it was going to happen again, and more seriously. "Once upon a time there was a younger son of the Prince of Syracuse who had one blue eye and one brown, and a charm of manner that made anyone who talked to him believe that—" This had to be left hanging because he who had always known everything about his characters, as God knows everything about human beings, didn't know, and tried to pretend that he meant this to be left hanging; but of course the listeners knew, and word got around that his memory was failing, his stories were not as good as they used to be, and fewer and fewer people stopped to listen to him, and those who did had to be content with fragments of stories, more interesting sometimes than the perfectly told stories had been, but unsatisfactory and incomplete.

Knowing that this was going to happen, his wife had been putting a little by to tide them over in their old age, and so they didn't starve. But he stayed home from the marketplace because it was an embarrassment to him that he couldn't tell stories anymore, and sometimes he sat in the sun and sometimes he followed his wife around and while she was digging a spider out of a corner of the ceiling he would say, "Once upon a time there was a girl of such beauty and delicacy of feeling that she could not possibly have been the child of the hardworking but obtuse couple who raised her from infancy, and although they seemed not to realize this, she had an air of expectancy that—" Here he stopped, unable to go on, and although his wife would have given anything to know what it was that the girl was expecting and if it really came about and how, she said nothing, because, poor man, his head was like a pot with a hole in it. Sometimes when her work was done she sat in the sun with him, in silence. They had been together for a very long time and did not always need to be saying something. But she would have liked it if he knew how much she did for him; instead, he seemed to take it for granted that when he was hungry there would be food, and when he was tired there was the bed, with clean sheets on it smelling of sunshine. She realized that it was not in his nature to be aware of small, ordinary things of this kind—that his mind trafficked in wonders and surprises. And it was something that she lived with the beginnings of so many wonderful stories she could think about as she went about her work: The story of the flute player's daughter, who picked up his instrument one day and played— although she had never to his knowledge touched it before or been given any instruction in the fingering or in breathing across the hole—better than any flute player he had ever heard. When he asked her how she was able to do this, she said, "I don't know. It just came to me that I knew how to do it." And when he asked her to do it again she couldn't, and this troubled her so much that she became melancholy and—and what? The storyteller didn't know. The thread of invention had given way at that point. . . . The story of the African warrior who was turned into a black cat, who at night wanted to be outdoors so that he could search for the huge moon of Africa that he remembered—the only thing that he remembered—from before his transformation. . . . The story of the old woman with a secret supply of hummingbirds. . . . The story of the brother and sister who in some previous incarnation had been man and wife. . . . With all these unfinished stories to occupy her mind, the storyteller's wife did not lack for things to think about. She wished that he could finish them for his sake, but she had come to prefer the fragments to the finished stories he used to tell. And in time she came to see that they couldn't be finished because they were so interesting there was no way for the story to go on.

The old man felt differently. "I would like just once before I die," he said to himself often, "to finish a story and see the look of thoughtfulness that a perfect story arouses in the faces of the people listening to me in the marketplace." Now, when he took his stand on the steps of the monument, the passersby hesitated, remembered that there was no use listening to him, because he always lost the thread of the story, and so passed on, saying to one another, "What wonderful tales he used to tell!"

Some vandal had chipped off the nose and two fingers of the statue to Unaging Intellect, and it had never been much admired, but he had told so many stories with the recognition that the monument was at his back that he had come to have an affection for it. What he had no way of knowing was that the monument had come to have an affection for him. What would otherwise have been an eternity of marble monumentality was made bearable by his once-upon-a-times. But why all these princes and talking parrots, these three wishes that land the guesser into a royal palace which is more marble, and uninhabitable, these babies switched in their cradle for no reason but to make a strange story, these wonders that are so much less wonderful than the things that are close to home? And because it is part of the storyteller's instinct to know what his audience wants to hear, one day when there was nobody around, the storyteller began: "Once upon a time there was an old man whose wits were slipping, and although he knew he didn't deserve it, he was well taken care of by his wife, who loved him. They had children but the children grew up and went away." Here the statue took on a look of attentiveness which the old man did not see because his back was turned to it. "The old couple had only each other, but that was a lot because with every year of their lives they had a greater sense of the unbreakable connection that held them. It was a miracle and they knew it, but they were afraid to talk about it lest something happen. Lest they be separated . . ." On and on the story went, with the monument rooted to its place by interest in what the old man was saying. Monuments do not have anyone who loves them. They exist in solitude and are always lonely, especially at night when there is no one around. The thought that human beings could undress and get into bed and sleep all night side by side was more beautiful than the monument could bear. The fact that she cooked for him because he was hungry and that his hunger was for what she cooked because it was cooked with love. That he was under the impression that, old and scatterbrained as he was, he was the one who took care of her and that she would not be safe without him . . . When the storyteller said, "From living together they had come to look alike," the monument said, "Oh, it's too much!" For there is no loneliness like the loneliness of Unaging Intellect.

9. The blue finch of Arabia

O N the evening of the twenty-fourth of December, an old
woman and an old man got off the train at a little wayside station on the Trans-Siberian Railroad and hurried across
the snow to the only lighted shop in the village, which was a
pet shop. In their excitement they left the door open, which
annoyed the proprietor, who was deaf, and they had a hard
time making him understand what they wanted. They had
come from Venice, they said, on the strength of a rumor that
he had a pair of blue finches. The proprietor shook his head.
He had had *one* blue finch, not a pair, and he had sold it that
morning.

"Tell us who you sold it to!" the old woman cried.

"We'll give you a thousand dollars," the old man said, "if
you'll just tell us his name."

"I didn't ask him."

"But how could you *not* ask him his name?" the old man
and the old woman cried.

"Did I ask yours when you came in just now and left the
door wide open?" the proprietor said. "Besides, it was the common blue finch of Africa, and not the one you are looking for."

"You know about the blue finch of Arabia?" the old man
shouted.

"Certainly," said the pet-shop proprietor.

"But I daresay you have never seen one?" said the old
woman slyly, in a normal tone of voice, hoping to test the pet-
shop proprietor's hearing.

"A pair only," the proprietor said, turning off his hearing
aid. "Never just one."

"We'll give you two thousand dollars," said the old man,
dancing up and down, "if you'll just tell us where you saw
them."

"Very well," said the pet-shop proprietor. "Where is the two
thousand?"

"What's that?" asked the old man.

"I say where is the two thousand dollars?" the pet-shop

proprietor shouted. "This is a very good hearing aid I am wearing. Here—try it, why don't you?"

The old man looked at the old woman, who nodded, and then he reached in his pocket and took out his checkbook, and she opened her purse and took out her pen, and then he turned to the pet-shop proprietor. "Name?" he shouted.

"Make it out to cash," the pet-shop proprietor said.

When the old man had finished writing out the check for two thousand dollars, he put it on the counter between the pet-shop proprietor and him, and he and the old woman leaned forward with their eyes bright and their mouths open and said, "Now, tell us where you saw them. They're worth half a million dollars."

"The pair of blue finches?"

"Are we talking about canaries?" asked the old man, drumming his nails on the counter.

"I saw them—" the pet-shop proprietor said, closing his eyes, "I saw them—" he repeated, looking tired and ill, and older than he had looked when they first came into the shop; "I saw them—" he said, suddenly opening his eyes and looking happier than the old man and the old woman had ever seen anybody look, "*in a forest in Arabia.*"

The old man shrieked with anger and disappointment, and the old woman reached for the check for two thousand dollars, which was already in the pet-shop proprietor's wallet in his inside coat pocket, though nobody saw him pick it up, fold it, and put it there.

The old man and the old woman ran out into the deep snow, crying police, crying help, and leaving the door wide open behind them. As it happened, there were no police at that wayside station on the Trans-Siberian Railroad. They rattled the door of the railway station but it was locked. On the outside, the schedule of trains was posted, and they lit matches, which they shielded with their hands and then with the old man's hat, trying to make out how long they would have to wait in the cold before another train came along that would take them back to Venice. When they did see, finally, they couldn't believe it, and went on lighting more matches and looking at the timetable in despair. The next train going in either direction was due in nine days. In the end, since all the other houses were closed and dark, they had to go back to the pet-shop, and this time the old man pulled the door to after him. The pet-shop proprietor, seeing that they were about to speak, adjusted his hearing aid; but though they opened their mouths again and again, no sound came out, and after shaking the apparatus several times, the pet-shop proprietor put it in his pocket and said in a normal tone of voice, "If you don't mind the conversation of birds, and if fish don't make you restless, and if you like cats and don't have fleas, there is no reason why you can't stay here until your train comes."

So they did. They stayed nine days, there in the pet shop, among the birds of every size and color, and the cats of all description, the monkeys and the dogs, the long-tailed goldfish, and the tame raccoons. At first they were restless, but they had promised not to be, and gradually, because whatever the pet-shop proprietor did was interesting and whatever he had in his shop was living and beautiful, they forgot about themselves, about the passing of time, about Venice, where they had a number of important appointments that it would cost them money not to keep, and even about the blue finch of Arabia, which they had never seen but only heard about. What they had heard was how rare and valuable it was, not that its song is more delicate than gold wire and its least movement like the reflections of water on a wall. The old woman helped the pet-shop proprietor clean out the cages, and the old man brushed and curried the cats, who soon grew very attached to him, and when the pet-shop proprietor said suddenly, "You have just time to walk from here to the railway station at a reasonable pace before your train pulls in," they were shocked and horrified.

"But can't we stay?" the old woman cried. "We've been so happy here these last nine days."

The pet-shop proprietor shrugged his shoulders. "It's all right with me if you want to spend the rest of your life in a wayside station on the Trans-Siberian Railroad," he said, "but what about the appointments you have in Venice?"

The old woman looked at the old man, who nodded sadly.

"Before you go," said the pet-shop proprietor, "I would like to present you with a souvenir of the establishment." He opened a door just large enough to put his hand through, and reached into a huge cage that went all the way up to the ceiling and the whole length of the room and was full of birds of every size and color, and took out two small ones, both of them blue as the beginning of the night when there is deep snow on the ground. "Here," he said, thrusting the birds into a little wire cage and closing the door on them.

"But won't they get cold?" the old woman asked. "Won't they die on that long train ride?"

"Why should they?" asked the pet-shop proprietor. "They came all the way from—"

At that moment they heard the train whistle, the train that was taking them back to Venice, and so the old man rushed for the door, and the old woman picked up the cage with the blue birds in it and put it under her coat, and they floundered through the snow to the railway station, and the conductor pulled them up onto the train, which was already moving, and it was just as the pet-shop proprietor said: The birds stood the journey better than the old man and the old woman.

At the border the customs inspector boarded the train, and went through everybody's luggage until he came to the old man and the old woman, who were dozing. He shook first one and then the other, and pointing to the bird cage he said, "What kind of birds are those?"

"Bluebirds," the old man said, and shut his eyes.

"They look to me like the blue finch of Arabia," the customs inspector said. "Are you sure they're bluebirds?"

"Positive," the old woman said. "A man who has a pet shop in a wayside station of the Trans-Siberian Railroad gave them to us, so we don't have to pay duty on them. The week before, he sold somebody a blue finch, but it was the common blue finch of Africa."

"We had all that long trip there," the old man said, opening one eye, "and this long trip back, for nothing. When do we get to Venice?"

"If they had been the blue finch of Arabia," the customs inspector said, "you would have been allowed to keep them. Ordinary birds can't cross the border."

"But they do all the time," the old woman said, "in the sky."

"I know," the customs inspector said, "but not on the Trans-Siberian Railroad. Hand me the cage, please."

The old man looked at the old woman, who stood up stiffly, from having been in one position so long, and together they got off the train, missing their appointments in Venice, and spent the remaining years of their life in a country where they didn't speak the language and there was no Commodities Exchange, rather than part with a pair of birds that they had grown attached to on a long train journey, because of their color, which was as blue as the beginning of night when there is deep snow on the ground, and their song, which was more delicate than gold wire, and their movements, which were like the reflections of water on a wall.

10. *The sound of waves*

ONCE upon a time there was a man who took his family to the seashore. They had a cottage on the ocean, and it was everything that a house by the ocean should be—sagging wicker furniture, faded detective stories, blue china, grass rugs, other people's belongings to reflect upon, and other people's pots and pans to cook with. The first evening, after the children were in bed, the man and his wife sat on the porch and watched the waves come in as if they had never seen this sight before. It was a remarkably beautiful evening, no wind, and a calm sea. Far out on the broad back of the ocean a hump would begin to gather slowly, moving toward the shore, and at a certain point the hump would rise in a dark wall and spill over. A sandpiper went skittering along the newly wetted, shining sand, the beach grass all leaned one way, the moon was riding high and white in the evening sky, and wave after wave broke just before it reached the shore. The woman said to the man, "What are you thinking about?"

"I was thinking about how many waves there are," he said, which made her laugh.

"Thousands upon thousands," he said solemnly. "Millions . . . Billions . . ."

He had been brought up far inland, where the only water was a pond or a creek winding its way through marshes and pastures, and though this was not his first time at the ocean, he could not get over it. No duck pond has ever yet gathered itself into a dark wall of water. Creeks gurgle and swirl between their muddy banks, but never succeed in producing anything like the ocean's lisp and roar. There was nothing to compare it to except itself.

The next morning he went for a swim before breakfast. The waves were high, but he waited, and the moment came when he could run in and swim out into deep water. He swam until he was tired, and then rode in on a wave, and dried himself, and went back to the house with a huge appetite.

There was no newspaper to remind him that it was now

Sunday the twentieth, and that tomorrow would be Monday the twenty-first. There was a clock in the kitchen, but he seldom looked at it, and his watch lay in his bureau drawer with the hands resting at one-fifteen. The only thing that kept him from feeling that time was standing still was the sound that came through the open windows: *Sish . . . sish . . . sish . . . sish . . . a-wish. . . . sish. . . .*

As always when people are at the ocean, the years fell away. The crow's-feet around the man's eyes remained white longer than the rest of his face, and then all the wrinkles were smoothed away during the nights of deep sleep and the days of idleness. He and his wife were neither of them young, and nothing could bring back the look of really being young, but five, ten, fifteen years fell off them. When they made love their bodies tasted of the salt sea, and when the wave of lovemaking had spent itself, they lay in one another's arms, and heard the sound of the waves. This year, and next year, and last year, and the year before that, and the year after next, and before they came, and after they had gone. . . .

The woman was afraid of the surf, and would not go past a certain point, though he coaxed her to join him. She stood timidly, this side of the breaking waves, and he left her after a while and went out past the sandy foam, to where he could stand and dive through the incoming wall of water. There was always the moment of decision, and this was what she dreaded, and why she remained on the shore—because the moment came when you had to decide and she couldn't decide. Years ago she had been rolled, and the fright had never left her. So had he, of course. He remembered what it had been like, and knew that if he wasn't careful diving through the waves he would be whipped around and lose control of what happened to him, and his face would be ground into the sharp gravel at the water's edge, his bathing trunks would be filled with sand, and, floundering and frightened, he would barely be able to struggle to his feet in time to keep it from happening all over again. But he was careful. He kept his eyes always on the incoming wave, and, swimming hard for a few seconds, he suddenly found himself safe on the other side. As he came out of the water, his face was transformed with happiness. He took the towel his wife held out to him and, hopping on one leg, to shake the water out of his ears, he said, "This is the way I remember feeling when I was seventeen years old."

While she was shopping for food he went into the post office and waited while a girl with sun-bleached hair sorted through a pile of envelopes. He came away with several, including a bank statement, which he looked at, out of habit—debits and credits, the brief but furious struggle between incoming salary and outgoing expenses—and then put in the same drawer with his watch.

All through sunny days, and cloudy days, and days when it rained, and days when the fog rolled in from the ocean and shut out the sight of the neighboring houses, the waves broke, and broke, and broke, always with the same drawn-out sound, and silently the days dropped from the calendar. The vacation was half over. Then there were only ten more days. Then it was the last Sunday, the last Monday. . . . Sitting up in bed, the man saw that there was a path of bright moonlight across the water, which the incoming waves passed through, and the moonlight made it seem as if you could actually see the earth's curve.

During the final week there were two days in a row when the sky was racked with storm clouds, and it rained intermittently, and the red flag flew from the pole by the lifeguard's stand, and only the young dared go in. Like dolphins sporting, the man thought as he stood on the beach, fully dressed, with a windbreaker on, and watched the teen-agers diving through the cliffs of water. The waves went *crash!* and then *crash!* and again *crash!* all night long.

This stormy period was followed by a day when the ocean was like a millpond, and the waves were so small they hardly got up enough hump to spill over, but spill over they did. *Sish* . . . *sish* . . . *a-wish* . . . Since the world began, he thought, stretched out on his beach towel. The I.B.M. machine had not been invented that could enumerate them. It would be like counting the grains of sand all up and down the miles and miles of beach. It would take forever. He could not stop thinking about it, and he decided that in a way it was worse than being rolled.

It was what reconciled him, in the end, to the packing and the last time for this and the last time for that, and getting dressed in city clothes, and the melancholy ritual of departure. It was too much. The whole idea was more than the mind could manage. Outside the human scale. Rather than think about the true number of the waves, he gave up his claim to the shore they broke upon, and the beach grass all leaning one way, and the moon's path across the water, and the illusion that he could actually see the earth's curve.

From the deck of the ferryboat that took them across the bay to the mainland, he watched the island grow smaller and smaller. And in two weeks' time he had forgotten all about what it was like, *this year . . . next year . . . last year . . . and before we came . . . and after we've gone . . .*

11. *The woman who never drew breath*
except to complain

IN a country near Finland dwelt a woman who never drew breath except to complain. There was in that country much to complain of—the long cold winters, the scarcity of food, and robber bands that descended on poor farmers at night and left their fields and barns blazing. But these things the woman had by an inequality of fate been spared. Her husband was young and strong and worked hard and was kind to her. And they had a child, a three-year-old boy, who was healthy and happy, obedient and good. The roof never leaked, there was always food in the larder and peat moss piled high outside the door for the fireplace she cooked by. But still the woman complained, morning, noon, and night.

One day when she was out feeding her hens, she heard a great beating of wings and looked up anxiously, thinking it was a hawk come to raid her hencoop, and saw a big white gander, which sailed once around the house and then settled at her feet and began to peck at the grain she had scattered for her hens. While she was wondering how she could catch the wild bird without the help of her husband, who was away in the fields, it flapped its great soft wings and said, "So far as I can see, you have less than any woman in this country to complain about."

"That's true enough," the woman said.

"Then why do you do it?" asked the bird.

"Because there is so much injustice in the world," the woman said. "In the village yesterday a woman in her sleep rolled over on her child and smothered it, and an old man starved to death last month, within three miles of here. Wherever I look, I see human misery, and here there is none, and I am afraid."

"Of what?" asked the bird.

"I am afraid lest they look down from the sky and see how blessed I am, compared to my neighbors, and decide to even things up a bit. This way, if they do look down, they will also hear me complaining, and think, 'That poor woman has lots to contend with,' and go on about their business."

"Very clever of you," the bird said, cleaning the underside of its wing with its beak. "But in the sky anything but the truth has a hollow ring. One more word of complaint out of you and all the misfortunes of all your neighbors will be visited on you and on your husband and child." The bird flapped its wings slowly, rose above her, sailed once around the chimney, and then, flying higher and higher, was lost in the clouds. While the woman stood peering after it, the bread that she had left in the oven burned to a cinder.

The bread was the beginning of many small misfortunes, which occurred more and more frequently as time went on. The horse went lame, the hens stopped laying, and after too long a season of rain the hay all rotted in the fields. The cow went dry but produced no calf. The roof began to leak, and when the woman's husband went up to fix it, he fell and broke his leg and was laid up for months, with winter coming on. And while the woman was outside, trying to do his work for him, the child pulled a kettle of boiling water off the stove and was badly scalded.

And still no word of complaint crossed the woman's lips. In her heart she knew that worse things could happen, and in time worse things did. A day came when there was nothing to eat in the larder and the woman had to go the rounds of her neighbors and beg for food, and those she had never turned hungry from her door refused her, on the ground that anyone so continually visited by misfortune must at some time have had sexual intercourse with the Devil. The man's leg did not heal, and the child grew sickly and pale. The woman searched for edible roots and berries, and set snares for rabbits and small birds, and so kept her family from starving, until one day, when she was far away in the marshes, some drunken soldiers happened by and wantonly set fire to the barns, and went on their way, reeling and tittering. The heat of the burning barns made a downdraft, and a shower of sparks landed on the thatched roof of the farmhouse, and that, too, caught on fire. In a very few minutes, while the neighbors stood around in a big circle, not daring to come nearer because of the heat of the flames, the house burned to the ground, and the man and the child both perished. When the woman came running across the fields, crying and wringing her hands, people who had known her all their lives and were moved at last by her misfortunes tried to intercept her and lead her away, but she would have none of them. At nightfall they left her there, and she did not even see them go. She sat with her head on her knees and listened for the sound of wings.

At midnight the great bird sailed once around the blackened chimney and settled on the ground before her, its feathers rosy with the glow from the embers. The bird seemed to be waiting for her to speak, and when she said nothing it stretched its neck and arched its back and finally said, in a voice much kinder than the last time, "This is a great pity. All the misfortunes of all your neighbors have been visited on you, without a word of complaint from you to bring them on. But the gods can't be everywhere at once, you know, and sometimes they get the cart before the horse. If you'd like to complain now, you may." The wind blew a shower of sparks upward and the bird fanned them away with its wings. The woman did not speak. "This much I can do for you," the bird said, "and I wish it was more."

When the woman raised her head, she saw a young man whose face, even in the dying firelight, she recognized. There before her stood her child, her little son, but grown now, in the pride of manhood. All power of speech left her. She put out her arms and in that instant, brought on by such a violent beating of wings as few men have ever dreamed of, the air turned white. What the woman at first took to be tiny feathers proved to be snow. It melted against her cheek, and turned her hair white, and soon put the fire out.

The snow came down all night, and all the next day, and for many days thereafter, and was so deep that it lasted all winter, and in the spring grass grew up in what had once been the rooms of the farmhouse, but of the woman there was no trace whatever.

12. The masks

ONCE upon a time there was a country where everyone wore masks. They were born wearing them. About twelve months they lasted, and were shed the way a snake sheds its skin, and for the same reason, and under the old mask there was a new one, at times all but undistinguishable from the old one, at times startlingly different. The first warning was a loosening of the skin next to the hairline, and as soon as he noticed it the person would retire for two days, and food would be left on a tray outside his door, and when he emerged with an entirely new mask his friends and family were careful not to stare openly at him until he had got used to it. The masks were not what we think of masks as being—for purposes of disguise, say, at a fancy-dress ball, or for purposes of concealment. In that fortunate country people had no need to conceal their feelings, and the masks let anger come through, as an ordinary face does, and joy, and sadness, and triumph. That is to say, the mask was their true face but they could not keep it for more than twelve months, and if you had said what a pity, they would have said, "Yes, but so is it a pity that my little grand-daughter cannot always stay five years old. Never to change one's mask is not in the nature of things." When that same little granddaughter, who had been wearing the mask of a strong and healthy child, emerged from her room with the mask of a child who is wan, tires easily, and is sickly, it struck terror to the old woman's heart, for the masks were sometimes prophetic.

People were fond of their masks and did not discard them when they were no longer of any use. Parents saved the masks of their children until they were old enough to take care of them themselves and realize their value. In the privacy of his own room, the person would go to the closet where the masks were kept and take out the mask of the period when he had been most happy, or sometimes the opposite of it, and try it on in front of the mirror, remembering old emotions. Sometimes they even went so far as to wear them in public, fastened on over their current mask, with an elastic under the chin, and the hair down to conceal the line where it had peeled from the face. And their friends would affectionately smile, remembering how they were at that period, and understanding why they chose to return to it for a brief moment. Ministers of the Gospel, professors, politicians and statesmen, official heroes of all kinds were obliged to wear the same mask year after year, no matter what new mask had formed under the old one, or how ragged the original mask had become with constant wear. When a great artist died, or a king, or a President, or a general who had changed the course of history, his masks, all of them, were hung in a museum that had been built for that purpose, and the idea was that they would hang there in perpetuity, for the edification of posterity. No doubt they would have if there had been such a thing as posterity. Or perpetuity. Instead, the masks of the great and famous were forever being shifted around—from the most conspicuous place in the main hall to some obscure alcove, and vice versa. Or even to a storeroom in the basement, where they were to be seen only on written request. When an ordinary person died, his masks were gathered up, usually by someone whose own mask was bathed in tears, and put away in a pine box. From time to time the box would be opened and the masks looked at longingly or with new understanding. They did not deteriorate, or suffer the slightest change. As year after year passed, the box would be opened less frequently, and sometimes when it was opened it would be by a person who had never actually seen any of the masks before, though he had of course heard of the person they belonged to. Or it might be someone who had the name and even the facts wrong, and, studying the masks, would arrive at all sorts of interesting conclusions that were occasionally taken seriously, and so muddied the stream of history.

The living masks of saints grew less distinct in outline the closer they came to the knowledge of God. Lovers, especially at the beginning of their rapturous exploration of one another's natures and bodies, would sometimes childishly exchange masks—as if it made the slightest difference to a heart overflowing with feeling. The masks of husbands and wives long married and deeply connected by subterranean knowledge of one kind and another grew to look more and more alike, so that if they had changed masks with each other it would hardly have been noticed. The discarded masks took up more and more room, inevitably, and people with imagination sometimes felt that it was hardly worth their while to grow a new mask every twelve months when there were so many of them in pine boxes in storeroom after storeroom stretching back and back into the distant past. They didn't expect anyone to take their carping seriously, but on the other hand change would never come about if people did not, for one reason or another, accept it as a possibility. In the case of the fortunate kingdom where everyone wore masks, it began with the young. Whereas people in their forties and fifties and upward continued to retire into their bedrooms at the appointed time and to emerge with a new face, it was said that fourteen- and fifteen-year-olds were passing the time when this should happen, and rejoiced in the thought that in failing to produce a new mask they were defying their parents. When several years passed and they still had not changed their masks, they knew they were part of a New Movement. "It's a fad," people said. "And like every other fad it will pass." But they saw nervously that the younger children had taken the idea up too, and finally it spread to children too young to know what it meant not to change one's mask ever. And, not wanting to appear peculiar, the older people did not retire when the twelve-month period was up, and, instead, kept their old mask, and so it became clear at last that Nature, not Fashion, was at work.

After that the discarded masks were taken out of the pine boxes and thrown out on the dustheap, and with time they became extremely rare, like authentic Chippendale and Chinese Export and gold coins from the reign of the Emperor Hadrian. They were studied by the historian and the moral philosopher. As for people in general, they seemed to grow old much faster than formerly, because having no mask they had to create one with the play of facial muscles, and this gave rise to crow's-feet, and wrinkles across the forehead, and deep lines etched from the corners of the nose to the corners of the mouth, and sagging flesh, which fooled nobody, of course, because the heart of the person underneath this simulated mask was either always young or never had been.

13. *The man who lost his father*

Once upon a time there was a man who lost his father. His father died of natural causes—that is to say, illness and old age—and it was time for him to go, but nevertheless the man was affected by it, more than he had expected. He misplaced things: his keys, his reading glasses, a communication from the bank. And he imagined things. He imagined that his father's spirit walked the streets of the city where he lived, was within touching distance of him, could not for a certain time leave this world for the world of spirits, and was trying to communicate with him. When he picked up the mail that was lying on the marble floor outside the door of his apartment, he expected to find a letter from his father telling him . . . telling him what?

The secret of the afterlife is nothing at all—or rather, it is only one secret, compared to the infinite number of secrets having to do with this life that the dead take with them when they go.

"Why didn't I ask him when I had a chance?" the man said, addressing the troubled face in the bathroom mirror, a face made prematurely old by a white beard of shaving lather. And from that other mirror, his mind, the answer came: *Because you thought there was still time. You expected him to live forever . . . because you expect to live forever yourself.* The razor stopped in mid-stroke. This time what came was a question. *Do you or don't you? You do expect to live forever. You don't expect to live forever?* The man plunged his hands in soapy water and rinsed the lather from his face. And as he was drying his hands on a towel, he glanced down four stories at the empty street corner and for a split second he thought he saw his father, standing in front of the drugstore window.

His father's body was in a coffin, and the coffin was in the ground, in a cemetery, but that he never thought about. Authority is not buried in a wooden box. Nor safety (mixed with the smell of cigar smoke). Nor the firm handwriting. Nor the sound of his voice. Nor the right to ask questions that are painful to answer.

So long as his father was alive, he figured persistently in the man's conversation. Almost any remark was likely to evoke him. Although the point of the remark was mildly amusing and the tone intended to be affectionate, there was something about it that was not amusing and not entirely affectionate—as if an old grievance was still being nourished, a deep disagreement, a deprivation, something raked up out of the past that should have been allowed to lie forgotten. It was, actually, rather tiresome, but even after he perceived what he was doing the man could not stop. It made no difference whether he was with friends or with people he had never seen before. In the space of five minutes, his father would pop up in the conversation. And you didn't have to be very acute to understand that what he was really saying was "Though I am a grown man and not a little boy, I still feel the weight of my father's hand on me, and I tell this story to lighten the weight. . . ."

Now that his father was gone, he almost never spoke of him, but he thought about him. At my age was his hair this thin, the man wondered, holding his comb under the bathroom faucet.

Why, when he never went to church, did he change, the man wondered, dropping a letter in the corner mailbox. Why, when he had been an atheist, or if not an atheist then an agnostic, all his life, was he so pleased to see the Episcopal minister during his last illness?

Hanging in the hall closet was his father's overcoat, which by a curious accident now fit him. Authority had shrunk. And safety? There was no such thing as safety. It was only an idea that children have. As they think that with the help of an umbrella they can fly, so they feel that their parents stand between them and all that is dangerous. Meanwhile, the cleaning establishment had disposed of the smell of cigar smoke; the overcoat smelled like any overcoat. The handwriting on the envelopes he picked up in the morning outside his door was never that handwriting. And along with certain stock certificates that had been turned over to him when his father's estate was settled, he had received the right to ask questions that are painful to answer, such as "Why did you not value your youth?"

He wore the overcoat, which was of the very best quality but double-breasted and long and a dark charcoal grey—an old man's coat—only in very cold weather, and it kept him warm. . . . From the funeral home they went to the cemetery, and the coffin was already there, in a tent, suspended above the open grave. After the minister had spoken the last words, it still was not lowered. Instead, the mourners raised their heads, got up from their folding chairs, and went out into the icy wind of a January day. And to the man's surprise, the outlines of the bare trees were blurred. He had not expected tears, and neither had he expected to see, in a small group of people waiting some distance from the tent, a man and a woman, not related to each other and not married to each other, but both related to him: his first playmates. They stepped forward and took his hand and spoke to him, looking deeply into his eyes. The only possible conclusion was that they were there waiting for him, in the cold, because they were worried about him. . . . In his father's end was his own beginning, the mirror in his mind pointed out. And it was true, in more ways than one. But it took time.

He let go of the ghost in front of the corner drugstore.
    The questions grew less and less painful to have to answer. The stories he told his children about their grandfather did not have to do with a disagreement, a deprivation, or something raked up out of the distant past that might better have been forgotten. When he was abrupt with them and they ran crying from the room, he thought, *But my voice wasn't all that harsh.* Then he thought, *To them it must have been.* And he got up from his chair and went after them, to lighten the weight of his father's irritability, making itself felt in some mysterious way through him. They forgave him, and he forgave his father, who surely hadn't meant to sound severe and unloving. And when he took his wife and children home—to the place that in his childhood was home—on a family visit, one of his cousins, smiling, said, "How much like your father you are."
    "That's because I am wearing his overcoat," the man said—or rather, the child that survived in the man. The man himself was pleased, accepted the compliment (surprising though it was), and at the first opportunity looked in the mirror to see if it was true.

14. *The old woman whose house was beside a running stream*

THERE was an old woman whose house was beside a bend in a running stream. Sometimes the eddying current sounded almost like words, like a message: *Rill, you will, you will, sill, rillable, syllable, billable.* . . . Sometimes when she woke in the night it was to the sound of a fountain plashing, though there wasn't, of course, any fountain. Or sometimes it sounded like rain, though the sky was clear and full of stars.

Around her cottage Canada lilies grew, and wild peppermint, and lupins, Queen Anne's lace taller than her head, and wild roses that were half the ordinary size, and the wind brought with it across somebody else's pasture the smell of pine trees, which she could see from her kitchen window. Here she lived, all by herself, and since she had no one to cook and care for but herself, you might think that time was heavy on her hands. It was just the contrary. The light woke her in the morning, and the first thing she heard was the sound of the running stream. It was the sound of hurry, and she said to herself, "I must get up and get breakfast and make the bed and sweep, or I'll be late setting the bread to rise." And when the bread was out of the way, there was the laundry. And when the laundry was hanging on the line, there was something else that urgently needed doing. The stream also never stopped hurrying and worrying on to some place she had never thought about and did not try to imagine. So great was its eagerness that it cut away at its banks until every so often it broke through to some bend farther on, leaving a winding bog that soon filled up with wild flowers. But this the old woman had no way of knowing, for when she left the house it was to buy groceries in the store at the crossroads, or call on a sick friend. She was not much of a walker. She suffered from shortness of breath, and her knees bothered her a good deal. "The truth is," she kept telling herself, as if it was an idea she had not yet completely accepted, "I am an old woman, and I don't have forever to do the things that need to be done." Looking in the mirror, she could not help seeing the wrinkles. And her hair, which had once been thick and shining, was not only grey but so thin she could see her scalp. Even the texture of her hair had changed. It was frizzy, and the hair of a stranger. "So long ago," she said to herself as she read through old letters before destroying them. "And it seems like yesterday." And as she wrote out labels, which she pasted on the undersides of tables and chairs, telling whom they were to go to after her death, she said, "I don't see how I could have accumulated so much. Where did it all come from?" And one morning she woke up with the realization that if she died that day, she would have done all she could do. Her dresser drawers were tidied, the cupboards in order. It was a Tuesday, and she did not bake until Thursday, and the marketing she had done the day before. The house was clean, the ironing put away, and if she threw the covers off and hurried into her clothes, it would be to do something that didn't really need doing. So she lay there thinking, and gradually the thoughts in her mind, which were threadbare with repetition, were replaced by the sound of conversation that came to her from outside—*rill, you will? You will, still. But fill, but fill*—and the chittering conversation of the birds. Suddenly she knew what she was going to do, though there was no hurry about it. She was going to follow the stream and see what happened to it after it passed her house.

She ate a leisurely breakfast, washed the dishes, and put a sugar sandwich and an orange in a brown paper bag. Then, wearing a black straw hat in case it should turn warm and an old grey sweater in case it should turn cold, she locked the house up, and put the key to the front door under the mat, and started off.

The first thing she came to was a rustic footbridge, which seemed to lead to an island, but the island turned out to be merely the other side of the stream. Here there were paths everywhere, made by the horses in the pasture coming down to drink. She followed now one, now another, stepping over fallen tree trunks, and pausing when her dress caught on a briar. Sometimes the path led her to the brink of the stream at a place where there was no way to cross, and she had to retrace her steps and choose some other path. Sometimes it led her through a cool glade, or a meadow where the grass grew up to her knees. When she came to a barbed-wire fence with a stile over it, she knew she was following a path made by human beings.

First she was on one side of the stream and then, when a big log or a bridge invited her to cross over, she was on the other. She saw a house, but it was closed and shuttered, and so, though she knew she was trespassing, she felt no alarm. When the path left the stream, she decided to continue on it, assuming that the stream would quickly wind back upon itself and rejoin her. The path led her to a road, and the road led her to a gate with a sign on it: KEEP THIS GATE CLOSED. It was standing open. She went on, following the road as before, and came to another gate, with a padlock and chain on it, but right beside the gate was an opening in the fence just large enough for her to crawl through. The road was deep in dust and lined with tall trees that cast a dense shade. She saw a deer, which stopped grazing and raised its head to look at her, and then went bounding off. The road brought her to more houses— summer cottages, not places where people lived the year round. To avoid them she cut through the trees, in the direction that she assumed the running stream must be, and saw still another house. Here, for the first time, there was somebody—a man who did not immediately see her, for he was bent over, sharpening a scythe.

"I'm looking for the little running stream," she said to him.

"You left that a long way back," the man said. "The river is just on the other side of those big pine trees."

"Is there a bridge?"

"Half a mile upstream."

"What happens if I follow the river downstream on this side?"

"You can't," the man said. "There's no way. You have to go upstream to the bridge."

Should she turn around and go home, she wondered. The sun was not yet overhead, so she walked on, toward the trees the man had pointed to, thinking that he might be mistaken and that it might be the running stream that went past her house, but it wasn't. It was three times as broad, and clearly a little river. It too was lined with wild flowers, and in places they had leaped over the flowing water and were growing out of a log in midstream. The river was almost as clear as the air, and she could see the bottom, and schools of fish darting this way and that. Rainbow trout, they were. Half a mile upstream and half a mile down made a mile, and she thought of her poor knees. The water, though swift, was apparently quite shallow. She could take off her shoes and stockings and wade across.

Holding her skirts up, she went slowly out into the river. The bottom was all smooth, rounded stones, precarious to walk on, and she was careful to place her feet firmly. When she was halfway across she stepped into a deep hole, lost her balance, and fell. She tried to stand up, but the current was too swift, and she was hampered by her wet clothing. Gasping and swallowing water, she was tumbled over and over as things are that float downstream in a rushing current. "I did not think my life would end like this," she said to herself, and gave up and let the current take her.

When she opened her eyes, she was lying on the farther bank of the river. She must have been lying there for hours, because her hair and her clothing were dry. In the middle of the river there was a young man, who turned his head and smiled at her. He had blond hair and he was not more than twenty, and he had waders on which came up to his waist, and his chest and shoulders were bare, and she could see right through him; she could see the river and the wild flowers on the other bank. Had he pulled her out? You can't see through living people. He must be dead. But he was not a corpse, he was the most angelic young man she had ever seen, and radiantly happy as he whipped his line back and forth over the shining water. And so, for that matter, was she. She tried to speak to him but could not. It was too strange.

He waded downstream slowly, casting as he went, and she watched him until he was out of sight. She saw that there was a path that followed the river downstream. I'll just go a little farther, she thought, and started on. She wanted to have another look at the beautiful young man, who must be just around the next bend of the river. Instead, when she got there, she saw a heavy, middle-aged man with a bald head. He also was standing in the middle of the river, casting, and a shaft of sunlight passed right through him. She went on. The path was only a few feet from the water, and it curved around the roots of old trees to avoid a clump of bushes. She saw two horses standing by the mouth of a little stream that might be the stream that went past her house—there was no way of telling —and she could see right through them, too, as if they were made of glass. Soon after this she began to overtake people on the path—for her knees no longer bothered her, and she walked quite fast, for the pleasure of it, and because she had such a feeling of lightness. She saw, sitting on the bank, a boy with a great many freckles, who caught a good-sized trout while she stood watching him. He smiled at her and she smiled back at him, and went on. She met a very friendly dog, who stayed with her, and a young woman with a baby carriage, and an old man. They both smiled at her, the way the young man and the boy had, but said nothing. The feeling of lightness persisted, as if a burden larger than she had realized had been taken off her shoulders. If I keep on much farther, I'll never find my way home, she thought. But nevertheless she went on, as if she had no choice, meeting more people, and suddenly she looked down at her hands and saw that they too were transparent. Then she knew. But without any fear or regret. So it was there all the time, an hour's walk from the house, she thought. And with a light heart she walked on, enjoying the day and the sunlight on the river, which seemed almost alive, and from time to time meeting more people all going the same way she was, all going the same way as the river.

15. The pessimistic fortune-teller

ONCE upon a time there was a girl who told fortunes by the roadside. She did not need to do this for a living. Her father was an entrepreneur who had made a great deal of money and was on the board of directors of so many companies and charities that only his secretary knew the full extent of them, but one day when he came home from his office there his daughter was, with a silk scarf tied around her head, and large earrings, and a long skirt, and looking in every way like a gypsy except her pale, pinched face.

At first people thought it was a game, and were suspicious, and either hurried past her or crossed to the other side of the street, but women cannot resist lifting the curtain of the future just a tiny bit, and so, pretending not to take it seriously, but actually with an open mind, somebody sat down at the card table and offered her open palm. Not for long, though. What she heard was nothing she wanted to hear, and nothing like so comforting as the prognostications of ordinary gypsy fortune-tellers: no tall dark handsome man, no sea voyage, no business ventures that must not be acted upon in the early part of the month, but instead a threat to the thing she held nearest and dearest. With a pale, pinched face she hurried home and shut herself in her room and began restlessly to clean out her bureau drawers in an effort to get what she had been told out of her mind.

Many combinations of circumstances can be reasonably dismissed as the result of coincidence, but not all. At some point the combination is so remarkable that it could not occur except by design, by some ultimate cause or Prime Mover. Though the woman made every effort to forestall the thing that the girl told her might happen, the events unrolled exactly as she had predicted, and the steps that were taken to prevent the calamity seemed, in the end, to have actually helped to bring it about.

Meanwhile other women stopped on their way home from the market or from the church or a call on a sick friend—never with their husbands, because they did not care to waste the energy it would require to defend their action, and because, also,

a woman who has no secrets from her husband is not a woman
but a child.

And what did they hear, sitting at the card table in front of
the rich merchant's house, with their hand lying palm upward
in the hand of the merchant's thin-faced daughter? Miscar-
riages, misfortunes, death in the family, financial reverses, ill
health, ill will on the part of those who were nearest and dearest to them. One would have thought that one experience with
so pessimistic a fortune-teller would have been enough, and
perhaps it would have been if the miscarriage had not actually
occurred, and the misfortune, and the death in the family, and
all the rest, exactly as predicted. And thinking always that if
they knew what was going to happen they could do something
to forestall it, the women went back. They told their friends, in
strictest confidence, and the friends came, looking woebegone
even as they sat down and before they had heard a word of the
fate that was in store for them.

The girl's father was not able to stop her from putting a
scarf on her head and dressing up in earrings and a long
Roman-striped skirt and sitting at the card table on the front
lawn with a pack of cards ready to be turned up one at a time,
in a sequence that was never meaningless and never optimistic.
She was of age, and had an inheritance from her grandmother,
and was sufficiently strong-minded, as he had every reason to
know, that she would simply have set up her fortune-telling in
some other place where he wouldn't even be in a position to
know what was going on, or to help her if she needed help.
And of course before very long she did. No one can consistently and successfully foretell disaster without being held in
some way responsible for it, no matter how much reason ar-
gues that it is not the case. The feelings know better. And in
time the women who sat down at the card table pressed their
lips in a thin line, clutched their purses tightly to their stomachs, and the hand that they extended was not relaxed but tense
and in some cases trembled. Or the eyes beseeched a softer,
kinder interpretation of what was to come, and when the
women did not get it, they fished through their purse for a
handkerchief, wiped the tears away furtively, and blew their
nose, and heaved a sigh as if their misfortune, the death in the
family, the financial reverse had already taken place. As indeed

it might just as well have, because take place it did, exactly as foretold, and whether you shed tears before or after an event in no way changes the event or how it affects you.

It speaks a great deal for the superior rationality of men over women that no husband succumbed to the temptation to have his fortune told, but if the entrepreneur's daughter had had any understanding whatever of business affairs, or of the stock market, or of real-estate values, who knows what might have happened? But she didn't. The only losses she understood were emotional. So the men were free to consider what to do about her. Social ostracism was considered and rejected. She had never been popular at parties and had reached the point where she refused all social invitations. They could have ruined her father financially, and seriously considered doing this, and decided against it, on the ground that it would not get at the root of the matter, or affect the income from the trust that had been set up for her by her grandmother. Clearly she had powers that people ought not to have, and clearly in earlier times she would have been regarded as a witch and burned. They got to her through her mother, with the help of their wives. And the girl, turning the cards over, foresaw what would happen as a result of her visit to the famous psychiatrist, and what the psychological tests would show, and kept the appointment and took the tests and allowed herself to be shut up in a hospital and treated with drugs that temporarily invoked such complete confusion of mind that for days she lost sight of even her own identity, let alone what was going to happen to the doctors and nurses who, with the best intentions, were doing this to her. Before being led away for her first shock treatment she asked to be allowed to use a deck of cards, but that was the last time. When she came home, cured of her melancholy and also of her talent for divining the future, there was a general feeling of relief, as if they had, by taking appropriate measures, indeed got at the root of the trouble and they could expect a long happy prosperous life, without a single serious misfortune or so much as a cloud in the sky. The young married couple who lost their first child did not know that it was going to happen, and so in the suddenness of their grief did not think to blame anybody except themselves, and since this was not reasonable, and similar sorrows could be pointed out to them and are clearly part of the pattern of human life, they came in time to accept the disaster, and were not surprised it did not repeat itself, but merely bent over their newborn child with loving and thankful hearts. Men suffered financial reverses and either shot themselves or went off to South America, depending on their temperament. The ill will of those who were close, people learned to live with, recognizing that an element of this could be found in a remote corner of their own hearts, and when a gypsy fortune-teller set up shop in an empty building on a back street at the edge of the business district, the women—in pairs, clutching their purses, and with an eye for roaches and bedbugs—sat down to have the curtain of the future lifted a tiny bit. The gypsy was a professional and knew her trade, and the fact that no tall dark handsome man came along and swept the stout middle-aged woman off her feet, that a business venture acted upon in the beginning of the month was as fortunate or as unfortunate as one postponed till the end of the month, that they did not go on a long sea voyage—all this didn't matter in the least. They paid what they were asked and went off in pleased expectation of good luck they were too old or too ill or too set in their ways ever to have.

16. The printing office

IN a certain large city, on a side street that was only two
blocks long, there was a two-story building with a neon sign
that read R. H. GILROY ♦ PRINTING. This sign, which was
strongly colored with orchid and blue and flickered anxiously,
was the crowning achievement of thirty years of night work
and staying open on Saturdays and Sundays. R. H. Gilroy was
a short, irascible man with a green eyeshade, a pencil behind
his ear, and a cigar butt in the corner of his mouth. The sign
didn't mention the printer's wife, though it should have. She
answered the telephone and did the bookkeeping and wrote
out bills in a large, placid, motherly handwriting, and knew
where everything was and how to pacify her husband when he
got excited.

From her desk by the radiator, Maria Gilroy looked out on
the Apex Party Favors Company and A. & J. Kertock Plumbing and Heating, directly across the street. She could also see
the upper stories of the Universal Moving and Storage Company, two blocks north. At odd times of the day, birds swooped
down out of the air and settled on the iron ladder that led
from the roof of the storage company to the cone-shaped roof
of a water tank. The people of the neighborhood—boys lolling
on the steps of the vocational high school, the policeman who
stood under the marquee of Number 210 when it was raining,
and others—took these birds to be pigeons. The printer's wife,
who was born and brought up in Italy, knew they were not
pigeons but doves. When her eyes demanded some relief from
the strain of balancing figures that were, at the same time, too
close to her face and too far from her heart, she would get up
from her desk by the radiator, and go outdoors and stand
looking up, shielding her eyes with her hand and straining for
the sound that she remembered from her far-off childhood,
and that she could sometimes almost hear, and might indeed
have heard if a truck hadn't shifted into low gear or a bus
hadn't backfired or if the children who lived over the Apex
Party Favors Company and whose only place to play was the
street had ever stopped yelling at each other. The silence that

810

was always on the point of settling down on that not very busy street never actually did, and the birds circling through the silence of the upper air never settled on any perch lower than the iron ladder of the water tank of the Universal Moving and Storage Company.

The printer's wife tried various ways of coaxing them down. She bought a china dove in Woolworth's and set it in her window. She tried thought transference. She bought bread-crumbs at the delicatessen and scattered them on the sidewalk. But pigeons flying to and from the marble eaves of the post office saw the breadcrumbs and swooped down and strutted about on the sidewalk, picking and choosing and making sounds that were egotistical and monotonous, and of course they kept the doves away. When it rained, the breadcrumbs made a soggy mess on the sidewalk and the policeman left the shelter of the marquee and crossed the street and told the printer he was violating a city ordinance, which made him ter-ribly excited. So she gave up trying to lure the birds closer and merely watched them. There was sometimes only one on the ladder, and there were never more than three. The business was open on Christmas Day, as usual, and on New Year's, and the birds were either on the ladder or in the air above it, but on the second of January she didn't see them all day, and when they weren't there the next morning, she said, "I wonder if something has happened to my birds."

The printer, who was reading proof for the sixth edition of a third-rate dictionary, bit into his damp, defeated cigar and reached for the pencil behind his ear. "Eeyah!" he exclaimed bitterly, and restored a missing cedilla. On the margin of the proof he wrote a sarcastic note for the typesetter, who was quick as lightning but not, unfortunately, a perfectionist. The printer's wife glanced over her shoulder and saw that the page he was correcting began with the word "doubt" and ended with "downfall." Her eyes traveled down the column of type until they stopped at "dove (duv)." In mounting excitement—for it must be a sign, it couldn't be just an accident—she read on hastily, through the derivation [ME. *douve*, akin to OS. *dūba*, D. *duif*, OHG. *tùba*, G. *taube*, ON. *dūfa*, Sw. *dufva*, Dan. *due*, Goth. *dūbo*, and prob. to OIr. *dub* black. See DEAF] and the first and second meanings, and arrived at the third.

The words "emblem of the Holy Spirit" flickered on the page, though the harsh white fluorescent light did not alter, and she felt a moment of fright. Turning her eyes to the window, she saw the orchid faces of A. and J. Kertock, who had just pad-locked the door of their shop and were about to go home to their dinner, content and happy with using brass fitting when solid copper was specified and the thousand and one opportu-nities for padding a plumbing and heating bill. She nodded, and they—quite ready to admit that it takes all kinds to make a world and even though honesty is not the best policy there was no reason why the printer and his wife shouldn't pursue it if it gave them any pleasure—nodded in return. She wanted to throw open the window and ask them if they had seen the doves, but it wasn't that kind of a window.

The next morning, while she was tearing January 3 off her desk calendar, the doves settled down on their perch. It was a very cold day, and she was concerned for them. If they only had a little house they could go into, out of the wind, she kept thinking, and she was tempted to pick up the phone and call the Universal Moving and Storage Company. By the next morning, the wind had dropped and the air was milder, and that evening orchid-and-blue snow drifted gently down on the sidewalk and on the stone window ledge, and on the tarred rooftops across the street. By eleven o'clock, when the neon sign was turned off, the street was like a stage setting.

At noon on the sixth of January, the printer's wife put on her coat and her plastic boots and trudged through the snow to the delicatessen and came back with three chicken sandwiches on white, three dill pickles, and a paper container of cranber-ries. Leaning against the garbage cans of Number 210, where it certainly hadn't been a few minutes before, was a Christmas tree with some of the tinsel still on it. It had seen better days, but even so, in a landscape made up entirely of brick, stone, concrete, and plate glass, it was a pleasure to look at, and all afternoon the printer's wife kept getting up from her chair and glancing up the street to see if the tree was still there. At four o'clock she put on her coat and her plastic boots and went out into the street. The policeman saw her pick up the Christmas tree and carry it into the fish market, but he took no notice.

When she walked into the printing shop a few minutes later
with her arms full of green branches which the fishman had
kindly chopped off for her, the printer saw her and didn't see
her. Words and printer's symbols were the only things he ever
saw and saw. She took the container of cranberries from the
top drawer of the filing cabinet and then picked up the branches
and went to the back of the shop and climbed the stairway to
the second floor, where the back files and the office supplies
were kept and where there was an iron stairs leading to a trapdoor that opened onto the roof. The roof of R. H. Gilroy ♦
Printing was flat and tarred, and it had a false front with an ornamental coping. In a corner where the wind would not reach
it, the printer's wife made a shelter and sprinkled crumbs (she
had eaten the slice of chicken but not the bread) and cranberries in among the green, forest-smelling boughs. The wind
whipped at her coat, but she did not feel the cold. And all
around her the rooftops were unfamiliar because of the snow,
with here a pavilion and there an archway or a garden house or
a grotto. The falling snow softened the sound of the trucks in
the street, and the children who lived over the Apex Party
Favors Company were indoors at that moment, playing under
their Christmas tree, which sometimes stayed up until Easter,
and was decorated with soiled paper hats, serpentines, crackers
without any fortune in them, and papier-mâché champagne
bottles. The street grew quieter and quieter and quieter and
quieter, and at last, out of a sky as soft and as silent as the
snow, three doves descended. They alighted on the ornamental coping and from the ornamental coping they flew to the
chimney pots, and from there straight into the corner where
the pine boughs had been prepared for them.

Aware that his wife had been standing behind his chair for
some time, the printer looked up impatiently. Something in
her face, an expression that he recognized as related in some
remote way to printer's signs and symbols, made him take off
his green eyeshade and place his cigar stub on the edge of the
desk and follow her. As they passed the typesetter, she motioned to him, and he stopped his frantic machine and came
too. At the top of the iron stair she turned and warned them
not to speak. Then she pushed the trap door open slowly. The
silence that had been coming and coming had arrived while

she was downstairs, and as the two men stepped out onto the roof, bareheaded and surprised by the snow alighting on their faces, they heard first the silence and then the sound that came from the pine boughs.

"*Zenadoura macroura carolinensis*, the mourning dove," the printer whispered, quoting from the great unabridged dictionary that it was his life's dream to set up in type and print. His ink-stained, highly skilled, nervous hand sought and found his wife's soft hand. The typesetter crossed himself. The doves, aware of their presence but not frightened by it, moved among the boughs, seeking out the breadcrumbs, and with a slight movement of their feathered throats making sounds softer than snow, making signs and symbols of sounds, softer and more caressing than lŭv and dŭv, kinder than good, deeper than pēs.

17. *The lamplighter*

J UST before dark, when it was already dark inside the cottages and barns and outbuildings, the lamplighter came riding up one street and down the next, on his bicycle, with his igniting rod. He did not answer when people called a greeting to him, and so, long ago, they had stopped doing this—not, however, out of any feeling of unfriendliness. "There goes the lamplighter," they said, in exactly the same tone of voice that they said, "Why, there's the moon." Through the dusk he went, leaving a trail of lighted lamps behind him. And as if he had given them the idea, one by one the houses began to show a light in the kitchen, or the parlor, or upstairs in some low-ceilinged bedroom. Men coming home from the fields with their team and their dog, children coming home from their play, were so used to the sight of the lamplighter's bicycle spinning off into the dusk that it never occurred to them to wonder how the lamps he was now lighting got put out.

No two mornings are ever quite the same. Some are cold and dark and rainy, and some—a great many, in fact—are like the beginning of the world. First the idea of morning comes, and then, though it is still utterly dark and you can't see your hand in front of your face, a rooster crows, and you'd swear it was a mistake, because it is another twenty minutes before the first light, when the rooster crows again and again, and soon after that the birds begin, praising the feathered god who made them. With their whole hearts, every single bird in creation. And then comes the grand climax. The sky turns red, and the great fiery ball comes up over the eastern horizon. After which there is a coda. The birds repeat their praise, one bird at a time, and the rooster gives one last, thoughtful crow, and the beginning of things comes to an end. While all this was happening, the villagers were fast asleep in their beds, but the lamplighter was hurrying along on his bicycle, and when he came to a lamp, he would reach up with his rod and put it out.

The lamplighter was not young, and he lived all alone, in a small cottage at the far end of the village, and cooked his own meals, and swept his own floor, and made his own bed, and had a little vegetable garden and a grape arbor but no dog or cat for company, and the rooster that wakened him every morning before daybreak belonged to somebody else. It was an orderly, regular life that varied only in that everything the lamplighter did he did a few minutes earlier or a few minutes later than the day before, depending on whether the sky was clear or cloudy, and whether the sun was approaching the summer or the winter solstice. And since at dusk he was in too great a hurry to stop and speak to anyone, and in the morning there was never anyone to speak to, he lived almost entirely inside his own mind. There, over and over again, he relived the happiness that would never come again, or corrected some mistake that made his face wince with shame as he reached up with his rod and snuffed out one more lamp. The dead came back to life, just so he could tell them what he had failed to tell them when they were alive. Sometimes he married, and the house at the edge of the village rang with the sound of children's excited voices, and in the evening friends whose faces he could almost but not quite see came and sat with him under the grape arbor.

The comings and goings of his neighbors were never as real to him as his own thoughts, and so the first time he saw the woman in the long grey cloak walking along the path that went through the water meadows, at an hour when nobody was ever abroad, it was as if an idea had crossed his mind. She was a good distance away, walking with her back to him, and then the rising sun came between them and he couldn't see her anymore, though he continued to peer over his shoulder in the direction in which he had last seen her.

He told himself that he needn't expect to see her ever again, because he knew every woman in the village and they none of them wore a long grey cloak, so it must be a stranger who had happened to pass this way, very early one morning, on some errand. He looked for her, even so, and the next time he saw her it was from such a great distance that he was not even sure it was the same person, but the beating of his heart told him that it was the woman he had seen crossing the water meadow. After that, he continued to see her—not often, and never at regular intervals, but always at some moment when he was not reliving the happiness that would never come again, or undoing old mistakes, or placating the dead, or peopling his solitary life with phantoms. Only when he wasn't thinking at all would he suddenly see her, and he realized that the distance between them was steadily diminishing. One morning he thought he saw her beckon to him, and he was so startled that he almost fell off his bicycle. He wanted to ride after her and overtake her, but something stopped him. What stopped him was the thought that he might have imagined it. While he was standing there debating what he ought to do and trying to decide whether she really had raised her arm and beckoned to him, suddenly she was no longer there. The early morning mists had hidden her. And in that moment his mind was made up.

Morning after morning, he peered into the distance and saw, through the mist, the familiar shape of a thatch-roofed cottage or a cow standing in a field, or a pollarded willow that had been there ever since he was a small boy. Or he saw a screen of poplars and the glint of water in the ditch that ran in a straight line through the meadows. But not what he was looking for. And as dusk came on and he got out his bicycle and his rod, there was a look of purpose on his face. If anybody had spoken to him as he rode past, stopping only when he came to a lamp that needed lighting, he would not have heard them.

And who said incontrovertibly that things are what they seem? That there is only this one life and no little door that you can step through into—into something altogether different.

One beautiful evening, when the warmth of the summer day lingered long past the going down of the sun, and the women stayed outside past their usual time, talking and not wanting to interrupt their conversation or the children's games, and one kind of half-light succeeded another, and the men came home from the fields and sat down to a glass of cold beer, and the dogs frolicked together, and finally there wasn't any more light in the sky, and in fact you could hardly see your hand in front of your face, suddenly a babble of voices arose all over the village, all saying the same thing: "Where is the lamplighter?"

People groped their way into their houses, muttering, "I don't understand it. This sort of thing has never happened before," and in one house after another a light came on, but the streets remained as dark as pitch. "If this happens again, we'll have to get somebody else to light the lamps," the village fathers said, standing about in groups, each with a lanthorn in his hand, and then, chattering indignantly among themselves, they set off in a body for the lamplighter's cottage, intending to have it out with him. A lot of good it did them.

18. The kingdom where straightforward, logical thinking was admired over every other kind

IN a kingdom somewhere between China and the Caucasus, it became so much the fashion to admire straightforward, logical thinking over every other kind that the inhabitants would not tolerate any angle except a right angle or any line that was not the shortest distance between two points. All the pleasant meandering roads were straightened, which meant that a great many comfortable old houses had to be demolished and people were often obliged to drive miles out of their way to get to their destination. Fruit trees were pruned so that their branches went straight out or up, and stopped bearing fruit. Babies were made to walk at nine months—with braces, if necessary. Elderly persons could not be bent with age. All anybody has to do is look around to see that Nature is partial to curves and irregularities, but it was considered vulgar to look anywhere but straight ahead. The laws of the land reflected the universal prejudice. An accused person was quickly found to be innocent or guilty, and if there were any extenuating circumstances, the judge did not want to hear about them.

In the fiftieth year of his reign the old king, who was much loved, met with an accident. Looking straight ahead instead of where he was putting his feet, he walked into a charcoal burner's pit and broke his neck. The new king was every bit as inflexible as his father, and after he ascended the throne things should have gone exactly as before, only they never do. The king had only one child. The Princess Horizon was as beautiful as the first hour of a summer day, and the common people believed that fairies had attended her christening. Her manner with the greatest lord of the land and with the poorest peasant was the same—graceful, simple, and direct. She was intelligent but not too intelligent, proud but not haughty, and skillful at terminating conversations. She was everything a princess should be. But she was also something a princess should not be. Or to put it differently, there was a flaw in her character, though it would not have been considered a flaw in yours or mine. Because of the royal blood in her veins, it wasn't suitable for her to be alone, from the moment she woke, in a room full of expectant courtiers, until it was time for her to close her eyes to all the flattery around her and go to sleep. But when the Princess's ladies-in-waiting had finished grouping themselves about her chair and were ready to take up their embroidery, they would discover that the chair was empty. How she had managed to elude them they could not imagine and the chair did not say. Or they would precede her, in the order of their rank, down some long, mirrored gallery, only to find when they reached the end of it that there was no one behind them. When she should have been opening a charity bazaar she was exercising her pony; someone else had to judge the footraces and award the blue ribbon for the largest vegetable and the smallest stitches. When she should have been laying a cornerstone she was climbing some remote tower of the palace, hoping to find an old woman with a spindle. When she should have been sitting in the royal box at the opera, showing off the crown jewels and encouraging the arts, she was in some empty maid's room reading a book. And when the royal family appeared on a balcony reserved for historical occasions and bowed graciously to the cheering multitudes, the Princess Horizon was conspicuously absent. All this was duly reported in the sealed letters the foreign ambassadors sent home to their respective monarchs, and it no doubt explains why there were no offers for her hand in marriage, though she was beautiful and accomplished and everything a Princess should be.

One summer afternoon, the ladies-in-waiting, having searched everywhere for her, departed in a string of carriages, and shortly after the Princess let herself out by a side door and hurried off to the English garden. She was in a doleful mood, and felt like reciting poetry. Everywhere else in the world at the time, English gardens were by careful cultivation made to look wild, romantic, and uncultivated. This English garden was laid out according to the cardinal points of the compass. Even so, it was more informal than the French and Italian gardens, which were like nothing so much as a lesson in plane geometry. Addressing the empty afternoon, the Princess began:

The wind blows out; the bubble dies;
The spring entombed in autumn lies;
The dew dries up; the star is shot;
The flight is past; and man—

At that moment she observed something so strange she thought she must be dreaming. A small white rosebush named after the Queen of Denmark was out of line with all the other small white rosebushes.

The Princess spent the rest of the afternoon searching carefully through garden after garden. A viburnum was also not quite where it should be. The same thing was true of a white lilac in the Grand Parterre, and a lemon tree in the big round wooden tub in the Carrefour de la Reine. So many deviations could hardly be put down to accident; one of the gardeners was deliberately creating disorder. It was her duty to report this to her father, who would straightway have the gardener, and perhaps all the other gardeners, beheaded. But he would also have the white rosebush and the viburnum and the lilac and the lemon tree moved back to where they belonged, and this she was not sure she wanted to have happen. It stands to reason, the Princess said to herself, that the guilty person must work after dark, for to spread disorder through the palace gardens in broad daylight would be far too dangerous.

That night, instead of dancing all the figures of a cotillion, she sent her partner for an ice and slipped unnoticed through one of the ballroom windows. There was a full moon. The gardens were entrancing, and at this hour not open to the public. Walking through a topiary arch, the Princess came upon a gardener's boy in the very act of transplanting a snowball bush. Instead of calling out for the palace guards, she stood measuring with her eyes exactly how much this particular snowball bush in its new position was out of line with the other snowball bushes.

The gardener's boy got up from his knees and knocked the dirt off his spade. "The deviation is no more than exists between the North Pole and the North Magnetic Pole," he said, "but it serves to restore the balance of Nature." And then softly, so softly that she barely heard him, "I did not know there was anyone like you."

"Didn't you?" the Princess said, and turned to look at him. After a moment she turned away. For once she found it not easy to be gracious, simple, and direct. She said—not rudely, but as she would have to a friend if she had had one—"I have the greatest difficulty in managing to be alone for five minutes."

"I don't wonder," he said. Their eyes met, full of inquiry. "When I look at you, I feel like sighing," he said. "My mouth is dry and there is a strange weakness in my legs. I don't ever remember feeling like this before."

"I know that when Papa and Mama and Aunt Royal and the others come out on the balcony and bow to the cheering multitudes, I ought to be there with them, and that I embarrass Papa by my absence, but I do not feel that appearing in public from time to time is enough. There are other things that a ruling family could do. For example, one could learn to play some musical instrument—the cello, or the contrabassoon. Or get to know every single person in the kingdom, and if they are in trouble help them."

"Your every move and gesture is sudden and free, like the orioles," the gardener's boy said.

"Also, I am very tired of wearing the same emeralds to the same operas year after year," the Princess said. "Isn't it nice about the birds. One says 'as the crow flies,' meaning in a straight line, but when you stand and watch them, it turns out that they often fly in big circles."

"If I had known I would find you here," the gardener's boy said, "I would have come straight here in the first place."

"Or they fly every which way," the Princess said. "And nothing can be done about it."

"I cannot tell you," the gardener's boy said, "how I regret the year I spent wandering through China, and the six months I spent in the Caucasus, and those two years in Persia, and that four months and seventeen days in Baluchistan."

By this time they were sitting on an antique marble bench some distance away. They could hear the music of violins, and the slightest stirring of the air brought with it the perfume of white lilacs.

"What made you take up gardening?" the Princess asked. "One can see at a glance that you are of royal blood. Was it to get away from people?"

"No, it was not that, really. At my father's court it is impossible to get away from people. There is no court calendar and no time of the day or night that anybody is supposed to be anywhere in particular, and so they are everywhere. I long ago gave up trying to get away from them."

"How sad!"

"Until I set off on my travels, I didn't know the meaning of solitude. In my country it is the fashion to admire any form of deviation. The streets of the capital start out impressively in one direction and then suddenly swerve off in quite another, or come to an end when you least expect it. To go straight from one engagement to another is considered impolite. It is also not possible. In school, children aren't taught how to add and subtract, but, instead, the basic principles of numerology. As you can imagine, the fiscal arrangements are extraordinary. People do not attempt to balance their checkbooks, and neither does the bank. No tree or bush is ever pruned, and the public gardens are a jungle where it is out of the question for a human being to walk, though I believe wild animals like it. About a decade ago, the musicians decided that the interval between, say, C and C sharp didn't always have to be a half tone—that sometimes it could be a whole tone and sometimes a whole octave. So there is no longer any music, though there are many interesting experiments with sound. The police do not bother men who like to dress up in women's clothing and vice versa, and the birth rate is declining. In a country where no thought is ever carried to its logical conclusion and everybody maunders, my father is noted for the discursiveness of his public statements. Even in private he cannot make a simple remark. It always turns out to be a remark within a remark that has already interrupted an observation that was itself of a parenthetical nature. As it happens, I am a throwback to a previous generation and a thorn in the flesh of everybody."

"How nice that there is someone you take after," the Princess murmured. "I am said to resemble no one."

"As a baby I cried when I was hungry," the Prince said, caught up in the pleasure of talking about himself, "and sucked my thumb in preference to a jeweled pacifier. Applying myself to my studies, I got through my schooling in one-third the time it took my carefully selected classmates to finish their education, and this did not make me popular on the playing field. Also I was neat in my appearance, and naturally quick, and taciturn—and this was felt as being in some oblique way directed against my father. From his reading of history he decided that the only way to make a troublesome crown prince happy was to abdicate in his favor, and he actually started to do this. But the offer was set in a larger framework of noble thoughts and fatherly admonitions, some of which did perhaps have an indirect bearing on the situation, if one could only have sorted them out from the rest, which had no bearing whatever and took him farther and farther afield, so that he lost sight of his original intention, and when we all sat down to dinner the crown was still on his head . . . I have never talked to anyone the way I am talking to you now. Are you cold sitting here in the moonlight? You look like a marble statue, but I don't want you to become chilled."

She was not cold, but she got up and walked because he suggested it.

"Two days later," he continued, "I saddled my favorite Arabian horse and rode off alone to see the world. When I first came here, walking in a straight line through streets that were at right angles to each other, I felt I had found a second home. After a few weeks, as I got to know the country better—"

Seeing his hesitation, she said, "You do not need to be tactful with me. Say it."

"My impressions are no doubt dulled from too much traveling," he began tactfully, "but it does seem to me that there are things that cannot be said except in a roundabout way. And things that cannot be done until you have first done something else. A wide avenue that you can see from one end to the other is a splendid sight, but when every street is like this, the effect is of monotony." Then, with a smile that was quite dazzling with happiness, the Prince went on, "Would you like to know my name? I am called Arqué. Before setting off on the Grand Tour, I should have supplied myself with letters of introduction, but I was in too much of a hurry, and so here, as in the other countries I visited, I knew no one. I could not present myself at the palace on visiting day because I was traveling incognito. I was free to pack my bags and go, but I lingered, unable to make up my mind what country to visit next, and one morning as I was out walking, an idea occurred to me. I hurried back to the inn and persuaded a stableboy to change clothes with me. Fifteen minutes later I was at the back door of the palace asking to speak to the head gardener. Shortly after that I was on my hands and knees, pulling weeds. The rest you know."

They were now standing beside a fountain. Looking deep into her eyes, he said, "In my father's kingdom there is a bird called the nightingale that sings most beautifully."

"A generation ago there were still a few nightingales here," the Princess said, "but now there aren't any. It seems they do not like quite so much order. This is the first time I have ever walked in the gardens at night. I didn't know that this plashing water would be full of moonlight."

"Your eyes are full of moonlight also," the Prince said.

"I feel I can tell you anything," the Princess said.

"Tomorrow," Prince Arqué said, glancing in the direction of the rosebush that was named after the Queen of Denmark, "I will move them all back."

"Oh, no!" the Princess cried. "Oh, don't do that! They are perfect just the way they are."

"Would you like to be alone now?" the Prince inquired wistfully. "I cannot bear the thought of leaving you, but I know that you like to have some time to yourself."

"I cannot bear to leave you either," the Princess said.

Since they had both been brought up on fairy tales, they proposed to be married amid great rejoicing and live happily ever after, but the Minister of State had other plans, and did not favor an alliance with a country whose foreign policy was so lacking in straightforwardness. The Princess Horizon was locked in her room, Prince Arqué was informed that his visa had expired, and they never saw each other again. According to the most interesting and least reliable of the historians of the period, Prince Arqué succeeded his father to the throne, and left the royal palace, which was as confusing as a rabbit warren, for a new one that he designed himself and that set the fashion for straight lines and right angles in architecture. From architecture it spread to city planning, and so on. King Arqué had a son who was terribly long-winded, and a thorn in his flesh.

As for the Princess Horizon, it seems she found a new and rather dreadful way of disappearing. From the day she was told she could not marry Prince Arqué, she never smiled again, and no one knew what was on her mind or in her heart. When her sympathetic ladies-in-waiting had finished grouping themselves around her chair, to their dismay she was sitting in it. When the royal family appeared on a balcony that was reserved for moments of history, the Princess was with them and bowed graciously to the cheering multitudes. She opened bazaars, laid cornerstones, distributed medals, and went to the opera. When the exiled King of Poland asked for her hand in marriage, the offer was considered eminently suitable and accepted. The exiled King of Poland turned out to have a flaw in his character also, but of a more ordinary kind; he had a passion for gambling. Ace of hearts, faro, baccarat, hazard, roulette—he played them all feverishly, and feverishly the courtiers imitated him, mortgaging their castles and laying waste their patrimony so they could go on gambling. The trees in their neglected orchards soon took on a more natural shape, and sorrowing elders grew bent with age. The common people aped the nobility as usual. New roads were carelessly built and therefore less straight than the old ones, the law of the land became full of loopholes, and only now and then did someone indulge in straightforward, logical thinking.

19. *The old man at the railroad crossing*

"REJOICE," said the old man at the railroad crossing, to every person who came that way. He was very old, and his life had been full of troubles, but he was still able to lower the gates when a train was expected, and raise them again when it had passed by in a whirl of dust and diminishing noise. It was just a matter of time before he would be not only old but bedridden, and so, meanwhile, people were patient with him and excused his habit of saying "Rejoice," on the ground that when you are that old not enough oxygen gets to the brain.

But it was curious how differently different people reacted to that one remark. Those who were bent on accumulating money, or entertaining dreams of power, or just busy, didn't even hear it. The watchman was somebody who was supposed to guard the railroad crossing, not to tell people how they ought to feel, and if there had been such a thing as a wooden or mechanical watchman, they would have been just as satisfied.

Those who cared about good manners were embarrassed for the poor old fellow, and thought it kinder to ignore his affliction.

And those who were really kind, but not old, and not particularly well acquainted with trouble, said "Thank you" politely, and passed on, without in the least having understood what he meant. Or perhaps it was merely that they were convinced he didn't mean anything, since he said the same thing day in and day out, regardless of the occasion or who he said it to. "Rejoice," he said solemnly, looking into their faces. "Rejoice."

The children, of course, were not embarrassed, and did not attempt to be kind. They snickered and said "Why?" and got no answer, and so they asked another question: "Are you crazy?" And—as so often happened when they asked a question they really wanted to know the answer to—he put his hand on their head and smiled, and they were none the wiser.

But one day a woman came along, a nice-looking woman with grey hair and lines in her face and no interest in power or money or politeness that was merely politeness and didn't come from the heart, and no desire to be kind for the sake of being kind, either, and when the old man said "Rejoice," she stopped and looked at him thoughtfully and then she said, "I don't know what at." But not crossly. It was just a statement.

When the train had gone by and the old man had raised the gates, instead of walking on like the others, she stood there, as if she had something more to say and didn't know how to say it. Finally she said, "This has been the worst year and a half of my entire life. I think I'm getting through it, finally. But it's been very hard."

"Rejoice," the old man said.

"Even so?" the woman asked. And then she said, "Well, perhaps you're right. I'll try. You've given me something to think about. Thank you very much." And she went on down the road.

One morning shortly after this, there was a new watchman at the crossing, a smart-looking young man who tipped his hat to those who had accumulated power or money, and bowed politely to those who valued good manners, and thanked the kind for their kindness, and to the children he said, "If you hang around my crossing, you'll wish you hadn't." So they all liked him, and felt that there had been a change for the better. What had happened was that the old man couldn't get up out of bed. Though he felt just as well as before, there was no strength in his legs. So there he lay, having to be fed and shaved and turned over in bed and cared for like a baby. He lived with his daughter, who was a slatternly housekeeper and had more children than she could care for and a husband who drank and beat her, and the one thing that had made her life possible was that her old father was out of the house all day, watching the railroad crossing. So when she brought him some gruel for his breakfast that morning and he said "Rejoice," she set her mouth in a grim line and said nothing. When she brought him some more of the same gruel for his lunch she was ready to deal with the situation. Standing over him, so that she seemed very tall, she said, "Father, I don't want to hear that word again. If you can't say anything but 'Rejoice,' don't say anything, do you hear?" And she thought he seemed to understand. But when she brought him his supper, he said it again, and in her fury she slapped him. Her own father. The tears rolled down his furrowed cheeks into his beard, and they looked at each other as they hadn't looked at each other since he was a young man and she was a little girl skipping along at his side. For a moment, her heart melted, but then she thought of how hard her life was, and that he was making it even harder by living on like this when it was time for him to die. And so she turned and went out of the room, without saying that she was sorry. And after that the old man avoided her eyes and said nothing whatever.

One day she put her head in the door and said, "There's somebody to see you."

It was the grey-haired woman. "I heard you were not feeling up to par," she said, and when the old man didn't say anything, she went on, "I made this soup for my family, and I thought you might like some. It's very nourishing." She looked around and saw that the old man's daughter had left them, so she sat down on the edge of the bed and fed the soup to him. She could tell by the way he ate it, and the way the color came into his face, that he was hungry. The dark little room looked as if it hadn't been swept in a month of Sundays, but she knew better than to start cleaning another woman's house. She contented herself with tucking the sheets in properly and straightening the covers and adjusting the pillow behind the old man's head—for which he seemed grateful, though he didn't say anything.

"Now I must go," she said. But she didn't go. Instead she looked at him and said, "Things aren't any better, they're worse. Much worse. I really don't know what I'm going to do." And when he didn't say what she expected him to say, she stopped thinking about herself and thought about him. "I don't care for the new watchman at the crossing," she said. "He stands talking to the girls when he ought to be letting the gates down, and I'm afraid some child will be run over."

But this seemed to be of no interest to him, and she quickly saw why. Death was what was on his mind, not the railroad crossing. His own death, and how to meet it. And she saw that he was feeling terribly alone.

She took his frail old hand in hers and said, "If I can just get through this day, maybe things will be better tomorrow, but in any case, I'll come to see you, to see how you are." And then, without knowing that she was going to say it but only thinking that he didn't have much longer to wait, she said what he used to say at the railroad crossing, to every person who came that way.

20. *A mean and spiteful toad*

A TOAD sat under a dead leaf that was the same color it was. Most toads are nice harmless creatures, full of fears, and with good reason, but this toad was mean and spiteful. For no reason. It was born that way. One day a little girl on her way home from school saw him and nudged him gently with the sole of her shoe to see him hop. Which he did, helplessly. But the bile churned in his ice-cold veins and he said—though not so she could hear it—*You will turn against the people who love you the most.* And for the whole rest of the day, under the leaf that was the same color he was, he was pleased. Of all the curses he had ever put on people and other toads, this struck him as the most original.

When the little girl got home, her father was sitting in the big chair that was sacred to him, reading the Sports section of the evening paper. He lowered his newspaper and said, "Did you have a nice time in school today?"

No answer.

"I see," he said, and went on reading the paper. He was an even-tempered man, and it is a fact widely acknowledged that little girls sometimes get up on the wrong side of the bed.

At bedtime, as she was having her bath, her mother started to go in and inquire whether she had taken a washcloth to her ears, and found that the door was locked. She started to call out and then thought better of it. "A new stage," she said to herself and went into the little girl's room and picked up her clothes and opened the window and turned the covers down. She had only this one child and her heart was wholly wrapped up in her.

This made it not exactly easy for the little girl to turn against her, but she knew all about Cinderella and the other little girls whose mother died and whose father presented them with a wicked stepmother, so by a careful reinterpretation and re-arrangement of whatever was said at the family dinner table and at other times, she convinced herself that *they* were not her true mother and father but just some people who were taking care of her until her rightful parents came to get her. When her father picked her up and sat her on his lap, as he was given to doing, she squirmed and got down. He waited for her to come and kiss him good night and she didn't.

Later, he said to his wife, "What's with Alice?"

"She's going through a stage. I think it makes her uncomfortable if we show any affection."

Once in a while she would lean against her father, but when he responded by putting his arm around her she was gone. It was all the work of the toad.

"What did I do?" the woman asked over and over again.

And over and over and over again the man responded, "Nothing."

The other toads in the neighborhood knew, of course, about the toad who was mean and spiteful, and they were careful not to sit under or on the leaf he considered his property. Their lives were full of dangers. People sometimes stepped on them without meaning to. Bad boys pulled their legs off. Cars ran over them and left them flat as a pancake in the middle of the highway. In the place where everything is known and recorded, there is a list of the human beings who have been kind to toads, and left a saucer of milk where they could find it, and carefully avoided stepping on them, and been distressed at the sound of the toads' cry as they were about to be hurt. It is not a very long list.

Sometimes the little girl broke down and allowed herself to treat her mother and father as she had before the mean and spiteful toad put a curse on her, but these periods were brief. There was hardly time for her mother to remark to her father, "Have you noticed how happy Alice is these days?" before they saw once more the closed look that meant *Don't touch me.*

One day the woman was on her hands and knees in the garden weeding a flower bed when a tiny voice said, "It isn't any of your doing. It's the mean and spiteful toad who sits under a leaf that is the same color he is."

At first the woman thought she had imagined this, but on reflection she realized that she couldn't have, and looked around to see where the voice had come from, and spotted a toad sitting under a big foxglove. "I didn't know toads could talk," she said.

"Oh yes," the toad said. "But they don't talk to people. At

least not very often. It's just that we—the toads who live in this part of the world—have noticed how much you and your husband love that child and we can't bear the way you are being treated."

"It's true that she isn't very affectionate these days," the woman said. "It seems to be a stage she's going through."

"She hates you," the toad said.

"Really?" the woman said, trying not to show how the words had struck her to the heart.

"Both of you," the toad said. "She nudged the mean and spiteful toad with her shoe and he put a curse on her."

If I tell George, the woman thought, he will never believe me. He will think I have gone crazy. . . .

"What's to be done?" she asked.

"By you, nothing," the toad said. "Something has to happen."

"To Alice?"

"No. To the spiteful toad. Wait. Be patient. Hope for the best."

So the woman did. And in the place where each thing that happens to every form of animal, vegetable, and mineral life is recorded, it was recorded that a mean and spiteful toad, with only a small provocation, had made a little girl turn against her mother and father who loved her. Immediately afterward, into the atmosphere was released a small drop of mystery, which during a heavy downpour was absorbed into a drop of rainwater that by a—you might say—miracle fell on the mean and spiteful toad. Feeling a pang of remorse he said to himself, *It's only what they deserve*, and tried to put the matter out of his mind. And couldn't. *If I remove the curse*, he said to himself, *I will be just like every other toad and somebody will step on me. Or my leaf will blow away. Or something. So I won't. I won't, I won't, I won't. I just won't. . . .*

Ordinarily the woman was careful not to touch the little girl but this day the little girl looked so strange and lost that she put her hand on her forehead, thinking she must have a fever. The little girl closed her eyes and shuddered, and then she burst into a storm of tears and threw her arms around her mother and said, "Oh, Mama, I really do love you!"

All the kindhearted toads sitting under leaves here and there in the garden set up a humming in their throats. "Watch out," they said to each other. "I never thought he would do it, but now that he has, he's bound to do something especially mean and spiteful to make up for it."

The leaf that the mean and spiteful toad was hiding under gave forth a faint glow, but that was because of the mystery.

21. *All the days and nights*

O NCE upon a time there was a man who asked himself, "Where have all the days and nights of my life gone?" He was not a young man, or the thought would never have crossed his mind, but neither was he white-haired and bent and dependent on a walker or a cane, and by any reasonable standards one would have to say that his life had been more fortunate than most. He was in excellent health, he had a loving wife, and children and friends, and no financial worries, and an old dog who never failed to welcome him when he came home. But something had taken him by surprise, and it was this: Without actually thinking about it, he had meant to live each day to the full—as he had—and still not let go of it. This was not as foolish as it sounds, because he didn't feel his age. Or rather, he felt seventeen sometimes, and sometimes seven or eight, and sometimes sixty-four, which is what he actually was, and sometimes forty, and sometimes a hundred, depending on whether he was tired or had had enough sleep or on the company he was in or if the place he was in was a place he had been in before, and so on. He could think about the past, and did, more than most people, through much of his adult life, and until recently this had sufficed. But now he had a sense of the departure from him not merely of the major events of his life, his marriage, the birth of his children, the death of his mother and father, but of an endless succession of days that were only different from one another insofar as they were subject to accident or chance. And what it felt like was that he had overdrawn his account at the bank or been spending his capital, instead of living comfortably on the income from it.

He found himself doing things that, if he hadn't had the excuse of absentmindedness, would have been simply without rational explanation: for example, he would stand and look around at the clutter in the attic, not with any idea of introducing order but merely taking in what was there; or opening closet doors in rooms that he himself did not ordinarily ever go into. Finally he spoke to his wife about it, for he wondered if she felt the same way.

"No," she said.

"When you go to sleep at night you let go of the day completely?"

"Yes."

As a rule, he fell asleep immediately and she had to read a while, and even after the light was out she turned and turned and sometimes he knew, even though she didn't move, that she was not asleep yet. If he had taken longer to fall asleep would he also have been able to let go of the— but he knew in his heart that the answer was no, he wouldn't. And even now when he felt that he was about to leave a large part of his life (and therefore a large part of himself) behind, he couldn't accept it as inevitable and a part of growing old. What you do not accept you do not allow to happen, even if you have to have recourse to magic. And so one afternoon he set out, without a word to anybody, to find all the days and nights of his life. When he did not come home by dinnertime, his wife grew worried, telephoned to friends, and finally to the police, who referred her to the Missing Persons Bureau. A description of him—height, color of eyes, color of hair, clothing, scar on the back of his right hand, etc.—was broadcast on the local radio station and the state police were alerted. What began as a counting of days became a counting of weeks. Six months passed, and the family lawyer urged that, because of one financial problem and another, the man's wife consider taking steps to have him pronounced legally dead. This she refused to do, and a year from the day he disappeared, he walked into the house, looking much older, and his first words were "I'm too tired to talk about it." He made them a drink, and ate a good dinner, and went to bed at the usual time, without having asked a single question about her, about how she had managed without him, or offering a word of apology to her for the suffering he had caused her. He fell asleep immediately, as usual, and she put the light out.

I will never forgive him, she said to herself, *as long as I live*. And when he curled around her, she moved away from him without waking him and lay on the far side of the bed. And tried to go to sleep and couldn't, and so when he spoke, even though it was hardly louder than a whisper, she heard what he said. What he said was "They're all there. All the days and all the nights of our life. I don't expect you to believe me," he went on, "but—"

To his surprise she turned over and said, "I do believe you," and so he was able to tell her about it.

"Think of it as being like a starry night, where every single star is itself a night with its own stars. Or like a book with pages you can turn, and that you can go back and read over again, and also skip ahead to see what's coming. Only it isn't a book. Or a starry night. Think of it as a house with an infinite number of rooms that you can wander through, one after another after another. And each room is a whole day from morning till evening, with everything that happened, and each day is connected to the one before and the one that comes after, like bars of music. Think of it as a string quartet. And as none of those things. And as nowhere. And right here. And right now."

A tear ran down the side of her face and he knew it, in the dark, and took her in his arms. "The reason I didn't miss you," he said, "is that we were never separated. You were there. And the children. And this house. And the dog and the cats and the neighbors, and all our friends, and even what was happening yesterday when I wasn't here. What I can't describe is how it happened. I went out for a walk and left the road and cut across Ned Blackburn's field, and suddenly the light seemed strange—and when I looked up, the sky wasn't just air, it was of a brilliance that seemed to come from thousands and thousands of little mirrors and I felt lightheaded and my heart began to pound and—"

She waited for him to go on and when he didn't, she thought he was trying to say something that was too difficult to put into words. And then she heard his soft regular breathing and realized he was asleep.

In the morning I will hear the rest of it, she thought, and fell asleep herself, much sooner than she usually did. But in the morning he didn't remember a thing he had told her, and she had great trouble making him understand that he had ever been away.

OTHER IMPROVISATIONS

Contents

1. The old man who was afraid of falling

ONCE upon a time there was an old man who was afraid of falling. He put handrails on both sides of the stairs and raised the turf to the level of his doorsill. He also had bars put across the lower half of the windows and the well covered over so he couldn't fall into it. At considerable expense he had a railing built all around the roof of his house so that if he should ever have to go up and clean the gutters he could not fall off. And gradually he stopped going to the village to see his friends because they lived in houses that had steps in unexpected places and were foolishly indifferent to the risk they took or the danger that awaited other people who came to their houses.

Rather than walk down the steep path to the village, the old man stayed at home and got his food from the farmers driving by with carcasses of lamb and young pig, or their carts piled high with vegetables. He was careful not to climb up on the back of the cart, but made the farmers drop the reins and get him what he wanted, since, as he explained to them each time, he was afraid of falling. As year after year went by, he stayed more and more in the house, letting his garden grow up in weeds, and making the farmers come to the door with their produce. When he went outside, something was always falling —in winter the snow, in spring the rain, in summer the flower petals, and in autumn the leaves, and it was more than he could bear to see this perpetual tragedy going on around him. In the end he drew the curtains and never looked on the outside world if he could help it.

Even indoors he was not altogether safe. A picture fell from the wall for no reason, or the cat jumped up on the table and he closed his eyes and waited for the crash that followed. He picked up the broken china and got rid of the cat. He took down all the pictures. And after that he felt as safe as anyone can feel in a world where people are perpetually falling from ladders and breaking an arm or a leg, until one night the chimney caught on fire. He was not seriously alarmed, but the roaring got louder and louder, and he was afraid that sparks from the blazing chimney might fall on the roof, and if he had to go up a ladder in the dark *he* might fall, so he put on his cape and rubbers and ran through the darkness calling for help.

The week before, a mountain lion had carried off a child, and the people of the village, horrified by this unheard-of accident, had dug a number of pits and covered them over with leaves and branches. Everyone in the village knew where they were and avoided walking on them, but because the old man never went out, nobody thought to tell him about the one that was two hundred yards from his house. Besides, it was in plain sight from his windows and he could have seen the men digging it, if only his curtains had not been drawn.

He lay at the bottom of the pit, sick with pain, and cried for help, and at last he heard a child's voice somewhere above him saying, "Is that you?"

"I've hurt my back," the old man said. "You must go to the village and tell them to come at once and bring some ladders and lift me out. Tell them to bring ropes, too, that they can tie around their waists as they are descending the ladders, in case somebody falls."

There was no answer, and for a long time the old man thought the child had run to the village for help, and he lay there expecting the men to arrive with ropes and ladders and rescue him. Then, to his dismay, he heard the childish voice again, singing a little song, the words of which the child made up as he went along.

"Oh, please!" the old man said. "Whoever you are, stop singing and run to the village for help before it's too late."

"Too late for what?" asked the child.

"My back is hurt," the old man explained patiently, remembering how hard it is to capture the attention of children, and also trying to keep his language as plain as possible. "I walked on some leaves and the ground gave way and I fell in this pit and hurt my back, and if I have to be here until morning, I'll die."

"It's never too late to die," the child said, and began singing again:

> "*Mercy, ride, my mare must know*
> *The holy tide, the turned-in toe*
> *They all must go . . .*"

"Go to the village," the old man said, "the place where all the houses are, and tell them—"

> "*Creep and hide,*" the child sang.
> "*The wall is down*
> *The scholar's pride, the satin gown*
> *They all must drown . . .*"

"Do as I say," the old man said, "and I'll give you a penny."

"Do you have it on you?" the child asked suspiciously.

"No," the old man said, "but I'll give it to you later."

"Promises don't interest me," the child said. "You're sure you haven't got a penny?"

"Go to the village or I'll tell your mother on you."

"I have no mother," said the child.

"I'll tell your father, then. Or don't you have any father, either?"

"No father," the child said. And then, "*No father, no bother; no murder, no matter; no wonder, no thunder; no answer, no blunder; no—*"

"Stop," cried the old man. "Who are you, child? Have you no heart in your breast that you can see an old man dying in a pit and not run to the village for help?"

"I'm your heart's young cousin, Courage," said the child. "I'm keeping you company until you die."

For long time there was silence and then the child said, "Are you still there?"

"Certainly," said the old man.

"I was afraid you'd gone," the child said.

"How can I," the old man said, weeping softly, "when I'm down at the bottom of a pit and my back is broken?"

"How can you be afraid of falling, then?" the child said.

"Am I really going to die?" the old man asked.

"Certainly."

"How soon?"

"Soon," said the child.

"Then I don't think I am afraid any more," the old man said. "I don't know why. I just feel calm and safe."

"If you'd like me to," the child said, "I'll come down there and keep you company."

"You're not afraid of falling?"

"No," said the child. "I just let go."

"Let go," the old man repeated after him. "Let go," and he did, easily and happily and without a care in the world.

2. The epistolarian

ONCE upon a time there was an old maid who was the laughingstock of the hamlet she was born, raised, and died in. All she ever did was write letters. Other old maids taught school or took courses in typing and shorthand, put up twenty-seven quart jars of tomatoes, crocheted table mats, carried baskets to the poor, conducted a Saturday Morning Bible Class, devoted their lives to caring for invalid fathers, or joined in the general warfare of all women against disorder and dirt. But this old maid wrote letters, fifteen or twenty a day, over a period of many years, and not one of them, so far as the postmaster knew (and he was certainly in a position to know), was ever answered. She wrote to all her relatives, naturally, and no doubt her nieces and nephews would have answered the letters she sent them if once in a while a check had been enclosed, but this was not the case. The letters piled up on mantelpieces, on hall tables, and were not only unanswered but unread.

The bulk of the old maid's correspondence was directed to strangers—to the farmer whose cow had just given birth to a two-headed calf, to the leading actress of the day, to the most popular bishop, to the head of an anti-missionary society, or to a great scientist whose name was a household word, though his mathematical formulae were not widely understood. Sometimes the letters were addressed to shady characters as well—to the heartbreakingly handsome young housebreaker, to the model boy on trial for larceny and rape, to the blond young woman suing for a huge share in an old man's estate, to anybody, as a matter of fact, whose name, picture, and address appeared in the evening paper.

The editors of all the newspapers in the capital and in the chief provincial cities were supplied with long letters for their contributors' columns, and even though these letters, all in the same small indefatigable hand, were signed by various pseudonyms ("A Constant Reader," "An Observer," "One Who Hopes to See Justice Done") there were always far too many of them for the available space, and they accumulated, gathering dust on copy hooks and in the cubbyholes of the editors'

847

roll-top desks. And at three minutes before noon each day the old maid hurried into the post office, her fingers stained with ink, her apron covered with ink blots, her hair untidy, her mind at peace as she thrust her morning's output through the wicket to be weighed, stamped, and disposed of in local and out-of-town bins. The people of the hamlet often gathered to count the fruit of her labor, and when there was an outsider present, somebody would make a circular sign with his forefinger, pointing at his temple. The stranger would grasp the significance of this gesture, nod, and smile. But it was always done behind the old maid's back, and not meant unkindly.

In time, the area covered by her letters increased until it took in all six continents (if you count Australia as a continent) and required such considerable daily sums for postage that the old maid was never able to afford new curtains or a new dress, and it was feared she might even be going without proper food. As proof of the contrary, it was sometimes pointed out that the addresses were rising rapidly in the social scale, and included countesses, dukes, then a grand duke, a lord chief justice (who would certainly not let a poor woman starve that he knew anything about), a lady-in-waiting, a court astrologer, a dowager queen (at this point the villagers were sure there would be trouble, that the police would come and take the poor silly thing away and lock her up), and eventually a king and an emperor.

The letters went on being mailed steadily and in quantity, and then one day the old maid did not appear just before noon, or after lunch; and that evening the postmaster kept open an hour after closing time, and finally sent a boy to find out what was keeping her. Death was. The boy knocked politely and, receiving no answer, pushed open the door of her cottage and saw her lying on a couch with her eyes closed, the nap she had lain down to having proved to be a longer sleep than she had anticipated. On her desk by the front window were the final letters, thirty-eight in all, in their envelopes, addressed, sealed, and ready for mailing. The boy gathered them up, tiptoed out of the room, closed the door softly, and found the letters in his coat pockets the next day.

*

The funeral was brief and modest. The nephews and nieces came and carried off the furniture, which was not worth much, the best pieces having been sold to provide postage for the letters that lay on their hall tables and gathered dust on their mantelpieces. Only the postmaster, passing the old maid's empty cottage with the "For Sale" sign on the door, felt that all had not been done for her that should have been done. Though she had never received any answers to the letters she spent her life writing, it was quite possible, he decided, that the people she wrote to would care about her, at least to the extent of wondering why the letters had stopped coming. So he took it upon himself to write a brief note to each of them, explaining that the village correspondent had passed on. Fortunately he was a methodical man and had kept a record of the names and addresses of everyone she wrote to, as a kind of curiosity and also to prove that an out-of-the-way part can be an important cog in the great machine. After he had reached the last name on the list and sealed the last envelope, an idea occurred to him. He steamed open the thousands of envelopes that lay in piles all over the post office, and to each of the thousands of notes he added a postscript, explaining that on such-and-such a day there would be a memorial service in honor of their friend.

He did not expect a living soul to attend, and he had difficulty persuading the assistant curate to prepare a short tribute for the occasion. But when the day came, the roads were blocked for miles around with all manner of carriages, many of them bearing coats of arms. Also farm wagons, delivery wagons, a dogcart, a gypsy wagon, and a hansom cab long out of use. Ten special trains had to be accommodated on the single siding. The village street was crammed with people who had come to the memorial service, and, the old maid's cottage being very cramped and small, the meeting was held out-of-doors. The curate's assistant, finding himself in the presence of a great multitude that included the highest dignitaries of state, aged members of the Academy of Arts and Sciences, the crowned heads of Europe and Asia, had stagefright and could not give his prepared speech, but there were many who did speak that day, extempore, from their place in the throng. The greatest living scientist, whose name was a household word, spoke of the old maid's letters—of what an inspiration they were to him, how intelligent and helpful her comment was, and how she had believed, long before the rest of the world, in his mathematical diagram of the five dimensions (length, breadth, thickness, time, and love). The greatest living poet praised her literary style (which was news to the village) and read a rather long poem in *terza rima*, the prologue to his unfinished epic, which he was dedicating to the old maid. The dowager queen said, with tears in her eyes, "So long as I heard from her, I knew I was remembered. Her letters gave me the courage to go on opening bazaars." The king said, "Through her letters I knew what my people were thinking, and that they were loyal to me. I always meant to write to her and never got around to it, more's the pity!" The emperor said, "Acting on her advice, I put off waging two very expensive wars. Every letter she wrote me is preserved in the Imperial Archives, bound in green vellum, for the use and admiration of a grateful posterity."

When the service was concluded, the criminal element, such as were on parole at the moment—second-story men, blackmailers, arsonists, dope peddlers, etc.—proceeded to the cemetery in a body and placed on the old maid's grave a floral tribute in the shape of a white quill pen made entirely of wired sweet peas. Attached to it was a florist's ribbon with the words "Yours very affy," in a raised silver-and-gold facsimile of her now famous handwriting.

3. The shepherd's wife

THERE was a shepherd's wife in Bohemia who was greatly saddened when, after twelve years of being married, she still had no children. Her husband was a quiet man, large and slow-moving and dependable, and she loved him with all her heart, but he had no gift for speech, perhaps from spending so much time with animals, and instead of the prattle of childish voices that she so longed to hear, the woman was forced to be content with the ticking of the clock and the sound of the teakettle on the crane, the singing of wet wood on the hearth. Sometimes her husband was gone for days at a time, and then the sound of her own footsteps grew unbearably loud, and she thought that if only her husband would come home, so she could hear his heavy sigh when he sat down and warmed himself before the fire, and the dog's tail thumping, she wouldn't ask for more—not even the children that had been denied her.

For every deprivation there is always some gift, and the shepherd's wife was famous throughout the village for her ability to make things grow. The windows of her cottage were full of flowering plants all winter long, and when other women had trouble with their house plants—the leaves turning yellow and dropping off and no new green coming, or red spider, or white fly, or mealy bug, or aphids—when their favorite plants were, in fact, almost ready to be thrown on the compost heap, they would bring them to the shepherd's wife and say "Can you do anything with this? It used to have masses of blooms and now look at it!" and the shepherd's wife would make a place for the sick plant on the window sill on the south side of the kitchen, where the sun poured in all day long through the thick, round glass. A month later she would wrap the plant up carefully against the cold and deliver it to its owner, in full leaf, with new buds forming all over it.

"What ever do you do to make things grow?" the other women asked her. "Do you water them very often, or just every other day, or what is your secret?"

"To make plants grow," the shepherd's wife always said,

"you have to look at them every day. If you forget about them or neglect them, they die."

The other women, whose households were blessed with children, never remembered this advice or quite believed in it, and there was even a rumor (for it was a very small place, and no one living there escaped the breath of slander) that the shepherd's wife was a witch.

Actually, there was more to it than she could ever quite bring herself to tell them. After all, they had their little Josephs and Johns and Mary Catherines, and she had only her Christmas cactus, her climbing geraniums, her white rosebush in its big tub, and her pink oleander. So she kept her secret, which was that she not only looked at every plant every day but also talked to them, the way some lonely people talk to animals or to themselves.

"Now," she would say, standing in front of the Christmas cactus, when the shepherd was out of the house and there was nobody around to hear her, "I know you're slow by nature, but so is my husband, and he has his happy moments and you should have yours. All you need to do is grow a little." Then she would pass on to the pink oleander. "What is *this*?" she would exclaim. "Why are your leaves dry and stiff this morning? Too much sun? Very well, behind the curtain you go until you are feeling better." Then, to the white rosebush: "Just because those great geraniums are almost touching the ceiling and crowding everything else out, you needn't think I don't know you are here. Besides, if you will notice, the geranium blossom has no scent. . . ." So she talked to the plants, as if they were children, and, like children, they grew and grew and blossomed over and over again all winter long.

One day, the old midwife who always took care of the birth of children in the village came to the shepherd's wife and, drawing her to the chimney corner where the kettle was boiling for tea, said "It's time somebody told you—you are with child."

At first the woman wouldn't believe it, although the midwife had never been known to make a mistake in these matters, and when she did believe that it was true, she was still not happy. "I've waited too long," she told herself. "If children had come when I was younger, it would have been very different.

Now I don't know what will happen to me. I may die. And if nothing dreadful happens to me, something will certainly happen to my Christmas cactus, my climbing geraniums, my rosebush, and my pink oleander as soon as I take to my bed and cannot look at them and talk to them the way they are used to."

She didn't confide these fears to her husband, not wanting to spoil his happiness, but he knew her moods, and when he saw that in spite of the blessing that had come to them she was still heavy-hearted, he stayed home with her more, and arranged with the other shepherds to mind his flocks for him. Wherever she went about the cottage, scrubbing and cleaning and putting things in order, he watched her, hoping to find out what was on her mind.

Having him around the house so much made her nervous, and when the plants began to drop their leaves and turn yellow because she couldn't bring herself to talk to them in front of anybody, she saw the fulfillment of her worst fears. She became pale, her shoulders drooped, she never spoke of the future, never discussed with her husband what they might name the child, or even whether it was going to be a boy or a girl. It was as if the child inside her were somebody else's plant that she could care for with her body but must not become attached to.

When her time came, the shepherd ran through the snowy night to the poor hovel that was all the midwife had for a roof over her head, and brought her hobbling back across the ice and snow. He put the kettle on the crane and built up a roaring fire and tried to stop his ears against the sounds that came from the bedroom—sounds that made his heart stop with terror. He felt a desperate need to talk to someone, but the midwife was too busy, coming and going with her hot cloths and her basins of boiling water, and she would not listen to him. At last he turned to the plants and told them his fears. Immediately before his eyes the limp leaves began to straighten, the stems to turn green. He went on talking to them without perceiving that anything unnatural had happened. His wife's secret was safe. He was a man, and so it didn't interest him.

In the terrible course of time, while the shepherd sat with his head in his hands and cursed the day he was born, the moans in the next room became screams and cries, and then suddenly there were two cries instead of one. A little while later, the midwife appeared with a baby, the smallest that had ever been seen in the village. She removed the soft woollen scarves it was wrapped in, and showed it to the shepherd, who sprang up with such pride in his heart and such happiness in his face that the newborn babe responded and began to wave its arms feebly.

"You have a daughter," the old midwife said.

"From God," the shepherd said.

"A very small, meachin, puny daughter," the old midwife said scornfully.

"She will be the most beautiful and proud woman that ever lived," the shepherd said. "She will be as beautiful and proud as the forests of Bohemia."

When the old midwife left him to care for the mother and child, he turned again to the plants on the window sill, and when the sun came up and lighted their leaves, he was still telling them about his newborn daughter.

Day after day the plants grew, but the baby did not, and the mother remained feverish and pale on her bed and did not love her child. When the shepherd knelt beside her and asked how she was feeling, she shook her head and did not say what she thought, which was, I shall never get up out of this bed.

She didn't dare ask about the plants—if they had died one by one, and been thrown out—but one day, after the midwife had gone to assist at the birth of another child, and the man had left the house for a few minutes to see about his sheep, the woman got up out of bed, intending to get back in again as soon as she had satisfied her curiosity. She tottered into the kitchen expecting to see the dry stalks of all her beloved plants, or maybe nothing at all, and what met her eyes was a green bower of blossoms such as she, who was famous throughout the village for her ability to make things grow, had never managed to have. The scent of the flowers was heavy in the low-ceilinged room, and as she stood there, looking at her Christmas cactus, her climbing geraniums, her white rosebush, and her pink oleander, the tight center of her heart opened, petal by petal.

She ran into the bedroom, where the child fretted, and brought it, cradle and all, into the room where the flowers were. "This is my very own daughter," she said. "She's very small, and she cries all the time, but some of you were sickly too, at first, and dropped your leaves, and showed every sign of not flourishing, and now look at you. Dearest heart," she said, pulling back the woollen cover until she could see the shadowy silken skin at the baby's throat. "Now you must grow. You must stop fretting. You must sleep," she said, unbuttoning her dress and helping the tiny pale mouth to find her breast. "You must grow tall and proud and beautiful, like the forests of Bohemia."

4. The marble watch

NCE upon a time there was a country so large that messengers journeying from the capital to the frontier were often never heard from again. The royal palace was immense, the palace grounds occupied thousands of acres, and rescue parties had to be sent out to locate important personages who had got confused and lost their way in the rose garden. The King's guard was made up entirely of men who were seven feet tall, and the horses that drew his enormous gilded coach were as broad as Percherons. And the courtiers often had trouble staying awake during the King's witty remarks, which, like his gestures, were modelled on those of his royal father, known in history books as Charles the Ponderous. At court concerts, the program listed various symphonies, concertos, *divertimenti* for strings and oboe, quartets, quintets, and what have you, but the musicians played only the largo and lento movements, omitting both the allegro vivace at the beginning and the presto at the end, in the belief that they were impossible to play and would no doubt be nerve-racking to have to hear. At the court balls, there was an interval of an hour or so between minuets, during which the dancers fanned themselves and recovered their breath. A simple audience with the King went on all day, without accomplishing anything. The royal proclamations, read in every square and market place in the kingdom, took up so much time and were so packed with polysyllabic words of Latin derivation that when the inhabitants were free to return to their plows and shoemaker's benches, their looms and churns and shops, they found that their minds were slow and listless, and very little work was done in this once prosperous kingdom. The imports exceeded the exports by several milliards of pounds sterling, and the currency was so inflated that arithmetic was no longer useful in settling accounts and bookkeepers had to resort to differential calculus and a slide rule.

It took the King a long time to realize that something was wrong and another five years to consider carefully what he ought to do about it. The council of state had not met since his father's time, and when it finally convened, at his order, the King's opening remarks took three weeks, after which the council adjourned and met again in the following autumn. The chancellor of the exchequer estimated expenditures for the next nine years at rather more than thirty times expenditures for the past nine years, and revenues at one one-hundredth of expenditures. The evening papers reported that in general the chancellor's tone was optimistic and appeared to satisfy the King and council. During the next three days the members of the council rose, one after another, and begged for a further adjournment, on the ground that they needed time and statisticians to consider the difficulty that had been placed before them. The only dissenting voice was that of the royal astronomer, who, with long, long pauses after each word, said, "My lord, the stars are moving much more quickly than they used to, or else we are moving more slowly, and it is my opinion that the root of the trouble lies—"

"Louder!" called a voice at the back of the council chamber, which held five thousand people. "We can't hear you back here."

"No one knows exactly what day of the week it is," the astronomer said. "And speaking for myself, I cannot say that I am even sure of the month. Every year the earth grows more out of touch with the sky."

"In your royal father's time," the astronomer continued, when the council convened the next morning, "many people had watches and could tell the time of day, and the clever ones were able to keep track of what day of the week it was, and even to predict more or less accurately the end of one month and the beginning of another. It is my opinion that we should, with Your Majesty's approval and encouragement, construct a timepiece."

"But if there were so many watches in our father's reign, why construct one?" said the King. "There must still be a timepiece somewhere."

"Your Majesty," said the astronomer, "I have inquired exhaustively into the matter, and while it is true that here and there, in remote districts, it is still possible to locate a timepiece, they have not been wound for decades, the works are corroded with rust, and they do not keep time at all, let alone the precise mathematical time that would serve our present purposes. What we need, in my humble opinion, is a watch that can be wound and will run."

"We seem to remember a watch heavily encrusted with jewels that was presented to us by a visiting potentate," said the King, "on our tenth birthday. But it was all so long ago. No doubt that watch has been mislaid."

The chancellor of the exchequer rose and stated categorically that the watch in question had not been mislaid. "I cannot put my hand on it at a moment's notice," he said, "but I know I saw it listed in a survey of the royal assets, five or ten years ago."

"If it was listed in the survey," the King said, "then it must be somewhere. In the sub-basement of the treasury, perhaps. But I dare say that, like the others, it has grown rusty. But tell me," he said, turning back to the astronomer, "were not the watches that people carried during the reign of our father very small—so small they could be carried in a man's vest pocket? And were not the works flimsy? And did not those watches have to be wound once a day?"

"Even so, Your Majesty. The cases were sometimes of silver and gold, but the works that hurried the hour and the minute hand round and round and in this way indicated the rushing of time were exceedingly delicate, and the watches had to be wound once a day, preferably at bedtime."

"That's what we thought," said the King. "And if you dropped one of these watches, did it not break, and have to be left at the watch-mender's for weeks at a time while it was being repaired, with the result that the person or persons who carried it had no way of telling the time?"

"There was that difficulty," the astronomer admitted. "And would be again, unless we constructed an alternate watch, to be referred to on those occasions when—"

"It seems hardly fitting that a kingdom the size of this be run according to an instrument so undependable and so unimpressive," said the King. "If you are truly convinced that a watch will bring the earth closer to the sky and, incidentally, improve the condition of the treasury, then we will construct a watch and see that all civil, ecclesiastical, and court activities conform to it. But we will construct this timepiece of some appropriate material. Something solid, durable, and rustproof, that will not need tinkering with or constant winding. Let the watch be constructed of marble."

The construction of a marble watch, the first ever attempted, so far as anybody knows, went on without interruption, diligently, for fifteen years, during which time the inhabitants of the kingdom grew threadbare, and the treasury used up its last resources on the quarrying and cutting of snow-white stone. The court astronomer had a nervous breakdown and was replaced by his assistant, who in turn died of a broken heart. The work was carried on by one person and another up until the very day the kingdom was invaded by an army from one of the very small but active neighboring kingdoms. The enemy troops were in possession of the capital before the people realized that their country had been invaded. The King escaped with his life and the blueprints of the great Timepiece.

He hid first in the hut of a fisherman on the shore of a lake so broad that even on a clear day you could not see the opposite shore. Then he was sheltered by a charcoal burner whose hut was in the shadow of a mountain so tall that the snow-covered peak was usually hidden by clouds. And finally he was driven to accept the hospitality of a poor poacher who lived by snaring rabbits in a wood so dense that no man had ever penetrated more than halfway through it. In the course of these successive flights, the King lost weight, learned to move quickly, to eat and sleep in snatches, and to speak sometimes with admirable conciseness, on the run. Since there was no court, there were no court proclamations that needed composing. The poacher's wife and daughter were busy with their own affairs, which were never affairs of state, and so he could not offer his opinion about the way they were conducted. The occasional messengers and spies brought only discouraging news, and the King devoted himself to the study of natural history. Many of the birds and beasts that he watched were, he could not help noticing, extremely small, and some of the insects were so minute that they might easily have served as parts of the old-fashioned watches that people carried during the reign of his father. Even so, it appeared that by their smallness and quickness they were often able to escape from or defend themselves against their natural enemies. The ants particularly commanded the King's respect and attention. After observing them for some time, he settled the question of the royal succession by marrying the poacher's quite charming daughter, and thereby rid himself of the only one of his problems that was at all pressing.

After a short interval, a mere nine or ten months, she presented him with a son, and during the baptism of the Heir Apparent at a forest spring a messenger arrived with mud on his boots and his horse in a lather. The enemy—never, it seemed, very large in number—had grown weary of subjugating so inactive a country, had provoked a war with another small neighboring state, and had not been heard of for nearly six months. It was presumed that either they had been defeated in battle and perhaps perished or else they had simply got lost somewhere between the capital and the frontier and were wandering around, helpless and incapable of further harm. At all events, there was no longer any reason why the King should not return and rule over his people. Unfortunately, the messenger added, the enemy's last outrageous act before they departed on their warlike expedition had been to pull down the royal palace, but the Royal College of Architects was already at work on the design for a new palace that would far surpass, in size and splendor, the one that had been destroyed.

The King and Queen and Heir Apparent travelled all the way through crowds that were half naked but not listless, and that indeed often cheered quite energetically. The King pitched a tent in the rose garden, now overgrown with brambles, and sent for the College of Architects. Together they went through the plans for the new palace, while the Queen looked over the King's shoulder.

"Much too extensive," he said, astonishing everyone by the quickness of his decision and the brevity with which it was conveyed. "By your own least conservative estimate, the quarrying and cutting of that much marble will take fifty years. Possibly longer. I am not a young man and this tent leaks. Since it is traditional that the king live in a marble palace, I must, I suppose, follow the custom of my ancestors, though wood, I have recently discovered, is easier to heat and less clammy on damp days— Did the enemy carry watches?"

"No, Your Majesty," said the Architect Royal. "They were so quick in everything they did that they seemed not to know or care what time it was."

"The great Timepiece was not destroyed along with the palace?"

The Architect Royal shook his head. "There was talk of destroying it, but the enemy general paid a visit to the site of this magnificent experiment and was so impressed that he said, 'Let it be. If we destroy it, nobody will ever believe that people are as foolish as they really are.'"

"I see," said the King, and for several minutes he remained deep in thought. At last he roused himself and said, "Fine. There ought to be just enough marble in that uncompleted watch to construct a palace the size of the poacher's hut, for which Her Majesty is, quite naturally, homesick. A week ought to be ample time for drawing up the plans and executing them. And if you can locate an ant's nest, will you transport that also to the palace courtyard, and then go on about your business."

All this, being the King's decree, was done, and in no time at all the want of equilibrium between exports and imports was a thing of the past. At court concerts, musical compositions were played straight through from beginning to end. At court balls, the minuet gave way to the waltz and the mazurka. The Queen got over her homesickness, and the King, observing the ant colony whenever he had some decision of great moment to make, soon brought on an era of such prosperity that he is referred to in all the history books as "Charles the Expediter" and by the common people, affectionately, as "Charles the Flea."

5. The half-crazy woman

ONCE upon a time there was a half-crazy woman who lived off the leavings of other people, who shook their heads when they saw her coming, and tried not to get in conversation with her. They wanted to be kind, but there is a limit to kindness, and the half-crazy woman was so distracted that anyone listening to her began to feel half crazy too. Since people avoided her, she talked to any stray dog or cat that came along, and sometimes even to the old willow tree that grew by her door. One autumn evening when the weight around her heart was too heavy to bear, she went outside to the sty where she kept her thin, disgruntled pig and said sorrowfully, "Pig, you won't die of hunger, will you?"

The pig said, "No, I won't die of hunger."

"Thank you for that," the half-crazy woman said, but she was not satisfied. The pig had had nothing to eat for three days.

She went back into the house and saw the fire burning low on the hearth and said, "Fire, you won't go out, will you?"

The fire said, "No, I won't go out."

"Thank you for that," the half-crazy woman said, and tried not to worry, even though there was only an armful of faggots to last all night.

But then she remembered the bread baking in the oven. She opened the oven door and looked in and saw the loaf baking from the heat of the stones in the chimney and thought, What if I should forget to take it out? What if the loaf should burn?

She said anxiously, "Loaf, you won't burn, will you?"

The loaf said, "No, I won't burn."

"Thank you for that," the half-crazy woman said, and thought, Now I have nothing to trouble me.

But the wind, rising, shook the walls and rattled the door of her poor cottage, and so she lit a candle and went up the ladder that led to the attic. The attic was low and she could barely stand upright. She heard the wind straining at the eaves and thought how old the house was, and how poorly built, and she put her hand up and said, "Roof over my head, you won't blow away, will you?"

The roof said, "No, I won't blow away."

"Thank you for that," the half-crazy woman said, and tried to feel happy, but happiness doesn't come for the asking, and there was a musty smell in the attic that she couldn't account for. It was not the smell of old clothes, or of dust, or of leather, exactly, but something of all of these things, and it added to the weight around her heart. It must be the smell of Death, she thought, and in that very instant felt his presence there, in her empty attic. He was standing behind her, close enough to make the hairs on the back of her neck stiffen and rise. "Death, you won't ever leave me, will you?" she cried, and was frightened at the sound of her own words.

"No, I won't ever leave you," Death said. "You don't have to worry. Go downstairs and take the loaf out of the oven before it burns and throw some wood on the fire before it goes out and feed the pig before it dies of hunger."

"Thank you for that," the half-crazy woman said, and climbed down the ladder and took the loaf, which was a golden brown, out of the oven, and threw some faggots on the fire, which blazed up brightly, and took some scraps that she had been saving for her own supper out to the pig. The wind had died down suddenly, and the half-crazy woman saw that it was going to be a calm clear night with millions of stars in the heavens. She found a stick and scratched the pig's back until it grunted with pleasure. Then she went into the house and cut a slice from the warm loaf and ate it by the fire. The weight was gone from around her heart. She thought of the presence waiting in the attic and listened but there was no sound. The house was still. And the half-crazy woman knew for the first time what it is to have peace of mind.

6. The woman who didn't want anything more

O NCE upon a time there was a woman who didn't want anything more. Tables, chairs, pictures, old china, potted plants, scatter rugs, washcloths, bookends, sewing scissors—there was nothing she needed beyond what she already had, and when people asked her "Isn't there something you'd like for your birthday?" she said "No, I really don't want a thing," which bothered them, of course, because there were a great many things that they wanted, and so they set about trying to find something for her. They gave her cookbooks, which she thanked them for politely and put on the shelf with the other cookbooks. They gave her hooked rugs, which she thanked them for and put in the attic. They gave her autographed copies of their own books, which she had already bought and read, but she thanked them and put the two copies side by side in the bookcase. They gave her woollen scarves, which had to be wrapped in newspaper and put away in the cedar chest, which was full. And they gave her a portable television set, a footstool, a fire screen, and a folding table, all of which presented a problem to her, though she managed eventually to put them away somewhere out of sight.

"If people only wouldn't give me things," she used to say to herself, without realizing for quite a long while that she had gone one step further and didn't even want the things she already had.

One day, she opened her front door, with her hat and coat and gloves on, ready to go out and get in the car and drive downtown, and there, lying across the welcome mat, was a man, sound asleep or dead drunk, she was not sure which. His clothes were filthy, he needed a bath, and he hadn't shaved, and it was obvious at a glance that he was a tramp, with nothing in his pockets, and no place of his own to go to.

Her first impulse was to step back into the house and call the police, but then he opened his eyes, which were so mild in their expression that she had another impulse instead, which was to go back inside and make him a pot of coffee. And then she had the third and most interesting idea of all.

She opened her purse and took out her house key and her car key and gave them to him. On second thought, she handed him her purse, too, and went off down the sidewalk without looking back to see what happened.

If she had stopped to think, she would have realized that you don't get rid of everything you own as easily as all that. She should have given him a deed to the house, and the registration certificate for the car, and a forwarding address to show to people who turned up asking for her, and a signed statement to show to the police. But she didn't think of any of these things, because she was so taken with the idea of giving away everything she had, three days before Christmas, when the hall closet was full of unopened packages and the mailman came twice a day with more.

There was snow on the ground, but she had her arctics on, and it did not occur to her to give them away, because she was not morbid or fanatical. She walked downtown, and tried not to see the store windows, which usually depressed her because they were full of things she already had, or had had until a few minutes ago, and one does not get used to the idea of being free of things all at once; it takes time. The people she passed were carrying all sorts of awkward parcels, sometimes two and three of them tied together, and these things they had bought and were carrying home, either to give to somebody or to give to themselves, did not seem to have brought the light of pleasure to their eyes. She came to a bakery, and the sight of the Italian fruit bread and French pastries and *croissants* and *brioches* and hard-crusted wheels and sticks of white bread in the window reminded her that there was no bread in the house. She didn't want any for herself; she was not hungry. But she remembered the tramp, who would probably be disappointed when he sat down at the kitchen table with a cup of hot coffee and found there was no bread and butter to go with it. So she turned and went into the shop, which was crowded with people buying bread and pastry and party favors and other fancy staples for the holidays, but she didn't mind waiting. There was nothing that she should have been doing at that moment, and the place smelled of fresh bread, which was baked on the premises, and it was a long time since she had smelled this happy smell.

When her turn came, she got as far as "I want—" and then stopped, because her arm was unnaturally light without the familiar weight of her purse on it. But she realized that the tramp could—and in fact would have to—go out and buy his own bread, because she had given him all the money she had, and her bankbook, in case he ran out of cash, which he eventually would, and needed to dip into her savings account. So, smiling at the woman behind the counter, she said, "I just want to stand here and smell the smell of fresh bread."

Unfortunately, there were a great many things that the woman behind the counter wanted, and so she didn't understand; besides, she had grown so accustomed to the smell of fresh bread that she didn't even smell it any more. And she suspected that the woman was a thief, or perhaps the accomplice of thieves, who, when she signalled to them that the shop was empty of customers, would rush in, with their faces masked and guns in their hands, and help themselves to the contents of the cash register. But if you are in business you never can be sure who you are dealing with, and one person's money is as good as another's, and so she pointed to a sign: "No loitering on the Premises."

"I see," said the woman, and turned and went outside. It was getting dark, and she had no place to go to, which pleased her, and no engagements, which also pleased her, but she found that she couldn't get the smell of fresh bread out of her mind as she walked along, with her collar turned up against the evening wind. Suddenly it occurred to her that she could go back home—only it was not her home any longer—and ask the tramp if he'd mind if she made some bread.

The front door was wide open and the oil-burner was running. The key was in the door. She called and there was no answer. The place, which she had expected to find ransacked from top to bottom, seemed to be in perfect order, except that the car keys were lying on the floor in the library. She saw, looking out of the library window, that the car was still in the garage. Nothing was missing; not the contents of her purse, which she did not want; not the typewriter, which she seldom used; not the portable TV, which she never turned on; not the pair of expensive binoculars somebody had insisted on giving her; not even the flat silver and her jewelry, which she would have been happy to see the last of. Apparently, the man she found lying on her doorstep didn't want anything either. With a deep sigh, she adjusted herself to the idea that she was not, after all, free of things, and with a shrug accepted the idea that she still had a roof over her head. "I wonder if he—" she said to herself, and started for the kitchen, which was in some disorder. The tramp had not stopped to make a pot of coffee for himself, but had sampled the contents of the liquor closet instead, and then worked his way rather unsystematically through the icebox, tossing wrappers and bones and anything in the way of leftovers that didn't appeal to him on the kitchen floor. "Surely he wouldn't think to—" the woman said to herself hopefully, and with a beating heart she put out her hand and opened the flour bin. Sure enough, the tramp had not stolen the flour; or, it turned out, the skim milk, or the butter, or the yeast, or the salt and sugar.

She got out the breadboard and the measuring spoons and the measuring cups, and put on a clean white apron, and began to measure and mix the ingredients, and when the dough had risen and the oven was the right temperature, she slipped the pans in and closed the oven door quickly and sat down to wait. For a short while she was afraid that the whole thing was an illusion, and that she would not really care any more about the smell of fresh bread baking than she did about hooked rugs there was no floor space for, or the woollen scarves in the cedar chest, or the money in her savings account, or the roof over her head. Then it began, faintly, ever so faintly at first, but unmistakable. She closed her eyes and caught the odor with a series of little searching sniffs.

"*Oh, bread, hurry!*" she said to it, and when the bread, all golden, was out of the pans and cooling on the kitchen table, she made herself a pot of good strong coffee. This is more like it, she said to herself. And indeed, from that time on, it was.

7. The girl with a willing heart and a cold mind

NOT everybody's heart and mind reside in their body. There was a girl whose feelings and ideas led so separate a life that they were to her always like a younger brother and sister whom she cared for anxiously, as if they had to be watched, and might, the moment she turned her back, fall and skin their knees, or wander, picking flowers, too close to the edge of some terrible cliff. When she fell in love with a young fisherman who went out every day, whether it was storming or fine weather, with five other men in a sturdy boat, and came in the evenings to sit beside her on her father's doorstep and plead with her to marry him, she consulted both her heart and her mind, for she didn't want to leave them behind when she went to live with the fisherman, and she didn't want them to be unhappy. Her heart was willing. It said, "Oh, let us go and live with the fisherman and keep his house clean and the fire burning all day on his hearth and have a good supper waiting for him when he comes home at the end of the day, half frozen with the cold. Let us go, by all means. The fisherman needs us. The very sound of his voice pleading is more than I can bear." But her mind was skeptical. It would not take a stand, not believing in one thing more than another.

After the girl and the young fisherman were married, and the girl kept his house clean for him and the fire burning brightly on the hearth and the kettle ready to boil the moment he came in at night, her mind gave them no peace. First it set upon the fisherman, who was a simple creature, not used to doubting, and when he drew the girl on his lap after supper, her mind came between them and said "Do you really love her, fisherman, or are you only pretending?" until the poor man grew vague and absentminded in his answers and sought comfort in sleep. Then her mind, not being at all satisfied with this small triumph, plagued and pestered the girl. When the fisherman lifted her in his arms and carried her off to bed, her mind said, "Why are you here? How did it ever come about?

Weren't you happier before, in your father's house, sleeping in your own narrow cot? Wasn't that what you really wanted?" And the poor girl, not being able to answer, lay awake hour after hour, listening to the sound of the fisherman's heavy breathing by her side. Her only comfort at such times was her heart, with its steady beating.

"Heart, are you there?" the poor girl would ask. "Heart, do you feel anything?"

"Yes, I feel something," her heart told her patiently. "Go to sleep. It's only your mind filling you with doubts. In the morning, in broad daylight, everything will be all right. Have trust in me."

And finally, out of weariness, the girl fell asleep. But even with the fisherman's arm around her, and his heart beating against her ribs, she had troubled dreams and cried out unintelligibly in her sleep and woke up exhausted in the cold morning light. The color left her cheeks and she grew thinner, and the fisherman quarrelled with the other men, his boat companions, and cut himself with his knife because his hands were unsteady, and neglected to mend his nets, so that the best fish sometimes got away. And when he got home at night, the fire on the hearth had gone out, the house was dark, and no voice answered his call, and he had to go wandering off over the moors, tired though he was, until he found his wife, her hair damp with mist and her lips tasting of salt spray, and a lost look in her great dark eyes.

If he didn't come back, the girl thought, walking home with him hand in hand—if some night it got dark and I were waiting with supper all ready on the hearth and I didn't hear his step outside but only the wind howling and the branches scraping against the window and no sound indoors but the ticking of the clock, and if I put on a shawl finally and went outside and found the other women waiting on the cliff, their faces stiff with fright, their eyes intent on the darkness, and no boat on the sand, then I would know beyond all doubt whether I loved him or not. Then I would know if my heart is feeling. And when her husband, noticing her silence, asked her what she was thinking about, she shook her head or told him some small lie: she was worrying about the peas, which had a burnt taste because the water had all boiled off while she was getting wood for the fire, or about the postman's little girl, who had rheumatic fever. But actually it was his own face that she was thinking of, when they brought him in, lifeless, his hair matted and wet, and laid his body across the bed—his beautiful, loving, dead face.

And when he suddenly gave up going out in the early morning with the men in their boat, and took a job with the peat cutters and came home at night smelling of the marsh grass instead of the sea, she felt that there was no hope of her ever being happy, no way that she would ever know whether she loved him or not. And things might have gone on this way all her life if her body, which had no traffic with either her heart or her mind, hadn't rebelled finally and said, "You silly girl, I will now show you. I will give you an answer that you can't argue yourself out of. You are already with child, do you understand? The fisherman's child is growing inside of you, and has the fisherman's eyes and hair and his patient, loving disposition. You can go home to your father now or you can stay with the fisherman. Now is the time to decide."

The voice of her body was so stern and uncompromising that the girl began to weep. "O mind," she cried, "what are you thinking? O heart, what are you feeling now?"

There was no answer. She thought for a moment that both mind and heart had deserted her and that she was a madwoman. But then she put her hand to her side and felt her heart beating there, like her husband's heart inside his rising and falling chest, and her thoughts came now from her head, not from outside her. She threw her arms around the fisherman so wildly that he woke and made a warm nest for her in the curve of his naked body.

"Go to sleep," he said. "You've been dreaming. You've had a bad dream. While I'm here, no harm shall touch you." She smiled in the dark at his childish pride and thinking about the child inside her, which had his sea-blue eyes and his clustering dark hair, she fell into a dreamless sleep.

When he woke in the morning and put out his hand, she was gone. His heart beat in terror until he heard her moving about in the next room, setting the table for breakfast, and singing softly so as not to wake him.

8. The woodcutter

O NCE upon a time there was an old woodcutter who lived in a hut in a clearing in the forest, far from any town. Behind the hut there was a pond with carp in it, and in the forest there were wild apple trees and blackberry brambles and rabbits and deer. With all this to draw upon, the woodcutter and his wife lived well enough until, on the doorstep of their old age, a young King, hunting in the forest, became separated from his court and rode up to the hut and saw the pond and the circle of tall pine trees around the clearing and said to himself, "Here if anywhere I shall find the meaning of life."

He got down off his horse and knocked on the door of the hut and explained to the old woman that he was lost.

"Now, isn't that a pity," the old woman said. "Come in out of the cold and warm yourself. I have lived so long in this hut that I don't remember any more how to get out of the forest, but my husband is cutting wood and when he comes home for his supper he will show you the way."

She was embarrassed to find herself alone in the company of the King, and so while he was warming himself at the fire she took an apple out to his horse, waiting patiently beside the door of the hut. When she came inside she asked, "Aren't you afraid to leave your fine horse without even tying the reins to a sapling?"

"No," said the young King, "the horse is well trained. He will not run away, and if he did, it would not matter. I have other horses."

He began to talk to the old woman about the subject that was dearest to his heart—the meaning of life—but she didn't understand a word he said. She saw that the King was sitting too near the fire, and the smell of burning wool was so strong in her nostrils that at last she had to speak to him about it.

"Hadn't you better move away from the fire? Your fine cloak is being scorched and that would be a pity."

"No," the King said, "I like the warmth. The castle I am living in at the moment is on a hill and often cold and drafty. If the cloak is scorched it does not matter. I have other cloaks."

871

The old woman glanced at the wooden peg by the door where her husband's old cloak of rough homespun hung when he was at home. In the room there was no sound but the crackling of the fire, and the King, glancing around, said, "Aren't you ever lonely here?"

"No," said the old woman. "My husband comes home at nightfall, and I know that I have to get his supper for him, and therefore I am never lonely."

"But what if something happened to your husband?" the young King asked.

"Nothing could happen to my husband that wouldn't also happen to me," the old woman said. "I am not afraid."

"In the castle I am now living in," the King said, "there are many people, all of them ready and anxious to wait upon me and be near me. If one of them gets sick and dies, there are always others ready and anxious to take his place."

The old woman noticed the wrinkles in the young King's forehead and the pallor of his face.

"You are not married?" she asked.

"No," the King said.

"That is a pity," she said, shaking her head.

"No," the King said, "it doesn't matter. If I could have two queens, I would have married long ago, but the archbishop will not permit me to have two queens, and I do not wish to be dependent on any one person, and therefore I have never married."

Just at dark the woodcutter came into the cottage, and when the two men stood side by side, the old woman saw that the King, in spite of his crown, was not as tall as her husband nor as broad in the shoulder.

The three of them sat down to supper, and afterward the woodcutter lit his lantern and the King leapt on his horse and they went off through the forest. As soon as they were out of sight of the hut, the King began to speak to the old wood-cutter about the meaning of life. The woodcutter listened respectfully, and when the King had finished he waited for the woodcutter's reply, for he was genuinely concerned about the welfare of his subjects and liked to hear their views on matters of importance. But instead of answering him, the woodcutter raised his arm and pointed. There in the distance the King saw the lights of the castle.

Early the next morning, the forest rang with the sound of marching feet, the trample of ox teams, and the creak of cart wheels. A thousand workmen surrounded the hut in the forest. They had brought their tools with them, and they began to dig a deep ditch around the woodcutter's hut and to widen the forest paths for roads. When the old woman came out of the hut and remonstrated with them, the workmen shrugged their shoulders.

"It is the King's will," they said.

"But why does he have to dig his ditch here?" the old woman asked.

"It is for a moat," the workmen said.

"But what good is a moat where there is no castle?"

"When we are finished there will be a castle where your hut now stands," the workmen said.

"But the King already has another castle," the old woman said, "and this poor hut is the only home we have under the sky."

"The King has many castles," the workmen said. "This castle is for him to come to when he needs solitude to consider the meaning of life."

Since she could get no better reason from them, the old woman threw a shawl over her head and ran off through the forest. By nightfall the moat was completed and the water from the pond let into it. The carp from the pond swam round and round the woodcutter's hut, and the rabbits and deer crossed and recrossed the new road that led out of the forest. It had taken the old woman all day to find her husband, and she was half crazed with calling and searching for him. When they saw their hut surrounded by a moat over which there was as yet no bridge, the woodcutter could not speak for despair, but out of habit the old woman gathered sticks for a fire, and they got ready to pass the night with neither food nor shelter.

"At least the forest is still the same," she said. "We still have the stars in the sky," and she fell asleep with her head in her husband's lap. The woodcutter stayed awake to tend the fire, but he was worn out from his day's work and from grief at losing his home, and his head began to nod and the heat of the fire made him drowsier and drowsier.

At midnight a procession of horsemen and men carrying torches came into the forest and arrived at the clearing. The two figures beside the ashes of their fire did not stir, and the King, dismounting from his horse, thought for a moment that they were statues brought by the workmen for his new castle. Then he realized his mistake and shook the woodcutter, but there was no response. The woodcutter had gone where no king's touch would waken him, and what had happened to the woodcutter also happened to his wife. In anger the King turned to the court chamberlain and asked, "Why didn't the men build a bridge so that the two old people, who, after all, were kind to me, could get to their hut?"

The court chamberlain hemmed and hawed and said, "The royal order was to build a moat. Nothing was said about a bridge over the moat."

"No," the King said thoughtfully. And then, "It doesn't matter. I have other woodcutters. Tell them to come and cut wood in this forest. If I don't hear the sound of the axe ringing in the distance I will be lonely here."

But it turned out, strangely, that there were no more woodcutters. All the firewood in the kingdom was cut by the old man who now sat with his chin resting on his breast, his gray hair whitened by new-fallen snow.

The King stood and looked at him a long time, while the torches burned down and the courtiers shivered with the cold and waited for their royal master to be of one mind or another. At daybreak he turned to them and said, "I have found the meaning of life."

They stood waiting for him to announce that life is good or that life is bad, but instead he took off his crown and handed it to the court chamberlain.

"From now on I will be the woodcutter," he said, "and live in this hut."

"But you are our king," the court chamberlain said.

"No," the King said. "And in any case it doesn't matter. There are many kings and many people ready and anxious to be kings. I am the only one who is ready and anxious to take the place of this poor woodcutter."

Bearing the crown carefully in his left hand, the court chamberlain mounted his horse and rode back into the forest, and the courtiers, in the order of their rank and according to established precedence, mounted their horses and followed him.

9. *The man who had never been sick a day in his life*

ONCE upon a time there was a man who had never been sick a day in his life. When other people were doubled up with stomach cramps, or lay in a darkened room waiting for a migraine to pass, or stuffed themselves with pills that had no effect on their coughing and sneezing, he was not unsympathetic, for he was a very kind man, but the look in his eyes gave him away. It said all too plainly that he didn't understand what pain and discomfort were all about.

When his wife took sick, she filled a hot-water bottle and made a collection on her bedside table of everything she was likely to want, and when he came to the door and said, with genuine concern in his voice, "Is there anything I can do for you?" she said, "Yes, close the door and leave me alone." So he did. A person who had ever been sick might have felt guilty for being so well when his wife was so miserable. All he felt was the kind of wonder people feel at some flourish of human nature that defies understanding.

But the thing about perfection (and what he had was a kind of perfection) is that one minute it is there and the next it's gone, usually forever. And so the day came when the man who was never sick a day in his life was too sick to get up out of bed and lay in an upstairs room roaring like a bull. The hot-water bottle and the extra pillow behind his back and the nice appetizing tray with the best breakfast china on it he rejected indignantly. And when he couldn't give voice to his indignation because of the thermometer under his tongue, he glared balefully at his wife, as if his swollen glands and backache and hundred-and-one-and-two-tenths temperature were entirely her doing.

"Don't go spreading it all over the neighborhood," he said when she took the thermometer out of his mouth. But it was too remarkable an event to be kept from people, and in no time at all nice nourishing soups and calf's-foot jelly and even flowers began pouring into the house. At the sight of each new offering the man closed his eyes and said, "For God's sake, take it away. What can they be thinking of?"

"You," his wife said.

She left the soup or the calf's-foot jelly or whatever on the bedside table and went out of the room and stayed out a good long time. When she came back, the invalid's food was untouched, so she went right out again and stayed even longer. No remarks were made on either side, but there was a look in his eye that had never been there before, and it was not pleasure in being sick or gratefulness for small attentions. He wouldn't answer questions—wouldn't even speak. So she called the doctor, who was busy, like all doctors, and didn't come until she had given up hope of his ever coming. In the downstairs hall, as he was leaving, he repeated his instructions: the large pills to be given every four hours, the smaller pills at bedtime, with the capsules, and said that it would take time and to do what she could to make him comfortable.

"You don't know what you're saying," the woman said.

Upstairs, the sick man heard their voices, which came quite plainly through the ceiling, and then—incredibly—the sound of suppressed laughter. The doctor was an old friend and the laughter was affectionate, but that didn't make any difference. In fact, it made it worse. A wave of hatred came over the man who had never been sick a day in his life—hatred not only of his wife and his friend but of life itself, which had lost its meaning and its virtue, and he realized that he had had enough of it and would just as soon not have any more. So he gave up, refused to lift a finger, stopped caring about anything, and with his face turned to the wall waited for the moment when they would realize that he had lost his hold on life and was going to die. He got well, of course. His body got well, in spite of everything, and rather sooner than his wife expected. His body got up out of bed and dressed and shaved and went to his office. There was a mountain of mail on his desk and the telephone was ringing. But it was a different man that answered it.

10. *The problem child*

O NCE upon a time there was a man with a very beautiful
and gentle wife, whose only thought was to cherish and
protect him, as his was for her, and their happiness was completed by the birth of a daughter, who, as she grew older,
showed every sign of having inherited her mother's beauty and
loving nature. It was easy enough to see what the future would
bring, except that it did not turn out that way. Suddenly, with
no warning, the woman took sick and died, and where then
was the man's happiness and the child's future?

For a time he was half mad with grief, and neglected his
affairs, and also neglected his child, though he didn't mean to
do this, and things steadily went from bad to worse, and people
shook their heads over the situation, and wished there was
something they could do. There was, and they did it without
realizing it. So many things were said in praise of the dead
woman's character that gradually, in the man's mind, she
changed, she became perfect, without a flaw. All his memories
of her, every affectionate and tender thing she had ever said to
him, fell away, and it was as if he had been married to a photograph. One does not grieve forever over the loss of an ideal person. The man threw himself into his work, the color came back
into his face, he smiled more often, and he was seen—dining in
expensive restaurants, or in his car, headed for the country on
a Saturday afternoon—with a pretty woman, a widow with
two nearly grown daughters. No one blamed him for this, or
had a word to say against her, except (and this was not really
against her) that she wasn't exactly the person they would have
expected him to show an interest in.

The wedding was small and quiet, and among the guests
were a number of people who had been devoted to his first
wife. He particularly wanted their approval and blessing on his
marriage, and it was not withheld. But there was, of course,
someone who was even more important to him. When the
minister had pronounced them man and wife and they turned
to face the wedding guests, the man's eyes sought out first of all
his daughter. After his wife's death, in their bewilderment, they

had clung to each other like drowning creatures, but during the last few weeks he had discovered that sorrow is more easily shared than happiness. Though she was docile about everything, he had no doubt but that in her heart she blamed him for not remaining faithful to her mother's memory. As he bent down and kissed her, he told himself that when she was a little older he would be able to put things in a light that she could understand and accept.

Unfortunately, children do not always want to understand, though sometimes, when one would prefer that they didn't, they understand all too well. The girl continued to reject her stepmother's affection, no matter how tactfully it was held out to her. Both the man and his wife had been prepared for this. What they did not expect was that it would go on so long. Since nothing was lacking to his happiness but his daughter's willingness to be a part of it, at times he could not help being exasperated with her. Up till now, she had never given him any trouble whatever, and so, as his wife pointed out, he was not used to being patient with her. When they were talking about the problem, late at night as they were undressing for bed, her conclusion always was that they should not add to the difficulty by exaggerating its seriousness. It would work itself out, with time. "Besides," she would say, as she sat at her dressing table putting cleansing cream on her face, "it isn't as if there was anything personal in the poor child's attitude. It's just a classical situation, and it has to be dealt with intelligently." Or she would say, "All that is perfectly true, and sometimes I feel like turning her over my knee and spanking her. But it doesn't help to get emotionally involved. Then you are fighting it out on her level, which is just what she wants."

When the man got home at night and his daughter threw her arms around him, he returned her embrace tenderly and kissed her on the cheek, and then after a second disengaged himself, for she was at an age when, the books all agreed, it was unwise to prolong demonstrations of affection. As one would have expected, the girl had no friends. She came straight home from school and went upstairs to her room and read until dinnertime. When the telephone rang it was always for her stepmother or her stepsisters. "Isn't there somebody you'd like to have come and spend the night with you?" the woman would ask, and the girl would shake her head and stare at her stepmother as if she were prying into something that was none of her business. "I know perfectly well I am exaggerating," the woman said afterward, as she and her husband were sitting together in their cosy little library, having their evening drink. "And in any case, I shouldn't let her get under my skin. It's just that it came on top of a long and rather difficult day. Let's not talk about it any more."

But they did talk about it, of course. It concerned them too deeply for them to be able to ignore—or forget about—what went on under their eyes every day. As she pointed out, it would have been far easier, when the girl did something she shouldn't have, to tell him and let him deal with it, but this was not really the way to break down her resistance. It was why so many women never succeeded in winning the affection of their stepchildren and were merely tolerated, when they were not actively disliked by them. Also the girl would know— how could she not know?—where the information came from.

She treated the girl exactly as she treated her own two daughters. If they had been disrespectful or disobedient, she would have had no choice but to punish them, for their own good. And since her stepdaughter was of an age when she could no longer be spanked, punishment had to take the form of withholding privileges and pleasures. So, when she was buying pretty new frocks for her own daughters, she chose something for her stepdaughter as well, and then, regretfully, put it back on the rack.

When the girl's behavior had been particularly flagrant, she was not allowed to eat with the family, and since it would not have done to have her confiding in the servants, she was made to eat in her room, from a tray. This was not a fairy tale, and so no fairy godmother appeared to change a pumpkin into a coach and all that, and send the girl off to a ball where the prince was waiting to fall in love with her. Instead, she cried herself to sleep, grew pale and thin, grew untidy in her appearance, and more and more obstinate in her conduct, and in every way possible confirmed her stepmother's view of the situation, which at times was close to despairing. They consulted an eminent child psychologist, who confirmed their fears and at the same time reassured them, for it was something of a comfort to know that the girl was like other emotionally disturbed children and not a unique case. He suggested that she would probably do better with a woman analyst. The therapist he recommended had studied with Anna Freud, and had a German accent, and was a chain smoker, and looked like a man, but she was very intelligent. The girl refused to play with the doll's house and the blocks, but she listened politely to what the woman said. In brief, what this amounted to was that the wicked stepmother of fairy tales is really a disguise—the child's repressed hostility toward its real mother, the rival for the affection of the father, becomes a projection. By forcing her stepmother into this role she had, in a sense, been keeping her dead mother alive and near her. The simple truth was that she did not hate her stepmother but was, if anything, too fond of her, and jealous of her stepsisters, who had a stronger claim on her stepmother's affection. Understanding this should have resulted in some change in the girl's behavior but it didn't. She kept the appointments with the analyst, though about other things she was very forgetful. But she answered all questions reluctantly and did not free associate. It appeared that she could not or would not believe that the analyst—that, indeed, anyone—was on her side. In the end, the analyst reported to her parents that there was no transference, and the treatments, which were, God knows, expensive enough were discontinued.

Those overtures that were made to her—as a rule, privately —by old friends of the family, women who had known and loved her mother, the girl also rejected, or perhaps misunderstood, and so after one or two attempts the women stopped trying to do anything for her, in the belief that there was nothing they could do.

"What I fear," her stepmother said, "above everything else in this world, is that she will run off with the first man who looks at her. The Fuller Brush man, or somebody who works in a filling station." And that was exactly what happened, only it was a second-hand car salesman, and he was neither well made, nor well brought up, nor mentally her equal. He was not even very young.

*

At first the girl's father was inclined to blame himself severely, and wanted to rush after the couple and make sure that they did not regret their action. But his wife convinced him that it was too soon for them to be anything but excited by what they had done, and he would simply be the villain who threatened their happiness. If it was the mistake that it appeared to be, then they must have time to realize it. If he made things too easy for them now, they would all the rest of their married life look to him to solve their problems. Reluctantly, he was prevailed upon to wait, to delay his forgiveness, to do nothing. And things did not turn out so badly as one might have supposed. Though the second-hand car salesman wasn't anything to write home about, the girl's only thought was to cherish and protect him, and for a time they were quite happy. When he took to drink and beat her, she left him and lived with someone else, for she had already experienced the worst that can happen to anybody, and knew that loving kindness can vanish overnight, and girls who lose their mother and are more handsome than their stepsisters have no one and therefore better learn to look after themselves.

11. *The woman who had no eye for small details*

ONCE upon a time there was a woman who had no eye for those small details and dainty effects that most women love to spend their time on—curtains and doilies, and the chairs arranged so, and the rugs so, and a small picture here, and a large mirror there. She did not bother with all this because, in the first place, she lived alone and had no one but herself to please, and, anyway, she was not interested in material objects. So her house was rather bare, and, to tell the truth, not very comfortable. She lived very much in her mind, which fed upon books: upon what Erasmus and Darwin and Gautama Buddha and Pascal and Spinoza and Nietzsche and St. Thomas Aquinas had thought; and what she herself thought about what they thought. She was not a homely woman. She had good bones and beautiful heavy hair, which was very long, and which she wore in a braided crown around her head. But no man had ever courted her, and at her present age she did not expect this to happen. If some man had looked at her with interest, she would not have noticed it, and this would, of course, have been enough to discourage further attentions.

Her house was the last house on a narrow dirt road, deep in the country, and if she heard the sound of a horse and buggy or a wagon, it was somebody coming to see her, which didn't often happen. She kept peculiar hours, and ate when she was hungry, and the mirror over the dressing table was sometimes shocked at her appearance, but since she almost never looked in it, she was not aware of the wisps of hair that needed pinning up, the eyes clouded by absent-mindedness, the sweater with a button missing, worn over a dress that belonged in the rag bag. A blind man put down in her cottage would have thought there were two people, not one, living in it, for she talked to herself a great deal.

Birds in great numbers nested in the holes of her apple trees and in the ivy that covered her stone chimney. Their cheeping, chirping sounds were the background of all that went on in her mind. Often she caught sight of them just as they were disappearing, and was not sure whether she had seen a bird or only seen its flight—so like the way certain thoughts again and again escaped her just as she reached out for them. When the ground was covered with snow, the birds closed in around the house and were at the feeding stations all day long. Even the big birds came—the lovely gentle mourning doves, and the pheasants out of the woods, and partridge, and quail. In bitter weather, when the wind was like iron, she put pans of warm water out for them, and, in a corner sheltered from the wind, kept a patch of ground swept bare, since they wouldn't use the feeders. And at times she was as occupied—or so she told herself—as if she were bringing up a large family of children, like her sister.

Her sister's children were as lively as the birds, and even noisier, and they were a great pleasure to the woman who lived all alone, when she went to visit them. She played cards with them, and let them read to her, and listened to all that they had to say, which their mother was too busy to do. While she was there she was utterly at their disposal, so they loved her, and didn't notice the wisps of hair that needed pinning up, or that there was a button missing from her sweater, or the fact that her dress was ready for the rag bag. Looking around, she thought how, though her sister's house was small and the furniture shabby, everything her eye fell upon was there because it served some purpose or because somebody loved it. The pillows were just right against your back, the colors cheerful, the general effect of crowdedness reflected the busy life of the family. Their house was them, in a way hers was not. Her house, to be her, would have had to be made of pine boughs or have been high up in some cliff. The actual house sheltered her and that was all that could be said for it.

Her nieces and nephews would have been happy to have her stay with them forever, but she always said, "I have to get back to my little house," in a tone of voice grownups use when they don't intend to discuss something.

"Your house won't run off," her sister would say. "Why do you worry about it so? I don't see why you don't make us a real visit."

"Another time," the woman said, and went on putting her clothes in her suitcase. The real reason that she could not stay longer she did not tell them, because she knew they would not take it seriously: she could not bear the thought of the birds coming to the feeders and finding nothing but dust and chaff where they were accustomed to find food. So home she went, promising to come back soon, and never outstaying her welcome.

But no woman—no man, either—is allowed to live completely in her mind, or in books, or with only the birds for company. One day when she opened her mailbox, which was with a cluster of other mailboxes at a crossroads a quarter of a mile away, there was a letter from her sister. She put it in her pocket, thinking that she knew what was in it. Her sister's letters were, as a rule, complaining. Her life was hard. Her handsome, easygoing, no-good husband had deserted her, and she supported herself and the children by fine sewing. She worried about the children, because they were growing up without a father. And though they were not perfect, their faults loomed larger in her eyes than they perhaps needed to. In any case, she was tired and overworked and had no one else to complain to.

Hours later, the woman remembered that she had not read the letter, which turned out to be only three lines long: "I am very sick and the doctor says I must go to the hospital and there is no one to look after the children. Please come as soon as you can get here."

All the time the woman was packing, she kept thinking now about her poor sister and now about the poor birds. For it was the middle of the winter, there was deep snow on the ground, and the wind crept even into the house through the crack under the door, through closed windows. She filled the feeders to overflowing with seeds and suet, and sprinkled cracked corn on the ground, knowing that in two days' time it would all be gone. It was snowing again when she locked the door behind her and started off, with her old suitcase, to the nearest farmhouse. She would have to ask the farmer to hitch up his horse and sleigh and drive her to the station in the village, where she could take a train to the place where her sister lived. Fluffed out with cold, the birds sat and watched her go.

When she came back she was not alone. The farmer's sleigh was full of children with sober, pale faces. They climbed down without a word and stood looking at their new home. The woman had left at the beginning of February, and it was now nearly the end of March. The snow on the roof, melting, had made heavy cornices of ice along the eaves, and the ice, melting, had made long, thin icicles. The woman got down, and thanked the farmer, and stood looking around, to see if there were any birds. The trees were empty, there was no sound in the ivy, and the cold wind went right through her.

"Come, children," she said, as she searched through her purse for her door key. "Let us go in out of the cold. You can help me build a fire."

Inside it seemed even colder, but the stoves soon made a difference. She was so busy feeding the children and warming their beds that she scarcely had time to go to the door and throw out a handful of seed on the snow. No birds came. The next day, she swept a bare place in the sheltered corner, and put out corn for the pheasants and quail, and filled the feeders. But she did all this with a heavy heart, knowing that it was to no purpose. And her sister's death had been a great tragedy and she did not see how she could fill her sister's place in the children's hearts or do for them what their mother had done. The corn on the ground, the sunflower seeds in the feeders were untouched when night fell.

Inside the house there was the same unnatural quiet. The woman did not talk to herself, because she was not alone. The children said, "Yes, please," and "No, thank you," and politely looked at the books she gave them to read, and helped set the table, and brought in wood and water, but she could see that they were waiting for only one thing—to go home. And there was no home for them to go to now but here. They did not quarrel with one another, as they used to, or ask her riddles, or beg her to play Old Maid with them. In the face of disaster they were patient. They could have walked on air and passed through solid walls. They looked as if they could read her mind, but theirs were no longer open to her. Though they cried at home, they did not cry here—at least not where she could see them. In their beds in the night, she had no doubt.

The next morning, exhausted, she overslept, and when she came into the kitchen the children were crowded at the window.

Something outside occupied their attention so they could hardly answer when she said good morning to them.

"Your birds have come back," the oldest nephew said.

"Oh surely not!" she cried, and hurried to the window. On the ground outside, in the midst of all the whiteness and brightness, it was like a party. The cardinals, the chickadees, the sparrows, the juncos, the nuthatches, the jays were waiting their turn at the feeders, pecking at the corn in the sheltered place, leaving hieroglyphs in the snow. Somehow, mysteriously, deep in the woods perhaps, they had managed without her help. They had survived. And were chirping and cheeping.

"We got our own breakfast," the children said. Though they didn't yet know it, they would survive also.

The tears began to flow down her cheeks, and the children came and put their arms around her. "So silly of me," she said, wiping her eyes with her handkerchief, only to have to do it again. "I thought they were all—I didn't think they'd survive the cold, with nobody to feed them, for so long." Then more tears, which kept her from going on. When she could speak, she said, "I know it's not—I know you're not happy here the way you were at home." She waited until she could speak more evenly. "The house is not very comfortable, I know. I'm different from your mother. But I loved her, and if you will let me, I will look after you the best I can. We'll look after each other."

Their faces did not change. She was not even sure that they heard what she had said. Or if they heard but didn't understand it. Together, they carried warm water in pans, they swept off a new place for the quail, they hung suet in bags from the branches of the hemlock. They got out the bird book, and from that they moved on to other tasks, and the house was never quite so sad again. Little by little it changed. It took on the look of that other house, where everywhere about you there were traces of what someone was doing, as sharp and clear and interesting as the footprints of the birds in the snow.

12. *The man who loved to eat*

ONCE upon a time there was a man who loved to eat. Two helpings of this, a little more of that, and when he was full, out of consideration for his wife's feelings, he had a little more of something else. Half an hour after he had got up from the table, he would pass through the kitchen and, seeing the remains of the roast on its platter, think regretfully, It won't be the same tomorrow. And then, after a guilty look over his shoulder, he would snitch a small piece of outside, not at all bothered by the fact that he was putting roast beef on top of prune whip. Oddly enough, it did not occur to him that he was greedy until this was pointed out to him at a dinner party by the woman who sat on his left and who, for one reason and another, did not enjoy seeing people eat. He thought a moment and then said, "Yes, it's true. I am greedy," and he decided to leave part of his dessert, but it was a particularly good strawberry mousse, and the next time he looked down, his plate was bare. He should have weighed three hundred pounds and waddled when he walked, but instead he was thin as a rail. He had always been thin. All that food did for him was keep up his appetite.

Though his wife ate sparingly, being mindful of her figure, she liked to cook for him, and his friends smiled as they watched him settle down to a menu. It is not moral perfection that most people find endearing but an agreeable mixture of strong points and frailties. His weakness was clearly the love of food, and he confidently expected to eat his way into his grave. But just when you think you know how things are going to be, it turns out that they aren't that way after all. "Will you have another helping of potatoes?" his wife asked one evening, and he started to say "Yes," as usual, and to his surprise he heard himself say "No." He had had enough. He couldn't eat any more, not even to please her. He wondered if he was coming down with something, and so, privately, did she.

The next morning he woke up feeling perfectly all right, and ate a huge breakfast, and that should have been the end of it, but there was a nagging doubt in the back of his mind; what happened once could happen again. He tried not to think about it. Four days later, when he sat down to the table, he found that once more he had no appetite. This time he was really frightened, and the nagging doubt moved from the back of his mind to the front, and stayed there. He ate, but out of the sense that it was something one must do. No real craving. At breakfast he did not find himself having just one more slice of buttered toast, with currant jelly on it because the other four slices had been either plain or with orange marmalade. He did not say, eying his wife's plate, "If that piece of bacon is going begging . . ." or "If you're not going to eat your English muffin. . . ." He—who was never melancholy—caught himself out in a sigh, and asked himself questions that are better left unasked.

When it came time for his annual checkup, his doctor announced that his heart was normal and so was his blood pressure.

"You mean normal for my age," the man said gloomily.

"Yes. For a man of your age you're in very good shape. Appetite?"

"No appetite."

"Why not?"

"I don't know. I'm just not hungry. I'd just as soon never eat anything again as long as I live."

"We'll have to give you something for that," the doctor said, and he did. Though the man who loved to eat had absolute faith in any kind of medicine, and as a rule showed marked signs of improvement before the pills or the antibiotic could possibly have had a chance to take effect, this time it was different. The liver shots did nothing whatever for him.

About once every month or six weeks his appetite would return, for no reason, and he would stuff himself and think, Ah, now it is over. I can go on eating. . . . But the next time he sat down at the table, no sooner did he raise his fork to his mouth than with a look of utter misery he put it down again.

One day, passing by a secondhand bookstore, he happened to see, on a table of old, gritty, dehydrated books, the "Enchiridion" of Epictetus. He bought it and took it home and sat down to read it. "Require not things to happen as you wish, but wish them to happen as they do happen, and all will be well," Epictetus said, on page 8. The man who loved to eat took a pencil out of his inside coat pocket and underlined the sentence. A few pages farther on, he marked another: "Everything has two handles, the one by which it may be borne, the other by which it cannot." Suddenly he stopped reading and sat looking off into space. The expression on his face was that of a person who has just been saved from drowning. "Umm," he said, to nobody in particular. He read on a few more pages, and then, having absorbed all the Stoicism he could manage in one dose, he closed the book and went about his business, thankful that his pleasure in food lasted as long as it did— though what is thankfulness compared to a good appetite?

13. *The woman with a talent for talking*

Iɴ the very olden times, in a village that was a whole day's march from the main road that led from Athens to Thebes, there was a woman who differed from her neighbors in that she seemed to have no special talent that reflected credit on her. As she continually observed, each of them had some accomplishment at which they so far excelled her and everyone else that there was no point in trying to match them. "I have a fool-proof receipt for stewing a kid in white wine," she would say to herself, "but what is the use of my trying to make appetizing meals when Cleome cooks by instinct, without ever looking at a receipt? . . . I could raise parsley and sage and sweet marjoram and basil and lavender, like Dido, but that takes a well-drained soil and a green thumb, neither of which I happen to have, and you have to be outdoors all day, and how would I get the weaving done? The weaving is more important. . . . Dorcas has been weaving since she was a child. Her mother taught her to weave, and now her cloth is fine and even throughout, whereas mine puckers. She doesn't even have to look while she weaves. Her hands do it for her. As for cutting the cloth that Dorcas weaves so beautifully, I could never do that as well as Sappho, who looks at her husband and cuts out a cloak that hangs from his shoulders the way the woodbine hangs from the oak. . . ."

So the woman considered and rejected the knacks and skills she saw all around her, and the more discontented with herself she became, the more she was compelled to communicate her dissatisfaction to someone, and so she went from house to house, saying, as she opened the door, "With all there is to do at home, I really shouldn't be here. What's that you're doing?" And they showed her what they were doing, and she was full of genuine admiration, which she had to express, being of an enthusiastic disposition, and then the cork was out of the bottle. For the woman did have a talent, and it was for talking. At first the other women wasted their time trying to get a word in now and then, which was barely possible and not worth the effort, because the woman whose talent was for talking had no more talent for listening than she had for weaving. Or they put aside their work, hoping that if they gave her their full attention, she would shortly leave them in peace. She didn't leave them in peace. Having admired what they were doing, she sat down in a nice comfortable chair and began to tell them what she was thinking of doing, and whatever it was, they knew from past experience that she was never going to get around to doing it, and it took real strength of character not to point this out to her. So they picked up their work again, and without meaning to, they stopped listening to her—except for a word now and then—and she didn't care whether they listened to her or not, so long as they allowed her to give voice to every stray thought that crossed her continually straying mind. She not only told them what she thought and how she felt about everything, but how they felt and what they thought. This she caught out of the air. Her talent was quite out of her control, like her tongue, and what she told them was, on the whole, accurate enough. It dramatized their monotonous lives, and relieved the feelings of those who were encouraging water to run uphill or trying to make a silk purse out of a sow's ear or remaining silent in circumstances where silence is golden. After she left, they went about their work serenely and did not provoke their husbands or scold their children or beat the kitchen maid.

For many years the village lived in something like harmony, far from the main road that led from Athens to Thebes, until one morning a stranger passed through the marketplace—a mischievous-looking young man with a white cloak, gilt sandals with little wings on them, a grey dove on his shoulder, and an oak staff in his hand. The stranger and the woman with the talent for talking met and fell into conversation at the well. That is to say, she talked and he listened intently to everything she had to say. After a time they left the well and sat on the steps of the Temple of War. After a time they left the Temple of War and sat on the steps of the Temple of Wisdom. After a time they left the Temple of Wisdom and sat on the steps of the Temple of Love. After a time they left the Temple of Love and went into the woman's house, and when night came the stranger was still there. When he left no one knew, but he was gone when the woman's husband came home driving his goats ahead of him.

A whole day and a whole night passed, and by the next morning the women of the village had become aware that something was wrong. One by one, they paused in the midst of their work and looked at one another and said, "Have you talked to Oenone? I didn't see her all day yesterday." No one had seen her. So they stopped what they were doing and went to her house. The floor was unswept, the cooking pots were unwashed, the cat was complaining. This was not unusual, any of it. What was unusual was the silence. They called and got no answer. And finally they peered into the room where the woman and her husband slept, on a bed that was seldom made before dark, and there she lay, with her eyes wide open and the cover drawn up to her chin.

That evening when the woman's husband came home from the hills, the other women were waiting for him. It had been a trying day, and they were cross as bears. "What's happened?" they demanded. "Is Oenone sick? Is she just too tired to get out of bed? Is she discouraged with life?"

"All I know," he said sadly, "is what she said in her sleep."

He started to turn and go into the house, but they stopped him.

"Tell us," they said. "What did Oenone say in her sleep?"

"It is of no consequence," he said. "And I don't know that she would like me to repeat things that she does not know she said."

The women swore they would not tell a living soul, and, looking around, he saw that there was not much likelihood of their telling anybody because they were all here, so he said, "It sounded like 'The stranger!'"

"And then?" the women said.

"That's all she said."

"Well, that's very interesting," Penelope said, "as far as it goes. But meanwhile, I cannot thread my needle, I am so confused and irritable."

"I'm sick of weaving," Dorcas said. "Even though I do it better than anybody else. Other women can move about while they are working, but I am chained to this loom."

"It is discouraging to have to cook with dried herbs that have lost most of their savor," Cleome said, "when I know that if I only had time—Oenone has often told me that if I only had time I could raise my own herbs like Dido, and pick a leaf or two fresh from the garden as I needed them."

"The garden," Dido said, "takes all my energy and prevents me from learning to play the flute, as Oenone wants me to do."

Because Oenone was not there to weave these complaints into her conversation and so dispose of them, dissatisfaction hung over the village like a cloud of devouring insects.

This situation lasted for two more days, and on the third night the woman once more cried out in her sleep. Now, to people who talk in their sleep all questions are a warning, and so the woman's husband was careful to speak only in statements. "Yes," he said quietly and evenly. "The dreadful stranger."

"He said—" the woman began.

"He said something," the man prompted.

"He said nothing," the woman said in her sleep. "That was what was so dreadful. If he had said anything, I would still be talking. But he was silent, and it was growing dark outside, and it came to me out of the air that he was a god and knew what I was thinking, and that I didn't need to say it out loud. The reason I talk is—"

The man waited.

"The reason I talk," the woman said, moaning, "is that there is something I don't want to say. I don't know what it is. I only know that if I hear myself saying it, something dreadful will happen."

"I see," the man said, in a voice hardly above a whisper. "I could be wrong, of course, but I always thought you did not listen to what you were saying."

"No," the woman said in her sleep, "I do not listen. I do not want to listen. If I did, I would catch nothing out of the air."

"I am with the goats all day and sometimes all night, and they never say anything but bla-aa, and so I am out of the habit of listening—to them, or myself, or you. And Dorcas and Sappho and Cleome and Dido and Hermione do not listen because they are too involved in their own affairs."

"That's true," the woman said, and fell into a deep sleep.

In the morning, she woke in her usual cheerful frame of mind and went about her talking. Wherever she appeared, the women were too busy to stop and listen to her, and a great deal was accomplished. The seedlings were thinned, the knitting grew longer and longer, the dough was kneaded and set to rise, the soiled clothes were washed on the riverbank. Toward nightfall, the woman heard a dove calling from the edge of the wood, and interrupted herself to listen uneasily. But common sense told her, and she told the person she was talking to, that any interest the gods take in the lives of mortals must be fleeting. By and by, having been everywhere else, she went home, fully intending to cook her husband a good supper, and found that he had eaten long since, and was keeping her plate warm by the fire.

14. Perfection

ONCE upon a time there was an elderly chicken farmer whose chickens, both white and red, gave perfect eggs. People came from far and wide to buy them, and he could have charged twice the market price but he didn't, because he was not interested in money—only in perfection. His chickens laid perfect eggs because, after a good deal of experimentation, he had found the perfect combination of feed for them, and he didn't leave the light on in the chicken house so as to make them lay eggs at night when they ought to have been sleeping, or keep them cooped up in the inhuman way that most chicken farmers do, and his hens were perfectly happy and laid so many perfect eggs that it was a problem to find boxes to put them in. But one chicken is very like another, in most instances, and having found a perfect strain of chicken, and the perfect feed for them, and word having got around that his eggs were better than anybody else's so that people came from far and wide to buy them, there was not a great deal for the farmer to put his mind to, until one day he happened to see, lying on the ground, a maple leaf. It was bright red and streaked with yellow, and without any imperfections, and he was so taken with it that he went to his workbench and got a can of varnish and a paintbrush, and stuck the leaf to the front gatepost, and varnished over it so that it neither lost its color nor grew tattered with the wind and weather. All winter it was a pleasure to him, and when the snow lay deep on the ground he would go out to the front gate and look at the red and yellow leaf. When September came around again and the leaves began to turn, he kept his eye out for other perfect leaves and found them. A perfect oak leaf, and a perfect elm leaf, and a perfect hickory leaf, and a perfect birch leaf. In order to find them he must have picked up and discarded hundreds of oak, elm, hickory, and birch leaves. And the perfect specimens he stuck to the same gatepost and then he varnished over them, and when winter came there they were, a reminder of other seasons, and a proof that perfection exists in leaves, if nowhere else.

But it does exist somewhere else, of course, as the farmer discovered by searching. Four-leaf clovers, mushrooms, blue-jay feathers. The perfect blue-jay feather he kept in a pencil box, the perfect mushroom wouldn't stay perfect even when he had varnished it, but the four-leaf clover did. And after that he began to experiment with the brook that ran through his pasture. The song of the brook was, even before he did any-thing about it, almost perfect, but it didn't stay that way, for it depended upon how much water was rushing over the stones and washing against the grassy bank. After a heavy rain it re-verted to mere noise, and during a drought he had to strain his ears to hear it at all, and the sound at the best of times was not quite on pitch. So he built a dam, in order to let the water through in a steady flow, and he found what stones were helping the sounds and what were hindering them from ar-riving at perfect pitch, and he moved them here and there, and dug pools at irregular intervals, and when he was finished he could walk from one end of the pasture to the other listening to the song of a brook that was never less than perfect. People came and leaned on the fence and listened to it and said what a beautiful sound and went away and forgot about it, because they were interested in perfection only up to a point. But the man would lie awake listening to it with tears of pleasure run-ning down his cheeks in the dark.

And after that he turned his attention to the sky, selecting and rejecting one sunrise, one sunset, after another, searching for the perfect moment between day and dusk and not knowing what he would do when he found it. Also the perfect star. The perfect patch of blue sky seen through pine branches. The odor of frost coming out of the ground. The smell of cows in a barn, feeding contentedly. The perfect spring day.

With so many things to occupy his mind, he hardly noticed that his hair was turning white, that he stooped when he walked, and that he needed less and less sleep, as all old people do when they are nearing the end of their life. But one day, walking through a strange house, he saw himself in a mirror when he was not expecting to, and perceived by the great changes in his face that he did not have very much longer to live. So he began to reflect upon the perfect death. Most people would have said that it was to die in one's sleep. After considering this carefully he rejected it. It was based on fear. He wanted to know when death happened. And he began to practice dying. But there are some things that can only be done by analogy, so he didn't cut himself badly or fall and break his hip, he merely practiced breathing in and out, and counting one two three four five six seven eight nine ten, one two three and so on, letting the air out of his lungs and waiting attentively for a kind of flip deep down in his chest, at which moment he stopped breathing out and began to breathe in. He became quite perfect at this, so that he could do it lying down or standing up or walking around and finally it just happened without his doing anything about it, or even having to count. And people thought he was growing deaf because he didn't hear what they said, but the truth was he had stopped being interested in anything they might have to say to him and instead was waiting for the day when he would come down with influenza and take to his bed, knowing he would never get up from it. And of course the day came, and so did the doctor, and in spite of the medicine he prescribed the old man's fever rose higher and higher, bringing images of the evening star or willow trees reflected in a still pond, and his breathing grew harsher and harsher, and in his delirium he counted soundlessly, one, two, three, four, five, until the moment came, as he knew it would, when he stepped out of this imperfect world into utter perfection and became one with the maple leaf, and the sound of the brook, and the blue jay's feather.

15. *What you can't hang on to*

ONCE upon a time there was an old woman who lived in a house by a river. The lane from the village ended at an old stone bridge half hidden by willows, a few feet from her garden gate. The river flowed around both sides of the garden and the house and came together just beyond the coal shed. Houses beside a river are always damp and subject to floods. And since it was often just as cold inside as out, she seldom bothered to close the front door until she went to bed at night. The cats never had to be let in or out, and the fish peddler never had to knock. He just stood on the back steps and hollered, and the old woman came to the door, and he showed her what was in his basket. The cats' meat man did the same. The house always smelled of the outdoors, and the old woman dressed warmly and didn't mind if there was a wreath of fog above the mantelpiece in the parlor.

The river was a little too wide for a boy to leap across and after the spring rains the current was swift, but for the rest of the year it was hardly noticeable. When the old woman leaned out of her bedroom window to see what kind of a day it was, she saw young boys and old men fishing, for it was only a short walk from the village. Usually they were staring so intently at the surface of the water that they didn't know anybody was looking at them, but now and then one of them saw her and tipped his cap or waved.

The old woman was the last living member of both sides of her family, and inevitably the possessions of one branch after another ended up under her roof. Some of them, if you were at all knowledgeable, were enough to take your breath away. She was so accustomed to getting letters from solicitors informing her of modest bequests of money and furniture that it came as a surprise to her that there was no one left to leave her anything. There was hardly room in the house for another object if they had. Old furniture wherever you looked. Old prints, old drawings, old paintings on the walls. Old books that people had to advertise for, often in vain. Old china and silver.

As always when someone has valuable possessions, there

were people who cast a covetous eye on the contents of that house by the river, and if they didn't know the old woman well, they said, "If you are ever of a mind to part with that settee in the upstairs hall . . ." Or that Boulle cabinet. Or writing desk. Or pencil sketch by Turner. Or battered first edition of *English Bards and Scotch Reviewers.* And if they thought they knew her well enough to come right out and say it—"If you haven't promised it to somebody, will you leave me that Crown Derby teapot in your will?" And if they knew her better still, they said, "That soup tureen—Minton, isn't it? Lovely!" and changed the subject.

The old woman was fond of her possessions but not as fond of them as she was of her cats, and people who live alone get strange ideas, of course, and she had come to feel that her death would not be any great loss to the world and if she lived past a certain age might be a merciful release to her. But in her mind's eye she saw the furniture standing around on the lawn and being knocked down by the auctioneer's mallet and the garden grown up in weeds. Maybe there is still some grandniece or nephew or cousin by marriage, she would think. There weren't any that she knew about and so she resigned herself to the inevitable and only now and then, when she was pruning the huge Belle de Crecy rose bush or on her hands and knees in the vegetable garden thinning carrots, she would straighten up for a moment and look around her and sigh at the thought that this place, which she was so attached to, would not survive her in any recognizable form.

In her thirties the old woman had published a book of poems which had been praised by Thomas Hardy, and the praise brought forth a letter of thanks from her, and this led to her being invited to Max Gate to tea, and to a further exchange of letters, and his letters to her she had naturally kept. A young American who was doing a critical study of *The Famous Tragedy of the Queen of Cornwall* came upon her letters in the Hardy papers and from them deduced that Hardy had discussed his feelings about the production of the play in a letter to her. So he wrote to the old woman and the upshot was an invitation to stay in the house by the river. In writing back, the American mentioned the fact that his wife would be travelling with him, and the invitation was amended to include her. When they stepped down from the train, in the railway station of a town that was three and a half miles from the village, a taxi was waiting and drove them through some of the most enchanting scenery in the whole of the south of England. "Look!" they kept exclaiming. "Oh just look!" As the old woman was greeting them the young man broke into a fit of coughing, which made the fishermen look up in irritation, for it was loud enough to frighten the fish. The old woman said, "I'm afraid there is not much that can be said in favor of the English climate."

The young man smiled wanly and said, "I have a slight temperature but I didn't want to miss seeing the letters and . . ."

While he was finishing his sentence the old woman was on her way upstairs, and before he quite realized what was happening to him he was in a big bed warmed by stone hot-water bottles, with a down comforter over him, in a bedroom full of things that had come down a long way through both sides of the old woman's family. He slept, and woke himself up coughing, and heard voices outside, and slept again.

His wife, thinking to keep out of the old woman's way while she was getting supper, went for a walk and came back in a state of rapture at what she had seen.

"The sign at the crossroads said TOLER FRATRUM—"

"There used to be a Roman settlement there," the old woman said, nodding.

"—and when the farmer called off his dogs it didn't sound as if he was speaking English."

"The Dorset dialect," the old woman said. "Reading it in Hardy is one thing and hearing it spoken is another."

They carried trays upstairs to the invalid and then sat talking over a fire, and at dusk they wandered out into the garden to look at the daffodils. It was quite apparent to the old woman that the young woman had lost her heart to the place, which was not surprising. What was surprising was that she didn't seem to covet anything. Perhaps in America they didn't care for old furniture, being a new country.

The old woman lay awake that night thinking, which she didn't commonly do.

On the third morning, the young man's fever broke and he insisted he was well enough to get dressed and come downstairs.

He sat transcribing the letters of Thomas Hardy in a room heated by a small stove, while the two women talked in whispers so as not to disturb him. At lunchtime the old woman said, "If there is anything in this house that you would like me to leave you in my will, just tell me." And when, after consulting together, they mentioned a book of no great monetary value but hard to come by, she was disappointed. "Are you sure there isn't anything else?" she said, and the young woman said, smiling, "There isn't anything in the whole house that we don't love." At that moment a car horn sounded. The taxi was at the gate, and the Americans said goodby, and off they drove, promising to come back next year.

The old woman went up to London to consult the solicitor who, over the years, had informed her of so many bequests, and he made notes of what she said. "On the condition that they live in the house," the old woman said. "No. Strike that out. There are to be no conditions."

When the American couple stepped out of the same taxi, a year later, the fishermen hardly bothered to raise their heads. The Americans went all through the house without touching anything, and then sat down in the cold little parlor. "I feel her presence," the young woman said, and a cat jumped into her lap and settled down there. "Pity we can't afford to keep it," the young man said. "I feel we'd be very happy here. But we have no choice."

He meant that, given their financial circumstances, they had no choice but to sell the house and everything in it—the Crown Derby teapot and the letters of Horace Walpole in fifty-four volumes, the Regency mahogany writing desk and the Sheraton tallboy chest of drawers, the pencil sketch by Turner and the pair of gilt elbow chairs designed by Henry Holland. Everything disappeared into the storerooms of a London auction house and a FOR SALE sign was planted by the driveway.

When the Americans returned to England two years later they drove south and west from London, in a rented car, to the Hardy country and made a detour to see what had happened to their house.

There was a NO FISHING OR TRESPASSING sign at the bridge, and the front door of the house was shut, there were curtains in all the windows, and the garden was grown up in weeds.

As they sat in their car, the young woman said sadly, "I keep thinking that there was surely something we could have done," and the river said, *No, there was nothing. The collecting of beautiful objects has to end ultimately in their dispersal. The old woman would have found the curtains odious, as indeed they are, but fortunately she doesn't know. What you can't hang on to you must let go of—that is the principle on which I operate, on my way to the sea.*

16. Mushrooms

ONCE upon a time there was a woman who dreamt that she found a mushroom in a wood. It had a violet cap and stem and pale yellow gills, and she took it home and sautéed it in a little pan and just as she was going to eat it she woke up. And after that she kept making excuses to walk in the wood.

She found red mushrooms with white stems, and white mushrooms with gray spores, and violet mushrooms with violet stems and white gills and sulphur-colored mushrooms with pale yellow gills. She borrowed a mushroom book but there was no such mushroom in it. She asked an old man who lived by himself and walked the woods, too, looking for mushrooms, which he put carefully in his basket, and he said he had never seen such a mushroom but that if he did he would save it for her.

She drew a picture of the mushroom in her dream and colored it, so she wouldn't forget what it looked like, and sometimes when she went to bed she composed herself and tried to dream of it, but instead she dreamed of examinations she was not prepared for, and trains that had left at a different time than it said on the time-table, and flying, and children, when she was not even married.

If she found the mushroom, she said to herself, she would be a different person and her life would be easier and happier, so she kept on walking the path through the wood, looking from side to side, and at all stumps and fallen trees carefully, and especially after it had rained. Sometimes she brought a basket with her, like the old man, and gathered the mushrooms that the book said were edible, and brought them home and then did nothing about them. For they were not the mushroom she had found in her dream and brought home and sautéed in a little pan and been about to eat when she woke up. The old man brought her a purple mushroom with a purple stem and pale yellow gills, but she said no, it was not purple it was violet. And later on, thinking she had got it wrong, he brought her a pale yellow mushroom with a pale yellow stem and violet gills, but of course she hadn't got it wrong, and this mushroom was deadly poisonous.

In the end she said sadly to herself that she wasn't ever meant to find the mushroom she dreamed about, and stopped looking, and shortly after that she met a man walking alone in the wood, and he wasn't like anybody she had ever seen. He was dressed in velvet, and had a big brimmed hat with a feather in it, and the under side of his hat was pale yellow and his stockings and shoes and knee-britches and doublet and cap and the upper side of his hat were all violet, and her heart beat violently at the sight of him and she said, "I have been searching everywhere for a—"

"Look there by your feet," the man said, and there it was. And three feet away, under an oak tree there was another, and farther along the road there were three more—all this in a place that she passed every day, and it hadn't even rained. But when she raised her face to ask how he knew what she was searching for, there was no one there.

She picked the mushrooms carefully and put them in her basket and took them home and cut them into fine slices and sautéed them in the pan she dreamed about and when she sat down to eat them she saw she was not alone. The man in the velvet costume was sitting at the kitchen table looking at her seriously, as if there was a riddle that she must solve, and without thinking what the riddle was or how to answer it she put the plate of mushrooms in front of him and he began to eat them slowly, still looking at her, and just as she was thinking *Perhaps he won't want all of them*, he said, "Look down at your place," and there was another plate of mushrooms just like the one she had put before him.

The clock went on ticking until some time the following day, and the spider in a corner of the ceiling went on waiting for an unwary fly, but there were no people any more. Or ever again. Though her acquaintances called the police, and they and everybody searched as hard for her as she had for the violet mushroom, they never found her. The house stayed empty for years and years, and a window blew open in a storm, and the birds and bats flew in and nested there, and the roof rotted and fell in, and finally it was a ruin leaning against the chimney.

When even that disappeared, it became part of the wood, as it was originally, and in time nobody knew that there had been a house there, because the doorsill was covered with creeping vines and the chimney had fallen, and it was known as the best place for miles around to gather mushrooms.

17. The dancing

ONCE upon a time there was a woman who was kept awake at night by the memory of what it was like to go dancing. She was well along in years but not yet old like her husband, and on Saturday night she used to stand by the window watching the couples go by on their way to the village hall, where there was a fiddler who could make almost anybody's feet start twitching. At the remembrance of the reels and the jigs and schottisches and hornpipes of her youth she would smile and turn away from the window without realizing that she had sighed for what was gone and would not return ever again.

Such sighs are always heard by the people who live under the Hill, and one night as she was lying in bed beside her old man, who was sleeping like a baby, she thought she saw something moving at the window, and was alarmed, and sat up in bed, and saw a child's face looking in at her. "What is it?" she asked, thinking that somebody must be sick and the child had been sent to get her. And then she saw the pointed ears and realized that it wasn't a child but one of *them*.

"You're not about to put a sickness on my old man's cow, are you?" she said, and when there was no reply she threw the covers off and went to the window but there was no one there. And if she hadn't been standing on her two feet she would have thought she had dreamed it.

The next night there were two of them, and she lay still and pretended not to know they were there, and after a while she heard a tiny voice say "We've come to take you dancing . . ."

"Oh, I'm too old for that," she said, and the fairies said "How old are you, exactly?"

"Fifty-nine last June twenty-seventh."

"I'm five hundred and ninety-seven, I *think*," one of the fairies said. And the other said, "I'm a thousand and something, I forget just exactly what. And you don't have to get dressed up the way the village girls do when they go to the fiddler, come just as you are."

So she did.

They were dancing in a ring in the sheep meadow and the

ring opened and made a place for her and then the music continued, so light and eerie that at first she had to listen hard to hear it. And she realized why they all had such long ears. "Do you feel your age?" the fairy who had come to get her asked, when they were catching their breath after a particularly fast set of Sir Roger de Coverley.

"No," she said.

"Neither do we," the fairy said. And she was about to ask why this was when she saw that it was broad daylight and she was in her bed and her old man was already up and a-doing. And instead of feeling tired after being up all night dancing, she was strangely rested. I mustn't do that any more, she said to herself. The dominie wouldn't approve. But when night came and she lay there stretched out in the darkness and no little head appeared at the window, she felt let down and disappointed. And after a time a voice said in her ear "So it's the dominie you care about and not dancing."

"Oh no!" she exclaimed. "I don't know why I thought that, I certainly don't mean it."

"Then why are you lying there in bed when you could be dancing with us in the dell?"

Off she went, in her nightgown, with her hair done up in rag-curlers. And never thought once about how she might look to the fairies, any more than they thought how they might look to her.

Night after night after night this happened, and finally the old man's sleep was disturbed by a dream that he was separated from her and walking in a wood calling her name. When he woke he said to himself, I had a bad dream, and put his hand out in the dark and found that she was not lying in the bed beside him. He called out and there was no answer.

When she wasn't in the other room, he looked around for a note, but there was nothing. And no wife. Such a thing had never happened in all the years they had been married. And he was standing there in a fright, wondering what to do next, when a voice from inside the milk pitcher said, "If you're looking for your missus, she's with us." He looked in the milk pitcher and it was full of pale sparks.

"Take me where she is," the old man said, and the voice

from the milk pitcher said, "If I take you there, you'll have to dance."

"I'm much too old for that," the old man said. "My knees aren't what they used to be."

"You can just shuffle, then," the voice said. "Only don't keep me waiting. The dancing has already begun."

When the woman saw her old man in his long white night-gown and nightcap, she let go of the hand of the fairy she was dancing with and made a place for him. And it was wonderful how lively he was. He kept up with dancers that were ten times his age.

The next morning while she was getting his breakfast he said, "I had a dream last night."

"Oh?" she said. "What was it?"

"I dreamt you and I were dancing with the fairies in Dead Man's Hollow."

"Were you enjoying it?"

"Very much. But my rheumatism is much worse than usual this morning." And she saw by the way he hobbled around that it was true.

That night, lying in bed in the dark, she thought how much she loved the dancing in Dead Man's Hollow the night before, and then she thought of her poor old man lying sound asleep beside her, and she thought I mustn't do that to him, he's too old, and I'm all he has and he's all I have.

"Once you say no, we can't come for you any more," a voice said, an inch or two from her ear.

"I know," she whispered. "But he might catch pneumonia. And in any case, I don't want him to wake in the night and not find me lying beside him. I hope you understand."

"How could I?" the voice said. "Fairies don't have any heart. Are you coming or aren't you?"

She wasn't sorry afterward. But people did say that she had aged considerably in the last few months. Which was the fairies' revenge, for she was a lovely dancer and they wanted her all to themselves.

18. The education of Her Majesty the Queen

ONCE upon a time, when airplanes couldn't be counted on always to rise into the air and the motorcar was still a novelty, there was a princess who married a commoner. Reluctantly her father put aside his expectations for her—she was intelligent and capable and would have made a wise and popular queen—and named his nephew, whom he did not like, as his heir apparent. The Princess was obliged to live on her husband's salary, though if she had married the ruler of no matter how small a state or principality, Parliament would have voted an annual stipend sufficient for her every comfort. Fortunately her husband had a salary, but this had its unfortunate side, for it meant that he was in trade, a thing which it would take several generations for the family to live down, and meanwhile she and her husband were not invited to houses where they would have been most welcome if they had been living at the expense of the Nation.

The house they lived in was hardly bigger than a cottage, and no one who was at all knowledgeable would have considered that one ill-tempered old woman in the kitchen and a lame man to clean the stable and fill the woodbox twice a day was keeping an establishment. But the Princess never tired of the view from her bedroom window, which was of a pond with geese on it, and willow trees. And if she found herself doing things that formerly were done for her, she did not mind. To gain her father's consent to her marrying, and the consent of Parliament as well, had required a great deal of obstinacy on her part, from time to time the shedding of tears, and even a certain amount of what in other circumstances would have been described as blackmail, and she did not care to give anyone an excuse for saying I told you so. To tell the truth, she did not by ordinary standards have much to complain of, and when she did allow herself to complain it was always to her husband and always about her mother.

She was an only child, and because the Queen did not have any other sons and daughters to visit or offer advice to, she came rather oftener than was tactful and sometimes she came rather earlier in the morning than it was convenient to receive her. The Princess, having kissed her husband good-bye and lingered over her second cup of coffee, would start to make the bed and empty the slop jar, and before she had done either one there would be a noise outside of carriage wheels and horses' hooves and she would peer out of the bedroom window just in time to see a footman in the palace livery jump down from the box and open the door of the royal coach, and Her Majesty would emerge from the cavernous gilt interior dressed as for a levee and with a little black boy to hold up her train, at a quarter of nine in the morning. Though the Queen was never alone from the moment she woke up or even at night, when she had to ignore the majestic snores beside her in order to fall asleep herself, she was lonely and missed her daughter. So she came and sat on a rickety chair in the tiny bedroom, and when the Princess put clean sheets on the bed the Queen would say, not in criticism, really, "You shouldn't have to do that"—for she had never lived anywhere but in a palace, with a staff of hundreds to dust and sweep, to light the fires and make the beds and polish the silver and wash the crystal chandeliers in soapy water and keep up appearances, and she judged everything from this rather special point of view.

Whether the Princess was hanging out the clothes or making an Easter cake or sewing a button on her husband's shirt, it was the same, so far as the Queen was concerned—for having always had someone to do these things for her, she could not help feeling that there was something improper about doing them for oneself. And when the babies started coming and the Princess nursed them, the Queen would shake her head commiseratingly and say, "You shouldn't have to do that. I had a wet nurse for you, and I am told that many women give their babies a bottle," and afterward she would complain to His Majesty that the Princess had been short with her.

Though the Princess had cut herself off from the line of succession by marrying a commoner, she continued to be universally admired. Her children grew up healthy and handsome, with, for the most part, A's on their report cards, and they never hesitated to bring their friends home—a thing that would not have been permitted if they had lived in a palace—and before the family sat down to a meal somebody always had to count noses. The Princess's husband had the look of a contented man and everything he put his hand to turned out well. Before long, instead of complaining to her ladies-in-waiting about the cramped quarters her daughter was living in, the Queen now complained about the stairs, and the way her grandchildren left their boots and cricket bats and clothing all over three floors of a rather large town house. Though she was not a stupid woman, she nevertheless had the feeling that in a properly run household toys did not stay in the middle of the living-room floor for people to trip over but reverted to the toy chest when children were tired of playing with them, and petticoats and dresses, of their own accord, either ended up hanging from a hook or a rod in the closet or found their way to the laundress.

When she first noticed a gray hair among the Princess's dark brown tresses, the Queen not only was disturbed by this not uncommon misfortune but attributed it to the fact that her daughter would do things that she should have allowed other people to do for her, though there were no other people but the ill-tempered cook and the lame man—the one now quite old indeed and deaf and half blind, so that she had to cook mostly by feel, and the other too feeble to keep the woodbox filled and clean out the stable and so he would bring his grandson to do it for him. On days when neither the lame old man nor the boy showed up, the Princess cleaned out the stable and filled the woodbox herself. Her hands were reddened from housework and she lost the soft look that people have who are continually waited on, but she was a fine-looking woman, with a proud carriage and a light in her eye that only those have who have managed to live exactly the life they wanted to live. Still, her mother went on saying, "You shouldn't have to do that," in a voice more than faintly tinged with sympathy, and the Princess eased her feelings by saying afterward to her husband, "I would love to know what she thinks I ought to be doing."

But naturally she knew the answer, which was: being a princess, being waited on. In the royal palace everything, or so it appeared, was taken care of by some chamberlain or lord-of-the-bedchamber or lady-in-waiting or flunky in livery—with one exception, and that exception was perhaps an oversight: there was no one to attend to the ill or the dying. The court doctor came and prescribed emetics and repeated bleeding, after which the personage grew much weaker and deathly pale from the loss of blood. And rumor of what was happening spread through the palace, and both the courtiers and the servants, fearing that they would lose their place at court, were so busy currying favor with probable successors that the invalid's slop jar went unemptied and his sheets unchanged.

When the Queen took sick, the King was out of the country on affairs of state. He sent ambassadors daily to inquire about her condition, when it would have been much better if he had come himself. The Princess left her house in the charge of her oldest daughter and went every day to the palace to look after her mother. The Queen was indeed grateful to have her. And when her daughter brought her a tray with a nourishing soup she had made the night before or fluffed up her pillows or drew the curtains to shut out the glare, she said in a weak voice, "You shouldn't have to do this." She said it largely out of habit, for by this time it was reasonably clear that if the Princess did not do these things for her mother, nobody else would. On the last morning of her life, the Queen opened her mouth to say something and the Princess, who was sitting at her bedside, holding her hand, bent down closer, expecting to hear the tiresome words once more. Instead, with an effort, her mother said, "It seems that nobody can die for me. I have to do it all by myself." She stopped, seeing that her daughter's eyes had filled with tears. When two tears ran down the Princess's cheeks, the Queen reached out and wiped the tears away, lovingly, with her hand. It was the first time in her life she had been moved to do something for somebody else, and she died quite happy.

19. *Newton's law*

O NCE upon a time there was an old woman who was much troubled by the pull of gravity. She would start to get up out of her chair and fall back twice and make it only on the third try. "I don't know what's the matter with me," she said. "Everything is so much heavier than it used to be," and she went and weighed herself on the bathroom scale, and to her surprise she weighed less than her normal weight, and so she knew the scale was wrong, and would have thrown it out and got a new scale except that she had had it for a very long time and was attached to it, the way people are to objects they are used to.

In the morning, when she woke, her mind was ready to begin the day, but the weight of her head on the pillow was so great that she continued to lie there with her eyelids closed— they, too, felt the pull of gravity, slight as they were—for sometimes twenty minutes. And when her daughter took to bringing her tea to her in bed, she tried to resist, because her daughter had small children that required a great deal of attention and she wanted to be a help to her instead of an additional burden, but the tea was a comfort to her and for a short while gave her the strength she needed to overcome the earth's pull.

She started to pick up something, some heavy object that in the old days she would have thought nothing at all of lifting, and her daughter said, "Here, Mother, let me do that, you'll strain your back." And it was true, she would have. Because that particular object and all other objects were heavier than they used to be. And she said to herself, "I marvel that nobody notices it; though perhaps they do notice it and just don't think it is worth commenting on."

Walking had always been a pleasure to her, especially walking in the woods, but she gradually gave it up. Her shoes were too heavy, and spoiled her pleasure, and she found that if she sat in a chair by the window—Granny's chair, it was referred to by the children, and nobody else ever sat in it, lest she would want to—and looked out of the window and let her mind roam wherever it wanted to, she got much the same pleasure she used to when she was an active young woman and would say, "Come, children, let's go for a nice long walk in the woods."

Words, too, had become heavier, causing her to speak more slowly. But that was, she knew, partly because of the weight of what she had to say. Her mind was full of comparisons, mostly of how things used to be with the way they were now—the clothes people used to wear, the food they used to eat, the things they used to enjoy, and what they cared about; all was so very different, and interesting to consider, for those who could remember what she was talking about. However, she couldn't help noticing that when her daughter had a party, the guests would take turns coming and sitting with her and drawing her out in conversation, and at first she enjoyed it and thought they were genuinely interested in what she could tell them of the past, until a heavy thought occurred to her: they were perhaps just being nice, and not really interested in her stories. Or perhaps had heard them before, since her memory was failing and she knew she repeated herself. So she tried not to hold them in conversation longer than they had any desire to be talking to her, and that in turn made her appear somewhat withdrawn.

The truth is, she was withdrawn. She was preoccupied with her own comparisons, and when something took her away from her thoughts it was likely to be something her grandchildren did or said. She loved to watch them playing outdoors. How they ran! As if they had no more weight than an autumn leaf! They had so much energy that they needed to work off, and they seldom simply walked but instead hopped and skipped or threw themselves on their bicycles and raced down the drive and out of sight, leaving her with a smile of pleasure on her face. For it was a kind of miracle, one of a whole host of miracles that people were so used to that they didn't think anything about them. Like getting into bed at night and falling fast asleep the minute your head touched the pillow. And not knowing anything more until daylight.

The only way she could go to sleep now was to read, sitting up in bed until the words became all mixed up and she could not remember the sentence she had just finished reading, and then she would turn the light out and slip down under the covers and drift off, only to waken between two and three in the morning and lie there for an hour or more, courting sleep. How many times had she heard Old people need less sleep? And other things like it, all of them perfectly true. Such as, When you are young the days seem so long, and when you are old they race by. For there was no lack of descriptions of what it is like to be old, and even, alas, of what it is like to feel that you are a burden to the earth.

As a young woman she had had a beautiful straight back, and when she caught a glimpse of herself in the mirror she saw that it was bent, as if she was holding two pails of water and pulled down by the weight. And though she straightened herself, and meant to continue to hold herself erectly, a minute later she was holding the pails of water again.

You cannot go around holding two heavy pails of water all day without feeling tired, and she was, and in fact did less and less because there was less and less that she could do. And when at last her legs gave out and she took to her bed, it was with a certain pleasure in giving up the struggle. She died in her sleep, leaving forever the dead weight of her body. The creature itself, light as an autumn leaf, lighter even, light as a wisp of smoke, as sunshine, as air, went to join the eternal lightness that makes all the rest possible.

NEARING NINETY

Nearing Ninety

Out of the corner of my eye I see my ninetieth birthday approaching. It is one year and six months away. How long after that will I be the person I am now?

I don't yet need a cane, but I have a feeling that my table manners have deteriorated. My posture is what you would expect of someone addicted to sitting in front of a typewriter, but it was always that way. "Stand up straight," my father would say to me. "You're all bent over like an old man." It didn't bother me then and it doesn't now, though I agree that an erect carriage is a pleasure to see, in someone of any age.

I have regrets but there are not very many of them and, fortunately, I forget what they are. I forget names, too, but it is not yet serious. What I am trying to remember and can't, quite often my wife will remember. And vice versa. She is in and out during the day, but I know she will be home when evening comes, and so I am never lonely. Long ago, a neighbor in the country, looking at our flower garden, said, "Children and roses reflect their care." This is true of the very old as well.

Though there have been a great many changes in the world since I came into it on August 16, 1908, I try not to deplore. It is not constructive and there is no point in discouraging the young by invidious comparisons with the way things used to be.

I am not—I think I am not—afraid of dying. When I was seventeen I worked on a farm in southern Wisconsin, near Portage. It was no ordinary farm and not much serious farming was done there, but it had the look of a place that has been lived in, and loved, for a good long time. I was no more energetic than most adolescents, but the family forgave my failures and shortcomings and simply took me in, let me be one of them. The farm had come down in that family through several generations, from the man who had pioneered it to a woman who was so alive that everything and everybody seemed to revolve around her personality. She lived well into her nineties and then one day told her oldest daughter that she didn't want to live anymore, that she was tired. Though I was not present

but only heard about it in a letter, this remark reconciled me to
my own inevitable extinction. I could believe that enough is
enough. One must also, if possible, reconcile oneself to life. To
horrors (the number of legless peasants in Cambodia) that if
you allowed yourself to think about them more than briefly
would turn your heart to stone.

Because I actively enjoy sleeping, dreams, the unexplainable
dialogues that take place in my head as I am drifting off, all
that, I tell myself that lying down to an afternoon nap that
goes on and on through eternity is not something to be concerned about. What spoils this pleasant fancy is the recollection that when people are dead they don't read books. This I
find unbearable. No Tolstoy, no Chekhov, no Elizabeth Bowen,
no Keats, no Rilke. One might as well be—

Before I am ready to call it quits, I would like to reread
every book I have ever deeply enjoyed, beginning with Jane
Austen and Isaac Babel and Sybille Bedford's *The Sudden View*
and going through shelf after shelf of the bookcases until I arrive at the autobiographies of William Butler Yeats. As it is, I
read a great deal of the time. I am harder to please, though. I
see flaws in masterpieces. Conrad indulging in rhetoric when he
would do better to get on with it. I would read all day long and
well into the night if there were no other claims on my time.
Appointments with doctors, with the dentist. The monthly
bank statement. Income tax returns. And because I don't want
to turn into a monster, people. Afternoon tea with X, dinner
with the Y's. Our social life would be a good deal more active
than it is if more than half of those I care about hadn't passed
over to the other side. However, I remember them. I remember them more, and more vividly, the older I get.

I did not wholly escape the amnesia that overtakes children
around the age of six, but I carried along with me more of my
childhood than, I think, most people do. Once, after dinner,
my father hitched up the horse and took my mother and me
for a sleigh ride. The winter stars were very bright. The sleigh
bells made a lovely sound. I was bundled up to the nose,
between my father and mother, where nothing, not even the
cold, could get at me. The very perfection of happiness.

At something like the same age, I went for a ride, again with
my father and mother, on a riverboat at Havana, Illinois. It was

a sidewheeler and the decks were screened, I suppose as protection against the mosquitoes. Across eight decades the name of the steamboat comes back to me—the *Eastland*—bringing with it the context of disaster. A year later at the dock in Chicago, too many of the passengers crowded on one side of the boat, waving good-bye, and it rolled over and sank. Trapped by the screens everywhere, a great many people lost their lives. The fact that I had been on this very steamboat, that I had escaped from a watery grave, I continued to remember all through my childhood.

I have liked remembering almost as much as I have liked living. But now it is different, I have to be careful. I can ruin a night's sleep by suddenly, in the dark, thinking about some particular time in my life. Before I can stop myself, it is as if I had driven a mineshaft down through layers and layers of the past and must explore, relive, remember, reconsider, until daylight delivers me.

I have not forgotten the pleasure, when our children were very young, of hoisting them onto my shoulders when their legs gave out. Of reading to them at bedtime. Of studying their beautiful faces. Of feeling responsible for their physical safety. But that was more than thirty years ago. I admire the way that, as adults, they have taken hold of life, and I am glad that they are not materialistic, but there is little or nothing I can do for them at this point, except write a little fable to put in their Christmas stocking. Our grandchild is too young to respond to any beguiling but his mother and father's. It will be touch and go whether I live long enough for us to enjoy being in each other's company.

"Are you writing?" people ask—out of politeness, undoubtedly. And I say, "Nothing very much." The truth but not the whole truth—which is that I seem to have lost touch with the place that stories and novels come from. I have no idea why.

I still like making sentences.

Every now and then, in my waking moments, and especially when I am in the country, I stand and look hard at everything.

APPENDIX

Contents

Preface to "The Château"

BEFORE the Second World War, when it was the best time to go to France, I went to islands, instead—Bermuda, Trinidad, Barbados, Martinique. When I finally did go to Europe, in the summer of 1948, it was to please my wife, who had been taken to France and England by her parents when she was twelve years old and wanted to see again places and things she remembered. To me, France was the tragedies of Racine, Proust's madeleine, *Le Grand Meaulnes*, *The Counterfeiters*, and Cyrano de Bergerac's white plume. I did not expect to feel any different toward the country of France than I would feel toward, say, the state of Texas, but at first sight of the coastline, before I ever set foot on French soil, I lost my heart. It didn't occur to me to hope that this attachment would be returned. Nevertheless we fairly often met with an affectionate response—from the cook and the concierge of the Hotel Montgomery in Pontorson, from a waiter in a small restaurant in the St. Sulpice quarter of Paris, from an old woman in the Touraine, and so on.

We wandered from place to place, drunk on the beauty of a country so much older than the U.S.A., and looked at every public building, every faded tricolour, every village street, every ticket-taker, every flame-eater, every boulangerie, every pâtisserie, every crémerie, as if our lives depended on seeing all that there was to see. It's a wonder we didn't go blind. Because of all they had lived through during the German occupation and because we were among the first post-war American tourists, the French were open and accessible in a way that was not, I think, usual with them.

After four months our money ran out. I walked into our house on a country road forty miles north of New York City, put the suitcases down, and with my hat still on my head sat down to my typewriter and wrote a page of notes for a novel. I thumbtacked it to the bookcase behind me and didn't look at it again. For the next ten years I lived in my own private France, which I tried painstakingly to make real to the reader. It was my way of not coming home.

The Javanese stone-carvers who somewhere around the year A.D. 800 covered the Borobudur with scenes in high relief and statues of the Buddha, enshrined in openwork bells, intended to delineate symbolically the material world and all human life, sometimes called The Thousand and One Things. I thought this was a worthy goal to aim at, though in a novel whose action contained nothing more dramatic than hurt feelings caused by misapprehension and a failure to understand the language, it would probably not be noticed. After the book was done I looked for the first time at the sheet of paper I had tacked to the bookcase and saw to my surprise that everything on it was disposed of in the book.

When I turned the manuscript over to the publisher, one of the readers felt strongly that Part Two was unnecessary and should be cut. From the point of view of classical form he was, I suppose, right, but it would have left a number of questions unanswered. Also there is, there has to be, a form inherent in the material, and it doesn't always follow the ideas of Aristotle or even Henry James. Losing my confidence I turned to Alfred Knopf, who was sitting on the sidelines during this discussion, and he said, "Have it whatever way you want." So I let it stand. I would not now be able to forgive myself if I hadn't.

1992

Preface to
"*So Long, See You Tomorrow*"

W HEN I was in the seventh or eighth grade the father of a
boy in my class at school committed a murder. It was
not a thing you could easily forget. The details floated around
in my mind and were considerably altered, as is likely to happen with a memory carried over a period of many years. The
first time I tried to deal with the situation in writing, it was in
the form of a short story in which a boy was wakened out of
a deep sleep by the sound of a gun going off inside the house.
It was still dark outside. He heard his mother's voice saying
"Don't!" and a second shot and then silence. He thought his
father was away and that he was the nearest thing to a man in
the house and must protect his mother. When he opened the
door of his room the hall light was on and his father was
standing there as if lost in thought. Indicating the room where
he and the boy's mother slept he said, "Don't go in there."
After which he went from room to room turning on lights and
opening and shutting drawers, and when finally he left, the
boy summoned the strength to telephone his grandmother
and say, "You have to come." "Can't it wait until morning?"
she asked and he said, "No." He was waiting on the front steps
when she got there, and told her about the shots and that his
father had said he was not to go in the bedroom. "Somebody's
got to do it," she said. The milkman making his rounds in his
wagon in the first morning light saw them, the old woman and
the boy, standing on the sidewalk, and heard the old woman's
story and took them in his wagon to the police station. It was
all very real to me, but when *The New Yorker* didn't cotton to
it I concluded that I didn't have the kind of literary talent that
can deal at close hand with raw violence, and put the manuscript in a drawer. One day, sitting at my desk, I found myself
thinking of the boy in my class, the actual boy, the murderer's
son, and how we met in the corridor of a high school in
Chicago, and I saw that there was the possibility of a novel.

I remembered reading about the murder in the Lincoln

Evening Courier but it turned out that their files did not go back that far. My cousin Tom Perry, who lives in Lincoln, got photocopies for me from the state historical society, and I was astonished to discover how far, in that short story, I had strayed from the facts. I have not departed from them in any way in *So Long, See You Tomorrow*. What I couldn't find in the newpaper account or what nobody could tell me, I have permitted myself to imagine, but the reader is given fair notice that I am doing this.

Christopher Isherwood once observed that in a novel the first person narrator must be as solidly done as the other characters or there will be an area of unreality. One can think of exceptions—*The Brothers Karamazov*, for example—but anyway I thought he had something. If I followed his precept it meant that I had two stories on my hands, which must somehow be made into one. Since any prose narrative is open, during the writing of it, to all the winds that blow—to anything that happens to the novelist, to what he happens to read, to any new idea that comes into his head—it is likely to be affected in some degree by accident. One day, waking from a nap, I sat on the edge of the bed in a mild daze, staring at a row of books. Among them was a book about Alberto Giacometti. I opened it at random and found myself reading a letter from Giacometti to Matisse in which he described a love affair that took place while he was working on a piece of sculpture now known as "Palace at 4 A.M." As literal autobiography I doubt if it is worth much, but it contained a perfect metaphor for what I wanted to say and a bridge between the two stories that made them hold together.

I came to have a considerable feeling for the farm boy whose character and daily life I invented. The actual boy who served as a model for him I knew only very slightly. After the novel was published I wondered if he (now, of course, an elderly man) would read it. Or if I would hear from him. I never did.

1992

Preface to
"All the Days and Nights:
The Collected Stories of William Maxwell"

THE four-masted schooner lay at anchor in Gravesend Bay, not far from Coney Island. It belonged to J. P. Morgan, and I persuaded a man with a rowboat to take me out to it. In my coat pocket was a letter of introduction to the captain. The year was 1933, and I was twenty-five. I had started to become an English professor and changed my mind, and I had written a novel, as yet unpublished. I meant to go to sea, so that I would have something to write about. And because I was under the impression, gathered from the dust-jacket copy of various best-sellers, that it was something a writer did before he settled down and devoted his life to writing. While the captain was reading my letter I looked around. The crew consisted of one sailor, chipping rust, with a police dog at his side. It turned out that the schooner had been there for four years because Mr. Morgan couldn't afford to use it. The captain was tired of doing nothing and was expecting a replacement the next day and was therefore not in a position to take me on. He had no idea when the beautiful tall-masted ship would leave its berth. And I had no idea that three-quarters of the material I would need for the rest of my writing life was already at my disposal. My father and mother. My brothers. The cast of larger-than-life-size characters—affectionate aunts, friends of the family, neighbors white and black—that I was presented with when I came into the world. The look of things. The weather. Men and women long at rest in the cemetery but vividly remembered. The Natural History of home: the suede glove on the front-hall table, the unfinished game of solitaire, the oriole's nest suspended from the tip of the outermost branch of the elm tree, dandelions in the grass. All there, waiting for me to learn my trade and recognize instinctively what would make a story or sustain the complicated cross-weaving of longer fiction.

I think it is generally agreed that stories read better one at a time. They need air around them. And they need thinking about, since they tend to have both an explicit and an un-spelled-out meaning. Inevitably, some of the stories I wrote, especially when I was young, are stuck fast in their period—or to put it differently, the material was not as substantial as it ought to have been—and I see no reason to republish them. When I was working on the ninth version of "A Final Report" I came on the seventh, in a desk drawer, and saw that it was better than the one I was working on and that I must have been too tired when I finished it to realize that there was no need to pursue the idea any further. On the other hand, "Love" came right the first time, without a word having to be changed, and I thought—mistakenly—that I had had a break-through, and stories would be easier to write from that moment on; all I needed to do was just *say* it.

The stories I have called "improvisations" really are that. They were written for an occasion—for a birthday or to be rolled up inside a red ribbon and inserted among the orna-ments on the Christmas tree. I wrote them to please my wife, over a great many years. When we were first married, after we had gone to bed I would tell her a story in the dark. They came from I had no idea where. Sometimes I fell asleep in the middle of a story and she would shake me and say "What hap-pened next?" and I would struggle up through layers of obliv-ion and tell her.

1995

Remarks upon accepting
the Gold Medal in Fiction from the
American Academy of Arts and Letters

WHEN I was a small boy, seven or eight years old, among my worries was the house I was born in. It wasn't as nice as the house we were then living in and it didn't look very substantial to me, and I was afraid it would no longer be there when the time came for them to put up the plaque.

Over the years my expectations moderated. And I came to realize that where I belonged, and where I wanted to be, was not in the White House but among the storytellers.

I rejoice in this honor, which I did not expect, and which comes as somewhat but not entirely a surprise that I could be thought to deserve. I wish that I had written *The Great Gatsby*. I wish that I had written "In the Ravine" and "Ward No. 6." I wish that I had written *The House in Paris*. I wish that I had written *A Sportsman's Notebook*. But the novelist works with what life has given him. It was no small gift that I was allowed to lead my boyhood in a small town in Illinois where the elm trees cast a mixture of light and shade over the pavements. And also that, at a fairly early age, I was made aware of the fragility of human happiness.

1995

CHRONOLOGY

NOTE ON THE TEXTS

NOTES

Chronology

1908   Born William Keepers Maxwell Jr., August 16, in Lincoln, Illinois, second child of William Keepers Maxwell (b. 1878) and (Eva) Blossom Blinn Maxwell (b. 1881). (Parents, both Lincoln natives, married June 2, 1903; first child, christened Edward but called "Hap" after the funny papers' Happy Hooligan, born March 25, 1905.) Baby William ("Billie"), delivered at home, is fragile and sickly, weighing only 4½ pounds at birth, at six weeks even less: "Mother's milk did not agree with me, nor did anything else until the family doctor suggested goat's milk." Coaxed toward health by constant attentions of Blossom, whom he will remember as a stout, handsome, brown-eyed woman "acutely responsive to other people's happiness or distress." Father, chief Illinois agent for Hanover Fire Insurance Company, travels the state every Tuesday through Friday for annual salary of $3,000. (Additional income will later come from renting out 360 acres of farmland east of town, purchased with small inheritance from his father, Robert Maxwell [1850–1904], a lawyer.) Brought up in the Christian Church, a fundamentalist American offshoot of Scottish Presbyterianism, William Sr. is thrifty, sober, practical, and emotionally distant; Maxwell will remember him as a good father but a man of his period, who "felt responsibility for his children rather than pleasure in them." Family lives in a small house at 455 Eighth Street; neighbors include many relatives, including the boys' maternal grandparents (Edward Blinn, a judge of the court of claims, and Annette Youtsey ["Nettie"] Blinn), paternal grandmother (Margaret Turley Maxwell), four aunts and an uncle (Annette, Edith, and Ted Blinn; Maybel and Bertha Maxwell). In 1908 the town of Lincoln —seat of Logan County, 165 miles southwest of Chicago, at the very center of the state—has a population of nearly 11,000. The neighborhood where Maxwell grows up is northwest of Lincoln's downtown but connected to it by an electric streetcar line. Elms, silver maples, box elders, and cottonwood trees canopy the brick and cobblestone streets, which in every direction trail off into dirt and gravel roads leading into cornfields.

1909   In front of the Eighth Street house, five-year-old Hap climbs onto a rear wheel of Aunt Annette's buggy. When she, not seeing him, starts her horse, his leg becomes tangled in the wheel and is later amputated above the knee. "By the time I was old enough to observe what was going on around me," Maxwell will write, "my brother had an artificial leg—of cork, I believe, painted an unconvincing pink." Despite his "affliction," Hap is an extroverted, irrepressible handful: throughout their shared boyhood, he plays with Billie "the way a cat plays with a chipmunk or a mole, hoping to produce signs of life," which usually come in the form of angry tears.

1910   Family moves into larger house at 184 Ninth Street, cater-corner to the Blinn residence. This comfortable late Victorian, with its 11-foot ceilings and, in winter, drafty windows, its cheerful white walls and woodwork, its many snug and semi-secret places to read, and its upstairs bedroom shared by the two brothers, will figure into much of Maxwell's fiction: it is, in his phrase, his imagination's home.

1911   In spring, parents build a cottage on extreme outer edge of 120-acre Lincoln Chautauqua Grounds, two miles southwest of town. Family will spend this and many later summers here. During the six-week Chautauqua season, from mid-July through August, they hear opera stars, jazz orchestras, and William Jennings Bryan, watch ball games, swim in the Wading Pool, and make nightly visits to the ice-cream tent. Mainly they relax in the shade of the overarching oak trees.

1912–13   In July 1912, William Sr.'s Aunt Ina, wife of a plantation owner in Mississippi, visits Ninth Street with her large extended family. After their long, delightful visit, a series of misfortunes: Grandmother Nettie suffers a massive stroke, Uncle Ted loses his left arm in an automobile accident, and Aunt Annette, impatient with a kitchen fire that will not stay lit, pours kerosene on the grate and severely burns her hands. In November 1912, Grandfather Blinn is bitten by a ferret and contracts blood poisoning; he dies in January 1913, at age 68. Nettie follows him almost a year later, at age 65.

1914   In fall, starts kindergarten at a private preschool run by
            two progressive-minded middle-aged women in rooms
            above a storefront near Lincoln's courthouse square. His
            daily escort to and from class is the pretty 25-year-old
            teachers' assistant, Grace McGrath. A parlor soprano with
            a taste for the popular songs of the day, she will come to
            play a leading role in the Maxwells' musical evenings at
            home, hosted by William Sr., a talented pianist.

1915   One January afternoon, Blossom takes six-year-old Billie
            downtown to pick up a book that she loved as a child and
            has ordered for him. "When we got home," Maxwell will
            remember, "she sat down on the divan and I sat beside
            her and she began to read the book to me. It was
            Toinette's Philip, by Mrs. C. V. Jamison, a writer of chil-
            dren's books who was once well known. It was set in New
            Orleans, around the turn of the century, and it had an
            elaborate plot and fully developed characters. And it had
            scenes that moved me, just as they had my mother. How
            much influence this moment had on my future I cannot
            be sure, but I would think a great deal."

1916   Enters Lincoln Central School (grades 1–8) and from the
            start is an avid but introverted pupil. Excels in art, and
            throughout his school years is convinced he is meant to be
            a painter or a picture-book illustrator. Physically slight,
            gangly and uncoordinated, he is always last to be picked in
            playground games: "I was born to describe boys playing
            baseball, not to do it." He and Hap, with their parents'
            blessing, attend not the Christian church but the less dog-
            matic Presbyterian Sunday school, where they dislike ser-
            mons but enjoy singing hymns and learning Bible stories.

1918   Beginning in late August, Spanish influenza sweeps North
            America, killing nearly 600,000 persons in the U.S. by
            year's end. Pandemic reaches Lincoln in early October,
            infecting some 2,000 and killing nearly 100 in just three
            months. On December 24, William Sr. takes Blossom,
            pregnant with their third child, on a 30-minute train ride
            to Bloomington, Illinois, to deliver in Brokaw Hospital.
            The boys are left in the care of Aunt Maybel, who lives
            with her husband and Grandmother Maxwell on Union
            Street, three blocks from the Ninth Street house. On
            Christmas morning, the boys suffer first symptoms of flu

and are confined to separate bedrooms. In Bloomington, parents, too, come down with flu, and are hospitalized.

1919   On New Year's Day, Blossom gives birth to third son, (Robert) Blinn Maxwell; weakened by flu and labor, she dies of double pneumonia on the morning of January 3, at age 37. Father phones Maybel, who tells the boys. ("My childhood came to an end at that moment," Maxwell will later say.) Next day, William Sr., still recovering from flu, returns to Lincoln with Blossom's remains: "His face had turned the color of ashes, and would stay that way a whole year." The funeral service is performed at home, with the casket resting in the angles of the bay window of the front room. "The worst that could happen had happened," Maxwell will remember, "and the shine went out of everything." Father and boys are watched over by Grandmother Maxwell, Maybel, Annette, and the first in a series of housekeepers, "who looked after the baby and sat in my mother's place at mealtime. . . . The light bulbs did not give off enough light, and the food had no flavor."

1921   On October 5, not quite three years after Blossom's death, William Sr. marries Grace McGrath. Family begins a new life together in a place with no associations with the past: a rented, semi-furnished house on Eighth Street. William Sr. sells 184 Ninth Street and buys a vacant lot on Lincoln's northern frontier; the two-story stucco house he builds there, 226 Park Place, will be ready for occupancy in spring 1922. Billie reads Waverley novels and popular works in Scottish history, delivers the Lincoln *Evening Courier* on his blue and silver bicycle, and finds distraction from sorrow through working hard at school.

1922–23 In September 1922 begins freshman year at Lincoln Community High School, and the following week is elected class president. When assigned *Treasure Island*, reads it five times before turning to something else: "I had read for pleasure all through my childhood, but this was my first encounter with literature." In spring 1923, his first attempt at short fiction, the story of an aristocrat who hides inside a grandfather clock to survive the French Revolution, is published in the school's annual literary magazine.

1923   Father accepts promotion to state office of insurance company; in spring he and Grace sell the Park Place house and move to a two-bedroom apartment in the North Chicago neighborhood of Rogers Park. Billie and Hap remain in Lincoln, guests of Grace's mother, to complete the school year; four-year-old Blinn is looked after by Aunt Maybel, her husband, and Grandmother Maxwell. In June older boys join father and stepmother in Chicago, but Blinn, at grandmother's desperate request, stays behind. In the end, William Sr. allows the Lincoln Maxwells to bring up Blinn, a decision he will always regret, as it results in a lifelong physical and emotional distance between him and Blinn, and decades of indifference between Blinn and Billie. (In contrast, Blinn and Hap will become close friends and, after World War II, share a successful legal practice in Oxnard, California.) In September, Hap leaves Chicago for Urbana and his freshman year at the University of Illinois, while Billie enrolls as a sophomore at Nicholas Senn High School, one of Chicago's largest, with a student body of 3,400, nearly six times that of Lincoln High. Billie soon becomes aware that he has "left a good enough school for a great one," remarkable for its dedicated teachers and strong *esprit de corps*. Draws and writes for school yearbook, whose sponsor, Miss Karssen, takes him to the Art Institute, the Chicago Symphony, and the theater (they see Mrs. Fiske in *The Rivals*). English instructor Miss Sedgewick directs his reading and chooses books for him from the Chicago Public Library: Shaw, Barrie, Galsworthy, H. G. Wells, Conrad. Meets Jack Scully, his class's top athlete, and Susan Deuel, the brightest girl in sophomore English, both of whom become close friends.

1924   Brings home from school library a copy of Mark Twain's *Mysterious Stranger* with the intention of testing his religious convictions: "They were not, it turned out, very strong." Calls himself an atheist, a label that, as the years pass, will mellow into "unbeliever."

1925   In June accompanies Jack Scully to Portage, Wisconsin, where Jack has a summer job as a lifeguard on Mason Lake. When job Jack had arranged for him falls through, finds room and board in exchange for doing chores at Bonnie Oaks, a nearby farm and summer artists' colony. Maxwell sees that the farm's owners, businessman Harrison Green and his charismatic, culture-loving wife, Mildred Ormsby Green, "were not ordinary people—that is, they were not

farmers. Only when I came to read *The Cherry Orchard*
years later did I find people who were anything like them."
His first chore is to deliver a box of strawberries to the
Greens' celebrated neighbor Zona Gale, a woman of
letters whose *Miss Lulu Bett* had won the Pulitzer Prize
for Drama in 1920. "She was wonderful to me," he will
later write. "She talked about art, music, books, and the
mystical aspects of daily existence. She also—and it is the
one thing that always makes an adolescent's head swim—
treated me as an intellectual equal." The visits to Zona
Gale that summer are many, and by the end of August she
has appointed herself his mentor: "It was understood that
I would make something of my life, but meanwhile it
was life that she talked to me about. . . . I had been
immeasurably enriched, in ways I didn't even try to
understand."

1925–26   In senior year is associate art editor of the school magazine, for which he writes a series of essays on American
paintings in the collection of the Art Institute of Chicago.
Spends most Saturdays in galleries and museums, and decides that, after graduation, he will enter the studio program at the school of the Art Institute. Friendship with
Jack Scully deepens into passionate attachment.

1926–27   At end of summer, Jack returns from lifeguard job on
Lake Geneva, Wisconsin, with acute pleurisy, almost too
weak to enroll as planned at the University of Illinois.
Maxwell accompanies him to Urbana to help him
through orientation, and Hap arranges a few days' room
and board in his fraternity house. Then, "what with one
thing and another, including the full moon," both boys
accept pledge pins from Hap's fraternity and Maxwell
revises his college plans: he will spend a year at the university before going to art school. Takes several English
classes, and is delighted that Susan Deuel is in most of
them. Finds faculty friend in freshman composition instructor Paul Landis, who suggests courses and recom-
mends him to fellow teachers. In spring, takes advanced
course, English Romantic Poets, taught by Bruce Weirick,
who requires students to write poetry—an ode, a ballad,
a sonnet—"so that they might have a less distant feeling
toward Coleridge and Wordsworth." In May, Weirick per-
suades Maxwell to abandon plans to transfer to the Art

Institute and instead continue at Urbana, develop as a poet and a scholar, and become a professor of English.

1927–28   In sophomore year joins Illini Poetry Society, a dozen or so faculty and student poets who meet on Sunday evenings: "Every week, you had to read a poem you had just written, and mine betrayed a fondness for Elinor Wylie and Walter de la Mare." Other members include Landis, Weirick, and junior faculty member Garreta Busey, who for Maxwell represents "the outside world": she has lived in New York City, and until recently was on the staff of the *Herald Tribune*'s Sunday book review. Finds himself increasingly attracted to Margaret Guild, stepdaughter of English department chairman Jacob Zeitlin. After weeks of courting (mostly with opera records) introduces Margaret to Jack Scully. When she and Jack become lovers, Maxwell is devastated: "I thought I didn't want to live any more, and cut my throat and wrists with a straight-edged razor." After release from the hospital, wears a heavy gray turtleneck sweater— "the only turtleneck sweater to be seen anywhere on campus"—to cover bandages. Receives note from Susan Deuel, inviting him to the Kappa Alpha Theta spring dance; he goes, wearing the turtleneck, and she and her sorority sisters see to it that he is never without a partner.

1928–30   Resumes friendship with Jack and Margaret, but in a lower emotional key. (After graduation the couple will marry, move to Wisconsin, and pay visits to Maxwell throughout their troubled marriage.) Continues studies in English, with a minor in French. In May 1929, Poetry Society votes Maxwell's "Sleeping Beauty" the year's Prize Poem; publication in *Illini Poetry 1924–1929*, edited by Landis, marks his first book appearance. Writes two one-act comedies, one of which, "Polly Put the Kettle On: A Mother Goose Phantasy," wins the English department's Play Prize for 1930. Graduates May 1930 with Highest Honors and as class salutatorian (second highest grade-point average among 1,200 students).

1930–31   At recommendation of Weirick, the Harvard Club of Chicago grants Maxwell a fully paid scholarship to Harvard Graduate School. In Cambridge makes friend of poet and translator Robert Fitzgerald, then only a sophomore but already being published in leading literary journals.

Takes courses taught by critic Theodore Spencer and poet Robert Hillyer, and is visited by Zona Gale, who urges him to pursue his own work as well as his formal studies. Enjoys reading Old English epic and Old French romance, but encounters psychological block against learning the required German: even the most common words remain unrecognizable no matter how often he consults the dictionary. Ends year with a B in German, which voids renewal of scholarship. Unable to afford tuition, leaves Harvard humbled but with master's degree.

1931–33   Returns to Urbana to teach freshman composition and take further graduate courses. Rooms at the home of Garreta Busey, where he meets Charles Shattuck, a self-taught Shakespeare scholar who will become a lifelong friend. (Later Shattuck will marry Susan Deuel, and eventually will become a professor of English at the University of Illinois.) In February 1932, through arrangements made by Busey, begins reviewing popular novels for the New York *Herald Tribune*, which will publish some 20 items through October 1933. In May, Busey is approached by a friend, Yale historian Wallace Notestein, to do research for a collection of brief lives of English "characters"; she enlists the aid of Maxwell, who reads a two-volume biography of Thomas Coke of Holkham (1754–1842), an eccentric M.P. and agriculturalist, and rewrites the book as a 40-page essay. "Working with Garreta I discovered the pleasure of writing prose narrative," he will remember. "To keep the pleasure alive I began working on a long story, which I hoped would turn out to be a novel." On assignment for the *Herald Tribune*, reads *One More Spring*, by Robert Nathan, "a silly novel" about a group of dreamers who keep house in an abandoned tool shed in Central Park. "The gist of the book was that life is to be lived—and, well, it is, of course. Anyway, that book made me restless with my prospects. I saw myself being promoted from assistant to associate to full professor, and then to professor emeritus, and finally being carried out in a wooden box. This was 1933, and only an idiot would have thrown up a job at that point. But I did anyway."

1933   In early May, travels to New York with vain hope of securing a job at the *Herald Tribune* book review. Returns to Bonnie Oaks at the invitation of Mrs. Green, who gives him free summer room and board and the leisure to write his novel. Works and sleeps in a room on the third floor of a frame building that was once the farm's water tower, leaving it only for meals with Mrs. Green and fellow guests. (Maxwell will later say that most characters in his first book "were largely, but not wholly, extensions of parts of myself; [others] were derived from people living on the farm at the time, so it was a handy place to be. I finished the book in four months, with the help of Virginia Woolf, W. B. Yeats, and Elinor Wylie . . .") In early September takes complete draft of novel to Zona Gale, who, despite reservations—she asks if it is missing a concluding chapter —offers warm congratulations and an unsolicited letter of recommendation to prospective publishers: "It is modernity come of age, mellow, intelligent, casual, done with enormous delicacy." Returns to Urbana, where book is read by friends and faculty. In November Jacob Zeitlin, who has friends in New York publishing, sends a copy to Eugene F. Saxton, editor-in-chief of Harper & Bros. Meanwhile, Maxwell, inspired by a travel book by Lafcadio Hearn, plans a tour in the West Indies: "I was in search of the next thing to write about." In New York in mid-December, boards a tramp steamer bound for Martinique: "I stayed in Fort-de-France. I spoke only rudimentary French and the natives spoke patois. I had nothing to do all day except wander around looking at what there was to see. That month seemed as long as a year. . . ."

1934   In late January, receives word that Saxton wants to acquire novel, pending decision by his boss, Cass Canfield. Upon Maxwell's return to New York, Saxton offers fall publication and an advance against royalties of $200, with which Maxwell finances a 10-month stay in the city. Living at the Y.M.C.A. near Grand Central, quickly revises novel to meet April 15 delivery deadline. Proposes many titles—"Snakefeeders," "Thundercloud," "Today Is the Day"—before Canfield agrees to *Bright Center of Heaven*. First printing of one thousand copies, released in September, sells out quickly, but the second thousand, printed in December, sells hardly at all. When money runs out, in mid-December, returns to Bonnie Oaks, where, through May 1935, he does small chores in exchange for room and board.

1935   In winter, finishes three short stories and hires an agent to
            place them in magazines; V. S. Pritchett, a reader for the
            London quarterly *Life and Letters To-Day*, recommends
            one to the editor, who purchases it for the Winter 1936
            number. Plans autobiographical novel about the death of
            his mother; writes seven drafts of the opening section but
            is happy with none of them. At the suggestion of Robert
            Fitzgerald, applies to the MacDowell Colony, an artists'
            retreat in Peterborough, New Hampshire, where Fitz-
            gerald has a summer residency; there, from early June
            through the end of September, he completes a successful
            draft of the first third of the book, using Fitzgerald as his
            sounding board. ("In Fitzgerald's view, life was tragic,"
            Maxwell will later recall. "Under his influence I gave up
            Galsworthy and Barrie and Wylie and accepted the idea
            that literature was serious business.") In October, returns
            to Urbana, where Garreta Busey proposes that, in ex-
            change for grading her students' papers, she give Maxwell
            room and board, $4 a month, and the privacy necessary
            to continue his work. "Without this arrangement," he
            will later say, "I doubt very much that the book would
            ever have been finished or that I would have continued to
            be a writer."

1936   In February, completes novel, *They Came Like Swallows*,
            which Saxton acquires for Harper's in early summer.
            Story "Remembrance of Martinique" appears in *Life and
            Letters To-Day* and is reprinted in the July *Atlantic
            Monthly*. Through Saxton's influence, Katharine S. White,
            fiction editor of *The New Yorker*, purchases Maxwell's
            other completed stories, "Mrs. Farnham Puts Her Foot
            Down" and "A Christmas Story," both of which she
            schedules for December publication. In late August,
            moves to New York and finds inexpensive lodging in a
            rooming house on lower Lexington Avenue. Writes syn-
            opses of bestsellers for Paramount Pictures, and inter-
            views for entry-level editorial jobs with Malcolm Cowley
            at *The New Republic*, Christopher Morley at *The Saturday
            Review of Literature*, and, in late October, Katharine
            White. During their meeting, Mrs. White asks what he is
            looking for in the way of a salary. "Some knowledgeable
            acquaintance had told me I must ask for $35 a week or I
            wouldn't be respected, so I swallowed hard and said,
            'Thirty-five dollars.' Mrs. White smiled and said, 'I expect

you could live on less.' I could have lived nicely on fifteen. A few days later I got a telegram from her asking me to report to work the following Tuesday"—November 3 —"at the salary agreed on: $35 a week."

1936–37   Initial duties at *The New Yorker* include informing cartoonists of acceptances and rejections; he especially enjoys conversations with cover artist Ilonka Karasz, a Hungarian-born designer and painter. By Christmas, Mrs. White and senior editor Wolcott Gibbs begin training Maxwell as an editor of fiction, memoir, and humor. In January 1937, becomes occasional book critic for the *Saturday Review*, which will publish 17 items through February 1940. *They Came Like Swallows* published in March to positive reviews. Christopher Morley, a member of the selection committee of the Book-of-the-Month Club, chooses the novel as the club's dual main selection for April; Maxwell's initial payment is the "overwhelming sum" of $8,000. Finds room-and-a-half on Patchin Place, in the West Village; at request of Mrs. White, installs a phone, but when it rings he refuses to answer it. By year's end has published three more stories in *The New Yorker*, the last of which, "Never to Hear Silence," prompts an admiring letter from a regular contributor, poet Louise Bogan.

1938   Stories "Homecoming" (January 1) and "The Actual Thing" (September 3) published in *The New Yorker*; edits work by Daniel Fuchs, Oliver La Farge, John O'Hara, Sylvia Townsend Warner, Joseph Wechsberg, and others. In spring, receives award of $1,000 from Friends of American Writers, a Chicago women's club, for *They Came Like Swallows*. In December, Mrs. White announces that she and her husband, staff writer E. B. White, are moving to a farm in mid-coastal Maine from where she will continue her editorial duties; she appoints Maxwell her office liaison. When Zona Gale dies suddenly on December 27, at age 64, Maxwell is bereft: "I am only beginning to understand how much, in the way of literary taste and craftsmanship, I received from her."

1939   Wolcott Gibbs is appointed *The New Yorker*'s theater critic, and Maxwell assumes most of his editorial duties; job becomes so burdensome that he writes almost nothing. Suffers insomnia and takes to walking the city late at night; is happy only at the country home of Ilonka

Karasz or in the company of his new friend Louise Bogan. In July, meets Sylvia Townsend Warner during one of the English writer's rare visits to America: "Her conversation was so enchanting it made my head swim. I did not want to let her out of my sight. Ever." Trains Gus Lobrano, a friend of E. B. White, as assistant editor, and is deeply hurt when Mrs. White quickly promotes him to Maxwell's salary level. Hurt lingers, even after Mrs. White chooses "Homecoming" for inclusion in *Short Stories from The New Yorker* (1940), her selection of the best fiction from the magazine's first 15 years. On April 8 *The New Yorker* publishes "Good Friday" (later collected as "Young Francis Whitehead") and on December 18 the first of eight "lighter" stories—formula fiction written mainly for Christmas and other occasions—that will appear, under the pseudonym "Jonathan Harrington," through August 1942. When, in November, Lobrano is given Mrs. White's old office, Maxwell is indignant: "I thought, If this is the way things are, I will leave and become a writer." Resignation accepted, with sadness and concern, by editor Harold Ross; Maxwell will quit office on March 15, 1940.

1940   On March 1, leaves the city for a rented saltbox in Yorktown Heights, New York, an hour from Grand Central and 15 minutes from the country home of Ilonka Karasz. Writes short stories, not all of which are purchased by Mrs. White. In June, drives to Santa Fe with friend Moris Burge, an official with the American Association on Indian Affairs, and works for five weeks in home of Burge's fiancée. Enjoys extended visit with *New Yorker* writer Oliver La Farge, who lives among the Navajo, and in mid-July returns to Yorktown Heights "with the whole state of New Mexico up my sleeve." Begins writing a short book, never completed, based on impressions of the Desert Southwest. Plants rosebushes, paints shutters, and enjoys keeping house in rural Westchester County; reads widely, especially in Russian fiction: Chekhov, Turgenev, Tolstoy's "Master and Man." Lobrano phones to ask if he would do some freelance editing, and by October, won over by Lobrano's sincerity, he returns to the fiction department three days a week. In fall, spends two months in Bermuda, which becomes the subject of his only Reporter at Large piece (January 4, 1941). In December, Saxton attends a party in honor of the new fiction editor of *Harper's Bazaar*, Mary Louise Aswell, who knows Maxwell's novels and asks to see his stories.

1941   In February, *Harper's Bazaar* purchases "Abbie's Birthday" (later collected as "Haller's Second Home") for publication in the August issue. In May, at a party hosted by Mrs. Aswell, Maxwell meets Eudora Welty, a young writer visiting New York from Jackson, Mississippi; they become instant friends and lifelong correspondents. Shows Louise Bogan a work-in-progress, an autobiographical story about two contrasting but complementary teenaged outsiders, one frail and bookish, the other athletic and inarticulate; she tells him it is not a story but the first chapter of his next novel. Maxwell immediately sees the book in the situation, but not how to dramatize the painful, personal material. Over the next four years, he will send Bogan everything he writes about these characters; she in turn will read it with critical attention, providing the encouragement he needs to sustain him in his work.

1942   Ilonka Karasz proposes a collaboration: Maxwell will write a novella based on his experiences in Martinique, and she will illustrate it with egg-tempera paintings. After 10,000 words and a few full-color studies, the project is abandoned as too expensive to print in wartime economy. They try again with an illustrated story for children in which the figures of the zodiac come down from the heavens and take up residence on a Wisconsin farm. Harper's agrees to publish the book, but only if the art is designed to print in one color: Karasz chooses the deep blue of the nighttime sky and makes experiments on scratchboard. Meanwhile, Maxwell pushes on toward the middle of his novel, tentatively titled "No Word for Anybody."

1943   In winter is called for military service, and obtains deferment due to "anxiety neurosis." In spring, uses savings to buy a small, sturdy house—an early prefab, built in the late 1930s—on Baptist Church Road, in Yorktown Heights; it will be his country place for the rest of his life. In June, Eugene Saxton dies following a heart attack; his successor at Harper's is Edward C. Aswell, Mary Louise's husband. Mrs. White returns to the *New Yorker* office and

Maxwell's daily workload lightens. By July, he has been at work on his novel for three years and is still struggling with the material. Lobrano, seeing that Maxwell cannot complete a first draft without a sabbatical, speaks to Harold Ross, who hands Maxwell an unsolicited five months' leave at full salary, beginning August 1. Works without interruption in Yorktown Heights, and completes second draft by New Year's Eve.

1944   Returns to the magazine in January, again on a part-time basis, and works on third draft of his novel. Doubting the quality of his work and convinced that, "like a tree whose central stem had been cut," he is no longer maturing, begins analysis with Theodor Reik, a protégé of Sigmund Freud whose practice includes many artists and writers. Reik reads all of Maxwell's work, including his novel-in-progress, and by March is meeting with him an hour a day, five days a week. Completes third draft of "No Word for Anybody" and submits it to Edward Aswell, who acquires the book for Harper's and sets a delivery date of November 15. Maxwell rewrites and revises until day of deadline, incorporating many suggestions made by Aswell, Reik, and Louise Bogan. While novel is in production, Bogan finds a better title—*The Folded Leaf*—and in gratitude for all she has done for him, Maxwell dedicates the book to her.

1944–45   In October 1944, phones Emily Gilman Noyes, a young woman he had met earlier that year, when, just graduated from Smith College, she interviewed for a job at *The New Yorker*: "She wore her hair piled on top of her head, and she had a hat trimmed in fur, and I thought I had never seen anyone so beautiful. . . . I couldn't get her out of my mind." He invites her to join him for a drink at the Algonquin Hotel, where they talk about poetry and painting, her childhood visit to France, and her current work with children at an Upper East Side nursery school. In November, he takes her to a friend's party, after which he surprises both her and himself by asking her to marry him. She says no, but invites him to call on her again after New Year's. In December, Maxwell sublets an apartment at Park Avenue and 92nd Street, mainly to be near her. Throughout January he sees her almost every evening, and in February her parents fly to New York from Portland, Oregon, to meet him. On March 20, he again proposes, and this time is accepted. He and Emily marry, in a private ceremony, in the chapel of the First Presbyterian Church, New York City, on May 17. The bride is 23, the groom, 36; Gus Lobrano and Emily's mother are witnesses.

1945   In June, Maxwell ends therapy with Reik, upon whose couch, he says, "the whole first part of my life fell away, and I had a feeling of starting again." *The New Yorker* publishes the story "The Patterns of Love" (July 7) and a signed book review of Reik's *Psychology of Sexual Relations* (September 15). In April, Harper's publishes *The Folded Leaf*, with a jacket design by Ilonka Karasz, one of several she will do for him over the next 25 years. Reviews are many and enthusiastic: Edmund Wilson, in *The New Yorker*, calls it "a quite unconventional study of adolescent relationships—between two boys, with a girl in the offing—very much lived and very much seen. This drama of the immature . . . is both more moving and more absorbing than any of the romantic melodramas which have been stimulated by the war." By year's end 200,000 copies are in print, including a Book Find Club edition and a digest-sized paperback distributed to the Armed Services.

1946   The Maxwells keep house in Yorktown Heights, and, in Emily's words, lead "a Wordsworthian life: long walks, reading aloud, organic gardening." She paints, writes poetry, and quickly proves to be Maxwell's most trusted reader: he calls her "the critic on the hearth." Writes long short story, "An Evening Party," set in 1912 in "Draperville," a semi-fictionalized Lincoln, Illinois. Because of its provincial setting, the story cannot be published in *The New Yorker*: "Harold Ross edited a cosmopolitan magazine," Maxwell once explained, "and had a map of acceptable settings for fiction" that included the East Coast, Hollywood, Florida, Paris, "but not the Middle West, which rather tied my hands." Sends story to Cyril Connolly, editor of the London literary monthly *Horizon*, who writes: "It is really the very exciting beginning to a novel . . . One wants another 30 chapters, and I hope you will do it that way." *The Heavenly Tenants*, Maxwell's collaboration with Ilonka Karasz, is published by Harper's in September; it will be named a Newbery Honor Book for 1947. Edits stories by John Cheever, Mary McCarthy, and J. D. Salinger. At Christmas writes fairy tale, "The woodcutter," as a gift for Emily; it is the beginning of tradition he will observe for many Christmases, birthdays, and anniversaries to come.

1947   Continues work on his Draperville novel, writing quickly but somewhat distractedly. Deciding that "the burden of living a double life, of working at a somewhat demanding job and trying to write a book, is difficult to sustain," again quits *The New Yorker*, effective May 1. Completes final draft of novel by Thanksgiving; Emily discovers title, *Time Will Darken It*, in the pages of the recently published anthology *Artists on Art*. Edward Aswell acquires the book and sets publication date of September 1, 1948. Maxwell plans a second Draperville book, which he intends to publish as a series of short stories and then rework into a novel; is discouraged when *Harper's* and *The Atlantic* reject the first installment, "The Trojan Women." The story is published in the winter issue of *The Cornhill Magazine*, a London quarterly.

1948   In January, Aswell resigns from Harper's, leaving Maxwell without a sponsor there. Revises *Time Will Darken It* in proof and approves final galleys by the end of May. He and Emily plan long-deferred honeymoon in Europe, mainly in Emily's beloved France. On July 1 they depart New York aboard the *Queen Elizabeth*, burdened with a typewriter, too many over-packed suitcases, and a four-month supply of goods then unobtainable in France—cigarettes, coffee, nylons, writing paper. Land in Cherbourg, visit Mont-Saint-Michel, and sunbathe on the coast of Brittany; live for six weeks with a family in Blois and explore the château country; attend the Salzburg Music Festival, make a tour of Northern Italy, and linger a week in Rome; sublet an apartment in Paris and make side trips to Nice, Cannes, Chartres, and Versailles. On October 19 they board the *Mauritania* for voyage home. For Maxwell Europe, and especially France, is a revelation: "I remembered every town we passed through, every street we were ever on, everything that ever happened, including the weather." Upon returning to Yorktown Heights, types a two-page outline for a book about a newlywed American couple's encounter with postwar Europe. Writing this book will be his chief literary project throughout the 1950s.

1948–49   In fall 1948, Maxwell, dismayed by poor sales of *Time Will Darken It* and by lack of enthusiasm at Harper's, returns to *The New Yorker* on a part-time basis. Is admitted to the Century, an exclusive social club for writers and artists whose clubhouse is just steps away from the *New Yorker* offices; he will be a lifelong member, having lunch there almost daily for the next three decades, attending events and sitting on committees for even longer. To ease commute from Westchester, rents a floor-through walkup in the building where Ilonka Karasz now lives, a three-story brownstone on East 36th Street at Lexington Avenue; the Maxwells will spend weekdays there, returning to the country on weekends and during the summer. After Maxwell sends her a copy of *Time Will Darken It*, Sylvia Townsend Warner becomes a constant correspondent: during her remaining three decades they will exchange more than 1,300 increasingly affectionate personal letters.

1950   Writes several versions of the opening scene of his book about France, but is undecided whether the material would be better treated in the first or third person, as fiction or as straightforward travel memoir. In fall he and Emily, after five years' trying to conceive a child, attempt to adopt, but Maxwell's age, 42, presents bureaucratic difficulties.

1951   *Perspectives U.S.A.*, a new quarterly financed by the Ford Foundation and edited by Jacques Barzun, Lionel Trilling, and others, reprints "The Trojan Women" (Spring 1952) and purchases a new Draperville story, "What Every Boy Should Know" (Spring 1954). In summer Harold Ross, diagnosed with lung cancer, begins long hospitalization; he dies after surgery on December 6. Ross's handpicked successor, former managing editor William Shawn, immediately widens the magazine's editorial compass and encourages Maxwell to solicit, acquire, and edit fiction outside Ross's definition of "a *New Yorker* story." Among Maxwell's earliest purchases for Shawn are "The Bride of the Innisfallen" by Eudora Welty, her first story in the magazine, and "Madeline's Birthday" by Mavis Gallant, her first story anywhere.

1952   Maxwell's satisfaction with editorial work deepens as he helps shape the fiction department's new direction. At the

office, friendships with colleagues grow stronger, especially with staff writers and local contributors including
Harold Brodkey, Brendan Gill, Philip Hamburger, Joseph
Mitchell, Francis Steegmuller, Natacha Stewart Ullman,
and the Irish-born short-story writer Maeve Brennan. Continues work on his French novel, with limited success.

1953   In January, Eudora Welty visits the Maxwells in New York
City and gives a private reading of her short novel *The
Ponder Heart*; Maxwell will edit it for *The New Yorker*,
and, when published as a book, Welty will dedicate it to
him, Emily, and Mrs. Aswell. In April, the Maxwells visit
England and Sylvia Townsend Warner. Story "The Pil-
grimage," based on experiences in France, published in
The New Yorker (August 22), while the manuscript of the
French novel grows chaotically, its many and various
drafts filling a large grocery carton in Maxwell's study.

1954   When Jack Huber, a psychologist and close friend of the
Maxwells, learns that the couple is desperate to adopt, he
uses his influence at a Chicago agency where friends are
on the board. In February, after a great deal of paperwork,
the Maxwells interview at the agency, fly home, and wait;
in May, as their case is at last moving forward, Emily is
amazed to discover she is pregnant. Daughter, Katharine
Farrington ("Kate") Maxwell, born December 19.

1955   When the brownstone becomes unaffordable under its
new owner, the Maxwells return to living year-round in
Yorktown Heights. Maxwell—upset by loss of apartment
and worried about his financial future, his books out of
print and his current novel stalled—decides to give up
writing and become a full-time editor. Accepts invitation
to speak at a Smith College symposium, "The American
Novel at Mid-Century," but dreads writing speech, whose
assigned topic is "the novelist's creative process." Avoids
starting draft until he boards the train to Northampton,
but then his words flow so freely, and he believes in them
so passionately, that he knows he cannot give up writing
fiction. On evening of March 4 delivers his speech, "The
Writer as Illusionist," to a receptive audience including
fellow speakers Saul Bellow, Brendan Gill, and Alfred
Kazin. In fall, John Cheever and short-story writer Jean
Stafford invite Maxwell and Daniel Fuchs to appear with
them, not in an anthology, but in the literary equivalent

of a group exhibition of recent work. The resulting volume, called *Stories*, will include three items by Maxwell: "The Trojan Women," "What Every Boy Should Know," and a new story, "The French Scarecrow."

1956   Gus Lobrano dies, March 1, at age 53, and Maxwell inherits several of his authors, including Cheever, V. S. Pritchett, and long-time acquaintance Frank O'Connor. Hires assistant, Elizabeth Cullinan, an aspiring writer whose stories of Irish-American life Maxwell will edit for the magazine from 1960 through 1975. "The French Scarecrow" published in *The New Yorker* (October 6). Second daughter, Emily Brooke ("Brookie") Maxwell, born October 15. *Stories* published in December by Farrar, Straus & Cudahy.

1957   In September, poet Robert Lax prints Maxwell's fairy tale "The anxious man" (later collected as "The old man who was afraid of falling") in his little magazine *Pax*. Encouraged by friends' response, Maxwell revises nine other fairy tales for publication in *The New Yorker*; they will appear throughout 1958, in four installments of two or three tales each, under the heading "Old Tales about Men and Women."

1958   In March receives a letter from publisher Alfred A. Knopf: "Brendan Gill tells me that all may not be well between you and Harper & Brothers. . . ." In June signs a contract with Knopf for his French novel, to be delivered by January 1, 1960; he also signs a contract for reprints of three of his previous novels, to be published in paperback under Knopf's new Vintage Books imprint. (Declines Knopf's offer also to reprint *Bright Center of Heaven*: upon reading it for the first time in 20 years, finds it "hopelessly imitative" and "stuck fast in its period.") In May is surprised and encouraged by a $1,500 grant in literature from the American Academy of Arts and Letters. In August is visited by Frank O'Connor, in whom he confides that, although he has promised to deliver his French novel in 18 months, he has reached an artistic impasse. When O'Connor asks to read the manuscript Maxwell is "appalled" but allows his friend to drive away with the grocery carton full of typescript. Within weeks O'Connor writes that Maxwell seems to have written two novels—one about the American couple, the other about the French family they lodge with—and suggests they be combined and told from the Americans' limited point of view. "My relief was immense," Maxwell later recalls, "because it is a lot easier to make two novels into one than it is to make one out of nothing whatever. So I went ahead and finished the book." Meanwhile, learning that the Vintage editions of his early novels will be newly typeset, Maxwell takes the opportunity to revise them, beginning with *The Folded Leaf.* "When I was writing [that novel]," Maxwell later tells *The Paris Review*, "I was in analysis with Theodor Reik, who thought the book should have a more positive ending. And Edward Aswell at Harper's thought the book would be strengthened if I combined two of the minor characters. I was so tired and so unconfident about the book that I took their word for it. Later I was sorry. And when the book came out in the Vintage edition . . . I put everything back pretty much the way it was in the first place."

1958–59   In September 1958, when Kate starts kindergarten at the Brearley School, family moves from Yorktown Heights to the convenient address of One Gracie Square, a 15-story apartment building near 84th Street and the East River. Father dies, January 15, 1959, while Maxwell is revising *They Came Like Swallows*; rewrites novel mainly to soften the portrait of the stern and disapproving father character. Works himself to near-exhaustion to finish his French book, provisionally titled "Leo and Virgo." Knopf extends delivery date to June 1960. Vintage edition of *The Folded Leaf* is published in September 1959.

1960   "Leo and Virgo" is read by biographer, translator, and friend Francis Steegmuller, whose many queries prompt Maxwell to write an epilogue, "Some Explanations." When Maxwell delivers the completed novel to Knopf, editor-in-chief Harold Strauss proves so unenthusiastic— he dislikes the epilogue, and urges Maxwell to cut it— that Mr. Knopf assigns the novel to Judith Jones, who will edit this and all of Maxwell's later books for the firm. Vintage edition of *They Came Like Swallows* appears in April, and the French novel is announced under the title *The Château.*

1961   In March, *The Château* is published to mixed reviews but strong sales: in May and June it spends three weeks on the *New York Times* bestseller list, and by October more than 17,000 copies are in print. Despite interest from foreign publishers, Maxwell forbids U.K. and Continental editions in an effort to protect the privacy of the originals of certain European characters. Katharine White retires from *The New Yorker*; Maxwell becomes senior editor in the fiction department and inherits several of her authors, including Vladimir Nabokov and John Updike. Mentors young writers Larry Woiwode, the gifted protégé of Charles Shattuck at Urbana, and Shirley Hazzard, whose first short story he discovers in the "slush pile." Begins light but thorough revision of *Time Will Darken It*.

1962   *The Château* is short-listed for the 1962 National Book Award in Fiction (won by Walker Percy's *The Moviegoer*). Vintage edition of *Time Will Darken It* published in September. Signs contract for a collection of fairy tales, to be delivered to Knopf in 1965. Writes "A Final Report," his first story set in historical Lincoln, not fictional Draperville, and narrated in his own voice: "I found I could use the first person without being long-winded or boring, and at the same time deal with experiences that were not improved by invention of any kind."

1963   "A Final Report" published in *The New Yorker* (March 9). On May 22, inducted as member of the National Institute of Arts and Letters; citation reads, in part: "His grace and wit delight his readers, while his wisdom enlarges their understanding of the human heart."

1964   *The New Yorker* publishes "The Value of Money" (June 6), Maxwell's fictional tribute to his father. At the request of the widow of Oliver La Farge (1901–1963), edits and writes a foreword to *The Door in the Wall* (1965), a collection of 12 La Farge short stories.

1965   On May 1, family moves to 544 East 86th Street, their final New York City address. Completes his book of tales, 16 of which are serialized in *The New Yorker*, in five installments of two to four tales each, under the heading "Further Tales About Men and Women." *The New Yorker* publishes "A Game of Chess" (June 12), a story dramatizing Maxwell's troubled adult relationship with his brother Hap; to protect Hap's feelings, uses byline "Gifford Brown."

1966   In February *The Old Man at the Railroad Crossing and Other Tales* is published by Knopf, with a dedication to Emily. Frank O'Connor dies on March 10, at age 62. In summer, Maxwell takes his family on a car tour of Wales, England, and France and revisits many persons and places of the 1948 trip. When Elizabeth Cullinan leaves the magazine, hires new assistant, Frances Kiernan; in 1972 he will train her as an editor in the fiction department.

1967   After reading family genealogy compiled by late first cousin William Maxwell Fuller, begins planning a non-fiction work that is part personal memoir, part family history, part imaginative re-creation of the folkways, religious life, and biographical particulars of four generations of Blinn and Maxwell ancestors. To collect facts and anecdotes, begins an extensive correspondence with distant family members and with archivists and local historians in Ohio, Kentucky, and Illinois. To find a narrative voice, rereads E. B. White and further refines the first-person persona previously explored in "A Final Report."

1969   "The Gardens of Mont-Saint-Michel," a story of France, is published in *The New Yorker* (August 9). In May, Maxwell is elected president of the National Institute of Arts and Letters; will serve through May 1972. During his term, the secretary of the Institute is the poet William Meredith, who becomes a dear friend.

1970   Louise Bogan dies, February 4, at age 73; Maxwell writes her obituary for *The New Yorker*. Finishes manuscript of *Ancestors*, his nonfiction narrative, and revises text extensively in proof.

1971   *Ancestors* is published in June by Knopf, to mixed reviews. In writing this book, Maxwell will later say, "I came to feel that life is the most extraordinary storyteller of all, and the fewer changes you make [in facts and details] the better, provided you get to the heart of the matter."

1972   Stepmother Grace McGrath dies, October 15, at age 83; returns home for funeral and discovers a friend in stepcousin Tom Perry, the executor of Grace's estate and manager of the Maxwell family farm. In Lincoln is reminded of a schoolmate whose father, in the winter of 1920–21, killed his wife's lover and then himself. Upon return to New York attempts a short story based on this tragedy; in need of concrete details, asks Tom Perry to research the files of the Lincoln *Evening Courier* for contemporary accounts.

1973   Charles Shattuck nominates Maxwell for honorary degree of Doctor of Letters from the University of Illinois. Upon accepting diploma at commencement exercises on June 9, Maxwell says: "Though I have lived in New York City for nearly 40 years, when I sit down at the typewriter and begin to write, it is nearly always of Illinois. I have no choice, really. Other places do not have the same hold on my imagination. I am very moved by the high honor the university has bestowed on me—how could I not be, when what it amounts to, in the logic of emotions, is that the place where I belong has laid formal claim to me."

1974   "Over by the River," a long story ten years in the writing, published in *The New Yorker* (June 26).

1975   Company policy obliges Maxwell, 66, to retire from the magazine on December 31; before doing so, hires and trains fiction editors Charles McGrath and Daniel Menaker.

1976   "I slid into retirement and hardly noticed the jar," Maxwell tells Charles Shattuck. "It is wonderful not having to break off writing after four days and pick it up again three days later. Also, I rejoice in the thought that I shall never again write a letter beginning 'I am very sorry, but your story isn't right for . . .' etc. . . . Shawn very kindly offered me an office to write in, but I like to go to the typewriter in my bathrobe and slippers, straight from the breakfast table, and anyway I feel it somehow not right, and perhaps not dignified, to hang around after you are gone." At home begins, but soon abandons, a novel drawing on memories of Bermuda in 1941. Prepares a collection of 12 short stories published over the previous 38 years, revising most from their magazine versions and arranging them, not chronologically but thematically, in the following order: "Over by the River," "The Trojan Women," "The Pilgrimage," "The Patterns of Love," "What Every Boy Should Know," "The French Scarecrow," "Young Francis Whitehead," "A Final Report," "Haller's Second Home," "The Gardens of Mont-Saint-Michel," "The Value of Money," and a new story, "The Thistles in Sweden," published in *The New Yorker* for

June 21. Dedicates collection, *Over by the River and Other Stories*, to Sylvia Townsend Warner, and asks daughter Brookie to create the jacket art.

1977   Mentors Alec Wilkinson, the 25-year-old son of a York-town Heights neighbor, coaching him through every draft of an account of his year with the Wellfleet (Massachusetts) Police Department, later published in *The New Yorker* and as the book *Midnights* (1982). Using research material compiled by Tom Perry, returns to subject of Lincoln murder-suicide but now treats the material in the first person, crafting a work part memoir, part fiction, part historical reconstruction of a "true crime." In September, *Over by the River* published by Knopf, to very good reviews.

1978   Aged and ailing, Sylvia Townsend Warner asks Maxwell to be co-executor of her literary estate. She suggests that certain friends and readers "might like a volume of letters," and asks that he collect and edit them. In late April, flies to England for a leave-taking, but is too late; she dies on May 1, at age 84. Maxwell feels poorly, and is diagnosed with lymphoma; responds dramatically to chemotherapy. Lincoln novel develops quickly; he plans to call it "The Palace at 4 A.M.," after the sculpture by Giacometti in the Museum of Modern Art, but *The New Yorker*'s poetry editor, Howard Moss, objects: he once wrote a play with that title.

1979   New novel, now called *So Long, See You Tomorrow*, published in two installments in *The New Yorker* (October 1 and 8). In fall, over lunch at the Century, an admirer, art critic Hilton Kramer, urges David R. Godine, a Boston-based publisher starting a paperback list, to reissue Maxwell's major works, beginning with *The Folded Leaf*. Between 1981 and 1989, Godine will reprint eight of the books, seven with new covers designed by Brookie.

1980   Dedicates *So Long, See You Tomorrow* to Robert Fitz-gerald; the book is published by Knopf in January to uniformly positive reviews. On May 21, Eudora Welty presents Maxwell with the William Dean Howells Medal of the American Academy of Arts and Letters; the prize, for *So Long, See You Tomorrow*, is awarded once every five years in recognition of the most distinguished work of American fiction published during that period.

1981   *So Long, See You Tomorrow* named a finalist for the
        Pulitzer Prize in Fiction (won by John Kennedy Toole's
        A Confederacy of Dunces). On May 26, Ilonka Karasz dies,
        at age 85, after a long illness.

1982   In spring, makes final visit to France: five weeks in Paris,
        with Emily and Brookie. Interviewed for *The Paris Re-
        view*'s "Art of Fiction" series (Fall 1982); is so pleased by
        the results of his painstaking collaboration with editors
        that he adopts the practice of giving only written re-
        sponses to questions from print interviewers and insisting
        on the right to correct proofs.

1983   In January, *Sylvia Townsend Warner: Letters*, edited and
        with an introduction by Maxwell, published by Viking.
        The New Yorker publishes "Love" (November 14), inau-
        gurating a decade-long series of first-person stories about
        figures and events from Maxwell's Lincoln boyhood.

1984   *The New Yorker* publishes "My Father's Friends" (January
        30) and "The Man in the Moon" (November 12). To
        honor Eudora Welty on her 75th birthday, writes a short
        story, "With Reference to an Incident at a Bridge," for a
        tribute volume privately printed by friends. On April 26,
        in a ceremony at the Guggenheim Museum, receives the
        Brandeis University Creative Arts Medal for Fiction;
        among the jury for this lifetime achievement award are
        John Updike and Irving Howe.

1985   Robert Fitzgerald dies, January 16, at age 74; Maxwell
        delivers tributes at the spring meeting of the National In-
        stitute of Arts and Letters, April 2, and again at a memo-
        rial reading at the Guggenheim Museum, November 5.
        Brother Hap dies August 23; as a tribute, writes story
        "The Holy Terror," published in *The New Yorker* (March
        17, 1986).

1986   "The Lily-White Boys," a story of New York, published
        in special 100th issue of *The Paris Review*. Co-edits,
        with Susanna Pinney, *Selected Stories of Sylvia Townsend
        Warner* (1988).

1987   Memoir of Zona Gale published in the winter issue of *The
        Yale Review*.

1988   *Five Tales*, a small book of previously uncollected fairy
        tales written for his family, is edited by Emily and privately

printed as surprise gift to Maxwell and his admirers on his 80th birthday.

1989   In April, Knopf publishes *The Outermost Dream*, 19 essays on literary subjects, most of them revised or entirely rewritten versions of book reviews published in *The New Yorker* between 1956 and 1987. None of the essays considers fiction; instead they appreciate the diaries, letters, autobiographies, and lives of favorite writers (Virginia Woolf, E. M. Forster, Isak Dinesen, Samuel Butler, Byron, Colette) and friends (Louise Bogan, Frank O'Connor, V. S. Pritchett, Sylvia Townsend Warner, Eudora Welty, E. B. and Katharine White). Story "Billie Dyer" published in *The New Yorker* (May 15).

1990   Edits, with Charles McGrath, *A Final Antidote* (1991), a 56-page selection from the journals of Louise Bogan, privately printed in an edition of 220 copies.

1991   Writes story "The Front and the Back Parts of the House," published in *The New Yorker* (September 23); submits it and six other recent Lincoln stories to Knopf under the title *Billie Dyer and Other Stories*. Barbara Burkhardt, a Ph.D. candidate at the University of Illinois writing her dissertation on Maxwell's work, helps plan a "special Maxwell issue" of *Tamaqua* (Fall 1992), the literary biannual of Parkland College, Champaign, Illinois. Maxwell writes "What He Was Like" expressly for *Tamaqua* but the story is published by *The New Yorker* (December 7, 1992), which enjoys the right of first refusal. Instead he prepares a long excerpt from the abandoned Martinique novella of 1942 ("At the Pension Gaullard") and, from October 1991 through July 1992, fashions a long interview, mainly through the mail, with Burkhardt.

1992   In February, *Billie Dyer* is published by Knopf. When asked by an interviewer whether the book is memoir or fiction, Maxwell replies: "For me 'fiction' lies not in whether a thing, the thing I am writing about, actually happened, but in the form of the writing. The important distinction is between reminiscence, which is a formless accumulation of facts, and a story, which has a shape, a controlled effect, a satisfying conclusion—something that is, or attempts to be, a work of art." Writes prefaces for a Quality Paperback Book Club omnibus comprising *Time Will Darken It*, *The Château*, and *So Long, See You To-*

morrow. Asks Barbara Burkhardt to help him catalog his papers for eventual donation to the University of Illinois Library.

1993   Maeve Brennan dies, November 1, at age 76; Maxwell writes her obituary for *The New Yorker.* Enjoys visits from, and correspondence with, brother Blinn and his family, and the attentions of young admirers including poets Michael Collier and Edward Hirsch, fiction writers Richard Bausch, Charles Baxter, Benjamin Cheever, and Donna Tartt, and literary scholar Michael Steinman. He calls these new, unexpected, and affectionate friendships "a gift from life."

1994   Arranges and revises texts for *All the Days and Nights: The Collected Stories of William Maxwell,* comprising 23 short stories (including the complete contents of *Over by the River* and *Billie Dyer*) and 21 tales or "improvisations" (mostly reprinted from *The Old Man at the Railroad Crossing*). In spring, publishes three improvisations in *Story* magazine, and, in fall, four more in *New England Review.* Becomes a client of agent Andrew Wylie, who untangles Maxwell's rights history and negotiates a deal with Vintage Books for a uniform edition of paperback reprints.

1995   In January, *All the Days and Nights,* dedicated to Emily, is published by Knopf. It occasions a year of awards and acceptances: Ivan Sandrof Award for Life Achievement in Literature (National Book Critics Circle); Mark Twain Award (Society for Study of Midwestern Literature, Michigan State University); Heartland Award in Literature (Chicago Tribune Foundation); PEN/Malamud Award for the Short Story; Ambassador Book Award (English-Speaking Union of the United States), and American Book Award. In March, *Mrs. Donald's Dog Bun and His Home Away from Home,* a story for children illustrated with watercolors by *New Yorker* cartoonist James Stevenson, published by Knopf. On May 17, Maxwell accepts the Gold Medal in Fiction from the American Academy of Arts and Letters, presented by Joseph Mitchell. In November, records *So Long, See You Tomorrow* in its entirety for the American Audio Prose Library, together with an interview by series' producer Kay Bonetti.

1996   In May, *The Happiness of Getting It Down Right*, Michael
            Steinman's edition of the Frank O'Connor–William Max-
            well letters, is published by Knopf. Writes a memoir of
            Maeve Brennan for *The Springs of Affection* (1997), a col-
            lection of Brennan's Dublin stories edited by Christopher
            Carduff. On his 88th birthday, is interviewed by Edward
            Hirsch for *DoubleTake* magazine (Summer 1997). Writes
            introductions to the Modern Library editions of Joseph
            Mitchell's *Joe Gould's Secret* (1996) and his own *They
            Came Like Swallows* (1997).

1997   Donates majority of personal and professional papers to
            the Special Collections Library of the University of Illi-
            nois. Writes memoir, "Nearing Ninety," for *The New York
            Times Magazine* (March 9); will revise it for inclusion in
            Best American Essays 1998, edited by Cynthia Ozick. Lym-
            phoma returns, and again Maxwell responds well to
            chemotherapy.

1998   Christopher MacLehose, of Harvill Press, London, pub-
            lishes a paperback edition of *So Long, See You Tomorrow*;
            over the next four years he will make five other Maxwell
            books available to British and Commonwealth readers. In
            summer, Emily discovers she has ovarian cancer, and
            undergoes the first of three rounds of chemotherapy. In
            October, the Century presents a gala dinner and literary
            evening in celebration of Maxwell's 90th birthday and
            his 50th year as a member of the club. An interviewer for
            Illinois Alumni magazine asks Maxwell to name the
            happiest and most significant moments in his long
            life and career: "Perhaps when meeting the Wisconsin
            novelist Zona Gale when I was 16. Perhaps when I looked
            through a porthole at age 40 and saw the coast of France.
            Certainly the day when my wife agreed to marry me. And
            the days when my two daughters were born. And when I
            first read Tolstoy's 'Master and Man.'" Story "The Room
            Outside" published in *The New Yorker* (December 28,
            1998/January 4, 1999).

1999   Writes introduction to *The Music at Long Verney* (2001),
            Michael Steinman's choice from Sylvia Townsend
            Warner's uncollected stories, and a postscript to *The
            Element of Lavishness* (2001), Steinman's edition of the
            Maxwell–Warner letters. On June 7 *The New Yorker* pub-
            lishes "Grape Bay (1941)," not a new story but the revised

opening of the abandoned Bermuda novel of the mid-1970s. Two final improvisations published in the fall issue of *DoubleTake*.

2000   Health begins to fail: suffers pneumonia, near blindness, anemia, and return of lymphoma. Meets with family lawyers, and asks Michael Steinman to be his literary executor. In spring, Emily refuses to undergo fourth round of chemotherapy; she dies at home, on July 23, at age 78. Maxwell, surrounded by family and friends, follows her eight days later, on July 31, at age 91. A joint memorial service, organized by daughters, is held on September 8, at the Cathedral of St. John the Divine, New York City, and attended by hundreds.

Note on the Texts

This volume presents a selection from the fiction that William Maxwell published between 1957 and 1999. It contains texts of the novels *The Château* (1961) and *So Long, See You Tomorrow* (1980), 18 short stories, and 40 of the tales that Maxwell called "improvisations," as well as the essay "Nearing Ninety" (1997) and, in an appendix, prefaces to reprints of *The Château* (1992) and *So Long, See You Tomorrow* (1992), the preface to *All the Days and Nights: The Collected Stories of William Maxwell* (1995), and the text of Maxwell's remarks upon accepting the Gold Medal in Fiction from the American Academy of Arts and Letters in 1995.

Maxwell made notes for what would become his fifth published novel, *The Château*, immediately upon returning to New York in October 1948 from a four-month tour in Europe with his wife, Emily. (In his preface to the Quality Paperback Book Club reprint, printed on pages 927–28 of the present volume, Maxwell gives an account of the trip and the novel's inspiration.) By the summer of 1950 he had made four or five very different attempts at writing the opening chapters but was uncertain which one was the most promising. By the time Maxwell signed a contract for the novel with Alfred A. Knopf in March 1958, the manuscript consisted of many loosely connected scenes, some in several versions, tucked into folders and stacked in a large grocery carton in his study. Over the years, Maxwell stopped working on the novel more than once; as he later told *The Paris Review*: "I hadn't been able to make up my mind whether it should have an omniscient author or a first-person narrator, whether it should be told from the point of view of the French or the Americans traveling in France. I was afraid it was not a novel at all but a travel diary." In the late summer of 1958 a friend, the Irish writer Frank O'Connor, read the various drafts of the novel and made comments Maxwell found perceptive and encouraging. Using the working title "Leo and Virgo," he rewrote and revised the novel throughout 1959 and completed a draft by January 1, 1960. Maxwell asked the writer and translator Francis Steegmuller to read this draft and improve his "wobbly" French; while doing so, Steegmuller asked a series of questions about the characters and events in the book that inspired Maxwell to revise the novel further and write the epilogue, "Some Explanations." On June 17, 1960, Maxwell submitted the finished manuscript, now titled "The Days of France," to Knopf, where he worked with Judith Jones as his editor; it is unclear who suggested using the title *The Château*. The novel was published in March 1961, and Maxwell made no changes in the work after the first Knopf printing. The text printed here is taken from the 1961 Alfred A. Knopf edition.

The seven short stories collected in this volume as "Stories 1963–1976" were selected from the nine stories that Maxwell published during the 1960s and 1970s. They first appeared in *The New Yorker*, where Maxwell worked with Robert Henderson and Roger Angell as his editors, as follows: "A Final Report," March 9, 1963; "The Value of Money," June 6, 1964; "A Game of Chess," June 12, 1965; "The Poor Orphan Girl," November 13, 1965; "The Gardens of Mont-Saint-Michel," August 6, 1969; "Over by the River," July 1, 1974; and "The Thistles in Sweden," June 21, 1976. Maxwell collected "A Final Report," "The Value of Money," "The Gardens of Mont-Saint-Michel," "Over by the River," and "The Thistles in Sweden" in *Over by the River and Other Stories*, published by Alfred A. Knopf in 1977, and all seven stories were reprinted, some with slight revisions by Maxwell, in *All the Days and Nights: The Collected Stories of William Maxwell*, published by Knopf in 1995. "A Game of Chess," an autobiographical story based on Maxwell's troubled relationship with his older brother, Hap, was published in *The New Yorker* under the pseudonym Gifford Brown; Maxwell waited until after Hap's death to reprint the story under his own name. "The Poor Orphan Girl" was originally one of two untitled "improvisations" published in *The New Yorker* under the heading "Further Tales about Men and Women"; Maxwell titled it "The poor orphan girl" when preparing his collection *The Old Man at the Railroad Crossing and Other Tales*, published by Knopf in 1966, and rewrote the opening sentence when preparing the setting copy of *All the Days and Nights*. "A Final Report" was thoroughly revised for inclusion in *All the Days and Nights*, partly to avoid an overlap with material in the later story "The Holy Terror," partly to bring certain details of the story into line with the related short fiction collected in *Billie Dyer and Other Stories* (1992). Three further changes have been made in the present text to bring it into conformity with the *Billie Dyer* stories: at 365.9, "Logan County" replaces "Latham County," and at 371.39 and 377.21 "*Evening Courier*" replaces "*Evening Star*." The texts of the seven stories presented in "Stories 1963–1976" are taken from the 1995 Knopf edition of *All the Days and Nights*.

In the winter of 1972–73, Maxwell wrote a short story based on memories of a boyhood friend whose father, a tenant farmer in Lincoln, Illinois, committed a murder in a jealous rage. The story was rejected by *The New Yorker*, but Maxwell did not abandon the material, which provided the inspiration for his sixth and final novel, *So Long, See You Tomorrow*. (In his preface to the Quality Paperback Book Club reprint, printed on pages 929–30 of the present volume, Maxwell gives an account the novel's composition.) Maxwell submitted the finished manuscript, under the title "The Palace at 4 A.M.," to Judith Jones, his editor at Knopf, in January 1979. After she accepted the work, he gave a copy of the manuscript to Roger Angell at *The New Yorker* for first-serial consideration. The novel was edited by Angell in consultation with William Shawn, the editor of *The New Yorker*, and was published in its entirety, under the title *So Long, See You Tomorrow*, in two consecutive numbers of the magazine, the first five chapters in the number for October 1, 1979, and the remaining four chapters in the number for October 8. For the Knopf edition, published in January 1980, Maxwell used the *New Yorker* text while restoring, in a few minor instances, diction he had changed at the insistence of Angell and Shawn. Maxwell made no changes in the novel after the first Knopf printing. This volume prints the text of the 1980 Knopf edition.

After the publication of *So Long, See You Tomorrow*, Maxwell published 11 short stories, most in the form of first-person memoirs of people and events from his Lincoln, Illinois, boyhood. He collected seven of these Lincoln stories in *Billie Dyer and Other Stories*, published by Knopf in February 1992. Six of the stories first appeared in *The New Yorker*: "Love," November 14, 1983; "My Father's Friends," January 30, 1984; "The Man in the Moon," November 12, 1984; "The Holy Terror," March 17, 1986; "Billie Dyer," May 15, 1989; and "The Front and the Back Parts of the House" (as "The Front and Back Parts of the House"), September 23, 1991. The seventh story, "With Reference to an Incident at a Bridge," first appeared in *Eudora Welty: A Tribute on Her Seventy-fifth Birthday, 13 April 1984* (Winston-Salem, North Carolina: Stuart Wright, 1984), a booklet edited by Cleanth Brooks and Robert Penn Warren and privately printed in an edition of 75 copies. The seven stories were reprinted in *All the Days and Nights* in the same order as they appeared in *Billie Dyer* and were copyedited to conform with the spelling and punctuation used in the other stories in the collection. This volume prints the texts that appeared in the 1995 Knopf edition of *All the Days and Nights*.

The section of the present volume titled "Stories 1986–1999" collects the remaining four short stories published by Maxwell at the end of his career. "Grape Bay (1941)," which appeared in *The New Yorker* for June 7, 1999, was his last published story but was written much earlier; Maxwell described it as "not really a short story" but rather the opening scenes of a novel begun in 1976–77 and soon abandoned. The other three stories first appeared as follows: "The Lily-White Boys," *The Paris Review*, Summer/Fall 1986; "What He Was Like," *The New Yorker*, December 7, 1992; and "The Room Outside," *The New Yorker*, December 28, 1998/January 4, 1999. Maxwell included "The Lily-White Boys" and "What He Was Like" in *All the Days and Nights*, and the texts printed here are taken from the 1995 Knopf edition of that collection. "Grape Bay (1941)" and "The Room Outside" were never collected by Maxwell, and are printed here in texts taken from *The New Yorker*.

The "once-upon-a-time" tales that Maxwell called "improvisations" constitute a body of work distinct from his novels and stories. Most of them were written as gifts for his wife; the earliest, "The woodcutter," was a present for Christmas 1946, with the typed sheets rolled up, tied with a ribbon, and inserted among the branches of the family Christmas tree. He began publishing the improvisations in periodicals in 1957, and continued to do so until the end of his life; some were published singly, but most appeared in clusters of two, three, or four under headings such as "A Brace of Fairy Tales" and "Three Fables Written to Please a Lady." The present volume prints 40 improvisations published between 1957 and 1999.

Maxwell selected 21 improvisations for publication in the concluding section of *All the Days and Nights: The Collected Stories of William Maxwell* (1995). Fifteen of the tales collected in "A Set of Twenty-one Improvisations" had previously appeared in *The Old Man at the Railroad Crossing and Other Tales* (New York: Alfred A. Knopf, 1966); the remaining six tales had appeared in little magazines and in private-press printings between 1988 and 1994. While making his selection Maxwell revised many of the improvisations and in some cases gave them new titles. The tales collected in "A Set of Twenty-one Improvisations" had previously appeared as follows:

"A love story" (as "A love story—by request"), *Five Tales by William Maxwell: Written for his family on special occasions and printed to celebrate his eightieth birthday, 16 August 1988* (Omaha, Nebraska: The Cummington Press, 1988), a small collection edited by Emily Maxwell and privately printed in an edition of 220 copies.

"The industrious tailor" (untitled, under the heading "Further Tales about Men and Women"), *The New Yorker*, November 13, 1965; published (as "The industrious tailor") in *The Old Man at the Railroad Crossing* (1966).

"The country where nobody ever grew old and died," *The Old Man at the Railroad Crossing* (1966).

"The fisherman who had nobody to go out in his boat with him" (untitled, under the heading "Further Tales about Men and

Women"), *The New Yorker*, August 7, 1965; published (as "The fisherman who had no one to go out in his boat with him") in *The Old Man at the Railroad Crossing* (1966).

"The two women friends" (untitled, under the heading "Further Tales about Men and Women"), *The New Yorker*, August 7, 1965; published (as "The two women friends") in *The Old Man at the Railroad Crossing* (1966).

"The carpenter" (untitled, under the heading "Further Tales about Men and Women"), *The New Yorker*, December 11, 1965; published (as "The carpenter") in *The Old Man at the Railroad Crossing* (1966).

"The man who had no friends and didn't want any" (untitled, under the heading "Further Tales about Men and Women"), *The New Yorker*, December 25, 1965; published (as "The man who had no enemies") in *The Old Man at the Railroad Crossing* (1966).

"A fable begotten of an echo of a line of verse by W. B. Yeats," *Antæus*, Spring/Autumn 1990.

"The blue finch of Arabia" (untitled, under the heading "More Old Tales about Men and Women"), *The New Yorker*, October 18, 1958; published (as "The blue finch of Arabia") in *The Old Man at the Railroad Crossing* (1966).

"The sound of waves" (untitled, under the heading "Further Tales about Men and Women"), *The New Yorker*, December 11, 1965; published (as "The man who took his family to the seashore") in *The Old Man at the Railroad Crossing* (1966).

"The woman who never drew breath except to complain" (untitled, under the heading "More Old Tales about Women"), *The New Yorker*, August 23, 1958; published (as "The woman who never drew breath except to complain") in *The Old Man at the Railroad Crossing* (1966).

"The masks" (as "Variation on a theme from *Time Will Darken It* "), *Five Tales by William Maxwell* (1988).

"The man who lost his father" (untitled, under the heading "Further Tales about Men and Women"), *The New Yorker*, August 7, 1965; published (as "The man who lost his father") in *The Old Man at the Railroad Crossing* (1966).

"The old woman whose house was beside a running stream" (untitled, under the heading "Further Tales about Men and Women"), *The New Yorker*, December 25, 1965; published (as "The woman who lived beside a running stream") in *The Old Man at the Railroad Crossing* (1966).

"The pessimistic fortune-teller" (as "The fortune-teller," under the heading "Three Fables Written to Please a Lady"), *Story*, Spring 1994.

"The printing office" (untitled, under the heading "Further Tales about Men and Women"), *The New Yorker*, December 25, 1965; published (as "The printing office") in *The Old Man at the Railroad Crossing* (1966).

"The lamplighter" (untitled, under the heading "Further Tales about Men and Women"), *The New Yorker*, October 16, 1965; published (as "The lamplighter") in *The Old Man at the Railroad Crossing* (1966).

"The kingdom where straightforward, logical thinking was admired over every other kind," *The Old Man at the Railroad Crossing* (1966).

"The old man at the railroad crossing" (untitled, under the heading "Further Tales about Men and Women"), *The New Yorker*, December 11, 1965; published (as "The old man at the railroad crossing") in *The Old Man at the Railroad Crossing* (1966).

"A mean and spiteful toad" (as "Alice," under the heading "Three Fables Written to Please a Lady"), *Story*, Spring 1994.

"All the days and nights" (untitled), *Five Tales by William Maxwell* (1988).

This volume prints the texts of "A Set of Twenty-one Improvisations" that appeared in the 1995 Knopf edition of *All the Days and Nights: The Collected Stories of William Maxwell*.

The section of this volume titled "Other Improvisations" presents a selection of 19 tales printed in books and periodicals between 1957 and 1999. They are arranged in the order in which they appeared and are numbered following Maxwell's practice in "A Set of Twenty-one Improvisations" and *The Old Man at the Railroad Crossing*. The following is a list of the tales included in "Other Improvisations," giving the source of each text and, where applicable, details of earlier printings:

"The old man who was afraid of falling": *The Old Man at the Railroad Crossing* (1966). Previously printed (as "The anxious man") in *Pax*, September 1957.

"The epistolarian," "The shepherd's wife": *The Old Man at the Railroad Crossing* (1966). Appeared untitled under the heading "Two Old Tales about Women (Found in a Rattan Tea Caddy c. 1913)" in *The New Yorker*, March 15, 1958.

"The marble watch," "The half-crazy woman": *The Old Man at the Railroad Crossing* (1966). Appeared untitled under the heading "Two Old Tales about Men and Women," *The New Yorker*, June 21, 1958.

"The woman who didn't want anything more": *The Old Man at the Railroad Crossing* (1966). Appeared untitled under the heading "More Old Tales about Women," *The New Yorker*, August 23, 1958.

"The girl with a willing heart and a cold mind," "The woodcutter":

The Old Man at the Railroad Crossing (1966). Appeared untitled under the heading "More Old Tales about Men and Women," *The New Yorker*, October 18, 1958.

"The man who had never been sick a day in his life," "The problem child": *The Old Man at the Railroad Crossing* (1966). Appeared untitled under the heading "Further Tales about Men and Women," *The New Yorker*, October 16, 1965.

"The woman who had no eye for small details": *The Old Man at the Railroad Crossing* (1966). Appeared untitled under the heading "Further Tales about Men and Women," *The New Yorker*, December 11, 1965.

"The man who loved to eat": *The Old Man at the Railroad Crossing* (1966). Appeared untitled under the heading "Further Tales about Men and Women," *The New Yorker*, December 25, 1965.

"The woman with a talent for talking": *The Old Man at the Railroad Crossing* (1966).

"Perfection": Tearsheet, with typed title and autograph corrections, in the William Maxwell papers in the Rare Book and Manuscript Library of the University of Illinois, Urbana-Champaign. Appeared untitled in *Five Tales by William Maxwell* (1988).

"What you can't hang on to": *The Element of Lavishness: Letters of Sylvia Townsend Warner and William Maxwell, 1938–1978*, edited by Michael Steinman (Washington, D.C.: Counterpoint, 2001). Appeared under the heading "Three Fables Written to Please a Lady," *Story*, Spring 1994.

"Mushrooms," "The dancing": *New England Review*, Fall 1994, under the heading "A Brace of Fairy Tales."

"The education of Her Majesty the Queen," "Newton's law": *DoubleTake*, Fall 1999, under the heading "Two Tales by William Maxwell."

The essay "Nearing Ninety" was published in *The New York Times Magazine*, March 9, 1997, in a version edited without Maxwell's final approval. He took the opportunity to correct the text when Cynthia Ozick chose the piece for inclusion in *Best American Essays 1998*, published by Houghton Mifflin in October 1998. The text printed here is taken from *Best American Essays 1998*.

The appendix to this volume contains four short prose pieces by William Maxwell. He wrote prefaces to *The Château* and *So Long, See You Tomorrow* for a 1992 Quality Paperback Book Club omnibus edition of *Time Will Darken It*, *The Château*, and *So Long, See You Tomorrow*, and a preface to the first edition of *All the Days and Nights*, published by Knopf in January 1995. The texts printed in this volume are taken, respectively, from the 1992 Quality Paperback Book Club omnibus edition and the 1995 Knopf edition. Maxwell's remarks upon accepting the Gold Medal in Fiction from the American Academy of Arts and Letters were delivered at the Academy's Annual Ceremonial in New York City on May 17, 1995. A version of the speech was published in *Proceedings of the American Academy of Arts and Letters*, Second Series, No. 46, 1995. The text printed in the present volume, which varies slightly from the version published in the *Proceedings*, is taken from a single-page typescript in the William Maxwell papers in the Rare Book and Manuscript Library of the University of Illinois, Urbana-Champaign.

This volume presents the texts of the printings and typescripts chosen for inclusion here, but it does not attempt to reproduce non-textual features of their typographic design. The texts are printed without change, except for the correction of typographical errors. Spelling, punctuation, and capitalization are often expressive features, and they are not altered, even when inconsistent or irregular. Except for clear typographical errors, the spelling and usage of foreign words and phrases are left as they appear in the original texts. The following is a list of typographical errors corrected, cited by page and line number: 47.32, monsieur!; 48.27, apparent.; 50.5, now had; 55.9, floor.; 65.11, this.; 66.37, cheerfully:; 69.17, There.; 71.8, French—' owe; 77.29, Rhodes'; 88.35, "'ut . . . doaks!"; 90.37, of; 104.21, et; 104.21, chocolat-praliné; 116.5, dancing.; 122.18–19, Velasquez; 122.19–20, La Belle Ferronière; 140.15, Eugéne; 172.2, Eugene; 172.9, said." I; 182.7, Allegret; 209.16, suit cases; 218.9, mantel piece; 228.1, The; 241.17, fil a; 286.7, *le*; 287.13, *le Roi d'Ys*; 288.1, dedication; 288.31, *them*); 288.40, *Bethanie*; 292.37, governent; 295.30, *you* . . ."; 330.40, Calaban; 345.40, whispered;; 370.16, $12, $16, $16; 391.27, 'Ned,; 409.10, Psis; 415.14, thought was; 412.26, get A; 435.32, herbs."; 505.38, hands; 771.14, woman's Then; 777.30, there no; 821.2, *dies*;; 821.18, virburnum; 845.17, *wonder no*; 845.35, Then; 847.16, mantlepieces,; 849.22, such-an-such; 846.19, then; 897.26, blue-jay's; 927.2, First; 927.9, Le Grand Meaulnes, The Counterfeiters,; 928.14, Part II; 930.1, Evening Courier; 930.6, So Long, See You Tomorrow.; 930.13, The Brothers Karamazov,.

Notes

In the notes below, the reference numbers denote page and line of this volume (the line count includes headings). No note is made for material included in standard desk-reference books. Biblical quotations are keyed to the King James Version. Quotations from Shakespeare are keyed to *The Riverside Shakespeare*, ed. G. Blakemore Evans (Boston: Houghton Mifflin, 1974). For references to other studies, and further biographical background than is contained in the Chronology, see *William Maxwell: A Literary Life*, by Barbara Burkhardt (Urbana and Chicago: University of Illinois Press, 2005); *A William Maxwell Portrait: Memories and Appreciations*, ed. Charles Baxter, Michael Collier, and Edward Hirsch (New York: W. W. Norton, 2005); *My Mentor: A Young Man's Friendship with William Maxwell*, by Alec Wilkinson (Boston: Houghton Mifflin, 2002); *The Element of Lavishness: Letters of Sylvia Townsend Warner and William Maxwell, 1938–1978*, ed. Michael Steinman (Washington, D.C.: Counterpoint, 2001); *What I Think I Did: A Season of Survival in Two Acts*, by Larry Woiwode (New York: Basic Books, 2000), *The Happiness of Getting It Down Right: Letters of Frank O'Connor and William Maxwell, 1945–1966*, ed. Michael Steinman (New York: Alfred A. Knopf, 1996); and *Ancestors*, by William Maxwell (New York: Alfred A. Knopf, 1971). Significant interviews with Maxwell, for which he provided written, not oral, responses, include those by Edward Hirsch (*DoubleTake*, Summer 1997), David Stanton (*Poets & Writers*, May/June 1994), Barbara Burkhardt et al. (*Tamaqua*, Fall 1992), and John Seabrook and George Plimpton (*The Paris Review*, Fall 1982).

The editor wishes to thank the Rare Book and Manuscript Library of the University of Illinois, Urbana-Champaign, whose award of a research grant through the John "Bud" Velde Visiting Scholars Program supported his work on this volume.

THE CHÂTEAU

2.1–5   E. B. . . . W. S.] "E. B." is the Anglo-Irish writer Elizabeth Bowen (1899–1973), a friend of Maxwell who read the novel in manuscript; "E. C." is Elizabeth Cullinan (b. 1933), Maxwell's assistant at *The New Yorker* from 1956 through the mid-1960s, who typed several drafts of the novel; "M. O'D." is Michael O'Donovan (1903–1966), the Irish writer who published under the pen name Frank O'Connor and who, in 1958, read the novel-in-progress and gave Maxwell invaluable advice and encouragement; "F. S." is the biographer, novelist, and translator Francis Steegmuller (1906–1994), who helped Maxwell with his French and whose questions about the story inspired him to write the book's concluding chapter; "W. S." is William Shawn (1907–1992), editor of *The New Yorker* from 1952 to 1987.

5.1–16   ". . . wherever . . . *Meudon-Val-Fleury*] The epigraph by Elizabeth Bowen (see note above) is from the novel *A World of Love* (1955); those by Rilke are from *The Letters of Rainer Maria Rilke, 1892–1910* (1945), edited and translated from the German by Jane Bannard Greene and M. D. Herter Norton.

9.2–3   red and black slanting funnels] Trademarks of the British Cunard Line.

13.5   Italian elections] The Italian general elections of April 18, 1948, were the first under the postwar democratic constitution of 1946. The center-right Christian Democracy Party, led by Alcide De Gasperi, won a plurality with more than 48 percent of the vote, edging out the pro-Soviet Popular Democratic Front, a coalition of communists and socialists, with about 31 percent.

14.12   S.N.C.F.] Société Nationale des Chemins de fer Français, the French national railway system.

14.22   *Volailles & Gibier*] Poultry & Game.

14.23   *Spontex* and *Tabac* and *Charcuterie*] Spontex is a French manufacturer of household cleaning supplies (sponges, rubber gloves, etc.); a *tabac*, a tobacconist; a *charcuterie*, a delicatessen selling prepared meats (sausages, pâtés, etc.).

15.38   *Rasurel*] French line of women's swimwear.

16.34   Cinzano] Italian vermouth apéritif.

18.22   "De ce côté-là."] "It's that way."

21.14–18   "Nous cherchons . . . Nous désirons—"] "We're looking for a hotel. . . . We have a lot of luggage, and there's no taxi. . . . My wife is ill . . . she is very tired. We want—"

21.28   "Simple mais assez confortable,"] "Simple but rather comfortable."

24.2   "Little goat, bleat. Little table, appear,"] In the tale "Little One-eye, Little Two-eyes, and Little Three-eyes," told by the Scottish folklorist Andrew Lang in his *Green Fairy Book* (1892), these are the magic words that, when spoken by the girl Little Two-eyes, make a hot meal appear out of thin air.

30.25–26   "rillettes de Tours"]   Shredded pork in aspic, traditionally sold in a small crock.

32.31–34   "En apparence . . . est sérieuse."]   "In appearance all looks well for you, but do not be too trusting; adversity is around the corner. Deaths, separations, are indicated. In lawsuits you would be found at fault. The illness is serious."

33.3–4   "C'est votre frère?" . . . "Non . . . mon mari."]   "Is he your brother?" . . . "No . . . he is my husband."

40.34   The *service* is probably *compris*,"]   "The tip is probably included."

42.23   Charles Morgan and Elizabeth Goudge]   Morgan (1894–1958) and Goudge (1900–1984) were prolific and popular English prose writers of the 1930s and '40s.

42.25   *La Mare au Diable*]   *The Devil's Pool* (1848), novella of French country manners by George Sand (1804–1876).

42.27   *Le Grand Meaulnes*]   Novel of youth and romanticism (1913; translated as "The Wanderer") by Alain-Fournier (Henri Alban-Fournier, 1886–1914).

42.28   Mme de Sévigné]   Marie de Rabutin-Chantal, marquise de Sévigné (1626–1696), a Paris-born aristocrat whose witty personal letters, posthumously published by her granddaughter, provide a vivid record of high society during the reign of Louis XIV.

42.31–32   Boutet de Monvel]   Louis-Maurice Boutet de Monvel (1851–1913), French painter and lithographer renowned for his illustrated books for children, including *Vielle Chansons et rondes por les petits infants* and *Chansons de France pour les petits français* (both 1883).

47.17–26   "Je ne comprends . . . dans ma figure."]   "I do not understand the directions that Mme Michot gave me, and so have to ask everyone: 'Where is the house of M. Fleury—this way, or this way?' Again I get directions . . . and again I do not understand. Then . . . I ask my question of a little boy, who takes me by the hand and leads me to M. Fleury's house, quite near the post office. . . . I say 'thank you' and I knock at the door. The door opens a very little bit. It is Mme Fleury who opens it. I start to explain, and she shuts the door in my face."

47.29–48.7   "Le garçon frappe . . . dans le radiator. . . ."]   "The boy knocks at the door . . . and the door opens a bit. It's M. Fleury's son, this time. He listens. He does not close the door. . . . When I finish, he says to me 'One moment! Wait, monsieur!' I wait, naturally. Wait and wait. . . . The door opens. It is M. Fleury himself, in stocking feet, without shoes. . . .

I explain that madame and the luggage are at the station and that we will want to go to the château. . . . He listens. He is very sympathetic, M. Fleury, very nice. He sends his son ahead with the key to the garage where the truck is. The garage is locked because it's Sunday. . . . And then, we begin. M. Fleury— . . . —M. Fleury pumps air into the tires, and I, I lift some bags of grain that are in the back of the truck. The truck is older than the Treaty of Versailles. . . . Many years older. And M. Fleury's son pours a liter of petrol into the tank, which is empty, and water into the radiator. . . ."

49.6   Adam mantelpieces] Mantelpieces in the neoclassical decorative style of the Scottish designer and architect Robert Adam (1728–1792).

52.28   Almanach de Gotha] Authoritative directory of European royalty and nobility, first published in 1763 and updated regularly through 1944.

56.29–33   The newspapers of 1906 . . . St. Cyr.] In October 1894, Captain Alfred Dreyfus (1859–1935), a French artillery officer, was wrongfully arrested on charges of treason and subsequently sentenced to life imprisonment. The legal, political, and social controversy that followed—known internationally as the "Dreyfus affair"—divided the French nation throughout the mid 1890s and resulted in Dreyfus's case being reopened. In September 1899 Dreyfus was pardoned by President Emile Loubet. He was fully exonerated by a military commission on July 12, 1906, and one week later publicly decorated with the Légion d'honneur.

58.7   Mr. Midshipman Easy] Sea adventure (1836) set in the Napoleonic era, by the English naval hero turned novelist Captain Frederick Marryat (1792–1848).

58.35   Raskolnikov] In Dostoevsky's Crime and Punishment (1866), an impoverished student who murders and robs a miserly pawnbroker, then rationalizes his crime as an act for the greater social good.

58.37   Mr. Micawber] In Dickens's David Copperfield (1850), a debtor who lives in cheerful optimism about his future prospects.

60.23–24   raveled sleeve . . . knits up.] Cf. Shakespeare, Macbeth, II.ii.34.

64.13–14   Un peu d'histoire] A little history.

69.35   poupées] Dolls.

78.13   "entre la poire et le fromage"] Idiom whose literal translation, "between the pear and the cheese," refers to the moment during the evening meal when talk turns away from serious subjects and toward the amusing and trivial.

78.27–28   "le saucisson . . . pain."] "A sausage between two slices of bread."

79.18   potager] French-style kitchen garden, both practical and ornamental, planted with fruit trees, vegetables, herbs, and flowers.

80.15   Guerre de Quatorze] War of '14 (World War I).

81.36   "Entendu!"] "Of course!"

85.34   "Ravissant!"] "Charming!"

87.16–17   Henry Ford's museum] The Henry Ford Museum, in Dearborn, Michigan, incorporates Greenfield Village, an outdoor museum-park complex to which more than a hundred historic American buildings have been relocated, including the Wright brothers' bicycle shop (from Dayton, Ohio) and Thomas Edison's laboratory (from Menlo Park, New Jersey).

95.9   mairie] Town hall.

99.36   "J'adore la jeunesse,"] "I adore youth."

101.15   *Personnes Isolées*] Persons living alone (i.e., single-person households).

102.24   "Qui n'avait jam-jam-jamais naviGUÉ!"] Second line of the French children's song "Il était un petit navire" ("It was a small boat / That had nev-nev-never SAILED!").

106.10   *hoch Deutsch*] High German.

106.29   General Weygand] Maxime Weygand (1867–1965), a commanding officer in both world wars and, during the summer of 1940, the minister of defense for the Vichy government. After the war, he was imprisoned as a collaborator with the Nazis until exonerated by Charles de Gaulle in 1948.

121.2   Guerlain] Paris *parfumerie* founded by Pierre-François Pascal Guerlain in 1828. Its signature fragrance is Shalimar.

121.8   Cultes] Houses of worship.

122.19–20   *La Belle Ferronnière*] Portrait of a young woman wearing a jeweled headband, painted in the 1490s and attributed to Leonardo da Vinci.

134.18   "deux" for "douze,"] "Two" for "twelve."

136.16   Schumann] Robert Schumann (1886–1963), prime minister of France from November 1947 to July 1948.

138.8   "Pas un mot."] "Not a word."

140.27–28   Saint-Simon]   Louis de Rouvroy, Duc de Saint-Simon (1675–1755), whose candid, voluminous memoirs of life in the court of Louis XIV, published posthumously, are a classic of French history.

145.3–4   "une espèce de miracle"]   "A kind of miracle."

155.37–38   the big painting . . . River Styx.]   *La Barque de Dante* (*The Barque of Dante*, or *Dante and Virgil in Hell*) by Eugène Delacroix, first exhibited in the Salon of 1822.

156.31   Nini]   Jean-Baptiste Nini (b. Giovanni Battista Nini, 1717–1786), Italian-born French sculptor who produced more than a hundred portrait medallions.

160.31   fonctionnaire]   Civil servant.

164.37–38   *Auge . . . Bicyclette . . . Cheval*]   Trough . . . Bicycle . . . Horse.

172.2   "Avez-vous bien dormi?"]   "You slept well?"

182.1   "Une table pliante,"]   "A folding table."

187.20–32   "Vous prenez . . . le long du mur. . . ."]   "You are interested in houses?" "I am interested in this house. But—" "Then. . . . Here is a picture of a hunt that took place here in 1907. The key indicates the identity of the people. Here is the Kaiser, and near him is Prince Philip von Eulenberg . . . Prince Friedrich-Wilhelm . . . Princess Sophie von Württemberg, carrying the black Amazon parrot, and the king of England . . . My father and my mother . . . Prince Karl von Saxe . . . with their hunters and their lackeys. The picture is painted from memory, of course. These antlers that you see along the wall. . . ."

189.32–34   "Au clair . . . écrire un mot . . ."]   "By the light of the moon, my friend Pierrot, lend me your pen to write a note . . ."

191.21–22   "In nomine . . . spiritus sanctus,"]   "In the name of the Father and the Son and the Holy Ghost."

191.33   mairie]   Town hall.

191.35   maire]   Mayor.

194.27   pommes de terre frites]   French-fried potatoes.

196.1   Note de Semaine]   Weekly bill.

198.11–12   "Oui, . . . je viens . . ."]   "Yes, Grandma. Right away. I'm coming, I'm coming . . ."

201.22–25   Si, par hasard . . . Indre-et-Loire. . . .]   If, by chance, Mr. and Mrs. Rhodes knew someone who would like French help, my son and I

would happily go abroad. Here is my address: Mme Foëcy, St. Claude de
Diray, Indre-et-Loire. . . .

201.32   *bluets*]   Cornflowers (*Centaurea cyanus*).

206.21–31   *A Passage to India . . . A Sportsman's Notebook,*]   *A Passage
to India* (1924), novel by E. M. Forster; *Fear and Trembling* (*Frygt og Bæven*,
1843), philosophical work by Søren Kierkegaard; *Le Silence de la Mer* (*The Si-
lence of the Sea*, 1942), short novel of the German occupation of France by
"Vercors" (the writer and illustrator Jean Bruller, 1902–1991); *Journey to the
End of the Night* (*Voyage au bout de la nuit*, 1932), novel by Louis-Ferdinand
Céline; *To the Lighthouse* (1927), novel by Virginia Woolf; *A Sportsman's
Notebook* (1852), linked stories and sketches by Ivan Turgenev.

206.26–27   "un petit livre poétique."]   "A poetic little book."

211.10   French painter and lithographer]   A monumental bronze bust of
Pierre-Joseph Redouté (1759–1840), official artist of the court of Napoleon,
for whom he created many prints and folios depicting the plant life of France,
most notably roses.

215.30   "Le petit déjeuner,"]   "A small breakfast."

216.11   fauteuil]   Armchair.

217.30–31   Lancret and Boucher]   Nicolas Lancret (1690–1743) and
François Boucher (1703–1770), favorites of the court of Louis XIV and
painters in the rococo style.

223.4   Good Humor Man]   Ice-cream vendor. The Good Humor Company, founded 1925, popularized ice cream on a stick and the neighborhood
ice-cream truck.

226.37–38   'Heureusement oui.' "]   "Fortunately yes."

241.17   "coup de fil à 6h½."]   "Phone me at 6:30."

251.26–27   mes enfants chéris. . . . qui vous aime tant—]   My dear children. I kiss you both. Your elderly friend who loves you so much—

252.12   "Elle est un peu maniaque,"]   "She is a little crazy."

254.19   *gentille*]   Nice, kind.

264.31   "Minou."]   "Pussy," "Kitty."

264.33   "Minou à tres ans"]   "Minou at age three."

264.39–40   Edmond Rostand]   French poet and playwright (1868–1918)
best remembered for his romantic comedy *Cyrano de Bergerac* (1897).

268.10–11   "Maria de Bahia" and "La Vie en Rose."]   French popular songs of the 1940s: "Maria de Bahia" (1944), samba by Paul Misraki, words by André Hornez, recorded by bandleader Ray Ventura; "La Vie en Rose" (1942), ballad written, performed, and recorded by chanteuse Edith Piaf.

268.24–25   Mme la Patronne] Proprietress of the hotel.

271.34   *L'Invitation au Château*] Play (1947) by Jean Anouilh (1910–1987).

272.37–273.5   "Bonjour, madame. . . . Rien du tout,"] "Good day, madame. We would like a room for two persons . . . for a month . . . with a—" "Ah, monsieur, I am very sorry, but there is nothing." . . . "Nothing at all?" "Nothing at all."

273.12–14   "Mais la prochaine semaine . . . dommage."] "But next week, perhaps?" "Not next week either, monsieur." "That's a pity."

273.22   "C'est un très joli hotel,"] "This is a very pretty hotel."

273.28–34   "Nous aurions été . . . De rien, monsieur."] "We would have been very happy here." . . . "Ah, monsieur, I infinitely regret that there is nothing. The U.N., you know." "Yes, yes, the U.N. . . . Thank you, madame." "It's nothing, monsieur."

275.12–14   pas une seule chambre . . . lit] No room for two with bath, no big bed.

275.20–21   "Ne quittez pas,"] "Don't hang up."

278.27   pâté en croûte] Pâté baked in a pastry wrapper.

278.32   fraises des bois] Wild strawberries.

279.38   *Boris Godounov*] Russian opera (1874) by Modest Mussorgsky (1839–1881), based on the verse drama by Alexander Pushkin.

279.39   Bakst] Léon Bakst (1866–1924), Russian painter and stage designer closely associated with Sergei Diaghilev and the Ballets Russes.

280.4–5   *Les Contes d'Hoffman*] *Tales of Hoffman* (1881), posthumously produced opera by the French composer Jacques Offenbach (1819–1880).

280.24   *Le Reine Morte*] *The Dead Queen* (1942), play by Henry de Montherlant (1895–1972).

280.28   *Les Parents Terribles*] Play (1938) by Jean Cocteau (1889–1965).

280.34   ouvreuse] Usherette.

281.21   *La belle au bois dormant* and *Cendrillon*] *Sleeping Beauty* and *Cinderella.*

283.39   *Ici est mort Racine*] *Racine died here.*

285.2   "crise" and "grève"]   "Crisis" and "strike."

286.7   *Le Roi d'Ys*]   Opera (1888) by Édouard Lalo (1823–1892), libretto by Édouard Blau.

289.9–12   *Mais c'est . . . tendrement. . . .*]   But that may perhaps be too tiring for you. . . . Good-by, good-by, my dears, I kiss you with all my heart and love you tenderly. . . .

289.23   *Louise*]   Opera (1900) by Gustav Charpentier (1860–1956).

290.26–28   "j'aime la France . . . pas beaucoup."]   "I like France and I do not use the black market." . . . "Monsieur, there aren't many."

291.5   pot-au-feu]   Large cast-iron or earthenware cooking pot with a lid; Dutch oven.

299.5   Gluck's *Orpheus*]   *Orfeo ed Euridice* (1762), opera by Christoph W. Gluck (1714–1787), Italian libretto by Raniero di Calzabigi.

303.13   Bossuet]   Jacques-Bénigne Bossuet (1627–1704), Bishop of Meaux from 1681.

305.27   spider]   Heavy cast-iron frying pan.

306.5–6   Bossuet, Fénelon, Massillon, and Fléchier]   Four eloquent Roman Catholic priests during the reign of Louis XIV: Jacques-Bénigne Bossuet (see note 303.13); François Fénelon (1651–1715), Archbishop of Camrai from 1695; Jean-Baptiste Massillon (1663–1742), Bishop of Claremont from 1717; and Esprit Fléchier (1632–1710), Bishop of Nimes from 1687.

309.39–310.2   the Simone Martinis in Siena . . . without knowing it.]   Simone Martini (c. 1280–1344), Italian painter in the early Gothic style whose earliest masterpiece, a fresco depicting the Madonna and child as queen and prince of the world (1315), was painted for the Palazzo Pubblico in Siena. The palazzo's bell tower, completed in 1334, was for decades the tallest structure in Italy.

311.31   *Un Coeur Simple*]   *A Simple Heart*, novella first published in Flaubert's collection *Three Tales* (*Trois Contes*, 1877).

313.2–3   *Le Diable au Corps*]   *The Devil in the Flesh* (1947), film directed by Claude Autant-Lara, based on the novel by Raymond Radiguet (1922).

328.2   douane!]   Customs.

328.13–17   qu'il est encore . . . grand plaisir. . . .]   It is even more difficult to direct one's good impulses than one's bad, because unlike the latter, one can never exactly foresee the results. In any case, know that you have given me great pleasure. . . .

330.38–331.1   One of the ways . . . sunk beneath the sea.]   See Shakespeare's *The Tempest*.

339.17–18   President Pinay]   Antoine Pinay (1891–1994), prime minister of France from March 1952 to January 1953.

341.15   muguets]   Lilies of the valley, a traditional French token of good luck and the coming of spring. Throughout France, May Day is known as the "Fête du Muguet" and observed by the exchange of sprigs of the flowers among loved ones.

341.19–20   *The boy learns . . . to skate in summer.*]   Cf. William James, *The Principles of Psychology* (1890), Chapter 4 ("Habit"): "[W]e notice after exercising our muscles or our brain in a new way, that we can do so no longer at that time; but after a day or two of rest, when we resume the discipline, our increase in skill not seldom surprises us. I have often noticed this in learning a tune; and it has led a German author to say that we learn to swim during the winter and to skate during the summer."

344.6   *Les Indes Galantes*]   Opera-ballet (1735) by Jean-Philippe Rameau (1683–1764), libretto by Louis Fuzelier, whose thematically linked songs and dances tell love stories set in France, Peru, Turkey, Persia, and the American South.

345.1   Irmgard Seefried]   German soprano (1919–1988) noted for her interpretations of Strauss, Mozart, and *lieder*.

346.2   prix d'ami.]   Reduced price.

350.22   "A nos amis, à nos amours!"]   "To our friends, to our loves!"

351.18–19   *Phèdre . . . Ciboulette*]   *Phèdre* (1667), tragedy by Jean Racine (1639–1699); *Ciboulette* (1926), comic operetta by Reynaldo Hahn (1875–1947), libretto by Robert de Flers and Francis de Croisset.

356.31   Fantin-Latour]   Henri Fantin-Latour (1836–1904), French painter known for floral still lifes.

STORIES 1963–1976

371.29   Chalmers]   The Chalmers Motor Car Co., of Detroit, Michigan, flourished from 1908 until 1922, when it was purchased by the Maxwell Motor Corporation.

387.23–26   *Hello, guest . . . each minute.*]   From "Welcome, Guest" by Edgar A. Guest (1881–1959).

392.9–10   "Fingal's Cave" . . . *Rosamunde*]   "Fingal's Cave" ("Die Hebriden," 1830), op. 26, symphonic overture by Felix Mendelssohn;

Rosamunde (1823), by Franz Schubert, incidental music to *Rosamunde, Fürstin von Zypern* ("Princess of Cyprus"), play by Helmina von Chézy.

396.22   the Reverend John Skinner]   The diaries of the Reverend John Skinner (1772–1839), rector of Camerton, near Bath, were edited by Howard Coombs and Arthur N. Bax and published as *Journal of a Somerset Rector, 1803–1834* (1930).

403.7   Tripler's]   F. R. Tripler & Co., "Outfitters to Gentlemen," was for decades a famous menswear shop at 46th Street and Madison Avenue, New York City.

426.40   Dantès]   Edmond Dantès, protagonist of the *Count of Monte Cristo* (1844) by Alexandre Dumas.

427.12   Marguerite de Valois . . . Louise de La Vallière.]   Marguerite de Valois (1553–1615), "Queen Margot" of France and Navarre; Louise de La Vallière (1644–1710), mistress of Louis XIV from 1661 to 1667. The lives of both women were fictionalized by Dumas.

428.5–6   an "*hôtel simple . . . dans la localité.*"]   A "plain but comfortable hotel," with "a good restaurant for the area."

428.29   Boutet de Monvel]   See note 42.31–32.

431.28   Hawkeye]   Kodak box camera of the 1950s.

432.28   Quimper]   Distinctive faïence pottery, decorated with traditional Breton motifs, made since 1690 in the town of Quimper (or Kemper).

433.12   the girl in the fairy tale]   Belle, in "La Belle et la Bête" ("Beauty and the Beast").

433.40–434.1   *pardon* costumes.]   A *pardon* is a Breton pilgrimage to a saint's tomb, usually to seek the saint's indulgence or "pardon." There are five *pardons* during the Roman Catholic church year, on which pilgrims wear traditional Breton costumes: the men, embroidered waistcoats, leather leggings, and wooden shoes; the women, colorful habits and elaborate headdresses.

435.18   "*Cinq,*"]   "Five."

438.8   "*Votre tour est très sensible,*"]   "Your tour is very sensitive."

438.10   Only connect, Mr. E. M. Forster said,]   See Forster's novel *Howards End* (1910).

440.20   "*n'est plus un restaurant sérieux.*"]   "This is no longer a serious restaurant."

442.6   "*Paris n'est plus Paris.*"]   "Paris in no longer Paris."

443.34   Viollet-le-Duc] Eugène Viollet-le-Duc (1814–1879), architect, preservationist, and guiding spirit of the Gothic Revival movement in France.

445.10   *tout simplement*] Quite simply.

447.14   Doctors Hospital] Hospital (1929–2004) at East End Avenue and 87th Street, absorbed in 1987 into Beth Israel Medical Center. The hospital buildings were razed in 2004 by private real estate developers.

449.17–22   "Emily . . . into the distance. . . ."] From *Emily, the Traveling Guinea Pig* (1959), by Emma Smith, pictures by Katherine Wigglesworth.

457.3   *Sartor Resartus*] Satirical, semi-fictional philosophical work (1833–34), partly an attack on empiricism, by the Scottish historian and social critic Thomas Carlyle (1795–1881).

462.31   *Middlemarch*] Novel (1871) by George Eliot.

467.30   'In Dulci Jubilo.'] Fourteenth-century German carol ("Good Christian Men, Rejoice!").

473.28–29   "The Tinder Box,"] Fairy tale ("Fyrtøit," 1835) by Hans Christian Andersen.

496.9   Redouté's roses] See note 211.10. Redouté's masterpiece *Les Roses*, a series of prints depicting the roses at Napoleon's country house at Malmaison, was printed in three volumes in 1817–24.

496.29–30   Isak Dinesen's story . . . perfect blue,] A tale told within the story "The Young Man with the Carnation," published in Dinesen's *Winter's Tales* (1942); the tale has been anthologized separately under the title "The Blue Jar."

499.31–32   Today is not the day . . . tay.] Cf. a soldier's ditty of the First World War era: "Today is the day / They give babies away / With a half a pound of tea. / If you know any ladies / Who want any babies / Just send them round to me."

500.24   *Ring Round the Moon*] Christopher Fry's 1950 adaptation of *L'Invitation au Château* (1947), a play by Jean Anouilh.

500.26   Adlai Stevenson's] Adlai E. Stevenson II (1900–1965), one-term governor of Illinois (1948–52) and Democratic Party candidate for U.S. president in 1952 and 1956.

501.10   Seigneur Dieu] Lord God.

501.26   out of Krafft-Ebing] Out of the pages of *Psychopathia Sexualis* (1886), a collection of case studies in sexual deviancy by the German psychiatrist Richard von Krafft-Ebing (1840–1902).

504.30–31   For every evil . . . there is none.]   From a traditional English rhyme: "For every evil under the sun / there is a remedy or there is none. / If there be one, try and find it; / if there be none, never mind it."

SO LONG, SEE YOU TOMORROW

508.1   *Robert Fitzgerald*]   Fitzgerald (1910–1985), poet, translator of the Greek and Latin classics, and, after 1965, Boylston Professor of Rhetoric and Oratory at Harvard University. He and Maxwell met in 1931, when Maxwell was pursuing graduate work at Harvard and Fitzgerald was an undergraduate, and they remained lifelong friends.

523.19–20   "The Shepherd Boy's Prayer,"]   American parlor song (1879) by A. W. Holt.

523.27   "Alice Blue Gown."]   Popular song (1919) by Harry Tierney, words by Joseph McCarthy.

524.26–27   Ortega y Gasset . . . shipwreck.]   The Spanish philosopher José Ortega y Gasset (1883–1955) often likened the human condition to a shipwreck (*naufragio*).

527.33–528.22   "This object . . . fear and confusion. . . ."]   From a letter of 1947 from the Swiss-born Italian sculptor Alberto Giacometti (1901–1966) to his New York dealer, Pierre Matisse (1900–1989), describing sculptures to be exhibited at Matisse's gallery in January–February 1948. The translation is uncredited, and was first published by the Pierre Matisse Gallery in 1948. Maxwell's source is *Alberto Giacometti*, the catalogue for a major retrospective of the artist's work organized by Peter Selz for the Museum of Modern Art, New York, in 1965.

534.19   Roughead]   William Roughead (1870–1952), Scottish criminologist, criminal lawyer, and, in such books as *The Trial of Dr. Pritchard* (1906), a pioneer of the true-crime genre.

538.30   storm buggy.]   Horse-drawn buggy with an enclosed cabin.

540.14–15   buried at the crossroads . . . heart]   Until the early 19th century, many western governments, including those of the U.S. and Great Britain, deemed suicide both a felony and a sin. The suicide's corpse was denied a Christian burial and was instead interred at a crossroads, sometimes with a stake through the heart and usually after sundown.

543.35–37   "Here's to the heart . . . the girl I love,"]   From "Heidelberg," a drinking song from the comic operetta *The Prince of Pilsen* (1902) by Gustav Luders, book and lyrics by Frank Pixley. Copyright 1902 by M. Witmark & Sons; renewed © 1932 by Warner Bros., Inc. Rights administered by Alfred Publishing Co., Van Nuys, California. All rights reserved.

549.23   Chalmers]   See note 371.29.

553.24   Octagon soap]   Brand of lye-based laundry soap.

555.40   Franklin]   The H. H. Franklin Manufacturing Co., of Syracuse, New York, made distinctive, technologically innovative luxury automobiles from 1902 to 1937.

557.37–39   "How glorious . . . dwell with thee. . . ."]   From "I Praised the Earth, in Beauty Seen," hymn by Reginald Heber, Anglican bishop of Calcutta (1783–1826).

558.32–33   "Sir Galahad" and "The Dickey Bird,"]   Two popular color lithographs of the early 20th century: *Sir Galahad* (1862), a Royal Academy painting by George Frederick Watts (1817–1904); *The Dickey Bird*, an illustration by Maxfield Parrish (1870–1966) for Eugene Field's *Poems of Childhood* (1904).

559.4–7   Blessed is the peacemaker . . . which it is.]   See Matthew 5:8–10.

560.8   Decoration Day]   Annual holiday, first observed on May 30, 1868, to honor the Union dead of the American Civil War. After World War I, the name was changed to Memorial Day and the observance broadened to honor all those who have died in service of the country.

582.6   roached]   Combed upward from the forehead and temples and held in place by hair oil.

593.3   *The rich man . . . needle,*]   See Matthew 19:24.

BILLIE DYER AND OTHER STORIES

618.35–36   president of the college]   Raymond N. Dooley (1909–1971), president of Lincoln College, 1948–1971. A prominent regional historian, he was editor of *The Namesake Town: A Centennial History of Lincoln, Illinois* (1953).

619.14   Missionary Ridge]   At the Battle of Missionary Ridge (November 25, 1863), Union forces led by generals Grant, Sherman, and Thomas defeated a Confederate unit led by General Bragg, effectively ending the Confederate siege of Chattanooga, Tennessee.

620.25   Decoration Day]   See note 560.8.

621.27   Shadrach, Meshach, and Abednego]   See Daniel 3:12–30.

623.18–19   a hand . . . *writing on the wall!*]   See Daniel 5:5.

632.8   "PG"]   French: *prisonnier de guerre* (prisoner of war).

637.35–36   *Foxes have holes . . . to lay his head.*]   See Matthew 8:20 and Luke 9:58.

638.28   *Aquitania*] R.M.S. *Aquitania* sailed for the British Cunard Line from 1914 through 1949. In 1939–48 she was requisitioned for war duties and transported British and Allied forces to and from the Atlantic and Pacific theaters.

644.3   Palmer method] Method of penmanship instruction developed by Austin Palmer (1860–1927) and popularized in his *Guide to Business Writing* (1894). The Palmer method was widely taught in American elementary and secretarial schools during the first half of the 20th century as the standard cursive hand.

645.5   *Hearts of the World*] Silent film drama (1918) about the German occupation of a small French village during World War I.

645.27   Sells-Floto Circus] From 1906 to 1932, a small competitor of Ringling Bros. and Barnum & Bailey.

645.29   Chalmers] See note 371.29.

649.13–14   Blackstone's *Commentaries* and Chitty's *Pleadings*,] *Commentaries on the Laws of England* (1765–69), by William Blackstone, and *Practical Treatise on Pleading, and on the Parties to Actions and the Forms of Action* (1809), by Joseph Chitty.

652.3   *folie des grandeurs*] Delusions of grandeur.

658.3   Defeat . . . Hazlitt said.] Cf. William Hazlitt, "The Indian Jugglers," in his essay collection *Table-Talk* (1821): "Danger is a good teacher, and makes apt scholars. So are disgrace, defeat, exposure to immediate scorn and laughter."

669.34   Ernest Thompson Seton] Seton (1860–1946) was a naturalist and nature writer, an enthusiast of Native American woodcraft and folklore, and a shaping influence on the Boy Scouts of America. His books include *Wild Animals I Have Known* (1898) and *Lives of the Hunted* (1901).

695.1   *Aurora*] Fresco painted by Guido Reni (1572–1642) for the Casino dell'Aurora, Rome. It depicts a cortege of nymphs following the car of Apollo across the Mediterranean sky.

697.6   I began to write a novel] *Time Will Darken It* (1948).

STORIES 1986–1999

724.16   Trimingham's] From 1842 to 2005, Bermuda's largest general retailer, with its flagship store on Front Street, Hamilton, and smaller branches dotting the islands.

725.26–31   "Seven for the seven . . . shall *be* so."] From the traditional English carol "Green Grow the Rushes, O."

729.14   *Gristede's*] Manhattan-based supermarket chain.

735.28   Cletus Oakley] Oakley (1900–1990), longtime professor of mathematics at Haverford College and, with Carl Allendoerfer, co-creator of the "New Math" curriculum that was widely taught in public schools in the 1950s and 1960s.

737.3   horse-and-rider fences] Rude, all-wood post-and-rail fences, with the rail-ends stacked in alternating fashion between double posts.

737.11–12   The view . . . Whittier.] See Whittier's long poem "Snow-Bound: A Winter Idyl" (1866).

A SET OF TWENTY-ONE IMPROVISATIONS

739.1–2   A SET OF TWENTY-ONE IMPROVISATIONS] Reprinted from *All the Days and Nights: The Collected Stories of William Maxwell* (1995), this set of "once-upon-a-time" tales consists of 15 of the 29 "improvisations" that Maxwell collected in *The Old Man at the Railroad Crossing and Other Tales* (1966) together with six later tales. In his preface to *The Old Man at the Railroad Crossing*, Maxwell described his method in writing these improvisations as follows:

These twenty-nine tales were written over a period of many years, usually for an occasion, and I didn't so much write them as do my best to keep out of the way of their writing themselves. I would sit with my head bent over the typewriter waiting to see what was going to come out of it. The first sentence was usually a surprise to me. From the first sentence everything else followed. A person I didn't know anything about and had never known in real life—a man who had no enemies, a girl who doesn't know whether to listen to her heart or her mind, a woman who never draws breath except to complain, an old man afraid of falling—stepped from the wings and began to act out something I must not interrupt or interfere with, but only be a witness to: a life, with the fleeting illuminations that anybody's life offers, written in sand with a pointed stick and erased by the next high tide. In sequence the tales seem to complement one another. There are recurring themes. But I did not plan it that way. I have sometimes believed that it was all merely the result of the initial waiting with an emptied mind—that this opened a door of some kind, and what emerged was an archaic survival, the professional storyteller who flourished in all the countries of the world before there were any printed books, a dealer in the unexpected turn of events, in the sudden reversal of fortune that changes a human being's fate; old, frail, led around by young boy, his voice now gentle as a dove, now implacable, as he approaches the moment of irony; half-blind, but having seen such wonders as will require all his talent to tell about, and the emotional participation of whoever stops to listen to him.

756.17–18   Lady Mary Wortley Montagu]   Lady Mary (1689–1762), an English aristocrat, traveler, poet, and writer, especially noted for her letters from Turkey, where her husband was the English ambassador (1716–18). She settled, alone, in Venice, in 1759.

756.19–25   William Beckford . . . (Leipzig, 1832).]   Beckford (1760–1844), English Gothic novelist whose second book, *Dreams, Waking Thoughts, and Incidents: In a Series of Letters, from Various Parts of Europe*, was part travel journal, part personal confession, composed during his Grand Tour of the Continent in 1780–81. Beckford published the book in London in 1783 but suppressed most of the original print run; he rewrote the text for incorporation into his book *Italy, with Sketches of Spain and Portugal* (1784). There was no Leipzig edition of 1832.

759.32–33   "There were three sisters fair and bright,"]   Cf. "The Riddling Knight," traditional Scottish ballad, in *The Oxford Book of Ballads* (1910), edited by Sir Arthur Quiller-Couch.

764.7   William Morris]   English designer, craftsman, printer, and writer (1834–1896) who was a spearhead of the British Arts and Crafts Movement and a pioneer of socialism.

778.2   *a line of verse by W. B. Yeats*]   See "Sailing to Byzantium" (1928): "Caught in that sensual beauty all neglect / Monuments of unageing intellect."

821.4   *The flight is past; and man—*]   The missing word is *forgot.* See "Sic Vita" ("Like to the Falling of a Star"), poem by Henry King, Bishop of Chichester (1592–1669).

OTHER IMPROVISATIONS

854.8   meachin,]   New England dialect word, now obscure, meaning "cowardly," "retiring."

881.5   Anna Freud]   Anna Freud (1895–1982), the sixth and last child of Sigmund Freud, was a psychoanalyst, researcher, and theorist specializing in children's psychological development.

881.34   Fuller Brush man]   Door-to-door salesman for the Fuller Brush Company, a manufacturer of household cleaning products.

889.37–38   "Enchiridion"]   "Handbook for living" by the Stoic philosopher Epictetus (c. A.D. 55–135).

891.12   receipt]   Recipe.

900.6   *English Bards and Scotch Reviewers*] Satire in heroic couplets
(1808) by Lord Byron.

900.31   Max Gate] Thomas Hardy's home, in Dorchester, Dorset, from
1885 until his death, at age 87, in 1928.

902.31   Henry Holland] English architect and designer (1745–1806) in
the neoclassical style.

908.6   Sir Roger de Coverley] Old English line dance for six to eight
couples. The Virginia Reel is an American variant.

908.17   dominie] Scots word for a Protestant clergyman, especially a
minister of the Church of Scotland.

NEARING NINETY

920.13   Elizabeth Bowen,] See note 2.1–5.

920.17   *The Sudden View*] *The Sudden View: A Mexican Journey* by
Sybille Bedford (1911–2006) was published in 1953; it was revised and reissued
in 1960 as *A Journey to Don Otavio: A Traveller's Tale of Mexico.*

921.2–8   Across eight decades . . . lost their lives.] On July 24, 1915, the
excursion ship *Eastland* capsized on the Chicago River, drowning more than
800 of its 2,500 passengers.

APPENDIX

927.9   *Le Grand Meaulnes, The Counterfeiters,*] *Le Grand Meaulnes,* see
note 42.27; *The Counterfeiters (Les Faux-monnayeurs,* 1925), experimental
novel by André Gide.

928.2   the Borobudur] Immense ninth-century *stupa,* or pyramidal Bud-
dhist shrine, in Central Java, Indonesia.

928.13–14   one of the readers] Harold Strauss, editor-in-chief of Knopf
from 1942 to 1966.

929.9–10   a short story . . . inside the house.] A fair copy of this story
exists among Maxwell's papers at the University of Illinois, Urbana-
Champaign. The four-page typescript is undated. It is here reproduced ver-
batim, with underscored words printed in italics.

Bloody Murder

He knew that it was a gun going off that woke him, and he couldn't
understand, in the dark, why he wasn't dead. His mother screamed,
and it was like no sound he had ever heard in his whole life. He knew

he ought to go help her, that she needed him, and he sat up intending to throw the covers off and couldn't. Something was holding him, and it was the fact that his father was in the next room talking to her in a perfectly ordinary voice, as if they were at the dinner table. Then her voice got small and she said, "No, no, no, don't don't, *don't!*" and the gun went off again and was followed by silence. He clasped his knees and could not stop shaking. He was still like that when his father came in and flipped the light switch by the door and glared at him. Neither of them spoke. The bright light hurt his eyes. He tried not to look at the gun. And there was just time for him to realize that he was going to die too, and to accept this idea fatalistically, when his father said, "Go to sleep," and left the room.

Every light in the house was turned on—at three o'clock in the morning. He heard water running in the kitchen, and then the knife drawer in the kitchen table being opened. His father must be standing by the table in the kitchen, but doing what? A creaking sound meant he had shifted his weight. Or it might be the house, which was old and full of unexplained noises. Whatever it was his father was hesitating about what was now decided. He heard rapid footsteps: his father going into the other bedroom. A feeling of great drowsiness came over him, and he let his head sink down till it was resting on his knees and thought, *If I go back to sleep, when I wake it will turn out I was only dreaming.* And knew by the rough feel of the blanket on his forehead that he was not dreaming, the shots were real. What would happen if he shouted, "You forgot to turn the water off!"

The blackness outside crowded against the windowpane like people looking in.

He asked his father if he could have an air rifle last Christmas and his father said, "When you are older. . . ." This wasn't an air rifle, this was a, was a—

He shuddered at the recollection of the sound.

In the other bedroom a drawer was pulled open all the way and fell to the floor with a crash. "Now what?" his father muttered, talking to himself. As if the drawer was one more in a series of annoyances.

The drawer being jammed back into place, in the dresser. And then a sound he didn't know what to make of, at first: he had never heard his father cry before. Softly. And like an animal. He thought, *I ought to get up and go to him.* And would have if his father hadn't said, "Don't go in there."

When?

When did his father say that?

He didn't. He was going to say it.

How did I know that, he wondered when, a minute later, it happened. His father, standing in the doorway, said, "Don't go in there, do you hear?" And then he went into the kitchen and turned the water off. After that, the sound of the front door closing. He waited for his father to come back. A long time. In a house so quiet he could hear his own breathing. And finally he pushed the covers aside and went out into the living room and called his grandmother, standing at the wall telephone. It rang and rang, and he began to be afraid she wasn't going to answer, but she did, in a voice fuddled with sleep.

"You have to come," he said. "Something has happened."

"Is that you, Ronny?"

"Yes."

"In the morning won't do?"

Though it was still dark outside, the birds were beginning—he heard the same four liquid notes, over and over. Then a different bird.

"No, now."

"Wait a minute till I put my teeth in."

She was gone a long time. Then: "Where's your mother? Is she too sick to come to the phone?" And when this question met with no answer she said, "Let me speak to your dad."

"He isn't here."

"All right," she said. "But no one ever seems to think anything is too much for me, and I'm an old woman. I'll be there as soon as I can make it."

She didn't even stop to put her corset on, but daylight arrived first, and from far down the block she saw him. He was dressed and sitting on the front steps. Afterward, though she knew it couldn't be, it seemed that the look of the house told her everything, right down to the—

When she was close enough to get a good look at him, the words that came to her mind were *Why, he looks like an orphan* . . . And then *They've both run off and left him for me to raise, and it's too much. I just can't do it. They'll have to make some other arrangement.*

"Well, I'm here," she said, and when he still didn't say anything she started past him up the steps. She felt a tug at her skirt and turned.

"Don't go in their room," he said.

After a quick look around the living room, where nothing seemed to be amiss, she went into the kitchen, saw the knife drawer open, and out of habit closed it. What did he want of her? To take charge, know what to do, since he didn't. And she seemed to know what she was doing, but it turned out she didn't. She believed she was taking the bull by the horns, since no good ever comes of closing your eyes to trouble. So she went over to the bedroom door and opened it upon a sight that nothing in her whole experience had prepared her for.

When she cried out, he said from the front steps, without turning around, "I told you not to go in there." But after that he wasn't un-kind to her any more. He helped her to a chair and brought her a glass of water and found the heart pills that she always carried with her in her pocketbook, and when she opened her mouth he said, "Don't try to talk," and gradually the blueness left her face. They were like two strangers being considerate of one another.

When the milkman came, it seemed that he had been sent there to help them. They got in his wagon, behind the plodding old horse, as if they were all three starting off on a journey, and he drove them to her house and called the police from there.

Copyright © 2008 by the William Maxwell Estate.

933.14–17   I wish that I had written . . . *Notebook.*]   *The Great Gatsby* (1925), novel by F. Scott Fitzgerald; "In the Ravine" (1900) and "Ward No. 6" (1892), stories by Anton Chekhov; *The House in Paris* (1936), novel by Elizabeth Bowen; *A Sportsman's Notebook* (1852), linked stories and sketches by Ivan Turgenev.

*This book is set in 10 point Linotron Galliard,
a face designed for photocomposition by Matthew Carter
and based on the sixteenth-century face Granjon. The paper
is acid-free lightweight opaque and meets the requirements
for permanence of the American National Standards Institute.
The binding material is Brillianta, a woven rayon cloth made
by Van Heek-Scholco Textielfabrieken, Holland. Composition by Dedicated Business Services. Printing by
Malloy Incorporated. Binding by Dekker Book-
binding. Designed by Bruce Campbell.*

OCT 0 6 2008